Adelsverein: The Harvesting

Book Three of the Adelsverein Trilogy

Geron GA *& Associates*

Celia Hayes

Watercress Press
111 Grotto
San Antonio, Texas, 78216
www.watercresspress.com

Adelsverein: The Harvesting

Book Three of the Adelsverein Trilogy

Celia Hayes

Celia Hayes

A Note of Thanks, Appreciation and Dedication

This second edition of *The Harvesting* contains the complete text and historical notes originally published in the first edition. As ever with my books, this was not a project created solely by me. I owe a debt, as well as thanks and acknowledgements to a great number of people who contributed advice, feedback, editing, and all sorts of support to the original individual editions of the *Adelsverein Trilogy*, beginning with Alice Geron of Watercress Press, and members of the Independent Authors Guild; Diane Salerni, Michael Katz and Al Past for the use of his gorgeous color photos for the covers.

Extravagant thanks are due to Barbara Skolaut and J.H. Heinrichs – generous patrons of the arts, literature and most importantly, genre fiction – and to Mary Young, for help in time of need. Thanks are also due to Friedrichsburg historian Kenn Knopp who kindly reviewed all three manuscripts in search of historical errors. Any which remain in are purely my fault.. Thanks also to my late good friend and computer genius, David Walsh. Gratitude is also due to the the staff of the San Antonio Public Library, Semmes Branch. They managed to find many of those books on various matters to do with historical events in Texas which I needed to research this historical novel.

Finally, this volume is dedicated as always; with love for my infatigable daughter Jeanne, to my Mom and to Dad, AKA *Vati* – the best dad ever. Dad was – as was only to be expected – a dedicated fan, in spite of not being much into historical fiction. But he loved what I wrote, and read and critiqued – and we miss him.

Celia Hayes

avery on U.S. soil. Carl is an abolitionist, as are most of the German
ettlers, and Jack warns him that he and his kinfolk might be in
anger. But Carl has lived in Texas for nearly all of his life and served
ith valor as a soldier and ranger; he does not think he is at risk for
s opinions. He has also built a fine stone house and planted an
rchard. Nothing would make him leave. Shortly after Jack's visit,
arl, Magda, and their children return to Friedrichsburg to celebrate
e Fourth of July. Magda becomes ill from a complicated pregnancy
d must spend the summer at Vati's house. Her younger sister,
osalie, has fallen love with Robert Hunter, John Hunter's cousin.
he summer is terribly hot, and Texas is plagued with an outbreak of
ysterious fires, blamed on abolitionists intent on fomenting a slave
surrection. It soon becomes clear that war between North and South
 close at hand.

Shortly after Texas secessionists vote to join the Confederacy in
e spring of 1861, Carl and his family journey to Austin to attend the
edding of Margaret's oldest son to the daughter of a wealthy rice
lanter. It is an awkward visit, as most of those they meet—including
any of Carl's old friends and Margaret's own sons—enthusiastically
pport the Confederacy. Carl has fought for Texas, and for the right
r Texas to be able to join the Union. He disapproves of slavery and
nows that, because Texas and the South have no manufacturing base,
 the end they will lose a war. By chance, Carl has a brief and heart-
nding meeting with Sam Houston. Houston reminds him about the
asy wrong and the difficult right, and encourages him to stick to his
rinciples, even though his old friends, and Margaret's sons and
usband, are rushing to enlist. Carl promises Magda that he would not
ave to serve with the Union, where he would have to fight old
iends, nor will he serve the Confederacy.

Magda's brother, Friedrich, joins the Frontier Battalion. They
erve as a defense against raiding Indians, now that the Federal Army
as withdrawn from the frontier forts. Charley Nimitz is raising a
ompany for local defense, which means taking an oath of loyalty to
e Confederacy. Carl's foreman, Trap Talmadge, is an old Ranger
ergeant and he also intends to enlist, but over age and crippled, his
nlistment is refused. Despondent, Trap returns to an old friend: the

Synopsis—Book 1: The Gathering

In 1836, teen-aged German-American soldier Carl Becker is
part of a Texian garrison taken prisoner by Mexican forces at the
Presidio La Bahia—the Goliad—shortly after the fall of the Alamo.
Through the actions of his older brother Rudi, he escapes the mass
execution of those who had surrendered, ordered by none other than
General Santa Anna, President of Mexico and commander of the
Mexican Army. Carl's brother dies, but he lives.

Eight years later, he has become one of Jack Hays' Texas
Rangers. As a friend and a commander, Jack asks a favor of Carl, who
speaks German well. A German prince has grandiose plans to bring
settlers to the dangerous frontier, under the auspices of the
Adelsverein (The Society for the Protection of German Immigrants in
Texas). Jack wants Carl to discourage the prince, unaware that
thousands of German settlers are already on their way.

Among those hopeful immigrants is the clock-maker of Ulm in
Bavaria, Christian "Vati" Steinmetz; his wife Hannah; daughters
Magda and Liesel; and his twin sons, Friedrich and Johann. Vati
Steinmetz is a craftsman in Germany, devoted to books, but he is
fearful for his family in his homeland's political atmosphere at the
time. He and Liesel's husband, Hans "Hansi" Richter, accept the
Adelsverein's offer of land in Texas. They sail on the brig *Apollo*,
packed into a single, windowless lower deck. The *Apollo* runs into
winter storms on the Atlantic, and an epidemic of typhus kills Hannah
Steinmetz and the Richters' baby son.

Their situation becomes even worse upon reaching Texas.
Stranded on a desolate beach, many of the Verein immigrants have
fallen ill and died. Vati adopts a young orphan girl found in the camp
among the bodies of her family, and names her Rosalie. Meanwhile,
John Meusebach, the prince's replacement as Verein commissioner, is
moving heaven and earth to find transportation for the immigrants,
including the Steinmetz and Richter families. On their way to the
settlement of New Braunfels they meet up by chance with Jack Hays
and Carl Becker. Magda and Carl are attracted to each other, but Jack

Hays is recruiting a company of rangers for service in the Mexican War. Magda and Carl part ways; each thinking of the other, but unsure of what they feel or might mean to one another, given the unsettled circumstances.

New Braunfels overflows with settlers. Vati Steinmetz and his family set out with a wagon party towards the site of a new settlement, Friedrichsburg, in the limestone hills and oak woods lying two weeks' journey farther west. Meanwhile, Carl has been badly wounded in the siege of Monterrey and returns to convalesce at his sister Margaret's house. He tells her about Magda. The death of Carl's brother fractured his own family, especially Carl's relationship with his father, but Carl feels a deep affection for Magda and her own father. Margaret wisely encourages him to seek them out when he recovers.

Vati and the other settlers eventually make their new homes in a pleasant valley filled with oak trees, by a clear-running small river. Each settler receives a small plot in the town proper, and ten acres to farm nearby. Hansi is ecstatic at finally getting what they have been promised. New settlers arrive, among them former merchant-seaman Charley Nimitz, who will become Carl's rival for Magda's affections.

Jack Hays returns from the Mexican War and finds Carl on the mend. He asks him to accompany John Meusebach on his planned peace-making venture to the Comanche Indians, in hopes of ensuring the safety of the German settlers. Carl accepts, although he tells Jack that it will be his last assignment. He wants to settle down, and secretly hopes to renew his friendships with the Steinmetz family. John Meusebach reluctantly accepts Carl as a member of his delegation, saying that he cannot afford any more bad advice. In Friedrichsburg, Carl tentatively courts Magda, before departing with the expedition.

Off to a rocky start, they are received by the Comanche with a proper and nerve-wracking ceremony. Journeying farther into the Comanche territory, Meusebach meets with three important chiefs and negotiates a peace treaty. On their return, Carl warns John Meusebach that peace will last only as long as the whims of the Comanche are inclined towards doing so.

Carl takes up property and begins building a house of hi Both he and Charley Nimitz propose to Magda. She choose after much soul-searching, deciding that his calm and reliable is more to her liking than the outgoing and irrepressible C They are married, with joy and some apprehension, and Car Magda to his home—which is now *her* home. He introduces he American neighbors, the Browns, and to the hands who work f including his foreman, Trap Talmadge, and his Mexican sto Porfirio.

Settlers continue arriving in Friedrichsburg, even thou Adelsverein organization has gone bankrupt. A U.S. Army fort offers work and a market for many of the settlers, but new bring cholera with them which devastates the town. C occasional encounters with a local gang of toughs whom he s of murder and horse-thievery. But he applies himself towards l his farm, and a life with Magda. They return to Friedrichsburg birth of their first child, as parties of '49ers seeking gold in Ca begin passing through. Among them is Jack Hays, who has war and Indian-fighting. He tempts Carl with the lure of ac and gold. Carl declines, having found deep contentment in life with Magda, and his newborn son.

Synopsis—Book 2: The Sowing

Although they are happily married and the parents of son, Magda and Carl shelter a friend of theirs from Friedri John Hunter at their farm from a mob of angry soldiers, ther man to safety in San Antonio. J.P. Waldrip, a tough wit reputation as a cattle and horse thief—and perhaps worse looking for John Hunter. Carl sends him off, but Magda i frightened. She tells Carl that Waldrip is envious of their p and will seek an opportunity to harm them if he can.

Some years after this incident, when Carl and Mag added two more children (Samuel and Hannah) to their fai enlarged their farm, Jack Hays pays a visit to their holding. H warning for his old friend: war is almost inevitable between soil states and those who vociferously back the continu bottle. In San Antonio he is seen drinking with J.P Waldrip by Carl's former employee, Porfirio, and by Magda's brother Johann, now a doctor in practice there.

In the second year of war, Texas is put under martial law when enthusiastic recruitment for the Confederate army begins to flag. A draft of men aged 17 through 50 is instituted, outraging those who are pro-Union and opposed to slavery. Late one evening, a mob of vigilantes, a dreaded "Hanging Band," comes to Carl's house. J.P. Waldrip and a drunken Trap Talmadge are with them. Thinking that Trap has come alone to ask for his job back, Carl opens the door. The mob takes him away, their leader telling Carl that he is under arrest. He agrees to go quietly if they will leave his family unharmed. His last words to Magda are for her to look after the children and to be happy. The next morning he is found dead, shot in the back.

Magda is devastated with grief, left pregnant and alone on the property with her children to carry on as best they can. Her brother Johann is outraged by the murder. He writes to Magda, telling her that he is resolved to give up his medical practice and travel by covert means to Union-held territory to join the Union Army. He asks that Magda burn the letter and tell no one but trusted family members.

Two months later, Carl's land and house are confiscated by the authorities, who loot the farm of all the food and livestock. By order of the military governor, Magda (still pregnant) and the children are thrown off the property with only their clothes and a few personal items. After a torturous journey in a rattle-trap cart pulled by their oldest horse, she and the children join her sister Liesel, who is also pregnant and living with their father Vati in Friedrichsburg. Liesel's husband Hansi is in hiding, evading the provost marshal and the Hanging Band, for he refuses to take the loyalty oath or serve in the army in any fashion. Captain Duff makes life miserable for the Friedrichsburg Germans.

Magda and Liesel almost simultaneously give birth to girls. Rosalie is still in love with Robert Hunter, who is serving the Confederacy in the east, in Hood's brigade—another cause to fracture the family. Carl and Magda's oldest son, Dolph, is desperately unhappy, both for the loss of the father that he adored and the property that they both treasured. He is also unhappy at living in town, in relative poverty among the German community. Dolph tells Magda that he is not "one of them," that he is a Texian like his father. Carl's sister Margaret writes to Magda, telling her that she has spoken to friends of hers who are men in power, but has had no luck with getting Magda's property returned. All the honest and honorable men are away fighting in the war. Only the fanatical, the venal and self-serving are left on the home front.

At Christmas in Friedrichsburg, 1862, the provost marshal comes to Vati's house, searching for Hansi. Charley swiftly disguises Hansi as Father Christmas. The ruse is successful and the provost's men leave, without discovering their prey. Rosalie shares a letter from Robert Hunter with Magda. The letter mentions Trap Talmadge, who was finally accepted into a company of Texas cavalry serving in the east. He has become a suicidally fearless scouting officer, and a teetotaler. He has hinted to Robert of some dark personal tragedy for which he bears guilt, but only Magda knows what that might be. Vati's oldest friend in Texas, Herr Pastor Altmueller, hesitantly offers marriage to Magda as a way of assuring some kind of position and shelter for her. She refuses, saying that there is no higher honor for her than to be the widow of her husband.

Far away in Pennsylvania, Carl's older nephews, the sons of his sister Margaret, fall at Gettysburg. Margaret's husband has also died. A party of draft resisters and Unionists are murdered along the Nueces River. There are more murders, more hangings, and more of the German settlers' menfolk take to hiding in the hedges and fields. Charley Nimitz finally tells Hansi that it is too dangerous now to stay in the area, and uses his connections to arrange for Hansi and for his oldest son to serve the Confederacy as teamsters.

An epidemic of diphtheria strikes the district. The younger children of Liesel and Magda all fall ill. Five-year old Christian Richter dies of the disease. Almost unnoticed, Liesel begins a slow descent into mental illness that will plague her for some years.

The schoolmaster, Louis Schultze, is taken by the Hanging Band and murdered. Pastor Altmueller defiantly preaches a sermon criticizing those responsible for this and other atrocities. He is threatened by a masked mob, with J.P. Waldrip as a ringleader, but certain men of Friedrichsburg—led by Charley Nimitz and Dolph Becker—have mounted a quiet guard over the old man. The mob flees, but Magda fears that J.P. Waldrip has recognized her son and will take vengeance. She sends Dolph to Margaret in Austin to keep him safe from the Hanging Band. Unknown to her, Dolph meets with one of Carl's old Ranger friends, who is recruiting a "last-ditch" defense, a cavalry battalion made up of old men and under-age boys. Dolph enlists, following in his father's footsteps.

Magda's only solace as the war draws to an end is her infant daughter Charlotte, who most resembles her father. The Indian raids have renewed, even as men come trickling home, returned from army service or exile, to a wrecked economy and ruined farms. Dolph and his unit return from the far frontier in a rainstorm, and camp in the ruins of a farmstead in the dark. In the morning, Dolphs sees a carved doorway and realizes that he is on his father's farm. The orchard is in bloom, and he vows to return and rebuild, someday. Hansi comes home with his oldest son, driving two loaded army supply wagons. He tells Magda that half of it is hers, in payment for what the authorities took from Carl's farm. Robert Hunter returns with Trap Tallmadge's sword and a dying message from him: *"J.P. Waldrip fired the shot that killed your man."* In Austin, Margaret is dying. In her last letter to Magda she apologizes for not being able to get the farm returned. She sends Magda a final gift, a picture of Carl taken while he was recuperating at her house after his injuries in the Mexican War.

Magda and Hansi resolve to earn a living for their families by opening a small grocery store and a freight hauling business, using the wagons and goods that Hansi brought home from the war. Robert Hunter, the man Rosalie has continued to love all throughout the war, returns to marry her and reclaim his neglected small farm nearby. Magda receives a letter of consolation from Jack Hays. Only at the end of the war did he hear of Carl's murder and the confiscation of their property. Jack still has political connections, and he vows to see that the farm is returned. With the end of the war, and the return of some kind of prosperity, there is some tentative hope for the future in the Hill Country.

Celia Hayes

The Harvesting

They shall beat their swords into plowshares

And their spears into pruning hooks;

Nation shall not lift up sword against nation

Neither shall they learn war any more -

Micah 4:3

Celia Hayes

Prelude: *A Time of Portents and Wonders*

The rain continued all of that afternoon and into the evening, falling from dreary and sunless skies. It wrapped the world in a shroud of grey, flattening piles of fallen leaves into sodden masses and pattering on the roof of the mansion on Turner Street—sometimes lightly and sometimes in a full-throated roar—as the gutter downspouts spurted like fountains. The world outside was in shadow, in more ways than one, as was the downstairs parlor where Magda Vogel Becker dozed in the largest armchair as she waited for her youngest daughter to return home. The mantel clock chimed a musical half past, and Magda's eyes opened. Mouse, the fat little Peke, was sleeping on the footstool by her feet with his blunt muzzle dropped across her ankle. He started awake.

"Half-past eleven, Mauschen," the old woman remarked, disapprovingly. "She's very late tonight." The little dog merely yawned, stretching luxuriously, before regarding her with bulging eyes liquid with adoration, then laying his head across her ankle again. "It's just as well I sent the cook home. It's not as if we are helpless without servants! She will want something to eat, even if she will not admit it at first. Health, Mauschen, it's a precious thing ...."

Magda sighed; here she was, ninety-five years of age and waiting up, hovering like a mother hen over Lottie, the youngest and last of her chicks; and that chick being a woman in her fifties and a grandmother to boot! Ruthlessly she evicted Mouse from his position on the footstool. Setting her feet to the floor, she rose and moved to the largest window, drawing the heavy curtains aside.

Outside the rain poured down with increasing vigor, casting a halo of silver around the street lamp opposite. The wind tossed the dark branches of the oak trees in the garden across the way. Along Turner Street there were a few lights burning in upstairs windows— doubtless those households in which someone lay ill of the influenza. This was a dreadful epidemic, coming as a bolt of thunder out of nowhere.

Magda regarded the lights, knowing very well what was going on in those rooms. Behind every window was a sickroom, sickrooms where someone labored to breathe and someone else watched tirelessly, while the wings of the angel of death whispered in the darkest corners. Magda knew this very well for she had often tended the sick and dying herself, during her own life. There had been such ravages of sickness when she was a girl and a young woman. It had been confidently assumed such things had been banished, defeated, driven back into the shadows by such great advances in medicine. Her own younger brother, Johann, was a doctor and had talked proudly of such miraculous advances. No more did thousands die ugly deaths from cholera, from the yellow fever, from agues and diphtheria, since science and medicine had entered the fray. And yet now they seemed as powerless as they had ever been before—so many stricken so suddenly that the hospitals overflowed. Her daughter had volunteered to nurse at the Army camp, for there were many young soldiers fallen—not by bullet or shell, but to something which had seemed at first to be nothing more than the grippe.

Magda would have volunteered herself. "I have often tended the sick," she had insisted to her daughter and son-in-law, "and I have already had the grippe this year. I am not made of spun glass." But Lottie instantly forbade her to even contemplate such a thing. And perhaps she was right to do so, for Magda walked with a cane most days and could not lift and carry anything heavier than Mouse's food dish.

There were lights at the end of the street, a pair of lights that flickered as they moved, accompanied by the roar of an engine; one of those new-fangled motor cars. Magda watched with interest as it came down Turner Street, slowing to a stop before the window where she waited for Lottie to return. "A noisy thing, "she remarked to Mouse, "noisier than horses, but not quite so prone to run away … and certainly not as much of a mess."

Lottie's husband was thinking of buying one. Magda's younger son, Samuel, had bought a Hudson Touring car eight or nine years before, a marvelous thing with padded seats as comfortable as a leather sofa in a gentleman's study. Once, Samuel had taken her, Lottie, Lottie's children and his own—all crammed in together—to an exhibition of a flying machine. It was a gossamer thing of wires and delicate wings of canvas stretched over an intricate framework of wood; a tiny, fragile machine, lifting off the ground, soaring like a bird and circling the oval parade ground at Fort Sam Houston, to the wonder of the crowds watching underneath. *"Fancy that, Mama!"* Samuel had cried. *"Heavier than air, and powered by an engine—what will they think of next!"* Such marvels and wonders as this new century had brought—and such horrors, also!

Magda could hardly bear to read the news in the papers. It seemed that even those tiny, fragile airplanes had become instruments of war. She found it disheartening to see the evidence that her new country and her old one were deadly enemies in a battle to the death. Her grandsons and great-grandsons went eagerly to the war, little recalling that those enemies they were so eager to slaughter were their cousins, their second cousins, those

2

grandsons and great-grandsons of the friends and kin that her family had left behind when first they departed their ancestral village of Albeck on a bright autumn day over seventy years before. All that time, Germany had still been home in their minds, "the old country." Truly they had come a long, long way from Albeck, farther than Magda had even comprehended when she and Hansi and her sister Liesel had arrived. And her new country had been torn by a dreadful war, one part pitted against the other. War was nothing new to Magda Vogel Becker, who had lived for most of a century.

A woman emerged from the back of the automobile, a woman in a long pale coat, holding an umbrella over her head. Her face could not be seen for the darkness, the rain, and the distance from the window where Magda watched, but there was no need for that; a woman knew her own child. The automobile rolled away, setting a tidal wave of muddy water splashing over the sidewalk. The woman hurried up the sidewalk towards the porte-cochere and around the side of the mansion. A moment or two later, the sound of a door opening and shutting echoed in the hall outside the parlor.

"Lottchen … don't forget to bar the door," Magda called from the parlor. There was the sound of a heavy latch falling into place, and a few seconds later, Magda's daughter Lottie appeared in the doorway.

"Honestly, Mama, you were sitting up waiting for me, with the door unbarred?" Lottie had shed her coat and umbrella in the hallway, and now began unpinning her hat and motoring veil. She was a tall and fair woman, whose pale-blond hair was fading imperceptibly from the color of ripe wheat into white.

"I had Mauschen and … other means to defend myself," Magda answered. "You look tired, my dear little duckling. How bad was it today?"

Magda's daughter let her hat and veils fall onto a chair by the parlor door, and dropped into the chair nearest the fire, pressing her hands to her face.

"Dreadful, Mama," she answered at last. "They are so ill. Our best, and strongest and bravest young men, and yet . . . they die, and nothing can be done for them! They suffer so, Mama. One of Onkel Johann's old friends is the senior surgeon. He tells me that they drown, from this dreadful plague. They drown on dry land, as their lungs fill up with fluids, in a matter of hours. None of his colleagues can find a reason why. All we can offer to them is to tend and comfort them in their last hours."

"And hold their hands," Magda nodded, acknowledging in sad resignation. "At the end, perhaps that is all we can offer. To know there is someone near, who cares for them . . ."

"And to write a letter to their mothers," Lottie added. "That is why I am so late, Mama, I was writing letters. It would mean something, I think, that their mothers hear something of their last moments, and be reassured that they were tended as lovingly as they would have been in the bosom of their own families."

"One does what one can," Magda offered dryly. "And I assume that, such have been the miracles of this age, even in an emergency as this, I presume the hospital is tidy and adequate to the needs of the sick?"

"It is, Mama." Lottie smiled sadly. "It offers every suitable convenience but that of a sure and certain cure. Every other comfort than that!"

"That is good." Magda nodded. "At least, you have something! For your cousin told me once or twice of his experiences in hospital. They had no drugs at all, when they cut off his arm. And nothing could be done at all for him, but that—"

"Oh, Mama," Lottie gasped, "Cousin Peter—but that was so long ago!"

"No, "Magda shook her head, "it was not that long ago at all. A mere blink of time, to me!"

Chapter One: *Homecoming*

In the late summer of 1865, Peter Vining came home from the War. Hatless and thin to the point of emaciation, he was a tall and fair-haired young man with a drooping mustache of which he was still rather vain. He had a pleasant and open face marred by a thin straight scar that slashed down across his forehead and cheek, courtesy of a Union officer's saber. When he thought about it at all, he was only grateful that it hadn't cost him the sight in that eye. Still, the scar pulled his left eyebrow up in a permanently skeptical expression. Like many another, he was clad in the ragged remnants of Confederate motley. The newest thing anywhere about his person was his shoes, which had been the gift of a kindly surgeon in a Union hospital that had been set up outside of Richmond to care for the human wreckage left in the wake of the fighting.

"Take them," Major McNelley, the Union surgeon, had urged Peter as he looked down over his spectacles. "After all, you cannot walk all the way home to Texas barefoot. The sutler will not miss them, after all. Take them. I would hate to see my good work wasted."

"I expect not," Peter had replied, accepting the brogans with mixed feelings. He had lain raving with wound-fever in a rough Confederate hospital, a hospital that seemed to be short of everything except the sick and dying, and had woken in a Union one, on clean sheets. There had been plenty of medicines, and a surgeon who probed the bandages crusted on what remained of his left arm had informed him that he would most likely live. And that the war was over. So far, he hadn't been able to feel much beyond numbness about either of those pieces of information.

Still, he had needed shoes, and Major McNelley was right. He couldn't walk barefoot from Virginia to Texas, and his old boots were more hole than leather. He came as far as Galveston with a straggle of Texan survivors, men of Hood's Brigade and Terry's cavalry. Most of them had been in hospitals or Yankee prisoner compounds when the fighting ended, too sick to travel with the ragged remnants of their units when the Armistice was signed. Peter, bone-thin and pale from the hospital stay and months of semi-starvation, had gotten as far as Houston, where he fell sick again, fevered and shivering with the ague. The family of one of his friends had looked after him for a few weeks. When he had recovered somewhat, he wrote to tell his mother that he was on his way home, but had never gotten an answer. Not that he expected one, the way that things had fallen apart during the death throes of the Confederacy.

When he was able, he had bidden his friend's family goodbye and taken to the road like all the other grey-clad stragglers returning home in ones and twos, halt and lame and heartsick. It had taken him some days, but folk were kindly inclined towards returning soldiers, and he had not had to walk very much of the way.

The last few miles to town he had gotten a ride in a half-empty dray. The teamster who had given him the ride was a dark-haired and bullet-headed Dutch lad, a little younger than Peter, who understood just enough English to tell Peter that he was from the Hills and had driven wagons for the army in Texas for the past two years.

"*Nicht soldaten,*" he had offered, shrugging ruefully. Peter let it go without comment, being only too glad for the ride.

When they reached town, Peter jumped down from the back of the wagon, waved casually by way of thanks to the driver, and hitched up his bedroll, haversack and canteen for one last march.

He trudged wearily along the road from town. His eyes were fixed on a line of low hills above Austin. A rambling white house ringed by apple trees, like a castle in its moat, sat on the nearest of the hills, that grove of trees his grandfather had planted years before. And now he took those last few steps slowly, along the graveled drive beside the row of apple trees, their boughs heavy-hung with hard green fruit. He was so very glad to be home at last. It had been a long way, to get to the roof that his grandfather built and his mother had extended every which way ever since.

Old Alois Becker came to Texas with his wife Maria, his two sons, and a daughter, following the promises of Baron de Bastrop who was looking for settlers, back when all of Texas belonged to Mexico and the wild Indians. Alois built his home place on a tract of land near a settlement called Waterloo, on the upper Colorado River. When Texas won independence and President Lamar insisted on building a new capitol there, Alois and his neighbors had willingly sold their holdings. Well, actually, the neighbors sold up willingly; Alois Becker didn't give a damn one way or the other. His wife and one of his sons were dead, the other son gone, and his son-in-law lay dying of consumption by then. He sold all the property but for a few acres around the home place and the apple trees, and spent the last few years of his life sitting by the kitchen hearth, a lost and broken man, venting spitefulness on anyone who came within reach.

His daughter Margaret ignored it pretty much, letting it roll off her like water from a duck's back. She was a capable and busy woman, Margaret Becker Vining, running a boarding house to support her boys, her bedridden husband, and the father who sat by the fire and stared gloomily into it.

"You mustn't mind your Grandfather," she said once to Peter, when he was about four years old. "He always thought he was the monarch of his world, that everyone obeyed his slightest wish and that he could order everything to his liking. It broke his heart to find out he wasn't, and turned him sour and bitter. Everyone that he really loved either died or went away . . . your grandmother, your uncles. And he can't bear thinking on that and it makes him angry."

"*You're* here, Mama," Peter had answered, much baffled. "Doesn't he love you? And Horace and Jamie and Johnny?" He was afraid of his grandfather, who scowled at him from under great, hairy frowning eyebrows and barked abrupt commands at him in the old language. His older brothers took every opportunity to escape the old man's baleful eye. His mother had sighed and flashed a wry little smile as she hugged him to her in a rustle of lavender-smelling fabric, the black widow's weeds that she wore for the burying of her husband the year before.

"Oh, I think he loves us when he thinks about it; he just doesn't think about us much, Peter-my-chick. It's the grief that makes him sad and distracted. Pay no mind to it." Then she had tousled his hair and added, "We're stuck in the world that we are given, Peter. No use breaking your heart over what we wish we had. We're happiest in the long run if we adapt to what we are given, rather than yearning after what has been taken away from us. I was grateful to have your dear Papa for the time I did."

Practical words. Peter wondered now just how much strength it took to hold to such generous thoughts and words. His mother was a strong woman. She ran her household like a general at the head of an army and always had, but now she had buried two husbands and three of her sons lay far away in hasty graves dug into the soil of a wheat field in distant Pennsylvania. Which was irony if you like, for that was where Alois Becker and his kin had come from, all those years ago.

A general at the head of an army; well, he was done with armies and generals now. He had his certificate of parole from the Union Army tucked into his near-empty haversack to testify to that, and an empty left shirt-sleeve pinned up above the elbow to prove it also. He twisted his shoulders under the blanket-roll and the faded grey uniform jacket slung over his shoulder, shifting the sweat-making burden just a little. His trousers were military issue, but also worn to colorlessness. They had been light blue once, taken off a dead Union cavalryman, but good stout cloth at that. Peter hadn't much cared for taking clothes off a dead man, but he and his brothers were tall and fitting garments hard to come by. By the last desperate year of the fighting he had gotten to be a lot less particular.

At the top of the drive he paused to catch his breath and rest for a moment, sitting on one of the great stones that set the gravel drive apart from the trees and the meadow below. He was thinking it was very strange there was no one about the place. His mother's house—he could not think of it as anything other than hers—had always been as busy as a beehive, a bustle of boarders, visitors and Doctor-Papa's patients, his friends and his older brothers coming and going at nearly all hours. Now hardly anything moved at all, save a light breeze stirring the tree leaves. The window shutters were tightly closed against the midday sun, patterned with a shifting shadow-brocade of leaves. Nothing stirred. The home-place was as somnolent as an old dog, curled up and dozing in the sun. Well, he didn't much mind a quiet homecoming, but the unaccustomed silence sent a prickle of unease down his back. Still, Peter told himself, the war had changed a lot of things; why should he expect his mother's house to be immune?

He hitched up his blankets and haversack again and climbed the steps to the front door, his footsteps echoing hollowly in the covered porch that ran the length of the house. But when he lifted a hand to try the door, it was locked, and that was a surprise to him. Never, since Austin had become a settled and safe place, had Margaret Becker Vining's door been locked during the daytime.

He rapped tentatively with his knuckles on the panel, and called, "Hello! Is there anyone at home?" No answer came from within. He sighed and came down from the porch; may as well go around the back to the stables and the kitchen yard.

There must be someone about, he told himself. The door brass was as polished as it had always been and someone had scythed the grass under the apple trees not long since. He followed the graveled drive around the side; oh yes, there was a drift of smoke coming from the kitchen chimney at the back, and the smell of food cooking. He paused abruptly as he came around the veranda at the side of the house, for there was someone watching him with wary blue eyes. A small boy had half hidden himself behind a white-painted turned-wood post and a brightly glazed urn full of geraniums, and stared at Peter as if he were something rightly to be feared. At least someone was around, Peter thought with relief. Several of the French doors on the lower floor stood open to the light breeze that fanned the shaded side of the house. The child wore a black knickerbockers suit, much disarranged with dust, which Peter thought with sympathy must have been uncomfortably hot for the boy.

"Hello there," Peter ventured tentatively, and tried to gauge the child's age. Not ever having had much to do with children, he guessed about four or five years of age, and the round little face bore some slight resemblance to his own. Maybe this might be Horace's boy. His older brother had married Miss Amelia Stoddard in a splendid but hurried wedding, during that breathless interval between Lincoln's election and the firing on Fort Sumter. He had got a son on her, before the Vining boys all went to join Hood's Brigade. Flushed with the excitement of great doings, they were. No one could tell them any different, although one had tried to warn them about what they were getting themselves into. Peter remembered Horace's quiet happiness at hearing of the child's safe birth. Where had they been when the letter caught up to them, and how long after? He made himself smile at the child and added, "Are you the only one about, then? I'm Peter. I would be your uncle, I guess."

The child's mouth rounded into an "o" of astonishment. Without a word, he turned and scampered into the nearest door, crying, "Mama, come quick! There's another sojer outside!"

A woman's impatient voice answered from the dim room inside, "Oh, Horrie, don't shout like that. Be a good boy! I expect he's hungry. Tell him to go around to the kitchen and ask Hetty for something to eat." That was Amelia's voice, weary and not sounding so sweet and tinkling as she always had when she spoke to Horace's brothers. *So that must be Horace's son and a damn cold welcome from his sister-in-law,* Peter said to himself and shrugged wryly. He'd always thought Amelia to be a bit of a shrew, for all her finishing school prettiness. No reason for the boy to recognize him as family, since he hadn't been home in four years.

The boy Horrie appeared in the doorway just as Peter hitched up his blankets and haversack one more time. "Mama says to go around to the kitchen," he said somberly.

Peter answered, "So I heard." He didn't expect the child to hop down from the verandah and follow after him, but the boy did, as cheeky as a sparrow once curiosity overcame his fear.

"Are you really my uncle?" Horrie questioned, breathlessly. He had to take four steps to match two of Peter's as they strode around towards the kitchen yard and the stables.

"If you are Horace Vining Junior, then I am," Peter answered.

Horrie looked dubious. "Mama calls me that when she's angry," he ventured, with an air of someone making a confession. He craned to look up at Peter as they walked, adding "But most everyone else calls me Horrie. You don't look much like Gran-Mere's pitchers of you. You have a long m-m-m'stashe. Are you *sure* you're my uncle?"

"Positive," Peter answered dryly. "Hetty will surely tell you so, and so will your Ma and Daddy Hurst."

"If you say so," Horrie conceded. And then with the frankness of the very young, he asked, "What happened to your arm?"

"A big piece of Yankee lead happened to it," Peter answered. "And there was nothing to be done but have the surgeon cut it off before the gangrene set in."

Horrie's mouth rounded into that "o" of astonishment again. He seemed torn between sympathy and curiosity when he asked, breathlessly. "Did it hurt?"

"Not much," Peter answered, which was a lie. It had hurt like the devil, and he was still plagued by phantom pains; pains in his hand and wrist, and in the forearm that was gone. How he could feel pain in a limb that wasn't there any more was a mystery to him, and also to the kindly Major McNeeley, although he had told Peter it was not, as he put it, an "unknown phenomenon."

Peter thrust away a memory of amputated limbs, piled up like shucked corncobs by the field hospital after one or another of the battles in Tennessee; and the sound of men screaming under the surgeon's saw because there was no laudanum, nor even any whiskey. He was one of them, at the end. No, he couldn't speak of that here, not to Horace's little son, or Miss Amelia. Maybe to Mama; Mama was uncommonly strong-minded for a woman. She had heard tell of practically everything in her time, no frail little magnolia flower like Miss Amelia.

Horrie looked up at him, with a child's open sympathy already writ plain on his face, and a touch of boyish hero worship, too. "I'm glad you're home to take care of us, Uncle Peter," he said and then he dashed ahead of Peter as they rounded to the back of the house. The sprawl of outbuildings, the stables and the smokehouse, the summer kitchen and the woodshed—all were baking in the summer noonday. A single horse dozing in the pasture beyond the stable switched its tail moodily; that and the boy running ahead were the only things moving. Behind them, Amelia anxiously called for Horrie again, but he had dashed up the stairs to the back porch and flung the door open with a crash.

"Hetty, Uncle Peter is here and Mama says you're to give him sommat to eat!"

From around the side of the house, Amelia called faintly, "Horrie! Where are you going? Who is that?"

Peter followed his nephew into the old winter kitchen. It was the room in the oldest part of the house, dominated by the enormous fireplace, where Alois Becker had finished out his last sullen and defeated years raging at the fate which had taken away his wife and sons. Now it was the domain of Hetty, his mother's Irish cook and aide-de-camp in the business of running a boarding house. The fireplace had long since been stopped up and replaced with a patent iron stove. Once the kitchen had been as familiar to Peter as it now evidently was to Horrie, but Peter felt awkward, an alien and a stranger. He hesitated in the doorway until Hetty looked over her shoulder and dropped the skillet she was lifting from the stovetop with a ringing like an iron bell.

"Oh, 'tis himself at last!" Hetty cried incoherently. "Oh, to look at you! What have they done! Hurst, 'tis the young master himself, creeping in like a beggar . . . oh the wickedness of it all! Hurst, take his things!" and she swept him into an embrace, which he suffered gladly. This was more like it, and he gave himself over to much-anticipated enjoyment. Hetty wept like a fountain and fussed over him, while Horrie jigged with excitement.

Daddy Hurst beamed all over his dark African face and quietly divested him of his haversack, canteen and blankets. "Oh, seh, seh! Such a sight for sore eyes you be, now you set yoursef down. We 'bout gave up hope of you, Marse Peter. Hetty, give the po' boy a plate w' some proper supper on it, he sho'nuff 'pears like he needs it mor'n you or me." He patted Peter on the shoulder with enormous affection—that shoulder with a whole arm still attached to it—though he had to reach up a good ways. The old man seemed terribly moved for all that he tried to sound so stern to Hetty.

Daddy Hurst had been his mother's coachman and man of all work for as long as Peter could remember. Technically a slave and owned by old Mr. Burnett, Daddy Hurst had worked for wages in Margaret's household for years. Peter could not remember a time when the man had not been there, gnarled and brown like a chestnut, patient and stern with him and his brothers. There was nothing the least servile about Daddy Hurst. Peter supposed he was a free man now, although what difference that would make he could hardly imagine. But it was enough that he was still here, he and Hetty both, wrangling over the reins of authority.

Predictably, Hetty fluffed up like a banty hen. "And who do you think you are to be giving orders? Listen to him, the black heathen savage that he is!"

"Give the po' boy some food," Daddy Hurst scowled. Just loud enough to be heard, he mumbled, "Po' shanty-Irish trash." At the stove, Hetty muttered some obscure Hibernian curse in his direction and Daddy Hurst made a warding-off gesture. Watching this familiar by-play between old and fond adversaries, Peter felt something tight and hard within him loosen. Oh, yes, he was home, and Hetty and Daddy Hurst still feuded.

He noted that there were two places laid at the long kitchen table. At distant ends, of course, which was only right . . . but still. Peter wrenched his mind away from the thought that they were like an old but contentious married couple. That wouldn't do at all.

Hetty set out another place, as Horrie chimed in, "Isn't it grand? I saw him first, you see!"

"You hesh up, child," Daddy Hurst chided him.

Amelia stepped into the kitchen, rounding the door from the hallway, her voice raised in annoyance, "Horrie, if I have said it once, I've said it a hundred times, a proper young gentleman should not consort—oh!" Her delicate fingers went to her mouth, in a pretty and dramatic gesture.

The voices of her son, Hetty and Daddy Hurst rose in chorus, "It's Uncle Peter, Mama!" Horrie had no compunctions about shouting, "Didn't you see him? Ain't it grand?" He had gone over entirely to admiration of his uncle, it seemed, standing at his feet and looking up worshipfully.

"*Isn't* it grand," Amelia corrected him, and her own eyes overflowed, very prettily. But then, Amelia always did things very prettily. His brother's wife was as delicate as a porcelain flower, and widow's weeds made her appear elegantly frail. She reached out her hands to Peter, saying, "I am so terribly sorry for this poor welcome, Brother Peter, when we had been looking for your return for so long! You must forgive us—Horrie, child, please, remember your manners."

"No matter." Peter kissed her hand with a flourish and said, "I am glad to be home, Miss Amelia. I've no complaints about my reception. It was my fault for not sending word to you all."

Amelia dabbed at her eyes with a lacy handkerchief, as she appeared to take in Peter's appearance for the first time. "Oh . . . your poor arm," she said mournfully.

Peter replied with wry humor, "Look at it this way, 'Melia—what it'll save on the making of shirts. I'll only have to pay for a sleeve and a half, now. Think of the money I'll save."

Which was exactly the wrong thing to say for Amelia's tears redoubled and Hetty exclaimed in horror, "Oh, sor, how can you make such light of it? What would your dear sainted mother say?"

"I'm sure Mama will get out her account book and work out the savings to the penny," Peter answered lightly. "I have no doubt of it." It annoyed him, that Amelia and Hetty made so much of the loss of his arm. It wasn't something that he wanted to dwell on, and he wished that people would not notice it. He couldn't bear the look of pity in their eyes when they did. He thought that Daddy Hurst would be at least a little amused, but instead the old man looked nearly as weepy as the women.

Something was wrong, he realized. Horribly wrong. At last, Daddy Hurst whispered, dolefully, "Marse Peter . . . you don't know?"

"Know what?" Peter asked, although in his heart he thought he already knew. "What's wrong, Daddy? Where's Mama?" Amelia began to sob in earnest and so did Hetty. Horrie looked in bewilderment from her towards the other adults, and Peter absently patted his nephew's head.

At long last, Daddy Hurst answered, in tones of deepest compassion, "I'se sorry to be the one telling you, Marse Peter. We buried Miss Margaret in the East Avenue burial ground three weeks ago. Miss Amelia, she did write you a letter." He shrugged helplessly as Peter stared at him in shocked disbelief. "She was that sick, Marse Peter, but she jus' didn't want anyone to know. You know how Miss Margaret was . . . a proud woman." To Peter's horror, it looked as if Daddy Hurst might join the women in weeping.

No, it couldn't be, he told himself, in that first shock of disbelief. Margaret Becker Vining Williamson was vital, strong, a force of nature. As irresistible as one of those Texas thunderstorms which swept in and lit up the night sky for seeming hours with incessant bolts of lightning, tossing the branches of sturdy trees and bending the grass against the ground. An indomitable monument before whom strong men made obeisance and lesser women gave way; imperious and intelligent, worshipped, feared and loved in about equal measure. She had been here before Austin began, when the capitol was a scattering of hastily constructed, ramshackle buildings just east of the river, a friend and hostess to everyone who mattered over the three eventful decades since. Death would not presume... and yet her last living son acknowledged to himself that it had. Daddy Hurst and Hetty would not be grieving so. Her house would not be so empty, so dreadfully silent, were it otherwise.

Peter did not recollect how he came to find himself in the room which his mother kept as the family or private parlor, sitting in the chair which had been his stepfather's favorite seat, with his head bowed to his remaining hand. He supposed that Amelia had led him there, for she was fluttering and fussing over him, Horrie staring like a basket of owls, and him feeling as stunned as he had been when a Yankee bullet smashed his wrist during the fight at Rice's Station early in April. He'd been foolish and not quite taking it in, the blood and the mess and him staring and thinking it wasn't really real. This was his own left hand; he must be able to move his own fingers. And now, his mother must be alive, with her particular and enduring mixture of practicality and affection.

But no; his left arm ended now in a scarred stump a couple of inches below the elbow. He had begun to deal with the limitations and all the tricks and strategies that a one-handed man must learn or work out for himself, to cope with the world and the tasks that it asked of him. He would have to deal with his mother's absence. He had not realized until then how much he had counted on Margaret's cool and common sense, an anchor in a world where everything had come adrift, gone sour, flown apart.

Amelia was talking at him, sweet fluttery nonsense, while Daddy Hurst hovered in the doorway. After some considerable time, he made his voice to work, asking in deceptively calm and level tones that they leave him alone for a bit. They did just that, Amelia shooing out her son. Horrie left with seeming reluctance, looking over his shoulder as his mother chided him in her implacable soft voice. The quiet of Margaret's parlor settled around her youngest son, as lightly as motes of dust swirled in a narrow blade of sunshine which had managed to slip between the drapes.

Nothing much was out of place in the room, although it seemed not to have been frequented much. Margaret's desk was closed, her account books neatly lined up on the shelves above the desk. Her sewing table and mending basket also seemed empty. Always, her basket overflowed when he and his brothers had been about. The hinged cover of her beloved piano was drawn over the ivory keys. It had been a Christmas present and wedding gift to her from her second husband, whom Peter and his brothers had always called Doctor-Papa.

How Doctor-Papa and his brothers and Uncle Carl had plotted, to smuggle the piano into the house without his mother knowing! Today he could have brought in a circus with a calliope and a brass band, too, and no one would have ever noticed—the house was that empty. Peter leaned back with a sigh, absently rubbing away the ache in the stump of his arm with his remaining hand. Here he was, home at last, but it hardly seemed worth the trouble of the journey. Two elderly servants in an empty house, a sister-in-law who set his teeth on edge, and a small boy he didn't know at all. His eyes fell on the little cabinet where his mother had kept her small collection of curiosities and treasures: some china figurines, a delicate arrangement of wax flowers under a glass dome, a Chinese fan carved of sweet-smelling pale wood. There were family portraits and daguerreotypes among them and a miniature on ivory of her first husband, the father of Peter and his brothers, with a locket of his hair under glass. There was a portrait of Horace and Amelia in their wedding finery, and one of himself, Jamie, and Johnny. He smiled, defying the dull pain in his throat, to think of how they had put on their uniforms and tried to look so earnest and martial.

Uncle Carl would have shaken his head over that, for sure. There was his picture, framed in an especially ornate case, in Margaret's cabinet of treasures. He sat stiff and unsmiling with his family, his mother's younger brother, with his three children and that slim, black-haired woman he had married in the German settlements. They must have had that daguerreotype done when they came to Austin for Horace and Amelia's wedding. That had been so very awkward, that visit. Uncle Carl's wife barely spoke English at all and he was a stiff-necked Unionist, which hadn't gone without comment, given how high feelings had been running in the spring of 1861.

Peter remembered with another pang that he had spoken heatedly, indeed had been unforgivably rude to his uncle. His mother had been furious and he had been rude to *her* as well; he cringed at the memory. Someone had draped a bit of black ribbon over Uncle Carl's picture frame, which meant that he must have fallen on the field in spite of his Unionist principles. He had been a soldier, too—and a Ranger, one of Jack Hays' men. Peter didn't doubt that his uncle must have taken up service one more time, and that was just another sorrow piled upon all the rest. He racked his memory, trying to recall when his mother had written to them, and what she had said when she wrote to tell them of Uncle Carl's death. Not much, Peter thought . . . just a brief postscript in a letter to Horace, which he shared with his brothers. So it must have been in the second year of the fighting. Peter dully wondered where. Was it in some great fight, or maybe some piddling little raid or ambush somewhere? Not that it mattered much; dead was dead. And the Vining brothers and their brigade had much more pressing matters attending them at the time. Home had seemed very remote, and its people quite unreal, by the second year of fighting in the East. Even Doctor-Papa dying of camp-fever had not seemed quite real.

That depressing recollection was interrupted by someone tapping lightly on the door. After a moment it opened and Hetty put her head around it to say, "Mr. Peter, Miz Amelia said we was to bring you something on a tray. We thought sure you'd be hungry, after coming all that way."

"I am," Peter answered. "But you don't need fuss, Hetty. I'll eat in the kitchen like always."

From behind Hetty came Daddy Hurst's voice. "Oh, but Miz Amelia, she says that ain't fitting." Hetty opened the door to let him pass, and he entered carrying a wooden tray and a folding stand. "You look tahrd, Marse Peter, an' that ain't no mistake. You jes' set youself in that chair. Miz Hetty an' I, we'll fix you right up." He set up the stand with a flourish, and Hetty proudly placed a folded napkin on it, with a setting of silverware.

As she bustled out, Daddy Hurst winked broadly at him and whispered, "I got me a bottle of fine sipping whiskey set aside jus' for you. Saved it special an' I'll bring it later!"

"And I'll drink a health to you for thinking of it, Daddy," Peter answered, touched with the care they were taking of him. The old man winked broadly at Peter, hearing Hetty call from the kitchen.

"Jes' you sit easy an' rest," Daddy Hurst advised. "Miss Amelia, she did say we was to make your ol' room ready, air out the beddin' an' sech. I put yore things up there, as ever. Might I ast a question, Marse Peter? Why ain't they no buttons on yore jacket, now?"

Peter gave a snort of disgust. "When we came into Galveston, the Yankee provost marshal met us on the dock, and told us to cut all them Army buttons off. It was a condition of our parole, he said."

"My, my, my." Daddy Hurst clicked his tongue and shook his head in commiseration. "Seems lak they didn' want y'all to be in no doubt as to who won out, didn' they?"

"No, I guess they didn't," Peter said indifferently.

Hetty returned with another tray, this one laden with covered dishes and a tall glass of lemonade. "Don't you worry none," Hetty added. She set out the dishes with a flourish: a plate of ham, all neatly cut up so that he could manage it one-handed, some little boiled potatoes, a dish of greens cooked with fatback, warm cornbread wrapped in a clean napkin, and a smaller plate with a slab of chess pie on it. "I'll take it and find some new buttons for it, don't you fret. Miss Amelia might not take the same care your Mama did."

"Thank you, Hetty," Peter answered in gratitude, for his mouth was already watering at the good smells rising from the plates at his side. "I am forever more grateful. I'm hungrier than I ever recall being, all the time I was away. Don't worry 'bout that old jacket. I'm sure my brothers and I left enough clothes behind."

"Bless you, sor, so they did indade," Hetty adjusted the placement of the plates on the tray more to her liking, while she and Daddy beamed at him with expectant approval. "Oh, the pity of it, that you weren't able to see your dear mither one last time! But still an' all, you're home at last, an' that's a blessing. I've been sayin' a prayer just for ye, every day since we heard that your regiment was away to home, safe enough."

"Let the pore chile eat, Miss Hetty," Daddy rumbled. "'Sted a tawkin' an tawkin' over 'im, like one 'o dem mockin'-birds."

"Heathen sauce," Hetty snapped, without any particular heat. "Don't worrit yourself!" And she and Daddy went away, closing the parlor door after themselves, although he could hear their voices as they wrangled cheerfully in the hallway, and then distantly in the kitchen.

So empty, the house was now. He could hear Hetty and Daddy quite well, with his nephew's voice chiming in now and again. He ate and his appetite revived with every bite of Hetty's excellent cooking. When he had finished the last scrap, even the crumbs in the napkin wrapped around the cornbread, he sat back with a sigh, replete with good food for almost the first time since . . . he couldn't remember. He wondered what he should do next and told himself he ought to get up. He ought to go find his sister-in-law, ask for an accounting of what his mother had left. He ought to have *some* notion. What was it Horrie had said, about him being back to take care of them all? Look after them all; that was a joke. He barely felt able to take care of himself, maimed and tired, half-starved and weak as a half-drowned kitten, after the exertion of walking up the hill and around the house. Well, Major McNelley had advised that he wouldn't be fit for much for quite some time. He had looked over his spectacles at Peter and advised, "Something outdoors in the clean air of the country. Nothing terribly strenuous, mind you. Had you trained for any such profession before the war?"

"I was reading law," Peter replied.

Major McNelley sighed and said, "You probably won't be allowed to continue at such for a while, having been a Rebel and all. Look to doing something vigorous, which keeps you out of doors. You're one of the lucky ones, after all." Major McNelley had sighed again and lifted his glasses so that he could rub the tired eyes underneath. Peter sniffed a bitter laugh as he

looked at his stump. Major McNelley let his glasses slip back over his face and added sternly, "You're young, lad. And you've lived through this murderous stupidity, which is more than can be said of many another. You've got the rest of your life and more of your limbs and faculties than most of the other poor lads in this place. Now sort out what you can do, and want to do, and go home and do it." At the time, Peter had wondered if Major McNelley—fat, grizzled and by repute the fastest and most adept operating surgeon in several armies—had ever met his mother. They both possessed a ruthless talent for discouraging self-pity in others.

Someone tapped on the door. Before he could answer it Daddy Hurst put his head around the doorframe and asked, "Yo' finished, Marse Peter? Miz Hetty, she wants dem dishes, if yo' done wid 'em."

"I am," Peter replied, and Hetty bustled into the parlor. Peter thought that he ought to get up, but he still felt tired from the day's journey in the heat, and so much food had left him sleepy. Doctor-Papa's chair was extraordinarily comfortable. No wonder his stepfather fell asleep in it of an evening. Something nagged at him as his eyes fell again on Margaret's cabinet. Almost idly, he asked, "Hetty, Daddy Hurst, do you recall if Uncle Carl's family came to Mama's funeral?"

"They did not, I must be fair to say," Hetty answered carefully as she gathered the dishes together. "There were ever so many mourners; the church could scarce hold them all."

"Onliest fambly was Miz Amelia and th' boy," Daddy Hurst added.

Hetty sniffed, disdainfully. "I don't b'lieve young madam even wrote to Mr. Carl's wife until *after* the funeral," she said. "They were left in a poor way, too. Remember, Hurst? Their oldest boy stayed for a wee while, before he went off with Colonel Ford's company. A fine tall lad." Hetty neatly assembled the dishes, and Hurst folded up the tray-table. "With such a look of your brothers and yourself about him, too! Miss Margaret remarked on it, she did! Didn't he tell us that Mr. Carl's property was taken by the Army – Mrs. Carl and the children had to go live with her family?"

"They what?" Peter sat up, all drowsiness banished in an instant.

"Burned them out." Daddy Hurst nodded sadly. "Miz Margaret, she was that riled up 'bout it. Pow'ful sorrowed, too, 'cause she couldn't pull no strings to get that prop'ty back fo' them, an' then she was too sick, an' ever' friend she ast for he'p had too much on they plate. Miz Margaret, she regretted that mo' than anything elst."

"That's the first I heard of this, Daddy! Why would they have confiscated Uncle Carl's land?! He had that for service with the Rangers, I

remember—who would do such a wrong to his family? Uncle Carl was one of Jack Hays' men, too! Who would dare, and by whose law—some damned politicking scoundrel, I'll be bound!"

"Lordy, Lord, I dunno." Daddy Hurst shook his grizzled head. "There was po'ful evil bein' talked of, Marse Peter, po'ful evil . . . of such goings'on as most white folk would'n believe."

"It was the martial law, sor. They declared martial law, when General Hebert said that all the German towns were in resistance; such a to-do there was." Hetty added dolefully, "We never knew what to believe at the time. The lad . . . your cousin would not say a word about it. A right cagey one he was. Miss Margaret, all she would tell me was that Mr. Carl had been murdered and the property confiscated for his sympathies. And she could find no one what would lift a finger, for all the true men of honor were away in the fighting. All that were left, sor, were weak men using the war to score off old enemies or profiteers feathering their own nests, that and bullying lickspittle politicians. That was her very words!"

"Miz Margaret had a way wit' dem," Daddy Hurst added. Although he didn't specify which he meant, he continued with an oblique look at Peter as he capably folded up the stand and tray and tucked them under his arm. For the life of him, Peter couldn't read Daddy Hurst's expression; it seemed to be something halfway between genuine sorrow and a grim kind of satisfaction. "They say dat men wid masks, they come to de door, take away *dis* man, *dat* man, dis *other*. Dey hang dem all from an ol' oak tree, fo' disagreein' 'bout de Confederacy. Dey say, 'Dis man, he a Union man. Cain't have dat, when our boys at de fightin' in Virginny or some sich place,' so . . ." Daddy Hurst shrugged. "Men wid masks, dey pay a call at midnight. Most white men, dey ain't useta guard dey tongues like dey black folk do."

"No, I guess not," Peter said. His voice was calm, but inside a cold unreasoning rage was building in him. Curious that when Hetty quoted his mother, about lickspittle politicians and profiteers, he should so suddenly think of Miss Amelia's father, Mr. Stoddard of Mayfield and his plantations of rice and cotton in Brazoria. Stoddard, who had been such a fire-eater for secession, had cheered the march of grey-clad volunteers and raised a toast to the Confederacy at his daughter's wedding. Aye, he was keen to serve the Confederacy with his mouth, and maybe some of his money, but not—as far as Peter knew—with his own body. The rage sat in him like a cold lump of lead. Politicians; politicians and cowards; Peter silently damned the whole lot of them. They had roused the whirlwind of secession, encouraged it with

19

torrents of words, shouted down men like old General Sam Houston who counseled against it. And now, if what Hurst and Hetty had to say was true, while true men of honor paid in blood, such low men had spitefully beggared his own kin; that after murdering Uncle Carl in cold blood for being a stiff-necked and stubborn Dutchman, unwilling to take any part in the madness.

Peter said some words then, words which had probably never been uttered in his mother's parlor. He recovered control of his own tongue with some effort after a moment, ruefully acknowledging the truth of what Daddy Hurst had said, and realized that the old man and Hetty had quietly gone, closing the parlor door behind them. Again he wondered what he should do next.

Chapter Two: The Death of Dreams

Peter Vining's patience with his sister-in-law Amelia Stoddard Vining lasted approximately three weeks; a period of time rather longer than he had expected immediately upon his return. He ate heartily of Hetty's good cooking at every meal, and slept deep and restfully at night in his own room. He was only a little troubled with bad dreams and the wistful conviction that he would step out of his room at any moment and encounter his mother, Doctor-Papa, or his brothers. The memory of their voices, their footsteps, echoed all the more loudly in the empty house where they had lived. For quite a few days his ambitions went no further than that, and to do nothing more strenuous than to put on some of his old suits of clothing which Hetty laid out for him. They still smelled faintly of the herbs and camphor in which they had been stored away.

He had wondered why Hetty and Daddy Hurst remained, when they obviously got on so badly with Amelia but a visit from Margaret's lawyer and executor for her will provided a partial answer: his mother had provided them with pensions, and the right to live on her property for as long as they cared to stay. Margaret had seen to that in her usual efficient manner; the will was air-tight and her bank account and investments secured, although— thanks to the war—pitifully smaller than they would have been otherwise. No wonder Amelia was on edge—Margaret had boxed her in very neatly, leaving her with no other place to live unless she wanted to return to her father's house.

On a morning about two weeks after he returned, Peter bundled up the tattered coat, shirt, and cavalryman's trousers he had worn home from the Army. He intended to tell Daddy Hurst or Hetty to burn the filthy and ragged things. Amelia intercepted him at the bottom of the stairs, popping out of the doorway to the dining room like a dancing figure on an ornamental clock at the sound of his descent. Lately she had begun doing that, turning up unexpectedly no matter what room of the house he was in.

"Oh, they shall do no such thing!" she exclaimed heatedly, upon cross-examining him over what he had planned for what remained of his uniform clothes. "How could you think to do so! They are relics—sacred relics of our gallant struggle for liberty and rights! Burn them, *indeed*. Give them to me, Peter!" She took the bundle from him, and to his astonishment, held the unsavory things to her as if they were something worthy of protection. "I will see to it they are mended and suitably preserved, dearest brother, in memory of our cause!"

"Fancy talk for a bunch of rags," Peter answered, nonplussed. He went out to the kitchen, shaking his head and thinking that Amelia was being damn sentimental over something he wouldn't have given to a tramp for charity. Daddy Hurst and Hetty were the only sensible people in the house, it seemed like.

Daddy Hurst chuckled knowingly when he said as much. "Miz Amelia cain't never do enough for the *cause*," he said, "'Specially now."

Hetty sniffed as if she disapproved. With a pointed look over her shoulder as she laid a place for breakfast for him she added, "You best beware, Mr. Peter—there are causes and there are causes. Once Miss Amelia sets her sights on sommat, she does not take no for an answer."

"Most assuredly, I do not," Amelia herself announced with enormous satisfaction, appearing in the doorway—again just like one of those mechanical dolls. Everyone started as she stepped into the kitchen, her skirts rustling indignantly. She looked at the single place at the kitchen table. Her lips trembled with crushing disappointment. "Oh, Hetty," she added, "I thought it was understood—we take our meals properly, in the dining room!"

"I'd rather eat in the kitchen," Peter answered mulishly. His sister-in-law only laughed, a pretty tinkling laugh as she took his good arm.

"Oh, don't be ridiculous, Peter. One can't take meals with the servants—even those who have ideas above themselves. It's just not proper!" Over her shoulder to Hetty she added, as she escorted Peter towards the dining room, "Another place—in the dining room, Hetty."

On the whole, Peter would have preferred the kitchen to the all-but empty table in the dining room, where young Horrie kicked his heels against the legs of a chair too tall for him. He and Horrie exchanged sympathetic looks. Horrie dogged his footsteps also, but it did not annoy Peter in quite the same way. His young nephew craved attention and he was lonely for company, over and above Hetty and Daddy Hurst who treated him with considerable affection. But they were old, and had their own work about the place. Peter wondered why Amelia did not want to send him to school. Privately he thought she wanted to make a constant display of her maternal devotion, for she really seemed to care little for the boy, other than as an intelligent pet who talked. Horrie did not seem to care all that much either, to judge by the way that he squirmed out of Amelia's lap when she took him up onto it, or the way he turned his cheek away from her kisses, enduring such demonstrations with a stoic face.

"You should rightfully sit at the head of the table," Amelia added, as a tight-lipped Hetty carried in a tray with a fresh pot of coffee and another place setting on it. "You may move my place to the right, Hetty."

"It seems very dull without any boarders." Peter took the chair at the head of the table from which his mother had always presided, feeling as though he were usurping a place to which he had no real right. Behind Amelia's back, Hetty's lips twisted soundlessly in agreement, with a silent Gaelic imprecation added for good measure. "Had you not considered continuing as my mother did? It always made for the most interesting meals."

"Oh, really, Peter," Amelia laughed, that irritatingly sweet tinkling laugh. "I couldn't possibly engage in a business as vulgar as running a boarding house! Imagine—all those strangers and their impositions! It's just not suitable for a respectable woman to do!"

"It was respectable enough for my mother," Peter answered.

Hetty added spitefully, "Aye, so it was, Miss Amelia—an' what d'ye say to that?"

"Hetty!" Amelia sounded desperate. "I am talking about family . . ."

"And we're not family?" Hetty answered crisply, and set down the coffee pot with a decided thump. "Sure and the mistress did not think herself too good to work in the kitchen next to me, or bargain with the tradesmen, while some as I could mention sat in the parlor, all airs and graces an' la-te-dah! Not family! 'Tis why herself did what she did, leaving Hurst and I our lifetime in wages and said clear that we should live here as long as we liked! No one otherwise would do a lick of work, Miss Amelia, while the house fell down around ye!" Horrie listened, round-eyed and wary. Peter wondered of he had often observed this kind of scene, while Amelia's eyes filled as if being berated by Hetty were the greatest tragedy imaginable.

Peter cleared his throat and asked, "Hetty, might I have some breakfast now?"

Hetty's ill-temper vanished magically, and she beamed fondly at Peter and Horrie, "Of course you may! Here I am, forgetting myself again, with you and the little lad waiting on me!" She bustled away.

Amelia dabbed at her swimming eyes. "She does so forget herself," she quavered. "I know that your dearest mama carried on so bravely . . . under such a tragic loss! But times were so different, Peter. No one thought the tiniest bit ill of her, then. But times have changed and I am helpless . . ." And quite willing to remain so, Peter thought cynically. Mr. Stoddard's gently raised daughter would rather sit in genteel poverty in the parlor of an empty house than carry on from where Margaret had been forced to lay down the labor of caring for her family.

He reached across the tabletop for the coffee pot. Amelia touched his hand and raised her eyes winsomely. "But now that you have returned, you shall be able to look out for our interests—all of our interests," she added. It took Peter more than a moment to take in the implication. "Mother Williamson reposed such confidence and trust in you, Peter. She had such hopes of you returning safely, and of all of us being a proper family again." Peter gently slid his hand out from under hers, carefully keeping his face utterly blank. Amelia, setting her cap at him? Good God, what a thought! He poured himself coffee, while Amelia continued artlessly, "I would so much rather be guided by someone stronger and wiser. I have no head for such worldly matters."

"There's always your Pa," Peter pointed out. He was amused to see a flash of irritation in Amelia's lovely eyes. "Man of business— none better to look after your interests."

"Not like a husband would," Amelia said.

Peter thought with annoyance, *As if her looking at me with eyes like a cow would make me change my mind—how much of a malleable fool does she think I am? That worked with Horace, but I'm damned if it will work with me!*

"No, probably not," he answered agreeably. "So promise me one thing, 'Melia: let me look over any of the suitors you are thinking serious about. I *am* Horrie's uncle, after all." On the whole, he thought later, he was lucky she didn't throw the coffee pot at him. She was that riled by him deliberately missing all the hints she scattered like handfuls of chicken feed.

But Amelia swallowed her considerable fury, saying only, "I shall be sure of consulting you, Peter—being that you are the nearest to a dear brother left to me," which said much for Amelia's powers of ladylike self-control. Still, Peter didn't think she would give up the matter entirely. His brother's wife was single-minded that way.

The largest portion of Margaret's property was left to him, including the house. Amelia was the second beneficiary. She was a widow with a small son, and with little inclination towards managing her own affairs. Looking around for someone who would masterfully take all these burdens from her, Amelia's eyes couldn't help but fall onto Peter. Against all those practical considerations and what she perceived as her overwhelming need, his disinclination was merely a small obstacle to be overcome. No doubt she thought it would be only a matter of time before she wore him down as she had worn down his brother, with tears, tantrums, and pretty displays of forgiveness and reconciliation. Peter had observed this from afar, indulgently thinking his brother could be forgiven that kind of soft-headedness; Horace *had* loved her, after all. But Peter did not, and he had no intention of being maneuvered into doing as Miss Amelia wished.

In the end, he took counsel with Daddy Hurst. He correctly figured that Daddy Hurst's little cabin, at the back of the house, behind the stables and the vegetable garden, was one place he was safe from Amelia's ambush. He went down in the evening, after supper. There was still light in the sky over the weighted boughs of the apple trees, and the sun went down in a dark red smear of sky and purple clouds behind them.

Daddy sat at ease on his porch, slapping at an occasional late-season mosquito. Peter waited below for permission to enter and said, "I've come for that drink of whiskey you promised." It was one of his mother's rules, instituted firmly when he was small and adventurous: *'Wait until you are invited,'* Margaret told him sternly. *'But why, Mama—he's jus' an old nigra slave.'* *'Nonetheless,'* Margaret said, *'Hurst or anyone else, black or white, is due the courtesy of deciding when and whom he might invite into his home.'*

"'Bout time," the old man chuckled richly, "Come on up, set a spell." He gestured casually at the other chair, before fixing Peter with a shrewd and stern look. "How long you think befoah Miz 'Melia, she track you down?"

"Don't much care, Daddy—long as I can face up to her with a couple of drinks in me first!"

Hurst shook his head, rising painfully and in several stages from his chair. "Marse Peter, it don't do you no good a'tall to pour sperrits on your problems."

"I guess not," Peter agreed with a sigh, "but it does render them temporarily more amusing!" He settled into the other chair—surprisingly comfortable it was—as Daddy Hurst vanished into the dim doorway of his little house. He emerged with a dark glass bottle and a pair of battered tin mugs, silently pouring out a tot for each.

"To home," Peter lifted the tin cup in a mock toast, and the old man echoed it. Peter savored it in silence.

After a long moment, Daddy Hurst added, "It ain't the place, so much as dey people in it, Marse Peter." Peter made a noncommittal sound, for Daddy Hurst had unerringly put his finger on it. He might be home, but the people who counted in it most—Margaret, Papa-Doctor, Horace, Johnny, and Jamie—they were all gone. Of all those who had fixed his mother's house in his memory, and for whom he cared, only Daddy Hurst and Hetty remained. And little Horrie was the only one of his blood family left.

"It's not as if I can send her away from here," Peter said, a little surprised to find himself thinking out loud. "She was my brother's wife, after all. And for Horrie, this is all the home he's ever had." Daddy Hurst nodded thoughtfully in the twilight. He silently topped up both of their tin cups, the bottle clinking gently against each rim, while Peter continued, "Suit me right down to the ground if she sets her cap at some other fellow. Let *him* marry her, the poor bastard."

"Meantime, thayer Miz Amelia be, like a cuckoo in a nest." Daddy Hurst sounded like he was savoring the whiskey. "Mebbe you might have some bizness of yo' own, tahk you away for a time. Might give Miz Amelia a notion that you ain't so much interested."

"Something that would keep me way for a while," Peter mused, thoughtfully. After a long moment he said, "I like that thought. I could say I'm looking for work, got itchy feet."

"Mmmm," Daddy Hurst topped up the cups again. "Got me jest the idee, now! You could say you wuz goin' up to Friedrichsburg, to see 'bout Marse Carl's fambly. They wus lef' in a hard way, Miz Margaret she felt real bad 'bout that. Don' know if they is all dat better, even if de war is ober."

"If they're still in a bad way, I can hang my hat there for a while and help them out," Peter ventured slowly.

Daddy Hurst chuckled again and nodded. "An if dey ain't—wal' dey yo' kin! Jes' stay wit 'em for a bit, and Miz 'Melia, she'll nebber know de difference."

"Any port in a storm," Peter agreed philosophically. The more he thought on that, the better the notion sounded; get away from his mother's house, haunted with the memories of old happiness. His uncle's children should not have been orphaned and left in penury. Peter cast his memory back to Horace's wedding, the last time he had seen Uncle Carl, the only time he had met his cousins. Rudolph—that was the oldest boy, they called him Dolph. He had been about twelve then, now he would be close to a man grown. But the younger boy, Sam, and the daughter, what was her name? Hannah, that was it. They had been a little older than Horrie was now, an age where they might still need help, and from one of their kin. He could not recall much about Uncle Carl's wife, only that she was dark and plain, nearly as tall as he was. But his mother had liked her very much, so there must have been *something* to her. He doubted very much that widowhood would have left her as helpless as it did Amelia.

"You can't be serious!?" Amelia exclaimed in horror the next morning when he broached the subject over breakfast. "Why should you pay the least mind to that foreign woman and her brats! Horrie—leave the table at once," she added. Horrie had barely begun eating, and he cast an apprehensive glance at his uncle. Peter nodded reassuringly. Without another word, Horrie slipped down from his chair.

As soon as the door closed behind him, Amelia continued, her voice rising with an edge of hysteria in it. "As for him—I'd think he had shamed us enough! He was a traitor to the cause, to everything that we fought against! I remember very well how he made a scene at our wedding! If you ask me, he got everything he deserved! My Papa said they didn't hang enough of those filthy traitors when they had the chance—" She continued for some moments, while Peter crumbled a piece of toast in his hand, not particularly listening but waiting for her to be finished. He felt nothing but a sense of weary distaste; mostly for her, but a little for himself and the hot-tempered fool that he had been. His Uncle Carl had been kind, a soft-spoken and honorable man. He had not deserved what had happened to him, he did not deserve this spiteful calumny now, and his family deserved better consideration from his kinfolk, even if his politics had differed from theirs.

"Are you done?" he asked when Amelia had quite run short of breath in mid-tirade. She nodded tearfully, and he spoke in that soft, dangerous voice that might have deceived someone who didn't know him well into thinking that he wasn't angry. "She was his lawful wife and his children are my blood kin. What I will do as regards their welfare is my own business and none of yours. Do not presume to lay down any rules for me, Amelia. You were my *brother's* wife, not mine. For which I thank God, several times daily."

Amelia sprang up, sending her chair falling backwards to the floor with a clatter. For a moment, he thought she would throw the coffee pot at him for sure; instead she flung down her balled-up table napkin. Her face was pale, distorted with fury. No one who saw her at a moment like this would ever have thought she was pretty, Peter noted with a sense of calm detachment. Her mouth worked as if she were trying out words vile enough to express what she felt, at war with how she had always schooled herself to appear.

"You—you are horrid!" she finally spat, almost incoherently. "A horrid, horrid man!"

"Most likely," Peter agreed, in a voice flat with indifference. That was the final straw for her. She burst into a storm of tears and ran out of the room, throwing the dining room door back so violently that it fairly bounced off the wall as she went by. Peter flicked the crumbs from his fingers, and found another piece of toast. He laid it on his plate and was laboriously spreading it with butter when Horrie peeked around the doorway.

"May I come back now?" he asked in a plaintive voice. "She . . . Mama . . . is upstairs."

"Best place for her," Peter remarked, heartlessly. "Now the both of us can have breakfast in peace. Have some toast, but you'll have to butter it yourself." With only one hand available, applying pressure to the butter knife sent it skidding all over the plate; he had not quite worked out a means of holding it steady. Amelia had always made a big show of offering to do things like that for him—another reason for being uncomfortable around her.

Horrie scrambled up onto his chair again. The two of them crunched toast in companionable silence. At last Horrie ventured, "Are you really going away, Uncle Peter?" Poor little lad, he sounded terribly dejected.

Peter sighed. "I'm afraid so, Horrie."

"Could I go with you?"

"I don't think so," Peter answered gently. "The place for little boys is at home, and this is your home."

"I wouldn't mind," Horrie replied, stoutly. "I don't like it much, anyway. 'Cept for Hetty and Daddy, an' Gran-Mere."

"Well," Peter thoughtfully chewed the last crust and ventured, "If you liked, I could see that you went to school. You could board at the Johnson's. That's where I went to school sometimes, over on Bear Creek—that's a mite south of here. The Professor, he runs a fine school. There'd be all kinds of other boys and girls to be friends with you. I'll fix it with your Mama that you should go there, if you like."

"Could I?" Horrie beamed, his face instantly transformed to cheerfulness. Horrie wanted to be away nearly as much as Peter did. Peter could only think that his mother must have had the greater part of raising her grandson into such a sensible and fearless little lad.

"There are a lot of older students," Peter warned, "and you might be one of the very youngest. But if you really want, I'll see what I can do."

Amelia put up no resistance to his suggestion that Horrie board at the Johnson school; cynically Peter concluded that having missed her immediate marital target, she was indifferent to what either of them might do now. He and Daddy Hurst saw Horace's son happily settled at school.

The very next day Peter took the stage for Friedrichsburg. He tugged at his shirt collar and neck-cloth and thought how, sartorially speaking, he had been more comfortable living the tramp's life. But riding in the stage was several leagues above walking and hitching rides on freight wagons. The stage stopped just long enough in New Braunfels for passengers to get out and stretch their legs and admire the pretty town with its wide streets and the gardens in front of the tidy plastered houses. Plants in pots hung from the eves of porches, and there was a smell of good bread baking and a general air of comfort and well-being.

"'Pon my word, it looks as civilized as any town back east," said one of Peter's companions. "How long has this part of the county been settled?"

"Hardly twenty years, if that." Peter answered the man as shortly as possible. He was not much in the mood for talk. The sound of German speech from the folk in New Braunfels reminded him uncomfortably of his grandfather Becker. And some of them also looked too long at him, or quickly looked away from his pinned-up sleeve, another reminder that he was not a whole man. As if he needed reminding, or anyone's swift and unthinking pity.

The place did look peaceful, though, bustling and prosperous in a way that he had nearly forgotten existed. New Braunfels was a place that the war had seemingly left untouched, at least on the surface.

On the final leg of the journey he sat in the corner of the swaying coach, leaning back with his hat pulled down over his eyes, and pretending to doze as he thought about how he would go about finding his uncle's family. How would be introduce himself, and what could he say, after all this time? Feelings still ran pretty bitter about the war, if Amelia was any indication. The German settlers had been on the other side, if Hetty spoke true—and Peter had little doubt she did. He might, with a bit of effort, put the war behind him, put it away with the ragged uniform that Amelia made such a show of cherishing. But things like a stump and a scar, or the brothers he had once—those things pulled him back. He needed something new to do, something that would fill the day with interest so that at night he could sleep without dreams. He needed to put a thousand of those days between himself and the things he had seen in Tennessee and Virginia.

The journey was tiring enough that eventually he slept for real, during the last miles into the hills. He woke to a land of rolling limestone hills, quilted in green and gold. Meadows of autumn grasses and wheat fields, some in harvest and some still luxuriantly long, were stitched with oaks and rivulets of clear green water. Cattle grazed in the river-bottoms, or stood switching their tails in the shade. Once there was a herd of sheep, drifting across a distant hillside like a ragged cloud. The steeples, rooftops and chimneys of the town ahead were embedded in more green trees, like raisins in one of Hetty's sweet rolls. The coach bumped and swayed through a creek crossing, and there they were: the houses of Friedrichsburg closing in on either side, pretty little plastered houses like New Braunfels.

The coach crossed a single wide street and pulled up next to a sprawling ramble of bigger buildings, set in a garden of roses and green vines growing over standing pergolas.

"This is the Nimitz place," cautioned the stage driver. "Last place in 2,000 miles for clean sheets and a good meal."

"And a hot bath," added one of the debarking passengers. Peter jumped down, and scanned the street. It looked like a big town; not as large as Austin, but large enough that it might take some time to find Carl Becker's family, or someone who knew of them. He took up the grip with his things and followed the others back along the street. A huge tree overhung half the road and a stable-yard. Beyond was a large bathhouse; even in late afternoon there were plenty of bathers making use of it. May as well get a room, and spend the next day searching town.

The hotel owner, Captain Nimitz, was a wiry, fair-haired man of middle age. His eyes looked as if he was accustomed to viewing things farther away than the scattering of dusty visitors in his tidy hotel lobby. He seemed a jolly sort, welcoming his guests in German and English. Some of them seemed to be well-acquainted, from the laughter elicited by his remarks. After Peter engaged a room for the night, he ventured the question uppermost in his mind. "I'm looking for some kin of mine—the family of Carl Becker." Captain Nimitz looked at him quite skeptically, and Peter hastened to add, "My mother was his older sister. She's dead now, but her friends all thought that Uncle Carl's family was living here in Friedrichsburg, or nearby."

"You're very much in luck," Captain Nimitz exclaimed. His whole mien had changed to one of genuine rather than professional welcome. "They are here right now, around in back. The wedding is tomorrow, you see. When I first saw you, I wondered what suddenly put young Dolph in mind! The two of you look like brothers. If they're finished loading dishes and gone already, I'll send you after them in the trap." He turned and called into a doorway behind the hotel's simple desk, "*Bertha, komen sie hier, bitte,*" He rattled off what sounded like directions to the pretty girl who emerged from the back room like a doe emerging from the woods and added, "I'll see that your bag is put into your room, if you care to leave it with me."

"*Komm,*" whispered Bertha shyly. She led Peter down the hallway, past the counter, past what sounded like a busy taproom, through a kitchen just as busy, and out the back of the Nimitz Hotel to a yard with a hitched wagon standing in it. Two young women and a small girl about Horrie's age hovered around a pair of young men carrying a heavy wicker hamper between them. The men lifted it with much effort into the back of the wagon. Peter waited by the back door and, as they came back for a second load, he saw that one of them was the German teamster lad who had given him a ride, weeks ago. The other had to be his cousin Dolph, grown nearly as tall as his father, with something of the same self-contained look and the same clear blue eyes. The girl, Bertha, said something in German to the two women, and they turned towards him, curiously.

Peter stood dumbstruck, for the taller of the two was the most beautiful woman he had ever seen in the flesh, a veritable goddess with a riot of red-gold curls around a perfect, heart-shaped face and eyes as dark as morning glory flowers. He could not help himself, staring at her and searching for something to say for one long moment. It did not escape him that his cousin and the others noted this with amusement, as if it happened often. Well, of course it did, he chided himself.

He tore himself away from contemplating the glory of her eyes, as his cousin Dolph gravely observed, "Cousin Peter? Peter Vining? It is really you? Been a while, hasn't it?" Dolph's eyes went very briefly to Peter's empty sleeve, as if it was noted but as something that did not matter very greatly. He spoke briefly, a quiet murmur in German to the others, evidently explaining who he was, before he continued in English. "This is my cousin Jacob—he says you've met already— Cousin Anna, and my Aunt Rosalie, and my little sister Lottie. I don't think you have met them at all. What brings you into Friedrichsburg?"

"Long story," Peter answered, still unable to look away from the beautiful woman. Aunt Rosalie? Whose kin was she? She looked as unlike Uncle Carl's wife as it was possible to be and still be female, and she was scarcely his own age. The little girl clung to her hand, neither bashful nor bold. Oh, the child was one of the Beckers all right; blue eyes, the color of the sky and hair so fair as to be nearly white. "I just got back from . . . from the east and thought I'd look for you. I was told that my mother thought you'd been left in a bad way."

"Not so much," Cousin Dolph shrugged, guardedly. Hetty was right; he wasn't one to give much away. "We're doing all right now. It's a bit scrambled at the moment, with the wedding tomorrow."

"Our little Rose is marrying her brave soldier boy," the other young woman explained, the one to whom he had paid hardly any notice, while the beautiful Aunt Rosalie blushed. "We have hardly enough plates for the multitude, so Mrs. Nimitz is lending us sufficient." She spoke English with a decided accent; a tiny woman with skin as pale as cream, and sleek brown hair. Anywhere else but next to Miss Rosalie, she would have drawn every male eye.

"I think my heart has just now been broken," Peter bowed gallantly over Miss Rosalie's hand and then Miss Anna's, "to know that Miss Rosalie has been here all this time, and now it is too late. Her husband to be is one very lucky man, but at least I have the chance to admire both of you!"

"From a distance," Miss Anna observed, tartly. Peter thought that Dolph and Jacob exchanged a look of amused commiseration. He quickly dropped Anna's fingers.

"I'd ask you to supper," Dolph said, "but that the house is in such an uproar—I think it would take a buffalo stampede to get any notice tonight or tomorrow."

"I don't wish to be a bother," Peter replied. "I've a room here for tonight, and no hurry at all to be anywhere else. There's no taskmaster standing over me, these days."

"Good for you," Dolph said. He looked at Peter with one swift summing-up glance. "We'll have nothing but cold meats and dry bread for supper tonight! Everything is for the celebration tomorrow—but you'll come to it, of course."

"I will, if Miss Anna will save a dance for me," Peter answered, boldly. He thought that Cousin Jacob shook his head in mock dismay, just as the little girl plucked at Miss Anna's skirts. She ventured a question in German but Peter had no need of translation. She was looking at his empty sleeve just as Horrie had. Cousin Dolph looked a little embarrassed.

"Tell her it was to save on the cost of shirts," Peter said.

Before Cousin Dolph could do so, Miss Anna opened her eyes very wide and replied, "Think of what you could save at the shoemakers if they had cut off one of your other limbs!"

Peter laughed in unfeigned delight. "A practical woman who keeps accounts," he said. "My mother would have liked that, Miss Anna!"

"She does keep accounts," Cousin Dolph remarked, "for the store." He hesitated as if he had just had a thought. "And the business in freighting that Jacob's father runs." He spoke in German to Jacob, and the two of them took up the second hamper of dishes and set it in the back of the waiting wagon. "Might I stay and talk with you, Cousin? We can go around and sit in the hotel garden for a while. Have you ever been to Captain Nimitz's place before now? He claims that it is the equal of any in Texas. Jacob and Uncle Hansi will come back and talk business for a while, if you don't mind."

"Not a bit of it," Peter answered. He saw with a faint pang of regret that Miss Rosalie and Miss Anna were already taking their leave, as Jacob capably gathered up the reins. A long-limbed brindle-colored hound dozing underneath the rear axle roused itself and sauntered over to Dolph, who absently petted the top of its head.

"Anything for a bit of peace and quiet," Cousin Dolph observed. "This is m'dog, Pfeffer; means 'pepper' in German." He whistled for the dog to follow, and led Peter around to the side of the hotel, opposite the bathhouse and stables, where roses and the last of the summer hop-vines hung from rough cedar pergolas and tables and benches scattered in the shade underneath. "And you can tell me of your real purpose, Cousin."

"Do I need one?" Peter asked, as they sat down. Pepper settled at their feet, underneath the table. The two of them sized each other up in silence, and Peter had the unsettling thought that there was appreciably more to Cousin Dolph than one might at first think. He couldn't be much more than seventeen, if that, but he bore himself with such an air of capability that he seemed older. According to Hetty he had gone off in the last year of the fighting with Colonel Ford's company of boys and old men. Probably saw a fair bit of the old elephant, Peter thought. He had the look of someone who carried responsibility and kept his own counsel. For himself, Peter found it curiously comforting to look across the table at his cousin and see the likeness and temper of Uncle Carl, or Horace and Johnny and Jamie, to see that and know there were still those of his blood alive in the world.

"Most men have more than one reason for doing what they do," Dolph answered. "The reason that they tell everyone and the real one." He gestured unhurriedly at a white-aproned waiter who appeared in one of the doorways leading out from the taproom into the garden. In a moment, the waiter appeared with a pair of tall stone-ware mugs.

"Let's just say that the home hearth no longer appeals," Peter said at last. His cousin sank a few gulps of beer and regarded him skeptically over top of his mug.

"And . . . ?" he prodded gently.

Peter continued, "As a former Reb, I can't do much of anything. I've been advised by a practitioner of the medical arts to work in the outdoors, at nothing too strenuous; plenty of fresh air, so the man said. You offering me a situation, Cousin?"

"I might," Dolph replied. "You know much about farming?"

"Not a lick." Peter shook his head. "And I thought you all had lost your land, anyway." That brought up another uncomfortable thought. Uncle Carl's wife would have no reason to look kindly on a fighting Rebel.

"We did," Dolph answered with utterly calm and unshakeable assurance. "But I'm going to get it back. I'm not sure how, but with the war being over, it's just a matter of time until I do. And I'll rebuild the house and go home. They didn't burn all of it, you know; just the barn and the outbuildings. It was my father's house, his land, and I will have it back, one way or the other."

Peter drank of his own mug; he found his cousin's certainty rather unsettling. "It must have been something prime!" he ventured and his cousin nodded.

"Rich bottom land, in the valleys," Dolph answered, as if he savored the taste of the words, as if he was looking at it instead of Captain Nimitz' beer-garden. "Oak trees on the hills and cypress along the river."

"Someone just might beat you to it," Peter said. "Some rich man with connections might have taken it up already."

"No," Dolph shook his head. "It's deserted—too dangerous for anyone to take a family to, the way the Indians have been raiding again. I've kept my eye on it. I thought of just going out and living on it alone, never mind it being upright and legal-like, but my mother and Uncle Hansi need help with the business. I'm just biding my time, hauling freight."

"Sounds no worse than anything else," Peter observed, and his cousin smiled, the same serene and confident smile that had been his father's. After some moments of companionable silence, he was bold enough to ask the foremost question on his mind, "How will it set with you, and the folk hereabouts, that I took for secession and served in the Texas brigade?"

"War's over now," Dolph answered curtly.

"That's not the answer to the question, Cuz." Peter watched as Dolph looked down at the table between them, drawing his finger through a ring of spilt beer. "Everyone knows about the secesh lynch mobs, and how the military governor looked the other way. How will your mother take it—me working at your farm, knowing that your father and I had words, before it all began? Or was she a secessionist, like my brother's wife?"

Dolph shook his head, and answered as though he were thinking it out very carefully. "Mama loved the farm because Papa loved it. And she was for the Union because it was what my father believed in. She was a stranger to this country; she took his word on matters like that. It's Waldrip and the Hanging Band that she hates like poison, and not because they were secesh. That was just the excuse they used to murder Papa." When Dolph said the name Waldrip, his face had looked hard and grim. Seeing Peter's confusion, he added, "He was a low-life horse thief and troublemaker who used to live close by our place, once. He and Papa had words—nothing to do with the war—'cept that when everyone went off to fight, the ones that stayed behind here in the Hills were scum like Waldrip. I don't believe Mama cared two pins about secesh or Union, otherwise." A renewed smile broke like a sunrise on his face. "After all, Mama's brother, Uncle Fredi—he enlisted in the Frontier Battalion at the very start and I joined up with Colonel Ford's company. You could say we both wore the grey if we'd had any uniforms at all!"

Peter acknowledged the truth of this with a short, grim chuckle and Dolph continued, "Aunt Rosalie's man that she's marrying tomorrow? He was in Terry's company, up to the end. My other uncle went out to California and joined the Union Army and Opa was mad for abolition. So make of it what you will, Cousin Peter—but it's over now. Papa said once that slavery was like a boil and once it was lanced, all the pus would come out, and things would start to heal. Me, I don't propose to start picking at scabs. I got better things to do." He drank a good few swallows of beer and Peter did likewise, reflecting that his young cousin had an astonishingly level head—sober and impartial, more like that of a professor of fifty than that of a boy only just beginning to shave.

That was good beer, too; no wonder the Germans were inordinately fond of it. He set down his tankard and asked, "So, what do you plan, Cuz?"

"To ask Uncle Hansi if he'll take you on, for now. If you can't drive one-hand, you can handle a double barreled shotgun, can't you? Some places, Uncle Hansi likes to carry an extra man, someone to stand guard beside the driver."

Cousin Dolph looked beyond Peter, nodding cordially at three men who had just come into the garden by the street gate, and stood looking around for someone: Cousin Jacob had returned with another boy who looked about Dolph's age, and a burly dark-haired man with shoulders like a bull-buffalo. At first the man looked like just another thick and hard-working Dutch farmer, but this Uncle Hansi had a shrewd spark in his eyes. His demeanor commanded instant attention. Peter found himself standing up as if in respect to a senior—which Uncle Hansi undoubtedly was.

"Good day," he shook Peter's hand, briskly. He spoke with a thick accent, but fluently enough and serenely uncaring of the fact that to Peter, he sounded like a comic Dutchman. "Hansi Richter. Our house is a madhouse today. We come to Charley's for peace and quiet. Maybe there will be a brawl over a chess game or some other matter. Will still be more restful than home. My nephew told Josef you might like to work. I know who you are, one of Becker's nephews. You have the look, indeed. Rudolph has spoken for you. No need for that. He was a friend to us." At his uncle's elbow, Dolph winked broadly and lifted his tankard again. His uncle added, "You will come to the wedding feast tomorrow. I will send the lads if you do not come willing." The big man's face brightened and he exclaimed "Aha! Charley! Four more!" He lapsed into German with the hotel proprietor. They sounded like very good friends.

So this was the formidable Anna's father, Peter realized; they had the same forthrightness, as well as the same dark eyes. Jacob and the other boy brought up more chairs, and they settled around the table, beaming expectantly at Peter.

"You said you wished to admire and dance with their sister tomorrow," Dolph explained, with much amusement.

He laughed when Peter answered, "Do they have any apprehensions about my attentions towards Miss Anna?"

"Not about your attentions to her," Dolph began to cough as a mouthful of beer went down the wrong way. "About what she might do to you!"

"An untamed Kate?" Peter asked.

His cousin grinned. "You've no idea."

Chapter Three: *Endings and Beginnings*

Magda Vogel Becker had been three years a widow and four months a storekeeper for the enterprise that she and her brother-in-law Hansi Richter had started out of spoils left from the defeat of the Confederacy. Each morning she took refuge from a noisy kitchen full of her children and those of her younger sister, Liesel, in order to go over the morning accounts. Between breakfasts, early chores, and children collecting their books for school, she could not do accounts anywhere else but in the little office behind the store that had been her father's workroom. She sat with her books, pens and ink bottle at a small table under a window that looked out into the garden. Hansi had promised to buy her a proper desk, but—like a typical man—he kept forgetting that promise.

"Margaret's son, Peter?" she exclaimed when Dolph reported that his cousin had come from Austin expressly to look after them. Dolph lingered in the doorway to the shop storeroom, a box of the Nimitz's dishes in his arms. Pepper the dog was trailing him as faithfully as a brindled shadow. "Why did you not tell me of this before? I saw him among the guests at the wedding last night. I thought he was someone I knew, but from the shop! Where is he now, Dolph? You should have said something to me!"

"Oh, but I did." Dolph sounded apologetic. "You were busy with the wedding and all. Uncle Hansi has hired him. He's bunking in the Sunday house with Jacob and Fredi and me." Her son braced the box of china against the doorjamb in order to shift his grip. "He's out in the garden now, Mama, helping Anna take down the lanterns."

Magda felt rather foolish; she'd heard the voices of Anna and the littler children already at work in the garden, but never thought to lift her eyes from the ruled columns of the account books. She loved the garden of Vati's L-shaped house at the corner of Market and San Antonio Streets. She had overseen creation of many of its features: the stone-paved terrace and pots of herbs, the rustic benches and chairs, set all about underneath a pair of towering bronze-leafed oak trees. Those trees alone were all that were left on Vati's town lot, out of the great forest that stood in this place when they had come out from Neu Braunfels twenty years before. Vati built his house and shop from timbers hewn out of the other trees. His small granddaughters gathered acorn cups underneath to make little dishes and cups for their dolls. Vati had also planted a pear tree sent by his naturalist friend, Mr. Lindheimer, and his daughters made conserve from its golden fruit.

Meanwhile Vati grew old and frail in a house which was as much a beloved refuge as the one they had left behind in the Old Country.

The War Between the States had forced Magda Becker, her sister Liesel, and their children to return to live under her father's roof, driven by the provost marshal, the Hanging Band, and Confederate Army agents brandishing orders to confiscate food stores and farm wagons, and to draft sons and husbands. They remained because of the store, which was as demanding as a colicky baby, and because Liesel flatly and irrationally refused to return to Hansi's deserted Live Oak farmstead.

Magda was a slender woman in her forties, with features that had always been thought too sharp, too forceful to be beautiful, but had mellowed with middle age into something usually described as handsome. Always, though, those features were animated by undoubted intelligence. She preferred to dress simply, having more important things to do than go mooning over her own reflection in the glass. Of late, the concerted efforts of Liesel and Liesel's daughter Anna, coupled with pointed reminders from Hansi about being in a position where it was necessary to look like a prosperous woman, had induced her to set aside the threadbare, black-dyed calico and homespun she had worn all during the war.

She thought she had put aside personal vanity when she buried the one man in the world that she ever wanted to look beautiful for, that one man who she believed had even thought her beautiful. This morning she had almost accidentally achieved a degree of quiet elegance. She had looked at herself in the glass that morning and felt a mild flicker of pleasure at her reflection, wearing the dress that Liesel had copied from the latest fashion paper. The new fashion for narrower skirts and long bodice cut with plain sleeves flattered her slim figure, as well as a bosom slightly more generous than it had been when she was a girl, thanks to bearing children.

As she tallied up the expenses of hospitality for Rosalie and Robert Hunter's wedding party, Magda had the last cup of the morning coffee at her elbow; not that she felt the need for a stimulant, but real coffee was a joy to be savored after shortages during the war. So was the satisfaction of hosting a merry and well-attended celebration. Rosalie—their dearest little sister, adopted but no less loved for all that—had married the man she loved. Even when she feared that he had died in the fighting in the east, all during those months that she had no word, no letters, not a whisper of assurance about Robert Hunter and his fate, Rosalie held on to hope. Robert would live and return to her. That he had was a matter of deep joy for her, and no small satisfaction for Magda Becker.

Rosalie and Robert had departed very early, impatient to at last begin their life together. They had headed for Robert's tiny farm on a branch of the Pedernales, some five or six miles from town. Magda recalled how, years ago after their own wedding, she and her children's father had driven away from Friedrichsburg on a fall morning, pearlescent with mist rising from the creeks and all of the promise of a happy future spread out before them. Just as well she had not known of the limits that a cruel fate had placed on that future. She prayed with all her heart that Rosalie would have a long lifetime with her man, and that they would be able to grow old together in a way that she had been denied.

Now Magda looked out into the garden, still thinking on weddings. She recalled her own, remembered also that brief and uncomfortable visit to Austin for another wedding and the generosity of her husband's only sister, Margaret. Now she watched as Margaret's son stood half-way up a sturdy ladder, unhooking a tin oil lantern from a hook set into a sheltering branch. Peter steadied himself with his maimed arm, and laughed as he handed the lantern down to Anna, waiting below. They were too far across the garden for her to hear what Anna was saying. Magda's little daughter, Lottie, and Liesel's daughter Grete and son Willi—all too young for school—helped by carrying the lanterns into the house. As many of them had been borrowed from neighbors, the older boys would return them after school.

"My God," Magda exclaimed to Dolph, pity and a kind of indignation warring in her. "That poor lad—take care of us? What a ridiculous notion! He looks like something we would hang old clothes on and put out in the cornfield to frighten the birds! And his arm—"

"Don't speak of it to him like that, Mama." Her son finally set down the box of dishes, and came to stand behind her at the window. "I don't think he cares much for pity. Which would be the true reason, I think."

"I do not understand. What other reason would he have?" Magda turned away from the window to look at her son, being reminded yet again and with another wring of her heart that he had grown so tall. Her eyes were on a level with his now, calm and meditative and very, very blue in the squarely Saxon features which unmistakably marked those of Becker blood.

As Pepper nudged at his hand he answered thoughtfully, "Papa told me once, of wildcats or some such which had taken a hurt. They went off to their den to lick their gashes, and not suffer any others to come near. Coming here . . . is a kind of den. He can't stand people fussing over him, making a thing about his arm."

Pepper whined softly, and Dolph affectionately patted the dog's head. Creatures followed Dolph everywhere—horses, dogs and cats, even the chickens in the yard. It had prompted Vati's dear friend Pastor Altmueller to make a humorous comparison to St. Francis and his animal friends.

"It doesn't look like Anna is doing anything of that," Magda ventured.

Her son looked mildly amused, "No. It's as good as a play to listen to them. They carry on like cats and dogs. I think he's a bit sweet on her because she doesn't carry on all girly."

Magda agreed. "Anna is the last girl in the world who could be accused of being missish."

"As soon as we take the dishes back to Captain Nimitz, Uncle Hansi has a wagonload of shingles for Neu Braunfels. Cousin Peter is going along, to get a sense of how things work." Her son hefted the box again.

"I presume he will take his meals with us, here," Magda asked. "And that you have told your Aunt Liesel to set another place for him?"

"Yes Mama, when we're not on the road," her son answered, pacifically. He took the box of dishes through the storeroom. Through the opened doors, Magda could hear the horses standing in harness to the smallest wagon, jingling their tack impatiently. The sound of laughter floated in from the garden as Dolph called to his cousin. Magda smiled to hear it. So good a thing, after the blight of the war and never knowing whom to trust, of half dreading to open a letter or the newspaper for fear it might bring bad news, leaping out like a wicked sprite. The war had taken so much from her—husband and home, and nearly the life of her youngest child. For a time she also had wanted to curl up like an animal in its den, grieving and licking those savage wounds. She knew what it felt like, to give in to that impulse, when life shattered into a hundred thousand pieces.

"Be happy," her husband had bade her, the very last words he said to her as the Hanging Band led him away. *"Take care of the children. Be happy."* And so she had tried. She forced herself out of her room upstairs and shouldered responsibility not only for her children, but for Liesel and for Vati. Over the endless empty days of the last three years she had been picking up and reassembling the tiny shards of her life, and her children's lives. *Be happy. Take care of the children.*

She let her gaze linger a moment in the garden. The younger children would be off to school shortly, and she must unlatch the door to the street to the cool of the morning and prepare for another day of business. Dolph and Peter clattered away in the little wagon, driving towards Main Street to return the Nimitz' hotel crockery. As soon as Anna was finished with the lanterns, she would sweep the sidewalk in front of the shop window, water the tubs of colorful oleanders sitting outside with a bucket of water from the well, and sprinkle some of it in the street to settle the dust. Magda bent her head over the books again; had they paid as much as six dollars each for beeves? Really, that was too much. Perhaps Hansi had done someone a favor, paying so much over value in the market, for only two of them.

The sound of Liesel's voice floated across the garden, chiding Anna's fifteen-year-old sister Marie about washing the last of the breakfast dishes. A moment later, Liesel herself burst into the office like a calico whirlwind, wringing a dishcloth between her hands and demanding breathlessly, "Is he here? Have you seen Vati? He was in the parlor a moment ago, and how he's not and the front door is standing wide open!"

"No, he's not come through the shop. Dolph or I would have seen him." Magda corked the ink bottle and laid down her pen, trying valiantly to hide her own concern. Vati had become forgetful of late, and terribly impulsive, apt to take it into his head to walk across town to visit his old friend, Pastor Altmueller, or decide to pick grapes from the tangled thickets beside Baron's Creek without saying a word to anyone. All three of his daughters worried about this, but Liesel worried the most. She had always been moody, mercurial in her feelings. As Vati often observed, she was either on top of the tallest tower or down in the cellar. Lately she had been more and more often in the cellar. "Maybe he went upstairs to his room."

"No." Liesel wrung the cloth in her hands, twisting it as tight as a length of wood. "I sent the boys upstairs to look. His room was empty."

"It's only been a few minutes," Magda answered, soothingly. Her sister had never looked anything like her; a plump pretty wren of a woman, with blue-grey eyes, apple-pink cheeks and fair curly hair that was fading almost imperceptibly to grey. More and more she resembled their mother, who had died of ship fever and been buried at sea before they'd ever set foot in this country. Vati slipped now and again, calling Liesel by her mother's name, another reason for concern. "Lise, I must open the shop, but he can't have gone very far. You and I can go look for him up and down the street. I'll look a little way along San Antonio, if you look along Market Square. Come along then, he should be in sight if he has only just gone."

She rose from her chair and took Liesel by the arm, but as they went through the shop and into the hall her sister pulled back from her, as if she were a reluctant small child no older than their daughters Lottie and Grete, the almost-twin cousins.

"Why can't Dolph and the boys go look for him!" Liesel stood irresolute.

Magda stepped out onto the front stoop, shading her eyes against the morning sun as she looked along the store fronts on Market Square. "They've already gone in the wagon," Magda answered. "I don't see him anywhere! What are you waiting for, Lise? Come along, you said yourself he can't have gone far." She caught Liesel's arm and pulled her out onto the sidewalk, wondering with no little exasperation what was wrong with her sister. "For heaven's sake, Lise, don't worry about your shawl and bonnet, just go look for Vati!" She shoved her sister in the general direction of Main Street and went in the other direction, around the corner and a little way down San Antonio Street, past her own store window. There were folk about, but none of them were Vati; none of them a slender, elderly man pottering about like a gentle, near-sighted gnome. Oh, where could he have gotten to, just when she had to open the shop!

She hurried a little way along the street; no Vati anywhere in sight. The children—yes, send out the children to search, before they went to school. She doubled back upon her footsteps. Upon rounding the corner again, she found her sister exactly where she had left her, frozen stock still on the sidewalk, her pleasantly rounded face now tinted grey from dreadful fear.

"What is the matter with you!" she cried, and shook Liesel's shoulders. "I told you to look for Vati!"

Liesel only shook her head, gasping, "I—I couldn't, Magda." She began to shake violently under Magda's hands, gasping as if she had just run a long footrace. "There's something . . . something . . . I can't."

Magda put her arm around her sister. "There's nothing out here, Lise, nothing to be frightened of! Look . . . Lise, little one . . . there is no one about on the street to give affright." Liesel appeared paralyzed with terror, trembling and stammering incoherently as Magda half led and half dragged her into the house. Magda's concern was only partially mitigated by the relief of seeing Vati, with her younger son and daughter Hannah, coming briskly from the direction of Main Street. Once inside, the walls of Vati's house as comforting as an embrace, Liesel's terror seemed to lessen, although her trembling did not.

Magda begged again. "What is the matter, Lise, what did you see?!" But Liesel only clung to her, as if a child, breathing in deep gasps. She recovered some composure just as Vati and the children appeared through the front door.

Sam's boyish good cheer vanished as soon as he saw them clinging to each other like shipwreck survivors. "Mama! What's the matter with Auntie?"

Hannah clutched her brother's hand as Vati exclaimed, "Lise-love, what has happened, what is the matter?" He took Liesel in a soothing embrace, murmuring endearments, as if Liesel were a child as small as Lottie or Grete who had newly awakened from a nightmare.

"I don't know, Vati, I don't know!" Liesel sobbed. "I was just so frightened! I felt like I couldn't breathe, couldn't move, and we couldn't find you, anywhere!"

"There, there," Vati patted her cheek. "Nothing to fear, Lise-love, nothing to fear. Let us go out and sit in the garden, my dear child...."

"No!" Liesel shook her head, a new spark of panic in her eyes. "No, I don't want to go outside!"

"Well, we'll sit in the parlor, then," Vati replied instantly. "I shall tell you the most extraordinary thing, Liesel-love. I thought I saw Son Carl!" He walked with Liesel into the parlor. "I was sitting and reading over my dear friend Von Roemer's account—such a clever young man—of his travels hither and yon, when I looked up through the garden window! Really, I was so terribly certain!"

Magda stood in the hallway with Sam and Hannah as if she had been rooted to the spot. Vati's voice floated out of the parlor and Liesel murmured something in reply, too softly for Magda to hear. She turned to her younger son. Sam was shifting impatiently from one foot to another, with his bundle of schoolbooks on a strap over his shoulder.

"What did Opa say to you?" she demanded. Eleven-year-old Sam bounced through life, unquenchably exuberant and seemingly as impervious to damage as an India-rubber ball. Compared to his older brother, he was as transparent as the clear green water in Baron's Creek.

Now he answered, "He came running after us and he said he had seen Papa driving a wagon down San Antonio Street and wasn't it splendid that he was home at last?" For a moment Sam looked heartbreakingly mature. "Don't cry, Nannie, you know Opa was mistaken." From the pocket of his roundabout jacket he produced a perfectly disgusting calico handkerchief, which he handed to her. Hannah, ten and timid, still had nightmares about the Hanging Band that had come to their stone house in the Guadalupe River valley and taken away their father. "Here, blow your nose. He couldn't possibly have seen Papa. Papa is dead. I think he must have seen Cousin Peter or Dolph. They both look a little like Papa, from the back. And I said so to Opa—'Opa,' I said, 'that's our cousin from Austin, he was at the wedding party, he's come to guard wagons for Uncle Hansi, don't you remember?' And after a while, Opa looked so sad, and he said, 'Oh, so it must be—you are right!' And then he began to laugh at himself for being so forgetful and running out of the house without his hat and coat. He said he was getting so old he was forgetting everything!" Sam tilted his head thoughtfully to one side. "Mama, that was something awfully big to forget, wasn't it?"

"Yes, it was, Sam," she admitted. Her heart was wrung with despair for Vati's growing infirmity.

Sam hitched up his book bundle and took his sister's hand. With a cheerful voice he said, "I guess I will just have to learn enough to remind him of everything he forgets." The school bell clanged across Market Square, and he added, in the tenacious and cheerful manner that he shared with Vati when they both were roused with a fresh thirst for enlightenment, "Still, Opa knows so much! I expect it will take him forever to forget it all."

"You'll be late, children," Magda chided them. She kissed Hannah's forehead. "There now, little one. You know it was only Opa's fancy. It was Cousin Peter that Opa saw." Hannah managed a wistful and watery smile. Sam hugged Magda with his own rough exuberance and clattered away, chattering to his sister and slamming the front door resoundingly after them. Magda sighed. So much put upon her every day; a hundred small tasks to begin and never any time to properly finish any of them. The parlor clock chimed gently as she looked around the door at Liesel and Vati. "I must open the shop," she said, as they both looked up. "But if it is quiet, I will ask Marie to make up some peppermint tea."

"Oh, splendid," Vati beamed happily. "Just the thing! Peppermint tea with honey, and then we shall take a little walk over to Bernard's."

"I'd rather not, Vati," Liesel demurred, and again, Magda thought there was almost a note of panic in her voice.

"Unless you don't feel up to it, my dear," Vati answered instantly, all calm and soothing reassurance. Magda went on into the shop, where Anna was just finishing the sweeping and putting away the broom.

"What was the matter with Mama?" she asked. She untied the duster knotted over her head and quickly smoothed her glossy brown hair, neatly coiled into a knot under a neat white house cap. She already had her dark calico apron tied over her dress: tidy, composed, and ready for a day in the shop. Magda's smile flashed a reassurance that Anna, level-headed and practical, hardly needed. Magda and Liesel's oldest daughter had always been close, being similar in temperament.

"Something frightened her dreadfully when we went to look for Vati, just now. I can't think what, Anna—there was no one about in the street."

"Indians?" Anna ventured. "Mama is frightened to death of Indians just now."

Magda shook her head. "I have not seen any, of late. They do not come into town as freely any more."

"So your bread baking is safe, Auntie!" Anna giggled deliciously, and those elusive dimples flashed in her cheeks. Boys were enchanted by those dimples, and wished to make her laugh again, just so they could see them. A solemn changeling child, Anna really looked like neither one of her parents but had taken features from each: dimples and creamy complexion from Liesel, and Hansi's dark hair and eyes.

Magda clicked her tongue as she remembered her first face-to-face encounter with an Indian. "Walked right into the kitchen and helped himself to every loaf! A naked Comanche with eyes like a snake, and paid about as much attention to me when I told him to give them back as if I had been a bird twittering in the tree...." She laughed to remember that day, when Chief Santanna's tribe had been camping in the meadows by the creek, and came and went among the new settlers in Friedrichsburg as freely as any other. Still, that memory came with a little twist of grief within her breast. Carl had been living in the old stable out in back, helping Vati build the house. He had seen how frightened she had been, and he had....

'You must never be afraid, Miss Margaretha.'

Magda firmly closed the door on that memory. "I was only apart from her for a moment, just long enough to go around the corner. I cannot see how even an Indian could have been near enough to frighten your mother so, unless . . ." Magda took down her own apron, pausing as she tied the strings around her waist. "Anna, have you ever thought, perhaps your mother might be afraid to go outside?

"Afraid?" Anna actually giggled again. "But she *is* outside, and in the garden all the time. And the day before yesterday, we walked down to the Sunday house to bring back the bedding to wash. What is it about men, to never consider washing the sheets, until they are so stiff with dirt you can prop them in the corner like a plank?"

Magda persisted, trying to stay on point. "Yes, but she was with you. Today she was all alone. It was just for a minute, but she was all alone, and—"

At that moment the shop door opened, the bell on its metal spring chiming gently. "Good morning, Mrs. Schmidt," she said by way of greeting. "What may we help you with today?"

"Good morning, Mrs. Margaretha. Such a lovely day!" Mrs. Schmidt bustled in and set her basket on the counter. She was one of Vati's neighbors, and had been his housekeeper when Rosalie was just a little girl. Mrs. Schmidt also had no little skill as a nurse and midwife. "And after such a wonderful party yesterday for little Miss Rose, here I am surprised to see you opening at the very same time as always! I've brought in some honey. My boys and I gathered some pecans this week, and I wondered how much would you take for them, shelled, if we were to make the effort?"

"It depends," Magda answered. "On whether they are sound and unbroken meats."

"I'll tell the boys." Mrs. Schmidt nodded, and asked for a small measure of coarse brown sugar in exchange for the honey. Magda thought of asking her if she had ever heard of a woman being overtaken by a sudden and unreasoning terror. The bell chimed again, another customer, and Mrs. Schmidt wished to gossip with the newcomer, so the opportunity was lost. The morning fled swiftly, the hours carried away by a flood of customers and well-wishers. It seemed like hardly any time at all had passed until Hannah, Sam, and their cousin Elias came from the schoolhouse, hungry and impatient for dinner. Magda and Anna gratefully put aside their aprons and joined them at the long table in the kitchen, scoured with sand and wood-ash. They had a stout soup of beans and cabbage, and loaves of fresh-baked bread from Wehmeyer's bakery on Main Street. That was one of the luxuries which running the store had brought to them—relief from the burden of having to make their own bread for such a large household, and not having to heat up the kitchen in summer.

Hansi, his sons, Dolph, and Cousin Peter came in from the back, disheveled and wood-dusty from loading bundles of shingles. "Almost done loading," Hansi said. "Let your Papa have that chair, little Grete!" He exuberantly lifted Grete and sat her on his lap.

Liesel exclaimed, "You might have washed before sitting at table, Hansi!"

"Why? I'd only be getting dirty again," he answered reasonably. He pinched her behind as she ladled soup into his dish. She squealed in surprised and slapped at his hand; oh, Liesel seemed quite recovered from her fright of this morning. Covertly Magda watched her bustling around the kitchen at the heart of Vati's house. The big room was as neat as a pin.

Polished copper pots and pans were kept over the fireplace, and bundles of herbs were hung to dry over the hearth, scenting the air with the resinous perfume of rosemary and sage. The cupboard shelves were edged with stiffly-starched crocheted lace, and laden with pottery and china. At the last minute, Magda's younger brother Friedrich appeared, taking off his good coat and declaring how hungry he was after a morning spent inventorying a wagon load of goods arrived from San Antonio.

Magda gathered her youngest daughter Lottie onto her lap. So many children now, with the older boys back from driving wagons, and Friedrich home from the Frontier Battalion! There seemed hardly room for them all some days. Jacob and his brother George gathered with Dolph and Peter at one end of the table, and Vati beamed the length of the table at them all.

"Opa, how many legs does a spider have?" Sam asked plaintively. "Because a longlegs has only six, but it looks like a spider, and Elias says that the schoolmaster told him that it isn't a spider at all even if it looks like one otherwise."

"Not at the table, please!" begged Marie with a shudder.

"Eight legs," replied Vati with great delight. "Arachnids, so they are called by naturalists, after the nymph Arachne, the splendid weaver! She hanged herself when bested in a contest with the Goddess, which is why they commonly hang from the middle of their webs!" Vati continued expounding on the insect world, to the infinite delight of Sam and the other boys.

Marie, squeamish about most crawling things, pushed her plate away. "Oh, Opa, must you?"

Liesel topped up the bowls all the way around, with an extra dollop for Peter, before sitting down at Hansi's side, collecting another pinch on her backside.

With a teasing grin on his face Friedrich said, "Marie, one morning out in the desert, I thought I felt something moving by my feet. I reached down and put my hand down and discovered a spider as big as my hat." Marie squealed in horror and dismay.

Diverted, Sam asked, "What did you do with it, Uncle Fredi?

"I let it stay for the warmth! It had hair like a boar's bristle, all over its legs! There was snow on the ground, up to my horse's hocks, and we needed all the warmth we could get!"

Marie shuddered elaborately, and her father and brothers laughed. Magda spared a look sideways along the table at Carl Becker's nephew. She remembered Margaret's grand house, but he looked at home eating in the

47

kitchen. He talked in a low voice, in English to Dolph, but at ease with the chatter of German flowing around them. He still looked gaunt, as if there were hardly any flesh stretched over his bones. What else had happened to him during the fighting in the east, besides taking his hand and half his arm, to set such a mark on him? There was a truth to what Dolph had said that very morning, that Peter took refuge here, like a hurt animal licking its own wounds and looking for no one's pity. He seemed comfortable with the boys and Hansi. Vati regarded him with vaguely affectionate interest and made an effort to speak English to him, although Magda was quite unconvinced of Peter's interest in the local gossip with which Vati regaled him.

Mr. Zink, who had come out to Texas with the foolish Prince Solms so many years ago, had divorced yet another wife, and been sued in court yet once again. "A coarse, blunt-spoken fellow," Vati explained. "He had a grist-mill here for a while."

"And I think a lawsuit has been brought against him at one time or other by everyone in Gillespie County," Hansi added with a chuckle. He wiped up the last of the good soup with a crust of bread. "Not such a good surveyor as it turns out. Me, I think he would rather fight duels and seduce other men's wives than pay attention to his figures. Can we finish loading the shingles today?"

"Another hour or so," Dolph answered. "We can start this afternoon and reach the Stielers' place a little after dark. Camp there tonight."

Liesel went as pale as a sheet, and made a tiny whimpering sound as she sought Hansi's hand on the table. "Oh, no," she whispered, "no. You must not . . ."

"Never fret, dear heart." Hansi shook his head and squeezed Liesel's hand in reassurance as he answered Dolph. "No, I think not, lad. It's close enough to the full moon and with those folk killed not two months ago, right here in the county, I'll rest easier not putting my horses or your heads within bow shot of a Comanche raiding party after dark."

"Makes you wonder who really owns these lands," Friedrich grumbled, "when we dare not venture out after dark without carrying an armory with us."

"Don't say such things, Fredi," Magda chided her brother, with a sidelong look at Liesel's ashen face.

"Why not?" he answered airily. "It's true enough, isn't it?"

"Yes, but you can see how it upsets Lise," Magda hissed, alarmed by the terror in her sister's eyes, and Fredi's thoughtlessness.

"Well, never mind, sister dear." Friedrich rose from the table, still chewing on the last crusty heel of bread that he neatly scooped from the breadboard. "You need have no fear on our account, or yours. We've learned well the lessons about the dangers of living here. I go nowhere outside of town without a brace of loaded Colts and the lads all have something of the same. There's no cause to fret over us, Lise—no cause at all."

The shop bell chimed gently. Someone had just opened the street door. Magda hurriedly excused herself and hastened across the hallway into the shop, carrying Lottie on her hip. It was not a customer, but a boy from Muller's, who kept the post office now, bringing their mail and newspapers. Now that the war was over, letters and newspapers had returned to their previous frequency and thickness—and of course, running the store alone had easily tripled the number of envelopes arriving in the mail.

Magda sat down in her little office to sort through it. Lottie, a placid and undemanding child, was accustomed to amuse herself at Magda's feet or sit unobtrusively in her lap. There were letters for Hansi from various merchants that he did business with, hauling freight, a letter from Ulm for Vati, from his old friend Simon the goldsmith, another from her brother Johann, Friedrich's twin who had gone to California during the war to join the Union Army. He had liked serving so well, he chose to remain. The letter was postmarked from an Army post in Kansas Territory; Magda's heart sank a little at the sight of it. Trained as a doctor, everyone had hoped that Johann would return to Texas when the fighting ended, but it appeared now that Johann and the Army had other plans.

Magda sighed a little, and kissed the top of Lottie's fair head. "Lottchen, I fear you will be all grown up before you ever see your uncle Johann!" She was in the habit of talking to Lottie, or rather talking to herself when in her youngest child's presence. "And here we hoped, with the Army returning, they would see fit to send him home to us."

"Onkel!" replied Lottie brightly, showing two new little teeth in front and only drooling a little.

There was a letter for Liesel from Sophia Guenther, her old neighbor in Live Oak. She had been Sophia Pape when she arrived as a child with her parents during those stormy first few years in Friedrichsburg. The Papes and Richters were neighbors. Sophia had married a striving and ambitious young man who had it in his mind to run a mill. And so he had, but in prospering he had moved his young family to San Antonio, just before the war. A letter from Austin, for Peter, was addressed in a child's scrawling hand. Another one in Spanish was for her son. That one was from their old friend, Porfirio, who still addressed Dolph as "the young Patrón." Porfirio was no doubt reiterating his promises to come and help when the property that had been taken from them was returned. Magda set the personal letters aside, and began slitting open the other ones, the ones that had everything to do with business. Quite a lot of them were in English. Well, that was what young Guenther had always said, and Charley Nimitz as well: that one must do business with the Americans as well as the Germans. Magda agreed, although reluctantly. After all, it was Americans who had murdered her husband and confiscated his lands. Once, Carl Becker had many American friends, but that was in the years before war savagely tore country and companions apart. With a single exception of their neighbor, Old Brown and his slatternly wife, only his German friends and Porfirio came and wept with her at his funeral.

There were voices in the hallway, the children returning to school. After a moment Anna came into the room, followed by her father, who said, "Good! The mail is here. Anything I should pay attention to?"

"These," Magda thrust a thick handful of invoices and merchant circulars at them.

Hansi grumbled. "God help us, the world runs on papers now!"

"Give me the invoices, Papa," Anna said masterfully, "before you lose any of them. I can't tell you how much trouble we had over that one that you used to draw the plans for the new barn on."

"You can and you have, dear little one," her father answered, pulling up his chair with a sigh. "Several times daily, and the shortened version just now. So, what are they sending us that looks of interest?"

"Practically anything one might desire, just come in by ship to Indianola and Galveston," Magda answered. "And to San Antonio from Mexico." She thought that of all of them, Hansi had changed the most in leaving his few poor acres in Albeck. When she was as old as Anna was now, she would have sworn that her brother-in-law had no interest in anything but his muck pile and his ox team. The journey to America had shaken him loose, turning that plain stubborn farmer upside down and inside out. Then the war had lit an adamantine fire inside him, like the fire at the heart of a coal, a fierce ambition never to be in want or run in terror of authority ever again.

"Aye." Hansi settled himself into his chair and leaned forward to take the stack of circulars from her. "They might very well desire it ... but can they afford it? And can we afford to haul it up from the coast?"

"Oh, Papa, Runge & Company has received a shipment of fine porcelain dinnerware." Anna was looking over his shoulder. "As used at the finest tables frequented by crowned heads and nobility! Mama would love showing that off to Mrs. Schmidt, and Sophie Nimitz."

"Yes she would love that, poppet," Hansi answered fondly. "But how much fine porcelain could we sell out here, when the trail season begins in the spring? Better we sell rope and flour and salt-meat to travelers heading west in the spring. Besides, they'd want good hard cash for fine goods like porcelain teacups, and good hard cash is something we're a little short of ... aren't we, Magda?"

Magda nodded in agreement. "Now, game, pecans, shingles, and cattle-hides ...."

Hansi gave a great bark of laughter. "I'll be paid in money for that load of shingles, though. Pity you can't sell cattle in Texas for anything more than four dollars a head. I read last week that buyers in the north are paying forty and more."

"Uncle Fredi said before the war in California, he saw them selling for a hundred," Anna mentioned thoughtfully. "Each."

"Aye, but they had to ask so much because they lost half the herd on the way and then paid the drovers their wages and fare back," Hansi pointed out. "I never heard Fredi claim that anyone made a profit out of that venture, not even Little Rothschild himself. Still, a four-dollar cow and a forty-dollar market—if there were any way to put them together any closer than California I'd be interested."

"The boys would like that, and so would Fredi," Magda remarked, wistfully. "We did well out of pasturing cattle on our land. But we sold the last with our brand three years ago. The Army commissariat would have taken any others, if they cared to look for them."

Hansi snorted derisively. "Nonetheless, the boys say the hills are crawling with unbranded wild beasts—free for the taking, if they were worth taking anywhere. Do you know what?" he leaned forward, thumping his fist on the pile of merchants' circulars. "I think that early in the spring, we should run both wagons down to Indianola for goods for this place. Oh, we can pack them full going down of whatever we have to sell, or I can freight anything that someone else wants to take to the coast, just to spare the expense of an empty wagon. Vati and Jacob can run the place for a bit. It'll be a little slow then, anyway, and you two and Liesel can take the stage down to San Antonio, and then to the coast and meet us there."

Anna clapped her hands in delight. "Oh, Papa, what a splendid idea!"

Magda held Hannah close to her. "Are you sure, Hansi?" she asked, hesitantly. Suddenly the world seemed too large, as if the little room in which she sat had magically expanded around her, become huge, limitless.

"Well, of course," Hansi answered reasonably. "You two are the ones in the store all day, you know what folk are seeking, especially womenfolk. Besides, we're almost prosperous folk these days. Prosperous folk can venture on a little holiday, can't they?" He added warningly over his shoulder to Anna, "As long as it doesn't get to be too much of a bad habit, of course."

"Oh, Papa, I should adore it," she answered exuberantly. "I have longed to go away for a time, and see something else, just for the change of it! I have lived here all this time, and never gone any farther than Live Oak, and Mama is frantic when we go any farther than the Nimitz Hotel!"

"Then so we shall go, and mix business and pleasure." Hansi's eyes lit with enthusiasm. "And taste ice cream and see the railroad and all these fine goods," he thumped the pile of circulars with his fist, "and pick and choose amongst them. Lise will like that, won't she, Magda? And I'll see about buying her one of those porcelain tea sets, whichever one she likes the best, eh?"

"Go through the circulars and make a list." Anna pulled up another chair, "Three lists: what we have to have, what we would like to have, and what we will settle for . . . and the prices that we should expect to be asked for them all,"

"That's my clever little nun," Hansi said, approvingly. "And one more list; what we'll take if we can get it for a good price."

"Oh, Papa, we won't know until we get there, what might be on offer! What if someone offers us an elephant?"

"If there is a better market for elephants than there is for cattle," Hansi laughed at his own wit, "we couldn't go wrong in making an offer, poppet."

Intermezzo: Magda and Peter

On one particular night in spring, the pain of the wrist and hand that were no longer there kept Peter from sleep. He tossed and turned on his pallet in the loft over the little cottage on Creek Street. He couldn't sleep, didn't want to sleep, and there was no one to talk to. His cousin Dolph was away on some mysterious errand of his own, and Jacob and George were off to New Braunfels with one of the wagons. He was wakeful and lonely, his arm pained him unbearably, and sleep was impossible under the roof of the windowless loft, where the sun had been baking the shingles all day long. He drew on his trousers and boots and went down the little staircase at the side of the building, so steep it was more a ladder than a staircase, and sat for a while on the porch. It was cooler in the breeze that rustled the trees along the Baron's Creek. He had been amused to learn that it was called so after a real baron and it was a man that he knew by sight. That tall gentleman with a faded red beard, plain Mr. Meusebach, they called him in Friedrichsburg, though he had gone and settled on his own place in Mason County, away to the north. That was a man that they all looked to in Friedrichsburg, a man of respect and standing. They looked after him with something of the same awe that Peter recollected folk looking after old General Sam when Peter was a boy. After living here so many months, he could only suppose that they had looked after his Uncle Carl in the same way. Dolph had about said as much, in his own quiet way of not saying.

He sat on the porch, while his arm that was not there ached fiercely, like the pain of a rotten tooth, like a bruise that went all the way to the bone. Only there was no bone—how could it pain him to this degree, when there was nothing there to hurt? He sat and looked at the lights that still glowed from some windows in town, the faint voices from Main Street that floated in on the night breeze. Soon it would be the trail season—the wagons and pack-train parties which would join the regular coaches going too and fro along that road to the west. He remembered that there was a party camped in the meadows on the other side of town, and wondered idly if Captain Nimitz's taproom might still be open. There was still a faint flush on the western horizon, so he did not think it was too late, not beyond ten of the clock, or so. Windows of the houses along Creek Street glowed saffron, and presently he heard the chiming of the clock-bell in the tower of the Catholic church—the Marienkirche, as they called it. Not so late after all, just past ten thirty. It came to him that he wanted a drink, of whiskey or anything else, and he wanted company also—wanted it badly, anything to dull his senses and distract him from that pain.

The spring evening was mild. He had no need of a coat and hat. Rather than fetch them from the loft, he walked in his shirtsleeves towards Market Square.

The night smelled of earth newly turned in garden plots along the creek, and of water sprinkled on streets in the afternoon to keep down the dust. Closer to Market Square he could faintly smell cooking, of roasted meats and good bread, mixed with the scent of wood smoke and the ever-present odor of horse-dung. It would be a good, long walk down Main to Charley Nimitz's place—already Peter started to think better of it. It was not so much the walk to, but the walk back. He came up to Market Street, to where the square opened around him, with early moonlight silvering the dome of that odd, octagonal little church in the center, and wagon tops and tents glowing like paper Chinese lanterns. There were lights still glowing in the Steinmetz house, most of them upstairs, but a single lantern could be seen in one of the lower windows in the back.

Peter considered for a moment, and on impulse turned his footsteps that way, onto the graveled path leading around the store-room and into the back garden of that house, with its great double door drawn closed and undoubtedly bolted shut for the night. He walked through the garden, where the children's swing hung motionless from the limb of one of the great post-oaks, past the little wash-house in its screen of shrubbery. Here, where there were rustic benches and chairs scattered under the trees, on the terrace among the pots of rosemary and other herbs, Dolph's family—all of them, from the gentle, near-sighted old grandfather, down to the little girls, Lottie and Grete—sat and took their ease here on a Sunday, or on an evening after a hard day of work. No wonder his Uncle Carl had taken so to this place, this family. Why could he not find something of the same contentment, an escape from the gnawing teeth of constant pain in his arm, and the worse pain in his heart? Peter hesitated on the terrace, suddenly reluctant to approach the door. It was late. And tonight, the memory of how he had behaved badly to Uncle Carl, when he and his family departed from his mother's house, was as clear and as tormenting as the other pain. He had refused to shake hands, or say a word of farewell to Uncle Carl. Peter had always looked up to him, so it must have cut cruel, but Uncle Carl had only bid him take care of himself, for his mother's sake. Peter had turned his back and gone into the house, hearing the wheels of the brake carry them all away. He never saw his uncle again, never had a chance to put it right.

He had just about decided against going in—he had no right here, after all. But the back door opened quietly and a wedge of saffron lantern-light spilled out onto the terrace.

"I saw you from the workroom window." Uncle Carl's wife stood there, a darker presence among the shadows, her face a pale blur like a mask. "I thought you would waken Vati if you knocked on the door. He is in the parlor, pretending to read a book. But he is actually sleeping."

Peter glanced into the parlor as she barred the door—yes, indeed, there he sat, with the light playing over his glasses and a book lying in slackened hands in his lap.

"He looks very peaceful, Ma'am Becker," he whispered. "I'd be sorry to disturb anyone who can sleep peaceful these days."

"And you do not?" she asked shrewdly. "Sleep peacefully, that is?"

Peter had not intended to admit as much; he would not have, but that he was weary and his arm still ached like a rotten tooth. And Ma'am Becker, she had the sound of authority in her voice. He could have no more kept a truth from her than he would have kept it from his mother. After some weeks of living in the Sunday House, and taking his meals and leisure here, he had realized that she was another one such as Margaret Williamson, someone not capable of being surprised or shocked by much. And as far as authority went, with the household and business affairs, Uncle Carl's wife took second to no one as far as he could see. Even Hansi Richter treated her opinions with respect and deferred to them regularly

"It hurts like hell, Ma'am," he answered. "I can't sleep nights, when it does. And when I do sleep, finally ...."

"You dream, of vile things," she nodded briskly. "So. I see. So have I, now and again. So did my husband, often. Come into the workroom, I would rather not disturb Vati. What would you do, when you cannot sleep?"

"A tonic," Peter replied. "Whiskey helps, sometimes."

"No," she shook her head, decidedly. Peter followed her. Brisk and businesslike, she strode through the store stacked high with goods; sealed tins of tea from Japan, boxes of fine soap, crackers, and dried fruit, crocks of pickles and cheese, sacks of beans, and little bottles of bitters and tonics. He cast a longing look towards the shelf where they stood—herb-tasting oblivion in dark glass bottles with labels that promised all kinds of surcease. "No," said Ma'am Becker sternly, "not those. My sister, she takes too many of these tonics and I do not think they do her good. I have half a bottle of laudanum drops. Should your pain become too much for you, come to me."

"What about whiskey?" Peter asked, as he followed her into the little office behind the store, where Ma'am Becker had her desk and shelf of ledgers.

She shook her head, decisively, in a mannerism queerly reminiscent of Daddy Hurst. "No, I think not. There is no good to come from pouring whiskey over your pain."

"What did Uncle Carl do," Peter asked, "when he could not sleep?"

"He worked," Ma'am Becker replied, austerely. "He worked. He would say that if he worked until he was—you would say— ragged tired, then he would sleep." And she smiled, her face soft with fond remembrance, as if Peter and the store had disappeared and only the past could be seen. "And sleep with his hand always touching me, as if to remind him that there was someone always near who cared so for him."

"I don't have that, Ma'am," Peter allowed, "nor am I likely to."

The thought of that kind of intimacy repelled him. First he would have to reveal his scars, his deformity, and then he would have to suffer the scarcely-veiled pity in the eyes of those who looked at him and then looked swiftly away. It would be so much worse with a woman. He couldn't bear that kind of sympathy. That would be like someone touching an open, ragged wound still oozing blood.

"You should," Ma'am Becker answered, with thoughtful dispassion. "And you will soon, I think." She spoke as if it were self-evident, not merely automatic comforting. "You are a young man, still. And alive, which is something." Oddly enough, he was reminded of that Union doctor-surgeon, who had visited him almost exactly a year ago. What had he said—*You have survived this murderous stupidity with more of your qualities than many another*! Now Ma'am Becker continued, "It has been how long?" she touched his truncated arm with a feather-light touch.

"Almost a year," he answered, and she nodded.

"Always it will take time." Ma'am Becker's voice was heavy with compassion and understanding. "Much more than expected. To heal and to live without pain and to become accustomed to being without—is always longer than people will tell you. A poultice I will make for your arm. And a drink of hot milk with laudanum in it, to make you sleep, once the poultice eases the ache. You should sleep here tonight. Upstairs, there is another bed in the boys' room. You do not mind sharing with Sam and Elias?"

"You are too kind, to take such trouble," he protested, "I should not impose."

"It is not kindness," Ma'am Becker firmly brushed his objections aside. "It is only fitting, to do so. Your mother . . . she was dear to my husband and so were you. So are you now dear to me, to my son Dolph and the other children." It seemed to Peter that there was a shine of tears unshed in her eyes, and now he felt even worse.

"I am undeserving, Ma'am Becker," he answered wretchedly. "I did not part with my uncle on good terms and never had a chance to make amends."

She clicked her tongue disapprovingly. "You should not torment yourself with such a memory as that! My husband—he was a noble and generous man. He would not have held such a matter to heart but forgiven you at once and thought no more of it. He did indeed speak of you after we departed from your mother's house . . . when the fighting began, but always with affection. You should think no more of this. Now, go." She pushed him gently towards the hallway and the stairs. "It is the second room at the top. The other bed in it is made up with clean sheets. Samuel is no doubt still drawing in his sketchbook. You will tell him it is now time to blow out the candle and go to sleep, not so? I will prepare the poultice and hot milk and bring them to you. Go!" she directed him again; nothing for it but to obey. He climbed the stairs slowly. He had never been upstairs in Old Steinmetz's house, and hesitated at the top of the landing, where two small hallways converged.

The sound of girls' voices could be heard behind one of the doors, and from a door at the far end of the hallway came the rumble of Hansi Richter's voice. And one that stood half-open, yes, there was still a candle lit in that room, and young Sam in his nightshirt was bent studiously over a sketchbook. There were two bedsteads in that room. Peter assumed he was to take the unoccupied one. The wall over Sam and Elias' bed was adorned with a number of drawings, carefully done in pencil, pen or water-colors, vivid things done with considerable skill; horses and dogs, Indians in full war paint, and soldiers in elaborate uniforms.

"Your Ma said that it was bedtime," Peter remarked and Sam started guiltily. His other cousin appeared to already be asleep with the covers pulled over his head. Jack the dog looked up from where he was curled on the rag rug between the beds, and thumped his tail apologetically on the floor.

"Is it?" Sam asked with a spurious air of innocence, but his eyes widened as Peter walked across the room and sat on the other bed to take off his boots. "Are you spending the night here, Cousin Peter?"

"I guess so," he answered. "Your ma says I need a hot poultice for my arm and a drink of hot milk to make it feel better."

That made Sam intensely curious. "Will that truly make it feel better, Cousin Peter?"

Peter sighed, "I hope so." He set his boots on the floor and hung his trousers over the foot of the bed. Oddly enough, he felt much more ready for sleep than he had an hour ago when he was in the loft of the Sunday cottage. Hearing a step on the stairs, Jack the dog dove swiftly underneath Sam's bed.

Ma'am Becker appeared in the doorway with a tray in her hands. "Samuel, you know it is bedtime." She spoke in German, which Peter could now understand fairly well, although he could not participate in the kind of abstract discussions favored by Old Steinmetz. "And is that dog upstairs in this room again?" she added with some suspicion.

"I do not see him, Mama," Sam answered with an air of conspicuous virtue.

Ma'am Becker clicked her tongue again, murmuring, "That dog, always that dog!" as she brought the tray to Peter's bedside. Peter very carefully avoided meeting Sam's eye. He was afraid he would laugh.

"This poultice, " Ma'am Becker handed him an object about the size of a ten-pound sack of cornmeal, wrapped in a towel, "is made of sand and herbs in a heavy bag, and heated on the stove, made to sooth the aches with heat, as hot as one can bear it. Rest it against the place of greatest pain. Now, drink all of this." She handed him a pottery cup, warm to the touch. Peter gratefully drank it down while she waited. It tasted as if she had added honey to mask the taste of the laudanum. It seemed that by the time he had swallowed the last drops, the warmth of the poultice and the potion were already spreading, dulling the edge of the pain. He lay back with a sigh, and Ma'am Becker twitched the quilt to cover him. *Oh, yes*, he thought muzzily to himself, *it's working already, I recognize that queer floating feeling . . . just enough to blunt the pain and bring sleep.*

"When it pains you again," Ma'am Becker commanded sternly, "then come to me and tell me. I will make you hot milk and another poultice . . . which will do better than all those tonics. "

"Yes, ma'am," Peter answered—or he thought he answered, for he was already yawning, barely aware of her telling Sam to blow out the candle. She closed the door firmly when she went.

As soon as the sound of her footfalls faded on the stairs, there was a faint scuffle as Jack the dog emerged from under the bed. Sam remarked with great satisfaction, "Cousin Peter, are you awake? Is Mama's poultice doing you any good at all?"

"Yes, I b'lieve it is, Sam," Peter answered, the warmth and the drowsy feeling spreading irresistibly through him.

"That's good," Sam sounded quite satisfied, "that Mama is looking after you, too. She always looked after us. It's what Papa wanted her to do."

"Go to sleep, Sam." Peter gave a huge yawn. There was something more he ought to say, he thought, but he was swooping and falling into soft feather-beds of slumber, as if an ocean wave were rolling him over and pushing him down. The last conscious thought he had was of gratitude for having a place where he could go, a place where someone understood that he was hurting in so many ways, a place where someone listened with kind comprehension and made him hot milk afterwards.

Chapter Four– *Doctor's Orders*

It was a wintry day after the turn of the year. Clouds were as thick and regular as rolls of grey wool, but a shaft of sunshine had slipped through a rift and bathed the hills below in a rich golden torrent, turning the river behind them to quicksilver and gilding the limestone crags above. He and Dolph in the lead wagon, and Fredi and Jacob in the second, rested the horses. It had been a long haul up from the river crossing at Kerrville on the upper Guadalupe, having delivered a heavy load of mixed goods to Mr. Schreiner in Kerrville, who had intentions of opening a general merchantile in the near future. At Schreiner's they had accepted a new shipment of heavy cypress timbers and some barrels of burnt lime to be hauled back to Friedrichsburg.

Dolph slapped the reins on the team's back. "Soooo, move on boys." The two teams leaned obediently into their harness collars. It was beyond Peter's ability to manage two teams one-handed. He rode on guard, cradling a cut-down double barreled Parker shotgun across his lap and a heavy Walker Colt in a holster at his side—in helpless unspoken envy of those having the use of two good hands. Dolph drove and Pepper the dog would ride on the load of timbers or trot underneath the axle, whichever he pleased. All of them, save for the dog, had worked at loading and unloading. Peter groaned faintly at the ache in his shoulders, and the tenderness in the stump of his arm, for he had tried to use his abbreviated limb as much as possible. He had added a fine collection of bruises to the ragged hem-stitched scars there. On the whole, though, he did feel more able to cope. Perhaps Ma'am Becker was right about hard work and hot poultices. He had only gone to her three or four times more, on those few occasions when the pain had been especially fierce, asking for the hot milk and laudanum.

"You know, Cuz . . . this is just what the doctor ordered," Peter observed.

"What doctor?"

"The Yankee doctor—he told me that I should work at something outdoors in the clean country air—but at nothing too strenuous."

Dolph grinned fleetingly. "All the clean country air you can breathe, Cuz."

The road below them was a pair of wagon-tracks worn into the grass and undergrowth. The path fell across the distant hills and through the steep tree-filled valley in between, as regular as something cut by machine. Peter's gaze was drawn abruptly, as a fish is drawn by a hook in its mouth, to a flock of birds bursting up from a distant thicket. The birds wheeled a short distance and settled into a tree, then roused themselves once more, as if the tree was not the least to their liking. Behind them, Pepper suddenly growled softly; the dog was staring in the same direction, on a particular place in the valley below.

"Someone down along the road," Peter said, knowing that Dolph's attention was also suddenly riveted to the birds, the branches they had abandoned and the twiggy thickets beneath. The golden afternoon, the empty land around them and the bare-branched trees reaching up from either side of the trail seemed suddenly full of menace. Pepper growled again, a deep menacing rumble in his chest, and Dolph bade him hush. No, the dog clearly heard, and sensed something more. Something he did not like.

"Keep looking," Dolph advised softly. "Whoa, boys . . . whoa." He pulled at the reins; the wagon halted. "I think there's men among the trees—there."

Behind them, the second wagon halted and Fredi called, *"Wie gehts?"*

Dolph half turned on the seat, and called back, "I think there's someone lying in wait, down below." He added some more in German, advice and instructions, it sounded like. In response Friedrich cursed, good-naturedly, in the same language. Dolph made a sign for quiet. But he did not urge the horses on for some time. He sat quietly, with the reins slack in his hands and his eyes keenly quartering the distant thicket and trees where the birds were most uneasy. Pepper came down off the load and nudged Dolph's shoulder with his nose, whining deep in his throat, as if something worried him.

The horses stamped in a restless manner, seeming impatient, and finally Peter ventured, "That's where I would set an ambush, were I planning to lay for a fellow. Who do you think is down there and what might be their business?"

"Indians," Dolph answered in a somewhat absent voice, as if every one of his senses was focused on the road below. "Comanche, mebbe. There were unshod horses crossing this way, a little farther back by the river. Doesn't mean much—it's not as if there is a law telling every white man to ride a shod horse. And ol' Pep here certainly sees something shifty in that thicket down below. But that's something to take notice of." He sniffed at the breeze, now and again restlessly stirring the trees. He licked his finger and then rubbed the end of his nose. "Didn't you smell that? Almost like wood smoke, and then like sweat and rendered tallow? Just a faint whiff, now and again when the wind blows towards us from down there. There's men waiting in that thicket down below and they've been there a while."

Peter shook his head, in admiration for his cousin's wood-sense. "I'll take your word for it, Cuz. I don't smell anything but horses. How many, or can't you tell by your nose?"

Dolph smiled in faint amusement. "I'm good, but not that good. Half a dozen, maybe more. On either side of the road. Enough they think they might have a chance of taking us . . . but now they know that we know they're there and waiting. They will know that we will be expecting an ambush . . . since we have taken so long, in sitting here, and looking at where they must be."

"So, Cuz, what do you do, when you're about to be ambushed?" Peter felt oddly quite calm, and yet preternaturally aware of every new leaf, of every branch of the thicket and the stony bank that Dolph had been studying so intently.

"Colonel Ford always said to ride into it, once you knew where they were," Dolph answered. "Charge in and ride them over—turn onto their flank and push their ambush back upon them."

"'Fraid you'd have an idea like that," Peter sighed. "Just give me a moment, Cuz. I'd like to even up the odds a little." He stood up, and laid the Parker shotgun atop the load of timbers. "Didn't your Colonel Ford ever say anything about the high ground?" Clumsily and one-handed, he scrambled over the seat back and boosted himself to perch on top of the load with the Parker at hand. "I never heard of a Comanche yet, who can shoot from below through a thick timber beam! If they choose to take the first shot, be assured I'll have the second!"

"Good notion," Dolph grinned at him, looking back over his shoulder, as Peter settled himself for an uncomfortable but hopefully brief journey, sprawled out flat on top of the timbers. "I reckon you did learn something back east with ol' Hood and his brigade, after all—besides how to forage for good food and flirt with pretty girls. Hold on tight, here we go."

Peter flattened himself on top of the timbers, bracing himself as the heavy beams still shifted against each other like living things, with every jolt of the wheels. He could actually not see very much but those tree-tops level with the tops of the timbers and the cloudy sky arching overhead. He did see that Jacob had also climbed onto the back of Fredi's wagon, taking advantage of the same cover as he had. As their two wagons followed the road down through the shallow defile, Fredi drove with the reins gathered into one hand and a revolver cocked in his other. Oh, yes, this was another man who had seen the elephant.

Peter pressed his body still flatter onto the shifting timbers, every nerve tightened like a fiddle bow, tensed to the snapping point as he listened for . . . what would be the first sound as the Indians ambushed them? A war whoop, or the wicked whisk-and-snick sound of an arrow hitting home? Dolph urged the horses to a brisk trot—they could endure that pace for some few minutes, drawing that heavy bulk of timbers. If anything were going to happen, Peter told himself, it would happen now. He gripped the Parker— damn, but it was a fine weapon, so much better than that old Harper's Ferry musket he had carried back then, no wonder the Yankees won— remembering all the other times where he stood elbow to elbow with the fellows, waiting for a shout from their commander, or that first shot cracking overhead with a noise like a thunderclap. Compared to advancing across an open wheat field, this wasn't much at all. Flattened against the timbers, Peter breathed in very slowly and counted to ten, then twenty. If it came to it, he could reload the Parker in the blink of an eye. His cousin had patiently worked out how he could do so one-handed and drilled him mercilessly: he would hold two fresh cartridges between his fingers, jutting out past his knuckles, brace the barrel of the Parker in his armpit, thumb open the catch and break it open with his hand, pry out the empty shells, make a fist and slam in the new shells, and snap it shut. Ten seconds, or less, and in a pinch, or if the Parker got too hot, there was always the Colt. Frankly, if it were a Comanche ambush waiting down there, Peter would prefer the Parker, for the authoritative spatter that shotguns like that would make, close in. He counted to thirty, then forty. Still nothing happened. Fifty, sixty. Presently the team slackened pace to a walk. Peter sat up, bracing himself with one hand.

"So . . . I guess they decided we looked too tough a nut, Cuz?"

"Expect so," Dolph replied. Peter scrambled down from the load, and resumed his former seat. Dolph added thoughtfully, "We'll send word to Captain Inman's Rangers as soon as we get to town that there's a raiding party out there, looking for sport and easy horses."

"You saw something?" Peter asked, and his cousin nodded, his fair hair blowing off his face. Dolph's shapeless grey hat lay next to him on the wagon bench. He put it on his head again and slowed the horses to a walk.

"Comanche, lying in wait. I saw a scrap of red, a blanket like what they favor, just where I thought they'd lay up—back among the rocks and trees. But I think there was someone sensible among them telling them to hold back. So they let us by. I saw a couple of young ones, ducking quick-like behind cover as we went past; just boys, looking to make name and fame among their people. That's how they need do it, Papa told me."

"What else did Uncle Carl tell you, then?" Peter settled onto the wagon-bench, torn between genuine interest and the relief of terror recently past. "'Bout the Comanche and the other wild Indians?"

"Oh, he was wood-crafty," Uncle Carl's son returned evenly, meditating like a man asked a question of mild and academic interest. "The best that Colonel Ford ever knew. So he told me, often enough. Papa took me riding all across his land from the time I was tall enough to sit on a horse. And he talked to me and showed me things, said that I should pay attention around me always. Showed me how to track, what to look out for, what to listen for. Papa was . . ." Dolph paused again, re-settling his hat over the fair and white-blond head. Had he removed it as a taunt to the Comanche, Peter wondered, or some kind of signal? *Come and take it if you can.* "Papa knew his own lands as Mama knew her own garden or her own store-place, now. He said that one should know the wilderness out in the Llano country, just the same. I should know it so well and pay such attention so that I would recognize a handful of broken twigs and a footprint in the dust as quick as Auntie Liesel sees a pillow out of place in the parlor."

"Uncle Carl, he knew the Comanche pretty well too, didn't he?" Peter allowed at last.

Dolph nodded. "He went with Mister Meusebach's treaty mission and met with some of their folk. I could not say he was ever friends with any, but he respected them. And they spoke of peace with the Germans back then—and meant it, too. Some of the Comanche still remember. We lost more folk to the Hanging Band during the war than we ever did to the Indians before it." Peter looked sideways at his cousin. In three months of close association, that was the nearest thing to a bitter word that he had heard Dolph utter.

He was reminded again of his own angry and thoughtless words to his uncle, and said by way of apology, "I reckon feelings ran pretty high, Cuz, because of the war and all. It's something that most men regret, now."

Dolph slapped the reins over the team's backs and answered curtly, "As they should, but men like Waldrip never will. The war was just an excuse for him to carry on a feud. I don't rightly know if he'll ever have the nerve to come back to the Hills. I kind of hope he will."

"Why is that, Cuz?"

Dolph looked straight ahead. When he answered, the certainty in his voice seemed all the more chilling for its very matter-of-fact flatness, as if he described the weather. "It'll save me the trouble of tracking him down and killing him. He ran to Mexico, after Captain Banta was arrested and tried, hadn't the guts to face up to what he done and the folk he wronged."

"Here, I thought the war was over," Peter said when he recovered his own voice. "Carrying on a fight like that is a dangerous business."

"Cuz, when it comes to killing Waldrip, I'd have to get in at the end of a long line." Dolph shrugged as if it was a matter of no moment. "And the war had nothing to do with it, save for giving him a free hand."

"I'd sooner see the law deal with that kind," Peter said.

"Oh, the law!" Dolph barked out a short and derisive laugh. "The same law that they used to rob my mother of everything my father had worked for and throw us out of our house like so many beggars! That law, you mean? The same law that put Captain Banta safe in a jailhouse, instead of strung up to a handy tree or dead in the dirt like the Itz brothers? They used the law for their own purposes, broke it when it was too much trouble to obey, and then whined for the shelter within the law when men sought to deal with them in the same like as they had dealt with others. Look for the protection of the law out here, Cuz, you'll wait a damned long time—if you aren't dead first." He looked straight out at the wagon track unrolling before them, the backs of the four horses pulling in harness, and added, "It's not your fight. But if I ever do meet up with J.P. Waldrip, I'd like to think you'd cover my back. He's a twisty bastard, mean as a snake."

"You don't have to ask, Cuz," Peter answered, but with a feeling of foreboding. He hoped that this Waldrip would stay in Mexico for a long, long time. He didn't like to think of his quiet, soft-spoken cousin caught up in a blood feud, even if he was as wood-crafty as an Indian. "Just for my information, though; how will I know this Waldrip, if he ever turns up?"

"Odd eyes—one grey and one blue," Dolph answered. "He wore a tall black beaver hat, almost like what the regular soldiers used to wear, and he has a liking for tormenting the weak." He paused for such a long moment that Peter thought he was finished, until his cousin added, "I saw him hold a pistol to Hannah's head until Papa agreed to go quietly with them."

And for that, Peter had nothing to say. But he silently resolved that if it came to that, it would be his honor to guard Cousin Dolph's back. They were all the blood he had left in the world and Ma'am Becker near about the closest thing to a mother. Of course he would take their part, especially against a low-life like Waldrip.

On their return to Friedrichsburg late that afternoon, all four of them walked back to Vati's house for supper, their footsteps light with anticipation. They had first delivered the timbers and barrels of lime to where a new building was going up along Main Street, then had unhitched the teams, brushed down the horses, and taken care of all the necessaries. They were cold, hungry, and well-tired.

Golden lantern light slipped between the curtains and the cracks in the window shutters of the big house on the corner of San Antonio and Market Street, looking as warm as a mother's loving embrace. Beyond the expanse of Market Square and the coffee-pot octagonal dome of the Verein-Church, the sun set in a blaze of purple and scarlet clouds edged with fire. Pepper romped at Dolph's heels, looking as pleased as if he had two tails to chase. The four of them talked of the non-encounter with the Indians and of other matters to do with horses, trade, and freight wagons. Peter sensed, though, that his cousin's mind was elsewhere.

As they crossed the street, Peter thought again of Waldrip and the Hanging Band. Most folk hereabouts seemed ready to put the war behind them, for which he could hardly blame them at all. But he had heard whispers enough about Waldrip, and the men from Kansas who had abetted him in the worst outrages during the last year of the war. The widow Feller had been pointed out to him; her husband torn from her arms as Waldrip and the men from Quantrill's band went looting and hanging from house to house along Grape Creek. Surely a man of such notoriety would not dare set foot in Gillespie County, Peter told himself, not with every man's hand turned against him.

They went around to the back of Vati's house, and let themselves in through the garden door. Ah, the welcome of a warm house, with supper waiting and the lamplight gleaming on the brass and china ornaments hung on the walls. Peter thought, with a pang, of his mother's house—it had once been as welcoming as this.

"You're late!" Miss Anna welcomed them from the kitchen door.

"Alas my lady, a thousand apologies." Peter swept up her hand and kissed it with an extravagant gesture, then made a smacking sound with his lips, as if he was trying to figure out the taste of something in his mouth. "Oh, my, you were chopping onions, just now. And celery . . . a distinct air of celery!" Anna pulled her hand away and Peter made a tragic face. "My favorite vegetable—may I not have another taste?"

"No!" Anna snapped. "Your taste in perfumery is most lamentable, Mr. Vining!"

Peter grinned. He derived a great deal of pleasure from verbally sparring with Anna. She had a crisp snap and savor to her wits and conversation. Once one was accustomed to it, most other women seemed pallid and dull.

"Such news!" the old grandfather called to them, from the parlor. "Such splendid news!"

"The property is returned to us!" Dolph's mother appeared in the doorway, her face alight with happiness. "Mr. Schuetze was sent to bring these—can you believe it? He is the brother of our Mr. Schuetze who was our schoolmaster. He brought these directly from the Governor's office."

"And such more good news!" Vati chimed in. "They have seen to it that my daughter shall have a regular pension, paid by the state! Can you imagine? And better yet—that they should make it start from the death of Son Carl!"

"So Colonel Hays came up trumps, after all!" Dolph seemed pleasantly surprised. "Well, it was only right, after all. He did promise he would write on Mama's behalf."

"His letters must have fair scorched the paper they were written on," Vati bubbled. "To think of how he shamed them into generosity just when we had given up all thought of justice ever being done! It was enough for the return of the land, but this . . ."

"So Mama has a nice nest egg." Dolph kissed his mother's cheek while Fredi embraced her, and exuberantly kissed the other. "I guess a Reconstruction government is good for something after all. It's quite splendid, Mama—what will you do with it?"

"Consult with your Uncle Hansi about investing," Magda Becker answered. "And I shall ask Captain Nimitz and Judge Wahrmund for their advice as well." She suddenly sat down on the chaise, clasping the papers in her hands, and the tears started to shine in her eyes. "It doesn't seem quite real—and now that we are making a success at last of the store. I am so torn, Vati!"

"I am sure you will work out something, my dear." The older man patted her hand, fondly.

"This must be good news for you," Peter observed quietly to his cousin. He felt more than a tinge of regret that he could not claim any part in seeing to this just outcome, and also because Uncle Carl's family were not in need of such services that he could render to them now. He had no real intent of returning to Austin, but his excuse for remaining away grew ever more transparent.

Dolph saw right through him, and answered in some amusement, "You do not think you might be well rid of our company and hospitality? Never! Don't you remember what we talked of, when you first came—about my father's land? Mama wishes to remain here with my sisters, and Sam. I think she has no real liking for returning to the farm. She loved it so only because of Papa. She will let me take it over. You and Fredi and I will run it, with the help of our old stock-man, Porfirio. No slipping away to a life of city luxury for you!" he teased his cousin, and then added thoughtfully, "Besides, Opa is getting very feeble. Everyone always looked to Mama to see after him."

Peter was quite pleased. He had no interest in being within proximity of Amelia—as fond as he was of Hetty, Daddy Hurst and little Horrie. "What about Miss Anna, and her mother, taking care of Vati? They are not eager to depart such a pleasant roof, either."

It seemed that a shadow fell over Dolph's normal serenity, for Peter added, "Is there something the matter, Cuz?"

After a moment his cousin answered, "Aunt Lise has had some pretty odd fancies and spells, lately. Mama and I and Anna—we do not think her incapable, mind—but she does not always seem equal to coping with Opa."

"He seems fit enough," Peter answered. "And not half as absentminded as Doctor-Papa. That's what we called my stepfather," He began to tell the story of how his stepfather returned after a round of medical calls, having forgotten successively his hat, coat, stethoscope, medical bag, and his horse. Before he finished the story, Uncle Hansi had joined them, a burly presence hanging up his good cloth overcoat from the ornate coat rack in the hall, jovially complaining that supper wasn't ready yet. Of course, he had to be told the good news, with everyone competing to tell him. Vati brought out some bottles of homemade mustang-grape wine for a toast.

The evening became quite merry indeed. Peter thought no more about the matter, for it seemed to be the accepted thing that it would be the young men who would return to the ruined house on the Becker lands.

"I wish you did not need to travel so often," Liesel Steinmetz Richter said to her husband later that evening. "I feel so much safer when you are present, my heart." She was already in bed, having planned this beforehand; that he should see her, plump and pretty under the candle-light. Her hair lay in loose ringlets across the snow-white feather pillow at her back. The strings of her shift were loosened so that the delicate fabric cupped her breasts. She had dabbled rosewater behind her ears and in the shadowy valley between her breasts. It pleased her to watch her husband, pulling his shirt out of the waistband of his trousers, standing before the washstand. The single lamp cast his shadow on the wall behind him as he washed.

Liesel had adored her stolid, bull-shouldered husband since she was a small girl in Albeck, and he was a stocky boy more than a little interested in her clever but plain older sister. How Magda could have been scornful of his interest and seemingly unaware of Hansi's qualities—qualities that Liesel counted up to herself as if they were a treasury—was a mystery beyond all rationality. A mystery and a miracle too; *"That blockhead of a boy"* Magda had called him, when she was sixteen and Liesel two years younger. Perhaps he had only asked Magda to marry him out of courtesy, she being the oldest, but his affections then turned to Liesel.

Liesel had desperately hoped and prayed they would, had worked the folk-spells and charms that would bring him to her. She had dared even more than that, in the hayloft of Vati's old farm in Albeck, things that maiden girls weren't supposed to do or even know about. And perhaps girls like Magda, with their heads in books and dreams, managed not to know about them; but Liesel did, and bound Hansi to her with thin and shining bands of steel and affection and vows spoken in the church. Nine children had she borne to him since, seven of them still living and all but Anna, the oldest, being born in America. Liesel supposed, when she thought about it, that her children must be counted as Americans. The older boys, Jacob, George and Elias, and their sister Marie—they were all nearly grown, working at a trade with the freight wagons or in the shop, helping their father, their aunt and grandfather.

She dearly cherished her two youngest, five-year-old Willi and three-year-old Grete. Liesel worried about them the most—so little, so many dangers to little children lurking around every corner! Accidents, wild animals and raiding Indians, and the sicknesses like diphtheria . . . she had lost a child to that plague, dear little Christian who died gasping for breath in spite of all that could be done. Liesel's pulse began to hammer in her throat—no, she told herself desperately, do not think on that.

The children, they were asleep in their beds, in the rooms they shared with their siblings and cousins. Vati and the oldest boys, Fredi and that scar-faced nephew of Magda's husband, they were downstairs in the house. She could hear their muted voices, downstairs in the parlor; there was naught to fear. Her husband had come upstairs to her, leaving whatever interesting conversation they were having. Business, Liesel supposed. Men's business. She was no more interested in that than Hansi was interested in cheese-making, or polishing the lamp chimneys until they gleamed like diamonds.

Now as he splashed water from the pitcher into the basin, Hansi answered terse and plain, "If we had returned to my farm, Lise, I would not need to travel." Liesel's heart felt as if it would stop. He was angry with her, she could tell. He continued, calm and implacable, "But since you will not countenance living out in Live Oak, then I must do something to earn our keeping. You cannot have it both ways, Lise; either we remain under your father's roof and I am away with the wagons for weeks and nights at a time, or we live under mine—out in the country, among all those Indians and wild animals and all those things you spend so much of your life fearing!"

"Hansi," her voice sounded as if a hand clutched her throat, half-strangling her words and her breath. "Oh, dearest, don't ask that of me, I cannot bear it! You promised that we should be safe, the children and I!"

"So I have not asked it of you," Hansi answered, his voice muffled as he toweled away water from his face, his shoulders, and waves of dark hair that still fell so thickly over his brow and ears. It was not for her own Hansi to grow bald with a pitiful straggle across his crown, like other men. "I let you have your way in this, Lise—even if the war is over, and we could return to our house—remember, the house I built for you, just as you would have it? But no, you want to stay in town, in your father's house! It's as if we had never come away from Albeck and dreamed of lands of our own!"

Liesel quailed against the pillows; he was angry, angry with her, and she couldn't bear that. She had never been able to endure Hansi's anger, or even Vati's—slight and ineffectual as Vati's displeasure usually proved to be. Such terrified her . . . but not as much as the emptiness of the sky and the endless hills all around; there was no way to cajole the sky, the wilderness, the wild Indians. She had always been able to use her wiles on Hansi and rest of her family.

"Hansi, heart's love," she begged tearfully, "oh, do not be so unkind to me, I only meant . . ."

"I know what you meant, Lise." Hansi neatly folded the towel and replaced it on the washstand, his voice sternly controlled. "Having made your choice you should not constantly complain to me of the results. It does you no credit."

"I am sorry, dearest." Hot tears gathered, spilled over her cheeks. "Truly, I don't know why I say the things I do, sometimes."

70

"I don't know either, Lise," Hansi answered patiently. She felt the bed shift slightly as he sat on the edge of it, next to her. He touched her cheek, and wound a tendril of her hair around his fingers. "But you are crying as if you are a child about to be punished and I am nearly out of patience with it." With that touch, she forgot all intent of what she had wanted when she crept upstairs to make herself ready for him. She had no wish for his lusty affections now and he was in no mood for them either. Liesel had been married long enough to be a fair judge of Hansi's desires. She sobbed in his arms while he held her close, and when she finally had done with tears, she saw that he had tucked his shirt in again and kept on his boots. That nearly set her off again, with a pain in her heart from dread, wondering if her husband's affection might be slipping away from her. What could she depend on in this uncertain and capricious country, if she could not depend on Hansi?

"Stay with me," she begged in a whisper, "don't go away from me. Not now!"

But he shook his head and answered, "I must talk to the lads, Lise—while I have a chance and they are here. Fredi and Dolph are all afire with this news about Brother Carl's land, but George and I have business in Neu Braunfels tomorrow. I'll be back upstairs soon enough, Liesel-love—dry your eyes and go to sleep. Shall I leave the lamp burning, until then?" He kissed her gently and settled the covers over her shoulders, seeming to disregard the hand that clung to his. "I wish you would consider changing your mind about accompanying us to the coast," he added. He reached towards the lamp, adjusting the little wheel that held the wick with deft strong fingers. "Your sister and the girls are so looking forward to it, Lise . . . and seeing Sophie Guenther and the children. Her husband says that San Antonio may as well be next to Friedrichsburg, for there are so many German enterprises there. You would feel quite at home, if you could but consent to come with us." And he smiled at her, a look that had always melted her resistance, that had challenged her ever since she was a little girl in short skirts and Hansi dared her to climb the tallest tree in Vati's garden.

"I can't." Liesel felt as if her lips were suddenly ice cold, incapable of forming words, and Hansi sighed again. Putting her hand aside from his, he tucked the covers over her as if she were one of the children. "Who would see to Willi and Grete, to Vati and the house?" she pleaded.

He turned away saying, "Ah, Lise—the children could come with us and Mrs. Schmidt can see to the house. We've talked on this a hundred times before and you have the same old threadbare reasons. You care not for travel and adventure and now I have a great taste for it, since it is presently my business. Go to sleep, Liesel-my-heart, I don't know how long our plans must keep me from bed."

And he went softly from the room, closing the door after himself. Liesel pulled the coverlet close about her and lay with her arm across the place where he would be, listening to the voices downstairs in the parlor, hearing the low rumble of Hansi's voice as he rejoined them. What must they think of that, or did they think aught of it at all? Liesel wept silently into her pillow and resolved to do something. She had to face up to it, to lift her chin as Magda did and take her fears in hand. Surely it could not be so hard, this thing that Hansi wanted of her, what everyone expected of her, that which she had not so long since thought nothing of doing. Town was perfectly safe.

Liesel schooled herself to breathe quietly, told herself the children were perfectly safe in their beds. Perhaps she did not need to take another of those bracing tonics, those strange-tasting dark brews that sometimes helped to damp down her fears, made her feel merry and giggling again.

Tomorrow, she decided, *I'll walk out tomorrow. I'll prove it to myself, and then I'll tell Hansi that I'll come with him on this grand adventure to the city. It won't be so bad; Magda is coming. Maybe we will see something nice in the shops, and I can make her put on something other than that eternal black that she always wears now.*

Yes. Think of bolts of pretty fabric, shimmering silk and gaily printed calicos, the rolls of cobweb-fine lace and silk ribbons that a mercer in the big city would have in stock, think of buttons as bright as jewels. Think of that and not the other . . . Liesel fell asleep at last, rousing only briefly into wakefulness when Hansi at last came to bed. She curled herself against his comforting presence as much as a cat settles itself against a new source of warmth, and drifted away into even deeper slumber.

She woke in the morning, still resolved upon the task she had set for herself. All things seemed possible in the morning, a bright winter morning such as this: the air crisp and cold, the sky above scrubbed clean of clouds and clear, clear blue. Every leaf and blade of grass in the garden was rimed with a crisp edging of frost.

She looked around the door to the shop, where Anna was busy with a broom and duster. "I'm taking some things to the Sunday House for the lads," she said. "Some bread and sausage and cheese, to have for when they hunger but not feel like walking over here, late at night."

"Very well, Mama," Anna replied. Liesel saw the brief flash of surprise on her face. "Did you want me to come with you?"

"No need," Liesel answered, although her heart gave a small skip in her chest. No, that was the whole point of this errand; to take the basket and walk out of the house, through the garden and . . .

It was perfectly safe, Liesel told herself. There was nothing out there, not in the streets, not in Market Square. The few Indians who visited came to trade, harmless wanderers selling baskets of pecans, or trading dried meat and cured skins. Those masked men of the dreaded Hanging Band, they were also gone, fled into Mexico or locked in a stone jail in another county. The yearly trail season, bringing crowds of strangers with their pack trains and wagons bound for California and the far west—that would not open for months yet. There was no one, nothing to fear in venturing outside.

Liesel tied her bonnet ribbons under her chin; fuchsia-pink silk, a casual present from Magda who had gotten them as a gift before her widowing but thriftily held on to everything for which there might be an eventual use. She looked at herself in the mirror of the elaborate hall rack. Mr. Tatsch had made it to Hansi's order when the freighting business began to prosper, a splendid thing in the latest fashion, with a rack for umbrellas and walking sticks, brass hooks, and an oval mirror in the very center. Hansi had paid so much money for it and brought it home as proud as a boy with a pretty fairing for the girl he loved. Liesel thought on this every time she looked at the fair polished wood, the brass and the mirror.

The woman whose face looked back at her in the mirror seemed a stranger, a pale stranger with a strained expression in her eyes. Liesel pinched her cheeks to bring out something of their customary pink and drew her heaviest shawl around her shoulders. There, that was better.

"I'm going now," she called tremulously into the shop and passed out through the garden door onto the terrace at the back of Vati's house. The trees lifted their bare grey limbs towards the sky, the rose bushes presented nothing but a clutch of bare, thorny sticks, and the vegetable garden beyond the bathhouse was bare and dug over, awaiting spring planting. Magda's pots of rosemary offered the only splash of green against the stone pavers. Liesel drew her shawl ever closer against the chill of the morning and the frost breathing off the stone. She walked briskly across the terrace, past Vati's cherished pear tree, and the limp and dry remnants of last year's bean bushes and squash plants strewn across the frozen ground.

George and Jacob busied themselves with the horses in the stable-yard beyond, along with Fredi and Peter Vining. Liesel's pace slowed just a trifle as her eyes followed after her sons. Such fine, sturdy boys, hers and Hansi's pride! They were not as clever as sharp-tongued Anna, but they worked so hard for their father's business interests. She wished those interests did not have to take them away so often . . . no, not that thought. It felt as if a cold hand squeezed her heart, made her short of breath.

Willi, the youngest of them all, was perched on a pile of timber beams, chattering like a magpie to his indulgent older brothers and cousin. She waved to the boys and called, "Willi, do not be a bother, when the men have work to do!"

"I'm being a help, Mama," Willi called back.

Dolph added, "Not to worry, Auntie, we'll get some hard work out of this little teamster, yet!"

Liesel nodded, although she wished she could tell Willi to come away from the busy stable-yard. He had overcome his babyish timidity in the last year or so. Now he followed his older cousins and his brothers everywhere, among the horses and wagons and the talk of men and their doings.

Past the new part of the house, the extension of the shop and Vati's old workroom, the new plaster crisp and still as white as chalk. Hansi and the boys had laid out flat stones set in white river gravel to make a pathway free of mud, going out towards Market Street. Liesel walked a little faster, wishing this errand to be already over and done with.

"Not that far," Liesel whispered to herself. "Not that far." Just along Market Street, down towards the Baron's Creek, then along to the Richter's town plot, where she and Hansi had first planted a vegetable garden in soil so rich and soft that a man could easily put an arm into it up to the shoulder. Later Hansi had built a tiny cottage for them to use when they came to town for Sunday services at the Verein-Church.

She briskly passed their next-door neighbors' house, then the one after that; all very well so far, and her spirits rose. She had walked from Vati's house to the creek thousands of times, bringing food to her husband when he was living in the fields and woods, evading those who would try and force him to serve in the Confederate army.

And just as she passed the fourth house along, Liesel shuddered and suddenly anxiety leapt through that widening crack of her resolve; fear, pitiless and clawed like a gigantic cat, striking without mercy or warning. She couldn't breathe, couldn't move. Her chest hurt, and it seemed as though an endless roll of thunder drowned out every sound. She made a tiny, pitiful moan, as feeble as a newborn kitten mewing. The whole world spun violently around her, sky and houses and the tall bare trees lining Baron's

Creek. The street itself reared up and smashed into her and Liesel went spinning down into roaring darkness for a long, long time.

When she floated up to the surface of awareness, it was to a murmur of voices in the next room: Vati, her sister Magda, Fredi, and Doctor Keidel. Their voices all merged together, but it hardly mattered to her, because Hansi was there with her. He held both her hands, entirely enveloped in his large one. She lay on the chaise in the parlor, still wrapped in her shawl, although someone had thought to take off her bonnet.

"… Nerves," she heard Doctor Keidel say, and added as if he were quoting someone, "Who can minister to a mind diseased…?"

"… Not anything of the sort!" Magda answered indignantly.

Vati chimed in, "… not of the most even temper, assuredly…."

"I'm not going mad," Liesel quavered, "am I, Hansi? Tell me I'm not … it's just that things frighten me so, things without reason!"

"Oh, Lise-love," Hansi rumbled comfortingly, "you should have told us…."

"I didn't think you would understand," Liesel answered, her voice wobbling with a mixture of reaction and relief. She ached all over, as if she had been beaten. Her hands, her shoulder, even her face—all bruised where she had fallen, fallen so hard on the hard ground. "Everyone says there is nothing to fear, but I can't help it. Suddenly I feel like something is choking me. It's a waking nightmare … the sky is too big and I am as tiny as an insect that you squash with your thumb without even noticing it."

"How long have you felt like this, my heart? Shush, love, don't cry again."

"Since we buried Christian." Liesel gulped. "It seemed to happen a very little at first. I was better when you came home, for at least a little while, but then it came on again. I tried to prove that I was the master of such fancies, but . . . "

"Such a fancy as would have killed you, dear-heart," Hansi sighed and ran his free hand through his hair, setting it wildly astray. "Doctor Keidel told us that such continued agitation would over-exert your system. He would prescribe another tonic, but that he fears such would not have nearly as good effect as a quiet life! And now I understand; you should not force yourself into such excursions, Lise. As your husband, I forbid it. If you value a home life, a home life you shall have. I didn't realize what I was asking of you, until this moment."

"Truly?" Liesel breathed, hardly daring to believe. It was as if a tremendously heavy weight had fallen off of her shoulders, the burden of denial and deceit, no longer having to pretend. No one would be asking of her what was not in her power to provide. "You would not ask me to go to the coast with you, Hansi?"

"No, Liesel-my-heart." And he sighed again. "I don't see how you would want to live your entire life between four walls, but if that is what you wish and what your continued good health demands, then that is what you should have."

"It is not much, when you are with me," Liesel ventured, "to venture a little way . . . perhaps to the Nimitzes, or out into our garden."

"Might I then persuade you to take the water cure some day?" Hansi asked. He clasped her hands again, "Oh, do not look so, Liesel-my-heart. That would only be if you wished it, and I promise I would accompany you every step of the way. Be easy in your heart, love—I will not ever force you to go against your feelings."

"Promise, Hansi?" Liesel nearly wept with gratitude; her faith in Hansi's devotion restored.

"I promise." Hansi enfolded her in a rough but fond embrace, repeating solemnly, "I promise, Liesel-my-heart. So I promised when we married, so I promise now."

Chapter Five: The Young Patrón

"So what was that all about, Cuz?" Peter asked quietly. Doctor Keidel's trap had rolled away from the front door of the house on Market Street. Peter had seen nothing much other than Liesel, in her cherry-red Turkey-weave shawl, walking around the end of the house, past the stable yard. He and Dolph had been busy loading supplies for a long scout to the Beckers' long-abandoned farmhouse, a project which Dolph had long had his heart set on. They had alternately been hindered and helped in this by the efforts of Hansi's youngest son, an agreeable little lad who had just lost his front baby teeth. When he heard a man shouting, farther down the street some minutes later, he'd thought nothing much of it, until Fredi flung aside an armful of tack with a mighty oath and vaulted the corral fence in one leap, followed by the younger boys.

"Just Auntie Liesel's megrims," Dolph answered, quietly, although he had been close at his uncle Fredi's back. "She fainted from fright, in the middle of the street. Mama says she's been more and more peculiar ever since our cousin Christian died of the diphtheria, especially with Uncle Hansi being away and all."

"Christian . . . which one was he?" Peter asked, mentally running his mind over the tally of the Richter offspring, all the stair-steps between the delectable Miss Anna down to the solemn toddler Grete.

"Halfway between Eli and Willi," Dolph answered. "Just about all the children in town were sick from it then. Madame Keidel drove the doctor's trap from house to house so he could sleep between house calls. Mama says that Auntie Liesel has always taken grief and misfortune hard. In her moods she is always on top of the steeple or down in the deepest cellar."

"Hard for Miss Anna, then," Peter commented, and he thought that Dolph's amusement was broad enough to skip stones over. "And for your uncle as well, I daresay."

"I don't think Uncle Hansi minds, too much." Dolph still looked amused. "He'll know she'll always be fluttering around the house, making it comfortable for him, and she'll sure as hell never run away with a Yankee soldier, the way Mr. Ransleben's first wife did."

"When was this?"

"Years ago, but the old folk still talk. Don't let on you know about his wife and the soldier if you should meet him. He married again and moved to Comfort, near my father's place. He's a decent old stick, but it prolly drove him wild, knowing that everyone was wondering if he wasn't enough of a man to keep her content."

"A Yankee? For damn sure everyone would be wondering," Peter answered. A tiny part of him questioned whether there was enough of his own self remaining to keep a woman content, him with his arm that ended halfway up from his elbow. *Maybe if she weren't real particular.*

His cousin laughed, not privy to Peter's inmost thoughts, and added a battered wooden toolbox to the top of a wagon-load of lumber. Seeing that, Peter added, "I guess you and Fredi are still serious about re-building. You got enough in this here wagon, you could just about head west to California, if you wanted."

Dolph shook his fair head, gravely. "Nothing out there that I need. Besides, Uncle Fredi's been there and he says it's hardly worth the trouble of getting to it. Nothing but crazy miners and holes in the ground and everyone mad for gold or silver. Me, I'd rather go home, even if I have to build it again from the ground up."

"Your choice, Cuz," Peter sighed.

Dolph slapped his shoulder. "All that fresh country air, and rounding up cows on a fine spring morning? Nothing like it in all the world and better than any cure the sawbones could prescribe. Besides, Cousin Anna will still be here," Dolph added with an impish sideways look at Peter, "being shrewish. Most likely, Uncle Hansi wants to take her to Indianola so's she'll have a chance to be courted by fellows who haven't heard about her yet."

Peter refused to be drawn into the teasing, answering with a tragic face, "Won't do me any good, Cuz—I am perishing with an unrequited and hopeless passion for that fair and unattainable Diana, "Mrs. Hunter" as I suppose I must think of her now. An angel beyond my reach, the fairest belle of the hill country . . ."

"A fountain of tears, you mean," Dolph answered, utterly unmoved. "I swear, during the last couple of years, our Rosalie splashed about in a constant puddle of salt water. At least Robert took her away and spared us all the risk of drowning in it."

"I cannot wait until you turn moon-calf over some girl," Peter retorted, "because then I shall have the opportunity to sit back and point at you, laughing heartlessly all the while."

"Never happen, Cuz," Dolph answered with his accustomed serenity. "Not to me. And if it does, I know better than to make a show of it." He seemed to notice something on the wagon. "Speaking of putting a brand on a fine young filly, I've just remembered . . ."

78

"What? Is there a single thing we haven't packed in this here wagon, Cuz? I don't believe the whole Yankee army packed so much of their trash when they marched from Atlanta to the sea."

"Irons with the new brand," Dolph noted. "Uncle Hansi was going to see to it today, but he prolly forgot in all the ruckus about Aunt Liesel."

"A new brand?" Peter followed Dolph as the latter strode determinedly towards the house. Willi followed. He had to run to keep up with his elders. "I thought you were using Uncle Carl's. That was your plan, anyway."

Dolph shook his head. "Mama and I and Uncle Hansi had a notion to form a partnership, with a new brand and all. Anna drew out the design. It's already registered for us and all, but we just need to get the irons made. You see," he looked over his shoulder at his cousin as he opened the door, "Papa's brand was tied to his name. But during the war, because Duff and Waldrip and their friends called Papa an attainted traitor, the military governor had a confiscation order against any movable property of Papa's, 'specially if the Army could make use of such. Now we have a company with a registered brand. It's a bit more work for outsiders to find out who has shares in that company, and who might be offended." Dolph added, still looking over his shoulder, "Think of it like an ambush, laid in place and ready. Just in case, you see."

"You don't trust anyone much, do you, Cuz?" Peter observed after a moment.

Dolph answered bleakly, "Not much, Cuz, aside from kin and those who proved themselves true. Anyone with the power to give something precious to you has the power to take it back again on a whim."

The shop was empty at the moment except for Anna. She sat on a tall stool at the back, with her sleek brown head bent over a long leather-bound book of columns, half of them carefully filled out in ink. Still, Dolph added softly, "No one will ever take away anything that is ours by rights, ever again. Uncle Hansi feels the same—he'll never be a hunted man living the brush and out in all weather, unless he has a damned better reason for it than running from the provost marshal!" In a louder voice he said, "Anna, did Onkel Hansi see to the branding irons and the new design?"

Anna looked up from the accounts. She put her finger on a column to keep her place and answered in distracted irritation, "No, he did not. He and Auntie Magda are all taken up with Mama. I kept the design most carefully. I was afraid that it would be forgotten, or that Papa would roll a cigar with it, or write out an invoice on the front, unless I took special care."

She hopped down from the tall stool and vanished into the back room of the shop, returning in a moment with a sheet of heavy paper in her hand. "Here it is." She handed it to Dolph, then looked to Peter and asked, "So what do you think of this design? Do you think it will assure our fortunes, Cousin Peter?" She shot him a meaningful look, and he relished it and considered it akin to the sound of foils clashing, the formal prelude to another duel of wits.

"Your artistic efforts rival the great Italian masters, Miss Anna. By such merits alone, we are guaranteed success."

Anna pursed her lips, crisply retorting, "A pity the world does not run like a millwheel on the endless flow of your flatteries, Mr. Vining."

"Everyone has a talent, Miss Anna; that one must be mine." Peter looked at the paper in Dolph's hands; truthfully a fair and draftsman-like sketch of a brand. A capital "R" was reversed and set against a capital "B" so the same down-stroke formed the vertical basis for both, then they were set over a sideways "S" like the lazy flow of a river bend.

"Becker and Richter," Dolph explained quietly, "for Mama and Uncle Hansi's investment. The "S" is Steinmetz, for Uncle Fredi. Like me, he can put no money into this venture."

"Only hard work," Anna observed. "And are you putting hard work into this venture, Mr. Vining, assuming you are capable of anything beyond pretty flatteries?"

Before Peter could reply, Dolph pointed out, "I'm putting in nothing but hard work myself." He sounded amused as he added, "For the purposes of this venture and this brand, Cuz, you are a Becker and bringing in nothing more than a strong back and willing hands."

"Well, one of them, anyway," Peter observed wryly. He noted that Dolph looked quite discomfited at that, as if he was abruptly reminded of something he had forgotten. Miss Anna only sniffed in disapproval, as starchy as a maiden schoolteacher.

"Tell Onkel Hansi that we have seen to ordering new irons, then." Dolph said. "And that we have taken Willi with us." Anna directed a chiding look at her youngest brother. She spoke to him sternly in German, something about chores and errands.

Peter interjected in Willi's defense, "Oh, let him play a little hooky, Miss Anna. He has been a help to us this morning with the horses." Actually, Willi had been more of a hindrance, but he had followed directions so faithfully and eagerly that Peter couldn't help but be amused.

Willi and Horrie were much of an age, and Peter thought they might probably become friends, if they ever met.

As they departed, with a delighted Willi trailing behind and chattering away in a mixture of German and English, Peter added, "It beats all, how hard your German settlers work, even the children. I had chores when I was Willi's age, but my brothers and I had plenty of time to play, too."

"Not if Opa Becker had much to say about it, I'd have been willing to bet," Dolph answered. "Papa said he was a terror for work. Papa and his brother were always running off into the woods and it sent Opa Becker into furies. He said once that Opa Becker swore if they wouldn't finish their chores proper, then they wouldn't eat at his table. So he wouldn't let them come to meals . . . not that it did any good, because they went hunting in the woods, and gathered nuts and such. Papa said they had a grand time. It was summer, you see. They stayed away for weeks, until Oma Becker put her foot down. Uncle Hansi isn't so bad, really. Give him a pair of horses, some cattle, and an empty field and he'd be as happy as Adam in the Garden of Eden. It's Mama and Cousin Anna standing taskmaster, these days."

"Enough to put a man off marriage," Peter grumbled.

They walked briskly the length of Main Street, shrugging their coats tight against the bite of the north wind, but relishing the mild warmth of the winter sun on their faces and the clear blue sky, scrubbed as clean of clouds as if Miss Anna had been at it with duster and broom. They passed storefronts pressing close against the roadway, and small tidy plastered houses sitting back comfortably in their gardens—or rather what would be their gardens, come spring.

Suddenly Dolph asked, "D'you recall Opa Becker very well at all, Cuz?" And then he added, almost apologetically, "It's just that we knew everything there was to know about Mama's kin, and next to nothing at all about Papa's. He never talked much about them, except for Aunt Margaret. And we knew of you, 'course; but nothing much else."

"He was a hard, gruff man," Peter answered, "with a tongue and a nature to flay the skin off a buffalo. He died when I was about the age of this little sprout here," he tousled Willi's fair head with careless affection, "so it's not as if I can recall much, either. I didn't like him much and I don't think he cared much for me."

"I don't think he cared much for Papa, either," Dolph observed. "But Papa never said so, outright. He was fair, like that. When he talked of his folk, he always sounded . . . well, serious, but fair and generous. It's only now it came to me that he talked of his father as if he didn't care the least for him but didn't wish to be thought rude and unfilial. How do you think of your father, Cuz?'

"Barely at all," Peter answered. "He was dead of consumption before I was even out of small-clothes. Mama married Papa-Doctor when I was about seven. He was the best of stepfathers but I always thought he often seemed a little surprised to look up and count us all around the dinner table."

"Then who did you have in between, Cuz?" Dolph was curious. "Who taught you to sit a horse and mark a straight line and mind your manners to a woman while still paying a gallant compliment? Papa had shown me all that long before I was that age. You are very good at all that, so someone must have taught you early on."

"Daddy Hurst, I suppose," Peter answered, after a moment of thought and a startled realization that, yes—Daddy Hurst had indeed been that reassuring and kindly presence, all during those early years. He laughed, short and with no little surprise. "Strange, to think I learned all that from a nigra hired man."

"Children look to be taught," his cousin replied, "and they look to those around them, who treat them gentle and with respect. God knows, there are far worse in the world to learn those early lessons from than Daddy Hurst. I think he did well with you, Cuz!"

"I suppose so," Peter answered.

They talked of other matters, until they came to Mr. Kiehne's business on East Main, the tiny forge crouching under a huge and spreading oak tree of the same sort that shaded Vati's garden. Mr. Kiehne had built a fine house for his family, next to his sprawling and rackety business under the magisterial tree. Peter, Dolph and Willi threaded their way between waiting horses, wagons, and men to where Mr. Kiehne labored in his shirtsleeves by the red-hot heart of his forge. Willi bubbled with excitement and chattered like a magpie, as excited as if it were Christmas Eve and Father Christmas had brought him the most splendid gift imaginable for a small child.

"My aunt fusses over the children so," Dolph explained half apologetically as Willi stared round-eyed with awe. Mr. Kiehne was swinging his heavy hammer against an incandescent bit of metal pulled from the heart of his forge with a long pair of tongs. Sparks showered like a fireworks show at every ringing blow. "She hardly lets them go anywhere, without her or Cousin Anna holding their hand."

"Pity that," Peter grunted. "Does no good, mollycoddling the little lad."

"Uncle Hansi's more sensible," Dolph answered, "but he's away so much. It was different before the war, when they lived out in Live Oak. Different for us, too. Papa had me on a horse and working cattle with Porfirio almost before I could walk. Thank God Mama was sensible about that. *Guten Tag, Herr Kiehne!*" he added. Mr. Kiehne plunged his metalwork into a waiting tub of water, which immediately bubbled over in great gouts of bad-smelling steam. The smith swabbed sweat off his forehead with the back of a sooty hand and grinned at Dolph. To Peter, it looked as if they knew each other well. Of course, anyone who drove a wagon for Hansi Richter would know the town blacksmith, but it looked like a deeper familiarity.

"For what are you looking for today, lads?" the smith asked in stiff English, out of courtesy, after Dolph introduced Peter.

"New branding irons," Dolph answered, taking Anna's careful drawing from his pocket. "We'll need a set of six, if you can finish them in the next day or so. We're hoping to leave by Tuesday morning."

"Not a problem." Mr. Kiehne cast a quick and professional eye over the drawing. "So, you think to make something by a venture in cattle?"

"We hope," Dolph answered. "As best I know, no one has held a round-up on my father's land since the second year of the war. The winters have been mild enough, many calves must have survived. Somewhere, someone must want to eat beef well enough to make it worth our while to round them up, and drive them to Indianola. Uncle Fredi says that they're shipping beeves to New Orleans for the market there."

"If not, there's always a market for hides." Mr. Kiehne took up his hammer again with a grunt. "Monday afternoon, no problem for me, and maybe sooner. Send someone to ask, if you're in a hurry before then."

As they walked away, Willi tugged at Dolph's shirtsleeve and piped a question in German, to which Dolph shook his head and answered in that same tongue.

"He wants to come with us," Dolph explained to Peter. "George and Jacob have talked of nothing else. Uncle Fredi made this sound such an adventure, like it was when he and Uncle Johann and everyone first came out in wagons from Neu Braunfels and the Indians befriended them."

"You told him no, I hope." Peter was somewhat alarmed at the thought of being responsible for a small and daring boy, especially one who seemed as likely to run headlong toward those breakneck adventures to which he and his brothers had been prone when younger.

His cousin grimaced. "Aunt Liesel would scarce allow it. She is fluttering about like a mother hen whenever I let him ride old Three-Socks. She carries on as if he is a wild mustang, instead of a staid old thing half asleep on his feet."

"Perhaps when he is a little older his Mama might be talked into permitting it," Peter ventured.

Dolph shrugged. "Uncle Hansi is the one who will say yes or no, however much Auntie Liesel fusses about her darling."

They got away late on Tuesday, in spite of Dolph fretting and Fredi constantly thinking of essential items to pack into the smallest of Hansi's freight-wagons, on top of a load of beams and sawn lumber. Dolph rolled his eyes when Fredi dove into the storeroom or the kitchen for the twentieth time, returning triumphantly with some small item such as an egg-shaped coffee-roaster, or a side of cured ham.

"We can always buy such in Comfort or borrow from the Stielers or the Steves," Dolph said patiently, after the latest of these excursions. "It's not as if there is no one out there at all but wild Indians and wilder cattle!"

Fredi slapped his forehead and exclaimed, "Lead and the bullet-mould! Better to take such and not need it, than be in dire need and not have it to hand, eh lads?"

"At this rate we'll need another wagon," Peter murmured. Dolph was patiently cinching up three bedrolls to be added on top of the load when Fredi pronounced their supplies to be complete. "I don't suppose I should suggest a tent and a patent traveling stove?"

His cousin shook his head. "No. Half the roof was still on the house eight months ago. I expect we'll be able to use the kitchen stove once we knock the bats and swallows out of the chimney." Dolph tossed the bedrolls one by one into the wagon, while the horses stamped impatiently in harness. "And the orchard wall was sound enough. We'll picket the horses there at night, until we re-build the stable."

Peter looked very closely at his cousin. Underneath Dolph's usual serenity, suppressed excitement ran through him like a swift current underneath the calm surface of a river. He was drawn through with tension, like a racehorse waiting for the command to run.

"We'll be on our way soon enough, Cuz," Peter said.

"I've been waiting on this day for over four years," Dolph noted. "I can manage another fifteen minutes."

"But not much longer than that," Peter said. His cousin rewarded that feeble witticism with a brief grin. Dolph's and Fredi's horses stood patiently, already saddled and bridled by the time Fredi emerged from the house. Anna and Marie followed him, each carrying a basket with a cloth over the top.

"We would not let you go without good bread," Anna said in her precise way. "For there is no one there to bake it for you, even if you have the means of baking such."

Peter took the basket from her with his one good hand and nearly dropped it from the unexpected weight. "There is more in here than bread, by the feel of it."

"Of course," Anna returned. "You should not need to cook for many days, while you apply yourself to the building of roofs and the branding of cattle."

"Your concern for our welfare is overwhelming, Miss Anna." Peter set aside the basket and kissed her hand before she could snatch it away. "I am almost—but not quite—rendered speechless with gratitude! Here I thought you cared nothing for me at all!"

"And what must I give, that you are then entirely speechless, Mr. Vining?" she answered crisply. "Pray tell me, so that I may present it to you at once!"

"Ah, my dear Miss Anna," Peter said, as Dolph hid an amused smile and Marie looked almost envious. "So you promise. Well, there is one thing that I would like from you which would take the power of speech entirely from me for . . . oh, at least an hour."

"And that would be?" Anna asked, sharp and suspicious.

Peter said with delight, "Promise me that you will grant it, Miss Anna. You said anything within your power, to buy my silence for an hour!"

"You did say as much, Anna," Dolph pointed out, hugely amused. "Anything within your power to grant."

Anna looked between them both and acquiesced, "Then so I shall ... anything for an hour of silence."

"Your company for that selfsame hour, and to promenade with me on the seashore at Indianola," Peter announced triumphantly. "I will be as solemn as a judge and as silent as the grave for at least an hour, as promised, Miss Anna! Am I granted the boon of your company?"

"Such a sacrifice!" Anna replied with a toss of her head.

Peter grinned. "Your promise, Miss Anna!" She made a show of indifferent consent, shrugging as if it was something of no matter. Peter continued, wooingly, "I shall hold to it, most assuredly—in three months, on the seashore."

Anna muttered something under her breath, something that made Marie ruffle like a startled guinea-hen and Dolph laugh outright.

When the girls had deposited their baskets on the wagon-tail and returned towards the house, Peter demanded of his cousin,"What was so funny?"

Dolph answered only, "Better than a play," and would say no more, for Fredi came from the storeroom, puffing and with his arms laden. "Let us go, Cuz . . . before he thinks of yet another thing."

"If he looks towards the house and says 'just one more,' I promise I will help you hog-tie him and throw him in the wagon," Peter assured him. But it seemed that action would not be required. Uncle Hansi himself appeared, trailed by Ma'am Becker, stern and proud as a Spartan woman sending her son away with his shield. Behind them was the kindly and forgetful old grandfather, polishing his thick glasses as if he would wear away the lenses entirely.

"In three months, we meet in San Antonio, yah?" Uncle Hansi said, then clapped Peter on the shoulder, a mighty buffet that nearly launched him into the horse trough. "After you search out what remains of the Becker herd and rebuild the house. But that will take much longer than three months, I am sure!"

"We'll do what we can," Peter promised him. "Dolph says it is not so much a wreck as all that."

The burly freight-master shook his head. The grief in his shrewd, coffee-dark eyes was genuine. "Fifteen years hard work by Magda and Brother Carl brought all to ruin in a single day? It will take more than a day to remedy. Foolish to think otherwise." He staggered Peter with another one of those fond thumps. "You will see young Rudolph is sensible, not so? It was good land, and he thinks of nothing else. No use to anyone until he makes something of it, or gives up dreaming of it. And," the big man shrugged philosophically, "There may be money in cattle yet."

"Fredi is sure of it," Peter replied.

Uncle Hansi chuckled. "He is sure of anything that will lead him like a will of the wisp—too eager to follow and too easy to give it up for the next. But you two lads, you will hold him to sense, I am sure. Be careful of my horses, though! Do not give them to the first Comanche that you see."

He lifted Willi to his shoulder, as Dolph embraced his mother and his little sister. Peter kissed Ma'am Becker's hand and then impulsively her cheek. She had been very good to him, with her poultices and the drafts of hot milk, in which she had only confessed of late that she had steadily reduced the number of drops of laudanum. Peter had been astonished, for the pains in his arm had yielded to her ministrations without fail. '*How much was in the last dose, Ma'am?*' he had asked, and Dolph's mother answered, '*I waved the open bottle over a pan of milk while it steamed.*' Peter had laughed inordinately over that. And everyone had always said that Ma'am Becker was entirely humorless! But he had slept well and deep and had no more need of such physics as she administered, and could do a full day of hard work, besides. His cousins were his family now and Ma'am as close to a mother as he would find in the world of the living. Peter was more content now than he would have thought possible, on the day that he came back to his mother's empty house.

"Time to go," Dolph said. It seemed to Peter that they did so with almost indecent haste, once his cousin said the words; as if they were impatient to be away from Vati's comfortable house, eager to embrace discomfort and hard work. Peter took the wagon as the others rode their horses. He slapped the reins over the draft horses' backs and laughed to see Miss Anna watching them from the shop window. He would have waved, blown her a kiss on the freshening breeze, but that his one good hand was full of leather reins. Never had he been so convinced of a day being full of adventure and promise, not since the bright morning when he and his brothers had departed with their company for Virginia: brass bands and fluttering flags to speed them on their way, hastened with speeches and celebration, kisses from pretty girls. For all that bright beginning, that venture had not turned out well. Peter hoped privately this one would turn out better. Lord knows it could hardly turn out worse.

They followed the southward road towards San Antonio; one heavy-laden wagon and two horsemen, with Pepper the dog trailing after when he wasn't pursuing interesting smells into the bushes at the verge or chasing the occasional rabbit among the winter-burnt thickets of bare sticks and shriveled brown leaves. A hawk wheeled ceaselessly overhead, a dark spread of wings in a jewel-blue sky. In the fields near town, Peter saw men already laboring with their plows, slowly turning the dark earth over and over.

"They'll be planting in a couple of weeks." Dolph rode closer to the wagon. "The last chance of frost around here is in mid-March, if they're lucky."

"Still colder than a well-digger's ass," Peter grumbled. A gust of cold wind shook the wagon cover from the rear, as if to hurry them on their way. "We may regret setting out on this so early, Cuz."

Dolph shook his head, the wind ruffling his pale hair. "I'd already sent word to Porfirio," he answered, "for any of his kin as wanted work to come to us at round-up time. We'll need to have some kind of roof over us by then."

"You're hiring hands from as far as San Antone?" Peter asked. "You're damn sure of them staying, then."

His cousin had one of those inscrutable looks to him then, his eyes as clear and blue as the sky and nearly as unreadable. "Porfirio was my father's friend," he answered, "and there is business unfinished, as far as he is concerned."

Evening found them still short of the Becker holdings; they spent the night at the home of a German farmer and herdsman, with extensive lands and a large house near to Comfort and the river crossing. Dolph and Fredi stayed up quite late, talking softly in German to Mr. Stieler, his sons, and son-in-law. Mrs. Stieler and her daughter brought out many dishes of bread and cheese and vegetable pickles. Peter fell asleep by the fire until Dolph woke him.

"You should not have let me sleep so long," Peter protested as Dolph steered him towards the Stielers' guest chambers. "The least that a guest can do in response to such generous hospitality is to be amusing company."

"Not required that you put on a show," Dolph answered, raising the lantern and opening the door to it with his other hand. "After I said that we were back, and intending to work my father's lands again, Old Stieler was pleased enough about that, I tell you. You'd have had to walk on your hands and juggle with your feet to make any impression after that."

"Well, if you say so," Peter yawned. "So it's good news to him that you are back?"

"Of the best," Dolph nodded. "Enjoy this fine feather mattress, Cuz— tomorrow we'll bed down on last years leaves, if we're lucky. No," he continued, choosing his words with care, "it's just as well you were asleep. Old Gottlieb's oldest boy was one of Tegener's Unionists killed in the Nueces fight and by Captain Duff's orders left unburied. I didn't rightly like to remind him of the war, you see."

"And I'd bring that all to mind, then," Peter said bitterly. His eyes went, as they always did, to his pinned-up sleeve. "Through having done what everyone said was the right and honorable thing for a true Texian.

There are things I want to forget also, but I remember every time I try reaching out for something to pick it up with fingers that aren't even there. Your friend Stieler can put his loss out of mind now and again, which is more than I can do."

"Perhaps." His cousin had that carefully unreadable look, as he set the lantern on a little shelf plainly meant for it. "I did not mean to reproach you, Cuz. Folk were as divided here as anywhere else. Most wanted nothing to do with the war at all. Duff and his partisans and the Hanging Band forced us into taking a side, one or the other. Old Stieler and his family, they'd think more of you for being Becker kin than anything you ever did in the East in the war."

"As long as I wasn't doing it around these parts," Peter answered cynically and his cousin nodded agreement. "Out of sight and out of mind, I suppose." But his missing hand was never out of his mind, he told himself as he sank into the featherbed, pulling Mrs. Stieler's fine guest-bed quilt over himself. He wondered wearily when he would ever be comfortable and accustomed to its absence.

The next morning dawned clear and chill, but the sun promised warmth. They took leave of the Stielers with gratitude for their hospitality, and continued along the road. It sloped down a long decline towards the river-crossing and the hamlet of Comfort: yet another one of those tidy German settlements, this one built in a grove of towering cypress trees.

"I went to school here," Dolph nodded towards a dilapidated log house at the edge of the settlement. "It was almost too far to come, most days—but Mama insisted, once they started a school. The schoolmaster was a bit strange, too. He was too lazy to use a switch—he threw pebbles at us when we weren't paying attention. Good aim, too. Some of the older boys would come home, all covered with red welts. One of Mr. Steves's sons taught school after that. I liked him better. I might have come to like school but he had to quit about the time that Papa was killed and the Army sent us away. I didn't go to school much after that."

They passed out of Comfort, following a rutted track along the northern bank of the Guadalupe River that looped north and west into the hills. Scattered stands of cypress trees, with their coarse feather-like foliage, lined its banks and leaned over the deeper pools. The water slipped quietly over pure white gravel, as perfectly rounded as marbles. The hills closed in on the track and the river, now and again opening on a vista of meadows and gnarled stands of oak trees, still darkly green even though winter still gripped the land.

They saw no one other than themselves, nothing living but cattle drifting like cloud shadows on the distant hillsides. Once they rounded a bend where the rush of water falling over tumbled stones disguised the sounds of harness, wagons and horses, and Pepper surprised a white-spotted deer drinking from the waterside.

"Supper," Fredi remarked in delight, unshipping a carbine from the holster on his saddle. "What do you say to a haunch of venison, lads?" He looked over his shoulder at them while urging his horse forward. The deer bounded away in fright and the dog gave chase until Dolph whistled for him to return.

"Too much work to skin and gut, now," he said. "We're almost there, Fredi—you can chase him down some other day."

"It looks a wild place," Peter remarked. "As if there had never been any white folk here. If it weren't for the tracks, I'd never believe there had been any settlement out here at all."

"Duff's partisans plundered and burnt out most of the Germans," Dolph explained stoically. "And the Comanche raiders drove away most of the rest. You'd see ten burnt chimneys between here and Kerrville for every whole roof standing. Most of the valley farms look like that one." He jerked his chin towards several dilapidated piles of half-burnt logs, in the middle of a clearing overgrown with cedar saplings. A single chimney stabbed upwards, like an accusing finger. "'That was our closest neighbors. 'Course, it didn't look all that much better when the Browns lived there."

"What happened to them?" Peter asked.

Dolph shrugged. "I dunno. Old Brown's brother-in-law was taken at the same time Papa was killed—hung from an oak tree with some other Unionist men from hereabouts, taken by the Hanging Band, all in a single evening. Some of their boys went with Tegener's company and the rest hid out in the bush country. Their youngest boy Nate used to work for Papa—he went to Mexico, meaning to join the Union Army. He's never come back, so he either got killed or liked where he went to much better. I know the old folks finally had a belly-full and went north to Missouri."

"Were they Unionists, too?" Peter asked.

His cousin shrugged again. "No. I don't think they cared one way or another. They just wanted to be left alone."

Left to himself and his admittedly sketchy grasp of woodcraft, Peter would never have found the track to the Becker place, not without casting up and down the river for a considerable distance, or knowing that the weather and fire-stained walls just barely glimpsed between the trees was not an outcrop of natural stone. If the apple trees had been in bloom, that might have provided a clue to him—but they were not.

It fell to his cousin, drawing rein midmorning at a particularly large oak tree and saying quietly, "This is it, Fredi." Fredi whistled between his teeth, and looked away from the riverbank, towards a knoll some half-mile distant and the line of taller hills beyond it.

"You'd never know, would you, lad?" he said, heavily.

Dolph shook his head. "I'd know it in daylight," he answered. "In daylight, from the line of hills and the look of the river." He whistled to Pepper, and plunged his horse off the track and into the knee-high thicket of dead grass and scrub that lined it. "Follow close, Cuz. There is a trail, enough for a wagon—less'n a tree has fallen across it."

Peter urged the team to follow close upon the two horsemen, a long looping track away from the river, across a gently sloping meadow that in summer would be a lush green sweep starred with wildflowers. Presently he discerned the remains of a zigzagging cedar-rail fence, peeping coyly out from the undergrowth. Weathered grey by age and exposure, the rails would have looked like something that had occurred naturally, save for the very regularity. Within its confines, Peter thought he could see traces of furrows and long-dead corn plants, bleached to a startling pale yellowish color, strewn amongst last year's dead grass and the tender green blades just peeping up from the ground.

The track curved around the base of the knoll. It followed a wall of natural stone, man-made but weathered to the color of old ivory, streaked and patched here and there with green, grey and black lichen and mosses. Peter saw that the wall attached naturally to the ruins of a house; not, as first appeared, a natural outcrop of the hills. It crowned the knoll on the riverside, overlooking the valley below on one side, and a cleared space on the other. The cleared space was overgrown with tall grass and cedar saplings, out of which protruded an occasional blackened timber. The empty windows of the house looked blankly out on that space, like eye-holes in a skull. Ragged wooden fragments of a door hung from a set of hinges in the center of a porch, lost in a drift of dead leaves and grass grown nearly to the same level. At the opposite side of the clearing at the crest of the knoll, a stone cistern held a pool of unhealthily still water, thick with livid green scum and dark dead leaves. Peter's heart sank into his boots—this was a ruin, a ruin beyond redemption.

In the middle of that space, Fredi and Dolph dismounted. Following their lead, Peter halted the team. For a moment they stood, looking around at the bleak desolation, the black-streaked ruins of the house. Pepper sat with his tongue lolling out, scratching luxuriously at a flea. He nudged Dolph's hand, for his master stood, holding the reins of his horse and looking at the ruined house, the bare knoll, the empty sky, and the ever-present hawk spiraling overhead. Although his cousin's face seemed carefully blank of expression, Fredi's was all too transparent and Peter recalled that he also had lived and worked here for a number of years. This had been his home, at least as much as Vati's rambling Friedrichsburg house was; the place he had always returned to between his wanderings with herds of cattle to California and other places. Peter thought of how he would have felt, trudging wearily up the hill to his mother's house, only to find it ruined, grass and scrub bushes already taking hold. One always expected places to stay the same, the same as they were when last seen, as if one's memory preserved them in amber.

Dolph fondled Pepper's head, patting the dog with absent-minded affection. He turned towards Peter, calm and serene as a marble saint in a Catholic church, and observed, "We'll repair the roof first, I think. Then build a stable for the horses. Porfirio's boys will be here in a month or so. Onkel Hansi thinks to begin improving the breed of cattle then, so this will have to serve as ranch headquarters."

"In the meantime, we'll have to sleep somewhere," Peter observed.

"There's enough roof left over the kitchen end," his cousin answered. "Even if it leaks like hell, the upper floor will give better shelter than open air. We'll picket the horses out in the orchard at night. There was a gate to it around the side."

Fredi appeared to be overcome by sorrowful sentiments; he silently clapped his nephew on the shoulder. Finally, he said in halting tones, "I can scarce take it in, boy. This was such a fine farmstead, such a fine place as is hardly seen in the west!" His eyes filled and he added, "And such a happy place, too!"

"It will be so again," Dolph said, with perfect assurance. He ruffled Pepper's ears affectionately, and repeated, "It will be so again. You'll see."

They picketed the horses and set to work before even unloading the wagon. In truth there was so much to be done that Peter could scarce decide where to begin—raking out enough rubble from the largest room, or building window shutters and a door to secure at least that one room at night? Clearing the chimney of bird's nests, or cleaning out the cistern? Reinforcing the stout gate in the orchard wall, or building a ladder to reach the roof? For much of the day it seemed to Peter that each task undertaken either needed or inspired another five or six. Labors in the house or in the other ruins on the knoll left all three of them grimy and smeared with old ash and black soot. The grass and undergrowth was everywhere mined with the remains of burnt timbers, of charcoal and unidentifiable lumps of pottery and metal—yet another dirty chore, sorting out that which might be reused, once re-forged or pounded back into shape. A faint odor of ancient fires hung over the knoll like a ghost as they worked in the house, vying with the fresher smell of newly sawn wood.

"Not much left that we can use, Cuz," Peter remarked after a grueling stint of hauling yoked buckets of rubble from the bottom floor.

Dolph answered, "What they didn't steal, they smashed before they fired the barn. I'll be surprised to find anything whole or useful besides the walls." Yet he seemed remarkably cheerful for a man laboring in the ruins of his family home; Peter could only think his cousin was so happy to have returned at last that the matter of its condition was secondary. He himself could never have managed to put on such a stoic face.

"I'll buy a drink for whoever finds something whole or undamaged," Peter promised. He stood up with a grunt of effort, lifting a pair of buckets on a yoke across his shoulders, full of blackened pottery and rubble, and carried them through the hallway. Fresh dust swirled through sunlight that slanted down through floor-beams above and the ruined roof beyond that. Seasons of rain had streaked the plastered walls with soot. He and Fredi had already evicted a family of owls from the chimney.

He carried the buckets across the clearing, tipping their contents into a shallow pit on the far side of where the barn had been. Something moved in the cedar thicket below, something smaller than a man. It watched him warily, a gaunt tan-colored hound with fearful eyes. It scuttled deeper into the thicket when he made as if to come closer, then skulked out to watch again as soon as he retreated.

"There's a dog outside," he said conversationally to Dolph, on his return. "Looks as wild as a wolf."

"If it was truly wild," Dolph answered, setting down the shovel he used to move rubble, "it wouldn't be hanging around." He took a piece of their luncheon bread and cheese, and followed Peter to the rubble dump. Peter watched as he went halfway towards the thicket, then knelt down, coaxing the dog closer with the food and many soft and wooing words.

The dog eventually crept out to snap up the food and allow Dolph to stroke its nose and ears. "If you courted pretty girls with talk like that," Peter observed, "you'd be the maiden's delight of two or three counties. As it is, they must be weeping for all the charm you waste on poor dumb animals."

"Perhaps," Dolph answered, "but at any rate, you owe me a drink now."

"For what?" Peter demanded. The dog flinched at the indignation in his voice, but Dolph reassured him with a gentle caress.

"Finding something whole and useful," he answered, appearing quite pleased. "Papa always said there was nothing more useful around the place than dogs."

Peter shook his head. "I swear, Cuz, you must have an invisible mark on you somewhere. Everything halt, lame or starving never fails in finding you."

Dolph shrugged. "Truth is, Cuz, I like animals better than most people. Feed a stray dog, give it a home—it would never turn around and show black ingratitude like a man would."

The new dog followed them hopefully back to the house, where Pepper sniffed warily and growled a little under his breath. The new dog cringed, showing its belly and every rib under its dusty tan hide. Dolph tossed them both a little dried meat, which both dogs fell on with eagerness. When Peter came out from the house again, both dogs had curled up—not quite touching each other—in a place where the sun fell warmly against a sheltered angle of the lime-plastered wall.

By afternoon, they had emptied out enough of the least-ruined room, the kitchen, and swept the floor clean enough to set up bachelor housekeeping. Fredi's hastily-constructed shutters hung only slightly awry from hinges salvaged out of the burnt remnants of the old ones, and a good fire burned in the stone fireplace. They had spread out their straw-filled pallets and bedrolls there, unloaded the wagon and bailed out the water cistern until the foul-smelling, slimy filth was replaced by a trickle of fresh water from the spring. Peter ached in every bone from exhaustion, as did Fredi and Dolph.

Late in the afternoon, Fredi looked around at what they had accomplished so far and sighed contentedly. "Ah, it's a good start, boys. More than I thought we'd do on the first day."

"Still a long way to go," Peter agreed. Outside, Pepper barked several times—the "alert" bark that he used for friends and acquaintances, rather than the "danger" bark for strangers and odd noises in the night. Someone called from outside the house at some little distance and Fredi went out to the door.

"It's Berg!" he said.

Dolph's face lit up. "So he's still around," he exclaimed. "I guess he was too odd for the Hanging Band to bother with. The Indians think he is mad, you know. Papa always thought that was why they left him alone. He lived in a tower that he built for himself, away back in the hills. He's a stonemason. Papa hired him to help build this house, but he tinkers with all matter of inventions and gadgets." Dolph hesitated and then warned, "He's a little strange. Don't take offense at his manner. He's a good sort, for all that."

"One of those proven friends?" Peter asked, as he followed Dolph towards the door. His cousin nodded in the affirmative. For a good sort in Dolph's estimation, Berg the stonemason proved to be a very odd man indeed—and Peter thought that he had seen all sorts, around his mother's dinner table, or in the Army. A middle-aged man whose uncut hair straggled to his shoulders, he wore rough workman's pants and a roundabout jacket patched in leather over a rough homespun cloth shirt so worn that it was impossible to tell what color it had been—if it had ever been any color at all. As Dolph and Peter joined Fredi, he fixed all three of them with an unnervingly direct gaze and said, "Good. I thought you would return sooner than this. Another season and the beams would be ruined. Even so, you must rebuild the north wall."

"How very pleasant to make your acquaintance," Peter said to the open air. "You must be Mister Berg. My cousin has spoken of you."

Berg's attention swerved to Peter. There was something almost mechanical about his regard like the mouth of an artillery piece transiting through an arc to fix on a new position. Dolph elbowed him warningly in the ribs. *You only said he was odd*, Peter told his cousin with a silent expression, *not as mad as a March hare. No wonder the Indians leave him alone.*

"This is my cousin, Peter Vining," Dolph explained, as if nothing were the least bit awkward about this exchange. "We're going to rebuild the house and run cattle again, once we sort out what is the best market for beef."

"And what of the orchard?" Berg still had his attention fixed unswervingly on Peter. "Your father had such a care for the orchard. I would not see it neglected."

"We'll take good care of the orchard," Dolph answered.

Berg nodded abruptly, apparently satisfied with this assurance. "You have lost your arm," he announced, dropping that flat statement like a man tossing his hat and gloves onto a table.

"Not lost," Peter retorted. "I know perfectly well where it went—the Army surgeon took it away. It saves on shirts, you know."

Berg stared at him, utterly without humor. "You have not a . . . what do they call it? A mechanical?"

"No," Peter answered. The man was mad, utterly mad—perhaps the best way of dealing with him was merely to answer the question.

"I can make," Berg nodded confidently. "Show me."

"What?" Peter stared at him, utterly baffled. "Make a mechanical arm? For me?"

"Of course," Berg answered, with considerable impatience. "Take off your shirt. I must see both."

"Do it," Dolph whispered. Fredi watched with enormous interest and nodded agreement. "He can build anything. I think he could even build a mechanical head, if it was required and he had the whim to do it."

"Can't we go inside first?" Peter asked.

The strange hermit, Mr. Berg, shook his head. "No. Light is better outside. Now show," and he made a gesture of pulling at his shirt. Peter had no choice but to obey, taking off his coat and pulling his shirt over his head. He stood shivering in the thin winter sunshine as Mr. Berg scrutinized his arms with close attention, the whole one and the abbreviated one, first holding them out straight in front, then hanging at Peter's sides as the mad hermit directed. Finally he said, "Good. I make to fit."

Peter hastily and gratefully donned his outer clothing again. "You don't need to make any measure?"

"No. I have the eye." Berg answered.

With that, he nodded curtly and strode away, leaving Fredi shaking his head and Peter saying, "That must be the strangest social call ever paid—I never met a person less acquainted with an etiquette book in my whole life."

"He's always been like that," Fredi said. "Wish I had thought to ask him for whiskey. He distills it himself, and after this day I think we might have done it justice."

"Not if we have to go up onto the roof tomorrow," Dolph said. Peter looked after Berg, now some distance away and nearly invisible among the cedar thickets, and wondered if he was really as good an inventor as Dolph and Fredi thought. And what it would be like to have people not staring at his empty sleeve.

Chapter Six: *Indianola*

It was a matter of some excitement and no little apprehension for Magda Vogel Becker to journey forth from the house on Market Street. In all of twenty years since coming to Texas as a settler under the Verein auspices, she had gone no farther than her husband's land on the upper Guadalupe, save once to Austin. Her brothers, her sons, her husband, her brother-in-law and many of their friends—oh, they had traveled widely, the length and breadth of Texas, to New Orleans, and Mexico, to California— even returning to Germany! Bound with household and children, for care of Vati and then by the dangers of war, she had always remained by the home hearth and been happy in the main to do so. The welfare of the shop tugged at her like a fretful and frail child. For worry over the daily care of stock, accounts and the needs of customers, she might have very easily given up this long trip of Hansi's contriving.

But this was the slow time, after the turn of the year and before the trail season opened. Hansi was of the opinion that they might cut better bargains among the merchants and in the warehouses of San Antonio or Indianola. It was resolved among them all that the shop could do without her care for some weeks, while she and Anna saw to purchasing fresh stock. Of late she had felt something of an urge, even the necessity, of seeing other horizons, other skies. Anna felt it even more urgently; and it was only the need to pacify her sister Liesel's fears and worries for her oldest child that she had consented to participate in this excursion. Anna had her heart sent on going. Magda could not withdraw now, or her sister would use the lack of a proper chaperone to keep her oldest daughter close at hand.

Magda now sat with Lottie on her lap, Anna beside her, on a bench at the back of the Nimitz Hotel, waiting for the mid-week stage to San Antonio. Hannah played hopscotch by herself on a set of squares she had scratched in the dirt nearby. There were a handful of men also waiting the stage, but they respectfully tipped their hats to the women and stood a little apart. Magda did not know any of them—Americans, she supposed, as they spoke to one another in English. She cringed inwardly at the extravagant cost of such a journey, first to San Antonio, and thence to Victoria and Indianola, but Hansi had insisted that it was actually a sensible economy. She and Anna could not be spared from the shop together for the length of time that a journey with his wagons would entail; better to travel swift and sure by the stage, and lodge with friends.

Anna looked sideways around the edge of her modish straw bonnet. "Auntie, you are fidgeting again! You should not worry so. Mama will manage, with the help of Rosalie and Vati."

"I am sure," Magda replied swiftly, but she sighed and added, "I wish that we had not heard about Uncle Simon."

"It was very kind of his nephew to write, and to return all of Vati's letters," Anna said. Magda thought again of how Vati had looked when he opened the parcel from Germany and learned of the death of his friend from the old days in Ulm. Simon the goldsmith, with whom he had exchanged letters for twenty years, dearest friend for another thirty years before that. Vati had looked like a withered old gnome. He had taken the parcel of letters into his room upstairs and not come out for several hours. When he did, it was to insist that nothing was wrong. He would dig in the garden for a while and then walk over to commiserate with Pastor Altmueller.

"It was always Uncle Simon's thought that Vati should do a book of his letters from Texas," Magda said now. "And Rosalie will cheer him up, as well as make sure he does not boil his socks in the soup and leave his spectacles in all sorts of places." Rosalie, blooming like her namesake in the first year of her marriage to Robert, had promised to come and stay with him for the duration of their absence from the store.

"I suppose Mama will be giving her all sorts of advice about the baby," Anna said, with another of those sideways glances. Rosalie had come flying down from her husband's light one-horse trap and into her sisters' welcoming arms, whispering the joyous news that she had been too happy to keep to herself for another moment. She would have a child late in the fall, around harvest time. Liesel, who brought forth all of her and Hansi's children with the happy insouciance of a mother cat bearing kittens, was immediately forthcoming with advice—helpful, practical and reassuring for the most part.

"It is wonderful news," Magda answered. Almost involuntarily her arms tightened around Lottie, youngest of those given to her and her husband; born six months after his murder, the only one without memory of him and his endless kindness and patience with his children. Of such crumbs of happiness from the lives of other people was her life made of now. She wore black widow's weeds for Carl and intended to wear them for the rest of her life. "I hope Robert is pleased just as well."

"Oh, you know he is," Anna answered. "Men always are unbearably smug when their wives prove they have done the man's part well."

"Anna!" her aunt whispered in shocked reproof. How did Anna know of such things—and worse yet, dare to speak of them!

Anna just laughed and answered, "Oh, Auntie, I am twenty-three years of age! If I had cared to, I would have been married long since, with two or three of my own by this time. I know how children are begotten and how men look for pleasure in bed, and how we maiden girls are supposed to look the other way and pretend not to see what is plain in front of us!"

"It is still not fitting that you should be so open about these things," Magda insisted, and Anna laughed again.

"Auntie, I am unmarried, not an idiot! Why should I pretend about these matters?"

"It is not proper," Magda repeated. "Really, Anna—you should be married."

"You sound like Mama," Anna replied. "She is always asking me why I do not find this man or the other pleasing, and chiding me for being too particular. I thought you would think better of me, Auntie!"

"Are you being too particular?" Magda asked, stung at the comparison. She had been the plain one, always compared—to her disadvantage—to her sister Liesel, pretty as a princess who would be lucky enough to marry her prince almost as soon as she put up her hair. She had worried about Anna, similarly overshadowed by Rosalie, but Anna seemed to have suitors and admirers enough.

"No," Anna shook her head so vigorously that the curls next to her cheeks and the ribbons on her bonnet bobbed. "For they all seem like boys. Like my brothers. I say something I think clever to them, and they look back at me with their mouths open like geese. All but Cousin Peter—I suppose I may call him a cousin of a sort. He at least has some kind of wit about him! But the nonsense that man talks, like water from a millrace! He cozened a pledge from me to walk by the seaside with him by promising to be entirely quiet for an hour! I can hardly believe that man to be serious about anything at all. That the Confederate Army saw fit to take him in and put a gun in his hands only proves how hopeless an enterprise that war was!"

"But he amuses you," Magda asked, with tenderness. "And I think he admires you, for he makes any excuse to pay his compliments."

"He is never serious," Anna complained. "He teases like a boy!"

Magda sighed, "There are men who can never say what they are feeling, Anna. He is like his uncle. He also made light of what he felt most deeply, when I first made his acquaintance. There were some matters he never could bring himself to speak of, but covered them with a jest instead. Pay little mind to the jest, but rather the matters underneath it."

"I would," Anna turned her head, as if she heard something far away, "if he gave any evidence of having a serious thought in his head at all. Listen, Auntie—there is the coach."

"I hope there is room enough that Lottie may sit between us." Magda rose and called for Hannah, for now she could hear the thunder of hoofbeats drawing the heavy coach at a gallop down Main Street. In a moment, the coach turned the corner by the hotel bathhouse and the great tree that overhung the road—six powerful horses and the great box of the coach body rocking gently on its leather springs. So much swifter and more comfortable than a farm wagon, whose heavy wheels found every rock and rut in the road! The coachman's assistant and guard leaped down at once to help Anna and Magda with their bags. The men waiting stood back and allowed them first into the coach, to take the best and most commodious places, those facing forwards as the coach traveled.

"You shall sit next to the window, so you may see everything," Anna promised Hannah and Lottie. "We shall travel as swift as the wind, and at the end of it we shall be in a town three times the size of Friedrichsburg and several times as old."

"We went on a coach once before." Hannah bounced on the cushioned seat and tried leaning back against the head rests. She was yet too short to sit comfortably that way, and drew up her legs to sit curled next to her cousin and sister. "We went all the way to Austin, in a whole day!"

"Shush," Magda bade her as the other passengers clambered up, and took their places opposite, or perched on the narrow padded bench across the middle. Above their heads, the driver cracked his great whip, and they were off with a lurch and a shout. The wheels spun in a cloud of dust, left mostly behind in their speed; the coach swayed in a gentle, regular manner like the rocking of a child's cradle, while the world seemed to whirl past the coach windows at an incredible speed: Charley Nimitz's grand hotel, a scattering of houses on Baron's Creek, the place where the Verein blockhouse had once stood.

"We built a great bonfire and danced among the trees," Magda said.

Anna looked at her, baffled. "What are you talking about, Auntie?"

"Remembering out loud," Magda replied.

The hills spun past, scattered with gnarled oak trees, patched with green pastures and ploughed fields, threaded with clear-water creeks trickling over limestone falls, all the way to the river-ford on the Guadalupe at Comfort. Passing familiar, for Magda and her husband and family had often come that way before the military governor had confiscated their lands in the second year of the fighting. She had last traveled that road riding in a decrepit cart pulled by their oldest horse, she and her children turned out with only the property they could carry. Her arms tightened around Lottie— she had been pregnant and feared that she would miscarry along the way. No, not a good memory. The stage paused in Comfort just long enough for some of the men to jump down and stretch their legs.

"Look around, and see if we see Dolph!" Hannah cried.

Magda shook her head. "No, Nannie-my-chick—the boys would have taken the cattle down from the hills weeks ago—they're already far ahead of us. But at this speed we shall catch up to them in no time!" And the stage whirled away once more, the white dust boiling up behind and the road uncurling like a ribbon before them, dropping ever lower until they left the hills behind entirely. In late afternoon, when the sun lay slanted and golden across the lowlands ahead, the coach rocked and jolted through another river crossing.

"Salado Creek!" bawled the coach driver. "San Antone, straight ahead!"

"Oh, look!" Anna breathed. "It looks ever such a big city!"

Magda peered over her two daughter's heads and around Anna's bonnet—yes, there were domes and towers ahead, patched with rusty tile rooftops, all clustered around one enormously tall grey stone spire. Thick hedges of some spiny, dark green bush lined the road on either side.

"There are hardly any trees," Magda observed. "I wonder what they have built it all out of?" The coach rolled past a scattering of tall stone houses, as fine as any in Friedrichsburg, with glass in every window. They were set back in tidy gardens laid about with fences, but a little farther on, the town closed in on the road. This part of San Antonio, or "Bexar" as Carl Becker had always called it, was all Mexican, low and single-storey buildings, constructed out of mud-brick and burnt-tile roofs or flimsy pole houses thatched with river rushes. Doors stood open to a wide dusty plaza, and a crumbling citadel with a façade like a carved bedstead loomed over it all.

"Surely there is more to it than this?" Anna murmured, but the coach only slowed without stopping. The wheels rumbled over a short bridge; they caught a glimpse of a deep green river, smooth and edged by tall rushes down below. "This is more like what I expected," Anna sounded much relieved and even a little excited. "Oh, look! Are those musicians? And I

Celia Hayes

have never seen so long a train of pack mules. Do you suppose they have just come from Mexico? I wonder what they have brought?"

The coach slowed even more, for now they were in a long and broad street. From the crowds of people and wagons in it, Magda thought it must be the most important thoroughfare in town. The buildings lining it were a mad jumble of stoutly-built German stone as tidy as dollhouses, others built of timber planks in the American style and gaily painted, or plain Mexican mud-brick, low to the ground and with few windows looking out to the streets. Magda did note that some of the mud-brick establishments had glass windows set into the street-front side and a pleasing miscellany of goods on display within. The coach came to a halt and let them down in another square, smaller than the first plaza and presided over by a grim grey-stucco cathedral with a towering spire.

"Almost as if it were a square in the old country," Magda noted. She and Anna looked around in some apprehension, for they had expected to be met on arrival. Here they were, women alone and newly arrived in a strange town. Magda would have felt even more apprehension but for having friends here: Doctor Herff, in whose practice her brother Johann had assisted; the Guenthers, Hansi and Liesel's old neighbors from their farm in Live Oak; and not least, the family of her husband's old stockman, Porfirio Menchaca. Besides that, in the very bottom of her small valise, was one of her husband's Paterson Colt revolvers, carefully cleaned and loaded and with fresh new caps on all the cylinders. Before their marriage, Carl Becker had seen that she knew how to handle it, to shoot and reload, for those circumstances when the innate chivalry of the frontier might be in rather short supply.

There was no need for it today. Hansi Richter, stocky and dependable as always, appeared among those milling around the stage stop. Magda saw her son a little apart from the crowd, his white-blond hair a veritable beacon among the darker Mexican and American heads. Dolph was talking to a man and a woman seated in an elegant barouche. *Who were they?* Magda wondered for a moment. The man—a grey-haired, aged gentleman of immense dignity—had his hand on Dolph's shoulder as if he knew him and merely detained him for a moment's conversation.

"Papa!" Anna shrieked happily to Hansi. And who was this standing next to him but Porfirio, grown stout and prosperous? He swept Anna's hand to his lips with the same old gallant gesture, managing to convey avuncular affection, sincere masculine appreciation, and a roguish propensity to flirt all together. Hansi stood by, much amused. And then with

102

perfect aplomb Porfirio did the same for Magda, enfolding her hand in his and pressing both to his heart, addressing her as "Señora Becker." Against her will she was amused—he had been a perfect scamp of a boy, but now the propriety of his conduct and address had twenty years of practice and polish upon them.

Upon the blood of his ancestors he had sworn an oath of vengeance on the man who had murdered her husband, the Patrón, as he had called Carl Becker. Porfirio had built the coffin, rattled his popish beads during the long vigil before burial, wept at the graveside, and sworn to the widow that her husband would be avenged. When the farm was confiscated and she and the children impoverished, Porfirio saw to it she had some money. He also had helped her brother Johann escape safely to California, where he enlisted in the Union Army. Yes, he was one of those true friends.

He kissed Hannah on each cheek, admiring how she had grown. "A young lady!" he exclaimed. "When shall you have a debut, come into society and leave a thousand admirers with broken hearts!? Now he took Lottie up into his arms and admired her extravagantly, "The very image of the Patrón! You were given a blessing, Señora Becker, a very generous blessing."

"I have always been assured of that." Magda could have wept for emotion. "I have never forgotten your kindness to us or your help when we stood in most need of it. I think I shall never be able to thank you enough!"

Porfirio looked at her with a serious expression and lowered his voice. "It was a matter of honor, Señora. And of the other matter," his voice took on a steely edge, "I have not forgotten, either. My blade and his blood, sooner or later. They say he went to Mexico—it is of no moment, Señora Becker. He will return. They always return. Until then, I wait. Think of Waldrip as a walking dead man." He patted her hand again, a dapper and prosperous Mexican merchant with his beautifully brilliantined mustaches, almost but not quite concealing the steely edge and the deadly promise of his oath. Magda shivered—yes, Porfirio meant every word. "They say," he continued blandly, as if he spoke of the weather, "that Señor Talmadge, who opened the door to the Patrón's enemy? That he also is dead. Is that true?"

"Yes," Magda answered, noticing that Dolph had managed to detach himself from the gentleman in the barouche and was making his way towards them. "He was killed in the fighting around Atlanta in the last year of the war."

Porfirio smiled then, a mirthless smile, his eyes as cold and dead as a predatory animal. "Good," he said with satisfaction. He tipped his hat to

Magda and Anna, kissed Lottie and Hannah once more and took his leave. He promised the hospitality of his family on any evening that they would care to accept it. Magda shivered again, for she remembered that Porfirio and Trap Talmadge had been friends of a sort, working together with her husband. It was the bottle which had led Trap to betray her husband. Knowing that, he had gone away to seek atonement and death with Terry's Company in the fighting in the east. She felt sorrow for the man, not satisfaction.

"I have the use of a cart for your luggage," Hansi said, exuberantly. "But there is no room for more than the girls. We should walk anyway; the way is short and there is much to see. Who was that who talked so serious with you, lad?" he added to Dolph.

"Lawyer Maverick and his wife," Dolph answered with a careless shrug. "They said they were old friends of Papa's when he rode with Captain Hays' Rangers."

"Indeed," Magda sniffed. She glanced across the crowded square, where the man in the barouche and his lady still looked after Dolph, their heads close together as if they were speaking about him. "I think not. All of your Papa's true friends came to the funeral—like Porfirio and Mr. Meusebach. Let us be away, Hansi—the girls are tired after today."

"He was a decent old stick," Dolph protested mildly. "I think after a bit he rather had me mixed up with Papa. He kept saying I ought to settle into a profession, and did he want Mary—Mrs. Maverick—to take me in hand and find a nice girl to marry?"

"I have only a day to spend here," Hansi interrupted goodnaturedly. "Here, little one, ride on my shoulder, hey?" He lifted Lottie onto his shoulders and took Magda's elbow with the other hand. "Fredi and young Vining have gone ahead with the cattle herd and Dolph and I, we have two loads of hides. Oh, the stink of them! You would not find it endurable, all the way to the coast. So we shall depart in the morning, and in four days you should follow us by stage."

Anna bubbled over with excitement as she took Dolph's formally proffered arm. "Four days! Will that be enough time? We shall need to see all the shops and consult with Mr. Guenther."

"He is a sharp fellow." Hansi lifted their bags into a small cart, and nodded to the man who drove it. "He saw all the possibilities here, after he moved from Live Oak; a mill and a fine big house for his family. He introduced me to many men of business! I have gotten more contracts from two days spent here than a month anywhere else. And the acquaintance of those I wish to do business with! Nothing like meeting face to face, to get an idea of true measure. Thank God that wretched war is over! In short order, all shall be as it was before—or nearly so," he said as he looked sideways at Magda. With quiet sympathy he added, "Alas, much was lost that can never be replaced . . . but this venture! Such opportunities, as we never saw back in Albeck!"

"What about these contracts?" Anna said, as suddenly alert as a farmyard hen when a hawk flew overhead. "You kept careful notes, I hope!"

"Of course," Hansi waved expansively and Lottie squealed as his rippling shoulders threatened to toss her off her perch. "Careful, Lottchen, that was Onkel's nose!" he said as Lottie clutched at his head in fright. "Yes, I kept most careful notes, although we should go over them tonight, you, me and Guenther. What would I do without my careful secretary, then!"

"I am sure I don't know, Papa," Anna sighed. Hansi grinned and led them away, striding energetically along the busy street, pointing out establishments here and there with many a tantalizing comment about what they had to offer, or firms they could possibly do business with. He had not wasted his time while in San Antonio or his long friendship with the Guenthers.

"I am thinking, it also might serve to establish a presence here. San Antonio is at the center of matters to do with trade, you see—being at a crossroads; the old road between Nacogdoches and the west meets here with the trade route into Mexico—so Guenther and his business friends have advised me. He says we isolate ourselves too much in the hills."

Magda thought of the cool green valleys, the water tumbling over limestone falls, and the meadows of wildflowers; and compared that in her mind to the bustle and the dust of the city around them, the unfamiliar babble of Spanish and English talk all around them—and the strangers, the constant stream of strangers. But then, she told herself, there are constantly strangers in the shop. And if they were truly in business, they might have to consider living in a place that would help it prosper.

She and Anna and the girls stayed for three days with the Guenthers. Their splendidly comfortable house was in the newest part of town, a neighborhood built on the banks of a placid clear river to the south of the settlement. It was a neighborhood of large and comfortable houses built by those German settlers who had done very well in various business enterprises.

"They live as well as if they were still living in Germany," she commented to Anna, on the day that they took the stage to the south. "But for nicer weather in the winter."

"They say in summer everyone swims in the river." Anna looked at the gentle green meadows flashing past the state windows. "And the finest mansions have bathhouses at the bottom of their gardens, and in the evening everyone sips iced drinks and listens to music. There is always someone interesting come to town. I don't think I would mind living here in the least, Auntie."

"There is music and there are interesting people in Friedrichsburg," Magda pointed out chidingly.

"Yes, but more of them and a greater variety here, Auntie!"

The road to the south unreeled like a white ribbon before the coach-team. The countryside undulated gently and gradually flattened into an endless green meadow, as even as a tea tray, with cloud shadows drifting across it. They stayed a night in Victoria, which Magda recalled—from that first slow journey years before—had been a scattering of log huts and rambling walls of plastered Mexican mud-brick. Now it boasted many tall buildings of sawn wood planks, painted cheerful colors and trimmed in white wooden fretwork as delicate as lace.

The next morning they set out again, accompanied in the coach by a pair of young men who vied with each other to be of chivalrous assistance to her and Anna. She took little note of them, thinking that it was probably Anna who held their interest.

Hannah leaned dozing against her shoulder, and Lottie slept at her other side with her head in Magda's lap. Her attention was drawn to the scenery outside, especially whenever the road veered close to the riverbank. She did not share with her niece or daughters, her reason for paying such close attention fearing to be thought a sentimental fool—and she could not in truth be entirely sure she would ever be able to recognize the place she was looking for. There must have been a million spots along the lower Guadalupe where the river made a gentle bend around willow thickets, where a clump of cypress trees dipped knobby knees into the water, where the birds made a cheerful racket and the setting sun painted slanted shadows on the meadows.

"A green meadow by the river, with the birds singing all around," said Anna suddenly.

Magda, startled out of countenance, looked at her niece. "You remember," she said with surprise. "You were very small at the time—I didn't think you would."

"I remember the ship," Anna answered calmly. "And the storm. You promised that we would sit by the river in a green field and watch ducklings and dogs and deer and never set foot on a ship again. And so we did, and it was a dream that came true."

"Do you remember playing with Fredi and Johann, by the river, and how they built a raft?" Magda's lips felt suddenly dry, but not from dust. She moistened them with her tongue as Anna frowned, thoughtfully.

"I actually don't think so, Auntie. I have been told of it many times, about how the current carried the raft away and how Uncle Carl and Colonel Hays came at that moment and stopped you from going into the water and they rescued me, but I cannot really remember it for myself. It happened somewhere along here, did it not?"

"Yes," Magda answered.

Anna gently squeezed her hand, properly gloved like a lady for traveling, and smiled. The elusive dimples she had inherited from her mother danced merrily in her cheeks. "Any man who rescued—oh, Lottie, for instance—and me from a raging river? I think I would fall in love at once and forever—and beyond!"

"Oh dear," Magda observed after a quiet glance across the coach at their traveling companions, who now appeared completely smitten, "I think those two may be terribly discouraged to hear that."

"You never know." Anna lowered her eyes slyly and tilted her head so that the brim of her bonnet hid her face. "They might find such a challenge to be irresistible!"

This time when they reached their destination, Indianola, Hansi met them immediately at the stage. He assisted Magda and her daughters down from the tiny metal step, while Dolph held up his hands for Anna and impishly kissed her cheek as she descended.

"What was that for?" she asked suspiciously. Magda noted the fallen faces of the two men who had ridden with them from Victoria.

Dolph laughed. "Oh, either to spare you the trouble of unwanted attentions, or your gentleman companions the pain of a snub! I haven't decided."

"What? I do not have a chance to be the outraged Papa?" Hansi demanded, as the coach-driver and his assistant handed down their luggage.

Anna said, laughing, "I will not put you to the trouble of attending to such little matters, Papa—not when you have important business affairs at hand!"

"A nice sense of priorities," Hansi proclaimed in approval, "but no talk of business, until we are settled. I have rooms for you at a hotel, a very nice comfortable one, too, with a private sitting room; nicer than Charley Nimitz's, although I would not say so to his face. The Casimir House, and it is quite splendid, with every modern convenience! We have a wonderful view of the bay from our rooms! Would you not agree, this place is much improved from the time we first came upon it?"

Magda looked around, shaking her head in disbelief. "I would not have known it, except for the harbor."

She could scarcely credit that this busy portside town, full of trim wooden buildings with galleried balconies and raised sidewalks lining the street, could have sprung up on the selfsame spot where she, Vati, and Liesel had landed from the sloop *Adeline*. This place had been called Karlshaven then, named for the foolish Prince Solms who had been the first Verein commissioner in Texas.

There had been nothing much but tents and brush arbors, a shoal of abandoned furniture rotting away among the salt-brush along the shore, an evil smell hanging over little clusters of huts where the Verein had unaccountably dumped thousands of immigrants on a desolate shore. Here they had found Rosalie, a nameless orphan scarcely old enough to walk, weeping by the bodies of her dead parents. They had mercifully stayed here only a few weeks, living in a cave hollowed out from a sandy bank, until Mr. Meusebach had come with a party of Verein soldiers and a great train of wagons (and Hansi with his two trusty carts brought from Albeck). They had taken the immigrants away, up to the limestone hills where they had made their home ever since.

Its main avenue was the heart of Indianola, a promenade that stretched the length of town, parallel to the shoreline. In those places where there were gaps between buildings, and where the streets ran down to the strand, the sea was a constant presence. Grey-green, blue-green, or merely plain grey, a thousand silver sparks danced and glittered across the tops of a thousand incessantly moving little waves. The wind, when it blew from the sea, brought a constant salt and sea-weed smell and the mewing of gulls circling over the masts of ships that were moored against the docks. The entire town looked upon the sea. No place in it was very far from water;

either the harbor or the rush-rimmed lagoon behind. The clamor in its streets never ceased, pausing only in the depths of the night.

Hansi had rented them rooms with windows facing the sea. A constant breeze ruffled the long gauzy curtains hanging on either side. Anna and Magda set aside their bonnets, washed, and came to the private parlor. The room was strewn with a miscellany of merchants' circulars in untidy stacks, crumpled newspapers, and dirty plates that had not moved from where Hansi and the boys had left them. Anna made a 'tsk' sound between her teeth and began to set things in order. Dolph and Hansi already had their heads bent over a new pile of correspondence.

"Well, shall we be tedious and talk of business matters first?" Hansi asked. "Or wait until after dinner?"

"Business is what we came here for," Magda answered as Dolph pulled out chairs for her and for Anna. "Where are Fredi and Mr. Vining? Were they delayed upon the road?"

"They are bringing a surprise for you," Hansi said with a smug voice.

Dolph sighed, in no mood to play games. "They were at the stock-buyers. They will be here presently. Mama, there is not good news as regards cattle prices."

"Bad?" Anna raised her eyebrows.

Dolph nodded. "The wretched things abound, everywhere. We brought a herd of the fattest and best-conditioned beasts and barely got five dollars each—just about enough to cover expenses and a little over."

"Don't look so discouraged, lad," Hansi said kindly. "It is only that demand here has been met, and met several times over, leaving us with a veritable Alp of beef! Our only hope would be for someone to start a fashion for beef at every meal and every course—beef eggs, beef bacon, beef puddings and beef sweets."

"Onkel Fredi says there might be a market driving a herd north to Missouri," Dolph mentioned, "but for the folk there being so feared of the cattle-fever. No farmer along the way that you must trail a herd will countenance passage of a herd of Texas cattle."

"What about California?" Hansi asked thoughtfully.

Dolph shook his head. "Too long and dry. He'd not chance it the way the Indians are raiding again. He says there are easier means of killing yourself or going bust. Or both."

"Ah, well," Hansi brightened, "at least I got a damn good price for the hides—well worth putting up with the smell, too. What with the year's profits from the store, we can buy stock here for the next two years, if we feel so inclined. And thanks to Guenther's friends in San Antonio, I have the assurance of contracts all this summer. So, on to cheerier business then! Where shall we go first tomorrow? Annchen, did you remember our lists?"

Anna replied with brisk affection, "Of course, Papa. Auntie Magda has them in her valise."

Magda unsnapped the catches on the little leather valise that she carried everywhere when removed from all of the business-related necessities neatly arrayed in her little office behind the store.

"That reminds me, Hansi," Magda said, "you owe me a desk, a proper desk, mind you!"

"So I do," Hansi laughed. "Well, if you do not see anything that suits your fancy at Seeligson's, then draw up something for Mr. Tatsch and have it made to order. Come along, my little nun—we're planning our grand strategy! I have secured space in a warehouse and the use of stables and yard for our wagons, through the offices of one of our old friends! Do you remember Schmidt, who came no farther than here, declared himself finished with the Verein and all its works and ways, and built a house for himself? Took root like an oak tree, he did—and now he is as rich as one of the Firsts! We are invited to dine at his house tomorrow evening, by the way. Ah-ha, there's Fredi and young Vining, at last! Sit, sit, sit! Everyone will have a task and a budget. The firm of Steinmetz, Becker and Richter is poised on the edge of great things!"

There was something different. Magda could not see what it was at first, but she knew there was something. Hansi watched hers and Anna's faces expectantly as Fredi and Peter lingered a moment in the doorway, then joined them around the table. Trail-dusty and in their plain work clothes—at first she thought that was it, for Hansi and her son were wearing more formal dark coats, proper for town and doing business. Peter set down a sheaf of newspapers on the parlor table. Fredi tugged Hannah's plaits and ruffled Lottie's fair head playfully, kissed Anna with the affection of a brother—which he all but was, due to the closeness of their ages and upbringing.

"Well, what do you think?" he asked.

"Of what? The market price of beeves?" Anna asked, much puzzled.

"No, not that!" Fredi answered. "And it's not to do with that, it's something about . . . well, us."

Magda's eyes went from her son—smiling triumphantly as if he had just unveiled a grand surprise of a Christmas tree—to Fredi, who truth to tell looked about the same as always, only somewhat dirtier—and finally to Peter, who hung back with uncharacteristic bashfulness.

She realized what the difference was in him, just as Anna exclaimed, "Oh, dear, Mr. Vining! There goes the cost of your shirts, again!" Peter laughed a hearty and uninhibited laugh as he held up his left arm. It appeared whole; the shirt-cuff was buttoned around his wrist, not turned back and pinned up. But that he wore a dark leather glove over his fingers, one would have thought his hand entirely restored.

"Old Berg, with his gadgets!" Fredi exclaimed, not able to contain himself any longer. "You know how he has the gift for building what is needful? He came to help with the house, but first he went straight back to his workshop and whittled an arm for Peter!"

Hansi sat back in his chair and slapped the table top, pleased with their reaction, and admiring the new arm all over again. "Now that does beat, does it not? I tell you, it looks nearly real! I could not tell the difference myself, at first! Isn't Berg the clever chap?"

"I can't do conjuring tricks," Peter said modestly, although he looked quite pleased. "The fingers are jointed, so they can be bent to hold any position, and there is a spring to hold the thumb closed against the first finger. I can set it to grip, as long as I don't need to hold things too tight. And it looks . . . well, it looks so real that most people do not think anything of it."

Anna raised her eyebrows. "And that is what matters to you?" she asked. "That people not stare and look away?"

"Anna!" Magda hissed reprovingly.

Peter shrugged; he still looked quite pleased. "I am surprised you didn't see it at once."

"Those who know you—they see *you*!" Anna replied. "They do not see the arm that is not there. Or that is there now. Are you your arm, Mr. Vining? Or are you yourself?!"

There was an awkward silence, broken by Dolph saying gravely, "In truth, Cuz—others do not make so much of it as you think, for there are many such men, missing that or another limb. But that you do not feel the loss as much now, that is good, and it was very clever of Berg to make it so you could hold a set of reins."

Hansi slapped the table again. "Aye, he's a clever man. Now, I see you have brought today's newspapers. Good—pull up a chair, for we have plans to make!"

Magda thought that she had worked hard in the shop, but that was nothing compared to the days spent going from warehouse to warehouse with Hansi and the younger men: traipsing through smoky offices and cramped showrooms piled high with crates and hampers that spilled over with dizzying quantities and varieties of goods. It amused her very much to see how the important men, with their golden watch chains arrayed across their fine and fancy waistcoats, would first speak to Hansi and attempt to divert her and Anna elsewhere. They would offer some little refreshment, sent for by an errand boy, and show them to some little anteroom with a couple of chairs and a table to wait while the men did business. Oh, their faces, when she and Anna instead calmly accompanied the men into the dim and dusty warehouses, looping up their skirts to step around mounds of excelsior and over piles of lumber and boxes! It was nearly as amusing as the expression on their faces when Hansi not only asked Magda and Anna for their opinions, but deferred to their judgment. Oh, that was delicious, that and the sudden new deference when those important men realized that within the firm of Steinmetz, Becker and Richter, Mrs. Becker and Miss Richter spoke with quiet but powerful voices.

At one warehouse, though, Hansi and the boys withdrew to the anteroom, claiming with much merriment that with regard to this particular class of merchandise, they preferred to leave it in the hands of the distaff side of the firm.

"You know your budget, Annchen," Hansi warned, for it was a dry goods merchant with a shipment of fabric newly received from the east. "And how much space we have allotted in the wagons."

"Yes, Papa," Anna returned sedately. She and her aunt spent a blissful morning with the merchant, his assistants unrolling bolts of calico, flannel, wool goods and linen for their perusal and judgment.

"We have not been the least bit extravagant!" Anna assured her father afterwards. "We only bought a few things for ourselves, Papa. The most of it is for the store."

"But the silk and bombazine..." Magda ventured.

"Auntie, since you will not wear colors, you may as well have your black dresses made of fine cloth." Anna looked sideways at her aunt and ventured, "You could wear grey, now, for half-mourning, trimmed with a bit of purple ribbon. That would look very elegant, I think."

"No," Magda answered firmly. She would not be moved.

In the afternoons she walked with her daughters along the seashore, Lottie and Hannah searching for shells as the waves lapped gently at the blinding-white sand that was packed as firmly as a dance floor underfoot. Sometimes she allowed the girls to take off their shoes and stockings and wade into the shallow water, especially when the sun had been shining all day upon it, making it as warm as bathwater.

At times she would see Anna walking arm in arm along the strand with Peter or with Dolph, although at such a distance she did not know what they talked about. She supposed she might be judged a very careless chaperone, but Anna—being so level-headed and formidable—made such a convention hardly required.

They dined in the Casimir House dining room, or sometimes in their parlor, which the management arranged as a private dining room for them as well, and relished very much the fresh fish and oysters available with the ocean so close. Dolph and Fredi talked of little else but their hopes for the farm. Dolph did seem content and happy, though he once complained of how slow work had progressed. The roof was repaired, but little else.

"How fares the orchard?" Magda asked him

"In bloom, but not much chance of a good crop this year," Dolph answered. "Every tree lacks careful pruning, and there are only so many hours in the day."

"I should return," she sighed. "Do you think I ought to?"

"No, not yet, Mama," Dolph answered practically. "There is still so much to be done. You would not wish to see it as it is now."

She left it at that, for in her heart she agreed with her son. One could not return to a riverbank. Places changed, no matter how dearly one remembered what had happened there. Perhaps it would be better to keep the memory green in one's heart, rather than attempt a return journey. And besides, there was the shop, and this new enterprise.

"I wish," Hansi often observed with regret, "that Lise had been able to accompany us. What a holiday, eh?"

On the last full day, she and Anna and Hansi went to one particular merchant and picked out a china tea set for Liesel. The porcelain was as thin and translucent as a sea shell, glazed a delicate pink and trimmed with gold.

Hansi had it all re-packed in straw and a stout wooden box. "Just room enough, in the wagon," Hansi said in satisfaction. "Don't tell Lise that we have bought this for her—I want to surprise her."

"It's perfect, Papa." Anna went on tiptoes to kiss his cheek. "And she will be surprised—shall we just bring the crate into the kitchen, or shall we unpack it ourselves and leave her to find it in the parlor?"

"Whatever you decide will surprise her the most, Annchen!"

Chapter Seven: *Vati*

For some days after Hansi and the boys departed with their heavily laden wagons, Magda, her daughters, and Anna remained in their rooms at the Casimir House. They enjoyed daily strolls on the hard-packed beach, and one day they attempted to locate the approximate site of the sandy declivity which they and the Altmuellers had shared as a camping place—without success, for although there was still a marshy and rush-fringed lagoon behind the sand-shoreline, it was much changed in shape, and the brush-topped dunes had long since been flattened and covered with warehouses and stores. Once they'd had enough of leisure, although Hannah and Lottie claimed they did not have nearly as many seashells as they would like, they set out in the regular coach for Victoria, San Antonio, and points north.

Anna sighed and settled back against the padded seat as they departed the rag-tag plaza in San Antonio. "I shall be so glad to be home, and to sleep in a familiar bed once again, even if Marie talks in her sleep. And snores, however much I toss hairbrushes at her. Was Mama as noisy to share a bed with, Auntie? Was it as restless as sharing a bed with a husband?"

"I couldn't really say," Magda replied with austerity. Her own husband had been a quiet sleeper; save on those occasions when he had nightmares and talked in his sleep. Of that, she felt herself obligated not to discuss out of loyalty and love. Anna sent her a sideways glance and they talked little as the coach began to skim along the road north, towards the blue shadow of the hills.

They anticipated their arrival home with joy, looking forward to sharing an account of their travel and doings with Vati, Liesel, and Rosalie. Around noon Hannah looked from the window and cried, "Oh, Mama, look! The wildflowers are blooming! Shall we take a walk down to the creek tomorrow and pick some?

"As soon as everyone is done with their chores," Magda answered. She lifted Lottie onto her lap so that her younger daughter could see out of the stage window. "But they are so beautiful, like a painting of the sea, all blue and white!"

Sam waited for them at the stage stop behind the hotel, and Charley Nimitz, too—as was his right as the owner of the finest hotel within two thousand miles. But as soon as she saw their somber faces, Magda knew that a joyful return was out of the question. Sam's normal ebullience had been quenched.

Charley took her hands to help her and the girls alight from the tall stage step. "Mrs. Magda, I'm afraid I bring you bad news."

Before Charlie could say another word, Sam blurted out, "Mama, Opa's awful sick. Doctor Keidel says he likely won't get better." He swallowed, looking as thought he were bravely forcing back the urge to bawl as if he were Willi's age.

"Oh, Samuel!" Magda drew him to her. Of her children, he was closest to Vati, as she had been in turn. Sam and Vati shared a love of books and matters of the mind. Magda also thought that perhaps Sam had looked up to his grandfather in ways that boys deprived of a father would look to a fair substitute. She looked over the top of his head—oh, when had Sam grown so tall, that he came up nearly to her chin?

"You are returned just in time, I think," Charley added. "We would have sent word to Hansi. I have sent a message to the Stielers in Comfort to watch for him and urge his return with all dispatch."

"Papa is naught but two or three days away," Anna said. Although her eyes were dry, her voice quavered. "He had planned a detour to Neu Braunfels, but Uncle Fredi and Dolph will receive your message in a day or so. How is Mama bearing up?"

"As well as may be expected, but I daresay all the better now that you have returned," Charley answered, although his face was set in lines of grief. He loved Vati as well as one of his own family, having visited their house almost from the first moment he arrived in Friedrichsburg, when it was nothing but a sea of stumps and half-built houses. "I've told young Sam that I will make the cart available to you, for your sisters have been looking for you every moment since the coach arrived. Such poor comfort, eh? The use of a cart?" he kissed Magda's hand, clapped Sam on the shoulder, and embraced the girls as if they were all of one age—and that very young. "We will see to what is necessary, don't you worry about that. Herr Steinmetz is someone we all hold in deep affection."

Without any more ado, he carried their bags from the coach and saw them away, in the light one-horse cart that he used for hotel guests and their business around town. All the joy and anticipation of homecoming on a bright clear spring day had vanished, smothered by a dark cloud of grief and dread. Yet the sight of Vati, deathly ill, could not be as wrenching to Magda as the sight of her own husband in his coffin, or that of her mother's canvas-wrapped body sinking into the sea with barely a splash. No, Magda told herself desperately—nothing could be as bad. And Vati was not that old, he had never been ill, the doctor must be mistaken. She and Anna, together with her sisters—they would nurse him back to health.

"What happened, Sam?" she asked her son as he took up the reins. "When did he fall ill?"

"A week ago," he gulped, steadying his voice with an effort. "No, about ten days. It was a fair day and he was reading in the garden. I was digging in fresh muck around the trees. Around midday he asked me when Auntie Liesel would have supper ready, and I went to ask. Almost the moment I turned away, I heard him cry out. He stood up, clutching at his head as if he was in pain and then he fell down. His glasses broke on the stones when he fell and," shamefacedly he added, "he had wet himself, like a baby. His eyes were open, but he was not there, not himself, and he did not know us for many hours, until the next morning. Doctor Keidel says that a blood vessel burst in his head and that was what pained him so."

"But did he speak, did he not recognize anyone?" Anna asked. She rode in the back of the cart with Hannah, sitting on top of the bags. Poor Hannah appeared so tearful and stricken; Anna held her close for the comfort of both of them.

"He knew us," Sam answered bravely, "But he can barely speak … and half of his face droops as if he cannot move it. Doctor Keidel told Auntie Liesel that he had a slight p-p-paralysis of his limbs, but that it is becoming worse instead of better. All that we can do is to keep him comfortable and wait."

"Oh, Sam," Magda said helplessly while her son stared straight ahead, struggling to master his feelings. "I so wish Johann were here … or even Doctor Herff!"

"It's not as if they could make it any better just by saying so," Sam answered, wretchedly. "They're all doctors, after all. They'd say pretty much the same—I know, because I asked to look in some of Opa's own books about what might be done for what was wrong with Opa."

"How have your aunts managed?" Magda asked, carefully.

Her son almost sounded cheered when he replied, "Aunt Rosalie cried simply buckets, but not when we worked in the shop. She was very brave, then—everyone who came in asked about Opa, of course. Mrs. Schmidt came to help Auntie Liesel nurse Opa. Everyone has just been waiting for you and Onkel Hansi to come home, including Vati." He reined in Charley's horse at the front door of the house. "You should go in from here, Mama—I must take Captain Nimitz's cart back to the hotel."

Carrying Lottie in her arms, Magda rushed through the door. The stair-hall was empty, but only for a moment. Rosalie appeared from the shop and cried, "Oh, thank God! He has been asking for you, so piteously I could not bear it!"

Magda whispered fiercely, "Don't you dare begin to weep, little Rose, for I could not bear it either!" Her sister smiled to be brave and took Lottie from her.

"Go up then—and hurry, for we feared that he only holds on to life for wishing to see you!"

Up the stairs, while the girls gathered around Rosalie. Her heart was wrung, for this should have been a happier welcome, with the girls telling stories of Indianola and the curiosities to be found there, and of walking by the sea and eating ice cream cooled with ice brought from faraway New England and dearest Vati would be drinking in every word. Silence hung oppressively upstairs, as well as the faint pervasive smell of a sickroom. As she reached the landing, Liesel opened the door to Vati's room, a basket of laundry in her arms. She looked old, Magda realized with a pang; old and strained. She looked even more like Mutti, now that she had nearly reached the age that Mutti had been when Vati cajoled her into agreeing to accept the Verein's terms of emigration.

"I thought I heard your voices," she said with relief. "I had told him a hundred times that today was the day when you were expected. He forgets everything!"

"Vati always does," Magda answered.

Liesel sniffled a little. She closed the door behind her carefully, and kept her voice to a whisper. "No, now he forgets from moment to moment. Oh, I so wish Hansi was here! If only . . . "

"It's not as if your husband can somehow fix what ails Vati," Magda observed tartly. Liesel's eyes filled and spilled over onto her cheeks. *Why did everyone in this house begin weeping at the slightest provocation?* Magda raged to herself. She wished that Hansi would hurry his team along and return as fast as he could, for at least he would not be dissolving into useless tears. "I am sorry, Lise, I didn't mean to sound harsh. Shall I go in and let Vati see that we are safely returned?"

"Yes, of course." Liesel gulped, and set the laundry down on a small table which had been moved to stand beside the door. Magda realized it was there for someone to set a tray or burden on whilst opening the sickroom door. "Let me take your bonnet and mantle. He's sleeping now, but never for long."

Within Vati's room was silence, and light pouring in from dormer windows on either side. When Hansi and his sons had extended the house to make a larger workroom and storeroom below, they had made the room above into a bedchamber and study for Vati, with views onto the street on one side and onto the garden on the other. Vati lay propped on white pillows, so tiny and shriveled, hardly larger than one of the children. Her heart was wrung anew by the sight and by the sight of his glasses, lying on the dresser nearby, folded like the legs of a delicate gold insect. One of the thick lenses was smashed and a thin crack ran across the other. Poor Vati, he could barely see without them! Kindly, clever and endearing, he may not have been her parent by blood—having married Mutti when she was a tiny child—but her own father could not have been more tender or careful of her. Now they were about to lose him, but she pushed that thought aside.

She sat in the chair by his bedside with a quiet rustle of skirts. She would have taken his slack hand in hers, but feared to wake him. Someone had thought to arrange the furnishings so that he could look out from his bed into the garden, where his precious pear tree held up a cloud of delicate white bloom against the dark wall of the smokehouse and the hedge of wild mountain laurels separating the garden from the stable yard.

Liesel had assured her that Vati slept lightly and never for long. He stirred at the hastily muffled sounds of voices and footsteps on the stairs, turning his head on the pillow and opening his eyes, wide and unfocused without his glasses and as grey as rain. She saw that what Sam had said was true, that half of his face slumped downwards as if he had not command of his own features. But his eyes were alight with the same interest and affection that had ever burned in them, as he struggled to speak.

"M-m-g-da," His words came out a hopeless mush. "H-h-m . . ."

"Yes, dear Vati—we're home," she answered, tenderly. "Don't try to talk. You'll exhaust yourself for nothing. Shall I tell you about our journey? Just nod yes or no to my questions, Vati. We are so glad to be home, although we had a wonderful time, visiting the city! Hansi has bought the loveliest tea set for Liesel. This year we have prospered, we really have. Not as much as young Mr. Guenther." She continued on, keeping her voice soothing as she told Vati all of what she had been longing to tell him. He listened at first with attention, but within a short while his gaze became unfocused, wandering about the room and finally fixing on the window beyond her shoulder.

"P—p-r . . . t-t-t-re—ee," he made a great effort, "b-b-b-l-o-m."

"Yes, Vati, the pear tree is blooming," she answered, humoring him. That answer seemed to satisfy him, and he drifted back into that light sleep. She moved to softly get up and leave the room, but he still had her hand.

"S-s-s-i-m," he said with the same heartbreaking difficulty, "l-t-t-t-r . . . r-r-r-e-d."

"Read Uncle Simon's letters?" she asked, tentatively; and he nodded, barely moving his head on the pillow. It was not as if he had much in the way of treasured material possessionss, aside from books and his watchmaking tools. The fat bundle of old letters sat in two stacks on the bedside stand, as if someone else had already begun reading them. She picked up one on top of the taller stack that was already open and read of it, puzzling out Uncle Simon's neat, regular pen-scratches until Vati's eyes closed again.

The door opened softly at the end of the room, and Liesel whispered, "He shall sleep for a little bit, then I shall sit with him." She looked critically at Magda and added, "And you should rest yourself, Magda—you must be tired, after coming such a long way."

Magda shrugged, but she was grateful for the relief. Suddenly she was aware of how very tired she was indeed—exhausted down to her very bones. "We have so much to tell you all, but it doesn't seem very important now."

"I have already heard most of it," Liesel said, giving her a little push, "from Anna and the girls. And I suppose Hansi shall tell me once more, with embellishments about his cleverness and perspicuity."

"And justly so, for he is very good at this merchandising matter," Magda observed, "and the freight business as well. Good old farmer Hansi—who would have thought it of him?"

"I would have." As always, Liesel rose up in stout defense of her husband. "Even back in Albeck, I thought he could do anything he set his mind at!"

"He would never have had a chance, if we had not come here," Magda pointed out. "And did Anna tell you of the bolt of fine lawn we purchased at Rouff's? We thought of making new baby-linen for Rosalie's child, for all we have to give to her is stained and nearly worn out."

"Well, at least all of mine got good use of the old baby things." Liesel's face brightened. "Rosalie's shall have new and fair. I am so glad you are back, now!" She embraced her sister impulsively, as if she were Hannah's age. "Between the shop and the household and nursing Vati, if it weren't for Mrs. Schmidt, I don't know how we would have managed!"

In the days following their return from the coast, life settled into a queer, suspended rhythm, orbiting around the quiet sickroom upstairs. The next day Fredi, Peter, and Dolph arrived on lathered horses. They had traveled light and fast, abandoning work on the house. As Dolph observed philosophically, they had put a pause on their labors to trail cattle to Indianola, and another week or so would hardly matter.

"And Opa might yet recover," Dolph added hopefully.

Magda sighed. "Doctor Keidel advises guarding against such hope. Vati might live for quite some time, but as an invalid needing tender care. He says that your grandfather will never be able to move from his bed without assistance, so severe is the paralysis afflicting him."

"At least we know that he will not wander away and fall into the creek," Dolph pointed out, with the air of someone finding a silver lining to the blackest storm cloud.

"Very true." Magda found herself able to smile at that observation.

Dolph and her other children were of great comfort and assistance to her during those days after their return, those strange days which continued to feel to her as if they were all suspended above a precipice. Anna, Liesel and the children were tireless in their attendance on Vati, taking turns reading to him or sitting at his bedside telling him of their lessons. Unasked, Sam slept at night in Vati's room, on a pallet laid on the floor at the foot of his bed, that he might be close at hand during the night. He and Dolph and their cousin Elias were of most welcome assistance when it came to the indignities associated with cleanliness and bodily wastes. Dolph, with his nearly-grown strength, proved to be a most deft and tender nurse, gently lifting his grandfather so Liesel and Rosalie could change the sheets.

When Magda made mention of it, her son answered mildly, "We often had to do such service in Colonel Ford's company, Mama. Who else would tend our sick and wounded, then, if not for each other? I looked after Colonel Ford for months when he fell ill after he got word about General Lee surrendering."

Rosalie went with Lottie and Grete to gather flowers from the meadows beyond Baron's Creek. She had comforted them in their sore distress at seeing Vati in his condition the one time they were allowed into the sickroom. Lottie remained grave and silent, but Grete whimpered and pressed tight against Rosalie's skirts when she tried to urge them closer to Vati's bed.

Even Willi turned obstinate. Finally Rosalie said, "Poor lambs, it is hard for them to understand what has happened, and that it is still Vati."

Magda and Lottie shared her little bedroom with Rosalie, so they might be close to the sickroom at night.

Rosalie gratefully yielded governance of the store and its accounts back to Magda. Sitting up in bed that evening with Lottie in her arms, she said, "Oh, my—you and Anna are welcome to it! How you ever can keep all that straight, I cannot fathom."

"It is a great task, sometimes," Magda sighed. She sat at the foot of the bed with her knees drawn up under her nightgown and pulled her treasured Mexican-silver hairbrush through the long spill of her hair. Curiously, it called to mind those times she had shared sleeping quarters with her sister and with the younger Anna. "But after managing business affairs for my husband's house, I have found it only a matter of degree. Margaret told me once that she found it all quite invigorating, to have a great work of your own. I did not understand, quite, at the time. My children were all young and hers nearly grown and more."

"Mine has grown, enormously!" Rosalie giggled. "Look!" Setting the almost-asleep Lottie aside, Rosalie slid from under the coverlet and stood up. She gathered the folds of her nightgown in either hand, pulling the fabric close against her body. "You can almost see that I am truly with child!" And to be sure, revealed by the tight-drawn fabric, there was the slightest of bulges above the jut of her hipbones.

"So it has, little Rose." Magda set aside her hairbrush. Rosalie giggled and let go her nightgown. She climbed into bed again and sat with the covers drawn over her knees.

"Robert will be so pleased," she added, as she curved her arm around the sleeping Lottie and tenderly wound a lock of the child's hair around her finger. "Do you not despair of her hair being as straight as a stick? I so hope our child will have curly hair, but I vow I do not care about that all that much, really. Boy or girl, curls or straight—it will be so fair to have a child of our own! I can hardly wait!"

Magda blew out the candle and climbed into her own side of the bed. "Nor could I, little Rose." They lay in almost-darkness for a little while, for there was a tiny oil lamp burning on the table in the hall by the door to Vati's room. "Will your Robert—will he be a good father? Will he see the child as proof of his being a proper man? Or will he look on it as being trusted with the care of some wonderful and unknown plant that will bloom and thrive in accordance with the care he lavishes upon it? Will he think of this child as being a wholly unique being, a precious thing only entrusted into our care for a little while? Children sometimes do not thrive in this world!" Suddenly, Magda's voice caught in her throat. Ah, God, her eyes overflowed unbidden, thinking of her first daughter and the babe she had lost at six months, and of Joachim—Liesel and Hansi's firstborn son, who died of ship-fever in his mother's arms and was buried at sea all those years ago. Children died and their parents mourned; parents died and their children put on mourning colors. It was the expected thing that children stand at their parent's graves and throw in that last sad handful of earth. Dust to dust, ashes to ashes . . .

In the dark, her sister reached out for her hand and said in tones of wonder and awe, "Just now, I felt the tiniest flutter. It was not a pang of digestion from Mrs. Schmidt's wonderful dinner. It was something moving in myself, which was not of myself! It was the baby, was it not, Magda? Oh, there it goes again! I do not think it likes stewed beef and cabbage!"

"Well, that is Auntie Schmidt's cooking." In the darkness, Magda reached under the covers and patted Rosalie's stomach, "Sleep, baby, sleep, your father is watching the sheep . . . ."

". . . Your mother is shaking the little tree, sweet dreams fall down for you and me, sleep baby sleep," Rosalie completed the verse, all the while fighting off a yawn. "I remember you singing that to me, and Liesel singing it to Jacob and Georg. And now I shall sing it to my baby." She turned, rustling the bedclothes in the darkness. "What a wonderful thought. Will Robert be pleased to hear that I felt the baby moving? Or is it one of those things that men don't care to hear much about?"

Magda had come to think well of her American brother-in-law; of his considerable qualities, the most important of them being that he made Rosalie so very happy. With wry affection she answered, "He may not boast of it to his friends, little Rose, but still, it would please him very much, I think. I never saw my own husband's face look as happy as he did on that day that he felt Dolph kick and move within me."

She heard Rosalie sigh, a happy sigh of perfectly delicious contentment. "Magda," she asked after a moment, "you know, he will be here on Saturday, and we had planned that I would be going home with him, the Sunday after you returned. But should I now remain here, since Vati is so ill? I am so torn, Magda. I long for Robert and our little house, but with Vati so declined . . ."

"No," Magda reached out for her sister, and stroked back those strawberry curls from her forehead, "No, little Rose. Your place is with your husband. I do not think Vati has declined much since our return and I do believe he is a little better. I think he can talk a little more clearly—or perhaps I am just better accustomed to understanding him. You should go home on Sunday. If need be, we can send one of the boys with a message. In any case," she added with a small sigh of her own, "it is a given, everyone has always thought that I should be the one to care for Vati eventually. Perhaps it is best to gracefully accept that responsibility."

In the dark, Rosalie intercepted her hand, and clasped it in hers. She responded in tones which mingled both concern and relief. "You are sure that you and Liesel will not need me to remain?"

"Go home to your husband, Little Rose," Magda answered with affectionate understanding. "Go home to your house and your husband— while you have such and they need you. Sleep on thoughts of that homecoming, then. I shall see to Vati and the shop, as it was always intended."

Hansi and his sons arrived midday on Friday, having been in receipt of an urgent message sent by Charley to Neu Braunfels. They had not dared to travel at night, for there had been reports of Comanche raiding parties roaming at will in the Pedernales river country, but they rose well before sun-up and drove their teams hard. At her table in the workroom Magda heard the shop doorbell chime, but before she could move, Hansi charged in like a bull and fairly lifted Magda from her chair.

"Vati—he lives, still? We are not too late?" He looked around, and seemed to come to himself. "Of course not. You would have not opened the shop, otherwise. I had the boys leave me in the street, while they took the wagons around back."

"He has lived for almost a fortnight in this condition," Magda answered, "and against Doctor Keidel's advice, we almost begin to hope. I think he is a little improved, or at any rate, not worsened."

"We hurried at such speed, fearing the worst when we received Charley's message." Hansi shook his head, and almost laughed in boyish relief. "I fear that the horses will not soon forgive us, for the pace we made them set! Where is Lise? Upstairs? Good, I'll have them unpack her tea-set first. Good news then, eh?" He embraced her, hurriedly, and departed in the same manner and at the same exuberant pace, galloping up the staircase and calling for Liesel, although Rosalie emerged from the kitchen and Anna from the garden, both of them pleading for quiet.

Hansi's exuberance over the bargains they had been able to strike in Indianola, the promised cartage contracts from various merchants, and his pride in showing it all off to Liesel, revived all of their spirits. Vati's condition even seemed a little improved—at any rate, he was not any worse. On Saturday, Robert Hunter arrived and Rosalie flew to his arms as a bird returning to its favored nest. He brought word that one of their neighbors was going to complete a whole new barn and had planned a grand party to which all of those living nearby were invited.

Of course there was no question but that Rosalie should go home with him. Liesel agreed on that as well; Vati seemed to be better, he was not on his deathbed after all. And then Rosalie was struck with one of her brilliant Rosalie-notions and begged for the younger children to accompany her for a week-long visit.

"They shall be company for me and a preparation for when I care for my own!" she pleaded. "Please—it would only be for the week and they would have so much fun at the Fischers' barn-raising." She held hands with Lottie and Grete, who looked at their mothers with identical longing expressions. They both adored Rosalie, who petted and spoiled them with affectionate attention. "And you are so much taken up with the care of Vati and everything," Rosalie added. "Having them with me would lessen some of the burden on you. Please, just consider it."

"Please, Mama? May I?" Willi echoed. "Onkel Robert will let me ride his horse!"

Magda knelt on the parlor floor, where she and Liesel were unpacking the tea-set, unearthing each delicate piece like a treasure and placing them carefully in the ornate set of shelves that Hansi had produced from the first of wagonloads of goods.

"Oh, no, never," Liesel replied. "I could not countenance my children being so far from me at this time."

"But Vati himself sent me to live with you during the cholera, and Fredi and Johann to live with Magda and Brother Carl," Rosalie pleaded. "And when the children were sick with diphtheria, Anna took the babies to the Sunday house. Surely you trust me as well as you trust Anna?"

"Of course we trust you, little Rose," Magda temporized.

Lottie whispered, "Please, Mama?"

Magda regarded her daughter, the youngest of her children and the one from whom she least wanted to be separated; Lottie, nearly four years old and yet so fair and sweet-tempered. She and her cousin Grete were constant playmates and shared everything, including a cot together in the bedroom they lived in with Anna, Marie, and Hannah. They were both very proud of having taken that indefinable step from being infants.

Magda allowed carefully, "I think that we should consider this."

Hansi came in from the back with his arms full of more boxes; boxes full of fine goods from Indianola, which he set down just inside the door. "Consider what?" he asked, as he kissed Rosalie on the cheek, ruffled the little girls' hair and neatly pinched Liesel's bottom.

"Hansi, she wants to take the girls and Willi for a visit!" Liesel sounded anguished.

"Only for a week, Lise, and I promise that I shall care for them as carefully as . . . as you cared for me, when Vati asked that I should live with you until the cholera passed by!" Rosalie pleaded again. As Hansi looked from his children and Rosalie with their bright and eager faces, to Liesel's anguished countenance, Magda realized that the choice had fallen to him, and only in hindsight would she come to know how fateful that small decision would turn out to be.

"Oh, let them go, Lise," he said. "They should have a little holiday. After all, you would not let them go to the coast. You wept tempests of tears at the thought of even allowing them to accompany us without you. Let them go to Robert's. You cannot object on that account! Our little Rose will care for them as tenderly as she has cared for them every day that you have been busy in the sickroom and Magda with the shop. Vati is not as ill as all that, but you and Magda still have a full plate, eh? Let them have their holiday, Lise."

"Oh, thank you, Papa!" said Willi happily. At last Liesel acquiesced, but her face was the very aspect of woe and unhappiness as she sat on the parlor floor with her lap full of fragile shell-pink teacups and saucers.

But on that very Sunday morning, Lottie complained of a pain in her throat. During church services she leaned on Magda's lap, sleepy and fretful, her face flushed with fever. Magda carried her home and put her to bed, deciding with an odd mixture of reluctance and relief, that she could not countenance Lottie venturing the carriage ride to Robert Hunter's farm while sick. No, not knowing how easily, how swiftly, small children could sicken and die. Lottie was the last and—although she would not admit this to another living soul—the most precious of her children by Carl Becker. There would be no more children of her body, she would not marry again as her mother had, coming to love another after that first and transient dear love. She would risk no threat to that child. All of her children were loved, but Lottie had that most particularly secure place in her heart. So, she tucked Lottie back into bed and came downstairs to tell Rosalie and Robert that she would not risk a worsening of Lottie's condition or any danger of illness to Rosalie herself.

Rosalie leaned down from the front seat of Robert's trap and kissed Magda with her usual exuberant affection. "Poor little lamb," she said. "Never mind, then, perhaps next week after church I shall take Lottie for a picnic in the meadows, and we will pick the most splendid flowers, just the two of us! It will be her very special treat!"

Robert snapped the whip over the back of the single horse which drew the little spring-trap that he used for trips into town. Some impulse led Magda to watch after them for a moment, as the trap bowled down Market Square and turned the corner. The last sight she had was Willi waving happily from the back, with Rosalie clutching the back of Grete's dress as the little girl stood up on the seat between her and Robert, also waving her little hands.

"Oh, the house shall be so very quiet without them," Liesel lamented. "Too quiet for my liking! I wish we had not let them go, Magda!"

"It was too quiet for them, Lise," Magda comforted her sister, "for we were always shushing them, telling them that they must play quietly, lest they disturb Opa. They may run and play as loudly as they like at Rosalie's house. And that will be good for them, and good for Rosalie, also."

"I suppose," Liesel sighed, "but still—I shall be glad when they are returned to me. I don't think I shall have a restful moment until my babes are home safe where they belong."

Magda sat in the parlor of her daughter's house, as midnight chimed. Lottie was eating the soup that Magda brought from the kitchen. "She was right, you know," Magda said. "All unknowing. I had never thought your aunt to be a prophetess. She did not have a restful moment for a very long time."

Skeptically Lottie answered, "But surely she did not know it when she said that, Mama."

"No, she busied herself in the parlor, cutting out baby clothes for Rosalie's little one. She . . . none of us knew anything of the fate that would befall, or the true use to which that fine white lawn would be put." In the firelight, Magda's eyes had the shine of tears unshed. "None of us ever considered such a thing, until it fell from the sky like a thunderbolt when there are no clouds in sight."

Wednesday dawned clear and mild, although a line of clouds in the western skies might yet promise rain. Hansi and the boys went out to the stable yard in a great lather after breakfast, for there were goods to be inventoried and loaded. Magda took advantage of a quiet moment in the store to slip upstairs and attend on her daughter, then to see if Vati should be need anything. The clock in the parlor chimed half-past as she looked into Lottie's room. Liesel, armed with a set of pins in her mouth, her measuring tape in one hand and shears in the other was preparing for a zestful campaign against the bolt of lawn which Anna and Magda had brought from Indianola. She had promised to step into the shop to help Anna if necessary, but her eyes and her mind were obviously inclined towards seams, tucks and ruffles. Magda thought ruefully that her sister would forget entirely about the shop within about five minutes.

Lottie was asleep, curled up in the center of the truckle-bed she shared with Grete, her thumb in her mouth. Jack the dog lay on the rug at the side of her bed. Jack made doleful eyes at Magda and thumped his tail apologetically—honestly, how that dog managed to slip into the house and creep upstairs without anyone noticing. Magda forbore to chase him downstairs again, for she thought that Lottie might be lonely for Grete, her almost-twin. And poor Jack undoubtedly missed Sam and Hannah, who would not be home from school for some hours yet. She tiptoed out of the girls' room and into Vati's room. He too was asleep, with his face towards the window. No matter; she would linger for a few minutes. If he woke, then she would read to him from Uncle Simon's old letters; if not, then she would have a few minutes of respite from her vast assortment of cares.

She leaned her elbows on the windowsill, and looked out into the garden below and the stable yard beyond the laurel hedge. There was Hansi with a copybook in hand, making marks in it with a pencil, while Fredi busied himself with walking one of the horses up and down. They both appeared to be closely observing the horse's off-hind leg, and as Magda watched, Fredi got down on one knee to tie a poultice around the bad leg and wrap it with a long bandage. Magda saw her son emerge from the barn, leading another horse and evidently talking over his shoulder to Peter. She marveled again at the likeness between them; so marked at a distance, with the same height and the fair hair. That likeness dissolved at close range, for Peter was as outgoing as Dolph was reserved and that dissimilar temperament stamped their features as markedly as Peter's mustache and scar.

She was startled by a stampede of hoof beats in the street outside; three or four horses being ridden quite fast. She could not move swiftly enough to the opposite window to look down and see who it was, or why anyone would be riding through the city at such speed. But it made no matter, for there they were—three men in haste came around the end of their house and rode into the stable yard. The first brought up his horse in a cloud of dust, dismounting in a graceless rush. It was Hansi they meant to speak to; she could see as clear through the glass window as if it were a stage pantomime and read the expressions on their faces, although she could not hear what they said.

A trickle of unease went down her spine, for the man who spoke to Hansi was John Hunter. Once he had come asking for shelter under her husband's roof, riding a lathered horse and fleeing men who hunted him, hunted him as if he were an animal. She did not recognize one of the two men who remained on their horses, but the other was Charley Nimitz. He looked towards the house and she lifted her hand to wave at him, but he did not appear to see her standing in the window. His face was set in grim, unsmiling lines—most uncharacteristic for Charley. The only time she had seen him so somber was when he told her of Vati's condition . . . and before then, during the nightmare of her husband's funeral. Again, he must be bringing bad news; that must be the only explanation. Her children? Fear clutched at her heart with icy claws and then slackened; no, her son was down in the yard, in plain sight—and Lottie in bed asleep in the next room. Hannah and Sam were at school. Surely she would have heard some alarm if there was a danger threatening the children there.

John Hunter spoke only a few words to Hansi. Magda almost cried out, for it seemed that those brief words struck Hansi and the boys, first to stillness and then to a fury of action. Hansi thrust the copybook into his vest, and Fredi and Peter turned and ran into the stable. John Hunter sprang back onto his horse; he, Charley and the stranger departed in a thunder of dust and little clods of dirt thrown up by the storm of their departure.

Down below, her son was already running across the garden towards the house. Hansi lifted his head and looked towards the house, at the window where she stood. She nearly cried out again, for his face bore an expression of horror and almost unbearable dread.

Chapter Eight: *Comanche Moon*

Magda ran downstairs, as quietly as she could manage it, and intercepted her son in the kitchen. Dolph was methodically rummaging through the pantry shelves and throwing certain things—smoked meat, dried fruit, bread, and crackers—into a gunnysack. He had a belt looped over one shoulder, a belt heavy with the weight of a pair of massive Navy Colts that he had brought back from his service with Colonel Ford, and in which he took as much pride and care as his father had in his fragile and slender Paterson five-shot revolvers.

"Rudolph Christian Becker, tell me what has happened!" she demanded, in her sternest motherly tones. "What did John Hunter come to tell you, in such a hurry that he must go around to the back and speak to your Uncle Hansi directly instead of coming to the front door like a civilized man?"

Dolph hardly looked aside from her face as he swept a little bag of sugar candy into the sack and responded with a question of his own. "Where is Aunt Liesel?"

"In the parlor, cutting out new clothes, unless she is in the shop with Anna." A horrible suspicion dawned and broke and Magda stayed her son with a hand on his arm.

"Good," he answered calmly, and with that air of sad maturity which sat so oddly on the countenance of so young a man. "You both should stay with her."

"What has happened? Tell me!" she demanded again, but he deftly slipped from under her hand.

He buckled the gun belt around his waist. "They have found Robert Hunter's horse wandering free with a Comanche lance stuck into it, and his trap wrecked by the side of the road. Him, they found dead nearby with his head bashed in and scalped." She gasped in horror and grief. Her son added calmly, "They have taken the children and Rosalie—but we have a chance to follow their tracks and rescue them if we leave now."

And with that, he was gone from the house. In the time they had spoken those brief words, Fredi and Peter had saddled four horses, including blanket-rolls and long holsters for rifles and carbines. From the kitchen window, she saw Dolph run across the garden and toss the gunnysack to Fredi, saw him leap into the saddle as a bird leaps from the ground into the air—and then the boys wheeled away with the same thunder of hoof-beats, the same desperate urgency that drove John Hunter and Charley.

Just like that, a few words, and Robert Hunter dead? That direct and gallant young man who had kept his love for Rosalie alive through four desperate years of fighting in the East and come home to marry her . . . dead? Near to his own house, in time of peace, and with their child on the way . . . of course, he would have protected Rosalie and the children to his last desperate breath. She heard the door to the garden open and shut again and shivered at the sound, for the way it thumped sounded like the thudding of clods of earth on a coffin lid. Hansi stood in the hallway, his face a mask of desolation and dread. As soon as she came out of the kitchen, he turned towards her.

"They've taken my children," he said. His voice almost sounded normal, but his eyes had the same look of bottomless grief in them as they had on that long-ago day on the *Apollo* when the canvas-shrouded body of his and Liesel's baby son had been tipped into the cold, deep blue water. He had wept in Magda's arms then, for they had been childhood playmates, their companionship older than his marriage to her sister. "I have to tell Lise now. Please, Magda—come with me. She will be distraught."

"Yes, of course," she answered. Yet another memory came to her mind, of how he had ridden over the hills to come to Magda's side during the second year of the war, even when there was a death mark from the Hanging Band against his name. Magda's husband had considered him a friend. She thought of how Charley Nimitz remained her friend though she had declined his suit of marriage. Yet Charley has also been Carl Becker's good friend. Men of quality had loved her. She may have married only one of them, but Hansi and Charley were still her dearest and most reliable of friends. What better affidavit to being a woman of strength and character could be asked? "She is in the parlor, Hansi. Let me call Anna and close the shop."

He nodded and sank onto the hall bench as if too wearied and heartsick to move, head bowed to his hands.

She stepped to the shop door and spoke into the room. Anna looked sharp and startled from behind the counter at the back, but obediently closed the shades and locked the street door.

"Auntie? Papa? What is wrong?" She lowered her voice to a whisper, "Has something happened to Mama?"

"Robert Hunter was killed by Comanche raiders, sometime last night or this morning," Magda answered, through lips that felt as cold and stark as death itself. "Rosalie and the children are missing."

Anna gasped, a tiny sound in the hallway, but seeming as loud as a scream.

Above their heads on the stairs Lottie quavered, "Mama, why is Onkel Hansi crying!" She stood on the landing, barefoot in her nightgown, looking uncertainly between the three adults.

"Oh, Lottie—you should not have gotten out of bed!" Magda cried, nearly struck insensible by the realization that mere random chance had kept Lottie safely by her. If her precious child had not fallen sick, then she would also have been taken. The thought of Lottie carried away by one of the barbarous Comanche warriors or worse yet, dead and mutilated, was nearly more than she could bear. She ran up the few stairs and snatched up her child. Oh, the comfort of that small warm body, the softness of Lottie's hair against her own cheek, those little arms reaching to clasp her lovingly. No, she could not have born that loss. She hugged Lottie close to her, then followed Hansi and Anna into the parlor, where Liesel and Marie bent their heads over a swath of white cloth and several opened fashion-papers.

Liesel looked up, smiling as the door opened. In delight she said, "This is lovely materiel, Hansi—a dream to sew! You chose very wisely, my dears—" But then she saw their faces, anguish in her husband's eyes and tears in Anna's. She continued uncertainly, "Is . . . is Vati gone, Hansi? He seemed to recover a little . . . ."

"No, hearts-love. Not Vati." Hansi's voice was heavy with grief and dread. "Vati is as he has been for weeks, no better and no worse. It is the children, Lise—Willi and Grete. They have been taken captive. The Indians raided near to Robert's neighbors sometime in the night. They killed Robert and maimed his horse." He took her hands in his.

Marie's pleasant round features crumpled in horror. Liesel stood as if struck to silence, her eyes huge with shock. She did not cry out immediately so Hansi continued, "Rosalie is also captive, we think. But they cannot have gone far, the boys and I and Charley and his Ranger friends are already following their trail. We have every hope, Lise-love."

"No," Liesel whispered, disbelieving, "no, it cannot be. Not my children!" Anna and Magda exchanged a swift look of relief that Liesel seemed inclined towards stoicism under this dreadful blow.

131

But then her face distorted, transformed with appalling swiftness into inhuman fury as she screamed, "No!" She tore her hands from Hansi's and sprang at him, ripping at his face with her fingernails.

Years later when they spoke of this, in the time of the great epidemic, Magda mused to her daughter, "I was watching her face, and I have always thought that she went mad in that instant. It was horrifying to see—for she had always been kind, merry and sweet. A little troubled with gloomy moods, as any woman normally is. But she went into madness then. I feared for a long time to leave you anywhere alone with her. I believed that in her rage of grief she might harm you."

"So I thought also," Lottie nodded in assent, and shivered a little. "She looked at us . . . as of there was some evil demon looking out of her eyes and hating us all with a most desperate passion. It relieved me enormously when Uncle Hansi took her away."

Burdened with her child clinging to her, stunned by Liesel's senseless fury, Magda could only stand there while Marie wept and Hansi vainly attempted to capture Liesel's hands. "Lise! Stop that!" he shouted, pleading to be heard above Liesel's hysterical shrieks. "I beg of you, Liesel—control yourself!"

Ugly words, poisonous words and accusations, spilled from her mouth, her face distorted like a harpy-mask. "It's your fault!" Liesel raged, shrieking. "It is your fault—they should have remained safe, safe here with us! But no, you sent them away!" Then Liesel turned to Magda with an expression of wild and hateful malice and cried, "You were swift enough, sister—to keep yours close by and yet urge me to send mine from me! God should tear her from you, as he has torn mine from me, and as you took Anna from me!" Magda stood riveted in place, hardly daring to believe she had rightly interpreted her sister's words.

In one wild, desperate lunge, Liesel pulled away from Hansi's grip and took up the sewing shears. Magda held Lottie close and stepped back, a single involuntary step, while Anna caught her mother's wildly flailing arm and twisted the shears away. Baffled of her intent for just a moment, Liesel looked around the parlor like a wild animal cornered and seeking escape. She seized one of the precious pink porcelain teacups and smashed it on the hearth, together with its saucer.

"Oh, no, Mama!" Anna cried. "That was Papa's gift!"

"You will take his part, won't you?! Liesel screamed and reached for more of the cups. "It is his fault, it is his fault my children are stolen!"

Hansi gripped her shoulders, lifted her off the floor and shook her as a child shakes a doll; shook her until her head snapped back and forth on her shoulders. "For the love of God, Liesel!" he shouted. "How can you say such things, even dare to think that of your sister or ask such an evil of God! Be still! They've not gone far, Charley said that Robert's flesh was hardly cold! We have a chance to follow after, chase them down and take back our children and your sister! Listen to me, Lise!"

His urgent words had no effect. She fought against his hold on her shoulders and continued screaming accusations until Anna stepped close in to their maddened struggle. With quite astonishing calm she commanded, "Let me, Papa." And without any further ado she drew back her hand and slapped her mother, twice. The forceful blows rocked her head back and left a bright-red mark on each cheek. This also had the effect of silencing Liesel. She gaped at her daughter with open astonishment for a split second, and collapsed onto the floor, wailing inconsolably. She was racked with sobbing that left her unable to speak—which Magda thought with grim humor was an improvement on the vileness that had spewed forth during her tirade. At least this was more like Liesel.

Hansi knelt clumsily and took her in his arms, rocking her like a small child and pleading, "Liesel-love . . . we'll get them back! I promise on my own heart's blood, I shall find them, ransom their return!"

"Marie, don't stand there like a tailor's dummy." Anna, crisp as a general in the midst of a disaster, commanded her sister, "Run, fetch Doctor Keidel—leave a message at his house if he is out—and bring Auntie Elizabeth, too." Marie fled, with one last look over her shoulder. Anna clicked her tongue against her teeth, as if some small thing had drawn her disapproval. Taking the broom and ash-pan from the hearth, Anna swept up the shards of broken porcelain. Dry-eyed and perfectly composed, almost to herself she said, "One of the children might cut themselves."

Hansi straightened, dropping his arms from Liesel's shoulders. "I must go with the boys," he said. "I must go now, if we have a chance. Anna-pet, Magda . . . look after her." His eyes were desolate pools of grief.

"Of course, Papa," Anna nodded calmly. "Take care of yourself and the boys. Auntie and I shall manage."

"We shall get the children back," he promised once more. Then he was gone, leaving Magda standing there with Lottie in her arms. She felt as battered as a storm-wracked ship, numb from the successive blows that had fallen upon her family, upon her. Not the least of those was a tiny splinter of fear in her heart that Liesel had gone mad from grief.

"I will go upstairs and see to Vati," she said, and her voice sounded tinny and breathless to her own ears. Anna met her gaze from where she knelt next to her mother, trying to coax her into rising, or at least some semblance of governing her tears. "He would have been waked, I think. And want to know what the fuss was about."

"We should not tell him what has happened," Anna replied. Her face grew serious, thoughtful, her mind obviously running ahead of the situation. "Especially about Rosalie. You know how much Opa loves her! Doctor Keidel warned us that any agitation or fretting might kill him. He must not know, so we must keep this awful news from him. Speak to the children when they come from school and I will tell Auntie Elizabeth. Tell him, if he heard, that Mama saw a huge rat in the storeroom and it frightened her into hysterics."

Magda nodded, too exhausted and battered by emotions to suggest any other stratagem. She climbed the stairs, Lottie still clinging to her. How swiftly this nightmare had descended upon them; by the parlor clock chiming the quarter hour it had been just a bare fifteen minutes.

Vati still slept, mercifully—but it came to her that he appeared even frailer, almost translucent. His breath came so lightly it hardly moved the bedcovers over him. Holding Lottie to her, Magda sat in the chair beside his bed, thinking that even to be in his sleeping presence was a comfort and refuge. Soon, they all would be deprived of it. Vati's unconditional love for them all had been a slender shelter of reeds, but it had held unexpectedly strong for all of their lives up until now.

He stirred a little, and opened his eyes, grey as rain and vaguely puzzled to see her. His mouth worked, but not even that jumble of sounds that passed for his speech these days came out. Magda took his hand, laying slack on the bedclothes, and forced herself to smile and say, "Did the fuss downstairs disturb you, Vati? Nothing much—just a rat startled Liesel in the storeroom. You know how she will carry on."

He smiled with his customary affectionate understanding, and she thought he might have tried to reply, but it was too much an effort for him. But he squeezed her hand, with barely the strength of a new-born kitten, and in a very short time had drifted off back into slumber.

When she came downstairs again, the house seemed full of whispers and people; Doctor Keidel with his medical bag and Mrs. Schmidt taking off her shawl and moving capably into the kitchen. Magda opened the door to a knock, and there was a tearful Sophie Hunter and her mother, filled baskets on their arms, and already wearing black. Other women came, bringing food, loaves of bread, and pots of jam. When Doctor Keidel came down from attending Liesel, she had no place to consult with him but in the shop office, for the parlor was full of women callers and Mrs. Schmidt was in the kitchen feeding Sam, Hannah and Elias their dinner.

"She is resting now," Doctor Keidel said, heavily. "I have prescribed a sedating preparation. You may procure more of it at Muller's pharmacy, if more is required. It is my hope that Mrs. Liesel may be in a more rational mood upon awaking—and all the better should the little ones be found and swiftly returned. Otherwise . . . "

"Otherwise . . ." Magda moistened her lips. "Doctor Keidel, please answer me honestly. Could my sister be driven so far out of her mind with grief that she be capable of harming herself or someone else?"

"In my considered judgment," Doctor Keidel began, but hesitated before finally saying, "someone with the balance of their mind unhinged by such an event as has afflicted your sister," Anna or even Marie must have told him something of what Liesel had shouted, "may say such things and make threats which sound quite mad, even dangerous. But for Mrs. Liesel to act on such a threat—no, I believe you should set aside any such fears, Mrs. Magda." But he did not say this with conviction, which led Magda to suspect that secretly Doctor Keidel shared her fear that Liesel might intend harm to Lottie. "You might," suggested Doctor Keidel gravely, "if you are so concerned, ensure that Mrs. Liesel is attended at all times, even when she is in her chamber."

The sound of hurried footsteps and men's voices beyond the shop door interrupted Doctor Keidel. The door opened and Charley Nimitz looked around it. "Oh, good, the doctor is still here. Miss Magda," He lapsed into what he had called her when he courted her, but his eyes had as grim an expression in them as she had ever seen. A younger man followed him, travel-dusty and sweat-stained. "Young Ernst here, he has been sent as a messenger from those who have followed the Indian's tracks. They think they have found your sister."

"Excellent news," Doctor Keidel exclaimed. "That you have need of me means that she lives, I take it?"

"Rosalie—she is alive?" Magda's heart seemed lighter, but only for a moment. Ernst was only a boy, a little older than Sam, and he looked half-sick with apprehension

"Just barely," Charley answered, and he nudged the boy. Magda thought he was one of the Fischers, who had a farm on the Pedernales and were neighbors of Robert and Rosalie's. "Go on, lad, tell her."

"We . . . we found a woman." The boy gulped, and he would not meet Magda's eyes. "M' father and the others, they thought she could be Mrs. Hunter. They're bringing her here, but slowly, in a wagon."

"Could be?" Magda looked from his face to Charley's. "How could they not be sure, not recognize my sister! She has red-gold hair, the prettiest girl in Gillespie County—anyone would know her in a moment!" The look of sheer horror on young Fischer's countenance struck her through and through, as she comprehended the meaning of what he had clumsily tried to tell her.

She thought she might faint, or vomit from the nausea which rose into her throat. Doctor Keidel caught her elbow, and she leaned against him for a moment, regaining her composure. "You mean," she gasped and her voice sounded faint and flat in her own ears, "my sister . . . this woman they are bringing to us was treated in such a brutal manner—that there is a question of her identity?"

"They took her hair," the Fischer boy said, miserably, "and her clothes, all but her drawers. Them as found her, they thought sure she was dead. She was run through with a spear and pinned to the ground."

Ah, Rosalie, Magda thought and swayed with another wave of dizziness—what refined cruelty was that! She had once said in jest that she would die if strangers saw her under-drawers! Now Charley was speaking, answering a question Doctor Keidel had asked of him. "… May assume she was treated in the usual vile and degrading manner these savages mete out to white women captives?"

Magda looked between Charley and the Fischer boy, unable to speak for a moment.

"But she . . . she was in a delicate condition!" she gasped, horrified and outraged beyond any measure.

Charley answered, grimly, "I do not think that makes any difference to savages, Mrs. Magda."

Doctor Keidel cleared his throat. "We have time at least to prepare a chamber for her, Mrs. Magda. Warm blankets before the fire, perhaps . . . and stone-bottles of hot water very definitely. Her injuries may be indeed grievous—but that she survived them long enough to be found, that is some reason for hope, then."

In a frenzy of activity, she, Anna, and the able Mrs. Schmidt set up another sickroom. It was simplest for her to move her own small things into the girls' bedroom and give up her own room for Rosalie, since it was the one farthest from Vati's. Assisted by many willing hands, they filled stone bottles with boiling water and put them between blankets to warm them.

In the middle of it all Pastor Altmueller came to Magda, bearing a tray with a covered dish on it. "Miss Anna says you should sit down and eat this," he commanded austerely. "I recommend the garden, my dear."

"I couldn't touch a bite," she protested. Pastor Altmueller gave her a stern look.

"Miss Anna and Frau Schmidt say that the house is full of food and you have not eaten a thing since breakfast. It is now well past two o'clock. To carry on with those tasks which have fallen to us requires fuel. Besides," he continued slyly, "I will go upstairs and sit with your father . . . but only as soon as I have seen you eat enough of Mrs. Nimitz's delicious ragout. You should not keep him waiting." True to his word, he sat with her in the garden, watching with a kindly and fatherly interest as she ate.

"Truly, I did need this," she admitted at last. "The last bites went down rather easier than the first. Oh, Pastor A.! How could this happen to Rosalie? She loved Robert so deeply, and he endured so much in the war for love of her! They had not even been married above a six-month! And Liesel—I fear she will not be able to bear the loss of Willi and Grete, even if they are returned at once! This is cruel, cruel enough to question God!"

"Our Father's ways are inscrutable," Pastor Altmueller sighed. "His purpose is sometimes unknowable . . . and the way to the foot of His throne difficult at the best of times. Sometimes we may not even know why we are given such trials and burdens, but be assured always of His love."

"What a way of showing it." Magda set down her fork.

Pastor Altmueller bent his sternest look upon her. "We are never sent anything beyond our capability to bear," he intoned. "And we are never alone."

Nonetheless, she was glad of what little comfort the meal and his words afforded when the wagon bearing her sister finally arrived. Two women, neighbors of the Hunters, had traveled with Rosalie to tend to her. One proved to be young Ernst's mother.

"She has spoken a little, and seemed to know us," she explained to Magda. Magda stood on the stone walk in front of the house door and watched the men lift down a still form, shrouded in quilts and carried on a makeshift litter. "But she could not tell anything of what happened—not that I think I would wish to recall anything of what had been done, were I in her place."

"Did she say anything about my brother and sister?" Anna demanded. "Was there any trace of them found?"

"No." Mrs. Fischer shook her head, regretfully. "Although we asked here, repeatedly. She asked for her husband. We told her he was being tended in another house. She does not know he is dead."

A house of secrets, thought Magda, preceding the litter and its burden up the stairs to the room where Doctor Keidel waited with his stethoscope and his bag of cures and potions. A house of secrets, sorrow and madness, transformed in the space of minutes; maybe she would think more of returning to her husband's house. Even half ruined, it was better than this.

"Little Rose, you are come home, you are safe now," she had whispered, though she could see nothing of Rosalie but her face, ashen and bruised, her eyes half closed and unresponsive, until they laid her on the bed. Mrs. Schmidt shooed away everyone but Magda and Mrs. Fischer. "Go and bring more hot water," Magda hissed to Anna.

As the door shut behind her, Doctor Keidel commanded, "Let me see what I may of my patient, yes?" He sounded determinedly cheerful, either for his own benefit or for that of Magda and the other two—even Rosalie, if she could hear anything at all in her stupor. Mrs. Fischer and Mrs. Schmidt gently folded aside the swaddling of quilts. The final, innermost covering adhered to Rosalie's flesh in places, for she had bled. Magda swayed, and gagged from a sudden up-rush of Sophie Nimitz's ragout in the back of her throat.

"Madam Becker, if you are going to faint, I must ask you do so outside this room." Doctor Keidel observed, hardly looking at her at all. The chill of his rebuke steadied her.

"I am not going to faint," she answered firmly; although her own feelings were mirrored in Mrs. Schmidt's face. *Ah, Rosalie, my dearest little sister—such cruelties were done on your living flesh! How could you have lived, enduring this?!*

But live she did. Her chest rose and fell evenly and her heart beat strong and regularly. With a cloth dipped in warm water, Mrs. Schmidt daubed at those places where blood crusted the innermost quilt, and gently tugged that last covering free. New red blood oozed sluggishly from dozens of gashes and abrasions and matted the fringe of hair left around her bruised face. The entire top of Rosalie's head was either a spongy red mass or scraped white bone. Mottled blue bruises covered those parts of her body that had not been cruelly slashed with some kind of quirt, or possibly a willow-branch. Her wrists looked to have been bound, bound so tightly with something thin that it had cut the flesh, so Magda began sponging warm water on them.

A thick wad of dressing was held around her middle by a twist of linen bandage, just above the curve of the child in her belly. "I wish to see what is underneath that," said Doctor Keidel. Mrs. Fischer produced a small pair of scissors and carefully cut away the dressing around the wound. Doctor Keidel made no reaction other than a short hiss of breath when he saw the jagged and seeping wound underneath. "What matter of weapon made this wound?" he asked, face impassive.

Mrs. Fischer answered, "A lance with a long metal blade, thrust all the way through her body and into the ground."

"Narrow, but long. And removed by the same method?" the doctor queried. Mrs. Fischer nodded. "So, madam, if I may ask you to assist me in turning my patient, so that I may see the accompanying injury? Ah—thank you." Mrs. Fischer and Mrs. Schmidt carefully lifted Rosalie's shoulder and hip, turning her so that the exit wound could be seen. Doctor Keidel bent to closely examine the wound which had transfixed Rosalie to the ground where the raiders had left her.

Magda took a fresh wad of cotton lint and pressed it against Rosalie's back before the two women let her lay flat again. She could see it plain in her mind and memory, one of those slender Comanche lances; a long metal blade the length of her forearm, barely wider than the shaft; slender as a leaf and razor-sharp on either edge. When they had first come to Friedrichsburg, Mr. Meusebach had made a peace treaty with certain of the Comanche tribes, and for several years their folk had come to trade and visit. She had often seen their warriors carrying such long lances, adorned with feathers and ribbon streamers. As a small child, Rosalie had clapped her hands and marveled to see them capering.

The spear blade had gone through her body two or three fingers' width below the cage of her ribs. Doctor Keidel bent his face even closer and sniffed at the gash in Rosalie's side, a gash with puffy and reddened edges, slashed deep into her flesh. She wondered if Doctor Keidel was going to stitch it closed, but he straightened with a sigh. He looked as old as Vati, suddenly, grey with fatigue. Poor man, he hardly got a good night's sleep any more.

Mrs. Schmidt, her face ashen, began to remove the once-white linen bloomers that were Rosalie's only garment. The young woman moaned piteously and twisted away from their hands, a feeble motion and an effort soon spent. There were more and even darker bruises concealed underneath the cloth, and an assortment of crusted stains on it—not all of which were blood—which provided unspeakable proof of violence and violation. Rigid with disgust and anger at the picture thus provided to her imagination, Magda gently sponged more warm water onto Rosalie's legs and thighs. Would that she could wash away more than the blood, the matter and the dirt! Would that it were only possible to wash away the bruises and the pain as well!

"Lives the babe?" she asked Mrs. Schmidt, who probed at Rosalie's belly with sure fingers.

"She carries it still," Mrs. Schmidt answered. "In spite of all that was done." But the midwife-nurse and the doctor still looked sorrowful.

In silence they bathed and anointed Rosalie's poor lacerated body with sweet-smelling herb balms, and dressed her in one of Anna's oldest nightgowns, rubbed as soft as down from many washings. They wrapped her head with more bandages, tucked in the warm stoneware bottles and bricks wrapped in towels, and drew clean sheets and blankets over her. Mrs. Schmidt said that she would sit beside her, and comfort her if she wakened. Mrs. Fischer rolled up and took away those of her own soiled quilts. She promised that she would burn the stained drawers. Magda did not want to even touch the dreadful rags.

As Magda and the doctor emerged, Anna sprang up from the windowsill on the stair landing, where she had obviously been waiting. "She lives? Has she spoken sensibly?" she asked, anxiously.

"Yes, Annchen," Magda replied, "and no. But I believe there may be hope."

"No," said Doctor Keidel gravely. The two of them looked at him, shocked and disheartened. "Very little hope, Madame Becker . . . Miss Anna. I would speak to you both privately. In the absence or the infirmity of your fathers, I have no other choice than to take you into my confidence."

There was, as before, no other private place than the shop office. Doctor Keidel gallantly gestured to Magda that she should take the only chair. Anna perched on the edge of Vati's old workbench and sat with her legs swinging under her skirts, and the Doctor stood with hands clasped behind him and his face schooled with much effort to detachment and formality.

Doctor Keidel was nearly Vati's age. Besides being a friend to many he had served as the district's doctor for twenty years. There wasn't a family for miles around that he did not know, having treated them all. "To begin with, ladies," he cleared his throat, "I would anything in the world to not have to tell you this."

"Rather than let us discover it gradually and day by day, as our Rosalie suffers?" Anna snapped. "Pish! I thought you had better respect for my intellect and my Aunt's strength of character. You may tell us what you foresee; you are the doctor with your little black bag, come for an hour or so to look grave and sober. But we are the ones who will hold her hand, change her dressings and her bedding and remain with her day and night."

"Very well, Miss Anna. You ask for honesty and you shall have it." Doctor Keidel cleared his throat once more; a gesture not unlike Vati endlessly cleaning his glasses, a play for time to compose his thoughts. "Of Miss Rosalie's injuries, that one on her body is of most concern to me, medically. Oh, I have known of patients who have survived passage of a blade or a lance-head through their bodies and it is not uncommon for a man or woman to survive being scalped. That process is, curiously, not often fatal in and of itself. Painful and disfiguring, of course, but one may live without hair, not so?" The Doctor passed a hand over his own head, balding somewhat at the crown. "But of an injury which pierces the body cavity and such viscera contained therein—even if the organs might be repaired with careful surgery—which has been done, I assure you, by no less than Doctor Herff—eventually the site of the injury begins to mortify. Matter which has been spilled within the body cavity or carried hence from outside cannot be prevented from poisoning the blood." his shoulders slumped hopelessly as he spoke. "The end is inevitable, neither swift nor painless, unless aided with sufficient morphia. There is already a faint odor of such putrefaction rising from the wound."

"And the child?" Magda asked, forcing her voice past the pain in her throat when she recalled Rosalie pulling her nightgown tight against herself to show off the slight bulge of her stomach. "It has just quickened." But no, that was a slight and useless hope, swiftly destroyed by a shake of the doctor's head.

"Alas, Mrs. Hunter's infant cannot be rescued by performing the caesarian operation. The child is nowhere near term. And in any case," he added with difficulty, "it is most likely, because of the injuries she has sustained, that she will miscarry. The human body is very like to a damaged ship in a heavy sea, Madame Becker. When in danger of sinking, a desperate crew will throw overboard everything extraneous to immediate survival, even valuable cargo and precious possessions. The body overrules our emotions, even a mother's love for a child-to-be."

Anna spoke first. "Thank you, Doctor, for being honest with us." Her face and her voice were perfectly controlled, but her eyes reflected Magda's own anguish.

To face the imminent death of a dearly loved sister, to know of the destruction of the happy life that Rosalie had begun with Robert, after such trials of separation and war—this was bitter, bitter. Magda thought on how she had dressed Rosalie for her wedding, seen her drive away with Robert, and pondered her own married life. She had recalled with grief how hers had been cut so cruelly short, hoping that Rosalie and Robert's would be longer, but now it seemed she had been the more fortunate after all.

"She was given to us as a gift—and now she is to be taken away!" she exclaimed in anguish and dropped her head to her own hands. She wept, tears trickling through her fingers and splotching the skirts of her black dress. Rosalie, the beloved and beautiful, cherished instantly by everyone who saw her! Magda had loved Rosalie unreservedly from the day Vati found her, a nameless orphan left with the bodies of her parents in the hellhole of the Verein landing-camp. Vati had brought her to their own camp, wrapped in his coat, and calmly announced that he would adopt her— that he and Mutti had always wanted another daughter.

"Auntie," Magda raised her head at Anna's calm voice. Her niece pressed a handkerchief into her hand. Doctor Keidel was gone. She and Anna were alone in the shop office. Anna's face looked deliberately calm, as if she had forced all expression clear from her countenance. She appeared as composed as a perfect porcelain doll. On that long-ago day when the fates gave Rosalie to them, Anna had been a child of three and some; already solemn, the apple of Hansi's eye, and in the manner of children, inclined to be self-centered. Dear wise Helene—Mrs. Pastor Altmueller had been so very clever—she had taken Anna by the hand and said, *"This is Rosalie. She is your baby and you must take care of her."* And so Anna had. She had taken Mrs. Helene's ivory comb and combed out Rosalie's red-gold curls. Magda wept anew, to think of the pulpy red mess of Rosalie's head, so Anna put the handkerchief to her eyes and dabbed at the tears. "Auntie," she said again, "they are left to us to care for—I will see to Rosalie and you to Vati. Are we agreed?"

"Yes, Anna-love." Magda sniffed and blew her nose. "Yes— since there is none left but us to see to things."

"Honestly," said Anna. "Do these men think of such matters when they leap onto their horse and ride away, leaving us with such a burden to deal with?"

Caught halfway between sobbing and laughter, Magda answered "They do. When they come home and wish for good bread and a hot meal, or to have their wounds tended and bandaged." Making a sour face, Anna spoke one of Hansi's favorite epithets, and Magda laughed again to hear that coarse expression coming from the dainty and porcelain-skinned Anna.

"Well, it's all left to you and me now, Auntie," she added. "Mama is sick and Marie is a silly goose. Of course, Auntie Elizabeth will be a stout aide and so will all of our friends, but this is not their house."

Magda wiped her face one last time and straightened her shoulders. "So to our duties then, Anna—with as brave a face as we can put on."

"Yes, Auntie." Anna hugged her briefly and Magda thought again what a comfort Anna was, a brave and stout ally in the days to come. Really, she seemed more like a sister, a woman of her own age rather than twenty years younger.

"It seemed to us like an endless waking bad dream," Magda said reflectively to Lottie. They were sitting together in the darkened parlor of Lottie's grand mansion on Turner Street, in the year of the great epidemic, the year that the Great War ended. "As if we struggled through quicksand or mud and never quite reached safe ground. Your uncle Hansi, your brother, and Cousin Peter; they were gone for many days, all throughout the very worst of it. I am surprised you recall much at all, Lottie—you were so very small. I was glad of that, at the time, thinking that you would be spared such memories."

"Oh, no," Lottie shook her still-fair head, "I only knew that something horrible had happened, but for some reason also, everyone was making much of me and giving me small treats and indulgences. But no one could tell me when Grete was coming home, or make me understand what had happened to her and Willi. I had the silly notion that it was only a kind of prank that would be sorted out as soon as Uncle Hansi spoke firmly to the Indians."

Magda laughed, a little ruefully. "I felt so badly, having to leave you to the care of Marie and Hannah. I do not think I slept for more than two or three hours at a time. We closed the shop for days. Mrs. Schmidt and Pastor Altmueller were so constant in their attendance, they practically moved into the house as well. No," she shook her head, "we were never alone—our friends were ever with us, especially as word spread throughout the district."

"How long was it?" Lottie asked, and Magda gently tousled Mouse's silken ears as he lay on the footstool and watched her every move adoringly. The dog grunted with contentment.

"They buried Robert Hunter three days later," she mused. "Or perhaps four; it was Sunday, for I remember the church bells tolling. The church was full. That was the only day, save for one other, that I left the house until it was all over. I wondered, sometimes, if God would judge me harshly for wishing sometimes that he would hasten the end, for I was so tired, so sick at heart. Vati did not suffer; he seemed to fade, to become insubstantial. It was a wholly natural thing and we would mourn him even as we accepted this. He had lived a long and wonderful life, full of experience. He had seen his children grow and make their way in the world. He had lived to see the same of his grandchildren, too. But Rosalie—our dear little sister! That was so cruel, such promise cut short! Her suffering would have been unendurable, but for Doctor Keidel coming every day, sometimes twice a day to administer morphia."

"How long?" Lottie hesitated, for her mother stared unseeing into the grate, and the clear flames dancing over the coals.

"Almost a week," Magda answered. "Six days."

Chapter Nine: *Gone Like a Shadow*

They pressed the horses hard and themselves even harder. They chased after ghosts, phantoms, elusive traces left printed on broken branches and sun-bleached stones turned weather-side down along the banks of streams. Hansi, his nephew, his brother-in-law, and his friends were driven on by twin scourges of hope and fury; hope that they could recover Willi and his small sister, fury over the murder of friend and kin. And within each one of them was the cold fear that they would be too late, that the raiding party had at least half a day's lead. And that lead would only be improved upon, unless they urged the company on, farther and faster and into evening.

Half a dozen volunteers from the scattered Pedernales farms had followed the war party across the few miles between the river and Friedrichsburg, searching for the children and for Rosalie Hunter. In addition to sending a messenger to John Hunter, they had also sent one north to Captain Inman's camp on Ranger Creek. Late in the afternoon, Hansi, Friedrich and the others caught up to the messenger. By nightfall they had joined with half a company of Rangers, led by a lean and brown and silent young man, who seemed to be familiar to both Dolph and Fredi. A latecomer brought with him a rumor that Mrs. Hunter and been found; grievously injured, but alive. It was about the only good news they had, throughout that punishing long day.

Peter Vining ached in every bone, for all that he had spent four months in and out of a saddle pretty constantly. He was pretty sure that Hansi felt worse, being older and more often driving a wagon than riding a horse.

"Captain Inman was a neighbor of ours before the war," Dolph explained at a hasty campfire that night. "His older brother married one of Brown's daughters. They moved to Castell, after the old folks went to Missouri during the war, but he was in one of the frontier companies. I dunno what else he did during the war. I don't want to ask."

"Why not?" Peter inquired.

Dolph grinned. "'Cause he might have spent some time searching for draft dodgers and bush-men, like Uncle Hansi! Remind me sometime, I'll tell you the story of how the provost came to Vati's house searching for Uncle Hansi, and he was in the parlor dressed up as Father Christmas the whole time."

"Don't seem like you all took the war all that serious," Peter said.

His cousin answered bleakly, "'Fraid we cared more about the Comanche raiders than we ever did 'bout states rights, Cuz, and maybe today proves we had it more right than most."

Captain Inman's party included a skilled tracker, a Lipan Apache they called Guillermo. He was older than all the rest, stringy and weather-scarred. Alone among Inman's riders he wore no hat, only a band of red cloth around his brow, and his hair hung down to his shoulders. He and Dolph rode well ahead, while Captain Inman and his men stayed a little behind and to one side or the other, so as not to muddle the trail should they have to re-trace it. This did not surprise Peter very much; he had known that his cousin was trail-wise. That he was nearly as good as Guillermo proved an eye-opener, though.

"It's an easy trail," his cousin said mildly, when Peter made mention of it. They had stopped to water the horses and refill their canteens in one of the clear creeks that ran into the Pedernales. "They're not making any effort to hide it. They're just pushing hard, racing to outdistance us. Until they reach the Llano."

"What will they do then?"

"Scatter," Dolph answered. "Like milkweed seeds in a stiff breeze."

He did not have to say anything more. This would be their best chance to overtake the war party while they were still in the settled lands; ambush them and rescue Willi and Grete. Once the Indians passed into the empty wind-haunted lands of the Staked Plain and scattered, every one to his lodge or village—wherever it might be— then the search would become something more than this pell mell rush. They must catch them soon; catch them with Robert Hunter's blood still wet on their hands, the scalps taken from him and his wife still fresh and raw and the horses stolen from those small farmers along the Pedernales and its tributary creeks still fractious and wary. Catch them with their captives still alive and unscarred, before it became a matter of long and patient search and ransom.

Dolph sat on his heels by the campfire, his hands cradled around a cup of coffee. At sundown when Guillermo and Dolph could no longer see enough to follow a trail with any certainty of keeping to it, Captain Inman had reluctantly ordered them to set up camp and rest until sunrise. "In one way, they've made it easy for us," Dolph mused. "And hard at the same time; taking so many horses, they've left a trail a blind man could follow. But it means they have remounts."

Captain Inman nodded in agreement. "They will keep going during the night, once they know they're being trailed." He was an oddly soft-spoken and courteous man for a captain of Rangers, hardly ever seeming to raise his voice. Now he looked across the campfire to where Hansi was lying on a bedroll and rubbing his thighs, groaning all the while. "It might come to that, and he ain't holding up too well. You might be thinking on how to ask him to stay behind, less'n he slow up all of us."

"Uncle Hansi won't slow us," Dolph answered in mild rebuke, "It's his son and daughter they have."

Captain Inman sighed, "When we catch up to them, we're gonna need every man-jack we have, and that's the only reason I haven't told him to go home and wait."

"He won't slow us down," Dolph repeated. "He promised his wife he'd get Willi and Grete back. Uncle Hansi never goes back on a promise like that."

"If you say so." Captain Inman sighed again. In the morning he looked even bleaker, because Hansi was so stiff that he could barely move. He needed help from Fredi and Dolph to even climb into the saddle, but once there he refused to even consider turning back. At mid-morning, they came up on the place where the raiding party had camped.

"Walk careful," Dolph said. "Guillermo thinks he found something. They were here two nights ago, for sure."

"My children?" Uncle Hansi looked as if every move of his horse was a racking torment for him. "What of my children?" Guillermo silently pointed to a small oak tree, twice the height of a man, with a circle of disturbed earth around its trunk. About two feet up from ground level, the bark was a little broken-in all the way around, as if a rope had been tightly knotted around the trunk.

"One of them was here," Dolph said, "Look at the footprints."

Peter looked closer at the earth around the tree, seeing for the first time the little bare footprints in the dirt, as if a small child had been tethered there for hours, walking hopelessly in a circle, around and around the tree. All he could think about was how cold it had been at night and how desperately frightened the child must have been. Guillermo spoke, a question in Spanish which Dolph answered in the same language before switching into English, "He was asking how old Grete and Willi are. I told him, the girl's almost four and the boy six and a half years. He says this was the smaller child, then."

"What of the boy?" asked Peter.

Captain Inman answered, "No sign, but we haven't found a body either. Consider that a hopeful sign, if you like."

"Might they have already split apart?" Peter asked.

Captain Inman shook his head. "We wouldn't have missed that, not with all the horses they took. No way would they have split up without dividing the loot first."

Guillermo spoke then, one of the few times that Peter heard him volunteer a remark.

"What did he say, Cuz?" Peter asked.

Reluctantly Dolph answered, "He said—the boy is of a good age. They will be testing him. If he is weak, they will likely kill him. If he is strong, they will make him one of them—a warrior."

Peter thought of Willi, his innocent friendliness and hero worship, of how he trailed after them to the blacksmith on the day when they went to have irons made with the new brand. To think of him being wrenched away from his family, to know that he would likely be killed—that was enough to turn Peter sick at heart. They must catch up to the Comanche raiders; they must find them, the tiny and deadly needle in this vast empty haystack of a land.

Pressing on, they followed the trail with ever more determined energy. It cut west along the valley of the Llano River, towards the dry and harsh uplands. No more the gentle curving hills; these hills were as flat as a table top, and the scrub trees along the sides were gnarled and knotted, dark green in color. This was not country to farm; and yet there were folk living here, wresting a living out of the earth. They came upon a small settlement in the afternoon, a scattering of cabins, some with a palisade of sharpened cedar stakes around them. Captain Inman detoured from the trail, to warn the folk there—as if they needed any additional reminders of their peril, living so far out on the frontier—and to ask if any might have seen the war party and their captives.

"They herd sheep out here," Dolph explained. "Cattle too, but mostly sheep. The herders are out and about during the day and likely to keep a sharp eye open."

Captain Inman returned, reporting that one of the sheep-herders had indeed noted a party of Indians at some distance the day before. "They had many horses," he said, "and raised a trail of dust for a good way. He told his wife he watched from the hillside—didn't dare go any closer than that. He thought some of them might be riding double. The children, parceled out to different riders, I guess."

"They're heading northerly now," Dolph noted quietly. "We're about a day behind. We've got to catch them before they cross the San Saba."

Another night, another day of headlong pursuit. In the middle of the second day they saw scavenger birds circling in the empty sky.

"Something dead," Captain Inman said quietly only to Fredi and Peter. "Dead and fresh, and left along the trail. Keep Mister Richter well back, 'til we're certain of what it is."

Peter nodded, sick at the pit of his stomach. Which one of them might it be? Willi or his sister? Or another captive? The Pedernales men had brought word of the war party before a careful search had been made. They might have killed or taken others. No one might know of it for days, until someone noticed birds circling in the sky, or found a straying horse, or realized that someone expected to be at a certain place was not present.

It was not the body of a man or woman. Rather it was a mare which one of the Pedernales men recognized as his own, having been stolen by the raiders.

"Went lame, would be my guess," Dolph ventured.

Peter wondered, "And they cut it open and left innards all over the place, for what reason?"

That the Indians had killed a lame horse rather than let it slow them down argued that they knew they were being followed. "Our dust trail," Dolph explained. "They've been watching their back. And they cut the horse open to eat. Of what they wanted to eat, you really don't want to know, Cuz."

"So, they know we're after them." Peter handed back his cousin's canteen, and Dolph nodded. "Now we have to move even faster," he said, and so they did. They pressed on, infected by urgency. The horse-kill had been fairly fresh; they were closing the lead. Their own horses were tired, but Peter thought that spirits were good.

In the afternoon, storm clouds began piling up along the north-western horizon; an iron grey band that grew into towering mounds of white clouds. Peter did not like the look of it. Lightning flickered within the cloud and arced to the ground, a split-second flash of white light, and a grumble of thunder that sounded like distant artillery.

"Hurry!" shouted Captain Inman, waving his arm at the horsemen following after, two and two, three and three. Their horses lengthened stride into a gallop, an exhilarating scramble over broken ground, a heart-pounding race against nature as the rain threatened to wash all traces away. The wind blowing against their faces, tossing their horses' manes, brought the damp smell of rain on thirsty soil. They pressed hard as the storm-line swept down upon them. The sky darkened, the very air seemed to take on a queer, twilight tinge. And then the rain came—first a wispy grey veil, hanging from beneath the clouds, then in silvery sheets, and finally in torrents that hit the ground and splashed up as mud. Within a few moments they were soaked to the skin, water running from their horses in rivulets, but they pressed on at a gallop. Finally, Guillermo and Dolph halted at the top of a small hillock, with the empty plain spreading all around, the patter of rain falling into small streamlets under their feet. Guillermo spoke, sounding infinitely sad, yet philosophical.

Dolph translated, "The trail is gone. He can follow it no farther."

"That's it, then," Captain Inman said, softly as was his way, "I am sorry, boys. There's nothing more to be done. We've lost them."

The other men caught up, some of them cursing bleakly under their breath—not for the wetting they had received, which would make for an uncomfortable ride as well as a cold night—but for the fact that it had destroyed the trail, beyond the skill of any man to follow. If Hansi Richter's face was wet, none could know if it was from tears or from the rain. His children and their captors were gone, gone like shadows into the Llano country.

"Mama," asked Sam with intense interest, "is it true that Auntie Rosalie has been scalped?" It was the evening of the day after Rosalie had been found and brought back to Vati's house. He had cornered Magda in the upstairs hallway. She was holding a plate of Sophie Nimitz's good ragout, well cut up so that Vati might be tempted into swallowing a few bites. Sam and Hannah and their cousin Elias had come home from school to a house suddenly disarranged, disrupted and turned upside down, filled full of women murmuring sympathetically in the parlor and kitchen, and suddenly absent of men—older brothers, uncles and cousins.

"Yes, it is true, Sam," she answered.

Most disconcertingly he brightened with intense interest and asked, "Might I see, Mama?"

"No, you may not!" she snapped; honestly this taste for the gruesome in small boys! Oh, but Sam was not so much the small boy who had been entranced with tales of the Emperor Napoleon and military glory. He was near as tall as she, and imbued with Vati's fearless intellectual curiosity. She marveled at how that quality had seemingly leaped, like lightning-fire from tree-top to tree-top across the gulf between.

"Mama," he asked again, staying her as she was about to go into Vati's room. "Opa is going to die, isn't he?"

"Yes, Sam-Love . . . I am afraid so." In this house of secrets, it was about time that someone was honest. "Doctor Keidel has always maintained that there is very little chance of his recovering."

"Well, everyone dies," Sam answered, with something of Vati's own intellectual detachment. "Like the poem of brave Horatius at the bridge: *'Then out spake brave Horatius, The Captain of the gate: 'To every man upon this earth, Death cometh soon or late.'* Opa knows. I don't think he minds too much, Mama." Her son looked particularly earnest. "It's just that we will miss him terribly. And that's the hurtful part."

"Yes, Sam," Magda sighed, "that is the hurtful part—knowing how you will miss them."

"Like we missed Papa," Sam ventured, and Magda's eyes filled suddenly. Seeing this, Sam hugged her clumsily but with care to avoid tipping the plate in her hand. "Don't cry, Mama," he promised bracingly, "I am here, still, and I will be for a good long time."

"I am sure of that, young man." Much comforted, she kissed his forehead, grateful that her son had not asked any more about his Aunt Rosalie.

"Such a strange time it was," Magda later mused to her daughter. "Sometimes I did not know if it were day or night, or what day it might be. There was no meaning or rhythm to the hours. I came downstairs once, and found Captain Nimitz wrapped in his overcoat, asleep on the parlor chaise, and in the kitchen Herr Pastor Altmueller and Mrs. Schmidt were drinking coffee and arguing over the proper time to set out garden vegetables."

"Rather like the hospital," Lottie agreed. "If it weren't for the sound of reveille or retreat from the parade ground, I would not know if another day has passed."

Night and day, days and nights and hours flowed past with hardly a ripple to differentiate them save for the necessity of a candle, as she and Anna attended to the needs of their patients. At irregular intervals someone, usually Mrs. Schmidt, presented her with food and insisted that she eat. Magda obeyed, it being too much trouble to object; for all that it tasted like sawdust and ashes in her mouth. At wider intervals, she would obey similar commands to lie down and sleep, most always fully clothed and on top of the bedding. Sometimes she woke at night to find Lottie and Hannah, in their nightgowns, curled up next to her. She found such comfort in their trustfulness and the ease of their quiet breathing.

Anna ate and slept as little she did, sometimes only at her word; for they wanted to be sure that one of them would always be available. In this effort, Magda was given aid from an unexpected quarter. Sleeping fitfully, and hearing voices from the room where Rosalie lay, she rose from her pallet. Downstairs, the parlor clock chimed three strokes for the hour. She opened the door softly and Liesel glanced up from where she sat beside the bed.

"Anna looked so very tired," she said. "I told her to lie down for a while and I would take her place. Our little Rose rests easier if I sing to her. The baby rhymes . . . those soothe as they ever did, when she was small. She is fevered and becoming worse."

Magda came into the room, studying Liesel with wary care. She appeared as loving and careful as she ever did with her children and Rosalie; as if the hysteria she had shown in the parlor when Hansi told her about the children had all been an evil dream. Nothing in her face or demeanor hinted at how she had withdrawn to hers and Hansi's chamber, weeping uncontrollably and refusing all comfort. This was indeed Lise herself, as she had ever been; but the little worm of fear and distrust in Magda's heart still niggled. Lise had always either been on top of the tower or down in the deepest cellar. When Hansi broke the news to her of Grete and Willi being taken, she had withdrawn farther into the cellar than she had ever gone before.

"Doctor Keidel will come in the morning," Magda mentioned. "He said we may give her a few laudanum drops if he is delayed on his rounds." Rosalie moaned, fretfully, her body moving under the covers as if she could not rest easily. "Do go on singing to her, Lise. Give me that basket of lint and I will change her dressings."

Magda turned back the covers, then recoiled at the sight underneath and from the putrid odor which rose from the lance's wound. Dark blood mottled the nightgown and pooled on the mattress around Rosalie's hips. "Hand me a towel, Lise, quickly! She is losing the baby!"

If it were to do with childbearing, at least Liesel could be relied upon to keep her head. Liesel rested her hand on the slight rise of Rosalie's belly; her lips moved silently as she counted and counted again. "Close together," she murmured. "Not long now. Poor little love, never having had a chance. If Mrs. Schmidt is still here, I think you should fetch her now." Magda hastily put a towel underneath Rosalie's thighs, in a vain attempt to contain the blood and matter that came out of her in a regular trickle.

By the time she came up the stairs again, with Mrs. Schmidt puffing heavily as she followed, it was all but over; the half-formed infant slipped out of Rosalie in a gush of blood and clotted tissue. It hardly looked human to Magda's eyes, more like a small skinned rabbit with delicate little hands instead of paws, and a face that appeared more like a monkey. It was also too soon to tell if it would have been a boy or a girl. Mrs. Schmidt wrapped it in a clean cloth and took it away.

Days later, Magda thought to ask her what she had done with the tiny corpse. "I took it over to the Hunters," the old midwife answered sturdily, "and asked them as they were laying out Robert Hunter, to put it in the coffin with him. It seemed the right thing to do, putting their child in the same grave."

She and the children went to Robert Hunter's burial. They stood with a knot of women in the graveyard, while the wind whipped their black skirts this way and that, and bowed the flowers growing up through the grass in ripples like waves on the ocean. She tried her best not to think of Robert and Rosalie after their wedding, dancing, in each other's arms and looking at each other as if there were no one else in the world. She tried also not to think of that other burying, when she stood with the children by her husband's grave and knew that if it were not for them, she would have willingly lain down beside his coffin and let the mourners shovel earth over them both.

Afterwards, when she returned with the children and Anna, she saw Liesel in the parlor. Her head was bent over the bolt of white lawn, the very same cloth they had intended for making clothes for Rosalie's baby. Liesel deftly sent the shears angling this way and that, but the stack of cut dress pieces lying next to her elbow on the parlor table were not for a child, but for a woman. Their eyes met and Magda realized the garment was for Rosalie; a dress to be buried in, white for a bride, white for a shroud.

In the following days, other women came to the house, girls who had been Rosalie's friends or older women who were Magda's and Liesel's. They came to console and sit in the parlor with Liesel, weeping and sewing together.

From then on, she and Anna burned sweet herbs in the sickroom, for the smell from the suppurating wound soon became nearly unbearable, even if they opened the windows to the fresh air during the day. Only once did Rosalie seem to be anywhere near rational consciousness, and that was after Robert Hunter was buried, two or three days following her miscarriage.

Shortly after sunrise, a towering line of thunderclouds blew in from the northwest, grey as cold iron underneath but shining as white as spun cotton on their crests. At midday Magda turned from closing the sickroom window against a sudden squall of rain outside, and the bright spring day turned suddenly as dark as twilight.

"Magda?" Rosalie whispered pathetically from the pillow. Her poor bandaged head turned to follow as Magda drew the curtain closed. "Magda . . . it hurts. Everything hurts." Magda sat down, swiftly taking up Rosalie's hand in hers, and stroking her forehead. Such care that needed to be taken, when there was hardly a place to touch her which wouldn't cause more pain!

"I know, dear heart," she answered, wrenched by the look of utter bewilderment in Rosalie's purple-pansy eyes. Tears leaked out from their corners, trickling down and back into the bandages around her head. "Doctor Keidel is coming soon. There is a potion he is giving you, something to take away the pain. You're safe at home. Liesel and I are taking care of you."

"Robert." Rosalie moistened her fever-cracked lips. "Where is Robert, Magda?"

"They took him to the Hunters to be cared for," Magda answered, with perfect truth. That answer seemed to content Rosalie, for she closed her eyes for a moment.

"The baby . . . what of the baby?" she whispered, just when Magda thought she had begun drifting away into half-consciousness again. "I can't feel him moving any more. And it hurts in my middle, Magda." She wept again.

"Shush, Rosalie . . . little lamb . . . everything is going to be all right soon," Magda crooned. "The baby is being taken care of." She talked, soothing and comforting talk, every word of it a lie—whilst praying for Doctor Keidel to come and soon with his little silver case of syringes and vials. She raged inwardly against the Indian raiders who had brutally violated and tortured her sister, seemingly on an impulse, the same casual unthinking gesture of someone squashing a beautiful butterfly.

When Doctor Keidel finally came, she took refuge in Vati's room. Sheets of rain washed against the windows and the lamp flame flickered in the wayward draft from the open door.

"R-r-r-ain," Vati stammered, fighting a gallant and losing battle against those muscles that no longer obeyed his mind.

"A spring storm, with thunder and lightening," she agreed. "I fear it will shred the last spring petals from your pear tree, Vati. Shall I read some more to you from Uncle Simon's letters?"

He moved his head in the way that had come to mean assent, but there remained a question. "S-s-m-lll," he got out the mangled sounds with no little effort, and Magda realized with a cold feeling in her stomach what he meant. The odor of putrefaction may have clung to her clothes, or was now so strong as to waft from the other room. Having been breathing it for some hours, she was past noticing it—but not so for Vati.

"There is a dead rat, somewhere in the garden," she answered, steadily. "Or in the storeroom, perhaps. I will have the boys look for it tomorrow." She began to read, for he seemed content with that explanation. The rain fell with a sound like pebbles on the roof and against the glass. Presently she saw that he dozed and when Sam came in bringing Vati's dinner on a tray, she had him set it aside for a little. She did not wish to disturb him, and so she dozed a little herself, while outside the rain lessened.

"Mama?" That was Sam's voice, and she opened her eyes, startled to have drifted into sleep. The room brightened as the clouds moved past, casting moving patterns on the scrubbed oak floor and the pale bed sheets. Vati's head lay tilted to one side, as if he had been looking out at his beloved pear tree and fallen asleep. She saw first that the storm had indeed knocked loose most of the pale petals to the ground beneath. Rather than appearing as a cloud of white blossoms, the tree now appeared mistily green, adorned with the first tiny new leaves of the year. "Mama," Sam ventured again, and his voice sounded unsure, even a little shaken. "I think Opa is gone."

"No," she answered at once, and unthinking, "He is right here. Vati?" But there was no question once she looked again. There was a difference in the very look of someone who was alive, and someone who was not. Without making any fuss, or asking that any fuss be made of him, he had slipped away between one breath and the next, without a sound. His flesh was still warm, elastic. Sam helped her take away the pillows that had propped him up and they laid him flat and composed his hands to lie over his chest.

"I suppose I should go and tell Mrs. Schmidt and Pastor A. now," Sam ventured. "And Auntie Liesel, too."

"Wait for a little, and let me tell your aunt first," Magda said. Inwardly, she dreaded telling her sister that Vati was dead. Liesel might withdraw so far into her dark, deep cellar that nothing would coax her out.

Also, she might go into one of her hysterical fits again, which Magda didn't think she could endure. "Let us open the windows and let in the fresh air—the air here always smells so wondrous after a good rain."

Mercifully, it was Pastor Altmueller who appeared first. Kindly and ever-composed in the face of grief, he held her hand and Sam's and said a brief prayer that seemed to be meant more for Magda's comfort than for Vati's benefit. Vati had long insisted on being a free thinker, in spite of two decades of friendship with Pastor Altmueller.

"I shall notify Captain Nimitz, of course," he added, "and see to the necessities. One would wish for your brother and Hansi to return at this moment, when you have such need of their support and familial affection—especially if they manage to free the little ones. You are in my prayers, my dear Margaretha—as much and more as you ever have been."

"It was most curious, Lottie," Magda mused, "that I was able to maintain such composure—I think I had already done my grieving for him beforehand. Once your Opa had left us, I had already accepted the loss to us all. But your Aunt Liesel reacted precisely as I feared. She was inconsolable, incapable of leaving her bed. Mrs. Schmidt remained with her and with Rosalie for the duration of the funeral." Magda laughed, but it was more like a short and unamused bark. "Only on one occasion during the war—the War Between the States, Lottie—and of late in this dreadful epidemic, or when old friends were carried off by extreme age, was I required to attend on three funerals within the space of a week!"

"I remember the house being filled with flowers," Lottie ventured.

Her mother nodded. "Since it was spring, I sent you to gather them from the woods and fields by Baron's Creek, with Sam and Hannah and Marie, too. Poor girl, I believe that was the only day that she was permitted to leave the house, and only because your Aunt Liesel was insensible from a dose of tonic that Doctor Keidel gave her and so was unable to withhold permission. I gave your brother one of your Papa's old revolvers, though. Troubled times," Magda sighed. "There was no danger from Indians, not so close to town, with the trail season about to begin."

"And Sam let us ride on Papa's old horse, too," Lottie added. "That was a great treat for me."

"Yes, it was," Magda allowed fondly. "Poor old Three-Socks! He was a great age for a horse and half-blind as well, but to Sam he was a fierce battle charger, a veritable Bucephalus." She sighed again, immersed in memories. "My dear little Rosalie! Doctor Keidel came twice daily, towards

the end. We did not tell her of Vati. It would have made no difference, for she was beyond any understanding. Her pain . . . it was dreadful, even with the drugs we gave her. She wept and groaned, begging us most piteously to make the pain go away. The only thing that calmed her in the least was for us to sing to her. All the old baby songs, the nursery rhymes. We sang to her . . . Liesel, Anna, and even Auntie Elizabeth and I, until we were hoarse. The fever burned through her, from the dreadful infection. She would not have died of it today, Lottie, but when you were a child, people died often of things that are of hardly any moment, now."

"No one has been attacked by Indian war parties, of late," Lottie pointed out with a flash of irony.

"True," her mother agreed with bitter satisfaction. "Indeed, Anna and I were never able to muster much sympathy for the trials of the Comanche tribes after they were rounded up and made to stay on the reservation, although we were often lectured about our lack of fellow feeling. We were supposed to have been at peace with them, too! It was the cruelty of her death which stayed with us—she, who was the kindest, the sweetest of young girls! She had never been unkind to anyone, had never endured anything harsher than your Opa's disapproval. She was our shining, golden child . . . and her life came to such an ugly end, all that bright promise shattered. He— Robert Hunter—had forgotten his carbine, at the house-raising dance. They came away, early in the morning, having danced all night while the children slept, and encountered the war party by chance. They had tried to steal a fine herd of horses at Burkheim's but were baffled of that by the barking of Dieter Burkheim's dogs. And so . . ." Magda made a sad little gesture with her hand, indicative of finality and hopelessness.

"The Indians were in an ugly mood, when they came upon them— although your father used to jest that there was no appreciable difference between that and a good mood when it came to a Comanche war party. So she died, your Aunt Rosalie and my very dear little sister. She was taken from us, as she was given, without warning. And we have never really known who she was, her parents or her origins. Only that she was ours for a time and we loved her, very deeply." Magda looked into the fire burning in the ornate tiled fireplace and polished metal grate in her daughter's ornate and comfortable parlor. "Hannah said something to me afterwards, which was of such comfort."

When the whole ugly business of dying was done, they washed Rosalie's body and clothed it carefully in the white dress that had been cut out by Liesel and tearfully stitched together by those who loved her. So, too, did those who built the coffin weep as they worked, or so Magda was later informed.

She and Mrs. Schmidt opened the windows, aired out the room, and burned the mattress contents. Even so, it was many nights before Magda experienced uninterrupted slumber there. She would be glad, at the end of summer, to move into Vati's room with its window views into the street on one side and the garden on the other.

"Mama," asked Sam as she and Hannah walked from the graveyard for the third time in a week, "is Opa in heaven, even though he didn't believe in it?"

Before Magda could even start to consider the question, Hannah answered firmly, "Of course he is in heaven! Opa was very good." Hannah looked up at Magda, her clear grey eyes as candid and honest as Vati's own. Magda realized that Hannah had outgrown her childish timidity. It had been replaced by a quiet reserve, which she had not noted until now, much as she had not noticed how tall Sam had become. She took their hands as they crossed the footbridge over Town Creek, regretting once more how little attention she had paid to them since returning home from the coast. Behind them, Lottie toddled between her cousins Anna and Marie, and Elias brought up the rear of the chief mourners. The fresh breeze fluttered the dark veils worn by Magda and the girls. Anna had already drawn hers back from her face as soon as they left the burial grounds, declaring that she was tired of seeing everything through a black fog.

Hannah squeezed Magda's hand comfortingly and said with perfect confidence, "And Aunt Rosalie is in heaven too, with Papa there to protect her always."

Magda smiled a little at that, thinking of the day that Carl Becker had returned, as suddenly as a comet streaking across the sky. *He had come to Vati's house, in the first year of their arrival at Friedrichsburg, during a gathering in the garden to celebrate Jacob's baptism. Little Rosalie had seen him lingering at the edge of that happy gathering, so she took his hand and announced, "Here he is, Vati—I found him!" Magda came out of the house with a tray in her hands, and there he was: a tall and fair-haired man, standing with Rosalie as she swung their hands and laughed up at him.*

"That is a most comforting fancy, Hannah-my pet," she said.

Hannah replied with careful dignity, "It is not a fancy, Mama. She is in heaven and Papa is there with her." She seemed perfectly confident in her conviction. Magda realized with a sudden sense of wonder that her daughter was good. Truly good; that pure and humble sort of goodness associated with saints, not in the ostentatious way of a religious tract that was so typified by those who did good things only so everyone would notice them.

"I think Opa would find heaven awfully boring," Sam announced. "And I'll bet Papa would, too."

"Heaven is not boring," Hannah insisted, again with an air of perfect certainty. She would not be drawn into an argument over this, although Sam tried, until Magda finally told him to hush. Fancy or not, Hannah's conviction that her Papa still watched over and protected those he loved was of considerable comfort.

And when they came to Vati's house, Sam and Elias ran ahead, shouting that they saw horses in the stable yard. The men had returned. Magda picked up her skirts and ran to meet them. The faces they turned towards her were tired, and from the slump of their shoulders, she knew already that their search had been in vain.

Late that afternoon Peter Vining was last to use the wash-house at the bottom of the garden, soaking every bit of trail-grime and sweat from his body and changing into a clean set of clothes. Ma'am Becker had seen to him as she had seen to the others, with calm and understated affection, upon their return from the Llano. She came straight away to the stable, following after the excited children, her black skirts lifted above her shoe-tops with both hands. No tears, no questions and no recriminations. She had wordlessly embraced Hansi and her brother Fredi, and brushed Dolph's face with a kiss as light as a butterfly's touch.

"You look as if your arm pained you," she said to Peter, then another light touch. "Do you wish another of my remedies, then?"

"No, Ma'am," Peter had answered. "I am so sorry," he began to say, but she touched his lips with a motherly gesture.

"They are in God's hands, now," she answered. "Dearest Vati, our little sister, her child, and Robert who loved her. You should wash now. There are clean towels in the bathhouse. We have many guests in the house. Just leave your dirty things there. We shall do the laundry tomorrow, of course." She appeared much as she usually did, in the black of deepest mourning; only a little more wearied, her mind half-distracted by thoughts of the many guests in the house.

Obscurely, Peter was grateful at not having to relate any of their frantic but ultimately fruitless pursuit. The storm had defeated them and the children were gone beyond reach. There was no need for Ma'am Becker to ask any further questions; she could see it plain.

The house was full of people, some strangers to him even after six months. There had been food in plenty, laid out in the parlor for the mourners paying their respects after the funeral. It had taken some time for his mind to accept that the black crepe hung from the front door and draped over the windows was for more than the kindly old man with the thick glasses, but also for the beautiful Rosalie, the prettiest woman he had ever seen.

He had lingered behind—he was only part of the family by remote connection. The other mourners would be speaking German to him, and in his state of exhaustion, he was uncertain of his ability to cope. He supposed Hansi was upstairs, making peace with his wife over their failure to retrieve the children. Dolph and Fredi had washed hastily and dressed, leaving him to be the last in the stone-floored bathhouse.

The garden was empty for the moment, but for one of the younger girls sitting on the swing with her back to him, pushing her toes against the ground just enough to gently move the swing back and forth. As he drew closer he saw that it was not one of the younger girls, but rather Miss Anna, tiny and almost doll-like. He usually didn't notice her diminutive size, as her formidable manner turned attention away from that quality.

"Miss Anna," he ventured carefully—today was not a day for their usual exchange of mockeries. "I wish to extend my regrets over your loss . . . your losses."

"Thank you, Mr. Vining," she nodded regally. Her eyes were perfectly dry. "And I would like to extend my thanks for your own effort. I know my parents will also be grateful for them, but Papa will not think to say so for days. And Mama is too inconsolable to consider any proprieties."

"Think nothing of it," Peter answered, in his most gallant manner. "I will leave you then, Miss Anna, to enjoy your moment of solitude. I apologize most sincerely for intruding upon it."

"You need not," Anna returned, the tone of her voice most particularly desolate. "Apologize, that is. Oddly enough, I was not enjoying my solitude."

He inwardly kicked himself for having made a poor choice of words. Touched by her obvious grief, Peter spoke on an impulse, "Then may I share your solitude with you, Miss Anna? On promise of not speaking, if that is your requirement?" By way of an answer, she slid a little to one side of the swing to make room for him. He sat down awkwardly; there was not enough room to sit together without touching, and he was almost painfully aware of her presence.

His legs were so much longer, it was impossible to swing as she had been doing. But they sat for quite some time, not speaking a word, until Anna broke the silence. "I have not been able to weep for her. It is very curious, you know. Women are supposed to cry at funerals. I cared for her for days, telling myself that I must not shed a single tear, that it would distress her immeasurably to see me crying over her."

She did not seem to expect an answer to that, nor was there one that Peter could think to give her. Finally, he said, "It was a hard road for you, Miss Anna—and here I was feeling sorry for myself, that we could not get your brother and sister back."

"You've no idea." Anna looked straight ahead, her face still perfectly composed. "They told me once that she was my baby and I should look after her. And so I did, up to the end. Do you know how long it takes someone to die and how much they suffer, after being run through with a lance?"

"No," Peter answered quietly, "but I've seen men die gutshot, after screaming in a field hospital for days. I don't suppose it was any prettier, Miss Anna."

"No." Her voice sounded just a little softer, her composure somehow less rigid. "I don't suppose it was." They sat with their own thoughts, side by side on the swing, swaying just a little. Peter found it unexpectedly restful with Miss Anna perched next to him, as light and delicate as a bird.

"At least you were there to hold her hand, Miss Anna. At least you could do that much for her." Impulsively he reached for her hand with his own good one.

Chapter Ten: *Day of Reckoning*

"It all seems very quiet," Magda remarked on the Saturday that she and Anna reopened the store. "And so empty!" It was a week after Rosalie's funeral, a week after Hansi and the boys had returned, empty-handed and covered in trail-dirt, on horses trembling from weariness.

"I still keep expecting to see Vati in his room, or sitting under the pear tree," Anna agreed, wistfully. "I wish Papa and I could induce Mama to leave her room, but she will not hear of it." Hansi had exhausted himself, pleading fruitlessly with Liesel. He had finally lost his temper and left with Jacob, taking a wagon load of goods to Kerrville. He had promised to deliver a load of cut timber to the Becker farm, where work had commenced on the house after the spring cattle round-up. Magda didn't know if Liesel would have forgiven Hansi by the time he returned and was herself too grieved over Rosalie to care very much.

"It's like one of those starfish," Sam observed earnestly. He plied a broom with great energy, although Magda thought he was merely stirring the dust around. "When it loses one of its arms."

"How is that, Sam?" his mother asked, much puzzled.

"It grows another one to replace it." Sam scowled, thoughtfully. "Or maybe it's one of those jellyfish things I am thinking of. It grows again into the shape it needs, even if it's not in quite the same shape as it was before."

"Clear as mud, Samuel," Anna said, but secretly Magda thought her son was right. The household, her family—it was reshaping itself, like a starfish. Wearily, she wondered if the starfish, or whatever Sam was thinking of, felt pain when part of it was cut off. For they all felt pain, but only Liesel was incapacitated by it, by the unbearable absence, the emptiness in the places where Willi and Grete should have been. She had withdrawn into her deep, deep cellar, leaving Marie to cope valiantly with the household, aided as always by Mrs. Schmidt in the mornings and by Magda and Anna whenever they could step away from the shop and Hansi's freighting concerns. She refused to come downstairs, and on many days even remained in her room.

Vati might have been able to coax Liesel to come forth, he had always been good with her; but then there was the Vati-shaped absence where he had always been, as well. Magda had the same sense that had haunted her in the months after Carl Becker's death—that he had not really gone, but was somewhere in the house or close by. When she looked into the parlor, or out to the garden, she half-expected to see Vati there, dozing over a book with his glasses slipping down over his nose, or deep in some abstruse discussion with Pastor Altmueller.

Hansi insisted she move into Vati's room; certainly she preferred that to her old room, which for her was marked forever as the place where Rosalie had suffered and where the miasma of death seemed still clinging to the walls. Still, there was something restful about returning to the shop, restful and yet exhilarating. All the plans they had made while in Indianola, which had needed to be set aside for Vati's final illness, could now be picked up again and moved towards fulfillment.

Very gradually, over the weeks and months of the summer, that summer of the first full year of peace, they were able to do just that. Lottie began school that autumn, walking to the schoolhouse between Hannah and Sam, blithe and eager, with not a backwards look to Magda lingering in the shop door watching after them. Her older brother and sister had earnestly begun teaching her letters, marking out the shapes on Sam's school slate, and challenging her to sound out the letters of the shopkeepers' signs along Main Street. Lottie stopped asking wistfully after Grete about that time. She was a sensible and sensitive child; Magda thought that her younger daughter had worked out for herself the connection between the absence of her almost-twin cousin, and her aunt's withdrawal into seclusion.

There had never been any news of the children, in spite of all the letters that Anna wrote in careful English on behalf of her father: letters to the governor, to the officer commanding Federal Army troops in Texas and the territories, to the Territorial Indian agency. They received replies, expressing regret and occasionally even sympathy, but nothing more effective than that. Encouraged by Charley Nimitz, they placed advertisements in certain newspapers in Kansas and the Indian Territories, asking for information and promising a reward should that information lead to the return of Willi and Grete Richter, seven and four years of age, taken by Comanche raiders from Gillespie County in the spring of 1866. They received some reply to those, but mostly semi-literate scrawls asking for money in exchange for information.

"They are extortionists, Papa," Anna said firmly. She burned the letters before Liesel could see them and frantically beg her husband to pay anything, anything at all, to anyone who claimed to know where the children were.

Liesel grew pale from confinement indoors, and thin—thinner than she ever had been as a girl. Hansi's dark hair began to grow out in streaks of gray, and the skin under his eyes increasingly appeared bruised, as if he did not sleep well. When he did sleep at home, he spent those nights less and less often with his wife. Magda thought that he made the excuse of not disturbing Liesel so he could stay at the Sunday House, or in the room that Sam shared with Elias and any of the older boys who were at home.

On a weekday in November, he was in the office going through circulars with Magda and planning another buying trip to the coast. Marie came into the shop, saying, "Papa, there is a man at the door, saying he has an appointment with you!"

"Well, show him into the parlor." Hansi ran his hand impatiently over his hair. "Thunder and lightning, is it Thursday already? Don't just stand there, Marie, go on! Show Mr. Johnson into the parlor!"

"Papa . . . Mr. Johnson is a darkie!" Marie pleaded, in an agony of embarrassment.

Hansi snorted. "Marie, my silly goose, I am hiring Mr. Johnson to do a job for me. If he does what he says he can do, I will be in such debt to him that he may make amorous advances towards you under my own roof and I will have no objection at all. Go! Say that I shall join him in a moment." Marie fled, crimson with embarrassment.

Hansi chuckled at Magda's expression of shock. "He wouldn't, of course; besides being one of nature's own gentlemen, he's married—and married to a woman that he all but moved heaven and earth for, when she was taken by the Indians, two years ago. Besides," Hansi stood from the desk with a grunt of effort and pulled on his good coat, "he's a sensible man and a bold one, too. He has connections among the friendly Indians, so they say. Tell Anna to close the shop for a bit. I want her to hear what I have to say. You too, Magda."

"Who is this Mr. Johnson, then?" Magda asked, as she followed after her brother-in-law. "What does he do and why do you think that he, of all people, can help you get your children back?"

"Because he did it before," Hansi answered. As Anna locked the door and followed them towards the parlor he explained, "He worked as a foreman, first for the family which owned him and then for another. His wife and two children were taken two years ago in the Elm Creek raid. He went and got them back, spent a year prowling among the Indian camps in the territories. He's a trusty man as well as having the very nerve! I made enquiries, you know. If you can send a man out to search and carry the

164

ransom money for strangers, then I think I may trust him with about anything else. Including," he added with a heavy attempt at humor, "the virtue of my own daughters in the parlor, under my own roof, eh? Think I can depend upon the wild African to restrain himself?"

"Papa, there are folk you must not make a jest like that to," Anna said in all seriousness.

Hansi laughed again. "I know, Anna pet. I know. You, your mother and your aunt are about the only ones to whom I might say something of the sort." His face sobered as he put a hand to the parlor door. "She would laugh, so much. I would give much to have her back again with us, in her own good temper once more!" He opened the parlor door, saying as he strode within, "Mr. Johnson—so generous with your time to come all this way. Please, do sit down. My daughter and sister-in-law I wish to be present."

Not a proper, formal introduction, Magda thought. Such was the way of this country, even such as Hansi had become attuned to it. Receiving a colored man in the parlor, having his daughter and sister-in-law touch his hand, acknowledge him in courtesy. No, Hansi had become a man of business; he would not offend against custom to that extent.

Anna stepped forward, her voice perfectly controlled. "Miss Anna Richter," she said, evenly in precise English. "I serve as Papa's secretary. He has asked me to be present, Mr. Johnson. He tells me you may be able to retrieve my brother and sister from the hands of their captors. Do make yourself at ease and tell us of how you expect to accomplish this, when so many others have failed us in this respect. This is my aunt, Mrs. Becker," Anna added with a challenging flash of her eyes. "My dear mother is indisposed; her sister takes her place as far as the proprieties are concerned."

Hansi's guest had not sat down. He stood by the parlor stove, not at his ease, yet seeming to be comfortable, assured. He barely brushed Anna's fingertips with his own, nodded courteously at Magda. "I cain't much promise anything, Miz Richter, only that I will do my bes'."

"So," Hansi rumbled, "do, please—sit, sit, sit!" He gestured Mr. Johnson towards a chair and the visitor perched on its edge. He was wary and watchful, as if unaccustomed to well-adorned and comfortable parlors; but not nervous. His eyes flicked once, twice around the room, making a swift assessment of his surroundings and of Anna and Magda, before fixing his attention on Hansi, who continued, "You did not say how you came to hear of our need?"

"A frien' tole me about your advertising in de papers." Mr. Johnson had a deep voice, like a bass viol. His dark hair was cut close to his scalp, but other than that and the set of his mouth, Magda did not think he looked particularly African. He was not even as black as some of the slaves she had seen since coming to Texas, but rather dark brown and well-formed. "They knew I was set on going to Indian Territory in de summer to search for Miz Fitzpatrick's youngest granddaughter. So dey says as I ought to send notice to you, since you have kinfolk taken captive. It might be of service if'n I look for your chirren as well."

"So it would be," Hansi answered.

Anna said in very precise English, "You seek payment of sorts, we presume?"

Johnson replied with immense and careful courtesy, "Your father said a wage in his letter to me, but money ain't a necessity, Miz Richter, not 'til I find the chirren, if the Lord 'lows it. Then I sees what ransom the Injuns want. I don't wants you to open your purse, 'til I come back from de territory and tell you face to face, an' dat be de truth." Magda, sitting quiet in the corner, thought it sounded like a dignified reproof and wondered what it was about him that seemed so familiar.

Hansi replied with his own dignity, "Since you are undertaking such an enterprise at least partially on our behalf, I insist you allow us to provide you with supplies necessary for your long journey."

"I wouldn't say no to that, seh, I surely wouldn't," Mr. Johnson answered. His reserve thawed a little, for he smiled, an unexpectedly sweet smile. Magda realized why she had been struck with such a feeling of familiarity. He reminded her of her husband. Not in any particular physical likeness between them, aside from height, but that they both reflected the same self-contained reserve and air of quiet competence. Men of the frontier, they were; used to being alone and supremely confident in their abilities to venture into the wilderness and survive against any odds they found there. If Carl Becker had sat in the parlor of Vati's house and calmly announced that he was going to go to Indian Territory to ransom Willi and Grete back from captivity, Magda wouldn't have doubted for a second his ability to do exactly that. So it was with this man. He listened with grave sympathy as Hansi spoke of Willi and Grete, of their ages and appearances, of the pale scar on Willi's back just under the shoulderblade and the tiny chickenpox scar in the very center of Grete's forehead. He spoke also of the circumstances under which they had been taken and the fruitless pursuit of their captors. Mr. Johnson listened and talked little of his plans, only that he had intended to seek out a chief who was a particular friend of his, who had served as a mediator on his previous quest into the Llano country and Indian Territory.

Finally, Anna tilted her head and looked at him skeptically. "And may we ask why you are so ready to undertake such a mission as this, for so little reward and so much risk to yourself?"

"'Cause I'm right good at it, Miz Richter," he answered. "An' mebbe the Lord has called me to use that fo' other folk, they as knows what it's like to ride like the very devil hisself an' come home too late . . . find they own son dead on the porch and the house afire, an' Mrs. Fitzpatrick's daughter scalped an' dead with a empty rifle in her hands. It took me pert-near two years to get my Mary back and the babies with her and Mister White's boy, but I did it. I found some Injuns an' made dem hep me fin' dose who had my fambly. I came back an' I raised de ransom my own self, an me an' Mister White, we went out an' we got our own back. So, I got de callin', Mister Richter, Miz Richter. De Lord, he say you got de talent, you cain't put dat under no basket. Miz Fitzpatrick, she say her lil gran'baby still out dere," He regarded them steadily, his determination a quiet thing, like the limestone that underlay the hills around them. "So, I'm goin' back, bring dem babies home where dey belong just like I brung my own home."

"You are the first to speak to us and offer hope," Hansi noted, his own voice deep with suppressed emotion. "The first to speak so, since we lost the trail of the party who took them."

"I ain't brought them back yet." Mr. Johnson shook his head, as if to warn them against expecting miracles, but his quiet certainty was as a tonic.

"None the less," Hansi stood, as if to indicate that he had made a decision on the matter, "we shall support you in this venture, Johnson— support you with whatever you need. If you come to the house tomorrow, my daughter will provide you with letters of credit and introduction. I have friends in certain towns along your way. With my good word, they will supply you with all you require." As they shook hands, Hansi gripped Johnson's hand in both of his, begging, "Bring them back to us! My dear wife is nearly destroyed at the loss of her children."

"Unnerstand." Johnson also appeared much moved. "The Lord will guide my feet, and set my eyes on the heavens."

"Good, good." Hansi pulled himself together with an effort and made as if to show Johnson out of the parlor. As they went into the hallway, Magda heard her brother-in-law say, "So, Mr. Johnson, what is your profession, then? A scout for the Army, or a huntsman of the buffalo?"

"I allus done a lil freight-haulin'," Johnson replied, "wit' my own wagon an' team. An' I useta manage Miz Fitspatrick's land fo her, but that wuz before she an' the chirrin an' my Mary was all took by Injuns. Now, I took my fambly an' settled in Weatherford, over in Parker County. I do some teamsterin' now, haulin' more freight out to dem Army posts."

"Ah!" Hansi sounded very jolly as he opened the front door, and showed their visitor out. "I've always thought, if you can trust a man out and about driving a wagon full of your own property, you can trust him with about anything else."

The next day Mr. Johnson came for Hansi's promised letters. He was going north, he said, and advised them gravely not to look for word or his return immediately. It would take months of patient search and negotiation among the skin lodges of the Comanche and the Kiowa. But in spite of his words, their hopes had been raised—only to gradually deflate over that long span of time.

As winter came on, Liesel still kept to her room, but she would emerge on occasion, come downstairs and busy herself in the kitchen as of old. She took to sewing, almost compulsively, doing all the household mending. Liesel seemed quite cheerful then, with her mouth full of pins and slashing energetically with the sewing shears, fashion-papers strewn all about the bedroom that she and Hansi did not share.

By degrees, Magda and Anna became accustomed to that state of affairs. "Really, I don't know if I should laugh or cry," Anna said, twirling around to show off a new dress that Liesel had pressed upon her one afternoon. "It's like having a fairy dressmaker locked up in the attic."

"Your Mama has always done beautiful work," Magda said as Anna tied her shop apron over the new dress. They were in the workroom, where Magda was sorting through the mail.

"Good that you think so," Anna replied, "for she has one for you nearly finished."

"In black, I hope," Magda said austerely. Anna nodded.

"Merino wool, with jet buttons. But I am worried, Auntie. She is also making clothes for the children, for Willi and Grete. For when they return," she says."

"Oh, dear," Magda sighed. "I wonder if that is wise, Annchen?"

"I don't see how we can stop her from doing so," Anna said, with an air of utter practicality. "After all, it is of somewhat more use than wringing her hands and cursing Papa."

"True," Magda sighed. "And doubtless, they will need new clothes."

"It has been nearly a year," Anna said. She would have sounded harsh, but for that she was holding her grief in firm check. She came and sat at Magda's side, pulling up Vati's old work stool. "And no word of them in all that time—Auntie, what do we tell her when it becomes clear to everyone that my brother and sister are really gone? That no one can find them, and they are most likely dead? How long can we hold on to hope before that hope becomes destructive?"

"I don't know, Annchen." Magda was heart-sore because she had begun to wonder the same thing. Death was final and grief . . . well, if not final, became a familiar thing, something that one grew accustomed to. Uncertainty and hope endlessly deferred; that was a wound freshly inflicted every day and every hour. "Mr. Johnson did warn us."

"A charlatan like all the others," Anna sniffed dismissively. As Magda slit opened another letter Anna asked, "That one's not from him, is it?"

"No," Magda answered, as she read the short missive within. "It's from Porfirio." She laid down the letter, her face as white as linen. "Auntie, what is the matter!?" Anna cried.

"He says that J.P. Waldrip has returned from Mexico! That he has been seen in San Antonio! Anna, mind the shop for a bit, I must take this to Charley Nimitz."

Magda crammed the letter into the leather valise that she carried with her always. She put on her bonnet and shawl, fairly running all the way down Main Street to Charley's hotel. Hansi was on the road with his wagons, and her son was trying to restore what his father had built with such care and labor, so Charley was the only one she could take into her confidence on this matter.

"I want to bring charges against him," she demanded, sitting in the Nimitz's little private parlor, "for murdering my husband! Tell me what I must do, Charley! You were his friend—cannot I demand justice, now that the war is over and his fine Confederate protectors may no longer look the other way?"

"My dear Mrs. Magda." Charley regarded her with deep sympathy, as he finished reading Porfirio's letter and the scrap of stained notepaper that she drew out of the valise and thrust into his hands. "The trouble is—they will look the other way. Anywhere outside Gillespie County, that is. Politically, it's an untenable situation, bringing charges against a Confederate sympathizer for what he did during the war. The Union might have won, Mrs. Magda, but most of Texas is still mighty full of Southern sympathizers."

"He murdered my husband!" Magda cried passionately. "Trap Talmadge said he shot him in the back! Not from anything to do with the war—he hated Carl long before the war ever began! Trap left this affidavit to say so and I saw J.P Waldrip in my own house with the Hanging Band! He held our children at the point of a gun in my own kitchen until—until my husband agreed to go with him! Surely a jury would hear me out—"

"I am sure they would, Mrs. Magda," Charley interrupted with a somber face. "And Waldrip was a very beast. But murdering Carl Becker is not the very least matter of which he can be charged. What of the Grape Creek murders, or that of Mr. Schuetze the schoolmaster? There is plenty to lay at his door, but the trouble is that it was all done in wartime and now the war is over. I fear that there is talk of an amnesty regarding any such deeds, Mrs. Magda."

"And those who benefited by such deeds, or justified them, wish not to have them thrown in their faces?" Magda asked bitterly.

Charley sighed. "Indeed, they wish to have them forgotten. Having connived at such wrongs, they wish to begin with a clean slate. I am sorry, Mrs. Magda. I would wish to also see him in the dock, and better yet with a rope around his own neck, for what he did to you and to all of us. Justice may yet be done for that, but I do not think there is much official stomach for it. But I will talk to Judge Wahrmund and see what he thinks can be done."

"Watch and wait." Magda visibly attempted to keep her emotions under control as she returned Porfirio's letter and Trap Talmadge's affidavit to her valise. "I have waited nearly five years for something to be done about that vicious man. I can wait a little longer."

Charley escorted her to the door. "If he returns to Friedrichsburg," he added almost cheerfully, "we will have the warm welcome we promised him before. But I do not think he will dare return here. Dogs may return to their vomit, but in my experience, criminals think twice about returning to the scene of their crimes—especially when they have been warned against doing so."

"I suppose you are correct," Magda agreed. She departed thinking bitter thoughts about the Confederacy and those men who had trafficked in rebellion, committed grevious crimes, and now wished not to face any more of the consequences.

She had all but put Waldrip out of her mind on the March day that she took Lottie by the hand and walked to the graveyard. It had been a year since Vati died, a year since Rosalie breathed her tortured last. Magda felt the need to be alone on that awful anniversary, alone but for Lottie who was finished with school for the day. Her daughter carried a little pail to dip water from the creek and Magda left Anna in charge of the shop for an hour or so. Peter Vining had come to town to bring back another load of lumber and supplies, so Magda thought that he might also pay some elaborate courtesy to her niece while he was at it.

Oh, to be out in the fields on a spring afternoon, while the wind chased dandelion-puff clouds in a faultlessly blue sky. It put Magda in the memory of how she had tended the cows in the last year of the war, leading Lottie by the hand, wandering with her valise full of knitting and useless wads of Confederate money should she run across anything worth buying from the shops as she returned. She had never worried about danger, from Indians or anyone else, in those last days of the war, for Jack the dog accompanied them and she had always carried Carl Becker's old five-shot Paterson revolver in the valise.

She and Lottie picked armfuls of sweet wildflowers from the fields beyond Town Creek, and from the banks of the creek, to add to the little handful of new-blossoming daffodils from their own garden. They walked among the stones and monuments; so many of them there were now, so many friends! Dear Mrs. Helene, Pastor Altmueller's wife; Liesel and Hansi's son Christian, dead in the diphtheria epidemic in the last year of the war; and now Vati, dearest of all. And Magda still felt tears coming to her eyes, to think of Rosalie and her Robert, dancing at their wedding and looking only at each other, little knowing how short their marriage would be.

She tidied the graves, kneeling and heedless of her new dress, which, true to Anna's words, Liesel had pressed upon her. The grass and the soil in her fingers felt wonderfully like working in the garden; how little of that she did these days. It was country-quiet out here, town was far enough distant that the sounds of it carried but faintly: horse hoofs, the regular thud of someone splitting wood in the backyard of a house on Town Creek, and once the crack of something that could have been a rifle shot. Magda wondered who might be hunting so close to town.

She and Hansi had paid for a fine stone for Vati, with a holder for a little brass vase at the bottom. She emptied out last week's dead flowers, and Lottie solemnly filled it with fresh water from her pail. They did the same for Rosalie and Robert. They also had a fine stone, a single one for both of them. Mr. Berg had come out of the hills long enough to do it, carving a single rose by way of ornament. Robert Hunter, Rosalie his wife, side by side throughout eternity.

Magda shouldered her valise when they were done, and took Lottie's hand. The child swung the empty pail as they walked towards Austin Street and the stage stop at the back of Charley's hotel. Magda considered walking by Pastor Altmueller's house and paying him a visit on the way back; after all, that was only a little out of their way, down Austin Street, where all the houses backed on a loop of Town Creek. It looked as if the stage had come in, for there was a small crowd of men at the stop. But something was very strange, for the driver stood gesticulating by the side of his horses. They should have been on their way almost at once. Magda wondered what had happened. Perhaps one of the team had gone lame; not surprising, for the coaches went at a fearful pace, uphill and down.

As she and Lottie crossed over the Town Creek footbridge, Magda observed there were two groups of people. Some of them stood around the driver, quite upset, adamant in demanding that their journey continue. Most of those were Americans. The other group was men of the town, Germans from Friedrichsburg and nearby. They seemed terribly agitated also, gesticulating and shouting at the first group and each other. Even as she approached, some of them scattered, with a purposeful air about them. Something had happened, something to do with the stage. If the war had still been going on, Magda would have thought the stage had brought great news of some battle, victory, or defeat.

She had no need to ask, for as she drew closer, one of the men shouted, "Madame Becker, have you heard! He's back! J.P. Waldrip, he was on the stage from San Antonio! He was in a great bate of anxiety, all the way here, so they say!"

Magda felt as if she had been turned at once to a pillar of ice, for the words struck her numb and silent. So she had been, when J.P. Waldrip's masked friends had taken away her husband, binding his hands with rope and leading him away to his death. Then Waldrip had put his hands on her and struck her senseless with a revolver in his fist. When she revived, she was already a widow, although she had not known that for many more hours.

"Waldrip! Come here to Friedrichsburg? Has he gone mad?" she gasped. "We must send for the Sheriff! I demand that he be arrested for killing my husband!"

"The Sheriff has already been sent for, Madam!" It was Fritz Ahrens, Charley's brother-in-law. He seemed most particularly exhilarated. "No fear, on that! He might be quite eager to surrender to the Sheriff, on all accounts!"

"What happened?" Magda demanded again, "Why did he even come back to Friedrichsburg? Where did he go?"

"It seems that he has enemies in San Antonio, also." Fritz Ahrens chuckled with great satisfaction. "Last night, some Mexican chased him into an alley near the Vaudeville Theater, threatened him and drew a knife! So in mortal fear, he bought a stage ticket for El Paso, thinking to get as far away and as fast as he could! Of course, he must have known that the stage stops here but only for a short time, so I imagine he thought to brave it out! But just as everyone was dismounting, up rides young Braubach on a lathered horse, shouting riot and murder and fire!"

"Philip Braubach?" Magda gasped. "That married Louisa Schuetze? Who was the sheriff here before the war?"

"The very same! He had ridden after the stage upon hearing that Waldrip was on his way here! Young Braubach took out his revolver and shot at him! Right here, on this very street not ten minutes ago!"

"Where is Waldrip, then!" Magda demanded. There was no body on the ground, no evidence of anything untoward, and yet it seemed as if the whole universe had suddenly turned upside down.

"He missed," Fritz Ahrens said regretfully. "The revolver turned in his hands, for they were sweaty. He missed and the bastard Waldrip—sorry, Madame Becker—ran like a hare. He ran towards the gardens, but he can't get far, even if he runs true to form and steals a horse. We'll find him soon, of that you can be sure!" He touched the brim of his hat to her, and went off to join in the clamorous search.

"We must get home," Magda said urgently to Lottie, "and send Mr. Vining with word to your brother! He must know of this! And see that the Sheriff arrests that vile murderer!"

She set off towards Main Street, towards where the large oak tree shaded the Magazine Street entrance to Charley's stableyard and the bathhouses that served his guests. When they had first come to Friedrichsburg, when it was nothing but a forest of oak trees with pegs and little flags of cloth marking the outline of where it would soon be built, Magazine Street was where the Verein blockhouse and stores had been and the communal gardens that had supplied them all in the very first days. Now, Charley's hotel and outbuildings lined one entire block, between Main and Austin Streets, facing a row of small homes and shops opposite. She held Lottie's hand tightly, all thought of a leisurely stroll down Main Street forgotten with this news. She urgently wanted to speak to Charley, to Mr. Vining, to her son, to the Sheriff—anyone! J.P. Waldrip must not be allowed to escape. As she swept past the oak tree, her skirts rustling like a storm in a bed of reeds, she heard someone scream, and the dark figure of a man ran out of the stableyard.

It was Charley's daughter Bertha who screamed, and screamed again as the man ran towards Magda and Lottie. "It's him!"

Magda stood rooted to the spot; fear, shock and anger warring within her breast. Yes, her mind told her with chill precision; that was J.P. Waldrip, stumbling as his eyes darted here and there, like a trapped animal seeking escape, a fox hearing the hounds baying all around. He did not look much changed, with those feral mismatched eyes and the tall black felt hat by which he was known. But he was caged, however loosely, by the hotel behind and the girl standing in the passageway between the main building and the bathhouses with a pile of towels in her arms. His eyes darted towards Magda. She thought that he did not recognize her at first. She was just a woman in widow-black, holding a child by the hand, a woman who stood between him and his escape. It came to her with a start that there were men at either end of Magazine Street; those standing at the stage stop, as well as those searching. There were men on Main Street as well, even if they were not in on the search.

His eyes darted this way and that, finally meeting hers and holding for a startled instant, as recognition flashed between them. Recognition and desperate calculation too—and in the blink of an eye, something in Magda's intellect read his impulse and reacted with cold and unthinking precision. He knew her. When his eyes slid down towards Lottie at her side and he took one step closer and made as if to reach into his coat, she was in no doubt about what he meant to do. She had no intention of letting him do it. *No,* her mind cried out. *No, not again. He will not hold my child hostage.*

On that single thought, she set Lottie behind her and took the Paterson revolver from her valise, marveling at how cold and composed she was, how pure of doubt and hesitation. She held the old long-barreled revolver straight out, locking her elbows as her dear husband had advised her so many years ago, and calmly aimed as he had also instructed her to do. *Aim for his breadbasket,* Carl Becker's voice whispered in her ears. *The shots rise up.* In that moment which seemed eternal, she was ice cold and aware of everything around her, and yet it seemed distant, as if everything else happened behind a great glass window. She and the man who had killed her husband, threatened her children, held that very same revolver to Hannah's head; they stood facing each other. Lottie huddled at her back like a chick sheltering under the mother hen.

The first shot crashed like a thunderbolt in her ears. She supposed that she was at least as startled as J.P. Waldrip was, for he looked with amazed horror at the spreading red mess on his vest-front, just below where his coat buttoned over his chest. Then his parti-colored eyes met hers.

He took one wobbling step forward and said in a voice that sounded queerly normal, "You shot me."

That was for my husband, Magda thought coldly, as she drew back the hammer. *My husband, my children's father, my lover and dearest friend in the world. You fired the shot that killed him, after molesting me within his sight, with your hands and your words. You are loathsome, and the most unforgivable thing you have done is to make me hate you so.* The Paterson's narrow trigger slid obediently open to her finger. Why did the man not fall? Was he a devil spawned from hell, impervious to lead and any weapon at hand? She fired again. *This one is for Trap Talmadge, whose weakness you used, whose guilt for having betrayed my husband to your gang led him to seek death in battle. Poor Trap, who sought oblivion at the bottom of a whiskey bottle only when it was put in his way . . . who worked happily at our farm in the hills, teaching our sons to ride, working for my husband. You led him to commit the worst betrayal of all—giving up a friend into the hands of his enemies!*

A second bloody mess blossomed on his vest-front. Waldrip clutched his belly and his mouth opened in wordless bewilderment. Yet he remained on his feet, and as Magda pulled back the Paterson's hammer once again, his coat fell a little back and she saw that he had a revolver also, in a leather holster under his coat. *What would make the wretched man fall?!*

That is for our children, Magda thought, as she shot him again. *You used his love for them as a weapon, in order to make him go with your filthy gang. You knew that he would do anything rather than see his children harmed. And yet they were—Hannah was plagued by nightmares for years . . . and Dolph—Dolph was nearly lost to us all, for he loved his father well! You wish to make enemies, Waldrip? Threaten a woman's children, and see what an enemy you have made, when she has the chance to repay in blood!*

Waldrip fell then to his knees, stark bewilderment on his countenance. What had he expected? Magda thought with vicious satisfaction; that he would be welcomed with rose petals into Gillespie County where his wolves had ravaged and murdered all during the war? That a woman he had wronged in every way but the worst way imaginable would allow him once more to threaten harm to those she loved? That little Mrs. Feller, left destitute to care for her children on charity and sewing, or Louise or Clara Schultze, would not do the same, if they had a chance—and if their husbands had taught them to shoot!

That's for Schoolmaster Schuetze, the kindest and cleverest of teachers, who made a jest one afternoon and the Hanging Band came to his house that very night. That shot hit high, and left him gasping from a gush of bright blood that came out of his mouth. She could hardly see his shirtfront and vest for dark blood, yet he still lived, racked in agony for every breath he took as he lay on the ground at her feet, in the dust under the tree by Charley Nimitz's stableyard.

"Oh, God, please don't shoot me any more," he gasped. Pitilessly, Magda pulled back the Paterson's hammer one last time.

This is for me, she thought. There was a tremor in her arms. No need to brace her arms out straight, no need to really aim, that last time. *You made many enemies in your whole wretched, thieving life— but never knew until your last moments that the deadliest enemy of them all was a woman.* With a final crash of the Paterson firing, the life burst out of J.P. Waldrip in a tide of blood.

Magda stood over him, trembling like a leaf. She felt nothing more than an enormous sense of satisfaction. It had happened all so very fast. She looked down at the body at her feet, thinking that she ought to feel something more than that. She had killed a man, five shots with a Paterson, out in the street in front of everyone. All that she could muster up by way of regret was a conviction that if she had more of a chance to think about it, she should have contrived to shoot him without any witnesses. There would be trouble over this. Hansi and her son would be furious with her on that account, especially if it affected the business.

"Mama?" Lottie's voice quavered from beside her. "Is that man dead?"

"Yes he is, little miss!" Charley answered cheerily. Magda looked up, startled out of all countenance. How on earth had he managed to appear, so neat and unruffled in his black town suit and carefully trimmed beard? He winked broadly at Magda, chucked Lottie on the chin and in one swift movement he took Magda's wrist and slipped the Paterson out of her grasp. Magda blinked; he had palmed it neatly and conveyed it out of sight with all the aplomb of a stage magician, somewhere underneath the tails of his suit coat. "I do believe," he added in a louder voice, "that this would be the infamous J. P. Waldrip. I'll leave it to Doctor Keidel to confirm the details, but he certainly looks dead to me." He looked around at the murmuring crowd, suddenly gathered from the stage stop, from within the hotel and from up and down Magazine Street. Many of them were men carrying weapons—among them young Philip Braubach, and the cobbler, Mr. Fischer, who had his workshop in a house opposite Charley's stableyard. Mr. Fischer clutched a long carbine and looked much put out.

Charley put his arm comfortingly around his daughter and added, "Bertha saw him in the stableyard. When she screamed for help, I came out and saw him running towards the street, in the direction of Madame Becker and her daughter. And suddenly," Charley looked exceedingly bland, although his eyes danced with suppressed mirth, "I heard gunshots, but couldn't see from whence they came. Waldrip fell dead, right in front of us, and I have no idea who shot him. Some unknown assailant, I suppose. Waldrip had many enemies hereabouts."

Young Braubach snorted; it sounded suspiciously like a stifled laugh and a rustle of agreement went through the gathered crowd. Charley looked straight at Magda and continued, "And he had friends and kin, as well. Knowing that he is dead at the hands of an unknown assailant," Charley emphasized that phrase again, "they might wish to avenge themselves against the person who killed him . . . if they knew who what person was, of course. Alas," Charley shrugged elaborately, "I have no idea who shot Mr. Waldrip. Did anyone see anything at all? Bertha?"

"I didn't see anything at all, Papa," Bertha took her cue demurely. Magda saw comprehension flicker from face to face around her, saw the idea move like witches' fire, like ball-lightning, saw the complicit acceptance on every face, even those who couldn't possibly have been where they could have seen her shoot J.P. Waldrop five times in his body.

"'Twasn't me." Philip Braubach was the first to speak. "I had a shot at the bastard, but I missed, clean. Everyone saw me."

"Some will do anything to keep from having to buy wine when they win the shooting competition," commented Mr. Fischer dryly and to a general laugh. "So, if anyone cares to ask, what did he die of?"

"Lead poisoning," suggested Charley sweetly. That elicited another round of laughter. "Still and all," he added, significantly looking at no one in particular, "I suppose we should bury him decently, lest his next of kin come to complain of our hospitality. If they have cause," he coughed, and sent another significant look, "they will come and complain. Dissatisfied guests always make that special effort. Just as well they know nothing of where to direct their complaints, eh? Bertha, Madame Becker looks quite shaken; would you conduct her to the little parlor, and tell your Mama what has happened?"

Charley looked indecently pleased with himself, Magda thought, as Bertha led her and Lottie into the family parlor. As soon as they were safe indoors, Charley presented her with the Paterson, saying, "I do believe this antique weapon belongs to you, Madame Becker—I found it in my stableyard. I can only imagine how it got there."

"Charley . . . I . . ." Magda began to say, her heart overflowing with gratitude and affection for Charley's quick thinking; and affection too, for all of those townsfolk who had seen her shoot J.P. Waldrip.

"Not a word, Mrs. Magda." Charley kissed her other hand, the one that did not hold the Paterson. "Not a word. I did not see anything, nor did you. But . . ." he held her hand just a fraction longer than necessary. "I can't tell you how long it has been, since something I did not see, gave me such an enormous sense of satisfaction!"

Chapter Eleven: *A Plague of Cattle*

"And truly, Mama—did everyone keep silent about Mr. Waldrip?"
Lottie marveled. *"That is a wonder, that so many people could have seen such a thing and without a word being said, all agree to a secret!"*

Magda nodded. "It was indeed a marvel, but all knew very well the wickedness done by Waldrip and his friends. Our neighbors, Charley, his daughter—everyone! They held my life in their hands! But I did not fear betrayal for we had all suffered so during the war. No one had forgotten the malice of the Hanging Band, or doubted for a moment that those who had been a part of it would seek vengeance—if they knew who to seek it from! So we all kept silent, knowing that justice had been exacted upon a murderer. Even you, Lottie; you kept my secret also."

"I believe I thought it had been a dream," Lottie mused, "because no one spoke of it afterwards. I came to think I had imagined being there and seeing you holding a revolver and with Waldrip dying at your feet. How very gallant and quick-witted of Captain Nimitz, too!"

"It was fortunate that he was present," Magda agreed, "the dearest and most loyal of all of our friends that day. He gave out that I was quite overwrought, not able to answer questions. He deflected what little official curiosity that there was onto himself, and managed in short order to muddy the waters so much that my name was never attached to the business. Not that much of an inquiry was ever made, once Waldrip was buried. They buried him with his hat, you know. Everyone knew him by it; I think they wanted to make sure the Devil would recognize his own."

"Did anyone ever make mention of it to you afterwards?" Lottie asked.

Magda nodded regally. "Twice, only. I told Porfirio, of course; much later, after your Uncle Hansi had moved his family and his business interests to San Antonio."

"What did he say?" Lottie asked, as if she barely dared to breathe.

Magda smiled as if the memory gave her pleasure. "Well, he had broached the topic himself, first apologizing for not fulfilling his oath. But he had been the means of driving Waldrip out of San Antonio. 'I regret that I am not as swift as I once was, Señora Becker. That Waldrip creature got away from me', he said. When I confessed to him that I had killed Waldrip myself, he kissed my hand most affectionately and fetched out a bottle of very fine old French brandy. He poured the last of it into two small glasses

179

and we drank a toast to your Papa. Then he drank a toast to me, took both glasses, and threw them into the fireplace. He is the only person I ever told. Your brother knew also. I assume that Cousin Peter told him.."

* * *

Sophie Nimitz clucked over Magda and Lottie, and her own daughter, making much of the terrible fright they had all suffered. She brought Magda a little glass of her own mustang-grape wine and took Lottie to the kitchen for a bite of gingerbread fresh from the oven. She insisted that Magda put her feet up on the tuffet, while Charley sent word to Peter and Anna.

"You must say as little about this matter as you can," Charley advised her in a low voice. "Do not elaborate. If you keep what you say as brief and as close to the truth as possible, then you do not have to remember so many small details."

"I thought he was reaching for his own weapon," Magda answered, faintly. "He was going to take Lottie. He planned to use her to escape from town. I know this, Charley. I could see his thoughts in his face. It was as if he shouted it from the rooftop."

Charley nodded, swift in understanding. "But say nothing of that, Mrs. Magda! Say only that you were walking past the stable yard when you heard Bertha scream. You looked up, saw Waldrip and recognized him. But then you heard shots and he fell. You did not see where the shots came from."

Magda repeated obediently, "I did not see where the shots came from, which killed Mr. Waldrip."

"Good. Say only that and nothing more." Charley patted her shoulder comfortingly. He left the little parlor, and Magda sat with her fingers curled around the stem of Sophie's little wineglass. How strange it was to feel nothing much at all over having killed a man. Surely, one ought to feel something of guilt or regret? It was a sin to commit a murder, a violation of God's commandments; but thanks to Charley's quick thinking, she would likely escape any punishment for having done so. She thought about J.P. Waldrip, lying at her feet in the dust of Charley's stableyard; the way that the blood came out of his mouth as he coughed his last agonized breath, how the manic light in his odd-colored eyes had faded with the departure of life. But he would not haunt her dreams, she was sure, no more than he would haunt her sons with his malicious envy. He was dead, never again able to threaten harm to her family. She ought not to take such a deep sense of satisfaction from that, yet she did. Waldrip had been repaid for his many evil deeds. Justice had been served and she had been its instrument. She sat in the Nimitz's parlor, wrapped in that satisfaction, while people came and went. None came to speak to her, although she recognized the sheriff's voice, and Judge Wahrmund also.

Peter Vining arrived with the small wagon. Charley handed her up to the seat as if she were something fragile, and he exchanged some few words with Peter. She thought they spoke English, but in tones too low for her to hear, and that was the moment when she truly comprehended what she had done, what J.P. Waldrip had tried to do. She clutched the valise to her lap and held Lottie close. Now she trembled, reliving those moments when she looked into J.P. Waldrip's face and read the intention writ so plain. That vile man! He would have snatched her precious child from her hands, pressed the end of his pistol to her head, held Lottie hostage in exchange for his own freedom. No one would have dared threaten him, lifted a hand to prevent him leaving, not with Lottie's life at risk. He would have left town somehow, carrying his hostage with him. And then? The very possibility made her feel sick with horror. She would have done anything to prevent that, anything, and with her bare hands if necessary.

The wagon seat jostled as Peter climbed up and took up the reins, deftly adjusting the leathers in his wooden hand and pressing his mechanical thumb closed. Magda thought distractedly how very adept he had become with his artificial limb; that very morning he had come into the shop and purchased a button-hook. With as great a pleasure as Charley had once taken in his magic tricks, Peter had demonstrated how he used the button hook, anchored between thumb and fingers in the very same way he held a pair of reins, to fasten the shirt-cuff buttons on his right wrist. Peter Berg's clever device had been a boon to his confidence. He seemed much as he had been when Magda first met him, an outgoing and spirited lad. Now he looked sideways at Magda as he slapped the reins on the teams' back and chirruped to them. It seemed to her that there was a new degree of respect in his expression. Always he had treated her with the proper courtesy due to an older woman, his uncle's wife and Dolph's mother, but this was different.

"Five shots," he mused, apropos of nothing, after the horses had gone half a block from Charley's hotel. "All on target and none gone wild; that was some practiced shooting—even if it was up close."

Magda parroted Charley's advice. "I did not see where the shots which killed Mr. Waldrip came from." The corners of Peter's eyes crinkled; no doubt he was smiling under that dreadful drooping mustache. His amused expression was so like to that which her husband had worn that her heart was wrung once again.

He looked deliberately straight ahead, remarking, "It saved everyone a passel of trouble, especially for Dolph and I, Ma'am Becker. If ever a man needed killing, it was that Waldrip for sure. Captain Nimitz remarked to me on how you and Lottie were just innocently passing by."

"I am inconsolable," Magda returned sedately. "It is most tragic. He should have been arrested and tried for his crimes."

"Less trouble this way," Peter answered, still looking straight ahead. "But still; there is a smell of black powder remaining about your person, Ma'am Becker. You would be advised to air your clothing carefully, lest someone else remark upon it."

"Of course," Magda nodded. So that was how Peter knew, if Charley had not told him. It went without question that Peter would also take part in this unvoiced conspiracy. He had come to care for them greatly, and it was in Magda's mind that Hansi and her own son returned that affection and respect.

"And that was all that was ever said to me," Magda told her daughter, "and all that ever came out of it, although now and again strangers came to Friedrichsburg, inquiring about the mystery. Everyone they met would point out the very tree on Magazine Street where it happened, and tell them most eagerly of how J.P. Waldrip was felled by an unseen assailant, how he ran out from the hotel yard after Miss Nimitz saw him and screamed and how as he lay dying he begged not to be shot any more. Of every incident and detail save one—and I have always fancied that those who went into the most detail were those who had not actually been present. But that satisfied all those who heard. And if they were not satisfied, they made little complaint in Friedrichsburg, where there were many besides our family who had good cause to hate Waldrip. Yes," Magda added, as she looked into the fire, "five shots. Your Papa would have been most pleased with my aim." At her feet, Mouse the Pekinese rolled and stretched, and settled himself with his head resting on the toe of her shoe, whilst looking up at her. Magda chuckled fondly, "Such a dog as your Papa would never recognize as such! Now, the story of how this Mauschen and the others came to be mine—that had the beginning of it that very same spring!"

"Did it, Mama?" Lottie asked, dubiously, "But I didn't think you met Princess Cherkevsky until much later..."

"I didn't," Magda answered, "but the road to that meeting—we put our feet upon that road when Anna read some curious news in the American newspapers. Your Onkel Hansi always called it 'the road of silver and gold.'"

Shortly after the death of Waldrip, they received a message from Mr. Johnson. He had seen a white girl in an Indian camp in the northern territories, a girl of Grete's age, with a tiny round scar on her forehead; although her hair appeared dark in hue and he had not been permitted to speak to her. He could not press to interview the child without betraying his interest, and before he could do so, those who guarded her had gone to another camp; no one would tell him where. Liesel had one of her spells again, for Marie had let word of this slip to her mother, with the result that Liesel had retreated weeping to her bed.

"Papa," ventured Anna thoughtfully, as she set aside one of the American newspapers, "there is something interesting that you should see."

"Is there, Annchen?" Hansi asked. He lazily sent a puff of pipe smoke upwards. "Is it to do with business?"

"If it is," Magda suggested, "read it aloud to us." She knotted a thread-end and sighed; the boys were so hard on their clothes, and Lottie seemingly had grown almost overnight. At her feet was an overflowing basket of garments that needed mending and the little square sewing box was next to her. It was a Sunday afternoon and she might be done with shop business but that of her household pursued her ever, especially when Liesel had taken refuge in her dark, deep cellar again.

She sat with Anna, Fredi and Hansi in the garden of Vati's house, while Hannah and Marie pushed Lottie on the swing hanging from a lower branch of the old post oak. Lottie giggled and screamed in excitement as the girls pushed her ever higher. Sam lay on his stomach at their feet, leafing through the *Illustrated Leslie's Weekly* that Anna had already finished and passed to him. Dolph and Peter were down in the stableyard, looking at a new wagon that Hansi had ordered from Mr. Arhelger. Jack the dog lay in a warm patch of sunshine, but the other dogs trailed hopefully after Dolph.

"I thought Sunday was our restful day," Fredi chided, "when we talked of anything other than business."

"We cannot help ourselves, Fredi," Magda reproved him.

Anna said, by way of explanation, "We had thought to place an advertisement in the Kansas newspapers about the children, and I found this notice." She read from it, "*As a result of the passage of this law, cattle may be driven into Kansas without being subject to the annoying difficulties which drovers in Southern and Texas cattle were subjected to last year. Agents for the Kansas Livestock Company of Topeka are prepared to purchase at least 50,000 head of cattle, once said cattle are conducted to an established Depot of the Union Pacific Railroad. Drovers are advised, upon crossing the Red River into Indian Territory, to take a direct route to Forts Arbuckle, Holmes, et cetera, and from thence a due northerly course to the southern boundary of Kansas.*" She folded the newspaper so the story was uppermost and passed it to her father, adding, "The company has been capitalized at $100,000 dollars."

Hansi raised his eyebrows skeptically. "So they say to the newspapers. Where is this railroad to the Western territories being built, hey?"

Sam looked up from his reading. "Across the northern great desert, Onkel Hansi. They have been building from the ends—one starting in California, the other from Omaha on the Missouri River. Opa had a book with a map in it." He rose and dusted his hands on the seat of his trousers then made his way indoors.

Hansi took the newspaper from Anna. "Oh, that." Hansi snorted. "You mean to tell me that the railroad has finally gotten out far enough from lands owned by the majority shareholder to do good for anyone else? An age of miracles is upon us, clearly!"

"They must be following the old Platte wagon roads," Fredi observed, stifling a yawn. "They say the winters are deathly. And so are the Sioux Indians. I wonder how much farther they will go, until they give it up as a bad job? They should have taken the southern route—it would have been done years ago."

"One more thing to blame the secessionists for," Hansi grunted. "Giving up on our chance to have a trans-continent railway pass through the South, where it might have done us good. Fools!" He began reading the newspaper story.

Presently, Sam emerged from the house, lugging his geographical atlas. "It's called the Great American Desert," he said thoughtfully, as he laid the book on the table, open to a large map. "See? Hardly any towns at all."

"It's an old map," Fredi mused. "Still. You are right, lad. It is hardly more than desert now. But in taking a herd of cattle north by that way—it's no more desert than the way to California and a great deal shorter. There are no farmers objecting to the passage of animals they claim are diseased. Only the occasional hungry Indian!"

"How big a herd of cattle might that be," Hansi ventured thoughtfully, "if you cared to venture north with them, towards this new railroad depot?"

Fredi answered readily, "A crew of fifteen drovers at least, per every three or four hundred head. A couple of wagons full of supplies and a cook." Fredi fell silent as he thought more on it. "How much are they paying for cattle at markets in the north, Annchen?"

"Tenfold what they'll offer here," Anna answered. "Less men's wages and supplies, that would still leave us considerable profit."

"In driving cattle to the north?" Dolph, shadowed by his cousin Peter, had come up from the stableyard in time to overhear this. "There was some talk of this in San Antonio last year. It's no good taking longhorns into Missouri. They're riled up good and proper about cattle fever. There were some drovers who tried it this spring and got met with a mob for their pains."

"No, to Kansas, to the new railway," Hansi explained. "Annchen has read in the American papers they will pay more than forty dollars a head for beef cattle upon delivery there." Magda, her hands moving swiftly with needle and thread, watched her son's face as comprehension dawned.

"That sounds like a better plan than selling them for next to nothing in Indianola." Dolph took the newspaper from his uncle and read it in turn. "I like it, Onkel. And," he admitted in a burst of honesty, "I could use the money. I want to expand the house and start enclosing more pastures. All of that costs. And I'd like to improve the breed, just as Mr. King is doing at the Santa Gertrudis. I can't do that at five dollars a head."

Magda looked upon him, upon her sons and their cousin, and comprehended their restlessness and ambition. Dolph and Peter; they were dissatisfied with the peace that came after the fighting had ended. Not with an end to the killing and the dying; of that, they had a sufficiency, especially Peter. What they longed for was a sense of the whole grand purpose, the adventure and camaraderie. Driving Hansi's wagons, that was not enough. Having gotten the land back had only contented her son for a while.

"If the money for drovers' wages and supplies are lacking," Magda ventured, "I would take such from my State pension."

"And I would also back this venture from out of our profits," Hansi rumbled. "One for all, all for one, hey? Our company—now we will invest in cattle?"

"We certainly have enough of them," Fredi said.

Dolph added, "Like fleas on the backs of m'dogs. When should we do this, Fredi? In spring, after branding?"

Fredi nodded. He stood, striding up and down as he spoke, as if too restless to keep still while they made plans. "We'll have the whole winter to plan this," he said, "and to search out and hire the right sort of chap."

"Good riders." Dolph had the bit between his teeth now. In a moment, he would be pacing beside his uncle. "Used to working cattle and taking orders, but can still think on their feet."

"Been cavalry scouts or some such in the war," Fredi interjected, and laughed shortly. "Doesn't matter for which army, I suppose. Just be accustomed to living rough. And not being paid until the end of the trail."

"Someone whom we know," Dolph added, with a look at his mother and other uncle. "Someone trusty and known to us: you and I, or Uncle Hansi, or Peter between us. Or someone who we trust vouches for them. I'll not hire just any tramp off the road; I'd not pay such one penny of Mama's investment."

"This could be the making of our fortunes!" Fredi exclaimed. Hansi's and Magda's eyes met. How many mad schemes had Fredi encountered in the last fifteen years which he thought would be the making of a fortune? A throw of the dice, a will-'o-the-wisp glimmering; her brother was ever impulsive when it came to money. But he was a trusty man, as long as someone else held the purse strings!

"No drunkards," Magda put in. "And I don't mean hiring only those who have taken the temperance pledge—just those who crawl into the bottle and hardly ever come out." She met Dolph and Fredi's gaze; clearly they both thought of Trap Talmadge, that old friend and comrade of Carl Becker's whom he had hired out of loyalty and pity. "It's a weakness which destroys. Not just the drinker, but anyone else with the misfortune to be around him. I do not want to risk other lives, Hansi. We have too much already at risk."

Dolph nodded in agreement. He had been thirteen that nightmare evening when the Hanging Band came to the Becker place. Trap Talmadge came with them, drunk almost to insensibility. His father had opened the door, thinking his old friend had returned to ask for his old job back.

"Who would be in charge of the herd, day to day?" Hansi asked. "There must be one man to be the commander of all daily affairs on the trail, you know. It's how it works best."

"Onkel Fredi," Dolph responded instantly, and appeared startled when all looked at him. He continued, with an air of defense and logic, "He has trailed cattle to California, he is the most experienced of all of us in this, so he should be the trail boss. I think he should have day-to-day authority. But I think Onkel Hansi is the best suited to sort out matters of the market at the other end, of course. Well, really—he is the best at beating the best market price out of a buyer." Dolph looked around at them all, stationed under the tree while the summer breeze stirred the leaves.

"If so," Magda allowed, "then perhaps we should purchase additional cattle. If we are going on this trail and the market in Kansas offers that much promise, any increase in our offering is to the better."

"We can arrange for purchase of cattle now." Dolph put his elbows on the table. "And the owners deliver them to us, very early in the spring."

"Pasture them on my Live Oak land, or on the Becker holding," Hansi mused, his eyes alight with enthusiasm. "When should we depart for the north, lads? When the grass is well grown?"

"Even before then," Fredi answered, pausing in his long strides up and down. "Last year's dry grass will suit well enough at the start. If we move them slow enough, they will graze as they go."

"And that was where it began," Magda explained to her daughter. "On a Sunday afternoon, with a story that Anna found in the newspaper. We had prospered with the store, and with your uncle's freighting interests, and those interests would continue to prosper. But that single investment in trailing cattle to the north—that changed everything."

All during that summer and autumn, they sent letters; most of them written by Anna and Magda at Hansi's dictation, offering to purchase cattle from those friends they thought might have cattle to sell by early spring but not the resources to trail them north. They wrote letters offering employment to such of Peter and Fredi's friends as they knew to be restless but ambitious and hardworking lads. Magda wrote also to Porfirio, offering the same to those of his cousins and younger brothers as he could recommend. Porfirio answered by sending a dozen nearly wild horses and his cousin, Alejandro, who brought the herd to the Becker ranch and set about taming the tough, wiry mustangs for cattle work. He promised that other young men of his family would follow in spring.

"He can tame the orneriest horse any of us has ever seen," Dolph reported, just before Christmas, "I don't know how he does it. I think he puts a spell on them. The dogs, too—they follow after him, if they're not following me."

Dolph had also added another dog to his household, a small black and white bitch from a litter of puppies produced by one of the Stielers' sheepherding dogs. He had brought the pup with him at Christmas, tucked into the front of his coat. Hannah and Lottie had made much of the little wobbly-legged creature. Over Magda's misgivings, Dolph had promised the girls another from the same litter.

"So a remount herd," Fredi mused, "and a horse-wrangler. What about a wagon and a cook?"

"Leave that to me," Peter answered. "I talked to a fellow last week in San Antone who offered me a two-horse Army ambulance for a good price. I told him I would consider it." He knocked out his pipe and refilled it, before continuing, "See, they ride easy, being on springs. Someone gets hurt or sick, they can be hauled along without much problem, along with all the bedrolls and tent-canvas and that. You could have Arhelger fit out the back with a hinged tailgate, some cupboards and shelves and all—and there is your rolling kitchen."

"I like that." Fredi grinned broadly. "So the work is hard and the cows are stupid, we can't pay the men until we reach Kansas and the cattle-brokers, but at least they eat good on the way!"

Hansi and Dolph gathered maps and advice, seeking out those of their acquaintance who had taken small cattle herds to the north before the war to serve the emigrant trade along the river between Independence and Council Bluffs. Hansi had already taken his oldest sons, Jacob and George, much into his confidence as regards the freighting business; now he gave them increased authority and responsibility, although Anna would have the last word on any unforeseen matter which presented itself in Hansi's absence on the trail. They spent much of the holiday season poring over their plans and Fredi's maps, and such accounts and stories in the Kansas newspapers that Anna had gleaned.

"So, it is agreed, then—to leave in the second week of March from Live Oak." Hansi presided over a council in the parlor of Vati's house, just before New Year's, with his older children, and Magda, Fredi, Peter, and Dolph. "That will give us three months to reach Kansas by mid-summer. Assuming that all goes as greased."

"No reason it shouldn't," Dolph said.

Fredi laughed, a weary and cynical chuckle. "Oh, lad—I can give you any number of situations that might come to pass, but I won't get into that now! It would only discourage us all. But be assured, I take it as my duty to foresee them all—and then do my best to keep the herd moving!"

"If it works out as we expect," Hansi continued, "I will pay the men, and we'll return as expeditiously as possible by any means available to us. Say, by July, then." He looked around at them all. The candlelit parlor was still decorated for Christmas, filled with the resinous green scent of cedar branches. It was late, and the young children had already been sent upstairs to bed while their elders made plans for this New Year, the third since the ending of the war. Magda was reminded piercingly of how much had changed.

Their families had recovered some of their former prosperity, her husband's lands were returned to her son's care, and his murder avenged. But as blessings were given freely with one hand, fate had also taken from them with the other. Vati was gone and so, too, was their dear little Rose. The absence of Willi and Grete had broken Liesel's heart and estranged her from Hansi. Magda wondered in despair if even their return would heal her sister and make her marriage with Hansi whole again. Hansi busied himself with his businesses, and now with this cattle droving. All of his interests and conversations were things of which Liesel knew little and cared even less. He was not even there to share his concerns with her from day to day, as Carl Becker had once been wont to do when he and Magda had lived a contented life in the stone house in the Guadalupe River Valley, the house with the birds' nest and apple branch carved over the door.

"I would have us drink a toast," Hansi was saying, as Magda returned from her own thoughts.

"Oh, Papa—in whiskey?" Anna said. She sat on the chaise with Peter beside her.

"It's a manly drink, Miss Anna." Peter winked at her solemnly and whispered something in her ear, at which she rolled her eyes. Peter and Anna seemed to have settled into a teasing companionship, which pleased Magda, even though there was no indication of any special regard which could be construed as courtship between them.

Vati's parlor had so many fine ornaments and furniture in it now, things of quality in the very newest taste, which came their way because of the store. One of the newest was a Bohemia-glass decanter and a dozen matching small cordial cups, all in jewel-colored cut-glass. Hansi poured out a glass for each of them with a generous hand. "To our venture!" he said, raising his own glass. "And to our fortune—may it prosper!"

Magda took a sip of the whiskey, liking the taste of it little but knowing it meant much to Hansi and the boys. Whiskey was what men drank when they did business, and she supposed that since she and Anna did business also, they should appreciate such things.

While Hansi and the boys were on their way north, she and Anna would be in charge. It was curious, she thought, how living in Texas had so changed things for her. Out here, a wife was the first partner in a man's business. In his absence or in the event of his death, it was his wife to whom everyone naturally looked. Such authority could be held by any woman willing to step forward and grasp it firmly. This was not the east, this was not the Germany of her childhood, or the world of the proper genteel novels where a lady sat in her parlor and waited for the men of her family to see to everything outside that sphere.

No—either the guardians of those proprieties did not have such a grasp here, or perhaps they were not so commanding after all. Perhaps all they had was a belief that they were powerful. A woman like Margaret, or Anna, or that Miss Johnson whom Peter spoke so highly of, even herself— all they had to do was to step forward and break those genteel conventions, as fragile as a spider web, do as they pleased, and as their consciences or their obligations to family commanded them. Might liberation be as simple as all that, of breaking those chains that one had welded onto one's own soul?

She took another sip, a bigger one, which did not taste as strong as the first. It tasted a little like water from a peat-bog, smooth and oily, and she felt warmth from it in the back of her throat. This was what men of business drank, she told herself; so perhaps she must accustom herself to the taste, but yet not become so fond of it that she forgot all else. Anna was grimacing from the taste she had taken from her own glass while Peter laughed at her expression. Something in the way their heads inclined together caught Magda's notice. Could it be that Anna had feelings for him, something deeper than cousinly affection, that Anna herself was not aware of? And Peter, who bore such scars but paid such gallant attentions to every pretty girl; of course, he would be the last to know that even such a one as the forthright Anna held him in special regard.

Magda caught Hansi looking speculatively at his daughter and Peter, the sleek dark head and the fair one bent so closely over jewel-colored cordial glasses. She intuited his own thoughts; such a match would please Hansi. He would put no barrier in their way, would approve it heartily; but if he made such approval obvious, there was a danger that Anna would be contrary, or that Peter would rebel. *No*, she willed her brother-in-law silently; *say nothing to them. Only watch and wait. If it is meant to be, they will come to that realization soon enough.*

In February, Peter took the stage to Austin, saying little of what he was about other than to see that his mother's house had been properly taken care of. Amelia Vining had moved her establishment back to her father's generous roof at Mayfield. When Peter returned, he was accompanied by Daddy Hurst, spry and brown and hardly looking a day older than he had eight years before when Magda and her children had gone to Austin for Young Horace's wedding. He came into the shop office as Magda, Anna and Hansi sorted through another tall pile of merchant circulars.

"I've found us our trail cook," Peter announced jubilantly. "Daddy says he was tired of sitting around an empty house."

"I allus wanted to go see de nawrth," Daddy said with a sly chuckle. "An' now go legal-like, an' free? Miz Hetty, she say I ain't in no danger of scalpin' from dey Indians, wid no hair on this ol' haid to put at risk!"

Hansi looked from one to the other. "You can cook?" he asked.

The old coachman answered with calm dignity, "I ken do mos' things well 'nuff, Mistah Richter. My mama was cook to ol' Mistah Burnett. She done taught me some cookin' that Miz Hetty ain't ever done. 'Sides, you ain't looking for no high-an'-mighty fancy Creole French dishes? Jes' beans an' pone, an' coffee an' that. Plain cookin' for de han's, thass all?"

"Maybe a little more than plain," Hansi observed wryly. "Something to look forward to, at the end of a hard day would suit! I'll leave it all to you then." He shook Daddy's hand firmly, adding, "There's a list of food stocks for the journey, somewhere about."

"Here, Papa." Anna handed him a sheet of papers, clipped together.

Hansi thrust them at Daddy Hurst, saying, "Look it over and see if there is anything else you think might be needed."

"I ain't got any use for dem lists, Mistah Richter," Daddy answered, with imperishable dignity.

At Hansi's look of complete bafflement, Peter explained with embarrassment enough for the both of them, "Daddy Hurst can't read. It didn't used to be legal to teach nigras to read."

"Indeed!" Hansi looked indignant. "What an appalling state of affairs. How anyone can expect to get anything done?" He looked as if he regretted hiring Daddy Hurst.

Anna ventured, "I will read the list out to him. And then I will see what I can do." She shifted her gaze from Hansi to Daddy Hurst. "Mr.

Vining will drive you out to Live Oak tomorrow. There are already men there, so you will wish to make sure of the proper inventory. And of your facilities as the cook for them." It had the sound of a threat about it. Magda thought Daddy Hurst's expression warred between amusement and wary respect. Anna had that affect on men; it was nice to know that age and color did not offer an exemption.

Miles from the beginning of the trail north, without ever laying eyes on the herd of cattle or many of those who had been hired to handle it, by spring all of those living in the house on Market Street were in a high pitch of excitement. Dolph, Hansi and Peter had snatched the last mouthfuls of a lavish breakfast cooked for them by Liesel and Marie and started to prepare to leave.

Sam was almost beside himself with eagerness to go with his brother, pleading with Magda that since he had just turned fourteen he was clearly old enough to go. "No," Magda repeated for the twenty or thirtieth time.

Dolph finished strapping up his unwieldy bedroll and lifted it to his shoulder. "Pipsqueak, you have to help Mama with the store, remember—and school. Don't forget school."

The hallway seemed suddenly too small for Magda, filled to bursting with her menfolk and what they were taking with them. They loomed large in their work clothes and rough coats. She saw with a pang that Dolph wore his father's old buckskin jerkin. He had done so before, but now it seemed to fit him, for he had grown tall and filled out through the shoulders. A boy no longer, following in his father's footsteps and wearing that old coat; now he had become a man himself. "Let's leave before Auntie Liesel commences to carry on like a fountain," Dolph added in an undertone. Liesel had been sniffling all morning as she piled up food on her husband's and nephew's plates. She had seemed more cheerful of late, agreeable to Hansi's plans. Magda hoped that she would not go into her dark cellar again as soon as Hansi's wagon was out of sight.

Jacob brought around the wagon. Magda, Anna, and the younger children were going to accompany the men to Live Oak, where all was in readiness for departure. Charley and Pastor Altmueller and some of their neighbors were also going to come along. The morning had the air of a holiday.

"It's like the Fourth of July processions, isn't it, Auntie?" Anna ventured, as they rattled past the familiar coffeepot dome of the Verein

Church. She sighed, pulling her shawl close around her against the morning chill. "I wish I were going with them—anything for an exciting time!"

"It won't be exciting, Anna," Dolph responded. He and Peter lay sprawled on the pile of bedrolls and baggage in the wagon bed. "It will be business. And work. A lot of work! Dirty, boring, and not very interesting. In fact, you had better hope that it isn't exciting, because excitement burns the fat off cattle and fat cattle mean more money for us. Skinny cattle won't bring near as much."

"Oh, that," Anna pursed her lips. "Still, I think it would be interesting to go north. Fredi always said there are marvels to be seen, even if they do call it the great desert."

"We shall tell you all about it, Miss Anna!" Peter promised extravagantly. "Upon our triumphant return, laden with riches unimaginable!" He had begun to understand German uncommonly well, although he still spoke it very haltingly. He kissed his fingers and blew upon them, saying, "Will you greet me as a conquering hero then and return my kiss to me, holy palmer?"

He laughed with huge enjoyment when Anna scowled and answered in English, "Triumph, fiddlesticks. Only return and with my father and cousin safe; then I would not hold a poor price for our cattle against you."

"Why Miss Anna," Peter smiled even more broadly, "I didn't think you cared!"

Anna turned her back emphatically, while Dolph laughed and buffeted Peter's shoulder.

Their wagon, followed by the hotel trap and a handful of out-riding horsemen, reached Hansi's old Live Oak farm after sunrise. Magda caught her breath. So many cattle! As if they had sprung out of the ground like dragon's teeth sown in the furrows of his neglected acres. It was one thing to write the numbers, to write the invoices and the letters of credit; quite another to see the tossing endless parti-colored backs and their horns, all crammed together on Hansi's old pastures and fields.

"How many of them?" she inquired, as Jacob drew up the wagon in the old farmyard.

Her son paused as he leaped down. "Eight hundred fifty-three, Mama, at last count; unless a couple of the heifers have calved in the last week. That is the thing about cows—they will multiply." Peter tossed him his bedroll, laughing, then took up his own and hopped down from the wagon.

They carried their burdens to a sturdy wagon, with two teams waiting patiently in their harness. It had been decided to bring a supply wagon in addition to the converted ambulance and kitchen, rather than depend on what supplies might or might not be available along the way. "If it's one thing I would hate," Hansi had observed, "it would be paying three times over for what I know we have in our own warehouse. Besides, I'll drive the wagon myself. We might even be able to sell it in Kansas for a good price."

If the cattle numbered so many, it seemed to Magda that there were almost as many people in the farmyard, men and their horses swirling in a grand and purposeful circus. Her brother Fredi was the ringmaster and center of the storm. He looked settled and calm in the saddle of a pinto pony such as he used to ride when he was a boy, working cattle under the tutelage of her husband and Porfirio, in the days when the house on the Guadalupe was new and the limestone it was built of fresh and unstained. The air smelled of cattle dung and dust, and crushed grass. There was Daddy Hurst in the driving seat of the converted ambulance, taking up the reins in his capable hands and nodding respectfully in their direction. Fredi waved his hat to Daddy Hurst, who slapped the reins on the back of his team. His wagon lurched away; heavy-laden by the way his draft-team leaned into their yokes.

"So, now it is time," Hansi intoned. The sea of cattle had begun to move, slowly yet inexorably, as the tide begins to flow. It spilled out of his pasture onto the tracks leading east and north, down the valley, urged by mounted drovers. Hansi embraced Jacob and George, carelessly saluted Charley Nimitz, who watched the river of cattle flowing past with great interest, and kissed Anna on both cheeks.

"Have a care for your mother," he instructed, "and the store. But mostly for your mother, Annchen. Try to make her believe I will come to no harm, with all these fine young lads just waiting for a chance to show their mettle in our defense."

"Yes, Papa," Anna assured him.

"I'll send you letters, when we are near to a place we can mail them." He kissed Magda, "Don't worry for your investment. I shall see a tenfold return on it, if it's the least I can do! That's my promise, hey?" His hat knocked to a jaunty angle, he clapped his sons on the shoulders once more and strode towards the supply wagon, as happy as a boy set free from the schoolroom.

Magda impulsively embraced her son—grown so tall, she thought again. "You are full of lumps!" she exclaimed, for all those hard objects in his vest pockets dug into her ribs.

"Sorry, Mama," he replied, his eyes as calm and blue as the sky. "It's all the things I might need—cattle liniment and my brand book and pocketknife and cartridge box."

"Be well, then," she said. "Be well and take care that you return to us in one piece, Rudolph Christian Becker!"

"Of course, Mama," he answered serenely. Magda let her arms go from around him and stepped back. No, no longer a child; her oldest son had not been a child since that certain night in his thirteenth year.

A young man rode towards them, the reins of a pair of saddled but riderless horses held carelessly in his grasp. The rider was dark, Mexican, and he had such a look about him of Porfirio that Magda knew he must be his cousin Alejandro. Comfortably in the saddle, a dusty chevalier in plain workclothes, he hailed Dolph in Spanish, his teeth a flash of white in his dark face.

"'Bye, Mama," her son said over his shoulder. He went up onto the first horse like a bird settling onto a familiar perch and exchanged what sounded like rude remarks with Alejandro. The two of them joined their fellows at the edge of the moving river of cattle.

Then it was just Peter, holding the reins of the other pony in his good hand. "Farewell, Ma'am Becker, Miss Anna." He nodded to each of them in turn. Magda thought it was as though he did not presume on anything more familiar. No, Margaret's son should not have that cold a parting, she thought.

On impulse, she took his other hand in both of hers, his wooden one, with its unyielding jointed fingers. "You return to us safely," she directed. "Safe and whole. You are one of our own, Peter."

"Yes, Ma'am," he answered, seemingly gratified by the fond interest. "Don't worry. I will look after Mr. Richter and Dolph with every care, until we return safely."

"See to yourself as well," Anna said with brisk affection. To Magda's astonishment, she went to him and, on tiptoes, reached and pulled his face down to hers so she could kiss his cheek. "For it seems you feel obliged to look after everyone but yourself."

"Why, Miss Anna," he said, with a broad grin, "I shall—and am amazed that you would think of me with such tenderness! Dare I think you have feelings for me?"

"Someone should!" Anna answered him. "As a matter of charity, Mr. Vining," she teased.

"I am gratified," he said, then proceeded to return her kiss with a more enthusiastic one—on her lips. She pulled away from him with a gasp, flushing as pink as one of the primroses that starred the un-trampled grass. She lifted her hand and Magda thought she meant to slap him for impertinence, but he stepped away laughing and vaulted up into the saddle of his horse.

He was gone in a moment, and Magda observed, "Annchen, did you mean to encourage him? He may want another kiss like that, upon his return!"

Anna fumed. "Ridiculous man! How dare he be so forward!"

"Well, you did kiss him first," Magda pointed out, inwardly amused. "He would see that as an encouragement, you know. Most men would."

"I only thought to kiss him in farewell, as I would one of my brothers, or cousins. He had no right to read anything more into it."

"But you did not kiss Dolph, or your father," Magda reasoned, "Only Peter. Why would that be, Annchen? Do you have a special regard for him?"

Still blushing pink, Anna answered, "I might." But then she straightened her bonnet and turned to climb back into the wagon, "If I thought . . . oh, never mind, Auntie. He's as faithless as a silly bumble-bee, going from flower to flower. Let's go back to town. At least we can open the store for this afternoon!"

Chapter Twelve: *Long Trail Winding*

"What was that all about, Cuz?" Dolph asked of Peter, as they rode away from Hansi's old farm. They drifted slowly at the edge of that sea of moving cattle, taking up their positions on the point, a little way behind Fredi. The kitchen wagon and Hansi's supply wagon had already moved far ahead. The other riders spread out, riding swing and flank on either side of the herd. Even heavy-laden, the wagons moved faster than the plodding cattle. Those youngest and newest to the drive were stuck riding drag at the herd's tail, choking on dust and chivvying the stragglers along.

Laughing, Peter answered, "Miss Anna? I think she might hold me in more than the usual regard!"

Dolph ostentatiously sniffed the air. "It's morning and you are sober, Cuz. And so was she."

"She kissed *me*," Peter insisted, "in front of your mother, and most fondly, also. What do you suppose she meant by it?"

"Truly?" Dolph began to laugh, "Oh, Cuz, if Anna meant it seriously, then you are a marked man. Once we get to Abilene your only escape is to just keep going north on as fast a horse as we can provide."

"That isn't funny, Cuz," Peter responded with indignation. "Supposed I quite liked being kissed by Miss Anna?"

"Then you've been branded as neatly as any of these critters," Dolph answered. "And since that was the last kiss you will have from a woman until we get to Kansas, it's just as well that you enjoyed it." He added a rude description of what else was done with young cattle at their first branding, at which comparison Peter protested with loud indignation. A handful of cattle near to them started at his raised voice, a sudden eddy in a placid stream.

Fredi wheeled his horse, reproving him in a low but tense voice, "Be still, then! These beasts panic and stampede at the least thing! Hell, I've even known a cow to begin stampeding at the sound of their own dung hitting the ground!" Chastened, Dolph and Peter dropped the subject of Miss Anna's intentions for the moment, being that she was the daughter of Hansi, a man still hale and with shoulders like a bull. They rode too far apart for conversation the rest of that day, as they would during most of those days following, their attention always on the herd—that exasperating, wayward, deeply stupid, and enduringly impulsive collection of almost completely wild longhorn heifers and steers. Of every color imaginable; white and roan, grey-blue or spotted black and brindle brown in every combination, all the cattle had by way of commonality was a pair of wide-branching horns and a collection of brands on hip and shoulder, or notched ears and a trail-brand. All were as wild as deer and nothing any sane man would want to approach on foot, not without a lariat in hand and a watchful friend at back.

Sometimes, Peter wondered if they had all gone insane, thinking they could take this herd all the way to Kansas, winding a slow and tedious way through Indian Territory and across all that howling wilderness in between. It would be like shepherding a handful of mercury, a thousand droplets all eager and ready to separate and roll away in a thousand different directions. Especially when they got out into the unsettled country; Peter did not like to think any farther ahead than that. He counted it fortunate that it was not his job—that was Fredi's. And it was also Fredi's burden to command the drovers, as if he were the captain of the company. Dolph and Peter rated as something a trifle lower, perhaps as sergeants. There were thirty-three of them, including the Mexican horse-wranglers, all young and single, some more foolish perhaps than others. They were clothed in motley of work clothes, canvas pants patched with buckskin, linsey-woolsey or homespun cotton work shirts. Those who had previous experience with cattle on the trail had calico kerchiefs tied around their necks. Their hats were motley also; wide-brimmed Mexican sombreros or home-made of plaited straw. Billy Inman had a black cavalryman's hat with a bit of tarnished gold braid around the crown. They all had brought along sidearms of one kind or another, as it had long been the custom among Texians to go armed. Daddy Hurst and Hansi equipped themselves with shotguns, short in the barrels and triple-loaded.

Nearly all of Hansi's drovers were American-born, either kin to Porfirio, sons of old Verein settlers, or formerly soldier-comrades in various military companies with Fredi or Dolph. Four or five were connections of the Brown family, the Becker's old neighbors from the Guadalupe holding. At twenty-three Billy Inman was about the oldest of the cowhands, a younger brother of Captain Inman, whose Ranger company had pursued the war party which had taken Willi and Grete. The youngest were too young to have served in the war at all; they hoped to earn enough money on this drive to help their families, left impoverished or homeless in the aftermath of the war. Hansi approved of this, in a fatherly way. He had arranged to send half their pay directly to their families, rather than see them tempted to go on a spree with it all once the end of the end of the trail was reached.

"We'll cross the Colorado tomorrow," Fredi advised them when they bivouacked one afternoon, bedding down the herd in a meadow below a ridge grown with oak trees. "Swim them across. Likely it will take all day. Then in the morning, we take them north. I'll scout on ahead."

"You want one of us to come with you?" Dolph asked.

Fredi shook his head. "No, we're close enough to Austin and the settlements along the river. I won't worry until we cross the Red River. Then, I'll want everyone to go two and two."

Days slipped past like beads on a string, indistinguishable from each other, endless under the blue sky that arched over them like a bowl. Like water, cattle followed a line of least resistance, pooling in the bottomlands, in the valleys, drifting out to graze a little apart from the line of their fellows, then coaxed into line again by a watchful and dusty horseman.

"That old blue steer with the broken horn; watch him," Dolph said to Peter as they began to turn the herd into their bedding-ground, one afternoon. "He's the leader. I been watching him, every day. He moves out as if he is the drill master, forges up to the front and stays out ahead."

"That does beat all," Peter chuckled, for sure enough, the big dark-grey steer with one horn shortened about five inches so that it ended in a blunt stub rather than a sharp point, was indeed stepping out as proudly as if he led a parade.

"If he were one of Stieler's goats, I'd have him wearing a bell around his neck, so that all the others would hear it and know to follow after."

They bent the mass of cattle into a curve, shooing the moving line of the herd into itself, until the narrow line joined and spread into a round mass, eddying and slowing like a whirlpool losing momentum, spreading out a little at the edges as individual cattle began to graze. The cook wagon and Hansi's supply wagon had been parked a little apart from the cattle herd's bedding ground, under the branches of a sparse grove of cottonwood trees. Daddy Hurst's cook-fire had already burned down to fine ruddy coals, and the smell of salt-bacon and beans came up to meet them. Alejandro and the other wranglers had set up a makeshift corral, running grass-rope between the wagons and tree trunks. Peter and Dolph unsaddled their horses and hobbled them to let them graze free for a while. They collected their bedrolls from the pile of them by the cook wagon, carried them a little apart, and dropped them with their saddles on a handy patch of ground in a rough semicircle around the fire. So it went every evening, assuming that it wasn't raining and neither one of them had night-guard on the herd.

Daddy Hurst handed them two plates, piled with beans and pone, and some kind of roasted meat. "Mistah Richter, he killed us some jackrabbits this afternoon, while waiting for you-all to catch up," he explained.

"Damn, that smells good," Peter said. "Daddy, I am so hungry I could about eat it raw."

"Ain't no call for that." Daddy wiped his hands on an indescribably filthy towel, tied apron-wise around his waist, and took back an empty plate from a drover who was already finished eating. "There wuz time enough to roast 'dem jacks."

"And a splendid meal did they make," said the drover, with elegant precision. "A Lucullan feast. My compliments to the chef, of course; I only wish we did not have to hurry so over this elegant repast." They called that man English Jack, to differentiate him from the wrangler Nigra Jack, a cousin of the Phillips family, free blacks who had settled a small farm near Friedrichsburg before the war and treated cattle with great skill. Like the Phillips father and son, Nigra Jack was a dab hand with cures and medicines.

"De other hans', dey need de plate, Mistah Jack," Daddy Hurst replied.

English Jack sighed, as if it were a great tragedy. "Alas, the sacrifices we make, bringing beef to the tables of — where the hell are we bringing it? After Abilene, of course. Does anyone know?"

"Chicago and points east," Dolph said. "But after Abilene, the herd becomes the buyers' problem."

"To which they will be more than welcome," English Jack drawled. If he had another name only Fredi ever heard it. He was a wiry, sunburnt man, slightly older than Peter, refined of manner in a way that would have made him the butt of much coarse humor if he had not also had a cold and assured way of looking at someone who had drawn his ire. He had turned up several days into the drive, when they passed close to Austin. A local dray appeared on a nearby road, bearing a passenger and all his trash slung on the back: a bedroll and saddle and a fine walnut stock carbine with engraved silver trim. One of the young drovers had fallen too sick to carry on, so Hansi had paid him what was due of his wages and sent him home that very day, scowling all the while and audibly worrying about where he was going to hire a replacement as trustworthy. English Jack's appearance had been providential. Better yet, Fredi knew him.

"He'll ride anything with four legs, as if he has no consideration for his own neck," was what Fredi said, "and dead aim with any weapon handed to him. The rumor is that he left England after killing a man in a duel—but there is also a tale that he stole silver from the regimental mess. Or stepped on the train of the Queen's dress."

Jack was nearly not hired at all when Hansi asked, "Do you drink?"

Jack looked down his nose and coolly replied, "Only to excess."

"Not while you're working for me, you don't." Hansi drew in his breath with a hiss and hired him anyway. It turned out that he could read and write—and he spoke German well. "There's a story in that man," Hansi had observed upon watching English Jack throw his bedroll into the back of the cook wagon and pick out a horse from the remuda.

Fredi said, "It's bad manners to ask, Hansi. Me, I'd bet that he's a younger son of a First. He has disreputable tastes or filthy habits and his family pays him a remittance to keep him the hell out of England. Not that I care," Fredi shrugged. "As long as he does what I tell him for the next three months and doesn't bugger the cows in the middle of the trail."

"I suppose he plays cards, then." Hansi brightened, for that was about the only common amusement among those who had any energy at the end of the day. That and talking about what they would do at the end of the trail, or what plans they had for such money as they earned. About the only variant on that was the ongoing and never settled dispute on whether grass-rope or braided leather made for a better lariat. Fredi and the Mexican wranglers insisted upon hide, insisting such was superior for length and accuracy, but the younger men held out for the strength and utility of grass-rope. Hansi and Daddy Hurst, when appealed to for settlement of this burning question, preferred to remain agnostic.

The cattle drive was, Peter reflected, uncommonly like the Army. The days combined lengthy and mind-numbing stretches of tedium interspersed with back-breaking labor and the occasional moment of innards-melting terror; all of it in the open air and in the exclusive company of men, day after day after day. Lazing around the cookfire in the evening reminded him of a bivouac in Tennessee or Virginia, save for the presence of cattle in their bed-down pasture providing a constant lowing and shifting in the background. Overhead the stars spun in glittering constellations in a dark-velvet sky; so close, Peter thought some nights, that he could reach up and pluck one from the sky, as easily as plucking an apple from the trees around his mother's home place. Again like the Army, all of them had forgone shaving; and those men who were of an age to have them boasted the beginnings of magnificent sets of whiskers. Hansi particularly resembled a large badger peering through a hedge.

Even the yarns swapped around the fire were the same. Improbable tales and speculative adventures about women figured pretty highly, until the evening that English Jack—appealed to by Billy Inman—drawled in his impeccable chipped-glass British accent, "A true gentlemen does not talk about ladies, in such company."

Not very much put down, Billy demanded, "What about whores? Can we talk about whores in company?"

"Of course not!" snapped English Jack, rolling himself into his blankets to signify that the conversation was quite definitely concluded.

"Who the hell said we wuz gentlemen, anyway!" Billy had the final word. After a couple of weeks of living rough on the trail, Peter rather agreed with Billy's assessment.

They slept in their clothes with their horses close to hand, penned in a rope corral. Peter took enough turns on night-guard himself; tirelessly circling the massed cattle, dark against the moon-brushed prairie, listening to the call of night birds and alert with every sense for some sudden movement, some sound out of the ordinary. They talked and sang to the cattle, to soothe and reassure them when fractious and unsettled. Most of the drovers knew a vast array of slow lugubrious-sounding ballads to serenade the cows with. Fredi swore up and down that any number of gloomy German Christmas carols had the same soporific effect. English Jack recited something he claimed was *The Iliad* at them—in Latin.

"Damn, these are going to be some eddicated cows!" commented Dolph when Jack enlightened him on this, one midnight when they passed, going in opposite directions as they circled.

"Almost a pity to eat them, don't you think?" English Jack answered, with a broad grin which could hardly be seen from the growth of beard on his face. "Ah, but that would negate the purpose of this exercise, wouldn't it? Forget I ever entertained such a heretical thought!"

"I would," Dolph answered, as he rode on, "if I understood what the hell you just said." He continued his lonely circular patrol. The night breeze kicked up a little, bringing with it the faint smell of rain. The distant northwest quadrant of the sky had begun to be blotted out by swiftly moving clouds, clouds that were becoming illuminated from within by brief pale flashes of lightning.

"Storm on the way," he said to English Jack, as they passed again. "With lightning," he added. The other man swore softly. "The wind's blowing it this way." Dolph listened admiringly as Jack added another couple of comments. "That's a right nice collection of cusswords," he said, "Wasn't a waste of education, I'd reckon. I'm going to waken Onkel Fredi, let him know to put on some more hands. They'll be right jumpy as that storm blows overhead."

"Don't take too long about it," Jack advised. Dolph nodded, angling his pony away from the edge of the herd and towards the pale glimmer of the wagon covers. Hansi and Daddy Hurst had gone to bed long since; their last act before sleep being to pull the wagon tongues around to align on the North Star.

The remuda ponies shifted and whinnied uneasily in their grass-rope corral, sensing the storm's approach. Dolph slid down from his saddle as he approached the camp, that eccentric circle of bedrolls spread out around the quenched cookfire.

"Señor?" A sibilant whisper from the cook wagon's shadow and the faint metallic click of a Colt hammer drawn back.

"Alejandro?" Dolph whispered in Spanish. "It's me. There's a storm coming. I'm waking up Fredi."

"Good," Alejandro answered. "The horses, they are restless also. How many more riders, Patron?"

"At least six," Dolph whispered. "And if the cattle stampede, everyone!"

"Ay, ya ya!" Alejandro sounded every bit as dismayed as English Jack. So far, they had been able to head off any potential stampede, quench any panic before it started and infected the entire herd. Fredi usually spread his bedroll near the supply wagon. Dolph found him, and gently nudged his foot. Gratifyingly, Fredi shot upright after a single shake.

"Storm coming," Dolph whispered; even more gratifying, his uncle needed no more than that and a swift glance at the sky. Very faintly, thunder grumbled in the distance, hardly louder than Hansi snoring, a few feet away.

Fredi threw off his blankets. "Right. Go on back, lad, I'll rouse—"

The rest of his words were abruptly cut off by a clap of thunder that rent the air like a cannon shot, seemingly directly over their heads.

"Ah, damnation!" said Fredi, as other sleepers also woke instantly, most with more colorful curses on their lips. His heart sinking within him, Dolph sensed a vibration in the ground under his feet almost before he heard the ominous rumble of distant hooves, and the bellowing of frightened cattle.

"Stampede!" he shouted, flinging himself towards his saddle as Fredi erupted from his own blankets. Out of the corner of his eye, he saw

Alejandro running from the remuda, leading four horses after him, his hands full of grass-rope and leather reins.

Peter shot out of dead sleep, instantly knowing what was happening. He caught up his hat with his good hand, and leaped for the reins of his horse. He had been supposed to relieve the night-watch at midnight, so his own horse had been saddled and close-hobbled at hand. Already panicking from the racket of the thunder and the noise of stampeding cattle, the pony danced restlessly as Peter tried to free it from the grass-rope hobbles.

"Damn ye, hold still!" Peter gasped, and swore as the frantic animal dodged at arm's length. There was no time for this; he wrapped the reins around his left arm and slashed the hobbles with his knife. He dropped the knife as he vaulted up—go back later to look for it, God if there was a later!

There was a rider ahead of him, perhaps two behind him, no time to look around and see who they were. He raked the horse's flanks with his heels, crouching low in the saddle as the beast obediently leaped ahead, oh God oh God, oh God, rough ground, broken with small gullies and animal burrows. If his horse put a foot deep into one, it was a broken leg for the horse for sure and a broken neck for him, hitting the ground at this pace.

Regardless of that peril, he sent his mount careening parallel to the mass of cattle, a tossing sea of horns and backs as they ran, silvered by starlight and eerie greenish flickers of lightning, their hooves shaking the ground, shaking his heart in his chest. Catch up, catch up to that leading edge of the herd, catch up and turn them, turn them at a run, run them back on themselves, crashing and buffeting their horns together in a storm of dust.Peter raked his booted heels along his horse's flanks again. Now there was a skein of horsemen flying alongside the herd; himself and Dolph, Billy Inman, and two of Porfirios' boys, a fragile net to catch and turn the hurtling cattle, catch and turn before the panicky beasts harmed themselves, gored each other with their enormous horns, broke a leg in a prairie dog burrow, hurled over the side of a ravine, rim-rocked themselves. Oh God, oh God, catch and turn them before it was too late, before Hansi and Ma'am Becker's investment turned into so much buzzard-meat, rotting in the hot sun.

He and Dolph reached the leading edge, neck and neck, that dark and dangerous edge, a knife-edge. He could feel his mount's ribs under his knees, shuddering with every willing breath, thanking God again that he was riding the better trained of his two, the paint-pony who minded the reins on his neck rather than the bit in his mouth. He had the reins wrapped twice around his arm just below his elbow, where his stump socketed into Mr.

Berg's clever wooden contraption. Moving the reins with his arm, rather than hand and fingers, he controlled with knees and heels. The paint-pony gallantly obeyed, plunging fearlessly toward that maelstrom of frantic cattle. Peter drew his Walker Colt from the saddle holster where he preferred to leave the heavy and unwieldy revolver. Shouting, he pressed the paint-pony closer, firing shots into the air, shots that he could barely hear.

"Turn them!" Dolph shouted. "Turn them!"

"Goddammit, I'm trying!" he shouted back. Another horse galloped by his flank, a horse with an empty saddle, flashing by in an instant and then out of sight in the dark tumult around them. "Who's horse was that!" he screamed into the dark, and Dolph shouted back, "I don't know, but if they're down in this they're dead!"

Wetness splashed on his arms, into his face. The storm had come upon them. Peter shouted curses at the cattle, at the wind rushing past, at the rain that fell chill and plastered his clothing to him as cattle and horsemen hurtled on into the darkness.

"They're slowing!" Dolph shouted. "Press 'em hard, damn you! Press 'em hard!"

Peter fired over the cattle, fired into the air until the hammer of his Colt clicked on empty chambers. Someone at his back still had a full load, though. A fusillade of shots crackled like fireworks, like the skirmish at Rice's Station in that last year of the war, the place where he took a bullet in his wrist. He shouted again, cursing, and Dolph shouted also. They pressed closer and closer. The mass of cattle, mindless and unreasoning, began yielding to their will, bending in their flight, turning to the right, turning again as they fled across the hummocky ground. A flash of lightning split the air, an eldritch and momentary light on the heaving wet backs of cattle and horses.

"Damn you all, hold them!" shouted a voice at Peter's back, then was lost in the crash of thunder. The cattle were mindless with terror, nothing could affright them even further after that, just men on nimble horses, waving their hats, shouting or firing their revolvers. After an eternity of galloping into the dark, it seemed to Peter that the mass of cattle had slowed in their headlong pace. They had run into a tract of wiry scrub. God only knew how far they had come, or where they were in relation to the camp, when they finally succeeded in turning the herd back in upon themselves. The land sloped gently uphill; Peter squinted into the dark, his face lashed by constant rain. He thought he remembered seeing higher ground to the west of them, just before they camped for the night. There was a seasonal watercourse on the far side of the sloping ground.

"Where are we?" Billy Inman called, out of the dark. The cattle were quiescent now, uneasy but standing bunched together as if to shelter against the rain, their sides heaving like bellows from the exertion of their run. Water ran hoof-deep around them; their horses sloshed through churned-up mud.

"I think we're west of camp," Peter shouted in return. "Who else is here? Call out your names, all who can hear me!"

"To me!" Dolph shouted in Spanish. "Alejandro! Marcos! To me!" Out of the dark and rain, voices answered them: Alejandro, Marcos and Diego, Billy Inman, young Frank Brown and his cousin Alonzo. Nigra Jack splashed out of the dark, leading a riderless horse he had found straying among the mass of cattle. "Whose?" Dolph asked quietly.

"Mastah Jack, de Englishmon," the wrangler answered. "He had dis ol' pinto, on watch 'dis night." The rain pelted down, fat water-drops as big as bullets. Peter could not see his cousin's expression. He was already soaked to the skin. The brim of his hat hung waterlogged like a dead leaf

"I'd guess he was moving around, on the other side of the herd, when they broke," Dolph said at last. "For I had just spoken to him, not three minutes before. They must have rolled right over him." He did not have to say anything else about the fate of English Jack, unhorsed and on foot among eight hundred head of fear-maddened cattle.

But Billy Inman said aloud what they all knew, in the tones of a man deeply shaken and only just beginning to recover himself. "Shit. They pro'lly stamped him as flat as a flapjack. Anyone know if he had anything on him worth going back and looking for?"

"Billy, you shut the hell up," Dolph spat. "And we'll sure as hell go looking for him, no matter what he had in his vest pockets. The man deserves a decent burial."

"In a cee-gar box, if nothing else," Billy replied. He barked a laugh in which humor warred with the kind of feelings that come from having survived some great exertion and terror.

"That's enough, Bill," Peter commanded. "Help us get them settled down—we can't look for him until it gets light anyway."

It wasn't that Billy was heartless, Peter knew as he knew anything else. They had all been in mortal terror, pounding after the herd in the dark and rain, fighting the elements, fighting for control and knowing that in a split second they might be unhorsed and trampled, as dead as English Jack.

No, Billy was just relieved to be alive as any of them—even soaked to the skin and lost somewhere on the night-darkened prairie north of the Red River.

A cold wind followed on the storm, blowing out of the northwest, chilling them all—cattle, horses, and men indiscriminately. Peter thought longingly of his bedroll, then even more longingly of a dry bed in the shelter of the little cottage on Creek Street, as he and the others watched over the dozing cattle. The cold bit deeper if they remained still, so Dolph, Peter, and the others tried to remain in constant motion to generate warmth. It was with no small relief after many hours of this that they saw the eastern sky gradually begin to pale to a glowing primrose yellow, and those few rags of clouds remaining after the storm turned the livid color of bruised flesh.

"How many are we missing?" Billy Inman asked.

Dolph replied, "'Bout half. We'll be all day searching them out and rounding them up." A bright thread of sunlight peeped coyly over the distant horizon. Peter, his cousin, and a few of the others had ridden towards the higher ground in an attempt to see where they were and where they ought to take the herd.

"Well, I reckon they'll have been too tired to run much farther," Billy observed, yawning hugely. As near as Peter could discern, the herd had run several miles west and north in a long arc, traced a line across the rolling prairie, mud and trampled vegetation left in their wake.

"Can you see the wagons?" young Alonzo Brown asked worriedly, his fifteen-year old countenance blotched equally with specks of mud and freckles. "Or any of the other hands?"

"Not to fret, 'Lonzo," Dolph answered, as the bright disc of the sun revealed more of itself above the far horizon. "I know they're dead east of us, somewhere along that little stream we had set up camp by. Look there." He pointed to a tiny, threadlike spiral of grey smoke rising from beyond a far line of dark green brush. "I'm thinking that's Daddy Hurst's cookfire and I could sure use a good hot breakfast, now."

"Me, all I care about is that it's hot." Peter nudged the ribs of his pony with his heels. The poor creature practically stumbled with weariness. "Let's get these damned animals moving in a favorable direction, Cuz. You ride point, I reckon—you know the way at least as well as any of us."

Moving slowly from exhaustion as much as care, Peter, Billy, and the others assembled the remnant of the herd and began chivvying it towards that rising wisp of smoke. It was several hours of tedious labor to do this. Peter reflected all the while on how during the night they had so quickly come the same distance, seemingly in a matter of a few minutes. Only a trifle less cheering than the smell of hot food and the odor of coffee was the sight of a good few head of cattle, grazing peaceably in the night pasture from which so many had run in a panic not six hours before. Either they had not all stampeded, or the other hands had been able to cut the rearmost off from the main body and force their return. Not even the sight of their drenched blankets and bedrolls, left scattered on the ground where they had been abandoned, could entirely quench Peter's feelings of relief and no little satisfaction at having retrieved something from a potential disaster.

Fredi rose from where he had been sitting by the fire in close conversation with Hansi. He looked as wearied as they all felt, but smiled with much the same cheerful relief, until he noticed English Jack's horse trailing after Alejandro.

"Not a sign of him," Dolph answered the unasked question. "We came back straight, though. As soon as I've had some breakfast, I'll take two of the boys and scout along the way the stampede went. How many are we short otherwise, Onkel?"

"About twenty head," Fredi answered. "We can rest the herd here for a day or two, while we search. I'll send out everyone who isn't minding the herd to go beating the bushes."

"Remember, lads," Hansi added, "every one of those missing cows is worth a month's wages in the cattle market in the north."

Daddy Hurst brought out hot bread, coffee lavishly sweetened with molasses, fat bacon, and apple duff made with dried fruit, which they fell upon as if famished.

"It ain't as if it's the best cooking I ever tasted," Billy Inman ventured with his mouth full, "but damn if it doesn't taste prime!"

"My grandfather used to tell us that hunger was the very best sauce." Dolph reached out for the coffee pot and poured a full cup for himself. "But as cooks go—sorry, Daddy, I think Auntie Liesel sets a finer table."

"Yo' auntie ain't tryin' to keep de fire alight, when it's coming down like Noah's flood," Daddy Hurst scowled, turning over another rasher of salt bacon with a long-handled fork. "Dis ol' nigra is all de cook you got, out here! You best 'member dat, when you want seconds, Mistah Rudolph!"

Peter nudged his cousin with his good elbow; it was never a wise idea to get on Daddy Hurst's bad side. "Cuz," he chuckled, "let me advise you of this one thing—never deliberately annoy someone who is alone with the food you are going to eat."

"One reason to keep your wife sweet," Billy Inman said.

Dolph retorted, "Fine advice from someone who doesn't have a wife, or any likelihood of a sweetheart. Ah, well, Daddy, you mayn't cook quite as well as Aunt Liesel, but you are right. You're here and she's not." His face took on a melancholy cast, as he downed the rest of his coffee. "And we may have to trouble you some more, Daddy, for the use of your shovel." No one needed to ask why. Dolph rose, tipping his plate and tin cup into the dishpan.

"I'll come with you," Peter said, and Billy Inman rose also.

"So'll I," he said, then added defensively, "He was a stuck-up sumbitch, but he was damn good at what he done. An' he was one of us."

"In a manner of speaking," Peter allowed, and Fredi nodded assent.

But before they could even draw fresh mounts from the remuda, a drover at the edge of the heard stood up in his stirrups, waving his hat and pointing towards something just out of sight of those in camp.

"What the—?" Peter ventured, for soon appeared a hatless man on foot, coming along the line of the creek bank towards them. "It's Jack!" So it was, although he was much more thickly daubed with mud than any of the rest, as if he had been thrown down and rolled in it. He sauntered casually into the circle of bedrolls like a man out for a stroll on the promenade.

"Glory be!" Daddy Hurst exclaimed. Dolph unobtrusively placed the shovel back in the toolbox on the side of the supply wagon.

"I see you found my horse and saddle," English Jack drawled. A broad grin split his unshaven and filthy countenance. At some point his nose had bled copiously into his beard, neckerchief, and shirtfront. "Don't tell me you chaps had given up hope on my survival?"

Billy Inman whooped and thumped his shoulders.

Peter exclaimed, "Well, we did at that, Jack. We were just setting out to see to whatever might be left after the cattle finished riding over you last night! Where the hell were you, all this time?"

"Extraordinary thing." Jack accepted a tin plate. "Thank you, Hurst. Coffee, too, if it's not too much trouble. I spent the night in a most uncomfortable ditch." Between ravenous bites of bread and bacon he added, "I see you were able to retrieve the herd. Excellent! 'Straordinary lucky, that; well done, all the way around."

"Yes, pretty much," Dolph said. "But what happened to you—when we found your horse and not you . . . ?"

"You assumed the worst?" Jack grinned again. "Don't blame you in the least. They broke and ran just about the place where I was, innocently and harmlessly sitting on Bonehead or Mush-for-Brains, or whatever my wretched horse's stable-name is. Stupid beast panicked, too, and then compounded the folly by stumbling over a badger hole, or whatever uncouth burrowing animal makes its home out here—and throwing me clear. Interesting experience—I don't think I've taken a fall like that in years."

"But if you were in the middle . . . ." Billy Inman's face was screwed up in an expression of baffled incredulity.

Jack continued, "When I came off my horse, I landed more or less astride the neck of one of the cattle, going at a fearful pace. As you may imagine, I hung on for dear life—steeplechasing in a mob doesn't have a patch on the experience. Oh, thank you, Hurst." He took a cup of coffee from Daddy Hurst, wrapping his fingers gratefully around it. "Truly ambrosial — that's the stuff the gods drink, Billy. Where was I?"

"Riding a cow through a stampede," Fredi answered. He was grinning also; even if they did not quite believe English Jack's story, it was still a damn good yarn.

"So I was," Jack continued. "And damnably uncomfortable it was for the both of us. Fortunately—I can only assume that bearing my weight must have had something to do with it—that particular cow fell back among the herd almost immediately. In very short order I perceived that I was being carried along at a point where it might be safer to abandon such a precarious position than to continue on. So with a prayer on my lips, and recollecting every blessed bit of advice I had ever received about disembarking at a dead gallop, I threw myself sideways. To avoid the hoofs—they say the trick is to cover your head in your arms and roll as soon as you hit the ground, you know. That being effected, nothing came to mind except try and curl up someplace out of harm's way and wait until morning. I found a commodious ditch." Jack shrugged elaborately, "Save for a small torrent flowing through the bottom, it was passably comfortable, although I confess I did not sleep all that well."

"You ain't gonna sleep all that well tonight, either," Billy Inman warned. "The rain wet all the blankets."

"And we're still short at least twenty head." Fredi stood up with a groan. "Which we must make an attempt to find, before moving on. Still, I can't tell you how glad I am that you survived last night, Jack. I'd have been in a hell of a pickle, otherwise."

"Oh?" Jack looked up from his coffee. "And how was that?"

Fredi answered, "I'd have had no idea of where to send all your things."

Chapter Thirteen: *Abilene, My Abilene*

Over the course of the day after the stampede, Hansi's drovers scoured the empty plains around their camping-place, while they left their mattress quilts and blankets spread on the grass in an attempt to get them thuroughly dried out. Dolph and Alejandro, of all the drovers most skilled at tracking, followed the trail of three cows for nearly fifteen miles. One of these presented Hansi with something of a dilemma upon their return.

"The heifer isn't ours," Dolph explained with considerable amusement. The cow in question was fawn-colored and leggy, ear-clipped and branded, but as wild as a deer. The newest brands on her looked to be recent, from the last spring round up. "And that looks like one of Withers' brands. They run cattle near Lockhart. One of their boys was taking a herd up the trail – she must have got away from them."

"It's not like we can easily return her to Mr. Withers," Hansi mused, "not knowing if they are ahead of us, or behind—as we would if we found a stray on our lands."

"Turn it loose?" Fredi suggested, but Hansi shook his head.

"No, it is something of value to an owner, as a wallet of money would be. Only less easily transported, eh?"

"Might make a right good supper," Billy Inman suggested. "'Specially if everyone else is as tired of sowbelly as I am. The Withers boys won't know 'bout their stray and I ain't planning to ever tell 'em."

Dolph shook his head. Hansi said, "I would not find a meal of someone else's beef sitting well in my belly, whether the true owner knows or not. So here is what we shall do. Put that cow among our herd, and when we reach the brokers in Abilene, I shall sell it with ours but send the money paid for that cow to the proper owner." Billy looked disappointed, but being that Hansi had the final say, he had no other choice but to obey.

The drive resumed the following morning, another endless string of days moving north, under a cloud of dust stirred up by the herd. Five miles or so in the morning, the same in the afternoon, letting the cattle graze as they wished, morning, noon and night. They did not stampede again so badly as that first time. Fredi spent hours out ahead of the herd, scouting for water and a good place to bed the cattle at nooning or at night, a place they could graze and not be tempted to wander from, with water close to hand.

In the middle of June, they swam the herd through the Washita River, fringed thick with cottonwood trees and thickets of willows with masses of bleached driftwood lodged high up in their branches. The leading cattle went into the water, swimming as confidently as waterfowl, with noses and horns just breaking the surface. Young Alonzo lost his hat when his horse went into a deep current-scoured hole in the middle of the river. The boy lost his hold on the saddle horn when his horse panicked and the river all but took them both. Fredi and Alejandro managed to pull them both to safety, with no loss save the hat.

Deeper into Indian Territory they ventured, that three-hundred mile long stretch through empty plains where no law held sway but the whim of those tribes who hunted there. Peter and those hands who owned long weapons took them from where they had been stowed in the cook or supply wagons and kept them close to hand in saddle scabbards. Those who did not possess such weapons polished and loaded their revolvers with great attention. The evening of their first night north of the Washita, Fredi put three men on night guard, fearing an attempt on the remuda.

"Those damned Comanche can no more keep their hands off horses than a drunkard can keep his from the bottle," he explained when he ordered this.

"So Papa used to say." Dolph agreed.

"Many a time, as I remember," Fredi sighed. He looked into the fire and mused, "I wonder what he would have thought of this venture, Dolph. Would he have joined us with the same alacrity as Brother Hansi?"

After careful consideration Dolph answered, "Truly, I do not know, for Papa loved venturing into the wilderness, but he loved his own land just as well. I think he would have backed our venture, sending his own cattle north to market. But I think he would have contented himself with sending us and spent his own efforts in overseeing breeding stock and his orchard."

"Leaving the hard work of it to us, then," Fredi observed with a wry laugh.

Some few days of slow travel north brought Hansi's cattle herd to another river crossing: the Cimarron River, or so said Fredi. Again, the herd plunged in almost eagerly, led by the big grey blunt-horned steer.

"I have half a mind to keep that one," Hansi said, after he and Daddy Hurst themselves had crossed. At the crest of a grassy knoll above the Cimarron, they both looked back at the piebald stream of cattle crossing over.

Daddy Hurst chuckled. "Make him de bell-mare, Mistah Richter? Foah de nex' time up dis ol' trail?"

"And the time after that," Hansi agreed, snapping the reins over his team.

The empty prairie rolled like an endless sea of grass spread out on either side and ahead of them, breakers and hillocks of grass, like an ocean billow frozen in the blink of an eye. The cattle plodded stolidly on, making little other noise than the creaking of their fetlocks as they walked. Sometimes they snorted or bawled a startled complaint as a jackrabbit started up out of the grass, a swift tan blur as it bounced away. Sometimes they saw the bleached white bones of buffalo, with the grass springing up lush and green between the bones.

"They say there used to be herds of buffalo, enough to cover all the country around," Peter observed one morning when he and Fredi had ridden ahead on scout. They were careful to stay within sight of Hansi and Daddy Hurst, and the drovers following behind. "My mother said there were buffalo around Waterloo when she was a girl, but they were hunted out, long since. Did you ever see any when you trailed cattle to California?"

"No, lad. We took the southern trail; nary a buffalo to be seen. What's this, then?" Fredi squinted against the dazzle of the sun. They had all gotten very brown and weathered, although Peter wondered just how much of the brown was dirt. Aside from being rained upon, and traversing a number of creeks and rivers, none of them had taken anything like a proper bath since crossing the Colorado below Austin. Movement stirred along the crest of the next rise in the prairie, the movement of men and horses, dark against the sunlit sky behind them. The silhouettes were of hatless men and lightly equipped horses.

"Indians." Fredi whistled through his teeth. "They probably want something of us and don't want to take the trouble of stealing it. Otherwise, we'd never have known they were there and watching."

"And they would want?" Peter inquired, nervous in spite of all his care to seem confident. Late one evening, when he was a small boy, Uncle Carl had once been brought to speak of what he had seen in the Llano, of what the Comanche did to white men they found in their lands. No one knew that Peter was listening. Peter had nightmares for months, and his mother had been very upset.

"What do we have most of?" Fredi grimly answered. "So many that doubtless they think we could spare some. The Cherokee charge a toll for herds crossing their lands over the old trail to Sedalia, but they were the civilized sort. They all but presented a proper bill."

One of the figures silhouetted against the sky raised an arm.

"Looks like they want to parley," Fredi added, taking his hat in his hand and waving it back. "You stay here, within sight of Brother Hansi, then. I'll see what they want." Fredi chirruped to his horse and with trepidation Peter watched him ride to meet the Indian, whose horse was carefully picking its way down from the heights above. They met at too great a distance for Peter to hear what was said. He waited, sweating with unease, painfully aware of those eyes upon him, knowing that only Hansi with his stores-wagon and Daddy Hurst in the cook wagon were within sight and close enough to come to his aid. The other hands were farther behind, strung out along the flanks of the moving stream of cattle, lost in the dust and the lie of the rolling prairie all around them. Peter moistened his lips, which were always dry—but his mouth was suddenly dry as well, considering what a vulnerable position they were in. Thirty of their own men, but all strung out along with the herd and not a good match for twice that many Indians, even ones armed only with bows and spears.

He fixed his attention upon Fredi, who was shaking his head and holding up his gloved hand with one finger raised. The Indian held up two fingers, but Fredi was implacable and Peter thought no end of his nerve for holding to it. Finally, they seemed to come to an agreement. Fredi returned, saying, "They're Kiowa, but inclined to be friendly. Ride back and tell Brother Hansi, I have agreed to give them one beeve in return for safe passage."

"Only one?" Peter asked, with no little relief. "That is all?"

"They're hungry," Fredi answered, "and they look it. If this is their hunting ground, they've had damn little luck with it. Their chief says that their women and children are mighty hungry." Peter thought that was just a story to elicit sympathy and maybe another cow.

Hansi said as much, when Peter relayed Fredi's words to him. "Go and tell the boys to cut out a steer for them," he said, "any but that blunt-horned grey beast. And not such a fat one; take one of those who straggles. We may as well get some good out of one of those which may not make it; not so?"

By the time Peter returned, driving a cow ahead of him, the wagons had caught up to Fredi and the patiently waiting Kiowa hunting party. Seeing them close up, Peter began to think Fredi right. These Indians appeared bony, ragged. Nothing of the proud warrior about this dusty straggle of weather-burnt men, and their ponies also looked hard-used. He drove the cow ahead of him, towards the half-circle of Indian hunters.

"One cow," Peter said to Hansi, who lounged against the side of the supply wagon. "So what are they going to do? Just stand there and look at it?"

Before Hansi answered, Fredi took out his revolver. Holding it by the barrel, he handed it ceremoniously to the Indian, who took it with an air of someone who had handled such only rarely. The cow looked around incuriously and fell to grazing, hardly aware of the Indian taking careful aim. One, two shots and the cow fell with hardly a twitch. Fredi took back his revolver and the Indians commenced to skinning the fallen cow.

"I think they eat now," Hansi observed with a shrug. With no little revulsion Peter saw that he was right. They were butchering it, cutting off strips of flesh and eating it raw. Hansi shook his head in pity at that. It was perfectly clear they had nothing to fear from these Indians, who paid them no more mind as they moved away, but gobbled the still-warm meat as fresh red blood ran down their faces and arms.

English Jack was on point that day. As he rode past Peter and the pitiful stripped carcass, with the hungry Indians clustered around like wasps around a savory blob of jam, he drawled, "I swear to you, Vining, we have all been most deceived in the Leatherstocking tales. Fennimore Cooper ne'er wrote of such a sight as this."

"I'd guess not," Peter answered. That evening, he quietly put away his carbine in the supply wagon, noting that the other drovers who had observed the scene were doing the same. A carbine in a saddle scabbard was one more awkward and unwieldy thing to bump against his leg, or against the side of the pony he rode, an extra weight at the best of times.

"Really, what have we to fear of the natives?" English Jack ventured that night, as they smoked and watched the sparks from their campfire rising to meet the stars overhead.

"Nothing much," Peter answered swiftly, before Dolph or Fredi could take issue. As far as he knew, English Jack knew nothing about the uncertain fate of Hansi's two small children, or the agonizing death of his sister-in-law. "'Less'n you're a couple of children, or a woman all alone or a man unhorsed and unarmed. Grown men with plenty of firepower among us? That's something else again!"

"How splendidly reassuring to hear so." English Jack lit his pipe with a twig held into the fire and reclined against his saddle. "Still, a bit of a comedown, what?"

"Oh, that party would be quick enough, if they had an advantage on us." Fredi took the twig from Jack and lit his own. "But they didn't—have

215

an advantage, that is. Still and all, keep a sharp eye out when you're on loose herd."

"Not to worry." Jack contentedly puffed at his pipe and looked up at the stars, a jeweled spangle scattered across the dark velvet of the sky. The Milky Way was drawn through it, like a dark veil trimmed with gems as tiny as grains of sand. Again, as he had on so many other nights, Peter felt as if he could reach out his hand and pluck a star out of the sky, as easily as taking an apple from a branch above his head.

"It is a sight to see, yes?" Hansi spoke out of the dark at the edge of the cook fire. "The sky so large and the land so empty. My wife has always feared this. A good thing I do not, eh?"

"You'd never have left Friedrichsburg," Peter answered. He had come to like Hansi during this long journey north. Peter had respected him before, not least for his ability to outwork men half his age. But now he liked him for his company on the trail, his knowledge of cattle, and his sure judgment of men as diverse as English Jack and young Lonzo Brown. If anything, it would be Hansi's cast-iron will which would bring this venture through all hazards to a successful conclusion.

Now the big wagon-master chuckled. "I would have never left Albeck. Albeck—did you know of that place? A little place of four streets and a church, near to Ulm. I was born there and never left my father's fields until I was drafted for service."

"I never knew you had been a soldier!" Peter said, with genuine astonishment.

Hansi snorted. "So I was, but not of my choice. Not much of a soldier or for very long, though I learned to shoot and drill and salute. When my service was done, I came home and married my wife, whom I had known since her sister and I were children together. Her father and mine were neighbors, although my father was a better farmer." Hansi puffed at his pipe until the tobacco glowed as red as coals in the cookfire.

Intrigued, Peter asked, "Why did you think to immigrate? Were you not happy working for your father?"

"I had two older brothers," Hansi answered, "and my father's fields were not enough for three of us or his house large enough for each of us to take a wife and beget children. Land," the big man sighed, "there was never enough of it. When the Verein promised us land—oh, they promised so many other things, if we would but sign their contract and come to Texas! But all they needed to say to me was 'land.' I had no mind for the other things. I think I knew that those promises were tinsel, things to promise to children and rash young men. But land that I could put my own work into, not my father's little plots and fields, nor my father-in-law's! Lad, that was all they needed to draw me away from everything I knew. My father-in-law, he was a clever man, full of books and notions. He thought it a grand idea so we came away together. But if he had not, I would still have gone with just my wife and our children. Only the two we had then." He chuckled again. "Oh, what I had to promise my wife—a house of our own, just as she wanted it." He drew on his pipe again, the coals flaring red in the darkness as the cookfire died down. "Just to get some peace! My dearest Lise knows well this one thing about me, you see."

"And what is that?" Peter asked.

"What I have made my mind up to do, I will." Hansi jabbed his pipe stem at Peter for emphasis. "All my life until coming to this country, I had never thought to do anything but farm, just as my father had. It was the way of it, in Albeck and the country we came from. Only my dear Liesel's father had any thoughts of doing different. And I tell you, behind his back some laughed at him for his ideas and his books. But once here, I began to look around and to see that Vati was right. There was nothing to stop a man from choosing his work, his business, and to work to better his station." Hansi gave a curt chuckle in the darkness. "I came here to be a farmer and once I would have been content to remain so. Then I began to drive wagons, and to see how the world works. Now I have ambitions, would you believe? I have decided to become a rich man, as rich as a prince."

"That's a lofty aim," Peter mused judiciously. "But didn't the preacher always say that a love of money is the root of all evil?"

"So swear those who do not have any," Hansi snorted. "Money is a tool—like a hammer, or a hay-fork. It is what I will use to ransom my children back from the Comanche, to make my wife happy again, and perhaps find a doctor that will make her truly well. And to build a grand house for us, and the same for each of my sons as they marry. That is what I want for me and mine. I will have it, so. I have set my mind on that! There was only ever one thing that I did not acquire for myself, once I had decided on it."

Around the dying campfire, most of the other hands had fallen asleep in their blankets. The night invited confidences. Peter felt himself rather honored that Hansi would share his thoughts and ambitions like this. "What was that one thing, sir?" he asked.

Hansi chuckled again. "A woman that I asked to marry but she said no; and rightly, too. It may be that I did not really want her that much and

217

she was wise enough to set me straight. I took her advice and married her sister."

"Ma'am Becker?" Peter nearly swallowed his own pipe-stem out of sheer astonishment. "You proposed marriage to Ma'am Becker?" he again asked in disbelief.

The big wagon-master sounded amused when he answered, "You wonder I had the nerve? She was the oldest, her dowry-field adjoined mine, and we had known each other since childhood. Why not, eh? But we are friends still and she a better sister and partner in business than a wife. Women know these things, sometimes better than we men. Especially clever ones like Sister Magda and my Annchen." Hansi paused, which gave Peter an uneasy feeling that this whole conversation had a purpose to which Hansi was just now coming.

But still, he did not expect the question which Hansi broached. "Had you thought of marrying? You are of an age to consider such matters. I had been a father twice, before I was of the age you are now."

"I had not thought of marrying," Peter returned warily. "My affections are not . . . they are not fixed at present."

"Ah," Hansi said, as if quite content with it. "So. There is something I should tell you. But I must beg your forgiveness for seeming to poke my long nose into your matters of the heart. It is only the interest of a father, or perhaps a kindly uncle. You and young Dolph alike, I take an interest in your happiness. Since both of you have no father still living, it is permitted, not so?"

"Yes, of course," Peter stammered. "It is kind of you to take such an interest. More than kind."

Hansi held up a deprecating hand, and the faint light from his pipe made a queer gargoyle shadow on his face. "It is only right, for family, you see." He drew deep on his pipe, and Peter waited with no little puzzlement as he brought himself around to the point. "My daughter, Annchen. She is a clever one, like her aunt. It is in my mind that she has a regard for you."

"We have no understanding," Peter blurted, before realizing how ungallant that sounded and that perhaps he should justify himself to Anna's father. "We have a friendship with one another. I hold her in deep respect. I was not aware of any particular favor on her part," he finished lamely.

Anna's father nodded, as calm as a magistrate on the bench. "I did not mean to suggest anything else, lad. Only you should know that I have observed. Know also that should Annchen's feelings for you prove to be serious and if you return them alike, than you have my approval. Without even asking for it, eh? A bit of a relief for you, not having to come to me, I think!" And Hansi puffed furiously at his pipe. It came to Peter that perhaps Hansi was himself somewhat embarrassed at having spoken so openly of such personal matters. Before he could say anything, Hansi added, "I wished to speak of this privately to you before anyone else, such as my wife, makes mention. And she would—women being like that, full of romantic fancies and suchlike. And I would not see you made obligated to profess feelings that you did not have. Embarrassing to be in such a spot." The darkness entirely hid Hansi's expression, but Peter thought that if it were light, he would have seen something of shrewd sympathy in that look. Doubtless, Daddy Hurst had exchanged gossip with Hansi, during all those hours when they made camp ahead of the moving herd.

"I am grateful for your consideration," Peter said.

Hansi waved his pipe dismissively. "Think little of it. Besides, this is my daughter Anna we speak of." And now Peter knew from the sound of his voice that he was smiling, "If she decides that she wants you and you want to wed, I do not think my opinion will have any weight at all."

Peter remembered how Anna's brothers had watched him with lively interest and amusement, that first evening in Captain Nimitz's beer-garden, when he had drunk with his cousin Dolph and this man who now took such a fond and fatherly interest. "Thanks for the warning, sir," he said, and Hansi laughed, rich and deep.

"Good night then, lad. Sleep deep, for we will be in Kansas in a day or so and on our way to be as rich as any of the Firsts."

Into Kansas they moved with the herd, into a sea of grass that swayed with the motion of the wind upon it, endless waves of tall grass bowing and rustling, green and silver where the sun shone upon it, starred with flowers. They passed out of Indian Territory and into new settled lands, here and there a scattered sod house or cabin of logs dug into the hillsides, or a solitary little lean-to, like half a house of newly sawn lumber, next to a garden bravely cut into the prairie. The people who lived there came out to see the cattle go past, watching with wary curiosity, and advising Hansi and Fredi of the proper trail to follow. Daddy Hurst traded some of their stores for eggs from the settlers' wives, knowing that they were within a week or so of reaching Abilene. Once, they left a newborn calf with a farmer who traded them a bushel of fresh greens for it; otherwise they would have had to shoot the calf, for it was too small to keep up with the herd, even at the pace they kept. They found handbills plastered to trees at the creek crossings, or pasted to stakes pounded into the ground, directing them to cattle buyers and advertising the stockyards at Abilene.

One day they saw a faint brownish smudge of smoke against the clear blue sweep of the horizon, a smudge that did not change position. "There's the town," Fredi said to Hansi. He had returned from a forward scout as the herd nooned in a lush pasture a little short of a creek that ran into the Kansas River. "About twenty or thirty miles ahead. Tomorrow we pasture the herd, and you and I and ride into town and find this agent."

"More than one." Hansi laid a finger alongside of his nose and looked sly. "Think you I promised to deliver this herd to only one buyer? No, our letters promised only that we would bring a herd to Kansas and discuss a final price upon arrival and depending upon the condition of the animals. And," he added, "I would like to see this place. It is in my mind to arrange for a purchase of good pasturage here, so that next year our herd may rest and fatten and that we may have leisure to wait on the best offer."

"You plan on doing this again?" Fredi asked in some astonishment.

His brother-in-law smiled. "Of a certainty, for I have made a most careful study of the market, whilst you were worrying about the condition of the herd and the quality of men to be hired and all these matters of the trail. There is a demand for beef cattle in the North that we hardly imagined! By our good fortune we have the means to deliver it, just at the moment when the railways make it practical. Next year, we shall bring another herd north." Hansi squinted thoughtfully towards the smudge that overlay their destination. "But by then, other men will have perceived the wisdom of what we have done. We will have competition, Fredi. But we have a head start and the field is very wide. I think that we should stay as far ahead as we can. I would like to meet with such men in the North as can best advise us. I should also like to begin improving our breed of cattle. As soon as the herd is sold and the drovers paid, I will go to Chicago. I should like to take some of my profits and purchase some fine eastern bulls and heifers. Young Dolph is in agreement with me, having already enclosed his best pasturage,"

"As am I," Fredi agreed hastily. "I did not know you entertained such grand plans as this, Hansi."

"You thought this was a gamble? That we would only throw the dice once, and be content with our winnings?" Hansi shook his head. "Perhaps I thought so at first. But the longer that I considered it, the better I perceived the advantages. This," Hansi waved his hand at the mass of cattle, grazing to their bellies in rich green grass, "to you it is an adventure, a day full of work to do and the chance to break your neck. But to me, it is business, a matter of providing goods at a profit to a customer, only not like a paper of pins or a wagonful of shingles. This is larger and of better profit as long as favorable conditions and the market for beef lasts."

"As long as it lasts?" Fredi raised an eyebrow. "You think it will not?"

"Nothing lasts under the same conditions." Hansi's teeth flashed white in the thicket of his beard. "All changes. And if we are shrewd and far-seeing, we change as well."

Hansi returned, jovial and beaming from ear to ear after that first foray into town. "They have arranged things very sensibly," he reported to Peter and Dolph, "stock-pens for the herds, so we need not pasture them for much longer. There is even a hotel—no need to sleep on the ground after tonight!"

"But what of the buyers?" Dolph asked, with some urgency. "What do they offer? Better than in Texas, I hope?"

"Aye, so they do," Hansi grinned. "You would not believe! Forty-seven dollars a head I was offered for the cattle, twenty-five for the horses."

Dolph whistled in amazement. "You took it, I hope?!"

"No," Hansi answered, "not since I have a chance to do better. There are many cattle buyers in Abilene, lads."

In the end, he did do better. Peter never thought he was so glad to see a town again, even one as muddy and rambling as Abilene, a sprawl of hastily built saloons along an impossibly wide street, each thirst parlor noisier than the other.

"Does anyone ever close their eyes?" he asked his cousin. "I can't see anyone getting a wink of sleep, between the racket from the stockyard and the trains, and the music from the gambling hells!"

"Fierce, isn't it?" Dolph agreed. "When I get home, that's when I'll sleep."

The two of them had repaired to a bathhouse near Abilene's largest and only hotel, named—with no small degree of humor—the Drovers' Cottage. Three stories tall and with splendid broad verandahs, it stuck up from the flat prairie like a tall plank-built thumb. They each carried a bundle of their best town clothes, creased from storage in the supply wagon. After removing their filthy work clothes they sank gratefully into tubs of gloriously hot water to scour off the accumulated layers of trail grime.

"Me, I think I'll go to the barber next," Peter ventured. But when he looked across at his cousin, Dolph looked to already be half asleep, with his head lolling against the tub rim.

Afterwards they hardly recognized each other. They walked down the wooden sidewalk that was elevated slightly above a sea of churned mud. This expanse was dignified by terming it a street.

"Texas Street," Dolph said to Peter.

Peter laughed and responded, "Do tell, Cuz."

A dapper gentleman in a fine pearl-grey suit sauntered towards them along the wooden sidewalk. The splendidly attired newcomer remarked, "I say, isn't this place most remarkably raucous?"

Peter blinked—the voice sounded familiar. "Jack?" He said in disbelief, for so it was. Gone was the grubby, bearded ruffian who had ridden with them since Austin. Here was a sleek and immaculately barbered Englishman in a faultlessly tailored jacket, and a silk waistcoat that was a miracle of quiet elegance.

Jack tipped his hat at them and smiled in wry amusement. "Quite a miraculous transformation, no? I hardly recognized myself. Extraordinary, the difference it makes, washing off most of Kansas! But now, if you'll excuse me, I have an appointment with a gentleman of parts who intends to relieve me of my purse by way of a friendly game of cards. Or so he hopes." Jack smiled, a fleeting and coldly calculating smile.

"A poker game?" Dolph asked.

Jack looked pained. "Really, chaps. Whist."

"He'll never know what hit him," Peter said, clapping Jack on the shoulder. "Good luck, then."

"Luck will have had nothing to do with it," Jack said as he took his leave.

They walked the entire length of Texas Street, crossed over, and walked back with Alonzo Brown and his brother. All of them were agog with excitement. They reveled in the noisy bustle of commerce of young men just like themselves, having come all the way up from Texas and now permitted liberty to blow off steam and enjoy all those things they had not seen for some three or four months. On one corner, a Negro minstrel band made merry music in the open air, competing with music spilling out from saloons farther down the street. A blanket spread out at their feet was half-covered in notes and coin, thrown down by their audience. A man came out from a photography parlor, and importuned them to have their pictures taken. To their amusement, the photographer offered to let them pose with their pick of some revolvers that he had on hand.

Peter, Dolph, and the Brown boys sat stiffly on a satin-upholstered settee and tried to look fierce. "I guess we should appear to be dangerous customers, Cuz," Peter ventured. They paid and promised to return for the developed pictures in a few days, although Peter wondered how on earth young Alonzo could look like anything more than a school boy, diffident and shy in his good town clothes and high-laced brogans. More than once, a longhorn cow galloped the length of the street, pursued by one or more laughing, shouting horsemen swinging their lariats overhead. At the next corner they skirted an excited group of hired drovers ringing a dogfight, a swirl of snapping teeth and brindle and fawn fur. Dolph looked pained as the losing dog yelped, a shrill and agonized cry.

"They oughtn't to do that," he whispered in distress.

Peter answered low, "Don't interfere, those boys are pretty liquored up, and there are more of them than us."

The dogfight broke apart. The loser fled, a young hound with a torn ear and a mangled throat oozing gore, as the ring of men around the fight exchanged truly amazing quantities of money. Dolph went after the hound, and his exasperated cousin followed after him, along a side street into the yard behind a grocery store. The young hound had taken refuge behind a stack of crates, snarling at all within reach.

"You and dogs," Peter said. "Don't you have enough of a pack at home?"

"I suppose," Dolph allowed, after the animal snapped at Dolph's gentle hand when he reached into that pitiful and insubstantial den. Dolph stood with some reluctance and dusted off the knees of his good town trousers.

"Let's go do what everyone else is doing," Peter urged him. "Getting a good meal and a better drink. If nowhere else promises better, we can go back to the Drovers' and Uncle Hansi will spot us dinner. He's a rich man, he can afford it."

"He's meeting with some buyers' agents," Dolph said. "Businessmen. I'd planned to be there, anyway."

"Then a drink," Peter said, "or hell, I vote we just go watch English Jack turn them cards." He drew his cousin back towards the main street, and one of the most splendidly imposing buildings there.

"Look at that," Dolph remarked as they peered through the glass doors. The interior was hung with mirrors and gold-framed paintings of elegant, if rather underdressed, women. "It's called 'The Alamo.' Guess they wanted us to feel right at home."

"They wanted to make our money feel right at home," Peter added with cynical cheer.

As they came through the door, a very lovely girl in a low-cut dress came up and put her hand on Dolph's cheek, cooing, "Why, you pretty Texas boys—won't you just go ahead and buy me a drink?"

"I don't think so, ma'am," Dolph replied. Before his cousin's eyes, Dolph put on his most innocent and blandest expression. "My mama don't approve of drinking and I don't rightly approve of such myself."

"But your mama ain't around to see what you do in Abilene," the girl replied winningly.

Peter said, "Yeah, but his big brother is, ma'am." He tipped his hat to her and took Dolph's arm. "Come along, Rudolph—you know what Mama said 'bout the demon drink."

Dolph tipped his own hat with a convincing display of shyness, and allowed Peter to take him back out the door. The pretty girl made a moue of momentary disappointment, but as the glass doors swung behind them, they heard her greet the next man to come through with a cheerful, "You pretty Texas man—are you going to buy me a drink?"

Dolph whistled, a sly expression of admiration, as they continued down the sidewalk. "I think we had a narrow escape, Cuz."

"So we did," Peter laughed, and fondly buffeted Dolph on the shoulder. "You did that well—the honest, country idiot on his first trip to the big city. Your father did the same; I once overheard Captain Hays saying as much."

"Did he, then?" Dolph suddenly looked as very young and unsure as he had pretended to be.

"He did indeed," Peter answered. "And Captain Hays insisted that such a pretense made him uncommonly good at games of chance, for he looked such an easy mark, that every sharper west of the Mississippi could hardly resist."

"So, that gave some advantage?" Dolph asked. Their boots thumped resoundingly along the wooden sidewalk. Dolph looked quite thoughtful and said, "I could use this, use it to advantage myself, Cuz, with buyers and all?"

"Uncle Carl surely did," Peter sighed. "Captain Hays said the first thing your father did when he left home was to win a horse playing at cards, and the second thing was to borrow a carbine from him so they could join a Ranger company together."

They paused to tip their hats courteously at a young woman elegantly dressed in flowered satin. She sailed down the wooden sidewalks as if she were a queen, the end of a delicate little chain leash in one hand, and what Peter thought at first was a tiny dog tucked into the curve of her arm. But it was not, as they saw at a closer glance. It was a plump little prairie dog with a collar around its neck. Peter realized that his cousin was staring more at the tame prairie dog than at the girl, who was indeed quite pretty, with very curly hair and a gap between her teeth which showed when she smiled at them.

"Hello, boys," she drawled. "Are you in town looking for some fun today?"

"Not much, ma'am," Dolph answered, still looking more at her pet.

"You boys surely can't go wrong in Abilene," she murmured invitingly. "Here, or down in the Addition. You'd be welcome any time."

"We'll keep that in mind, ma'am." Dolph finally took his eyes from the prairie dog. "Might you direct me to a general store, ma'am? One that might have some fresh meat scraps or something of that sort?"

Oh lord, Peter thought with an inward sigh, *he's still fretting over that dog.*

With a baffled but amused look the young woman answered, "Hazelett's General is back that way, boys."

As they continued on Peter said, "Speaking as a man of the world, Cuz, I find that I rather prefer the company of respectable women. And the temporary separation from such is not so unbearable that I must seek out the services of the other sort."

Dolph's eyebrows went up, nearly to his hair line. "Was she the other sort, Cuz? I hardly noticed."

"Of course not, you were too busy staring at her pet prairie dog. What kind of woman would be offering hospitality to just-met strangers on the street? Of course she was. You weren't interested in engaging her services, were you?

"No," Dolph shrugged. "Still, there's something finer about her, being kind to animals and all. I like people like that. I'd mind about the other thing, though." Peter thought his cousin was flushing a little pink. "It's like taking a room in one of those cheap boarding houses, sleeping on one of their straw-ticks? You don't rightly like to think of how many have been there before you."

"Interesting way to think of it," Peter sighed. "Come on, then, Cuz. Let's go find that poor mutt of yours, and have a quiet dinner with Uncle Hansi and the cattle buyers. At least, you and I will get out of Abilene with most of our wages still in hand."

"The sooner we leave, the better I'll like it," Dolph answered. "I figure they've made enough money off us as it is."

225

Chapter Fourteen: *What Once was Lost*

Cannily, Hansi sold the supply wagon and the team that had pulled it and found a purchaser for all the remuda horses. He kept out the stump-horned steer and the team that pulled the cook-wagon. He sent Peter, Dolph, and Daddy Hurst to drive it all—wagon, team and blue steer—back to Texas. They took the long road to Kansas City, and then south along the old Shawnee Road. They wrote triumphant letters home, telling Anna, Magda, and the rest of the family about the success of the cattle drive north and of their immediate plans.

After helping to prod the cattle onto railcars, the other hands took their pay and loaded their saddles and bedrolls onto a train headed east to St. Louis. From there, they would take a Mississippi riverboat south to New Orleans and return to their homes in Texas by stage, rail, or coastal packet. Hansi went with them as far as St. Louis, to arrange for their fares home. Only English Jack had no intention of returning to Texas, graciously declining the offer of his fare.

"Fascinating experience," he drawled to Fredi over dinner in the Drovers' Cottage ornate dining room. "Wouldn't have missed it for the world, and I wouldn't repeat it for another one, if it's all the same to your good self."

"What will you do here, then?" Fredi asked.

Jack looked blandly around the room. "This and that," he answered with deliberate vagueness.

Once the cattle were loaded, and the hands paid off, there was no reason to remain in Kansas. Fredi remained a few days after everyone else scattered to the four winds. There were some small matters like bills and fines to be sorted out, and a large disgruntled townsman who came to the Drovers' Cottage one morning insisting that one of Fredi's men had absconded with his dog.

"That was the finest fighting dog in Kansas!" said the man. He had buttonholed Fredi in the lobby of the Drovers' Cottage as he was on his way to breakfast in the dining room. "And I want to know what you're going to do about that thieving rascal who stole it!"

"A fighting dog? Didn't seem to have all that much fight left in it," Fredi grunted. He was almost sure that was the same light brown hound, with the flesh of its throat carefully stitched up and bandaged by Dolph. Fredi's nephew had departed Abilene several days before, the dog perched high on the seat of the cook-wagon next to him. Apparently others had seen it too.

"I demand payment for that dog!" the man snapped. "Or I'll see the law on you!"

Fredi sighed wearily. "How much?"

"How much? How much for a good fighting dog? Ten dollars, at least!"

Fredi took out a roll of bills from his vest and silently peeled off five of them. "That dog couldn't fight his way out of a rotten gunny-sack. Five dollars."

The man began to protest, but Fredi, hungry and impatient to dig into his breakfast, retorted, "You folk make a lot of money off my men, and our cattle. I think you should be content with five dollars for a dog that don't fight worth a damn." He leaned closer to the man, lowering his voice to a menacing growl. "Next year, maybe my men and our cattle, and our money—we go somewhere else? Some other town on the railroad with a fine stockyard and a big hotel! Nothing stays the same. Take the five dollars and be damned."

Fredi shouldered his way past the man without a backwards look; a small-town bully, in Fredi's experienced estimation. Five dollars for a scarred and beaten mutt was generous indeed, especially since the poor little beast was presently several days gone on the road east. He thought that might be the last of his business here, and tucked into breakfast with appreciation. The Drovers' Cottage offered a lavish bill of fare for every meal. After nearly four months of campfire-cooked beans and cornbread, Fredi relished every bite.

Still, he felt a certain amount of regret, for in his own mind he sensed that this trail drive enterprise was done and complete—at least for the present. Fredi, unlike Hansi and Dolph, cheerfully lived in the moment, thinking no farther into the future than the next day, or the next challenge; in fact, not a moment farther ahead than necessary. Also, unlike his more fastidious nephew, Fredi had quite enjoyed all the various pleasures that Abilene had offered, especially once the herd had been dispatched into cattle cars headed east. All those responsibilities he had carried as the trail boss had been banished. But of his close friends and acquaintances, only English Jack was still in town, and he was a flint-hearted bastard, as cold-blooded as a snake. Fredi had just about concluded that it was time to follow the other fellows and go home. He had not made up his mind whether to go by train and steamer as the other boys had—a long but rather dull prospect—or see if he might hitch a ride with an Army supply wagon going south, and rustle up a little excitement on the way.

"Mistah Steinmetz, sah?" The colored boy who carried messages and waited tables hovered over him, a heavy silver-plate coffee pot in hand. "Miz Gore tole me to tell you, dere's a message foh you at de desk."

"A message?" Fredi brightened. Maybe there was something worth remaining in Abilene yet another day for. "Who from—do you know?"

"Jus' a telegram, sah," the boy answered. "Jus' come from de office, I doan' know."

"No matter." Fredi drank the last of his breakfast coffee, reflecting that although it tasted very nice, with cream and fine sugar, Daddy Hurst's coffee from a tin pot and sweetened with molasses still was better for waking a man up. A telegram? It must be from Hansi. Perhaps he had bought a hell of a fine bull in the east, but Fredi couldn't think for the life of him why Hansi would spend money on a telegram to tell him all about it. At the desk in the Drovers' Cottage lobby, Fredi opened the folded paper with the telegram office's insignia printed at the top. It took him only a second to read the terse message, and several seconds longer to comprehend its implications.

Grete freed stop Fort Larned stop Come at once stop J Steinmetz sends end message.

Fredi refolded the telegram with hands that felt like they belonged to another. Mrs. Gore, the proprietress of the Drovers' Cottage, looked at him with apprehensive eyes.

"I hope it's not bad news, Mister Steinmetz."

"No." Fredi shook his head, feeling as stunned as if he had been thrown from the back of his horse, or a lightning bolt has crashed to earth just at his feet. "Its wonderful news, but I must leave immediately. And I must send a telegram in reply. I did not know my brother had gone to Kansas. How far from here is Fort Larned and what is the fastest way to get there?"

"Coach," Mrs. Gore answered. "The railway hasn't reached that far yet. If you weren't in such a hurry, you could go with an Army supply wagon, for they send goods out there all the time, for the Indian Agency."

"No, I can't wait for that, my dear Madam Gore. The coach it is, and today if possible."

"I'll send one of the boys to buy a ticket," Mrs. Gore offered. Fredi gallantly took her hand as if he would kiss it.

"I'll even ride on top with the driver, if so required," he mentioned, "as long as it's today."

Fredi packed his meager belongings, putting on his rough working clothes once again. This was like a miracle come out of the blue. Johnson's foray into Indian Territory the previous year had been unsuccessful in obtaining Grete and Willi's return. Since then, the Army had forbidden the paying of ransoms for white captives, on the very fair grounds that it only encouraged the Indians to take as many as possible in further raids. Nonetheless, Hansi had encouraged the search, heartened by occasional reports of captive girls among Kiowa and Comanche villages who were of the right age and appearance. But it had been two years since Willi and Grete were taken. Fredi had been long enough with the Frontier Battalion to know that not every captive would be redeemed, and the longer that those of a young age remained with their captors, the greater likelihood that they would choose willingly to stay.

Three days later, he swung wearily down from the stage when it pulled in at Boyd's ranch, on the crossing of the stage road over Pawnee Creek. He took down his saddle and bedroll from the luggage boot, arranging to leave them in the station office. Boyd's ranch looked a small and ramshackle place, one long sod building with many additions and extensions. The fort itself lay further on, a rough square of low buildings made of dark limestone, painted white and raised above the level of the parade ground. Fredi supposed the longer buildings to be barracks. The parade ground itself was a busy place, with wheels and the feet of blue-uniformed men churning up fine clouds of dust continuously. From somewhere the notes of a bugle fell, and Fredi stepped hastily aside as a long train of heavy freight wagons rolled past.

"I'm looking for Major Steinmetz," he asked of the first Yankee soldier he came close enough to speak to, a tall Irishman with yellow sergeant's chevrons on his sleeves. "Where would I find him?"

The sergeant squinted down at Fredi, a quizzical look on his face, as if he suspected a joke was about to be played upon him. "And where would I look for a foine doctor and surgeon like the Major, but in the post infirmary?"

Fredi scowled. For four years, a blue Federal uniform had meant an enemy, even if his own brother wore such. He had no patience for a battle of wits with a blue-belly sergeant who appeared to have little of his original issue of them.

"He's my brother, if you must know. I've come to take my niece home. Three days ago I'd a message that she was ransomed back from the Indians."

The tall sergeant's face brightened. "Ah! So that is why you have such a look of the Major, indade! The little maidy is staying with Colonel Wynkoop, for sure he is the Agent for the tribes in these parts. That is their house, over there," he pointed. "You can't miss it, for the Indians, y'see. The Major would be there."

"My thanks," Fredi nodded stiffly. He didn't know which made him more uneasy, the blue-clad soldiers all around, or the handful of Indians. He skirted the edge of the parade ground, walking towards that house which had been pointed out to him. It had an indefinably comfortable air about it, as if a woman might live there, not a single man batching it. A short distance from the stone house, an Indian woman sat on the ground, weeping in inconsolable grief. Fredi spared a glance. The woman had cut her hair off short and it hung in ragged black locks around her contorted face. Her deerskin tunic was unfastened from around her shoulders, hanging to her waist, and she was slashing at her bared breasts with a knife. The blood ran in trickles and splattered into the dust. Two boys hovered around the weeping woman as if they offered solace; but they seemed embarrassed, too, as if they wished the woman would demonstrate her grief anywhere else but in front of the white colonel's house. She cried out, wailing loudly, as Fredi walked past. He wondered vaguely why she was making such a fearful noise and spectacle.

A Yankee officer walked up and down the veranda of the Colonel's house. Now and again he glanced at the wailing woman as if he also wished for her to go and mourn somewhere else. There was something familiar in the set of his blue-clad shoulders and Fredi's heart jerked in sudden recognition: Johann. They had not seen each other in nearly seven years; an astonishing thing, for they were twin-born and inseparable until the age of sixteen, when Johann went back to Germany to study medicine. He had returned just at the start of the war. When the fighting began, Fredi volunteered at once for the Frontier Battalion, but Johann went to practice medicine with Doctor Herff in San Antonio.

Then J.P. Waldrip murdered Magda's husband. Up to that moment, Johann held abolitionist sympathies but considered Texas as home, the place to which he owed loyalty. But after seeing how the authorities had turned their backs on such a brutal injustice, he could not countenance serving the Confederacy in any way. Hearing that Johann had gone to California to join the Union Army, Fredi had sworn a heartbroken oath to Vati that when his unit ever encountered Union soldiers, he would fire into the ground, or above their heads. Now, looking across the dusty front garden of Colonel Wynkoop's house, Fredi recalled that promise. He never did have to do such a thing. In the remaining three years of the war, he had mostly fought against Indians or Mexican bandits.

He stepped up on the verandah. Hearing his footstep, Johann turned towards him, his face reflecting momentary annoyance and distraction. Fredi cleared his throat. "Hullo, Johann."

"Fredi!" In three long strides his brother was embracing him with fierce affection. "Ah, God, Fredi, it's good to see you. I didn't think you'd be here for another day. You must have traveled without stopping!"

"I did, brother, I did," Fredi answered. "I didn't know you were in Kansas!"

"I wrote two months ago, but you had already departed with the cattle." Johann's eyes sparkled with good humor and affection. "I thought to leave word in Abilene for you and Hansi and Dolph, but my letters must have gone astray. Oh, 'tis good to see you again." He seemed deeply affected by emotion.

Fredi felt much the same. So much had happened since that evening when they had last been together at Vati's house, on that spring evening the year that the war finally broke out. Johann was but newly returned from Germany, and Fredi had come up from Carl Becker's farm to drive Carl and Magda and the children home. They had gone to Austin for the wedding of Margaret's oldest son, and returned to find Vati's house in an uproar. Vati had just forbidden Rosalie to marry Robert Hunter. Fredi's throat tightened, thinking of that evening in Vati's parlor. Vati was dead these two years gone, and so too Rosalie the beautiful and beloved little sister, buried under a single stone with Robert who adored her. Buried also was Magda's husband, Carl Becker. As boys Fredi and Johann had practically worshipped him. It seemed hardly believable, that of those who had sat in Vati's parlor on that summer evening, only three remained to remember.

"'Tis good to see you also, brother," Johann said huskily; so he had the same memory in his mind. They always had always been able to sense each others thoughts. Doing so again was as heady as a deep draft of good wine. "I sent my message to Hansi. I thought he would come for his daughter if he had to walk all the way."

"Hansi is gone to the east, to search for better breeding stock," Fredi explained. "So I thought I should come. I would have anyway." Halfway between a laugh and a sob, he added, "So, you look well— for a blue-belly officer. I vow you must have been better fit than I by the end of it all!"

"So we did," Johann answered, with a merry look in his eye. "For we won. You should have come to Mexico with me, Fredi!"

Fredi laughed. Johann had never been one to stand up to teasing when he was a lad—too shy and tender-hearted. He stood back a little and looked critically at his brother. This was good. He was brisk and assured as he had never been when they were boys; a trim and confident young officer.

"By God, you do look well, Johann. You should come to Abilene and walk down the street with me. You'd never see the ground, for all the prairie nymphs throwing themselves at your feet!"

"True. But isn't there something to be said for quality over quantity?" Johann replied.

They laughed and embraced again, as Fredi recalled what he had come to Fort Larned for. "Little Grete—is she well? Who contrived to free her and how did they manage it?" he asked.

Johann led him to the front door of the house. He let himself in without any ceremony, by which Fredi assumed that he was a familiar and expected guest. "This last year has been a harsh trial for the tribes," Johann explained. "The hunting has been bad; most have no choice but to come and agree to accept a government subsidy. But the Army has made it a condition that white captives must be yielded up. Colonel Wynkoop saw her in a camp nearby about two weeks ago. He told them they must bring her to the fort before he authorized any supplies for them. Four days ago, they did."

The house was rough-plastered on the inside, not quite thick enough to hide the gaps between the stones from which it had been built. A few pieces of ornate furniture sat in the hall, as if refugees from a finer, daintier dwelling. Johann opened an interior door and said to someone within, "Madam Wynkoop, this is my brother Friedrich. He has just now arrived, to bring the little one home. Grete, little one, do you remember your uncle Fredi?"

A very pretty woman looked up and set aside an ivory comb, for she had been combing and arranging the hair of a little girl who sat on a parlor chair before her. Again, the furnishings had the look of something fine and fashionable, brought into this roughly-finished place. The woman was saying something about how many times she had washed the child's hair but

Fredi had no thought for anyone else in the room but his niece. He greeted Madame Wynkoop absently, all of his attention on the child.

He had feared for one wild moment that it was not Grete, but another child. After all, she had been only four years of age upon capture and now she had been with the Indians for half again that time. She was sitting rigidly motionless on a tall chair, clutching a large china-headed doll in her arms. Her feet, in new high-buttoned shoes, hung with her toes just barely touching the floor. She wore a dress slightly too big for her and bunched around her waist with a wide sash of hare-bell blue ribbon. Madame Wynkoop had tied a ribbon of the same color around her freshly-washed hair, which floated around her face like dandelion silk. It was Grete—no mistake about that—the same grey-blue eyes, faint pock-mark in the center of her forehead, and solemn round face framed in the same light brown hair as her mother and sister Marie.

"Grete." Fredi knelt on one knee before her so that his head was at the same level as hers and made his voice as soft as he could. He spoke in German, "Grete, I've come to take you home. Don't you remember me? Onkel Fredi?" She stared at him, her soft little face perfectly blank of expression, but he thought that her eyes rounded momentarily. From outside, the Indian woman wailed on a higher note, and the child's gaze flicked briefly in that direction. Fredi tried again, "Grete, sweetness, I've come to take you home to your mama. You remember your mama?"

Her lips moved very slightly, as if she were saying a word to herself. Her eyes filled briefly with tears, but within a moment it seemed as if she had willed them with un-childlike firmness not to fall at all.

At his side, Johann said softly, "She does not seem to understand anything but the language of the tribe she was with. When she was taken, she was old enough to speak well, wasn't she?"

"Four years old," Fredi answered heavily. "Chattered like a little magpie, she and Lottie both. Grete, do you remember Lottie? Your cousin Lottie, just your age? She has missed you these last two years, but your Mama and Papa, they have missed you terribly. Don't you want to come home?" Fredi wondered if perhaps she did understand, at least a little. She looked almost bewildered for a second; then a very tiny movement of her head, a defiant "no." She clutched her doll ever more tightly against her body. The parlor door behind them opened and shut, admitting another person and, briefly, the lamentations of the Indian woman outside.

"There you are, Curtis," Johann said in English, with some relief. "This is my brother, come to take her home, but she does not understand a word we say in German, either. Mr. Curtis is the interpreter for Colonel Wynkoop, Fredi."

Mr. Curtis was a slight and weather-browned man, with a beard that hid most of his face. He took a place kneeling next to Fredi, who had a sudden vision of how it must look, all these tall adults, looming over the silent child. To her it must feel as if she were some tiny defenseless animal, cornered by a pack of hunting dogs. Of course, no one wished to harm poor little Grete, but she must be absolutely terrified nonetheless.

"Cannot someone get that woman to leave?" Fredi asked, thinking that might be one thing giving the child a fright. "Who is she and why is she carrying on like that?"

"She is the one who cared for the child," Mr. Curtis answered, softly and with a sideways look at Fredi. "She was most reluctant to yield her up and protested the decision of her brother and the warriors."

"Good God!" Fredi exclaimed. "As if my niece belonged to her! Did she not think of my sister's grief when Grete and her brother were taken? She was deranged with sorrow! Her husband and the rest of the family nearly despaired, fearing that the balance of her mind was unhinged! My brother-in-law, my nephew, and I—we tracked the war party for days, hoping to free her and her brother! For two years, we have sent searchers into the Territories and never stopped praying for her safe return!"

Grete flinched back in the chair, as if she were frightened by his sudden and vehement tones. Mr. Curtis murmured soothing words to her, in the Indian tongue, and at last she spoke, seeming in the same language.

"What did she say?" Johann demanded.

"Her Indian mother told her that her mother and father were killed and that no one among the whites wanted an orphan. She promised that if no one came here to claim her, then she would take her back home to their lodge."

Mrs. Wynkoop made a wordless exclamation of pity and distress, and Fredi answered, "Ridiculous! Not a word of it true! My sister and brother are alive and very well, too! Tell her that, tell her I have come to take her home to her mother, her sisters and her cousins! We have been looking for her all this time and that her mother—my sister—loves her very dearly! Her fondest wish is for her to be at home where she belongs. Tell her that, Mr. Curtis, make her understand that!"

Mr. Curtis nodded, speaking again and at considerable length in that incomprehensible Indian tongue. Fredi and Johann watched her face intently and Mrs. Wynkoop whispered, "So it has happened often before. The small children are sometimes treated kindly once among the tribes, you see. They come to love those who care for them very deeply indeed. And speaking to no one of their kind for months or years, it is no wonder that they lose the power of their native speech almost at once."

"Will she remember?" Fredi asked, much distressed. He feared that Liesel would not cope well, knowing that the little daughter whose return meant all the world to her had placed another first in her affections. "Remember her own language, her parents?"

"In time," Mrs. Wynkoop sighed. "And with kind treatment, I am sure she will recall her own associations and family, and take up our ways once more. It is well that she is still so young."

Mr. Curtis finished speaking. A last soft-voiced question, and Grete bobbed her head in assent, precisely once. Her countenance was fixed in an expression of stern resignation. She hugged the doll even more tightly to her, as if it were a lifeline, and spoke a few brief words in such a dull and hopeless tone that Fredi's heart was wrung for her obvious sorrow.

"What did she say, then?" Johann whispered.

Mr. Curtis replied, "That being a good child, she has always obeyed."

"And she has been a good child." Mrs. Wynkoop patted Grete's cheek, with fond affection. "She has been a dear, good little girl—no wonder that woman cared for her! You should have seen how she was dressed, when Edward, my husband, brought her to me! She wore three brass bracelets and a deerskin dress sewn with shells and silver drops—but, oh, her hair was in a frightful state! It had been rubbed thoroughly with tallow and soot, to make it dark, you see. I must have washed it three or four times before every speck was out."

"Did you ask about her brother?" Fredi interrupted. "Her older brother was taken at the same time. His name was Wilhelm, everyone called him Willi? Was he living in the same camp, with the same tribe?"

Mr. Curtis spoke again, Grete listening with grave attention while the others almost held their breaths, which continued throughout her soft reply.

"She says they were together at first. Although they were made to ride with different warriors, they were permitted to speak to each other. She says when they first came to the village, everyone was amused by their talk. She was given by the chief to his sister and taken to her lodge. Her brother was given to another family; she did not see him so much. He was with the boys and men, she was with her Indian mother. She says the last time she saw him he had hurt his leg, being thrown from the back of a wild horse. He could not go with the tribe when they moved to a new camp. That was the last time. She has never seen him again."

"When was that?" Fredi hardly dared breathe, waiting for Mr. Curtis' translated reply. "How long ago?"

"In the first winter, before the grass began to grow."

About a year and a half ago. Fredi let out a deep sigh, thinking on how he should tell this to Liesel. No, best tell Hansi first. Surely he would be home from his cattle-buying trip to the East. He did not wish to be the one in the room, telling Liesel that her youngest son was almost probably dead and had been for that long. Not after what Anna and Magda had said of her reaction when the children were first taken. Fredi, being a happily uncomplicated man, had very little experience with female megrims and even less of a desire to acquire any more. No, that was more Johann's line of work, being a doctor-surgeon and all.

He did not feel quite so helpless in the face of little girl terrors. She was a dear little thing, as much of a twin to Lottie as he was to Johann. And besides, he had known her all of her life, up until her capture. Surely that counted for something, Fredi thought, and his spirits rose. Children were no more complicated than any small and relatively helpless little animal. Feed them when hungry, see them bedded down for the night in a safe place, sing to them when they were lonely, reassure them when frightened. He had gotten eight hundred and fifty-odd cattle and eighty horses safely to Kansas from Texas, doing pretty much that. How hard could it be, taking one small girl-child in the other direction, aside from the additional requirement to keep her in clean and dry clothes?

"I'd like to take her home, as soon as transportation can be arranged," he said at last. "Assuming she is fit enough to travel?" He looked questioningly at his brother, who nodded. "Although, I should like to have passed more time with you," he added to Johann with very real regret.

"Understood, brother," Johann responded. "Our sister must have her child returned without delay. The mail stage would be fastest, if that is acceptable. And shall I send word that you are returning, although you might very well arrive in Friedrichsburg before it does?"

"We did very well with the cattle, this year," Fredi answered. "I think I may spree a little bit. Send a telegram."

The next morning, when he took his niece by the hand and departed from Colonel Wynkoop's house, the Indian woman was still there. She began to howl again with grief and despair, as soon as she saw them emerge from the house. He and Johann walked on either side of their niece and Johann carried a small bag of clothes and necessaries which Mrs. Wynkoop had generously given to them for the journey. Grete hung back a little, tugging against his hand as they went past her, clutching her doll with the other hand. She turned her head a little, but her expression was the same unchildlike stoic mask.

"Perhaps now she will go back to her lodge," Johann said, "knowing that Grete's family did come to claim her."

"I hope so," Fredi said. "I'd sure as hell hate to be in the Wynkoop's parlor and have to listen to that for much longer."

By the time they had walked around the edge of the parade ground, her cries could be but faintly heard. By the time they reached Boyd's ranch and the stage station, they could not be heard at all.

"Safe journey, brother," Johann said. Standing by the stage steps, they embraced one more time. Fredi climbed into the coach and Johann handed Grete up to him. "You also, little one. Give my love to Magda and Hansi and all."

"Always." The coach was crowded on this day. Fredi took the child onto his lap, an awkward burden because she sat so stiffly and never relinquished her grip on the china doll. She looked out the window with the same stoical detachment with which she regarded everything else for many hours.

The coach swayed like a boat on the open sea, and presently Fredi began to sing, very softly, "Sleep baby sleep, your mama is watching the sheep. . . "

Later he would insist that he sang baby rhymes to his niece most of the way back to Texas, as the coach rumbled down the wagon road to Red River Station, to Austin and Neu Braunfels, and finally through the gravelly ford of Baron's Creek. Grete had begun to relax against his shoulder by then, and now and again to experiment with saying a word or two in German. She clutched the china doll that the Wynkoops had given to her, all the long dusty days of that journey, and clung to it for many months thereafter, even after she began to speak German again.

* * *

"Poor Grete," Magda sighed to Lottie, as cold rain splattered against the glass windows of Lottie's front parlor. It was after midnight, but neither of them was sleepy. Heavy velveteen curtains were close-drawn against the winter chill that breathed from the glass. "She was terrified. There was such a crowd, such a commotion at the store, when Captain Nimitz drove her and

Fredi home from the hotel. People recognized her in the street. It had already been printed in the newspapers—the German papers and the American alike—that she was freed from captivity and returning home. There were so many people who wanted to speak to her, so many people who thought she might know of other captives still in Indian hands."

"Auntie Liesel could hardly bear to let her out of her sight," Lottie added. She had finished her supper. Now she took up her needlepoint, deftly drawing lengths of worsted through the holes in the mesh fabric stretched in her embroidery frame, as she talked to her mother. "I wondered sometimes if Grete had felt more free among the Indians, and a captive when she was returned."

"Did she speak of such to you, Lottchen?" Magda asked. "It seemed at first that she was as silent as a ghost. Fredi told us it was not uncommon for such children to forget their native language, and have some small trouble in learning it again. Did she recall her old fondness for you, as she remembered her own language?"

"Oh, she recollected me at once, and Auntie Liesel and Onkel Hansi," Lottie answered. "But there was much I think she did not wish to remember."

"About Rosalie and Robert." Magda's eyes shone with the tears that a half-century of passing time could not banish. "We did not press her to tell us what happened that morning. There was no need and she was only a child. Did she ever confide in you?"

"Oh yes, Mama," Lottie answered, "We whispered at night under the covers of the trundle-bed."

"What did she tell you, then?" Magda asked, curiously. "We were always afraid she must have seen or heard such dreadful things!"

Lottie answered slowly, "When she first told me, I did not think she had, Mama. She told me that she and Willi were asleep, at first. They woke up when the Indians began chasing the trap, and Onkel Robert shouted in English. They did not understand. And then either the trap was wrecked, or Onkel Robert shouted for them all to get out and run, run as fast as they could. She said that a great many Indians on horses came after them. She and Willi were holding hands and running . . . and one of them just grabbed her by the back of her dress, and another caught Willi. She heard Auntie Rosalie screaming and screaming again, but the Indians put a blanket over her face then. She always claimed that she didn't see or know anything more after that, but upon her return, she knew without asking of me that Auntie

Rosalie and Onkel Robert were dead. I came to believe she had seen what had happened to them both."

"She did not wish to remember," Magda said softly. "For the woman she lived with afterwards had nothing to do with any of that, and she was kind to our little Grete."

"Such tales she wove for me!" Lottie sighed, reminiscently. "I think now, it was a way to reassure herself that it had all really happened and to her."

"Yes," Magda nodded, "Hansi and Liesel—they thought it best to expunge that memory. People would point and whisper and tell tales, and also they feared she would be bothered by newspaper reporters seeking sensational stories. So they tried to live for a time as they had before, but it didn't work. Hansi already had bought property in San Antonio, thinking it would be advantageous doing business there. He also thought it better for Liesel to be closer to such doctors as specialized in troubles such as hers. Poor Doctor Keidel was so harried; he had no time or patience for her maladies. So Hansi moved his family to San Antonio, thinking it might also be better for Grete to go to the German School with the children of his friend Mr. Guenther. I let Hannah go with them, for Grete seemed to trust her, and the poor child so needed a companion and champion!"

"She was teased at school," Lottie nodded, "for all the care taken. I do not know if she merely appeared to be odd, upon her return, or if she withdrew into herself for fear of being treated badly. She would never hear any ill spoken of the Indians, though. They were just fighting for their people, their lands and their way of life, she always would say."

"But not to your Cousin Anna," Magda snorted, "except that once. Do you recollect that occasion, Lottchen? You were then about twelve or so."

"Oh, my!" Lottie laughed and half-groaned. "I never really thought of Cousin Anna having a temper, merely a sharp tongue. She picked up the cream-jug and threw it at her, in the middle of family tea. 'Fighting for their people!' she shouted, 'Those brave warriors, fighting for their lands! Do you have any idea of the vile things they did to a defenseless woman, a woman with child! Or for what reason?' Then she told Grete—told us all, as a matter of fact, at the top of her lungs—and what it was like to watch someone die of a septic wound. Cousin Anna began to cry, she was so angry with Grete. Then her husband picked her up in his arms and carried her out of the parlor, and that was that."

"It was very educational," Magda agreed, austerely. "You had some very improper questions to ask of me, afterwards. I could hardly forget that. Your aunt and Marie and Grete all crying! I could hardly blame your Uncle Hansi for withdrawing to his study. Hannah was the only one to remain calm."

"Nannie," Lottie rested her hand with the needle in it, against the side of her embroidery frame. "She always seemed a little apart, a little pool of calm and serenity. I'd always wondered what it was like to have a saint in the family. Not as uncomfortable as it might seem, as it turned out. She was always so very protective of Grete. Was that why Onkel Hansi thought to send her to the Ursuline school, too?"

"It was very well thought of," Magda answered. "And Porfirio recommended it to me, as the best and most proper school for young ladies, in the care taken of the students. Hannah was happy there, so it seemed that Grete's difficulties might be best cared for there—among the Sisters and students who knew nothing of what had been her unhappy captivity from the age of four to six years."

"She was not unhappy, Mama." Lottie took up the slim steel needle with a tail of bright worsted hanging from it. "She was quite happy, in fact. She told me once of her most pleasurable memory."

"And what memory might that have been, dear child?" Magda tenderly asked. Although Lottie now was herself a grandmother and Magda the great-grandmother of many other children, Lottie still remained the most precious to her; the child to whom she remained the closest.

"When she had been with the Indians for many months," Lottie answered, "her foster mother gave her a headdress made of many trailing ribbons with silver adornments on the ends. And she could ride any of the horses that she liked, and so she would ride as fast as the wind across the prairie, she said. Above all, she loved to watch her hair, mixed with those ornamented ribbons, stream back with the speed of the horse running. Such a memory!" Lottie sighed. "I do wonder, how many times Grete has thought of that. Onkel Hansi saw that she went to school and Auntie Liesel that she had proper clothes and the manners of a lady and that everyone except for the sensational papers forgot about how she was a captive of the Comanche for the space of two years! Such a tiny space of time, considering that we are the same age and married with considerable success and happiness. But still, Mama . . . I am sure she does still think on that memory."

"It is a fine one to have," Magda answered, "and one that not many others can share. After all, this is now the twentieth century."

Chapter Fifteen: *Kissing Kin*

Fredi waded through a jostling crowd in the street in front of Vati's house, carrying Grete in his arms and demanding room and for quiet. Some of the faces Magda saw beyond the door were neighbors, many of them friends, but just as many were strangers. She thought their curiosity was ghoulish, frightening. How could they think this homecoming any of their business!

"She's frightened as hell, hasn't seen her family in two years," Fredi demanded as he shouldered a particularly insistent man out of his path. "Let her have a little time—let us have a little time, for the love of God. What is this, some kind of circus?" Grete buried her face in his shoulder, clinging to her doll with a death-grip as Fredi sprang up the steps and into the hall with her.

"You heard him," Charley Nimitz snapped as he briskly followed him from the cart with their small luggage. "No melodrama today— well, not in the street anyway."

"Mama!" Anna called from the stair landing. "Mama, they're here! Will you come down now?!" Liesel appeared at the top of the stairs as Anna and Magda exchanged a significant look.

Liesel had been on the highest tower since receiving the message from Johann, a letter which had preceded her daughter's return by just a bare three or four days. She had unpacked all the garments she had sewn for her lost children, laid them all out on her bed, then would rush into Magda's room or into the shop with armfuls of them, breathlessly asking for her sister's opinions on one or the other. She fretted endlessly over the size, holding up the various dresses against the puzzled but patient Lottie; a series of lovingly-sewn calico garments, creased from being folded into a trunk and fragrant with the scent of orris-root and lavender. It did no good for Magda to point out that Lottie most resembled her father, and that he had been a tall man. When Grete had been taken by the Indians, Lottie had been then almost half a head taller.

"She would have grown, Lise, but not taller than Lottie," Magda said, at last.

Lise was already ripping out a hem and replied with difficulty through a mouthful of pins, "But still, she will have grown, dear little Grete!"

"Lise, Hannah is as tall as Marie, even though she is four years younger," Magda said with a sigh of exasperation. Nothing damped Liesel's hectic spirits, knowing that her smallest daughter was free, after two years of uncertainty and despair. Hansi and the boys were on their way home, little knowing yet of Grete's release, although both Fredi and Johann had sent messages to the various rooming houses and to friends that Hansi might be seeing whilst considering fine pedigreed stock. Dolph and Peter, with Daddy Hurst and the cook-wagon, were probably still somewhere along the Shawnee Trail, north of the Red River. No one dared speak of Willi to his mother, lest her joy be dimmed.

That afternoon Fredi shouldered through the door, beaming with delight and his arms full of an exhausted child. Liesel almost flew down the stairs, torn between happy tears and incoherent and joyful exclamations.

"Oh, Grete . . . little Grete, my darling . . . look at you! Oh, my dear darling, how you have grown!"

Fredi set Grete on her feet and Liesel swept her into an embrace, kneeling in a pool of skirts so that she could kiss the child's solemn face.

"Mama?" she ventured tentatively. Liesel began to cry and laugh at the same time. Hovering with Anna and Lottie, Magda met her brother's eyes, tired but triumphant. Charley's merry grin seemed to light the house; no matter that Hansi and the boys were not home, possibly didn't even yet know of this joyous return. Hannah, Anna and Marie gathered closer around Liesel and her youngest while Sam and Elias hovered, fascinated and full of questions—some for Grete, who appeared quite overwhelmed, but many directed at Fredi.

The latter finally said, "Ah, Lise, take the poor babe into the kitchen and feed her oatmeal porridge. Our last few meals were truly awful and we are both starving. Not your place, Charley," he added as Charley made a mocking protest, "for I wished to get the girl back where she belongs!"

"Does she understand a word we are saying?" Charley asked softly, for it appeared as if she did not comprehend more than a few words. She stared at her mother, her cousins and sisters with eyes that were as round and as apprehensive as a baby owl's.

"Some," Fredi answered in the same tone, and unsuccessfully tried to stifle a jaw-crackingly wide yawn. "Your pardon! We came very far today and hardly slept at all last night for the noise in the stage hotel. I have been reciting every baby rhyme and children's song I can think of for the last five days. I think she does understand, for sometimes she sings along with me. She will remember, as we talk to her."

Lottie took her cousin's hand, after a wary look at Liesel and another in her mother's direction, as if to reassure herself that Magda was still there and she had nothing to fear from Liesel. "Do you want some gingerbread?" she asked in the most sweetly earnest tones. "Auntie Schmidt made some for us. You remember, you used to like gingerbread. Is that your dolly? May I see her?" Magda held her breath, for Grete still clutched her doll very firmly. "Do you have a name for your dolly, Grete?"

"Go on, get something to eat for the child, before she falls asleep in it," Fredi commanded heartily. Liesel kissed her daughter again and rose from the floor, shooing the children before her like chickens in the farmyard.

"She does seem to understand at least a little." Charley sounded much cheered.

Fredi yawned again. "She's a good girl. I have so much to tell you all. All the way to Kansas and back—by the gods, it all went well! Nearly lost a man in a stampede, but it turned out well! We wrote you about the sales of the cattle and horses! And your son has found himself another dog."

"How many pets does that make for him now, Madam Magda?" Charley laughed with very real affection. "Four or five by my count!"

"What of Willi?" Magda asked in a low tone as Liesel and the children vanished into the kitchen. "Was there any news of him? When Liesel regains her composure after this joy, she will think to ask about her son. What should we tell her?"

With a wary glance towards the kitchen Fredi answered, "Colonel Wynkoop and the other folk at the Fort Larned Agency had received no intelligence regarding him at all. Grete last saw him as the tribe they were with prepared to move to a new camp in the spring of the year after they were taken. He had been hurt, riding one of their wild horses. Wynkoop and his translator—sensible chap, knew a lot regarding their ways—he thinks it was likely he was left behind, being injured too badly to move." Fredi added, grave of face, "I think that he is most likely dead, poor little chap. But I would rather not be the one to tell Lise." He looked from Charley to Magda, both of them nodding sad agreement, and added, "I'll tell Hansi of this when he returns, but if she asks . . . ."

"Leave it to Hansi," Magda said. "Willi was his child also and Liesel is his wife."

Hansi arrived two weeks later, exuberant as a schoolboy and driving a fine new trap drawn by a lively but disciplined team of horses. He had brought presents from the east for everyone, but left the horses in the corral and the trap sitting in the barn while he rushed into the house empty-handed;

first through the storeroom and into the workshop, where he swung Anna up into the air as if she were still Grete's age.

"How's my little secretary and commander?" He kissed her cheek with affection.

Anna pleaded, "Put me down, Papa! Please! Dignity—there are customers in the shop!" She eyed her parent with affection and no little wariness, as he set her feet on the ground again. "You're inordinately pleased with yourself, Papa. What have you done?"

"Put our feet on a road paved with silver and gold, my dear little nun. How is your mother? Where is she? Where is your aunt?"

"Mama is upstairs." Anna straightened her skirts and smoothed stray tendrils of her hair back into its usual sleek knot. "She is in a good mood, Papa; almost as merry as she used to be. And Auntie is in the shop. Papa, did you get our letters? Fredi's and mine? About the children?"

"Yes, I did, little nun, and I talked to Fredi, too." Hansi's face was briefly shadowed. "I know what they told him at Fort Larned about Willi. Leave it to me to handle your Mama, if she asks. Out of the cellar and onto the topmost tower with having her little chick returned to her, I presume?"

"Yes, Papa, very much so," Anna returned sedately. "She has been over the moon with happiness ever since. She has not yet come to allow Grete out of her sight—to attend school, for instance! But she will let her go play in the garden with Lottie. They are out there now. Did you not see them when you came from the stables? Mama watches from the window above."

"I was in a hurry," Hansi answered, "but I will take your word for it!" The bell over the shop door chimed and Anna tilted her head, listening intently, "I must go, Papa, there are more than Auntie can manage. But you can see Grete and Lottie from this window. I … I watch them also. I think she is happy to be home now. She talks now. A very little and to Lottie mostly, but more than before."

"All to the best, my little nun." Hansi sighed and kissed her cheek once more. "All to the best. You said that your mama is upstairs? Good, for I have something splendid to tell her!"

"What are you planning, Papa?" Anna asked suspiciously.

Hansi smiled broadly. "Never you mind, but it will put the roses in her cheeks for sure to know that I have contracted to build her a fine new house of our very own—in San Antonio!"

"Oh, Papa!" Involuntarily, Anna clapped her hands. "Truly? How wonderful! Do you think Mama will consent?" The joy in her face faded a trifle, but Hansi nodded.

"She will, I think. If I persuade her, and you and your aunt back me up and hold her hands all the way. I think it might be accomplished with some little trouble. Annchen, I went all the way to Kansas with a herd of cattle and horses, I think I can easily get your Mama's consent to ride in a closed coach to San Antonio. She will not fall to her fears as long as we are all with her."

"True, Papa." Anna agreed. She smoothed her hair again. As she went towards the front of the shop she asked a carefully casual question. "Of my cousin and Mr. Vining, how did they fare in Kansas? Are they returning soon?'

"Yes, Annchen," Hansi replied with a broad grin. "They should return very soon. I think they fared very well in Kansas; neither of them had much of a taste for such delights as were on offer—which you should not know about anyway! Anyway, neither of them was charged with offending against the civil authorities. Always good, hey? They should return very shortly, since I need to consult with them about the care required for the stock animals I purchased! Young Vining has a good head on his shoulders! Will you be as pleased to see him as your mama is to see me?"

"Really, Papa!" Anna exclaimed, with a blush pinking the cream of her cheeks. Hansi laughed, and ran up the stairs.

At the top of the stairs was the room that Liesel and Magda had shared during the war, and that he and Liesel had shared after it. The door stood half-open, and he crashed through it with an exuberant thud. Liesel, looking out the window at the little girls playing in the garden below, spun around. She cried out, half joyous and half startled, her hand at her throat.

"I'm home, sweeting!" Hansi said only, and swept her into his arms.

Some considerable time later, she murmured from the shelter of his side, "In the afternoon, Hansi . . . whatever will people think?"

"Whatever they like," he answered nonchalantly. Liesel sighed. It had been so long, waiting for things to be as they had used to be. Hansi, her husband, so solid and comfortable, pulling the pins out of her hair and scattering their clothing over the floor, undressing them both with such eager haste! She had ached for this, alone in this bed for so many months, and now she felt exultant. She stretched out her arm, embracing the solidity of his chest, feeling the steady thud of his heart against her face. Her hair was spread across them both; she could feel him toying with a strand of it, knowing that he wound one of her curls around his fingers. "Lise," he ventured and she almost purred with contentment. "Lise, I had a notion.

Would you like having a house of your own again? I had a thought that if I had a house in San Antonio to run the business from . . . then we could spend more afternoons like this."

"You're a wicked man, Hans Richter," Liesel told him with mock severity.

He pinched her breast lightly. "And you love every minute of it," he whispered, as his hand ventured lower, lower still. "And every inch too, I warrant."

"Don't ever leave me," she whispered, welcoming him again into her body; ah, the dear and familiar way of it, the dance of married folk, easy and accustomed to each other's bodies, dear and content to touch and embrace every part.

"Never," he answered confidently. "Never again . . . well, maybe in the summer while I take another herd up to Kansas. But until then," he smiled at her and whispered as his body pressed hers lovingly into the featherbed, "I shall stay here with you, Lise. The boys will take care of the wagons . . . and I will spend the days minding the business, and the nights with you."

And with that, thought Lise as she pulled her husband to her and he whispered endearments into her ear, she must be content. After all, next summer was a long way away, and her husband lay with her, bare skin to bare skin, and what was closer than that?

Even so, there were things to say. "Hansi," she whispered tentatively after another considerable time. His callused hands on her back pulled her close against his body. She thought he might have dropped off to sleep, for that was his way after happily exhausting both of them in the pleasures of the marriage bed. "Hansi, there is something I must ask."

"Ask away, then." No, he was not asleep; his voice was alert, thoughtful.

"There is something that no one has told me," she ventured. "About our little boy, about Willi." She felt her throat tighten, and firmly willed her voice to remain steady, the tears not to fall. "Amidst all this joy, it seems that no one can bring themselves to speak of him. Was there anything said to Fredi, nothing that Johann could find out at this fort place in Kansas . . . about his fate?"

His arm tightened comfortingly around her, and his voice was thick with compassion. "Lise," he ventured at last, "from what your brother told me, and I have no reason to doubt, our boy was last seen alive in an Indian camp about six months after capture. No one has seen him since. Johnson brought me only reports of a girl, never a boy of his description."

"So he is dead, then," Liesel said, brokenly. "I have begun to fear such."

"I think so, Lise," Hansi agreed. His voice sounded solemn, as if he sorrowed but his grieving had long been done. He touched her face with his free hand, smudging the tears that had begun to trickle down her cheek. "I think he has been lost to us for some time since. Lise-love, it is a sorrow, but one that we can bear. Think on this, my dear—we have been given nine children, of which fate or the Gods or whatever took four from us. Yet one has been given back and the rest thrive. We are fortunate, more fortunate than perhaps we deserve. Let us bend our minds toward the children we have, Lise, not the ones taken from us."

"I shall try," she whispered, between sobs. "But . . . such a grief!"

"Must be endured," he answered, "as do others grieve. They bear it, and go on. Lise, dearest; Grete has been given back to us. Think on that gift! Think on our boys, and on Anna and Marie! Come downstairs, out of this room and be well again. Come to San Antonio; such fine amusements for you and Anna to partake in. Madame Guenther will take such enjoyment in your company. Think of how you shall decorate our new house there! Grander than ever, bigger than the house at Live Oak! Will you consent to this, Lise?" he begged.

Her arms went around him, as far as she could reach. She could never deny him this, or anything else he wanted of her, not since she was a girl. *Love me, my husband*, she begged silently, communicating through her embrace. *Love me and never leave me again. This place is so large, so empty. I am lost without you.*

* * *

"Not only had your uncles had success with the cattle drive that year," Magda explained to Lottie, *"but they had made many friends and even found some interested in investing in western cattle. The stock that Hansi brought back from the east went into pasture under your brothers' care. Fredi took over management of the Live Oak property. And after the turn of the new year, Hansi took Liesel and his daughters to San Antonio. His grand new house was nearly finished."* The parlor clock chimed gently—neither Lottie nor her mother felt like sleeping. It seemed as if the memories of the old days held them in a spell. Lottie was entranced, for her

mother had never spoken so freely of those matters of which she herself possessed only a child's limited recall.

"I remember," Lottie answered. "You and Nannie went with them and she remained there, to go to the Ursuline School. I would have been a little jealous, but even with Grete returned, Auntie Liesel still frightened me. She behaved so strangely, sometimes. But Onkel Hansi was so attentive to her."

"He loved her very much, Lottie," Magda explained gently. "Everything that he did in life, I think Hansi thought first of whether it would please her or not. Moving his business concerns to San Antonio was advantageous to him, but he also thought it would be better for her. She might feel safer living in a city, far away from the frontier and Indian war parties, and there would be doctors that might better advise them. She would go into the garden on her better days. If he and Anna accompanied her, she would consent to go in a carriage to the finest shops or to the gardens around the marvelous San Pedro springs. She was content for some months, until spring..."

"Time for the cattle herd to go north again," Lottie said.

Her mother nodded. "They planned again, the same as the year before; only this time, two herds. Each with a crew of thirty drovers and a cook wagon, traveling two or three days apart, along the same trail as the year before. Your uncles thought Cousin Peter was experienced enough after the first drive to be the trail boss of the first herd, and Hansi intended to travel with them, driving a supply wagon as he had before. Fredi and Dolph would follow with a second herd. We had taken much care with the arrangements, Lottie!" Magda exclaimed, reminiscently. "But there was only so much that we could do! So much depended upon what waited at the end of the trail, in Kansas! There were decisions that only Hansi could make, decisions that would have to be made on the spot! Just when everything was in readiness, two days before they were to depart—disaster!"

"I remember it seemed most romantic, at the time." Lottie smiled over her needlework.

Her mother clicked her tongue against her teeth, disapprovingly. "Nothing romantic about a leg broken in two places," she retorted. "Your uncle was in agony."

* * *

Magda had been working in the store with Sam, listening with half an ear as Anna read off a list of merchandise in the storeroom, and thinking with some surprise how contented she felt. Anna and Hansi had arrived on the stage; Hansi to prepare for the long drive north, and Anna as ever his secretary and right arm. Jacob and George arrived with a wagon of goods for the store, thrilled with the excitement of seeing the beginning of another cattle drive. Peter had also come up from the Becker ranch, ready to spar with Anna after a winter of overseeing cattle. He came in riding a brown horse, and Magda's heart turned with a pang of sorrow seeing him from a distance. So like Carl Becker, back when he would slip quietly into the house, in those months after they had been affianced and he was busy at building a proper stone house for her! She put those memories out of her mind almost at once, for Peter was merry and bold, in the way that she remembered him being before the war. Mr. Berg had done him well, with that mechanical arm.

It was almost like it had been in the first year after the war, with Vati's house full of family; not the sedate and quiet place that it had become with only herself and her own children in residence. She had missed Anna— so pleasant to have her back again for a long visit. And how beautifully and modishly turned out she was! Magda supposed that the shops in San Antonio must have recovered extraordinarily well from wartime shortages; that, or Liesel was reveling in the fashion-papers and her needle again.

Outside in the street, a wagon rattled past, turning the corner into their stableyard and halting on the gravel just outside the store-room's outside door.

"There's Papa with the stores wagon," Anna called from the other room. "Good, we can have the boys begin loading." From outside came the sound of a horse whinnying in distress and the shout of a man, abruptly cut short by a thud, the kind made by something heavy striking the ground. "Papa!" shrieked Anna at once. Magda picked up her skirts and abandoned Mrs. Arhelger, halfway through a request for a sealed tin of that nice tea from Japan and a sack of bread flour. Her heart was already in her throat as she ran through the workroom, and into the storeroom, towards the double doors at the opposite end. She could see the wagon on the gravel drive, the dark form of a man lying there, crumpled as if he had fallen, and Anna bending over him with a face as white as milk. Hansi's face was nearly as pale, already beaded with sweat from agony, but he tried to smile in reassurance to his daughter and sister-in-law.

"Damn beast . . . shied at a dove starting up under its nose as I was climbing down . . . I'd sell the God-be-damned beast for that, if we didn't have to leave tomorrow!"

"Let me help you up, Papa," Anna pleaded, but Hansi shook his head.

"The brake didn't hold. I fell badly—broke a bone by the sound of it! God in heaven it hurts! Send for Doctor Keidel, Annchen." Hansi let his head fall back, and said his favorite oath, then groaned. "And not at a worse time! All our plans depend on the herd leaving in two days!"

Magda sent Hannah for the doctor, while Peter and the boys made a litter out of some spare timber and their coats to carry Hansi inside—not without some difficulty, for he was no small weight. They laid him on the chaise in the parlor. By that time Doctor Keidel arrived, upbraiding them querulously for the clumsiness of the splint Peter had thought to affix to Hansi's leg.

"You are not fit to travel," Doctor Keidel opined at last, before putting his coat back on. "Not for many weeks."

"But we are to take the trail north with the herd in two days," Hansi said, thickly. The pupils of his eyes were already huge and he looked glassily cheerful, for Doctor Keidel had administered a good quantity of syrup of laudanum.

"And so will pigs grow wings and begin to roost in trees," Doctor Keidel responded. He held up his hand as if to block their fruitless protestations. "No, this I cannot approve for my patient!"

"But our plans depend on this!" Anna cried, wringing her hands. "There are decisions to be made that only Papa might make!"

"Well, then, someone else will have to make them," Doctor Keidel insisted. "There is not enough laudanum in Texas to spare a man the pain of a broken leg, riding in a jolting wagon all the way to Kansas."

"We might hire someone else to drive the supply wagon," Peter spoke up, from where he stood by the window. "And Mister Richter might go by stage two months from now, and meet us in Kansas, when we arrive."

"No, no," Doctor Keidel shook his head. "The break is bad, and will hardly have begun to have knitted well. I must advise against that, medically speaking."

"Then someone else must meet the Kansas buyers," Magda said. "Someone capable of bearing much responsibility."

"It's not just at the other end," Peter said earnestly. He looked troubled, for which Magda could hardly blame him. The onerous duty of trail boss would have been sufficient challenge, but now it would also fall to him and Fredi to negotiate with buyers, to step in and perform what Hansi had done so ably. "There are matters all the way along . . . matters involving money, which may only be decided by an owner, or someone of a better knowledge of the owner's mind than mine."

"Then I should go to Kansas with the herd," Anna announced, her chin lifted defiantly, before anyone had a chance to scoff. "And why not? I know Papa's business better than anyone else, save perhaps Auntie Magda."

"That's my poppet!" Hansi said with muzzy approval, amid a chorus of dismay from everyone else. "S-she does that, my clever little nun. To Kansas with the herd—just the ticket!"

"But a respectable young woman alone and unmarried among all those men!" Magda exclaimed. "Even if she is chaperoned by one of her brothers, you know what people will be saying? Oh, what will they think of her? And what will they think of us and our businesses? Even people who know us, who respect us; they will wonder. No, Hansi—that wouldn't do at all."

Anna was composed and thoughtful, the quietness in the heart of the storm around her. She merely tilted her head speculatively.

"Well then," she offered, "what if Mr. Vining and I married? Then I might accompany him and the herd to Kansas without any shred of impropriety attaching to us."

"Splendid idea!" Hansi agreed with such hearty exuberance that Magda wondered if Doctor Keidel had given him entirely too much of the drug. "Sp-splendid, Annchen! Solves the problem in one fell swoop, eh?"

There was a brief and horrified silence in the parlor for the space of a breath, or the length of time it took for everyone to draw theirs in. Peter looked stunned, as if he had been poleaxed.

Dolph leaned against the door, his eyes meeting Magda's. He would be no help, for he started laughing as if it were a fine joke upon everyone. "Oh, Cuz, you should have taken my offer seriously—there's no escape for you now!"

The color rose in Anna's cheeks. The longer this went on, Magda realized, the more hideously embarrassing for all. She raised her voice, commanding, "Enough! Enough of this! What are we thinking, to even entertain such a mad notion as this! Marriage is not a matter of convenience, something to solve a temporary reversal of our plans!"

"Well, I can't think it would be all that disastrous," Hansi insisted, even more glassy-eyed as the laudanum took deeper effect. "He's a good trusty man and she could do worse!"

"Hansi!" Magda hissed. "Don't make it worse! Doctor Keidel, did you have any notion it would affect him like this?"

"Not any in the world," Doctor Keidel returned with suave amusement. "But it does make for a more than usually interesting house call. I bid you good evening all. And if there is a wedding resulting from this, I will be enormously disappointed if I am not invited."

"See the doctor out," Magda ordered Dolph through tight lips. She directed a quelling look at her nephews, then took in Anna and Peter with another. "Now, you two, go into the garden, and sort out in privacy what you want to do about this ridiculous notion. And if you come back to the house and agree with me that it is a ridiculous notion, no one will ever say another word about it. Does everyone understand?"

Anna, her face scorched from blushing, looked across at Peter. "Will you join me in the garden, Mr. Vining?" She held out her hand, and like a sleepwalker, Peter offered her his arm. Everyone else, even the boys, murmured some kind of obedient assent to Magda's command and fled; all but Hansi, who lay on the chaise with an absurdly cheerful expression on his face.

As soon as the garden door closed, Magda shook her head, "Oh, Hansi! Whatever possessed her to make such an offer! And for you to approve? That will just make it worse, especially if he doesn't wish to marry! Now he can hardly turn it down without seeming most unchivalrous. And Anna—she will be so embarrassed!"

"Not to worry," Hansi answered cheerily, seemingly afloat on a high tide of laudanum, "He's a decent, trustworthy sort—quite sensible. Think she likes him too, so that's all right. Nothing like an old-fashioned arranged marriage, y'know! No matter that my little nun has arranged it herself! At his own pace, it would have taken him forever to get to the point!" He lay back on the chaise, but moved too abruptly for the comfort of his broken bones. "Ah, Goddamn, that hurts. 'S better this way, Magda. Lise'll be disappointed, though. I think she wanted a grand wedding at the new house. N'er mind. All her friends are here, and all the family gathered for the start of the drive. A splendid start for them, hey?"

"I do hope so," Magda answered, deeply pessimistic. She could see through the parlor window into the garden. Dusk filled it up like a cup, the bare tops of the oak trees brushed with the gold of the setting sun. Anna and Peter sat side by side on the children's wooden swing, their backs to the windows.

"What are they doing now?" Hansi asked, querulous with pain and frustration. "'Can't see from here."

"They're just talking," Magda answered with a sigh.

Peter was too stunned to do anything more than what Ma'am Becker commanded. It was as if he had taken a fall from a horse, straight and flat onto the ground, all the air knocked out of his lungs by the impact. He had offered Miss Anna his elbow, and they walked sedately out of the house. That time of the afternoon the garden was silent but for the chatter of birds high in the oak branches. Anna went towards the swing, which was rocking a little at the end of its suspending ropes. Silently Peter held it steady as she sat on it, then moved enough to one side so there was room for both to sit, squeezed closely together on the wooden seat. Marriage? Had she really suggested such a thing as a practical solution to the situation they all faced in Hansi's injury? Such a life-changing step suggested in such a calm and modest manner; it beggared his imagination. Him? Marry Anna Richter? It would be like suddenly adopting a fierce hawk as a pet, expecting it to sit tamely on your finger like a parakeet.

"I am sorry, Mr. Vining," she blurted suddenly. "It seemed like a very sensible notion. I spoke without thinking, or considering your own feelings." He could see the color rising in her cheek, between the wings of dark brown hair over her ears and the high neck of her practical day dress.

"Well . . . it doesn't happen every day to a fellow," he answered. "Although 'tis said that Queen Victoria was the one that put the question to Prince Albert. The rank, you see. She outranked him. 'Course," he added with a laugh which rang a little awkward, "it wasn't as if he could say no. She was the Queen and all. Probably came out as an order, even if she didn't really mean it that way."

"Exactly." Anna pushed her toe against the flagstones beneath, sending her end of the swing to gently sway back and fourth. "I gave no consideration to how it would sound—in front of Papa, and everyone. I expect Auntie Magda is giving us a chance, giving you a chance to think. And to speak honestly, without embarrassing either of us any further."

"It is an idea deserving of consideration," Peter ventured thoughtfully and sat silent for some moments.

"Had you thought on marriage?" Anna asked, carefully. "At all? With . . . with anyone? Such a station is not something you are disinclined towards? Or are you intent on another party?"

Peter thought back to that night by the campfire, when he and Hansi had talked long under the stars, and Hansi had let it be known that he might approve of Peter courting his formidable daughter. When they returned from Kansas, Peter had fairly held his breath every time he had encountered Miss Anna. Few enough occasions they were, too—but if there were a change in her manner towards him, he was damned if he could see it.

"I'd thought on it, in a general way, of course," he answered, "As something that might happen . . . oh, around the time that I could support a wife and a family. I was not set on anyone in particular, Miss Anna. But it was occasionally suggested to me that you and I might eventually develop an understanding. Your cousin Dolph was very often humorous about the possibility."

Anna said a very rude word; Peter laughed outright. Curiously, the idea of a pet hawk had a certain appeal. It tickled him, like a smooth drink of whiskey, the fumes of it rising into his brain. "We would always have something to talk about," he pointed out. The more he considered, the more the whole notion appealed. Anna was pretty, clever, strong-willed, and the apple of her father's eye. He liked her family, respected her father, and when he looked at the matter honestly, he liked her. Rather more than liked her; there was an edge to her that made most other girls her age seem tame and spiritless. And that brought to mind an agreeable side effect. Marrying her would, without a doubt, remove him from any chance of falling prey to his sister-in-law's marital schemes.

"Miss Anna," he said at last, "you know, I think I like the idea. I like it fine. More than fine." He smiled. "Let's get married."

"Really?" she breathed, looking sideways at him, still blushing as pink as one of Ma'am Becker's roses growing at the bottom of the garden. "Do you want to indeed, Mr. Vining?"

"I do," Peter answered stoutly. He took her fingers in his good hand, raising them to his lips. "It's a grand idea. I may as well do it proper. Miss Richter, will you do me the very significant honor of consenting to become my wife, and going with your father's cattle herd all the way to Kansas the day after tomorrow?"

"Why, Mr. Vining!" Her eyes sparkled with demure laughter. "This is so unexpected, I hardly know what is proper to say. But of course, I accept your very honorable proposal. Of marriage and cattle-herding, both." They both chuckled at that, and sat for a moment in the gently swaying swing, taking in the enormity of this commitment. Now that it was done, the better Peter thought of it, and obscurely wondered why he hadn't earlier ventured to take the bull by the horns, as it were. "We shall have to go and tell Papa," Anna said at last. "He and Auntie Magda must be on tenterhooks, wanting to know what we have decided. Poor Auntie Magda will have to set up a wedding party for us on practically no notice at all."

"Wouldn't you miss not having a splendid turnout with all the trimmings?" Peter asked, diverted. He was recollecting all the grand to-do about his brother Horace's wedding. Their mother and Miss Amelia's mother had planned for simply months.

"Oh, no," Anna shook her sleek brown head. "Too much of a fuss. And an expense. I never thought to be married at all, you see." That sentiment came as a shock to Peter, but he said nothing. "Whatever Auntie Magda may contrive in the next day will be enough for me. Enough for us, I mean." She reached for Peter's other hand, the wooden one, and curled her fingers around his. She looked very young at that moment, so terribly serious, and her voice sounded quite small.

He looked closely at her. "I promise, Miss Anna—to try and make you as happy as any woman could be."

"You will," she answered simply and rested her cheek on his shoulder. Again he thought of a hawk, settling as tamely as a pet parakeet. "Make me happy, I mean. You are everything I would have chosen in a husband."

Chapter Sixteen: *The Road of Silver and Gold*

"*I always thought it was so wonderfully romantic.*" *Lottie sighed wistfully as she and Magda sat in the parlor of the mansion that Lottie's husband had built on Turner Street, so many years later. "To marry so impetuously and to spend your honeymoon trailing the herd north! Almost as romantic as eloping, even if Auntie Elizabeth kept croaking about marrying in haste and repenting at leisure! Most folk did not even think that Cousin Anna and Cousin Peter even liked each other, so they were at least spared the usual sort of venomous gossip.*"

"*They would not have dared say anything of the sort to any of our faces.*" *Magda looked into the fire, with the austere assurance of a Roman matron or a Vestal priestess. "For your Onkel Hansi, he gave his approval most cheerfully and Pastor Altmueller agreed—although with some reluctance—to perform the marriage. I think he consented only on the account of our long friendship. Anna herself swore faithfully that she was under no duress and she had no other reason for hasty vows other than the necessity of departing according to schedule.*"

"*It still seemed very romantic,*" *Lottie said again. "But I suppose it did deprive Auntie Liesel of those excitements attendant to marrying off a daughter.*"

"*We never fussed as much, in my day,*" *Magda said, still austere. "We did things very plainly. And Anna had them as plain as I ever did; or more! She did not even wear Liesel's white silk dress, or carry flowers…*"

* * *

Magda looked in astonishment and horror at her niece and Peter Vining when they returned from the garden, swinging their hands like a pair of truant schoolchildren.

Anna spoke first, while Peter appeared as fatuously pleased as if it had all been his idea to start with. "Yes, Papa, Auntie—we have decided to be married."

"Splendid, splendid!" Hansi boomed from where he lay on the chaise. "You'll never regret it, not for a moment. Let me shake your hand, lad! You'll be happy, especially if she is as merry a wife to you as her mother is to me!"

"Papa!" Anna remonstrated, a pink blush rising in her cheeks.

"Oh my!" Magda looked from one to another of them. "Tomorrow? There is barely time to invite everyone, let alone prepare for a celebration! I suppose I should send Sam to fetch Herr Pastor Altmueller. Will he consent to perform the marriage, since there is not time enough to post the bans?"

"I'm sure he would," Hansi answered, still hearty in spite of the discomfort of his broken leg and a considerable draught of laudanum. "And ask Charley Nimitz about lending his cook and another basket of crockery to us for the day! What good to own a hotel, with a fine kitchen, if you cannot help out old friends? We'll have a fine party for you, my little nun—don't you fret."

"I'm not fretting, Papa," Anna replied. She knelt in a soft rustle of skirts so that Hansi could kiss her forehead. "I am just thinking about what I should pack and take with me on the journey. I have only a day to prepare, and the herd is much more important than some silly wedding party."

"Anna!" Magda protested, while Peter said, "Miss Anna, can you drive a two-horse team?"

"I can learn," Anna answered, unruffled. "Why do you ask?"

Peter laughed; he sounded fond and delighted. "Because William Arhelger is nearly finished with our new cook wagon. The ambulance we used last year was too light to carry all the goods necessary, so I had thought to sell it back to him; but with a little work, it can serve as a wagon for you to travel in. Very comfortable, a little private caravan on wheels." He helped Anna rise from the floor and Magda thought for the very first time that Anna's mad notion to marry might actually work.

"I should like that." Anna looked thoughtful. "Can you arrange it in time?"

"I will go to his shop and see to it right this instant," Peter answered. There was a breathless moment when they looked at each other, excitement kindling like summer lightning, flashing pale in the nighttime clouds.

"You should call me by my name," Anna said after a moment, "since we are to be wed."

"Of course, Miss—Anna." Peter still sounded rather dazed. "And you should call me by my own name, as well, since we need not maintain such formality as all that, after tomorrow."

"I will send Sam for Pastor Altmueller," Magda interjected.

Young Sam was sitting behind the counter, kicking his heels against the legs of a tall stool. He'd been so happily engrossed in his book that he came up from it with a sigh as he marked his place with a thumb. "Pastor A.? Is something the matter, Mama?" he asked.

"No," Magda answered, "only that Anna and Cousin Peter wish to marry before departing with the herd."

Sam's eyes widened artlessly. "Poor Cousin Peter—I did not think she cared two pins about him."

"Go, Sam," Magda commanded before Sam could venture any more tactless sympathy for his cousin within Anna's hearing. "And run—we have not much time. As soon as you return, I must go down to the Nimitz's, so do not take your time talking with Pastor Altmueller about books!"

As her son departed with his hands in his pockets, whistling merrily and tunelessly, she looked towards the chaise where Hansi had become suddenly very quiet. He lay with his head back, snoring gently. "At last, some good from that dose. I had begun to doubt it had any efficacy at all. What about a wedding ring, Annchen? It is the custom."

"We'll take one out of stock," Anna answered, all practicality.

"And put it on my account," Peter answered grandly. "I'm sure I can afford it."

Anna tucked a blanket around her father's shoulders. "Dearest Papa, I hope he wakes up in time. It will be so undignified, having a wedding with him snoring away in the corner."

Magda took down a small ring of keys from the hook just inside the workroom door. The tiniest of them unlocked a small glass case which Vati had once used to display his best handiwork on a little tray lined with dusty purple velvet. They still had several of Vati's old pocket watches in that case, as well as a selection of plain gold wedding bands *("We might as well have a stock of them, people are always getting married," Hansi had pointed out reasonably)* and some modestly jeweled rings and pins which customers had used to pay off an account, or traded for goods. She opened the case as Peter and Anna came in from the parlor.

Peter was saying, "If you can sort out what to bring along by this afternoon, I'll bring the wagon over from Arhelgers and give you a driving lesson."

"If Auntie can spare me from the store," Anna looked composed and demure. "Oh, any of the plain gold rings that fit me will do. I think they were all priced the same."

Peter looked over her shoulder. "What about an engagement ring, then? Will that little one fit your hand?"

"This?" Magda lifted out the one he pointed out, a narrow gold band set with a chip of garnet and two miniscule pearls. Anna slipped it onto her finger; it went on easily enough.

Peter said grandly, "Add it to my account, then. Can you see to the other? I must go to Arhelger and let him know about the wagon." He beat a hasty retreat after Sam.

Anna put the gold band into her apron pocket and took down the account book. She opened the ink bottle and made a careful entry, remarking as she did so, "Well, that was fortunate. How long had you had that little ring in Opa's case? It's not the sort of thing that anyone would buy, ordinarily."

Magda shook her head, in disbelief. How could Anna be so casual, so very level-headed about this matter? She was about to tie her life, her happiness, her whole future to another person, yet seemed to see it as a matter for the account books.

"Anna . . . Annchen," she began to say, choked with an emotion she could neither define nor give proper voice to. "Are you sure of this—this decision to marry? And to marry not for love, but to maintain proper convention?"

"Yes, I am, Auntie." Anna wiped ink off the pen and re-corked the ink bottle, before setting both carefully away. "I am sure." She clasped her hands together and appeared very serious. "I have given it much careful thought, you see. I cannot claim to love him extraordinarily well at this moment . . ."

"Oh, Annchen!" Magda was revolted at the cold-blooded way that her niece considered these things, but Anna merely held up her hand and continued, ". . . but I like him very well and think that I could come to love him, as much as Mama cares for Papa, or you for Uncle Carl. As he would come to love me in time, as we share our lives as all married folk do. He suits me, Auntie! He does not speak to me as one speaks to an idiot child. When he sets aside mockery, he is very kind. After our little Rose," for a brief moment Anna's eyes looked bright with unshed tears, but there was a wistful smile on her lips, "on that day that we buried our Rosalie, he was most especially comforting. I had not expected such sensible consolation as he offered me on that day. But so he did, and I began to think most favorably of him. Besides," Anna sniffed, "he cares so little for himself! Like a man, never thinking of eating well, or putting a coat on his back when it is nearly freezing outside. Like one of Dolph's poor dogs, all skin and ribs. I do want to care for him, Auntie. I think I would be well rewarded for doing so. And," her eyes were now as bright as stars, "oh, to go north and share in the same adventures! I would like that extraordinarily well . . . almost as much as being married to him! Think of it, Auntie—and Mama might not be able to use her fears and megrims against me going, for I would be with my husband! How marvelous that would be!"

"You are sure of this?" Magda asked with enormous tenderness. "And that you are certain you will come to love him, as is proper in marriage? He is as dear to me as you and deserves no less a chance to be happy in marriage."

"I am certain, Auntie." Anna went on tip-toes and kissed Magda's cheek. Her hand closed on the pocket of her apron, as if she felt the weight of the gold band there. "I will take such care of him as he needs and deserves. Oh, my, I must pack! There is so much to be done, if we are to leave the day after tomorrow. I expect I will need to take a straw-tick and bedding for myself! Will you be able to manage in the store without my help, for the rest of the day?"

"So have the children and I managed all along," Magda answered with a sigh, for there would be much to do, even to invite those old friends who would be in town at mid-week.

So much indeed; it seemed that the next day and a half passed in a frantic dream, an exhausting yet oddly exhilarating dream. Magda's feet and shins ached from constantly running: from the shop to wait upon customers, to the parlor to tend Hansi, into the kitchen to placate Mrs. Schmidt, up the stairs to advise Anna on what to pack for a three-month long wagon journey north, and back down the stairs again at the silvery jingle of the shop bell. She suspected that everyone else in the household felt much the same, for there was something of the same look of exhausted triumph on all those faces in the candle-lit parlor. Even Fredi, who arrived at the last minute reeking of trail dust and horse sweat; even he looked tired. He, Charley, Dolph, Magda and her children, and Hansi lying on the chaise with his leg propped up on a heavy bolster, witnessed the marriage. Herr Pastor Altmueller's aged and beautiful voice read out the vows as if it were the first time he had ever read them or they all had ever listened to them.

Anna wore her best afternoon dress, blue satin with a darker blue draped overskirt and tight-sleeved jacket. It was set off with a small modish hat that sat rakishly tilted forward by a high-pinned knot of her hair gathered at the back of her head. The curled ostrich-feather trim on her hat barely reached as high as Peter's cravat stickpin, as the two of them stood side by side. Peter's hair and mustaches gleamed as pale as polished ivory under the candle-light. Magda thought he looked a little dazed, distracted by the rush of events and the last-minute emergencies attendant on their morning departure. She, herself was so weary that the wedding party, under lamplight in the garden, passed in a blur of faces, music, and happy voices. There was dancing under lanterns that swayed gently in a cool spring breeze that sprang up at twilight. Hansi, carried out on the chaise so he could enjoy as much of his eldest-daughter's wedding party as possible, had sent for bottles of champagne; cool and dry, straw-gold and full of tiny fizzing bubbles that rose from the bottom of Charley Nimitz's hotel glassware. Magda drank enough of it to feel mildly elevated and to muddle this evening with other celebrations held in Vati's garden, with the last of the pear-tree's delicate blossoms falling to the rich earth below.

Out of the corner of her eye, she thought she saw Rosalie and Robert, ghosts in wedding white and Confederate grey, dancing in each others arms as if there were no one else present. There were her sons, Dolph at twenty and fifteen year-old Sam already as tall and fair-haired as their father—and was Carl not there also, smiling his gentle and reserved smile at her on their own wedding day? Hannah, grave and serene, danced under the nearest lantern with Charley's son, the boy who had caught the diphtheria and nearly died of it during that last year of the war. Hannah laughed at something young Chester was saying to her. Poor lad, his health was still very delicate; Sophie and Charley worried quietly over him.

Lantern light gleamed momentarily from a pair of someone's spectacles and reminded her of Vati. Dearest Vati, whose love for them was the constant bedrock underlying all their lives. Vati would have adored this celebration, this gathering. He would have sat in his favorite wooden garden chair with the other greybeards, watching with approval as his oldest granddaughter married an American, kin to Magda's own husband, whom Vati had loved as a son. So would Mrs. Helene, who had dressed Magda for her own wedding, taken her firmly in hand and led her downstairs. *"Who would you wish to grow old with?"* Dear Mrs. Helene had asked her, during that breathless and fraught period when she had been caught between two suitors, two men of honor whom she had held in equal affection, who had both tendered offers of marriage.

How confused she had been, how uncertain; until her sleeping mind had told her which man was her soul mate, the man she wished to grow old with. It turned out not to be Charley, the charming man of business, everyone's friend and no man's enemy, who had threaded an easy way between opposite parties in the late war, the war whose conflicting loyalties had tormented the man she had chosen to marry. She never was given the opportunity to grow old with him, after all. His implacable enemy had found an opportunity to murder her dear husband. *"Be happy,"* Carl Becker had said to her, as the Hanging Band led him away. *"Look after the children."*

And so she had, obedient to his last wish. How she had come to love him, to give her heart unreservedly to him. Oh, that Anna could come to know that kind of love, but be spared from the devastation that came when love was no longer there.

She had so looked forward to growing old with him; so cruel that it would have been denied to her. But Vati had not been given the gift of growing old with Mutti, nor Margaret with either Peter's father, or Doctor Williamson. Perhaps love was all that was given, love for a time and conditional upon larger events. If love was all that there was, best to take it and squeeze all the juice of happiness, like an apple in the press, or an orange with the little olive-wood reamer. Love, a gift that is there for a time, take it up with both hands and savor the sweetness of the juice. Savor the day, and the sweetness, every day; for at the end of things, that may be all that the fates have granted to you! That and the children that came of that love; her brothers and Liesel, Dolph and Sam, Hannah and Lottie, Peter and Anna.

Love and today—all that could be counted on for a certainty, love and the constant affection of old friends. Anna, dearest of kin, almost a daughter of her own, friend and ally; would that she would find happiness in this odd marriage, in this strange land! Magda took another drink of the champagne in the glass in her hand, hoped that it would work for her niece and the man Anna had chosen for herself, hoped that Anna knew well her own heart and Peter's, too. He was a good lad, whom the war had treated most cruelly and marked for life with scars that would never fade.

* * *

With thoughts of morning's departure and a day of regular work looming over all, Anna's wedding party did not last as far into the night as Rosalie's had. It dwindled to a handful by midnight, as guests made their excuses. As the party slowed to a small and exhausted scattering of family, Dolph came and fetched Peter. On a last quiet check of the packed kitchen wagon and the ambulance fitted out for Anna, Dolph had discovered that one of their saddle horses, intended for the remuda and eventual sale in Kansas, had chewed a hole in a sack of grain and eaten enough to have given himself a case of the bloat. By the time they had dealt with this emergency and returned to the house, the garden was darkened. Mellow lamplight glowed faintly behind the upstairs windows. Peter heard voices from the kitchen; Ma'am Becker and Mrs. Schmidt, accompanied by the clatter of crockery. He looked around the corner of the parlor to bid a good night to Hansi, who was settling with a groan on the chaise to sleep. Doctor Keidel had forbidden him to attempt the stairs.

For about the first time that day, it sank in on Peter that he and Hansi were now kin; that stubborn, ambitious Dutch teamster and man of business was his father-in-law; he and Anna were legally man and wife. All the elation, the excitement that he had felt over the last two days abruptly drained away.

Oh, lord, thought Peter, *Was that such a good idea after all?* He assured himself it was as he trudged wearily up the narrow staircase, but he hardly felt convinced. It had seemed like a fine impulsive notion when the two of them agreed to marry two days ago. It had even seemed quite the thing when they stood up before Pastor Altmueller some hours ago, Anna trim and tidy in dark blue and her cheeks the delicate pink of primroses. He felt a fine and fierce affection and pride; such a clever and beautiful woman, a woman he could be honored to introduce as his wife!

A complexion like fine rich cream she had; that afternoon, his heart had skipped with a strange sort of excitement—soon he would know if the rest of her was as luscious. But then she would see him, see him entire, see that scarred stump of an arm; and he couldn't banish away that little niggling fear that she might be revolted, would think less of him, knowing that he was not whole.

He paused on the landing at the top of the stairs. Sometime during that interminable day, Ma'am Becker had asked him something about whether they wished to spend their first night as a married couple in the little Sunday House on Creek Street? He couldn't think why it would matter, and anyway, the wagons and horses were here. What was the sense of going all the way over to that tiny cottage, when they would just have to return here in the morning? He couldn't think why Ma'am Becker had even suggested it, or why she seemed disappointed when he said no.

A band of faint light showed underneath the door of the large guest room that he and Dolph had always shared after Hansi had removed his family to San Antonio. Dolph, with much ribald comment, had moved his small luggage and his possessions into Sam's bedroom.

"You're lucky we're away in the morning, else I would have the fellows give you a right good chivaree," he threatened, with a grin from ear to ear. "I may yet, Cuz!"

"Better not," Peter scowled. "Think of what your ma would have to say about that!"

"We'd be on the trail to Kansas, before she could say much," Dolph answered. "No, I'll take mercy on you, Cuz. What Anna would say doesn't bear thinking, not when you'll be spending the nights with her from here on out," Dolph added with coarse good humor.

Thinking on that, Peter sighed most wretchedly. Here it was, and the bride was supposed to be the one dreading the wedding night. Again, Peter wondered what mad recklessness had led him to this.

He tapped on the door very lightly, but the catch was not set and it slipped ajar under that slight pressure. He stood hesitantly in the doorway and gaped at the sight of Anna. She sat unconcernedly in the middle of the bed, two ledgers in her lap and a pen in her hand. She was in her nightgown, and her brown hair tumbled around her face and down her back. She looked all of twelve years old.

"Is the horse fit for the trail tomorrow?" she asked with great interest, "or shall we have to leave it behind? Auntie and Porfirio will be so disappointed. He was counting on a good price for them all."

"Dolph thinks the wretched beast will be fit in a couple of days," Peter answered, taken aback. "We'll go slow, of course . . . and use it gently, if at all."

"Good," Anna sighed, utterly practical. She corked the ink bottle and closed the topmost ledger, placed them on the night table, and regarded Peter with a coldly assessing eye. "You look tired. You should come to bed."

"I . . ." Peter began, but she clicked her tongue against her teeth.

"Close the door, then." She slithered to the side of the bed and stood up, aswirl in an ocean wave of muslin ruffles and lace. He couldn't help briefly seeing her bare feet and legs as she did so—creamy and perfect, like the rest of her. "A long day, and a longer one tomorrow, and all the days after that, looking after Papa's cows!"

Utterly confident, she came to him and calmly took his good coat from where he held it, draped over his wooden arm. She put it onto a wooden hanger and set it on a peg in the wardrobe, and then—to Peter's astonishment—she began undoing the buttons of his best waistcoat, as calmly as if she performed the duties of a gentleman's valet every day. Clever woman, she perceived his feelings at once and said with an exasperated yet fond sigh, "Mr. Vin—Peter. I know about the duties of a wife, in the marriage bed. Truly I do, although I have not experienced them.

I know . . . of those things that a loving husband and wife are supposed to do, and I do not think you are disinclined. This is true?"

Peter laughed, a short and wry bark of laughter. "You've no idea," he began, but Anna interjected, "But I do! You are tired and this has all happened so very suddenly." To his astonishment, she had slipped his good waistcoat off his shoulders. "Will you want this in Kansas?" she asked. "I think so, to meet with the cattle buyers. You shall need to be at your best. Alas, clothes do make the man, in the eyes of the world. Papa tells me so and so does Captain Nimitz. The stories he can tell, about the people who have come to his hotel! And the secret things that their clothing and bearing may tell to the observer with a knowing eye!" She found a hanger for the waistcoat and set it away, adding, "Of course, I can tell the same of the many customers who came to our shop! I will pack these in the morning—clothes should air after being worn. Sit. Sit, sit, and take off your boots."

Peter obeyed, thinking that it was a strange thing, beyond his knowledge of the world, to accept ministrations of the sharp-tongued and ferocious Miss Anna. She took his boots—his work boots, worn for his duties on horseback—and put them in the wardrobe. He had not thought when he came to Friedrichsburg this time, that he would have any social obligations, so he had left his good town shoes at the Becker place. Dolph had the house rebuilt over the winter, between cattle-drives, and Peter had a room in the new stone-built wing overlooking the white cloud of the apple orchard. Berg, that strange and abrupt-speaking stonemason, came out of the hills in his ragged work clothes and his tools in a pack on his back and stayed at the place all winter to oversee the work that Dolph could now pay men to do. Berg, who had made Peter's arm for him, the arm that made him nearly whole again; at least, folk did not stare at him in the street any more, stare at the pinned-up sleeve and the hand that was there no longer, as they had ever since the day that a harried Army surgeon had ordered him to bite down on a thick leather strap and went to work with his shining sharp surgical saw.

Oh, God—what to do next. They were married, and married folk shared such intimacies! He cringed, to think of Miss Anna . . . to think of Anna seeing such things and being repulsed! But instead, she came back from the wardrobe and sat on the bed next to him, swinging her feet like a small child, saying in such a candid and earnest manner, "I told you once, I think. You were not your arm. When I see you, I see you, yourself—your character and intellect, your conversation. I do not see that limb which is not there. It is not relevant. Auntie Magda has a scar on her cheek, but it does not change the person she is. Opa was so near of sight that he could hardly see farther than the book in his hands. Yet that did not change anything about him. It is merely some aspect, hardly worthy of consideration save in passing. So we are married." She looked sideways at him, her eyes as dark in the low lamp-glow as Daddy Hurst's trail-coffee. "You should not fear that I should be so shallow. I know who you are and accept that without reserve. Did I not say vows, before my family and friends? Then let me add another vow, a private one, between the two of us." She reached for his hands, the live and the wooden together, holding them together and clasped between hers. Peter looked at her fingers, soft childish hands, well-tended although her fingertips were stained somewhat with ink, which not all scrubbing could remove entirely. "I promise," she seemed to search for words and choose them carefully, "that from this time forward, I will not use sharp and clever words to tease and bait you in front of others. Not my family or friends, or even my cousins. I did so, ever since the day we met, part for my own amusement and because it amused others. I never considered that you might find such wit to be cruel or hurtful."

"Never, Miss—Anna," Peter shook his head, oddly moved. "Never— for I also took pleasure in our contests of wit and words."

"Oh, good," Anna laughed with uninhibited relief. The dimples showed in both her cheeks and Peter thought how much delight he took in seeing her laugh like that. "I had hoped you did, but I also considered that you might be dissembling, hiding such pain from us all. So," she continued, "I shall never torment you in front of other people. And on matters in which we disagree—and I know that we will, since we are two people of divergent experience and opinions—I would take care to make our discussion of such matters private."

"Ah," said Peter with a wry chuckle, "you would only take me out behind the woodshed for a whipping . . . discretely. I appreciate that . . . Anna. Less embarrassing all the way around!"

"I would ask you for reciprocal courtesy when it comes to our disagreements," Anna continued. She wore a slight frown, either of displeasure at being interrupted, or of concentration on the care she took with her words. "It is no light thing to be married, for a woman. And I have seen it to go very badly where there is neither liking nor respect between husband and wife. We should, I think, be like sword and shield for each other. One to protect, the other to defend against such woes the world inflicts upon us, as we stand together."

"I the sword and you the shield?" Peter was touched by her care and honesty, also that she would hit on that very chivalrous simile.

Anna nodded. "Or the other way around; you have no notion of how women may be so quietly vicious over the teacups. Are we agreed, then?" Peter nodded and she sighed rather happily, taking both his hands closer to her breast. She smelled deliciously of rose-water. Perhaps they had done well with this marriage after all, although for the life of him he still could not believe this was really happening to him.

They sat so for some minutes, until Anna said at last, "You should not put off preparing for sleep, you know . . . dreading to show me those scars which I know you must have." Such honesty fair took his breath away, her accurate reading of that fear he did not even dare voice to himself. "I shall not flinch," Anna added, soft but implacable. Without further fuss or ado, she began unfastening the buttons on his shirt-cuffs and those at his throat. There was no going back, Peter told himself. No going back, no more than he could have turned around at the edge of that Pennsylvania wheat field, in that breathless moment when the fortunes of the South were at high tide mark. He pulled the hem of his best white linen shirt out of his trouser waistband, pulled the garment over his head, knowing with a kind of despair that she would see . . . everything, and not be able to look upon him without horror or disgust. No matter how well she schooled her expressions ... how could she help feeling anything else? He did not want to look at her, but could not look away.

To his utter and continuing relief, Anna took the shirt from him, turned it right side out again, and folded it carefully, her face lit with nothing other than a mild and clinical interest.

"Oh, so that's how Mr. Berg designed it," she commented. "How very clever—with buckles so that you can put in on and fasten it with one hand. I would have thought some kind of lacing, almost like my corsets . . . but then you couldn't manage it, with only one hand, could you?"

"I suppose not," Peter answered. His chest felt tight, frozen, as if he dared not breathe.

Anna touched the first of the buckles, very lightly. "I can help you with it," she offered, "if you don't mind. It must be rather uncomfortable, at the end of a long day."

"It aches, sometimes," Peter ventured, past the tightness in his chest. "Hot compresses help with the worst. For months afterwards, I could feel my wrist hurting. Even though it wasn't there any more, it still hurt."

Anna unfastened the last of the buckles on the straps that held the upper part of Berg's creation close around what the surgeon had left of his forearm. Even though the inside was padded with a knitted, sock-like garment, there were still alternate red or pale welts on the flesh beneath.

"It's heavier than I thought," Anna observed, holding the wooden arm as he slipped it off. "Where should I put it? Close by?"

"Yes," he answered. He always felt a little strange putting the arm off, superstitiously nervous about having it out of his sight, as if it were some kind of talisman that he could not bear to let go of. And perhaps it was, at that. He peeled off the sock-padding, feeling that he may as well be hung for a sheep as a lamb, feeling her curious eyes upon that scarred truncation. "So, what think you of this, Mrs. Vining?" he asked bleakly.

"I think it is truly the most ghastly and hideous mutilation of human flesh that mankind ever suffered," she answered, seriously; but there was a humorous glint in her eyes. Peter gaped for one endless moment and then he began to laugh. It was as if a great bubble of morbid self-consciousness had been pierced. He had been fixated on his amputated limb, worried to a ridiculous degree about it, but Anna had unerringly put it into the right proportion again. He whooped with laughter until his chest ached, laughed to tears, knowing that Anna laughed also. He held her close as they lay across the bed, convulsed with shared laughter. It didn't matter that he didn't have two whole arms, only that she was there.

When he could finally speak again, he whispered, "'She loved me for the dangers that I had pass'd, and I loved her that she did pity them . . .'"

"Oh, I believe we shall do better than they did," Anna answered firmly. "Much, much better."

"In the morning, they began the trip north," Magda said to Lottie. "And several days after that, Fredi followed after with the second herd. From that day, our feet were set on a path of silver and gold, as your Onkel Hansi promised. He did well with cattle—in the years after we prospered, as if everything turned to gold at our touch. Our store, the freighting business, the cattle and horse herds . . . those all worked together, like the legs of a sturdy stool. Hansi considered such ideas for business as your cousins and your brothers had, and invested in them. In some years our own cattle were only a small portion of those that we sent north. Hansi and Fredi would contract to take this or that owner's herd to Kansas. They would hire the cook, the drovers and the wranglers and negotiate the selling price at the

end of the trail—all for a percentage of the profits. Anna and Peter went up the trail often, or as often as she could, before their children were born."

"I remember how she did not sing nursery rhymes to Henry when he had the colic," Lottie smiled, reminiscently. *"Rather, she recited the multiplication tables to him. Do you recall when we visited Onkel Hansi's house after Christian was born? There she was in Onkel Hansi's study, nursing Christian, holding him with one arm as she wrote a letter for Onkel Hansi with the other hand, while Henry made paper boats out of merchant circulars at her feet."*

"I have always thought, how very happy they looked, the day after their wedding." Magda looked into the fire, while rain whispered against the windows. *"How strange and ill-omened their wedding seemed to be at first, and yet they seemed so content with each other—he sitting next to her on the wagon-seat with his pony trailing behind, showing her how to drive, his hand over hers on the reins."* Magda laughed, short and wry. *"Your Aunt was frantic, of course—once she heard of this mad adventure and madder marriage. She dashed off letter after letter to me and dispatched Jacob and George at once, with a spring-wagon, to bring Hansi home. She would have sent them after Anna, as well, but Hansi put his food down. Or he would have, if he had been capable of standing. 'I'll have to talk sense to Lise' he told me as they carried him to the wagon on a litter, 'for she will be out of her mind with worry. As if our little nun didn't have a cooler head on her shoulders than any three young misses her age! Why don't you come to San Antonio and hold her hand for a while?'*

"'Why not indeed?' I told him. "What of the store?'

"'What of it?' he told me. 'Come in the winter, when the trail season is over. Let young Sam and Jacob run it for a while. Sam is a good, steady, reliable lad and Jacob is courting young Miss Schultz. He would, I think, like to settle down, and she helps her Papa in his store. Be a good help to you, she would.'

"'Everything is changing,' I said to him, 'and I don't think I like it much.'

"Your uncle looked at me and growled, 'Everything changes, Margaretha. It's to our advantage to know that, and change to meet circumstances. What would we be now—and where would we be if we had never dared to leave Albeck?'

"'Home,' I said to him. When the boys settled the litter in the back of the spring-wagon, your uncle looked down to me and said, 'Well . . . you

should see the fine place your boy made of Brother Carl's place. There's a home, if you like it.'"

"I loved it at once," Lottie said, softly. "Was it very changed, Mama? When we returned at last?"

"It was," Magda answered. "It was changed, but I loved it as much as ever."

"Whose idea was it that we should move to San Antonio, to Onkel Hansi's house?" Lottie bent her still-fair head over her embroidery frame as she and her mother talked. "I cannot recall, was it before Jacob married Miss Schultz? I thought it quite unfair at the time, as if just because he married, you should give up the store and Vati's house to him!"

"I did nothing of the sort," Magda answered, sternly. "Generally it is accounted a good thing not to have two mistresses in the same house! And Jacob marrying was not the reason. I fell ill of the grippe that winter and was a long time recovering. There was so much work in the store; it seemed as if those tasks were endless and never done. I felt so wearied all the time! Finally, your brothers and Onkel Hansi insisted that you and your sister and I come and spend the summer at your father's house. Dolph would be away on the trail north, and he would take Sam with him, while we would manage the property in his absence. It would be perfectly safe, for he employed many hands and not all would join him on the trail! Then in the fall, we would go to San Antonio so that you and Hannah could go to school there."

"That was more to comfort Auntie Liesel with our company, was it not?" Lottie asked.

Her mother nodded. "Not entirely; Grete benefited by your companionship. I think she was terribly lonely, then. Such a sweet child, but her sojourn with the Indians had left her with very odd manners and habits. Hannah had already attended the Ursuline school and had been very happy there, so it seemed quite natural that you two should join her when you were old enough." Magda sighed. "Your Aunt was more cast down, not by Anna marrying so suddenly, but because Peter took her afterwards to Austin, to live in his mother's house. She and your Onkel Hansi both felt her absence."

"Onkel Hansi always had trouble keeping a secretary who could keep up with him!" Lottie giggled. "I see then . . . he trusted you."

"I was certainly kept busy enough," Magda answered, and Lottie giggled again.

"It seemed perfectly splendid, Mama. Those years—summers in the Hills, Christmas and school holidays at Onkel Hansi's, or visiting Cousin

Anna and Cousin Peter and Opa's old house for the Fourth of July! But I loved Papa's house the best. I felt as if I knew it well, before I ever set foot in it."

"So you would, my dearest child," Magda answered tenderly. "For you listened to us all speak of it . . . but still, it was much changed when we returned at last."

"It seemed like a palace to me." Lottie's face glowed with nostalgic fervor. "An enchanted palace in a forest of flowering trees! But I had not seen a real palace, so I believe I had nothing for comparison then!"

Her mother snorted. "It was but a simple farmhouse—a palace only because your father built it for me and I loved him so very dearly! Dolph turned it into a true palace."

* * *

Dolph was busy with organizing the spring roundup so he sent Daddy Hurst at the reins of the trusty two-horse ambulance for Magda and the children. A freight wagon, heavily laden with such things as Magda wished to take with them, had already departed some days before that blustery March afternoon. Two young Mexican riders—nephews or sons of Porfirio—also came to escort the ambulance as outriders.

"Mistah Dolph, Mistah Peter, dey take no chances," Daddy Hurst explained with grim austerity, "'bout dem raiding Injuns. Dey inclined to b'lieve de worse . . . even if dere be plenty o' sojers along de Santone road. We leave fust ting in de morning, Ma'am, we be dere by twilight."

Dolph had also sent a pony for Sam, to that young man's inexpressible delight. In the morning, Daddy Hurst solicitously handed Magda and her daughters up to the little door at the back of the spring wagon, and stowed their many carpet bags and valises in the places set aside for luggage. They had kept one of the beds with which it had been originally fitted, now piled with quilts and pillows against the cold, and a narrow padded bench along the other side. Magda wearily swung her feet up and reclined as Hannah covered her with some of the bedding. The canvas wagon cover was drawn tight against the chill.

"You look tired, Mama," she said. Magda smiled at her oldest daughter's concern. At sixteen, Hannah was sweet-faced and serene, as composed and curiously mature as Anna had been at that age. "You can rest all the way, if you like."

271

Magda patted Hannah's hand. "You were always happy to be going home, weren't you, Hannah-my-chick?"

Hannah settled herself on the padded bench opposite, her head tilting thoughtfully as Daddy Hurst chirruped to the horses. "Is it really our home, after having stayed away so long?" she asked. "We were sent away before Lottie was born and she is almost nine. I have lived longer at Opa's than my father's house, so I wonder now, Mama—where is home, really?"

"Where we're going, Nannie!" Lottie bounced in excitement next to her sister, whom she called by the baby name that she used when she was small and couldn't speak clearly. "I can hardly wait! We've been as close as Comfort, but Dolph said then that half the inside didn't have a roof and last year he said the bunkhouse wasn't finished and so there was no room for us! He sounded as if he didn't wish us to come."

"Until it was all as perfect for us as he could make it," Hannah said, with perfect assurance. Magda smiled at her daughters and lay back on the pillows. Hannah and Dolph had been much in conference this last year, two heads bent together above the catalogues and circulars every time that Dolph had come to visit Friedrichsburg, if the two of them were not slipping away to Mr. Tatsch's workshop to order this or that bit of fine furniture for the house. She felt a rush of affection for them—they were good and loving children, all those she had born to Carl Becker; all of them different, all of them loved with the same knowledgeable affection. And now they loved and cared for her with something of the same solicitude. She was so tired, so weary, so hopeful of setting down those burdens and resting for a while!

She had felt this same dreadful lassitude, the same empty exhaustion, just before Lottie was born. The Confederate Army had confiscated the farm, thrown them all off Carl Becker's property, told them to take what they could carry and leave. Those soldiers had let them pile a few things into the ramshackle cart they hauled muck in, and hitched it to their oldest horse. This, on top of her husband's murder, was almost too great a blow to endure for Magda; not one tragedy but the accumulation of all of them. She had withdrawn to an upper bedroom of Vati's house for weeks.

This time, the weariness that followed upon the grippe had held her paralyzed with exhaustion. She dreaded the thought of being confined by her weakness to upstairs, like Liesel, and forced herself, over and over, to do business as she had always done. Until she fainted one mid-morning in the shop; Hansi had come roaring in like a winter gale after Sam and Jacob sent for him. "You will kill yourself," he said sternly, "with lack of rest and caring consideration for all but yourself."

"But the store!" she had pleaded.

"The store will care for itself in the hands of Jacob and my new daughter, sister Magda. It is no longer a delicate child demanding constant attendance." He looked beyond her, "Besides, our interests now have greater needs than you being available to measure out half a pound of sugar for Mrs. Arhelger and dance attendance upon Mrs. Schmidt as she makes up her mind between six yards of blue calico, or six yards of red. What do you think of another store, Magda? Or more than one?" Magda thought of the obligations she had to deal with in keeping a single store, of running between the shop and the house; Hansi read the expression on her face and began to laugh. "No, not for you to run it, you silly goose! To establish it, to organize the stock and the goods, to train Sam and Elias to run it . . . and then if you like and it does well, to do it again!"

"Where?" Magda asked.

Her brother-in-law only put on his most thoughtful and speculative expression. "Well, wherever you would think would make us the most money. But only when you are rested and fit!" Hansi had promised expansively. "Go home," he had then urged her. "Go home and rest. Potter and garden about the place that your son has reclaimed, enjoy the cool weather of the hill country! Then come to San Antonio in the fall, when the heat of the year has broken, and be useful once again. You wish for work, Magda—there is work enough! We are rich enough now to be able to pick and choose among the work that pleases us to do, not that we must to, in order to put bread and meat and milk on the table for our children!"

"We are rich?" Magda gasped. Of all he had said, this was the thing that had taken her attention.

Hansi had laughed again. "Yes, we are rich. That is one thing. But staying rich—that is another! These Yankees, they have no idea! Rest you then, Magda. In the fall when young Dolph returns to his father's land, come to San Antonio and I will show you what work it is to remain rich!

Thinking on that, Magda pulled the covering closer, against the north wind that seeped around the edges of the wagon cover. They would be home by the end of the day at the brisk pace that Daddy Hurst set to the horses. Home, as fast as the spring-wagon ambulance and its swift, swaying passage could take them—how much swifter than that torturous plodding journey on that dreadful day when they had been cast out! Destitute, hungry and harried, with her children heart-broken and carrying their particular pets and possessions, she with Lottie in her belly and fearing that this dreadful journey might make her miscarry of that last of her husband's children . . .

'*Take care of the children,*' he had told her, his last words to her as the Hanging Band took him away. "*Be happy.*' And he had looked over his shoulder and softly sung a verse from one of the Sangerbund pieces, the prisoners' chorus from *Fidelio*. How he had loved Sangerbund! How he had loved his children and her, and the place he had built for them. Now they had reclaimed and rebuilt his loving work. At last, after nine years, she and the younger children were returning.

By afternoon, Lottie vibrated like a taut fiddle string with excitement. Magda, who had dozed most of the way rocked gently by the swaying ambulance, finally permitted her to sit next to Daddy Hurst on the driver's bench, so that she could see ahead, over the backs of the horses, past Sam and Dolph's mounted escort.

"The shops are newer than I recall—and there are many more houses," Magda observed, as they rolled through Comfort. "When the war was over, I thought that many might not dare return. Even the Altgelts went to San Antonio. At least the Stielers and the Steves remain. Poor Mrs. Boerner, to lose a brother and a husband both! She died, you know. In childbirth, when she heard of what had happened on the Nueces to Tegener's company. They did not want to take the loyalty oath, so they meant to go to Mexico and join the Union army...."

"Like Uncle Johann," Hannah nodded, somberly.

"Yes," Magda answered. "I wouldn't have blamed any of them for never coming back. We're almost to the Browns. They went north, to Missouri. Their place was never much to look at!" Magda laughed, past the ache in her heart at that memory. "Your father took me to see them, when he first brought me here. I was horrified! They lived like the poorest sort of peasants, with a pig in the yard, and no glass in the windows, nothing of any kind of beauty or comfort."

"I expect that would be theirs." Hannah craned her head to look out the front of the ambulance, where the canvas was rolled back. "Over there, to the north of the road in a clearing between the trees. It looks like there was a stone chimney, and a pile of logs. It's all quite ruinous, Mama."

"And very little worse than when the Browns lived there," Magda pointed out. "I am surprised you can tell the difference. That was cruel of me to say, Hannah-my-chick, when Mrs. Brown was the only one to have been kind to us on that awful day." Her eyes filled, and Hannah patted her knee, under the quilts laid over it.

"I remember," she said, simply. "I remember. We were so hungry and she came after us on the road and brought us food. Mrs. Brown had the courage to be good. It's funny, Mama—everyone talks about such virtues, and what a wonderful thing they are, and yet, so few people actually have the courage in the face of such adversity. Isn't it curious, they are rarely the people we have been led to expect such exemplary virtues from! She did look so funny, Mama," and Hannah laughed, not out of unkindness, but rather fond affection, "so funny, in her ragged dress and bare feet, on the back of a mule! And she bullied the soldiers into fetching us water and to let us go slowly afterwards! She was fearless and so kind!"

"She and her husband were good friends," Magda responded. "Your father thought much of Brown—though I could scarce think why! I was shamed that I had thought so ill of them, and yet alone of all of our neighbors . . . "

"The spirit was with her," Hannah said, "and made her strong, daring to walk among the lions on our behalf, trusting that they would not harm her."

Startled by the fervor in Hannah's voice, Magda looked at her daughter's face, thinking—not for the first time—that there was something a little otherworldly about Hannah, as if she heard voices that no one else could hear, knew things that no one else could know.

From beside Daddy Hurst, Lottie called, "Oh, Mama, Nannie, look! There's ever so many cows! And horses, too! Are they all ours?"

"I think so, Lottchen," Magda answered, putting back the covers. She sat up, turning in the seat so that she could see through the front of the ambulance. "Although our property begins in another mile or so. The road was never so fine before, it was little more than wagon tracks worn through the grass. There were some places where your father and some of our neighbors rolled stones into some of the low places to make a level crossing . . . but nothing so level as this."

"Ben' a lot o' folk movin' 'long dis-here road," Daddy Hurst chuckled. "Not all foah de R-B Ranch, neither! Look you dere, Miz Lottie, Miz Becker! Round dat next bend, Mistah Dolph, he had dat stonemason fella put up two gateposts, to mark de road to de ranch foah stranger folk dat come dis way!"

"How very important that must make it seem," Magda remarked breathlessly, remembering how the track to Carl Becker's place had been marked when she first came to his house as a new bride: the bleached skull of one of those wild long-horned cattle hung from the nail driven into the trunk of an oak tree. Comfort hadn't been built then. It was a clearing by the river and the road to San Antonio that crossed it by a ford. The Indians once had one of their skin lodge villages there and when Carl Becker first built his house and orchard, the country was wild enough that he warned her about going very far alone. But he had often said that his father's farm had been once as wild and dangerous; his place in turn would become safe and settled.

Magda counted back: in the fall it would be twenty-three years since her husband brought her along this very road, driving a wagon with her bride chest in it and his saddle horse, old Three-Socks clumping along behind, tied to the wagon's tailgate. She thought at the time that it was the end of a long journey; that long journey that brought her and her family from Albeck, across the grey cold Atlantic to a promised paradise in Texas. And paradise it had truly seemed, especially after it had been forbidden to her. But no archangel with a flaming sword stood barrier now. She caught her breath, seeing the fine new stone gateposts on either side of a well-traveled drive, the low places filled in with river gravel.

"The trees are grown up thicker," she ventured. "We used once to be able to see the house from here."

On the day they had been sent away, she and Hannah and Sam had sat on the back of the cart, bumping down the road towards Comfort and watching a grey column of smoke rise into the pure blue autumn sky. The soldiers were firing the barn as they left, looting the farmyard and their stores of food, for the greater benefit of the Confederacy.

The two outriders and Sam spurred their ponies ahead as soon as they reached the gate. Daddy Hurst looked over his shoulder, "Dey go now, tell de folks that you heah at las' Miz Becker."

She hardly heard his voice, for she eagerly drank in the sight of her husband's old pasture and fields. The fences that he and Trap Talmadge had built with so much laborious care were repaired and stout. Someone was plowing; the scent of new-turned soil rose like perfume from the damp earth, as rich and dark as plum-pudding. That had been the cornfield, most years; enriched with stable muck. Now she saw that it was larger than ever before. The cedar thickets were gone, all but the largest trees. The wide pasture that stretched from below the orchard wall nearly to the river was dotted here and there with tall oaks, their leaves new and brightly green in the afternoon sun which slanted golden. Horses grazed there, more horses than Magda had ever seen on her husband's land.

"Dey been roundin' up an' breakin' ponies foah de remuda," Daddy Hurst commented.

"Oh, look, Mama!" Hannah breathed just as Lottie turned and asked, excitedly, "Is that the house, Mama? The big house, on top of the hill?"

"Oh!" Magda had been holding her breath, without realizing. Now she let it out. "I . . . I scarce recognize it! So much larger. And the orchard in bloom, so fair and white! Oh, Hannah, Lottchen, we are come home at last!"

Carl Becker's stone-built house had always crowned that low knoll above the wide meandering Guadalupe. The white limestone from which it was built had aged over time to a mellow honey color. It rose out of the orchard below like a sea cliff, and against it billows of white apple blossom foamed like waves. It had been a small house, shaped like an L, with a long covered porch in the angle of the L. Carl had built into the slope, which provided it with a tall basement dug back into the hillside. His house was as stout as any fortress in the old country, with tall shuttered windows that looked out over the orchard and the meadow beyond it, down to the river road. The other side had looked into the farmyard and the rising folds of hills that lined the river valley, hills that went from green to blue and violet with distance, sometimes clear and sharp as a paper outline against the sky and sometimes misty and softening indistinguishably into each other.

The house appeared nearly twice the length of what it had been, the new work fresh and white, and the shingles were dark, not weathered to silvery gray. Daddy Hurst clucked to the horses; they leaned into their harness, for the ground began rising at the place where the orchard wall began.

"Stop the wagon," Magda commanded him, overtaken by a sudden urgent impulse. "Stop the wagon and let me down."

Daddy Hurst pulled his reins and looked over his shoulder at her. "Miz Becker? We 'mose there, now."

"I know," Magda answered, breathlessly "Take the girls up to the house, just let me down here. I'll walk up through the orchard."

She was already throwing aside the quilts and standing up, resettling her bonnet on her head, vaguely aware of Lottie's puzzled voice and Daddy Hurst mumbling under his breath. He set the brake and came around to hand her down to the ground. She told herself to be sensible, to wait until Daddy Hurst delivered them all to the house, to be greeted by her sons, made welcome home—but she could not deny this sudden inchoate longing for her husband's presence. This she must do first, although she could not know why; and she would prefer to do it alone.

"Tell your brothers I will be along in a moment," she said. "Dolph cannot have changed the place so much that I cannot find my own way from here!"

"She is going to Papa," she thought she heard Hannah's gentle but confident voice telling Lottie.

She walked swiftly along a path at the foot of the orchard wall that had been worn by feet and wagon wheels. The ambulance continued on with a lurch and a crunch of iron tires on gravel. Here was the lower gate, made wide enough to admit a wagon into the orchard. The heavy wooden gate stood open; there was no need to protect the tender young trees from deer and cattle. She supposed that with so many settlers returning to the Hills and the Federal Army returning to their forts in the north and west, and so many hands hired to work here, that there was not much need to keep the gate closed for fear of Indians either.

The orchard! She walked through the gate and stopped short. Tears welled in her eyes, blurring the white cloud drifts of apple blossom; how she had loved this place above all! How her husband had loved it, tending the trees that he had collected with such care, making such farsighted plans. So many plans, some of them made in the knowledge that it would take more than one lifetime to see them to fruition! A lifetime, she thought, oh, that God had granted that Carl's had been a longer one. The ache of his loss at that moment was as fresh and lacerating as it was on the day that Carl Becker was buried in his own orchard, buried and mourned by those few friends who braved the Hanging Band and the provost marshal.

She walked swiftly among the trees on the lowest terrace, hardly aware that they showered white petals upon her black dress and shawl as she brushed through low hanging branches. By the end of summer, when they would have to leave for San Antonio, these branches would be hanging ever lower, heavy with fruit. Apples—how he had loved apples! They had shared an apple on that long-ago day when they met. He had peeled a winter-withered apple from his sister's trees, cutting it into quarters and making a small jest about the Garden of Eden.

In no time at all, Magda reached the farthest corner of the orchard. There was an open space there, in the angle of the wall. To her surprise there was now a low iron fence marking off a tiny enclosure around the two graves. The grass within was clipped tidily short, the little gate stood closed. Magda unlatched it and stepped within. The stones stood straight and clean, scrubbed free of any dirt that birds might have left on them. Here lay her first daughter, the baby who barely lived a month . . . and her children's father. Someone had even brought flowers, two small jars with water and field-flowers. Magda's eyes filled again and overflowed. She sank to her knees on a little square of green before the stones. Such tranquility was in this place, as if peace and sunshine filled it like a cup. She patted the ground over Carl's grave as gently as if she stroked a sleeping child and said, "Dearest dear, we are home at last!"

She had the oddest conviction that somewhere, somehow he heard her, that he welcomed them home with his customary quiet affection, a brush of a kiss on her lips as light as a feather. "The children are safe, safe from the malice of Waldrip. I saw to that, dearest dear—you would have been very proud of my aim. I have missed your companionship so dreadfully—we would have returned before now. Your son has been seeing to things." She sighed; what would Carl have thought of all this? As long as his treasured orchard was tended, Magda did not think he would have cared much. "And now I suppose," she added in a stronger voice, "I must go and see what the Confederacy and our son together have done with this house!"

It came to her, as she climbed the steps to the second terrace and then to the topmost, that although she had traveled all day and had felt quite tired until five minutes ago—now she felt as refreshed as if she had gotten a good night's sleep in a comfortable bed.

At the top of the slope, near where the orchard wall joined the house, there had long been a gate. In times past, it had opened into the farmyard, in the space between the house and the barn where the vegetable garden had once been. When Carl Becker had first begun to build, the house, barn and bunkhouse had been connected by a rough palisade of logs the height of a man; above all a careful and wary man, he sought to protect his family, his hired hands, and his horses against Indian raids or brigandage. Now it appeared that possibility was no longer to be feared; or at least, not so much feared as before. She stepped through the gate into a relatively open space, a forecourt to the house with a number of other buildings set around it: a pair of newly plastered cabins of logs and stone, both of them much larger than the old bunkhouse had been. One of them even had a covered porch. There was also a large barn of sawed planks, with an adjacent corral and a number of saddled horses hitched to the fence. There was even an open shed with a brick forge-fireplace inside, an anvil set before it.

Where the stone cistern had been there was now a neat white-washed shed, and water dripped into a stone water trough outside. She could scarcely find the place in the farmyard where she had stood and leveled a

Paterson at a Confederate soldier. They had come, a whole company of undisciplined young louts, to strip the Becker farm bare of all the foodstuffs, the stock, and their wagons. Having done that, three of them had amused themselves tormenting Jack the dog by shooting the ground near him. She had come running out into the yard, heavy with child, to find Sam holding Jack in his arms, crying frantically for her to make the soldiers stop. With his childish faith in her capability, just as they were being robbed of everything!

A soldier held his musket trained on her son. Whether he had meant to shoot or not, she did not know. But she had in turn held the Paterson on him. She had gone beyond all fear in those moments, somewhere beyond anger. No man would threaten her children. Magda had felt something of the same cold rage when she had killed Waldrip; so she would have killed that young Confederate soldier. In the end, his officer had called him away, and had ordered Magda and her children to go. So they had obeyed; now they had returned at last.

She barely had time to take in much else, for her children were gathered around the ambulance, with Dolph and Daddy Hurst and a Mexican woman with a shawl over her head all clamorously greeting the younger children. A fair of dogs orbited the humans, including Pepper, that Kansas hound with the scarred throat, and the little black herding dog, now grown to maturity. Only Hannah seemed composed, smiling at her mother with serene comprehension.

Sam shouted, "Oh, Mama, Dolph says that I may have three horses to ride on the trail!"

"You'll need every one of them, squirt," Dolph said easily, "For you'll be riding drag and eating dust with all the rest of the new hands. I can't do you special favors just because you're my brother! Hello, Mama." He embraced her warmly and kissed her cheek. With sudden shy uncertainty he waved his hand around, asking, "Well . . . what do you think?"

Magda realized that not only was it more substantial than before—it was also busy. Smoke rose from the forge building, along with the clear regular ringing of hammer on metal. A kitchen wagon, larger and heavier than the one they had used on that momentous first trail drive north, sat in the barn doorway, already half loaded with sacks of flour and barrels of salt-meat. Horsemen rode into the yard at a great pace and a cloud of dust before they dismounted.

"It's . . . very grand," Magda answered, breathlessly. "I would hardly have recognized anything at all."

"It's the show-place that Papa intended it to be," her son affirmed. She marveled once more at how easily he bore authority—for the property and the cattle, and all the men he had hired. Hard to believe that he was the same being as the plump fair-haired baby, chewing on rusks, fussing to be let out of the baby-pen to be spoiled by his father. He then looked at her critically, adding, "Onkel Hansi said you should not kill yourself with work this summer—only that which you really wish to do around the place. This is Tia Leticia, Alejandro's mother . . . you know my head horse wrangler? She's a cousin of Porfirio's, of course. She's a widow, too . . . and didn't want to marry again. She and Alejandro's sisters do the cooking and laundry, and look after the housekeeping." He spoke to the Mexican woman in soft Spanish, obviously performing introductions. "She'll look after you and the girls while we're away, and Frank Inman—my ranch foreman— he'll see to everything else. His younger boy is one of Onkel Fredi's top hands."

Magda was abruptly smothered in an affectionate embrace and a flood of Spanish. Tia Leticia looked to be about her own age, plump and bossy. She patted Magda's cheek; her voice sounded sympathetic. Dolph added, sounding amused, "She knows you were ill. Now she is upbraiding us for having you stand around. You should come inside, she says, and wash off the dust of travel. If you do not want to have supper in the dining room, she will make you a tray and bring it upstairs. You really should see the inside, Mama."

Sam and Daddy Hurst quickly gathered up the small luggage they had brought with them. Magda allowed her son and Tia Leticia, one on either side, to escort her into the house. Sam and Lottie ran ahead, Lottie almost incandescent with excitement. Once her house, she thought with a pang— still her house, she supposed, even if Dolph and Tia Leticia between them had already decided on its management.

The front door and the entryway were little changed; still the bird's nest on the apple branch and the date carved on the lintel; another one of Carl Becker's quiet jests. *The bird in the nest for Miss Vogel.* The house had been furnished sparely but appropriately, in simple taste, with furniture that Margaret sent from Austin as her wedding present, vowing that for all she knew, her brother would be content with a simple bedroll in the corner of the kitchen. The hallway looked much the same—stairs to the upper floor directly opposite, with the door to the parlor underneath, and the kitchen to the left. The kitchen, the heart of the house, where all the work of it went on—Tia Leticia's domain now, Magda supposed. There was a new doorway, to the right, into the new portion of the house.

"Dining room," Dolph explained. "You should see it, Mama. Mr. Tatsch made the buffet special. Beyond it there's an office and a little sitting room. I had them put your desk from Vati's house in there. I thought you would like it. There's glass in all the windows now, no more shutters keeping out the light!"

Tia Leticia patted Magda's hand and gestured towards the stairs. Sam had already gone halfway up, chattering to Lottie and asking over his shoulder if he could stay in the bunkhouse with the other hired hands. He and Hannah had been children, when they had been sent into exile. To both of them, Magda supposed that this return had something of the unreality of a fairy tale, a fable and a memory that grew thinner and more insubstantial with each passing year; overtaken by the worries and realities of school, the disruptions of the war, and the slow coming of peace with its attendant new concerns. As Hannah had observed, they had lived longer at Vati's than they had here.

She stopped cold at the doorway of the biggest bedroom, the one over the kitchen. This had been theirs, the heart of their kingdom. All of their children had been conceived here, she and Carl had laughed and loved here, talked of their future, of the future their children would have. Here was where she was told sorrowfully by her brother Johann that Carl had been murdered, treacherously shot in the back by J.P. Waldrip as he was arrested and taken away by lawless men who did the bidding of the Confederate authorities. No, she couldn't bear to sleep in this room alone.

"I think the girls should have this room," she said breathlessly.

Dolph looked startled. "But it was yours and Papa's before," he protested. Tia Leticia's eyes went shrewdly from her face to his, seeming to comprehend as Magda shook her head.

"So it was, but I cannot sleep there now. Let Hannah and Lottie share it."

Tia Leticia spoke, a quick and authoritative rattle, seeming to scold Dolph while she patted Magda's cheek again. *She knows,* Magda realized— *she knows and she understands my feelings on this. I think she rather expected such, being another widow without a wish to remarry.*

Dolph shrugged, still somewhat puzzled. "There are three more bedrooms; the smallest has a fine view of the orchard, all the way down to the river."

"I would like that," Magda answered quickly. "I'd love to look out on the orchard."

That room was plastered pale yellow, a color that held the sunshine and glowed in the afternoon like a Chinese paper lantern from the sunlight that poured in through a pair of tall windows. *Yes*, Magda thought, *this will do very well. This room is new; it will not haunt me with memories of vanished happiness. We will sort out the things that we brought from Vati's house, and it will be our home again. Not quite as it was—but ours.*

"Oh, there was a letter for you from Onkel Hansi," Dolph recalled suddenly, when she came downstairs that evening and joined her children in the parlor. That room was very fine now, with a tall tripartite glass window that had the same aspect as her bedroom: the orchard and the meadow beyond. Mr. Tatsch's workshop had excelled in providing the furniture; so comfortable and commodious, in simple and modern taste.

"So, now I know what you two were plotting, all last fall, after the cattle drive," Magda said to Dolph and Hannah. She opened the letter that he brought her from what he grandly described as his office, a small room that had its own door onto the covered porch that now ran the length of the house front, tucked between the kitchen and dairy on one side, and the new addition on the other.

"I left most of it to Hannah," Dolph admitted carelessly, as Magda skimmed her letter, a page and a half in Hansi's inelegant but readable hand. "I just wanted it to be as comfortable as Vati's house and for visitors not to worry about wiping their feet, or if they had mud on their clothes. What does Onkel Hansi have to say?"

"He will travel north on the third," Magda counted the days on her fingers, "so expect him here in four days time. He will travel with your herd, then meet up with Fredi at Live Oak. Anna and Peter will already have started north with their herd—how many parties will we have on the trail this year, Dolph?"

"Five," her son answered. "We have contracted with Captain King to bring one of his herds to the Kansas markets. And Billy Inman has arranged with another group of ranchers to buy their beeves outright. We have staked him the purchase money. When he gets to Kansas, he repays us out of what he gets for them, pays his drovers and keeps the rest for himself. He is going to rendezvous with the sellers in Mason and start towards the Red River from there . . . is something the matter, Mama?" he asked anxiously, for Magda had read farther down in Hansi's letter and made a small involuntary cry.

"Hansi writes that Mr. Johnson—you didn't meet him, only Anna and I—has been killed by Kiowa Indians. He came to Friedrichsburg to meet with Hansi, promising to look for the children and ransom them if he could. He had been able to find and return his own family, you see. And so he did go twice, and a most perilous journey it was, each time. He would have gone a third time, if Hansi had asked it, but having Grete returned and being assured, " Magda swallowed bravely past the pain in her throat, "that Willi was beyond all aid, Hansi did not want to put him at such a risk again, especially since he had a family of his own. Mr. Johnson was a teamster by profession, owning his own wagons and teams, although he was a Negro. He and three of his men were," the letter trembled in Magda's hand, "ambushed and besieged on the road to Ft. Griffin in January. Hansi writes that Mr. Johnson made a gallant stand sheltered by the bodies of his horse team, and nearly two hundred spent cartridges from his weapons were found nearby. The Indians mutilated his body most hideously, most likely in revenge for his courage and efficacy against them."

Dolph took the letter from her and straightened the pages that she had crumpled in her distress. "I am sorry to hear about this, Mama. Sorry for him of course—but even sorrier that it would so distress you so."

"He was so very brave," Magda gulped, "but so modest in his demeanor. So very like your father, I thought at the time they had something of the same spirit in them, though otherwise they could not have been less alike. Oh, I wish I had not heard of this on the eve of your departure! It seems like the worst sort of bad omen!"

"Oh, I wouldn't worry, Mama." Dolph smiled, sunny and cheerful. "For we all go armed and there are more than four of us. Moreover, north of the Red River crossing, the trail is like one long river of cattle and men, each one of us but a few hours removed from the next party on the trail. And the Army keeps a careful watch now. Onkel Fredi and Onkel Hansi will be the first to tell you. Don't worry about us, Mama. We'll be as safe as if we were sitting right here in the parlor."

"And besides, Mama," Hannah added softly from where she sat reading to Lottie, under the golden glow of the oil lamp, "if Mr. Johnson was truly as brave and honorable as Papa, than I can't help being certain that he would be in the same heaven also."

"I am sure he would be," Magda spoke with swift vehemence. "But it is still an ill omen!"

"But it did not turn out to be any such thing," Lottie said to her mother, long afterwards. "Only an ill chance hearing of another's tragic end on such a happy day for ourselves. It turned out to be a splendid summer."

"It was so, after all." Magda looked out at the rain, pouring down in Turner Street, beyond the ornate curtains in Lottie's parlor. "Your father's last words were to bid me to be happy. I think I came closest to such as I ever would, during that summer."

Five days later, she stood on the porch with her daughters and Tia Leticia, waving goodbye to her sons and Hansi, Tia Leticia's sons, Daddy Hurst, and a cavalcade of horses, men and boys. The kitchen wagon and the ambulance creaked slowly down the road towards Comfort as the herd was assembled for the long drive north. Their departure left the Becker place quieter, save for Dolph's dogs, howling disconsolately and shut up inside the barn. Magda watched pale grey dust settling in their wake, listened to the noise of their passage fade into distance, the shouts and whooping cries from the drovers, the occasional bellow of an angry cow. She tried very hard not to think of Mr. Johnson or the lonely trail across Indian Territory and into Kansas.

"What will we do now, Mama?" Lottie asked. Her daughter seemed a little deflated, now that the excitement of their journey home and the departure of the herd were over.

"Now, Lottchen?" Magda smiled at her. "We will do as I always did in the spring—put on my oldest clothes and work in the garden!"

Mr. Inman had ploughed up the vegetable patch, but done nothing else, what with the press of work attendant on spring roundup. Magda clicked her tongue disapprovingly against her teeth and zestfully took up a spade and a rake. She and her daughters went to work with a will, breaking up clods and digging in rotted muck, raking it all smooth and setting out seeds in the velvety-soft soil. There was a peace to be found in working out of doors, in the sunshine, even though Mr. Inman appeared to be either amused or disapproving of the sight of the Patrón's mother and sister hauling stable muck in buckets. That was nothing compared to Tia Leticia's remonstrations over the three of them digging in it, wearing only plain faded calico wash-dresses turned up to the knee, and no petticoats. She appeared to want the men to do that kind of work. When Magda courteously declined their services, Tia Leticia burst into floods of angry Spanish.

Magda finally blurted to Mr. Inman, and blushed as Hannah repeated what she had said in English, "Tell her kindly, no, this is our garden. I don't think the hired men know anything of vegetable gardens save for eating the harvest of it."

Tia Leticia apparently held very strong views of what was a proper morning occupation for a lady. Hard work in a vegetable patch was not among them. She simmered with disapproval for days, until the neat furrows and mounds began to come out in green sprouts. A bit of gentle weeding was apparently acceptable. By the end of summer, Magda had won her over by teaching her the art of making various sorts of cheese that were especially relished among the German settlers. The resulting garden bounty also made the crude labor of preparing and planting a little more acceptable.

At mid-summer, they received letters from Dolph and Sam; the latter amusingly and lavishly ornamented with pencil sketches of horses, cows and drovers working at various tasks. They had brought the herd safely to the great terminus for the cattle trail, this time at Dodge City, which the railway had reached at long last. Within a few weeks Dolph and Sam returned, weather-burnt and brown, full of tales of their adventures. In hardly any time at all, the oak trees had turned bronze; autumn had come, and the apple boughs hung heavy with fruit.

Hansi sent Daddy Hurst to bring Magda and the children to his San Antonio house. They brought two bushels of apples with them, and the fruit held their slight sweet perfume all the way there.

Chapter Seventeen: *In the World But Not Of It*

In early spring of 1875, Hansi's daughter Marie married a clever young man, the son of one of Hansi's San Antonio business associates. Both families—and indeed the entire German community in San Antonio—approved heartily of the match, and attended the lavish wedding ball which Hansi and Liesel gave at the sprawling and gaily painted mansion that Hansi had built with the profits of his various enterprises.

It was very much to Magda's astonishment that Marie had not wed as soon as she was old enough, for she was as pretty as Liesel had been at that age; and besides, she was given to sentimental over-affection for many a handsome youth. But aside from being handsome, Hermann Menges was a practical young man and inclined to work hard, which quality recommended itself to Hansi. He also possessed a puckish sense of humor, which ingratiated him with practically everyone else in Marie's family.

"She's done well for herself in him, our flighty little romantic," Hansi pronounced. He sat with Magda, Anna and Peter, at ease around one of the little tables that had been set out on the lawn under a cheerfully adorned canvas pavilion. Planks had been laid out for a dance floor, since the largest parlor in the house was too small to accommodate all the guests. An orchestra played music from the summer house; the girls whirling around the dance floor in their full skirts looked like moths dancing in the twilight.

"Better than I expected, Papa," Anna remarked. Peter teasingly made the sound of a cat meowing. The look that Anna sent her husband was more fond than annoyed, "And at least Mama finally got to put on a marvelous wedding with all the trimmings and baubles. I think I am forgiven for an elopement."

Hansi groaned comically and Peter said, in a way meant to bring comfort, "It might make you feel less pain on the matter of economy, sir—to just make an average for the costs for our nuptial celebration and this."

"And by this exercise you gain yet another able son, Hansi," Magda said, then as soon as the words were out of her mouth hoped that Hansi—bluff, practical Hansi—would not take them amiss, would not be reminded on this happy day of the sons lost to him. Magda knew that Liesel still secretly mourned for them—most of all, mourned for Willi. He, along with Christian, and Joachim who died as infant on board the brig *Apollo*, would have been beginning the business of being men; old enough to dance and flirt with a pretty girl, just as Sam was doing this very minute.

Hansi did not take it amiss at all. He smiled broadly and with very real affection at them all. "Aye, that's the thing to consider. He's good with figures, too. Mariechen wants to settle in Friedrichsburg for a time, so I thought I'd offer him a position in the old store. If Jacob says he's up to it, we'd set him up in Neu Braunfels. What do you think?"

"That would give him a year of experience," Magda ventured, "and if he has no aptitude for shopkeeping, we'll have enough time to find and hire someone who is."

"Your little lads can't grow up soon enough," Hansi jested to his daughter, "or else I'd put them to work in the new store, eh? They behaved well today, damned well."

Both Anna and Peter glowed with quiet parental satisfaction. Magda reflected that Anna had acted on a sure instinct, abruptly jumping into a marriage of convenience, when Hansi broke his leg and couldn't go on the spring cattle drive as planned. Against all initial forebodings, their marriage had worked out marvelously well. Anna had accompanied Peter up the trail to Kansas several times. Serenely and without fuss she provided a home for Peter's nephew Horrie and her own children; Henry—called Harry—who had just turned five, and Christian, who was almost four. Liesel had dressed them for the wedding ceremony in matching black velveteen knickerbockers suits with Battenberg lace collars, and tasked them with carrying velvet cushions upon which the wedding rings rested.

"I must confess that I bribed Harry into behaving by telling him he may pick his very own horse out of the remuda next spring," Peter noted. "Otherwise I think he might have taken shears to that velveteen abomination! What was your mother thinking, Anna—did she want the other lads to beat him up at school? They will, when they see him next!"

"The other boys' mothers and grandmothers make them wear the exact same thing for this kind of occasion," Anna returned calmly. "So they have very little reason to torment our son especially. Besides, I bribed him also. I promised him a saddle of his choosing for his next birthday."

"Well worth the effort and a bargain at any price," Hansi guffawed, as Harry's parents laughed in mutual appreciation for their eldest's cleverness. "I tell you, I have always said to beware of any enterprise that demands a suit of new clothes . . . unless you are a merchant, of course!" And Hansi laughed again; he had quite a fondness for Anna's sons. Harry was a bold and fearless urchin, possessed of nearly limitless supplies of charm and persistence. Anna and Peter between them usually did not let him get away with much, but on this occasion he clearly had the advantage of his parents.

It pleased Magda that her niece had fallen, all unexpected, into such a contented and affectionate marriage. Her eyes sought out her own children. Lottie and Hannah, along with Anna and Grete, had all been pressed into service as bridesmaids, draped in gauzy pink silk with crowns of silk rosebuds in their hair. The younger girls were dancing, tremulous with excitement at being allowed to participate in such a grown-up party. Hannah was dancing in a small circle with Peter's nephew Horrie and Anna's little boys, showing them the steps. Magda smiled with tender affection. Her daughter was so good with children. She had taken Grete and Lottie in hand, taught them how to waltz, and shown them how to handle gallant compliments and the ungallant kind with equal courtesy and aplomb. She had an aptitude for teaching and a gentle way of winning confidence in her from the shyest and most timid. Magda did not think she had any particular suitors that she held in special affection. That did not worry her; neither she nor Anna had scampered headlong from the schoolroom to the marriage bed. There was time enough for her soft-spoken Hannah to find her own way, her own beloved.

Sam of course, was in the middle of another laughing circle—mostly of girls in flower-colored dance dresses that showed their shoulders and their pale pretty arms. He had a pencil and the ragged notebook that lived in his coat pocket wherever he went. He was amusing those around him by making sketches; Magda could not see what they were of, but they made the girls squeal with laughter. Sam split his time between San Antonio and Hansi's many businesses, and helping his brother with the land. It was a proper ranch, now, Magda supposed. They had gone up the trail to Kansas with a herd every year for the last five. There also, Sam amused his fellows with sketches. "He's all but useless as a cowhand," his brother observed with a sigh, "but everyone likes him for those drawings and the yarns he can spin about kings and crusades and things." Sam had also done splendid oil paintings for Hansi's study, scenes of cattle drives and round-up times, with every drover and wrangler—and every horse as well—clearly identifiable.

Dolph himself was not with the dancers, or among the merry gathering of younger people. Magda thought he was in the dining room where a cold supper had been laid out for guests to partake of as they wished. Dolph, still serious and self-contained, held a kind of quietness to himself, even in the liveliest gathering. She had seen him talking quietly with Porfirio, who looked splendid in a black suit of Mexican cut, trimmed with silver buttons. Porfirio's family did not attend such social gatherings among the Americans and the Germans; only Porfirio himself, suave and gallant and with enough of a cold steel edge to put off anyone who thought to make trouble.

"Your son is talking business again," Liesel announced, as she came tripping down the steps from the house. The French doors between the big parlor and the terrace stood wide open this evening. Guests washed back and forth, like water in the tide pools and lagoons on the coast. "Make him stop, Magda. He is supposed to dance and flirt with all the pretty girls who have come to the wedding . . . not talk of wars and business with the dry old sticks."

Liesel's cheeks glowed hectically pink from excitement and exertion. Magda studied her covertly and carefully, alert for any sign that she was descending from her tall tower into the cellar again. No, she thought, not now, not tonight, with a house full of guests and the orchestra playing so delightfully. Liesel giggled, delicious as ever, as Hansi pulled her into his lap, careless of her elaborate dress with its complicated draping and overskirt. In spite of her squeals of protest, he kissed her very heartily. Anna exchanged a look of fond exasperation with Magda.

It was amusing, thought Magda, how Hansi's earthier qualities had been transmuted in the eyes of others by wealth and success. The hardworking cattle drover and teamster, with his dislike of formality, his open affection for his wife, and his shrewd eye for profit, was no longer seen as crude and rather vulgar, but instead, as endearing and eccentric. She had said something of the sort to him; Hansi had laughed uproariously and made a remark about the thickness of the gold plate on a pile of cattle turds.

It had been good for Hansi to bring Liesel to San Antonio, even better for Magda to heed Hansi's urgings to join them there for all but the summer months. He had a small guest cottage built for her use at the bottom of the garden adjacent to the cool green riverbank, calling it the "Rest of the Week House." Magda most often joined Liesel and Hansi for meals, especially when Hannah and Lottie were at school; she loved the little house and rejoiced to return to it, even if she had only been writing letters for Hansi all day. Now she thought of how wonderful it would be when the party was over, to walk across the garden and take off her shoes, to undress and slip into the little bathing cabin that overhung the riverbank and soak in the cool water for a while. The river flowed quiet and green; all the nicest houses were built on its banks, so that people could take advantage in the heat of summer. Liesel had a housekeeper and three maids who would see to washing the dishes and sweeping up after the party. This must be, Magda thought, what being rich meant; that you could hire someone to see to the mess.

There was a soft step behind her as Liesel gave one last squeal and wriggled out of her husband's arms. "I must see to my guests!" she gasped, patting her elaborately curled hair and the decoration of flowers and feathers in it, while Hansi begged for one last kiss. When she bent over to give it to him, he made as if to kiss her breasts, bulging up like pillows of rising bread dough against the force of her corset. "Hansi! For shame, you are awful!" she cried, and escaped; a fat busy wren in peacock's raiment.

"Auntie said I was being bad," Dolph said, from behind his mother, "and that I should bring Porfirio out to the dancing."

Porfirio bowed gallantly to them all. "I am to be a good example to the young Patrón, and show him how it is done," he said. "You also should also be guided by your lady mother, who has the care of your household and long knowledge of your qualities when it comes to selecting the woman you would wish to honor with your name, your property and the upbringing of your sons."

"Make Auntie Liesel happy," Dolph answered with a careless wave toward the dancers. "Go and dance with someone. That waltz is finished but they'll start up another in a minute." He pulled a chair from another table and sat himself on it, backwards, with his arms and chin resting on the spindly back. "Don't worry, I'll watch from here."

Peter sat back in his own chair, grinning under the drooping mustache that he still wore. "Oh, Cuz," he drawled, "watching doesn't get you anywhere!" He turned towards Magda, adding, "Ma'am? You must promise me, that when you have selected the proper matrimonial candidate among young ladies for my cousin here, please let me know, for I intend to tease and chaff and torment him until his life is a misery for love!"

"And why would I do that?" Magda asked, hugely amused.

"For his coldness and lack of sympathy for me, when I was tangled deep in the coils of unrequited and tragic affection—I owe him much for that!"

"You also owe me a dance, husband," Anna remarked, and although her voice held the satiric edge of old, her eyes were soft with affection.

Peter laughed and rose from his chair, holding out his hands for her. "Dance with me then, my lady wife! Let us show our dear Cuz the fruits of connubial bliss!"

"Humph," Hansi remarked as Peter and Anna went to the dance floor. "I'd have expected such of those two little bratlings of theirs, being afraid to set foot on the dance floor for fear of not having the nerve to speak to a pretty girl. But for a grown man to act that way!"

"Onkel Hansi?" Dolph said very sweetly and when Hansi looked at him, Dolph uttered one of Hansi's favorite directional obscenities. Hansi roared with laughter while Magda thought, *Honestly—men!*

Meanwhile, almost unobserved, Porfirio had claimed the next dance with Hannah. Magda would not have noticed, but that her eyes followed Peter and Anna, their hands intertwined as they walked towards the dance, her hand curled so casually around his wooden one. She saw how, with loving and unobtrusive grace, Anna deftly bent the wooden joints of wrist and fingers, before he set it around her slender waist. They swung into a lively waltz, seemingly without a care, the tall man with the grace of a horseman and the tiny woman in rose-bud pink, the top of whose head scarce came up to the stick-pin in his fine cravat.

Her eyes were on the dancers and her grave and graceful daughter just beyond Anna and Peter, as Porfirio came up and bowed with such elaborate courtesy! It caught her eye, Hannah's face with a look of happy welcome upon it. Porfirio was someone she was glad to see, a welcome partner in the dance. But as Magda realized upon closer look—not a suitor. Well thank God for that. He was easily twice her age, had tickled her feet as an infant, guided her staggering steps as a toddler, and was married besides. No, Porfirio was as much the indulgent and loving uncle as Hansi ever was. He held Hannah's hand respectfully—the hand on her waist was as kindly and as devoid of courtly intent as an uncle's or a brother's would be. And they talked as they danced, Hannah asking something of him and he responding with careful courtesy—no, he was surprised by what she had asked, shocked even, although he hid it well.

"What are you watching?" Dolph asked with sober amusement. "The bride you would have picked out for me, according to Tito Porfirio's instruction?"

"No, your sister," Magda answered without thinking.

Her son's gaze followed hers. "I am only glad that he is following Auntie Liesel's instructions," her son observed wryly, "with a demonstration and not an actual candidate for marriage. Marrying sisters and cousins is ill-advised and usually illegal, according to what I have been told."

"The children of such usually turn out to be idiots," Magda observed with austere authority.

Dolph laughed. "Like royalty and dogs bred too close," he agreed. "Nice conversation for a wedding party, Mama!"

"You should consider Porfirio's advice," Magda stated. "He only says what your aunt has been deafening my ears about for the last five years."

"Auntie Liesel has seen all of her children wed but Elias and Grete," Dolph answered. "And she adores a party and wants the excuse to plan another. I don't see the need of getting married just to satisfy Auntie Liesel's social calendar. I'll wed when I've met a nice girl who doesn't mind dogs and cows—and not a minute before. Besides, it's the bride's family who has the biggest to-do over the wedding. If you follow her example, you should be pushing Hannah towards every eligible and well-led suitor there is at this ball."

"There is a very ugly word used towards mothers who do such to their daughters," Magda replied. "Your sister has such fine qualities; I do not need to hunt a husband for her. But you should—when this dance is done, ask her to dance. She should not be embarrassed by a lack of partners tonight."

"Yes, do so," Hansi interjected as he rose from the table. "It is a party; we should dance. As for me, I go in search of my own beloved wife. I think we should dance at least once, if I may tear her away from the demands of a hostess!"

"Good luck with that, Onkel," Dolph said, with very real affection.

"My house, my party . . . I pay the bills, why not?" Hansi said. He rose from his chair with some difficulty. He had grown a little stouter with prosperity—and also had drunk more freely than usual. But he stepped up the stairs briskly enough and vanished into the house.

"Dolph," Magda asked, as a sudden thought occurred to her, "do you know if your sister has any particular favorite among the young men who pay suit to her?"

Dolph frowned thoughtfully, as if this were the first time he had considered the idea. At last, he said, "From what I have observed, Mama, she does not seem to favor any one over another. And she does have admirers, just that they are not the flashy and reckless young sports. Mostly of an amiable and responsible sort, and of a temper complimentary to hers; she takes a mild enjoyment in their company, but nothing more. She is not like Marie," and his voice dropped sadly, "or like Auntie Rosalie—with no eyes for anyone else in the room save that favored one. Anyone could tell, save for maybe a blind man or someone like Mr. Berg, who cares more for his mechanicals than any living human. When I take the next dance with her, Mama, I will ask her. No, I will not press her hard, I will merely ask as a brother. She will tell me, and if she will not, she will have told Sam. They were ever close."

And with that, Magda was content, being not all that concerned in the first place. Hannah was no flighty and romantic girl, given to reckless impulse and unsuitable affections. Dearest Vati had never had worries on that score about Magda herself; Hansi had never entertained such fears regarding Anna.

Sometime after midnight, with the orchestra still playing cheerfully away, she thought to take Lottie back to the cottage. She tracked Lottie and Grete down in the little parlor, each of them picking unenthusiastically at a plate of cake. Both girls were drooping like cut flowers and Grete couldn't stop yawning.

"Oh, Mama, please! We want to stay awake for breakfast at sunrise," Lottie pleaded, but the shadows underneath her eyes looked like bruises. "We're not the least bit tired, aren't we, Grete?" she appealed to her almost-twin cousin, who stoically shook her head.

Magda easily saw through them. "No, Lottie, you are beyond tired. You are exhausted, both of you. You're only fourteen, there'll be parties enough and dancing until dawn when you're older—especially if your aunt Liesel has anything to say about it! I'll strike a bargain with you, Lottchen; you may spend the night here, rather than come back to the cottage. That way, you may listen to the music for a little while—and if you lie down and sleep now, you may rise with the sun and attend the breakfast. Do we have a bargain?"

"Mama!" Lottie began to protest, but then her own face was split with an enormous yawn. Both she and Grete came, unresisting, when Magda led them upstairs. She helped them out of their outfits, those ruffled pink dresses that Liesel had taken such care over, and unpinned the circlets of silk rosebuds from their hair. She was quite sure that Lottie was half asleep even as she pulled the nightgown over her head. Grete certainly was; she crawled into bed as soon as she had divested herself of stays and petticoats, leaving them in a heap on the floor as if they were the discarded skin of a snake. Magda stayed long enough to comb out Lottie's straight fair hair and braid it loosely for the night, thinking fondly how long it had been since she had done this for her child.

"Good night, my dears," Magda added tenderly as Lottie pulled the light coverlet over herself. She stooped to pick up Grete's petticoats, wondering if the girl's carelessness of her clothing was something left over from her captivity, or merely that she had become accustomed to Liesel's lady's maid picking up after her. She draped the discarded clothing over the bedroom chair, blew out the lamp flame and went downstairs again.

"I've put the girls to bed, upstairs," she told her sister when she found her. Liesel stifled a yawn herself, but her eyes still sparkled hectically. "Lottie insisted that they would awake early and come down for the dawn breakfast, but I doubt it. I doubt that even I will, Lise. I'm exhausted also. Would you and Hansi miss me if I take refuge in my own feather bed?"

"Of course not!" Liesel reached up and kissed her swiftly on her cheek, "You were so kind to oversee matters all this morning. I am not tired—I confess I went and rested in my room on occasion. And once," she giggled knowingly; "I made Hansi come with me! I don't think anyone noticed!"

No, thought Magda in resignation, *only anyone in the next room, like your maid! Or anyone who saw you coming downstairs again with your dress all rumpled and Hansi five minutes later trying to saunter as if he had just gone out on the balcony to smoke. That act may very well have fooled me before I married—but it has not fooled me since!* Out loud, she said, "I think if I had someone I loved to dance with, as we used to do for the Fourth of July dances, I would easily manage the night. I will tell Sam and Hannah and Dolph that I am going—and not to make much noise when they come to bed."

That was the thing about widowhood, she thought to herself, slipping as unnoticed as a shadow around the edge of the dance floor—no one to dance with. This was one of those nights that she particularly missed the company of her husband. The Fourth of July dances in Friedrichsburg had always extended until dawn. She had loved to dance with him, a man all grace and power on horseback, and grace and assurance moving through the complicated steps of a schottische or a country-dance. She had loved the feel of his hands on hers, on her waist, and then afterwards . . . no, she wrenched her mind away from that, the memory of the little Sunday house on their own wedding night, and he as beautiful as a Greek statue, naked in the golden candle light. No, best not to think on that.

The little cottage had a small kitchen, with a new patent stove which heated water in a small reservoir built into it. The fire was burned down to coals, but the water was still hot. She took some and made herself a small bedtime tisane of chamomile and honey, then lay in bed and listened to the pleasantly distant sound of music, floating through the night air, until she fell asleep with the half-drunk cup of tisane at her elbow.

When she woke, the sky behind the filmy curtains was pale grey. The air was cool in a way that never lasted long after sunrise, once out of the high green hills. Her oldest son was shaking her elbow, his eyes shadowed with worry.

"Mama, where is Hannah gone?" he asked.

She sat up; she had fallen asleep with her wrapper still on. She clutched it around herself and answered, "Is she not here? In her room?"

"No, Mama—did she say anything to you last night?"

Magda clutched at her son's hands, stabbed to her very heart with a sudden memory of the morning she'd looked down from Vati's sickroom and saw John Hunter on a lathered horse, bringing the news to Hansi and his sons and nephews that Rosalie and the children had been taken.

"Not here!" she managed to say. "Not Indians, not here in the very heart of the city!"

"No, Mama, not Indians." Dolph shook his head, but his face still looked grave, "We were partaking of breakfast, not fifteen minutes ago, she and I with Sam and Onkel Hansi. She finished and left us, saying she was going to come here and sleep for a few hours, then she would return and begin helping Auntie Liesel with sorting out the wedding gifts and receiving calls. You'd better get dressed, Mama—she came and changed out of her gown, but her bed is empty. Not even crumpled the counterpane."

"Go tell your uncle," Magda gasped, bringing her feet to the floor. A look into Hannah and Lottie's bedroom was enough to convince of what her son said; the pink dress, the pretty dance slippers that matched it were all neatly put away. The circlet of pink silk rosebuds lay carelessly discarded on the dressing table, with a set of long gloves and an ivory fan which had been a Christmas present from Sam. Hannah had been carrying that fan at the dance, Magda recollected now. The bed had not been slept in, the coverlet still smooth, the fine linen pillow shams uncreased by the weight of a head.

Why would Hannah lie to her brother? Magda's heart hammered in her throat. Why would she tell him she was going home to sleep, then change clothes and leave? Perhaps she had gone back to Hansi and Liesel's?

"Go see if she went to the house," she gasped to her son. "Perhaps she changed her mind, decided to go and begin with . . ." But she knew, as soon as the words were out of her mouth, that it was ridiculous. She and Hannah had been awake at the break of day on the day before, preparing for the wedding. Hannah would have been exhausted attending on the bride, then the wedding and dinner to follow, the ball and dancing all night through. Only a matter of urgency would have kept her from doing as she had told

296

her brother that she would do—especially since Liesel would doubtless sleep the day away, not minding whether she had help with wedding presents and calls or not. There was a jangling wrongness about all of this; she could feel it in her bones. It was too much like the day when news was brought to them about Rosalie and the children, or much like the morning after the Hanging Band had visited the stone house with the bird and apple bough carved over the door, the morning when her husband's body was brought home, lying bruised and already cold in the back of the Browns' farm wagon.

She dressed hastily with trembling fingers, an old loose dress she used to garden in, not wanting to call for one of Liesel's maids to do up her stays and button her into one of her fashionable black dresses. She thrust her feet into shoes, did up half the buttons, and snatched a shawl from her chest of drawers without looking at it. Ah, the certain freedom of being a widow and always wearing black; everything always matched. Dolph met her halfway across the lawn as she ran panting through the detritus of the ball, past the deserted dancing floor, the pavilion with its ornaments and flowers already hanging limp and discouraged, as if they knew their hour was long past.

"She did not come back to the house," he reported. "Uncle Hansi has already looked. And he sent the maid to look again, but she's nowhere to be found in the rooms she's like to be; not in the bedrooms, not with the girls, and not in the parlor. He went to the stable to harness the trap himself, no time to wait on the coachman."

As they came up the steps to the terrace, where they had sat and watched the dancers just a few hours before, Sam emerged from the dining room, yawning between bites of a piece of toast spread with butter and jam.

"'Morning, Mama," he said cheerfully. "Sorry I didn't make it back to the cottage, seemed easier to just make camp on Auntie Liesel's parlor sofa. Now, that was a proper shindig—makes all the dime dance halls in Kansas seem awful pale, next to Auntie Liesel's hospitality." For the first time, he saw Magda's haphazard dress and Dolph's grim expression, and started up short. "Why, what's the matter? Who died?"

"No one yet," Dolph said. "Something's happened. Where's Hannah?"

With considerable difficulty, Sam appeared to either wake up or come down from his cloud of post-celebration elation.

"She left with Porfirio, about five minutes ago. Pulled up to the porte-cochere in his two-horse, she got in and off they went." A bit of the good-morning cheer vanished from his face as Dolph swore viciously. "Look, there's no need for talk like that, Dolph, not in front of Mama! This is Porfirio! It's like thinking ill of Onkel Hansi or Captain Nimitz!"

"You didn't see them dancing together last night." Dolph's face was cold, angry, like his father's on those certain rare occasions when Magda had been reminded of what Carl Becker had been and seen, reminded anew of that soldier's steel hidden under the gentle manner.

"No," Magda cried, "you are wrong! There was nothing amorous in his address to her! They danced, but it was no more than a family friend dancing with a young daughter—it was if I had danced with Pastor Altmueller, dearest of Vati's friends! Surely there was no ill in that, no intention as what you think! Nothing but proper familial affection! Surely, you cannot believe . . ." Magda choked on her own words, aghast that anyone—least of all her own son—would believe that Porfirio, who had buried her husband and sworn an oath of vengeance on his murderer, who had sent her money when her family was exiled, impoverished, and thrown on the charity of their true friends and Vati—No, this was too vile for belief, that he would seduce his Patrón's oldest daughter.

Hansi appeared, coatless and with the sleeves of his white dress shirt rolled up to the elbows. He had managed to set aside his cravat.

"Where to?" he asked, with grim cheer. "I hope this is not a fool's errand—that she took it in her head to go pick wildflowers or shop for ribbons. That doesn't sound like our Hannah-chick, though. Not the flighty thoughtless sort of wench at all."

"She went with Porfirio, not five minutes ago," Sam blurted.

His uncle cocked his head to one side and asked, "Right then—what was he driving?"

"A pair of brown geldings," Sam answered, swallowing the last of his toast. "Not matched—the off had white feet on the fore and a blaze on his nose. Hitched to an open barouche, painted dark green with black trim. Are we going after?"

"Of course," Hansi answered curtly.

Sam dusted off his hands and muttered, "Well, the finish to a heels-up in Kansas was never this interesting, unless there was gunplay involved." Disbelieving he added, "You can't possibly think that our Hannah has gone off with Porfirio!"

"I don't think," Dolph said between his teeth, "until we catch up to them and we know!"

"Hannah?" Sam laughed out loud. "Oh, this is a joke indeed! Somber and psalm-reading Hannah with Porfirio, the ladies' delight of two nations and God knows how many counties? Pull the other leg; that one has jingly spurs on! He's twice her age! If you want to spin a jest for me, at least make it one that is credible!"

"The sooner we go, the sooner we will sort this all out," Hansi observed. The three of them followed him through the house and past the maids, the household staff sleepily going about their duties, cleaning up the detritus of the party. Dolph handed Magda up into the light trap, Sam scrambled into the back, and Hansi took up the reins.

As they bowled briskly down the gravel drive, Hansi said, "Into town, first. It's early, yet, and they have just a short lead."

"Try Commerce Street," Dolph ordered, "and then Porfirio's house— the little place in the old village." At Magda's raised eyebrow, Dolph added, "He has another place there . . . for entertaining his friends." Magda kept her thoughts on that to herself, but Hansi grunted knowingly.

In the end, they had gone no farther than halfway down Main Street and the main square overlooked by the grand new Cathedral edifice with its half-constructed towers, trimmed with gothic stone lace. Among the carriages waiting at the foot of the steps was a green barouche, drawn by a pair of brown and white horses. The great wooden doors stood open to admit a scattering of the devout on this Friday morning.

"There!" Sam said breathlessly. "Over there!"

"I see!" Hansi responded. He jerked on the reins, sending the trap plunging across traffic, narrowly missing a dray with a load of barrels and eliciting a storm of curses not only from the driver but several pedestrians picking their way carefully across the middle of the square.

Porfirio sat on the barouche's driver's seat, smoking one of those little Mexican cigarillos. His head turned at the sudden noise of their passage across the square. Tossing the cigarillo aside, he leaped down and faced them, smiling—not a trace of unease or guilt on his face, only his usual assurance.

He called out jauntily, "Good morning, Madame Becker, Patrón. And how amazed I am, that you should be here so early after the ball!"

Dolph shot out of Hansi's trap before the wheels even stopped rolling. "Where is she!" he shouted, in response to Porfirio's greeting.

"Rudolph!" Magda cried out in horror, not waiting for Sam or Hansi to hand her down from the trap. "What are you thinking!? How can you even think this . . . this vileness!"

"Where is she!" Dolph demanded again. "Damn it, what have you done—"

"She is within," Porfirio answered quietly. He caught Dolph's arm as the younger man raised it as if to strike him. "Patrón, control yourself. This is not what you think." It seemed to Magda that he regarded Dolph not with anger, but with a kind of resigned sorrow.

"What am I supposed to think, when my sister tells me a blatant falsehood and departs five minutes later with you?" Dolph was pale with rage, would have wrenched himself free from Porfirio's hand, but that the older man held him with such strength.

"Alas, if it were any other young lady, you might have rightful cause to assume . . . what you have assumed." A flash of amusement lit Porfirio's face, as brief as a flash of summer lightning, but then he shook his head with seeming regret. "And a sweet flattery it is, Patrón—but no. Señorita Hannah is as a daughter or sister to me. She asked of me a favor this morning."

"What kind of favor!" Dolph snapped, and lowered his voice from an angry shout. "Why did she ask it of you in particular? Tell me that!"

By that time, Hansi had set the brake and tethered his team to a nearby railing. "Yes, tell us," he rumbled, taking Magda by the elbow. Looking shrewdly at Porfirio, at the ornate stone bulk of San Fernando rising up behind them, he added, "You would not be helping my niece run away with some penniless suitor—no more than you would run away with her yourself. Be silent, lad," he admonished Dolph, as the latter opened his mouth. "Let him speak—what is the meaning of this sudden excursion?"

"I think," Porfirio replied, with suave confidence, "the explanation should best come from Señorita Hannah. I had often begged her to share her confidences with you."

A small group of worshippers emerged from the Cathedral door at the top of the stairs. Hearing their footsteps and soft voices, Porfirio turned his head. "She is here," he added quietly.

Hannah rushed towards them and exclaimed, "Mama—Onkel Hansi!" Then to Porfirio she said worriedly, "What did they do to you! Oh, Dolph—you didn't strike him, he was only doing as I asked!"

"Nothing, little Señorita Hannah," Porfirio answered. "I am untouched; slightly bruised by the Patrón's mistrust, but undamaged. Señorita Hannah—querida," he added with infinite tenderness, "you really must tell them."

"Yes, I suppose I must." Hannah was eerily composed. "Only please don't blame Porfirio; none of this is anything to do with him, except that he sometimes enabled me to come here secretly."

"But why?" Magda took her daughter's hands. "What was so secret, that we must not know of it?! You left us to assume the worst, Hannah-my-chick."

"I have been taking instruction in the Catholic faith," Hannah answered, with quiet strength. She looked levelly at all their faces, "And that I wish to take vows as a religious."

"Oh, child!" Magda felt as though she wanted to weep, but couldn't. This was too deep, too sudden for tears. "Why could you not have told us, straight away?"

"Because I did not want to cause you worry, until I was entirely sure." Hannah returned their gaze, tranquil and composed, utterly at ease. "And yesterday as I watched Marie and Mr. Menges exchange their vows, it came to me that I was not meant for that. I have been called to a vocation. It was as someone was speaking to me, had been speaking to me for many months. And once I knew this and accepted that calling—then I was at peace, seeing the path laid out straight before me. I could but follow, Mama, Onkel Hansi. I am sorry to have distressed you all; I had only one thought this morning—to come here to confession and then to the convent."

There was a sudden silence, as if they were in a bubble, the morning bustle in Main Square unheard, even as they stood in the middle of it. Dolph looked abashed, mumbling an apology to Porfirio.

Sam said, cheerily, "Oh, sister—that sudden faint rumble coming from under the earth to the north of us—that will be Opa, rolling over in his grave."

"Sam!" Magda hissed, chiding him for such levity.

"You are resolved on this?" Hansi asked with careful consideration. "It is not some sudden rash impulse?"

Hannah shook her head. "No, Onkel. Be assured that I had considered long and carefully. It is a life vow." Her eyes, clear and grey-blue, without a speck of artifice in their depths, met theirs honestly. "And taken before God. Be assured, Mama—Onkel Hansi—I am resolved upon this course. I am of age, so whether or not I have your consent and blessing, I mean to do it. I would rather have it," for a brief moment, Hannah looked very young, as if pleading for that one thing, "but if I do not, then I do not."

"You mean to lock yourself away from the world." Magda wept to think of Hannah, in a coarse black robe, her head covered with a wimple and veil.

But Hannah smiled in fond amusement, "Oh, no Mama, not locked away from the world! We are very much in the world. I shall be a teacher, with a schoolroom full of boys and girls; in the world, just not of it!"

"It is no less an honor," Porfirio murmured, "among the old families, to have a daughter in one of the holy sisterhoods. In old Spain, there was a convent in Burgos where the mother-abbess was second only to the Queen herself."

"Nonetheless, I think we should be discussing this matter," Hansi interjected, "at length and elsewhere than the street. No, don't look like that, child," he added as Hannah looked towards Porfirio. "We shall not lock you up and feed you only bread and water hoping you will repent of this notion."

"It is not a notion," Hannah returned gravely, "I am quite resolved on it."

Hansi held up his hand, "No one has argued anything of the sort," he answered. "But such an irrevocable step, child! Your mother and I, your brothers—may we be entirely sure of your commitment to it? After all, it was news to us, not two minutes ago. Can you allow us a little longer to become comfortable with it?"

"Of course," Hannah acquiesced and allowed Hansi to hand her up into the trap. "But I shall not be discouraged from this purpose, Onkel. I have delayed long enough."

Porfirio tipped his hat to her and said, "I will send word to the convent this very hour, telling them of your wish to enter." He also accepted Dolph's rather embarrassed apology, "Think nothing of it, Patrón—you thought only of your sister and her safety."

* * *

"In the world, but not of it," Magda mused, when she and Lottie talked of this. "She was indeed quite fixed upon that purpose. Of course, we realized that at once. We talked to the Mother Abbess, to the priest who had given her instruction. They, like us, wished that she be firm in her dedication, and have every opportunity to turn aside. She went into the religious life so joyously, never looking backwards."

"Nannie was truly happy," Lottie said. "I visited her often, when my children were small. She was so very good with them, I used to think it such a waste, that she would not have her own children! But then I was very young myself, and did not understand."

"She did have children," Magda said. *"A whole orphanage full of them. She was very much loved, your sister."*

"So she was." Lottie threaded her embroidery needle. *"Her face was most serene when they found her, after the great storm passed. I talked to one of those who searched for the bodies of the sisters and the children. Nannie had a baby in her arms and seven other children tied to her with clothesline. Some of the older boys survived. They told their rescuers that as the great storm crashed in onto the building, they were singing a hymn to Mary, Queen of the Waves."*

"Your sister understood about children's fears," Magda said. *"Understood very well—for once she had been afraid herself. One is often haunted by the past,"* she added, almost irrelevantly.

"Haunted, Mama?" Lottie asked. *"How do you mean?"*

"Now and again, when I have ventured into town, or to the ranch, I think I see fleetingly, the face of one whom I loved or knew, someone who has gone from this life . . . like your Opa, in the face of an old man playing chess, or your sister, in the habit of a nun, coming down the steps of the San Fernando cathedral. I could have sworn a man I saw in the lobby of the St. Anthony was Hansi, a big man with dark hair! And then he turned his head, and he was as much a stranger as he had been familiar a second before."

"That is very curious, Mama," Lottie said, after a moment. She sounded as if she tried to hide her concern. *"Does this happen often?"*

"Not often," Magda answered, though she did so untruthfully. Of late, the momentary illusion of a dear and familiar presence had occurred with increasing frequency. That very afternoon, she had looked out from the parlor window into the street outside, and thought she saw a young man with the reins of a brown horse in his hands; a tall young man in an old-fashioned fringed leather coat, whose wheat-pale fair hair gleamed briefly in the twilight under the trees across the road. It seemed that he smiled at her with serene affection, and that the vision lingered for longer than the usual eye-blink of time. Curiously, she found these brief illusions, these visitations, rather comforting, but felt it wiser to make no mention of them to Lottie. The child would worry so. Lottie had a horror of mental afflictions, a lively fear of what that might portend. She had loved Carl Becker very much, and he had loved her—loved her so deeply that he gave himself up to his enemy rather than endanger her and the children. It made perfect sense that he would make these fleeting appearances.

"We have been so long apart," Magda remarked out loud, but fortunely not loud enough for anyone but Mouse to hear.

303

Chapter Eighteen: *The Cattle Baron*

"It seemed so very odd to have a sister going to become a nun!"
Lottie remarked, drawing Magda out of her contemplations. "The sisters at
school all seemed so very otherworldly, so mysterious, in their dark
medieval robes. Almost romantic. Really, most of us girls were quite sure
that each of them had been tragically disappointed in love. Well, the pretty
ones, at least. And the homely ones were too plain to have had a romance
and what else might they do with their lives, anyway? And here was Nannie,
as ordinary a girl as could be found anywhere, set on becoming one of
them!"

"I hope you and Grete did not quiz her with too many questions,"
Magda chided her daughter.

"In truth, Mama, we did not! Only the ones that we truly wondered
about! She was very sensible and straightforward about it all. She told us
she wanted to be a teacher and she did not think she was suited for
marriage. All of the dancing and flirting and holding hands and whispering
in corners, it bored her. It just wasn't something she felt an enthusiasm for.
And that the convent always felt like a home to her, a home that drew her in,
where she felt safe." Lottie threaded her needle with a new color of wool
worsted and continued, "She said that she felt as protected at the Ursuline
school as she had as a child, when Papa looked after you all; that the love
of Christ gave her strength to face anything in the world. She said several
times that she felt drawn to the religious life, that it was something that she
must do. Not because anything forced her obedience, but because it was
right for her do so. She told us it was a joy to take up that work that had
been set for her to do, and we should not think of her vocation as a
tragedy."

"And so it was," Magda agreed, "for she went joyfully to vows as
postulant as ever a bride ever went to her wedding. With more joy than I
went to my wedding, for I was having second thoughts about the whole
matter! I had never seen your sister look so happy. She glowed with it, as if
she were lit from within."

"A bride of Christ," Lottie mused. "And I do not think she ever looked
back with regret. She was truly one of the chosen, although it made all the
rest of us very sad, to know that she would spend the rest of her days apart
from us, more apart than if she had married and gone to another part of the
country with her husband. It was quite saddening for us, wasn't it, Mama?"

"Not for myself so much," Magda agreed. *"I came to see the matter through her eyes, of course—she was my child and I loved her very dearly. What she wanted to do with her life was by her choice. It did leave your brothers quite baffled, being men and young and not as well-acquainted with the hearts of women as they assumed themselves to be!"*

"And Auntie Liesel?," Lottie deftly sent the blunt steel needle through the mesh of the Berlin wool-work she had on her hoop, *That set off another of her spells, didn't it?"*

"Oh, yes," Magda answered. *"She took to her rooms. Not so much because of Hannah, but because Marie had married and gone to Friedrichsburg, and she was done with the grand distraction of planning the wedding. Only Grete was still at home to console her. Your Aunt was always at an extreme in her emotions."*

"I know." Lottie deftly anchored the end of her yarn, snipped it short and threaded the needle with another color. *"Always on top of the tallest tower or in the deepest cellar, as you and Opa always said. So Onkel Hansi then came up with a means to divert her from her imagined woes?"*

"Yes, Lottchen. He also meant to remove her entirely from where she might hear so much about campaigns against the Indians. That was about the time they were at last being forced to submit to the Reservation, to cease their constant raids into settled country and to disgorge the many captives they held. Each time there was a great to-do about this or that child or youth being returned to his or her home, your aunt was. . ."

"Distraught," Lottie agreed. *"I remember, so many scenes where she would begin to weep and wail herself into hysterical palpitations, begging us to send yet more letters or to call upon anyone who might have more intelligence of Willi's sad fate. Grete and I took to coming and hiding in the cottage, when she had those spells—for of course, it had been more than ten years by then. Poor Grete could hardly recall much more than a sketch of small details, more like the memory of a bad dream than anything else. But Auntie Liesel would fruitlessly quiz her over and over again."*

"Her doctors finally advised Hansi to take her away, as far away as possible," Magda nodded. *"To take a cure, and he had already begun thinking of a long visit to Germany, to our old home. Dolph and Peter talked much of buying pedigreed blood-stock in England, so it seemed to your uncle that such purposes could be all agreeably combined. Also, he thought to divert me; Hannah was in seclusion for her novitiate. 'It's like a caterpillar, weaving a chrysalis for itself, in peace and quiet,' Sam said to me, by way of explaining, 'and at the end of it, becoming a butterfly. But you*

305

can't go peeking into the chrysalis! It ruins the whole thing.' He and Hannah were always close. Of all of us, he understood her best and accepted her vocation most readily."

"At the time, we did not know of all that," Lottie said. "It just seemed like one of Onkel Hansi's notions—just more splendid than any of the others. To go to Europe, for a grand tour with the family, to travel in splendid luxury, and remain there for almost a year, seeing all those sights that we had only read of! It was like a dream come true!"

"Yes, you and Grete and Horrie were beside yourselves with excitement," Magda smiled, reminiscently. "And I admit that for me, it was terribly exciting. The very journey itself was so different. Such a contrast between our first arrival in this country, and our return to where we started, could scarcely be credited. Still," the light fled from her face, and she looked quite melancholy for a moment, "I found myself thinking constantly of your father—what he would have thought and said. He was so much a man of this place, of the frontier as it once was! What would he have thought of matters so new and foreign to him?!"

"I am certain his opinions would have been quite diverting," Lottie allowed. "And rather akin to what Dolph or Cousin Peter felt on most matters."

"Ah, but your brother usually kept his thoughts to himself," Magda pointed out.

Lottie giggled fondly. "Most of the time and in courtesy, Mama—lest they scorch the walls and furniture!"

* * *

They took passage on a Morgan steamship from Indianola, early in the summer after Marie's wedding and Hannah's decision to enter the religious life; Hansi and Liesel with Grete, Magda with Dolph and Lottie, and Peter and Anna with their two boys and Horrie. Magda had thought sure that Sam would accompany her, but at the last he declined, saying that he had the ranch to oversee.

Fredi had declined at the very first when Hansi broached the subject a week after Marie's wedding. He sat in the parlor of Hansi's grand painted mansion, turning his hat in his hands and looking at his sisters and brother-in-law with worried eyes in a weather-burned face.

"It's not a place that means much to me any more. Sorry, Hansi, Magda. I've got too much on my plate here. I want to take one more herd up the trail this season—I can't let the lads down, now that the arrangements are all made. Sorry, Hansi."

Sam did accompany them as far as Indianola, though, by coach as far as Cuero and then the train. "Maybe I'll regret not seeing all the noble paintings and art collections," he said, as he came with them to the long dock reaching out into the gray-blue waters of Matagorda Bay. "But I can't see getting a proper enjoyment of them while hand-holding Auntie Liesel and fetching her smelling salts and handkerchief."

"Don't be silly, she has a maid to do all that," Magda said.

Dolph grinned. "And Onkel's manly shoulder to cry on whenever necessary."

"Well, you and Peter don't buy any three-legged horses while you are at it," Sam advised. "I'll go myself next year, maybe—the museums and statues and all, they'll still be there!"

Over their heads the warning steam whistle blew, startling the gulls soaring on still wings on updrafts of warm air in the brilliant summer sky. Under their feet the wooden dock seemed to tremble with the force of the engine that turned the steamship's great wheels. At their back, Indianola sprawled along that brilliant white shell-sand beach, pastel colored houses with their ocean-front galleries and balconies like some kind of wooden Venice on the sea. The ice warehouse loomed like some strange fortress tower at the edge of town.

"Don't worry." Dolph took up the small grip which was his personal luggage in one hand and Magda's elbow with the other. "And don't lose any of my cows, little brother. It's time, Mama. We'll see you in the spring!"

"Bon voyage!" Sam shouted from the dock, waving his hat. Magda could see her son's fair hair and the pale straw of his summer hat for a long time, as the band of water widened between dockside and ship. She and her children, with Anna and Peter and their sons, remained on deck for as long as the town could be seen.

Peter and Anna each had a firm grip on the backs of the boys' coats. Anna sighed with a look of mock despair. "Auntie, I am going to be run ragged, long before we reach New York. Harry makes a bee-line straight for every dangerous thing imaginable. What are we going to do?"

"Tie a lariat to each of them," Peter said with an air of practicality, "with one of us or Horrie holding the other end!" He hoisted Christian up underneath one arm, holding him with his head down, while the child wiggled and squirmed.

Anna laughed. "Don't tempt me with that thought," she said.

"How is Ma'am Richter holding up?" Peter turned Christian upright and set him on his feet—but maintained a strong one-handed grip on his collar. The freshening sea breeze ruffled the boy's hair, and the ends of Anna's and Magda's bonnet ribbons.

"She had a bad moment on the dock," Magda answered, for Liesel had turned deathly pale as she stepped out of the closed coach which had carried them from the Casimir House. "Hansi picked her up and carried her straightaway below to their cabin. I think she shall stay there until we reach New York."

"Pity, that." Peter sniffed the salt-smell of the ocean with relish. "It's a guarantee for the worst sort of seasickness, to stay below all the time. A brisk turn around the deck in any weather is the best cure for it."

"Don't I know that!" Magda answered feelingly and shuddered, remembering the dank and reeking passenger deck of the brig *Apollo*, how she and Anna and the rest of her family had lain on their open shelf-bunks as a fierce winter storm violently pitched the ship, as roughly as a dog tossing a toy. How dark, how filthy that cramped space soon became; the wooden timbers creaking and groaning as a thing alive, while the wooden hull sweated moisture and radiated sea-cold upon them. She had held the three-year-old Anna in her arms during that long dark purgatory, praying for survival, dreaming of sitting by a river in a green meadow while birds sang in the trees overhead. "I swore after we landed in Galveston, that I would have to stay in Texas, for never again would I set foot on a ship to cross that ocean," she recalled.

Anna briefly set her arm around Magda's waist. "This is not anything like the old *Apollo*," she said to be comforting. "I have been reading the circulars; we have private cabins with every possible modern convenience and adornment, quite as fine as the best sort of hotel. And the Hamburg-America is even more luxurious. We shall all have private cabins. The ship companies now spare no expense when it comes to seeing to the passengers' comforts!"

"They certainly took no effort in that respect before!" Magda observed with some asperity. "Save for offering fresh straw for our beds, halfway through the voyage, and to sew the dead up in canvas for burial at sea! Oh, yes, our comforts were very well seen to!"

"It's not like that now, Auntie," Anna reassured her. "Papa says there is much competition between the steamship companies, offering luxuries to the traveler, especially those who travel for pleasure or enlightenment, and not because they must emigrate. Every care must be taken, lest we unhappy travelers go elsewhere, or stay at home!"

"That would have suited me," Magda said and when Lottie and Anna chorused their dismay, she smiled and added, "Oh, do not chide me! It has just been so long since we departed from Germany! So much has changed since our coming here, I am sure that what we left behind has changed as well! I do wonder if I shall see anything familiar at all."

"Ne'er mind, Mama," Lottie said with exuberant affection. "It will all be new to me, and I will enjoy it at least!"

They reached New York in good time, but waited there almost a week, for the regular packet-liner to Hamburg upon which Hansi had arranged passage did not depart until Thursday. Hansi booked a suite of rooms for them in a hotel recommended by a fellow passenger. Magda had been dreading to find that the hotel would be a low, dirty place, for she was not impressed at first by the city; so crowded, the streets piled with every sort of filth, with grimy tenement buildings leaning over streets that seemed like canyons teeming with people.

"As awful as the beach at Karlshaven was," she said to Hansi, "I rejoice now that we went there, and not here! Can you imagine Vati and the boys and I, marooned in this awful place?"

"Grim, is it not?" Hansi agreed. "Yet there would have been something for us to have made, through coming here. This is the fountainhead, where all the markets flow. I daresay I ought to know it better."

Magda shuddered. "I cannot imagine seeing only this dull grey sky and nothing of wildflowers."

"Well, there are sights to be seen, and many fine shops," Hansi told her. "Take notes and do not let Lise and the girls spend too much money!"

Peter and Dolph came back from an excursion to a bookseller in a state of amused disbelief. "You would not believe the dime novels which they represent to be about the West," Dolph said, shaking his head.

Peter added, "Utter bosh, every word of it! Apparently we cattle drovers spend all of our time in gunfights with the Indians or bandits or some such!" Peter chuckled, shaking his head. "Aside from shooting into the air to head off a stampede, I don't think I've ever had much other use for my six-shooter!"

"I killed a rattlesnake with mine," Dolph added, self-deprecatingly. "And I tried to tell them that there are probably more dangerous bandits around these parts than there ever are in old Abilene or Dodge, but I don't think they believed a word of it."

"Well, Cuz," Peter was still laughing, "do you think they'd have believed it if you told them that the only one among us who has ever faced down an armed desperado was your mother?!"

"You did not make mention of that, surely?" Magda pleaded.

Both Peter and Dolph laughed again. Dolph replied, "No, Mama, but I spun them some other fine yarns, since they were so disposed to believe them. I would have shown them some roping tricks, also, but I did not have my lariat with me."

"Good thing Papa Richter was not there," Peter added. "He would have seen there was money to be made in an exhibition! He would have hired a hall and some horses and put us both to work at it before we could count to five!"

With but a few days before their ship departed, Magda and the children went for many long walks in the nearby city park; at least there was something of the sky to be seen. The park was a grand creation which had only been lately finished; Magda privately thought that although the landscaped paths were very fine and the trees and plantings cunningly arranged, the meadows and banks of flowers thus displayed were not half as beautiful as the flower meadows in the valley of the Guadalupe in springtime, nor the ponds and streamlets nearly so fair as the clear green waters flowing over banks of white gravel.

In the evenings, she and Anna went to lectures, to concerts and once to the opera. "It's all very fine," she mused thoughtfully afterwards, "but I almost think we had just as fine in Friedrichsburg—certainly for music and concerts. And we did not have to dress up so much for it!" She added, with a sigh, they all felt very much at a disadvantage, comparing themselves to that portion of the bon ton of New York who attended such. Magda had always thought she was dressed plainly but elegantly enough for San Antonio, but in New York she felt quite as drab as a country sparrow.

"East or west, home is the best," Anna remarked, sinking into a soft chair in their little shared sitting room, and carefully unpeeling her long gloves. "Here, Auntie—I'll undo your buttons, if you undo mine. Thank God we are on our way tomorrow—if we stay here much longer, we shall have to hire a maid."

"I wouldn't mind, someone to see to laying out my clothes, and the laundry and that," Magda said. "But I hate to think of myself as so helpless that I must have someone help me put on my clothes."

The packet-steamer was larger than the steamship that brought them from Indianola, roomy and every bit as luxurious as Anna had promised it would be. Magda shook her head, thinking that it must be fully three or four times the length of the *Apollo*—and that the first class salon was itself as large as the *Apollo*'s passenger deck. No expense had been spared when it came to fitting out the first-class cabins, even if the considerable luxury of the appointments did not make them seem any larger. She and Lottie shared a tiny bedroom with Grete, and Hansi and Liesel shared another, with a miniscule sitting room in between. Horrie and Dolph shared a similar suite with Anna and Peter and the children. As soon as they were conducted aboard, a hovering steward, a deferential middle-aged man in a tidy white uniform, made sure to point out that the doors between the two suites were unlocked, so that they might come and go as they pleased. He brought them little cups of broth and some biscuits on a silver tray, pointed out the electric bell to summon assistance, and showed the children where the wash basin and the other facility was cunningly built into the wall, concealed by a carved wooden panel that pulled down to make a washstand above and a close-stool below. Daylight streamed in through small round windows set into the ship's side; nothing of their accommodations hinted that they were on a ship, save for the gentle, almost imperceptible motion of the deck under their feet.

"Not much like the *Apollo*, eh?" Hansi remarked with a broad grin, as Harry and his brother romped throughout the suite of connected rooms. "Did you notice? Our accommodations are amid-ships, so as to reduce the noise from the steam engine. What an invention! If we run into a storm, we'll just barrel straight through, like shit through a goose! None of this being tossed about by storms for weeks on end, at the mercy of every wind that blows! We'll be in Hamburg before another week is past. Think on that! What marvelous times we live in, not so?"

"Mama!" Lottie called from the other room, as she bounced on the edge of her bed. "The mattress is so soft and springy and the coverlet feels like silk!"

No, thought Magda that night, as she lay under her own coverlet, rocked into a pleasant drowse by the motion of the ship as she had never been on the *Apollo*, thirty years before. *This is not anything like it was before. We are lapped in comfort, every need attended to and every discomfort swiftly banished. This is not anything like that dark and protracted misery that was their passage before.* She had wept to remember it, sitting on the bank of a green river not long after her arrival in Texas, that new land. She had sat beside Carl Becker and poured out all her fear and grief while he listened quietly, cleaning and oiling those old Paterson revolvers that he carried as a Ranger at Captain Jack's bidding. And when she was finished, he handed her a bit of calico to dry her face with and shared an apple. She had loved him from that moment but not realized it for some time afterwards. Now she felt his loss so very keenly! What would he have thought of all this—fine mattresses and silk coverlets, an electric bell to summon a steward with a tray of china cups of tea and a plate of sandwiches cut into fancy shapes—that soft-spoken man who thought nothing of venturing into the Llano for months on end with no more than a single Mexican blanket and sufficient ammunition?

Oh, he would have been mightily amused, she told herself. In the darkness she reached out across the bed, across that place where he would have lain. What an adventure it would have been, this journey to the country where his people had come from, to show him those places that she could barely remember herself. And what an adventure it would have been to grow old with him. On that thought, she fell asleep, dreaming of flower meadows and a clear stream of water that wound through a grove of golden-leafed sycamore trees, through which she walked, never quite catching up to the man who was always just ahead of her.

On the morning of the tenth day after departing New York, they arrived in Hamburg, going from one marvel—the speed of their passage—to another: the modern and orderly bustle of a harbor that made Indianola seem as primitive and simple as an Indian skin lodge by comparison. Street after street of tall terraced houses surrounded the harbor basin, as forests of masts and spindly cranes darkened the sky. The main avenues within the city afforded a princely prospect, lined with imposing stone and plastered buildings. Prosperity hung like a fog in the air, along with smoke from unimaginable numbers of households burning coal.

"There are ever so many soldiers," Horrie remarked interestedly from the coach that bore them all from quay to railway station. "Is there a war going on, Uncle Peter?"

"Not at present that I know of," Peter answered.

Hansi snorted contemptuously. "There was a war, once King William of Prussia had finished uniting all Germany under one ruling house. Against the French, so it turned out to be very short."

"Who won?" Horrie asked.

Hansi snorted again. "The Prussians, of course—and now a united Germany has a place in the sun. So many of our folk in America were cock-a-whoop over that! For the life of me, boy, I couldn't think why. We left thirty years ago, not wanting anything more to do with kings and conscription. My father's house was about the size of the garden shed, and as hard as we worked, we couldn't get a scrap of land any bigger than a lady's pocket handkerchief—and on top of that, I had to go and spend two years of my life being a toy soldier so that the sons of the Firsts could swank around in a fancy uniform and pretend to be Julius Caesar. The only thing I wanted from Germany was out; the only thing they gave us freely was permission to leave."

Horrie looked a little taken aback by Hansi's vehemence, so Magda explained softly, "And so we did. It's just that some of the older settlers, they kept an interest in our homeland—for sentiment, more than any thing else."

"Sentiment." Hansi looked very keenly at the children. "Aye, that's all right then. Sentiment—but we made our future and our fortunes in America. That's where our interests truly lie; never forget that, lad."

Magda pondered on Hansi's words then and again, in the days that followed, puzzling out some kind of meaning, some kind of guidance. She thought at first, when Hansi proposed this journey, that it would be a homecoming; the return of the prodigals. For all those years of living in Texas, she and the other Verein settlers had always been seen as Germans, as outlanders, set apart by language and habits as clearly as the Indians, as the Mexicans like Porfirio were set aside—marked by those differences. Her husband, born in America and never having known anyplace else, even he bore the nickname of "Dutch" among his fellows in the Rangers.

They came from Germany, bearing Germany with them; their music and love of order and education. But in time that exile Germany was worn away, as the wind wears away a sandstone cliff. Only she and Hansi and Liesel remembered the old ways clearly. The new country had claimed their children; she could tell from observing Anna's and Lottie's frank address and bearing, the way they walked briskly, striding like women with a purpose. Such qualities were even more marked with the boys. Dolph and Peter carried themselves with the assurance of aristocrats but none of that swaggering arrogance that she saw among these men of her homeland in their elegant coats, those officers with their splendid decorations, to whom everyone deferred.

"Ma'am Becker," Peter asked her curiously, as they settled themselves into the elegant first-class waiting room at the main Hamburg train station, "why is it so many of these fine officers have so many scars? You could have run a fine-mesh sieve through my company after four years in the War and not found half so many scars as I have seen in the last three hours."

"From fighting duels," Magda explained, helplessly. She was rather startled by the frequency herself. "It is quite the fashionable thing to engage in duels and sword-play, or so my brother Johann told me, when he came back to study medicine here."

"Sword-play," Peter murmured, absently running his right thumb along the pale line that slashed across his eyebrow and down across his cheek. "So that's what they call it, over here. Back in Hood's command, there's two things we'd think of a chap scarred up like that one over there," he nodded towards the imposingly uniformed officer across the waiting room from them, "that he was damned unlucky—sorry, Ma'am—or damned clumsy. Neither of which excited much confidence in those around him in the line."

Magda allowed a slight, ladylike giggle to escape her lips. The gentleman to whom Peter referred was a miracle of military splendor striding impatiently up and down, all polished boots and gold braid, hung with ribbons and orders. She could imagine all his medals a-clank in symphony along with his dress sword and ornamental spurs.

She stifled another giggle. "My husband once said," and she felt that familiar tug of grief which his memory always brought to her, "that an officer in a uniform as resplendent as that, wouldn't move him to take two steps off of a rock ledge."

"Well, that was Uncle Carl." Peter's face lit with affectionate reminiscence. "No respect for authority at all, God rest him. So, what do you think of this all now, Ma'am? Is it what you remembered?"

"I am not entirely sure," Magda answered, thinking of how they had left Albeck in Hansi's carts on an autumn day, and gone to Bremen to sign the Verein contract, staying in simple guest houses or camping among the hedges. She had lived better than half of her life in Texas; been courted there, married her husband, buried him and one of her children, buried her father and sister and many friends, seen to the building of two—no, three houses—and several businesses. And she had killed her husband's worst enemy. No, Texas had made its marks on her. She looked at the other ladies in the First Class waiting room, elegant and tightly-corseted, attended by their maids and children, and wondered how many of them habitually

314

carried a revolver in their reticules and knew how to use it, or even had the need for that knowledge anyway.

They went to the spa at Baden-Baden. Johann had reccommended it for the curative properties, adding in his advisory letter that there were many amusements to be found and anyway it would be convenient to pay visits to Ulm from there. Hansi had made enquiries when he planned the grand excursion and booked rooms for them at the Stephanienbad Hotel on the park in Baden-Baden. They would stay there while Liesel took the water-cure. He and Peter and Dolph would venture to England, searching for blood-stock, cattle and horses alike, although Peter had allowed cheerfully, "Cuz will come home with some dogs—bet what you like on that, Ma'am Becker."

Magda had acknowledged that likelihood; it was as if her son had an invisible sign on his person, inviting the halt, the lame and the hopeless of the canine breed to impose freely upon him. "Would that he would come home some day with a wife," she said, feelingly, as Peter laughed.

"Oh, he will, Ma'am, he will! Personable, hard-working, possessed of a large land holding and not unappreciative of the ladies? He will marry! He is just not in any hurry!" And Peter gave an affectionate squeeze to her hand. "Uncle Carl was not and neither was I and you would know how well those marriages turned out! You should have no fears for my dear Cuz; he will marry when he finds the right girl."

"One who doesn't mind dogs and cows," Magda sighed. "I know—he has said as much to me."

"I believe we have arrived, Ma'am Becker." Peter stood as the train began to slow. "Alas, I don't think Cuz will find her here." He whistled softly in amazement as the train cars rumbled slowly into the Baden station, a miracle and a fantasy of wrought-iron lace and sparkling clean glass, hung with bright baskets of flowers. It was a tiny place; they could look out and see green trees and meticulously groomed parkland, all around. The banks of the river were set with small ornate villas, all plastered the colors of marzipan confections: pale pink, yellow, light blue.

Hansi stepped down onto the train platform, with Liesel clinging to him as if to a rock amid a flood—which he was, in a way. Magda took her other arm. No need to see to their bags, for two porters appeared instantly with barrows as soon as Hansi snapped his fingers.

"You do that very well," Magda whispered to him. "Very lordly, as if you had been born a First!"

"Practice," Hansi grinned impishly over Liesel's bonnet. "Although I have to say, these chaps are quicker off the mark than porters in the States. Must be all that talk about equality—spoils the hell out of the help!"

"Hansi, we are expected, aren't we?" Liesel quavered. "I am really quite exhausted."

"Yes, we are, Lise-love." Hansi patted her hand. "They're sending a coach for us, and a van for the luggage. I expect they're waiting for us outside."

They waited for a moment, allowing another party to pass from farther along the platform: an enormous retinue led by an elderly lady with improbably and garishly red hair, wheeled along in an invalid chair. Two manservants pushed the chair, and a lady's maid carried a muff, and a shawl, and a pigskin jewelry case. Another maid led a number of small, pudgy and long-haired dogs on leashes. The dogs romped excitedly at the ends of their leashes, barking in a shrill soprano chorus and jerking the maid's footsteps this way and that. As this procession passed by, the elderly lady called out a harsh command in a language none of them recognized. In response, one of the manservants lifted the fattest of the dogs into her lap. The lady and her servitors were followed by a dozen porters with handcarts and barrows, piled high with trunks, boxes and cases, most all of them expensively covered in leather and adorned with a discrete gold crest.

"I wonder where she is going." Dolph easily swung his little valise over his shoulder, declining their porter's offer to add it to the pile in his barrow with a swift shake of his head.

"To the graveyard in several easy steps, by the look of her," Peter answered with cynical cheer. "Looks like she is taking most of her trash with her, too."

Both Anna and Magda shot warning looks at their menfolk. "Really," Magda said, "she did not look as old as all that. I wonder what that language was that she spoke and who she is?"

"Sounded like Russian," Hansi observed, unexpectedly. "The Tsar's grandmother, I expect. Baden has always attracted the ton and the nobility."

The Richters and the Beckers followed slowly after the old lady's retinue; slow going, even if everyone else on the platform gave way. Magda was intrigued to see that many of them bowed or curtsied to the old lady, and the station master himself came forward and spoke to her most respectfully.

In the station forecourt there were carriages waiting on the new arrivals. The old lady was being helped into the grandest of them; an amusing spectacle, with all the dogs jumping about like furry wind-up toys. One of them escaped in the melée, the old lady shrieked imprecations and instructions as her servants, and the porters instantly dropped whatever they were doing and gave chase. The dog was agile and faster than might have been expected, given its short bandy legs and podgy form. It ran with happy energy, ears and long fur flapping and the leash trailing loose after, seeming to look over its shoulder and laughing at those in fruitless pursuit. Magda's breath caught in her throat, for the station forecourt was busy, full of horses and heavy wagon wheels, and no place for a small plump lapdog. In another moment it would run out into the road, past Hansi and the children. As it did, Dolph stepped onto the trailing leash. The running dog jerked up short, suddenly arrested in midstride. As Dolph scooped it up, one of the maids came running up, gasping out thanks and apologies. Dolph handed her the dog and from the carriage the elderly lady nodded regally.

Dolph sketched a bow in her direction, just as a dapper young man came up to them, saying, "Herr Richter and party, for the Stephanienbad Hotel? Of course, right this way, if you please." In hardly any time at all, he had seen them into another carriage, their collection of luggage loaded away while the elderly lady's staff and baggage were still being sorted out.

"It is the Princess Cherkevsky," the dapper young man explained, as they bowled away from the station forecourt, "a distant connection of Russian royal family. She is accustomed to spending summer here in Baden-Baden. Spring in Paris, winter in Italy, I believe."

"Does she ever spend any time in Russia?" Hansi asked, jovially.

The dapper young man gave a delicate shudder. "I don't believe the Princess cares very much for Russia, sir. She is only one of them by marriage to the Prince, so they say. It was kind of the young sir to retrieve her dog—she thinks much of her pets. They travel with her, everywhere—even into the baths!"

"Our pleasure," Hansi rumbled; he seemed enormously amused. Magda had a mental picture of that herd of pot-bellied, bandy-legged little dogs, swimming in the hot-baths in constellation around their mistress. She met her son's eyes and knew that he was thinking the same thing.

The Stephanienbad Hotel sat in the middle of a park of trees, a grand and ornate pile of towers and galleries.

"I shall be glad to stay here for a while," Liesel said, fretfully. "It seems like we would never stop traveling."

It seemed a busy place; Magda suddenly felt very tired herself. How could that be, when she had been sitting all day in the train? Yet she felt even more exhausted than if she had been carrying muck and digging in her vegetable garden all day. She and Liesel were conducted to a comfortable settee in the lobby, deep in a window embrasure full of potted ferns and ornamental palms, while their luggage was brought up and Hansi settled on their rooms. He had strict requirements as regards their rooms; that they all be adjacent, connecting into a single suite if possible. It took some few minutes for those wishes to be accommodated, and while his family waited the children chattered excitedly in English. Christian and Harry raced across the lobby; they had the energy that their elders lacked. Horrie looked around with the studied air of a boy trying to look older and worldlier than he really was, while Grete and Lottie teased him affectionately.

". . . Becker and Richter," remarked a voice close by, in German, and Magda startled, alerted by mention of her name. Two men stood nearby, in plain livery coats; they must be hotel staff, servitors. "American," continued the voice. "He's a cattle baron, from Texas. Rich as Croesus, so they told me when he made the booking. Don't expect he'll be too demanding, these self-made men usually aren't."

"Rotten tippers, though," remarked the other man, "but then he might give you some inside hints about cattle markets!" Magda realized from the manner in which they spoke so freely, that they didn't expect what they said to be understood. All those two men observed were the children speaking in English, knew that their family was from America. She thought she might laugh, at how readily they assumed that none of the family understood German. But then the second man drawled, "So, who's the fat cow and the black crow?" Magda listened in horror to the first man's reply, realizing that the men spoke so slightingly of herself and Liesel, thinking that they did not understand although they sat within clear hearing.

"The fat cow is his wife and the black crow is a sister-in-law. You know the drill; how the poor relation dances constant attendance!"

Liesel gasped, and Magda felt as if she had been slapped. How dare he speak so rudely, so insolently! How stupid did he think they were? She looked sideways at Liesel, whose eyes were full of tears. She was not fat, only a little plump. And Magda wore black like many another women, for mourning the man who meant all the world to her! How dare those men make mockery of that! Black crow, indeed!

Magda's chin went up; she couldn't abide that sort of thoughtless cruelty. Back in Friedrichsburg, Charley Nimitz would never allow his employees to speak of guests so slightingly in their very faces! Almost without thought, the perfect response to it sprang fully armored into her mind, like Athena from Zeus' forehead.

"Please, you," she said in English, "we would like some tea, please."

"Yes, madam," the first one straightened to attention. As soon as she saw that, she switched to precise and casual German, adding, "The fat cow and this black crow would like our tea served here, while we wait for our rooms to be ready, if that is at all possible."

She relished the expression on their faces for quite some time, that look of sudden realization and horror. It was cruel and unladylike to take such savage pleasure in their discomfiture, but she told herself they richly deserved it. And the tea was very good. It appeared almost instantly. The servitor brought a plate of little jam tarts and asked, in a trembling voice, if everything was satisfactory.

"Yes it is, quite," Magda answered with composure. Liesel did not touch the tarts, but the children enjoyed them enormously.

Chapter Nineteen: *Dreaming Under Summer Skies*

The staff of the Stephanienbad set aside a generous suite of rooms for them on the first floor for Hansi's and Magda's family.

"Perhaps they are just grateful that we did not bring as many servants as did the Princess Cherkevsky," Anna ventured.

Hansi laughed. "Or that your aunt did not make complaint to the management about those men of theirs who did not think we understood German."

"You should have, Magda," Liesel said tearfully from where she lay with her feet up and a handkerchief moistened with rosewater across her brow. The exhaustion of a long day's travel, capped by overhearing such rude remarks, had brought on a sudden terror-fit. She had clutched Magda's hand with painful strength, until they were shown to their rooms. "You should have reported them for their appalling bad manners! They should have been given the sack!"

"I suppose," Magda allowed, "but this way, they have learned a very salutary lesson. And I can remind them of it, each time I see them or they see me, merely by bidding them in German to do some errand for me. And each time, they are reminded that I could have made a complaint to the hotelier—but I didn't. I expect that they shall give exemplary service, do you not agree, Liesel?"

"Good God," Peter murmured to Dolph, "and they claim that it is Indian women who practice the most refined tortures upon their captives. I wouldn't have believed that, until now!"

"It is not vengefulness or cruelty," Magda insisted primly, "merely a correction of incompetence and bad manners. Really, you must give people credit for the capacity to learn and improve."

"Whatever you say, Mama." Dolph leaned down and kissed her cheek. "Crack your whip and watch your slaves fall to! Are we going to dine in our rooms tonight, or go to the dining room? It looks very fine," he added, as Lottie, Grete and Horrie chorused their eagerness for the dining room.

"You may," Magda answered.

Hansi added, "I think we will eat in our room and turn in early. You young pups may do what you like; just don't wake us when you return!"

"It was a lovely place," Lottie reminisced to Magda, *"such a beautiful, beautiful town—every prospect as lovely as a set for a stage play!*

One almost expected the chorus and ballet to appear from out of the wings, and commence to sing and dance. Such lovely gardens and baskets of flowers everywhere! My favorite walk was the Lichtenthaler Allee and being able to look into the gardens of all those lovely houses. Almost as entertaining as sitting in the public square listening to music. Every afternoon, such beautiful music under the sycamore trees! How horrible to think of how we have been at war with them for these last few years, Mama—when I found everyone so kind, so hospitable! Auntie Liesel began her course of treatment almost at once, didn't she?"

"Oh, yes," Magda sighed, "it was very protracted; soaking for hours in the mineral waters, baths and massages and constantly drinking of it, and special meals. Tedious for the rest of us, but it did her much good."

"I think it was the effects of everyone fussing over her constantly," Lottie observed.

"For shame, Lottie," Magda chastised her. "That was most uncalled for!"

"No? Oh, Mama—you hardly ever left her side! While Grete and I and Horrie enjoyed ourselves, you hovered over her like a nurse, like a mother hen with one chick! Even Onkel Hansi eventually got bored and went to England to buy horses with Dolph and Cousin Peter!"

"Before that—we did return to Albeck, though," Magda pointed out.

"Yes, but you traveled thence in a stuffy closed carriage with her, while the rest of us rode in an open barouche!" And she added with a shudder, "And what a place it was! Grete and I could scarce believe the wretchedness of it! Those tiny houses and that awful, awful man!"

"Lottie, it was not like that before," Magda exclaimed with some heat. "It was our home once before and we remembered it very fondly."

"With advantages," Lottie interjected. "So when did Onkel Hansi decided on dragging us all to that backwards little village?"

Magda laid her arthritis-knotted hand on Mouse's head. The Peke roused from sleep and looked at her with his bulging eyes almost liquid with adoration. Magda had always felt the cold quite dreadfully, and now she felt it even more. "We made an excursion to Ulm almost as soon as we had rested from our long journey! We were so eager to see our old home; I still cannot decide if we hoped it had changed, or remained exactly as we remembered in every detail! In Ulm, much had changed. Aunt Ursula's children had long since emigrated. And Uncle Simon, your Opa's dearest friend? He had died also, his children and his nephew scattered to the four winds. We could not even find the street where their shops had been, for that

321

part of town had all been new-built! The more we tried to recall where
everything had been, the more those memories escaped us, like water in the
palm of your hand! But Albeck . . . Albeck was the same," Magda sighed
bitterly, "just the same. Hansi had written to his brothers, Jurgen and
Joachim—his parents were long-dead, of course. His father died the year
after we departed, his mother sometime during the War Between the States.
But his brothers still lived in Albeck."

* * *

And so they went out from Ulm on a late summer day, a day achingly
like the day when they had departed, over thirty summers before. The
children were mad with excitement, although Horrie and Peter stood a little
apart from all this. Their connection to the homeland was slight at best.
Heinrich Becker, Margaret and Carl's grandfather, was from Kassel in
Hesse. A soldier in the Landgrave's regiments that had been brought to
America to serve the British, he had deserted amd married the daughter of a
Pennsylvania family of Anabaptists, and never regretted either action. Those
ties and memories the Beckers had of their ancestral heritage had long
decayed by the time Alois Becker crossed into Texas with his children, his
ox teams and Conestoga wagon—all but the language they spoke among
themselves and the songs they sang to the children. This new land had
claimed them, just as it had claimed her children in turn. Magda looked from
the narrow slit in the curtains drawn over the windows of the closed coach,
which was all that Liesel could bear, on this hottest day of mid-summer. Oh,
at least it wasn't as hot as it would have been in Texas, she thought
resignedly.

Her breath caught in her throat; this was the very place, the place
where Hansi had stopped his cart and held three-year-old Anna up in his
arms.

"Look," he called to them all at that moment, as their carts halted
beside the road out of their village, "look back, for that is the last sight of
Albeck! Look well, and remember—for that is the very last that we will see
of our old home!"

They had looked back obediently but with no small emotion, looked
back at the tiny huddle of roofs around the church spire, a little ship afloat
in a sea of golden fields; Hansi and Liesel with baby Joachim, the child who
was fated to die at sea, and Magda with her parents and little brothers in

the second cart, on their way to a new life in a new country. 'Gehe mit uns in Texas' was the slogan: Come with us to Texas!

"I never thought we would return," she said to her sister, the two of them in the stifling coach. "I never thought anything would induce me to set foot on a ship again."

"Are we almost there?" Liesel asked, almost wistfully. "I would so like to see Vati's old house again, although I suppose it is much changed. Do you suppose the new owners would let us go inside? We lived there so happily. I would like Grete and Harry and Christian to see. Do you remember how we milked the cows in Vati's barn? The morning after Vati and Hansi decided that we would accept the Verein's offer of lands and transport?"

"Yes, and I told you that Vati and Hansi had already decided upon it, so all we could do was to put the best countenance upon it and be brave," Magda answered. She found her sister's hand, neatly gloved and lying in her lap, as the coach swayed down the narrow road. She gave it a comforting squeeze and added, "You were brave, Lise—as brave as you could be."

"No I wasn't," Liesel gulped. "I could only put on a bold face as long as you or Vati and Hansi were with me. As soon as I was alone, such fears crept out of dark corners to overwhelm me! I could not bear it when Hansi went to drive for the Confederate Army—and then to lose my little boys and Grete to that cruel frontier!"

"But Grete was restored to you," Magda answered swiftly. "And Hansi and your other sons have had such success as they never dreamed of, that Vati never dreamed of! Surely that must be added to the ledger-book, Lise! Do you not also remember how you also had dreams, that you would marry Hansi and I would marry a prince and live in a mansion full of books and come to visit in a fine coach? That was your dream, sister. Does it not seem to have come true?"

"Oh yes," and Liesel laughed a little, "but at such a cost! But Hansi says all such things have costs. Until the race is completed, one may not even begin to know if the cost was worth paying!"

"No, one does not," Magda agreed. "But I would never have married if I had remained in Albeck; my children would never have been born—so for me it was worthwhile!"

"I suppose." Liesel sighed again, as the coachman reined his teams to a stop. The coach rocked forward and then swayed as Hansi opened the door.

"We're here, Lise-love! Your father's house! It's owned by a man in Ulm and there's tenants living in it now! There doesn't seem to be anyone about, so I don't suppose we should venture any farther than the yard." He helped Liesel down, and Dolph reached up to take Magda's hand.

The sunlight dazzled her eyes as she stepped down from the coach. The barouche was stopped a little beyond the gate into Vati's old farmyard; Anna and the girls stood under the archway, looking curiously within.

"Needs a fresh coat of whitewash," Magda said at once, her heart in her throat. The wooden gates stood wide open. She was struck with the sudden notion of how incongruous they all appeared, in their bright fashionable dresses and neat leather shoes, standing in the trodden muck of Albeck's narrow street, like butterflies lighting down on a dung heap, while hens picked at odd bits of greenery and grain between the cracks of the cobbled yard within.

"It's so much smaller than I remembered," Anna ventured at last. "I thought it as large as a mansion and the stable a good distance from the house. I did not recall everything crammed so tightly together!" Her nostrils flared delicately as she added, "Truly, Papa, how did we endure the muck pile so close to the house windows, especially on a hot summer day?"

"Muck was gold to us then, Annchen," Hansi answered exuberantly. "Every shovelful was precious, spread on the fields in the spring."

Beside Magda, her son shook his head in mild amusement. "Oh, Lord, Uncle Hansi—all I need do is pasture the cattle in one of my fields until they have added enough muck to it, without the bother of the hands carting it around."

"We did things differently, back then," Hansi answered. It seemed to Magda that he had a catch in his voice, as if he too had just realized how far he had journeyed from this place. The cattle baron, they had called him at the Stephanienbad, in his fine-cut coat, waistcoat with a heavy gold watch chain spread across a rich expanse of silk brocade, and elegant leather boots that had never stepped through a freshly spread layer of muck in the fields.

"Oh, look, Hansi, they have put pots of geraniums by the door, just as Mutti used to do!" Liesel exclaimed.

The door to the house opened, and a woman in a plain dark dress without any hoops, and a vast dirty apron tied around her waist, stepped out of the dim doorway. She stared at them, mute with astonishment for a moment before calling nervously, "Did you have need of something from us, madams and sirs?"

"Yes and no, madam," Hansi answered, cheerily. "For we are old residents of Albeck. This house was once my father in-law's; my good wife and her sister once lived here! Do you have any recollection of Christian Steinmetz and his kin?"

"Old Steinmetz the watchmaker?" the woman answered warily. "Whose daughter married the younger Richter boy and they went all off to America? I came here with my husband from Erbach on the other side of Ulm ten years ago; we knew them not. They were gone years before that." She shrugged her shoulders, as if it was of no note to her; and of course it wasn't, Magda realized. She and her family were tenants. They weren't of Albeck in the way that Vati had been. "They say," the woman added with indifference, as she threw a handful of grain towards the chickens, "that most of them either died of disease or were carried away by Indians. What were they thinking, going off to that place? Full of barbarians it is. Why would any sensible body leave here and go to there, my man says! What's the matter with being content with what you have right here?"

"Nothing much, madam," Hansi agreed with a cheery smile, "unless you aren't content with it and want better! I am Hansi Richter; Jurgen and Joachim are my older brothers!"

"Aye?" The woman looked skeptical, "Jurgen Richter never said much about a brother in America, then."

"I don't suppose I spoke all that much about him either, once I was in America." Hansi's cheer looked a bit dimmer. "But may I ask a favor, Madam? My wife and her sister once lived here and we had thought to show our children this very house. Might we come inside so that they might see?"

"Only as far as the kitchen, mind," the woman answered, warily. "The upstairs is let to another tenant and my youngest is asleep in the other room so you mustn't make any noise—I'll have no peace until she goes back to sleep." She patted her hair, uncomfortably, as if suddenly and most embarrassingly aware that it was falling out of its pins. "Let me have a moment, sir, madams—I left something on the fire." She dove into the doorway again, untying her apron as she did.

Magda said, "Oh, dear. She's in the middle of her work, and the kitchen is all disarrayed. We have embarrassed her, asking to see all that."

"Well, I'm not her landlord or her husband so why should I care?" Hansi asked reasonably.

Anna laughed, "Oh, Papa! You should know, any proper housewife hates for strangers to see a mess in her house! We should wait for courtesy, at least a few minutes."

"But not for too long," Hansi replied, "for my brothers are expecting our arrival shortly."

"Mama," Lottie whispered tremulously to her mother, "must we go inside? I really don't want to, it looks awfully squalid."

Magda reproved her. "Lottie, this is your grandfather's old house, where we all lived until we committed to immigrate to Texas."

Lottie replied, "Mama, I think Opa improved himself no end; this place is awful. It may be quaint but it is tiny and it smells!"

Magda sighed. Vati's old house in its present condition did indeed suffer by comparison in her memory, not to mention compared to the Becker ranch house and to Hansi's grand San Antonio mansion. But surely, Mutti and Vati, they had kept it in better condition than this. She and Liesel had scoured the stoop and swept the courtyard daily; Hansi had white-washed the walls every couple of years. Surely Vati's house had not seemed so humble and plain when it was their home!? Surely Mutti had kept it to a higher standard than it presently was, with an indefinable air of air of poverty and neglect?

"We will not stay long," she said. Lottie and Grete immediately appeared much cheered.

It was not so bad within, when the woman of the house finally made a welcoming gesture, inviting them to step across the stone threshold of the main door. Five hundred years and more of human activity had worn an achingly familiar gentle declivity into the doorstep. Magda thought of how often her own footsteps had carried her in and out of that door, busy about the business of Vati's farmhouse when she was a girl. She stepped through that oh-so-familiar door—so much the same, so much different!

A fire burned brightly in the hearth, gleaming from the copper pans hanging over it; but those pans were not as brilliantly polished as Mutti would have had them. Reassuringly, the kitchen was not a pit of slovenly disorder. Bunches of herbs still hung in their accustomed places, and the pieces of rustic furniture were not any fewer, or of worse quality, than what had been before. Indeed, the dish cupboard was the same, as Magda thought when she looked at it closely. It had been too large, too heavy to remove from the room without taking it to pieces, so Vati had relinquished it with all the other household fittings. Now it was filled with someone else's dishes, not the blue-and-white plates that Mutti had packed so carefully in wood shavings and put into the back of one of Hansi's sturdy farm carts. Now those very plates, which had survived the long journey and the years afterward, filled the shelves of the dish cupboard of Vati's Friedrichsburg house.

"Vati, your grandfather, he used to read in a chair set in this very place," Liesel was pointing out the deep-set fireplace, almost an inglenook in itself, to Anna's sons and Grete. "Late into the night, after supper. In winter, it was the warmest place in the house. And when he was in Ulm, at his shop in the city, there I would set and nurse my children."

"Our room was upstairs," Magda said softly to Dolph and Lottie. "Lise and I shared a little room under the eaves. From when we were children, until Liesel and Hansi married."

"It seems very cramped," Dolph pointed out, ducking his head under one of the age-darkened roof beams that spanned the fireplace end of the kitchen.

Peter added, and Magda could tell that he was smiling under his heavy mustache, "How many times would I have concussed myself, Cuz, before I took to walking around like a hunchback?"

A window filled with small roundels of bottle-green glass looked out from the kitchen, into the street. Like a sleepwalker, Anna moved towards it. "It is so very small," she said in a voice of wonder. "This window was above my head, once. It seemed to be as tall as a church-window, but I could not see out of it."

"You still cannot, Anna-my-heart," her husband pointed out with dry wit. "That glass is as thick as a pot lid." He took her hand, and placing his other arm around her waist, added softly, "Yes, I daresay this quaint little place has charm enough for the sentimental—but all the same I am glad you came away." Magda saw that Anna leaned towards his embrace, as if she were glad of it.

"I think we should go, Hansi," she said to her brother-in-law. "We are in the way of this good woman's work of a morning. This is not our house. It has not been such for years."

"I wish we could have seen upstairs," Liesel said, wistfully, with a look of longing over her shoulder towards the little door that led into the stair-hall.

Hansi answered, "No sense in it, Lise. I don't think the children are much interested, and Magda is right—we have been enough of an interference. Let's walk down to my brothers', though, hey? It's not such a long way, we'll tell the coachmen to meet us there."

They bade the woman of the house good day. Hansi lingered behind and Magda thought he gave her a little money. "For your trouble, good madam," he said.

As Magda went out into the farmyard, her son took her arm. "Now I see what Vati and the others were thinking of," he remarked.

"Thinking of?" Magda asked, much puzzled.

Dolph explained patiently, "What they were thinking of, when Vati built his house, and the other old settlers built theirs." Dolph waved his hand around the courtyard, and the little street beyond. "A place like this, mostly. Solid and close together. That kitchen was the pattern for the one in Vati's house, and the one that Berg built for Papa. Only," he added in a rush of candor, "I think ours are better. Not so cramped."

"And windows one can see out of," Peter added. In the bright sunshine outside, Anna opened her parasol, as did Lottie and Grete. Magda watched Liesel carefully; no, no sign yet of her descending in a rush to her deep dark cellar, or one of those fear-inducing megrims.

"I am glad to have seen Vati's house again," she announced, cheerfully breathless, "but Annchen is right; I had forgotten how very small it was!"

"You live in a mansion now, Lise," Magda was quick to point out.

She took Liesel's arm as Hansi emerged from the house and took her other, saying jovially, "Ah well, at least we can hope for a warmer welcome from my brothers, hey?"

Magda recalled Hansi's older brothers very well; they were as like to him as Hansi's older sons were like each other, stolid and stubborn, good company when they felt like it, with the same temper that never came out until provoked beyond reasoning. They had teased her roughly, as boys would, when they were all at the village school together. She was not pretty and meek like the other girls, and so gave back as good as she got, but Jurgen and Joachim had come and bid them farewell from this very courtyard, on the day the departed to take ship from Bremen.

There were few enough people in the streets of Albeck; only themselves, and once or twice someone looking out warily from a house window, as if they did not dare approach such a party of well-dressed strangers. There was not room enough for them to walk more than two and two. Liesel seemed to be without care or fear, chattering to Hansi with cheerful anticipation of a nice visit with his family, so Magda took Dolph's elbow and walked ahead.

There was the church, a blunt stone tower and an onion-shaped dome of tarnished green copper, reaching farther into the sky than the tallest tree. "When I was a girl," Magda whispered to her son, "I knew every stick and stone of this place."

"That would have been easy enough," Dolph smiled. "It isn't all that large."

Harry and Christian romped fearlessly ahead of them; the cheerful racket of their voices alleviated some of the brooding quiet of midday.

"I don't remember it being all so quiet," Magda ventured.

From behind her, Hansi said, "I suppose most are out in the fields . . . or mayhap most did as we did and immigrated to America, hey?"

"There is Hansi's father's house," Magda whispered. "Just past the church, with the oak tree before."

"Now I see where Vati had the notion to have a garden under the oak trees," Dolph observed. "I guess that those must be Onkel Hansi's brothers."

He sounded doubtful, and Magda could hardly blame him. Although in true age they were only a few years older than Hansi, these two men sitting in the dooryard outside the Richter cottage farmhold appeared so very much older. One of them—she thought it must be Joachim, the oldest—had gotten very fat. Although they still resembled Hansi in something of their coloring and features, Magda found the differences to be marked, even shocking. Hansi, immaculately barbered, cheerful of countenance, dressed like a man of prosperous circumstances—appeared half their age. Even more surprising was the lack of real welcome on their faces, as Hansi crossed the road, sweeping Liesel along with him in his haste to greet them.

"Jurgen—Joachim! Here we are then, all of us! Well, not quite all of us, since I've only brought two of my girls! Such a to-do, I can't tell you, the boys were all taken up with their own businesses and with young Marie just married! Did I tell you, I have three fine sons, five if you count my daughters' menfolk! This is one of them: Peter Vining, married my oldest, little Annchen who was just a child when we came away! Don't mind him, he's an American but good old German stock, he speaks now like one of us! The little boys are his and Annchen's! And you remember Margaretha, old Steinmetz's oldest daughter?" He was exuberantly clasping first one brother's hand, then the other, embracing them both, while Magda stood a little aside with the children.

"Welcome, Brother Hansi," Joachim said, sounding anything but welcoming. "Something to see you back after all this time. Your last letters to Mother didn't sound as if all those fine Verein plans had worked out very well for you at all!"

"Some of them worked out better than others." Hansi smiled; buff, hearty Hansi—the jibe went sailing straight past. Or did it, Magda wondered? She looked between the brothers, covertly. No one ever looked much at a woman in widow-black, so she felt secure in doing this. She observed Hansi, sucking in his comparatively smaller gut as he noted the spread of Joachim's own. Really, Hansi's brother looked like an inflated bladder on legs. She took a certain vengeful pleasure in that. Hansi was a good, honest man; he did not deserve being the object of this jealousy and malice. The years sat well and comfortably on him, whereas Joachim's cheeks were hazed by gray stubble, and the knuckles and fingernails of the hand that he held out to Liesel were ingrained with grime so deeply embedded that it could never quite be washed away.

"Welcome, welcome!" Joachim said, turning his attention to the others, although something in his gloating expression belied his words. "Come in, come in . . . although there are so many with you Brother Hansi—perhaps we shall be more comfortable in the garden, under the trees!" There were benches and rustic chairs enough, under the trees; Magda, remembering how small the Richters' cottage had been, thought it all for the better. Joachim's eyes lit with recognition, but there was still that avid, gloating look on his face, as he said to Magda, "You . . . I remember, you were the plain one, with all the brains. Margaretha, wasn't it? And who is this fancy-boy then?"

"My son, Rudolph," Magda answered quietly. She found Joachim repellant.

"Looked too young for a husband," Joachim laughed, greasily, "but then you never know. Sit—sit, sit! So you did marry, after all. Quite surprise all around, I'm sure! So who was the lucky chap—anyone from Albeck?"

"No," Magda answered, giving a Dolph's elbow a warning squeeze.

"Looks like you had bad luck with him anyway," Joachim observed. "Eternal mourning, just like the Widow of Windsor Palace, eh? Well, at least you had a chance to do a couple of turns around the paddock." Joachim winked, suggestively, while Magda stared straight over his head. Really, she thought; Hansi might be crude on occasion, but he was jolly with his remarks. Joachim was just crude, and cruel with it, although she was hard-put to tell if he was being deliberately boorish. "And this is Annchen . . . little Annchen! How you have grown!"

Joachim reached out, almost as if he would pinch her cheek as if she was still a little girl, but Anna deftly caught his hand. "Onkel Joachim," she exclaimed, "why, so I have! Nothing gets past you, does it?" She smiled with sweet venom, adding, "This is my husband, Peter—he was a nephew of Auntie Magda's husband."

"Keeps it all in the family then!" It seemed to Magda that Joachim leered very unpleasantly at them all. She could tell from the tension in her son that he disliked this man, this place very intensely. But he had disciplined his face to that bland expression that she knew so well. Still, she prayed that his visit would be short. "Sit, sit, I beg you!" Joachim cried, and when they had obeyed, sitting all in a row like birds on a branch, he sank back into his own chair and regarded them with one of those expressions that Magda could not fathom.

"You look well," Joachim remarked at last. "Better than I had expected, once we heard of your return. What did I say, Jurgen—here they are, coming back again! Back to Albeck! Here we thought, well, must not have done so good for themselves after all!" *What to say to that?* Magda wondered. *What kind of notion about their lives in Texas did his brothers get from Hansi's infrequent letters?*

Finally Hansi said, "This is just a visit, Joachim, not to stay for good."

His brothers looked immeasurably relieved by this reply and Peter whispered in English, "Cuz, something tells me that they aren't really that pleased to see the old boy. They're acting as if he has come to borrow money."

Anna's lips moved in one of Hansi's favorite oaths; she whispered in the same language, "What nonsense! Papa used to send money to Oma Richter all the time; not much but what he could. She would write and tell him how mean and cheeseparing Onkel Joachim was, once he inherited everything from Opa Richter. He couldn't send money during the war, of course, and Oma Richter died then. She was the only one who wrote, ever."

A woman emerged from the front door of the cottage, bearing a tray with some jugs and plates upon it. She placed them on the little table, and cast a resigned look upon them all. She also looked grey and careworn. The years had treated her with as little consideration as it had Hansi's brothers.

"That must be his wife, I suppose," Dolph whispered.

Magda said, "Yes . . . he was wed to a cousin of ours, Mathilde—at least I suppose it must be she. She was a little older than I and never good friends." She raised her voice a little, saying with affection and good cheer, "My dear Mathilde, how well you look! Don't you remember us? It has been such a long time, and we are much changed. I am Magda, Liesel's sister."

"Aye, I remember well enough." Mathilde used a corner of her apron to brush some fallen leaves off one of the chair seats, "You were the one supposed to wed our Hansi, not your flibbertigibbet sister." She vanished into the house again, leaving Magda startled out of all countenance; what was it to Mathilde who her husband's younger brother had married?

"M'wife and her sister wanted to see what had become of their father's house," Hansi said, by way of explanation. "And we wished to show the children a little of where we came from."

"Come back to see of there's any crumbs to be snatched out of our father's inheritance, you mean," Jurgen spoke for the first time. Oh, that was open malice, rather than the sniveling backstabbing kind. Joachim had the grace to at least look a little embarrassed.

Hansi exclaimed, "Oh for the love of God, what made you think such a thing?!"

"You'd lost the land, didn't you?" Now that she thought on it, Magda remembered that Jurgen was the one for really nasty schoolhouse pranks. *That manner of boy, that manner of a man,* she thought. Jurgen was all but gloating; that made her skin crawl. "All that land you went haring off to Texas for, believing all those fine stories. But one of those letters you wrote to Mother was all about how you were thrown off the land and all your stock and property confiscated. And we read of the war in the newspapers," Jurgen added with what seemed to be an indecent degree of satisfaction. "Of how the Confederate government then ran rough-shod over your rights."

Magda could not but think of how she had always been welcome at the Browns' ramshackle cabin in the early days of her marriage; how Mrs. Brown, sloven and slatternly, had always made much of her as a guest, even if all she had to offer was cool water in a battered tin cup. She could recall, also, how Porfirio's family spared no effort in making her warmly welcome at his rambling but windowless mud-brick home in San Antonio; neither of them with any other thought but the comfort of their guests. *"Rather bitter herbs and friendship,"* she recalled Pastor Altmueller saying often, *"than a stalled ox and hatred within!"* And this, she saw to her confusion and discomfiture, was not honest welcome and affection. This was bitter envy, a grievance all the more bitter for there being no reason for it. Why on earth should Hansi's brothers offer such grudging hospitality? This was a cold welcome indeed, in a place that she and Hansi and Liesel had expected to find warmer—at least warmer than the professional welcome of a place like the Stephanienbad towards the family of a very rich man. She sat in the shade of the oak tree in the garden of Hansi's father's cottage wishing that they had not come; wishing that they had rather kept Albeck in their memory, captured in amber and drowsing under the summer sun, mellow and golden, untarnished by the passage of time.

Meanwhile, Hansi laughed uproariously. "Oh, Jurgen, always grasping the wrong end of the stick! No, 'twas not my land that was taken! That was m'brother-in-law's property! And it was returned after the war, as soon as the Federals began putting things to right again! Young Rudolph here made a show-place out of it—he has the finest stud-farm in all of Texas."

"Save for Captain King at the Santa Gertrudis," Dolph murmured. "You have to be honest, Onkel—Captain King is years ahead of me!"

"Lost m'land!" Hansi was chuckling to himself. "Ah, that is a rich jest! No, nothing like that at all—in fact, I own more of it than ever before!" And buff, hearty Hansi had just the faintest touch of steel in his glance, the deft edge of a stiletto as he added, "I went into cattle, you know. Whatever property Father left to you, that was honestly yours as the eldest, Joachim. I've no claim on any of that. No need for it, either." And he shrugged broadly and smiled. "All I came here looking for was the chance to show my grandsons where I grew up and mayhap a bit of hospitality?"

"Eh, you always were a cheeky beggar," Joachim grumbled, "always with your hand out asking for more."

Dolph looked sideways at his mother, his eyebrows raised in disbelieving arches—Onkel Hansi? Asking for more? Magda pressed her lips together and shook her head warningly at her son. He and Peter exchanged puzzled looks while Anna's hand sought her husband's. Hansi either paid for anything he wanted, or he just took; there was no asking with his hand out to anyone.

"How well does he even know Onkel Hansi?" Dolph whispered in English.

Magda answered, "Not well at all, I think!" There was a feeling in the air like a thunderstorm, Magda thought; almost like the greenish tinge to the sky when sudden pale flickers of lightning flash behind the clouds. All of it was centered on Hansi and his two brothers, glowering with sullen resentment . . . that's what it was, resentment and envy. With a shiver, Magda recalled J.P. Waldrip, the look in his mismatched eyes on those few times he had visited Carl Becker's holding and looked around at what had been built with such care. Joachim and Jurgen, Mathilde, all looked at them in the same way. *They don't know,* Magda realized, *they don't know about the cattle, or the store, or they put aside whatever Hansi wrote about such things. They thought we were coming back as beggars! Cannot they see our clothes? Or were they so set upon our failure they cannot see anything else?*

"I've worked like a dog for everything I have," Hansi meanwhile was saying, still with enough of an amiable expression that anyone would take his reply for an affectionate jest.

"I'm sure you have, little brother," Joachim said, "but still . . . you should have stayed here with the family, instead of putting credence in all those wild tales of riches! We could have used your help, especially after Father died, couldn't we, Jurgen?"

Jurgen sucked on the end of his pipe and replied, "Aye, so we could, Brother. But some of us felt an obligation to our own blood."

"You mean, work for you as an unpaid laborer for all of my life?" That was the final straw. The amiability dropped off Hansi's countenance. He had a dangerous growl in his voice and Liesel squeaked in dismay. "Just because I worked so for Father, didn't mean I wanted to do also for you." And at that moment, Hansi's temper snapped. "Wouldn't be nice, Joachim," he snarled through clenched teeth, "to act as if we were old enough to be out of small-clothes? I've been away for thirty years; don't you think you ought to say something like 'Well, speak of the devil, isn't that our little brother Hansi?' You probably did say the 'speak of the devil' part! What about saying something like, "Well, well, what have you been doing with yourself, Hansi?! Is that your family, Hansi? Oh, tell me about the cattle business, Hansi, what is that like?"

"I think," Dolph murmured quietly to his mother and cousins, "that I will take Lottie and Grete to the coaches and tell them that we are nearly ready to depart. Something tells me that this sentimental visit will not last very much longer."

"Good idea, Cuz," Peter agreed, adding irreverently, "oh, Ma'am Becker; if you could only pick your relatives the way you can choose your friends and your spouse, how much less awkward that would make the world!"

Dolph nodded an abrupt courtesy to his uncles and strode back along the way they had come. Lottie and Grete opened their parasols, fleeing with him. No, the girls were not enjoying this at all, and Magda didn't blame them in the least.

Meanwhile, Hansi's voice was rising as his temper got the better of him. "How about, 'Well, Hansi, tell us about what it was like in Texas!

Well, how did you get along with those wild Indians?!' Or how about, 'Glad you didn't drown on the boat going over, Hansi!' Better yet, tell me about what it has been like here! Tell me about what you have been doing with yourselves all this time! Not bloody much, by the look of it! Thirty years and neither one of you have taken a step to better yourselves, better this place! I swear to God almighty, is that still the same leaky patch to the roof that has left a smear of mold all the way down the wall? So the roof still leaks and you have done nothing about it but complain?" He stood up so abruptly, his chair skidded backwards with the force of it. "Well this is the nub of it, Joachim, Jurgen—so listen good. I will not repeat myself. I did not return here to beg of your charity. I do not come back to beg of anything at all. I thought to show my grandsons the town where I lived when I was a child, the house I was born in, nothing more. Instead I find that my brothers are so set on gloating over me, so certain that I have been a failure—"

Abruptly he stopped, as suddenly as if he had run into a wall in the dark. "That's it," he added softly, "that's what it is. Not that we have failed, taking our lives into our own hands and venturing into the world, and come crawling back to beg charity from you. But that we have not. And you—that is what you cannot endure." He stared down at his brothers, breathing as hard as if he had just run a footrace. Joachim tried to rise, but Hansi pushed him, a hand on his chest, so firmly that he sat down with a jolt. Jurgen made a movement to rise, but Hansi glared him down. "No, sit and listen, the both of you. This I will only say once. I own three cattle ranches—the largest is the size of Bavaria. I also own four general stores, the least of which brings in an income of . . . how much yearly, Magda?"

He snapped his fingers impatiently and Magda said, "Twenty thousand dollars yearly . . . gross, not profits."

"I pay regular wages to about four hundred and twenty men the year around," Hansi continued. "They drive my wagons or tend my cattle and horses. There are half again as many hired in the trail season, when we send herds north. Two months ago, I dined with the Governor of Texas and his family; an amiable chap, very obliging. If I complained to him that my ass itched, he would dispatch one of his flunkies to scratch it for me. I own a mansion of twenty rooms in San Antonio; it would have solid gold doorknobs on it if I wished. My wife's boudoir is as big as my father's whole damned house and when I pleasure her in bed, we do it on silk sheets. Yes, I'm as rich as one of those damned Firsts."

He looked contemptuously at his brothers. "At least you have enough pride not to abase yourselves by begging for any of it. Good day to you both—and go to hell." He patted Liesel's hand—she had been clutching at his arm. "Lise, my dear, I think we should depart. Goodbye, Joachim . . . Jurgen. You should have enough grievances now about your rich American kin to keep you grumbling for years."

In frozen silence, Hansi led his wife towards the carriages. Peter offered his other elbow to Magda and whispered impishly to Anna, "Silk sheets . . . interesting."

"Shush!" Anna hissed in reply and called for Christian and Harry to follow. Magda did not look back; she assumed the two brothers were still sitting there, under the tree in front of that tiny cottage.

Hansi lifted Liesel into the coach and stepped up himself, saying, "Magda—I will stay with my wife and solace myself with her company this time. You should enjoy yourself in the open air, for once." He pulled the little door closed after himself with a bang and the coach was away with a lurch.

"Oh, yes, Mama, come with us," Lottie said gaily as she and Grete climbed into the barouche and settled their skirts. "I felt so sorry for you, not seeing anything around! How Onkel Hansi and Aunt Liesel can endure it on a day like this!"

"Guess he doesn't always need the silk sheets, then," Peter whispered, and laughed as Anna struck her closed parasol against his shoulder. They talked of practically anything else on their return to Ulm, and Harry insisted on sitting up with the driver.

"It was so small," Anna said only. "I didn't think it would be so small, or so shabby."

"Everything looks large and grand to a child," Magda said, adding to herself, *And sometimes to an older person, also.*

Chapter Twenty: *The Enchanted Island*

Magda rejoiced at returning to their comfortable rooms in the Stephanienbad; almost like returning home, after that uncomfortable interlude in Albeck. How peculiar it was to feel so, when she had always thought of Albeck as home. No matter how far they had traveled or how well they had lived, there was some corner of her mind that considered it as such, always some thought that someday they might return and step into those rooms again. But now they had returned, and discovered that not only was Albeck small and poor, but they were no longer welcome. *We are not the persons we once were,* Magda thought. She picked up her treasured silver hairbrush and began brushing out her hair in front of the dressing table mirror. *We have changed into someone else, without recognizing this until now.*

Behind her, she could see the heavy velvet drapes that closed over one of the tall windows in her room, fashionable sage green, and underneath it were filmy embroidered net curtains that turned the sunshine spilling through the glass into something misty and insubstantial. Her bed was made with fine linen and an elegant coverlet that matched the drapes; everything within sight being of the finest quality and most exquisite taste. How could she be one and the same as the person who had shared a tiny room under the eaves with her sister, slept on a mattress stuffed with straw and milked cows every morning, scattered grain to the chickens in the afternoon?

Her thoughts were interrupted by a light tap on the door. "Mama, are you dressing for dinner?" Lottie asked.

"Yes, I am, dear-heart," she answered. "Come in, help me do up the back of my dress, as soon as I have done my hair."

Lottie opened the door further and slipped inside. "You know. Auntie Liesel's maid will help you put yourself together, Mama," she said with affection.

"I know that, dear-heart," Magda replied. "I suppose I hate to think that I need help getting dressed, or that my clothes are so complicated that I need anyone's help . . . other than to do up the buttons I cannot reach! You look very elegant, Lottchen—almost a young lady."

Over her shoulder, Lottie smiled at her own reflection in the mirror. She wore a ruffled dress of pale yellow, with a modest neckline and elbow-length sleeves; appropriate for a girl of her age, dining in an elegant spa-hotel. Her hair was tied back with a matching silk ribbon.

"When might I put up my hair and wear long skirts, Mama?" she asked. Lottie's own skirt reached only to halfway between her knees and ankles.

"When you are sixteen, Lottchen," Magda answered. "And I would advise you to enjoy the freedom of not having your skirts trail after you, all through the dust."

Lottie took the hairbrush out of Magda's hand and drew it through the spill of her mother's hair. "But you look very nice in your faille evening dress," she said, and she tilted her head to one side and surveyed her parent critically. "And I think you could wear colors, Mama; half-mourning at the very least. You would look so well in dove-gray or lavender."

"No, Lottie, I think not," Magda answered with a sigh. "Lise vexes me endlessly on this matter; I had hoped I would not hear such from you as well."

"Yes, Mama," Lottie yielded in good temper. "But may I do your hair with some clips that Dolph and I bought for you last week? They are trimmed in jet," she added hastily as Magda opened her mouth, "and look so very elegant, in the latest fashion from Paris, so they said in the shop! We must hurry then—Peter and Anna have already gone downstairs!"

Magda acquiesced; it would please the child that she loved so dearly to do so. Lottie floated away to fetch the clips from her room. For a moment, Magda stared at her own reflection in the pitiless glass, wondering exactly when it was that she had become old. She was fifty-three, and her hair was still mostly black, although lightly sprinkled with gray in places. She had never been thought beautiful, so she did not have the fear of seeing her looks melt away in the face of passing years. There were shadows under her eyes and a faint dark scar on her cheekbone shaped like a half-moon. Her eyes themselves were still the same, dark gray—nearly black in some lights—and shrewd; but not even in kindly candlelight would anyone think her any younger than she was. Sighing, she stood and shed her loose wrap. The gown she would wear to dinner was already laid out across the foot of her bed; a princess-cut gown that Liesel had insisted she have made for her in New York while they were waiting for the packet. The back of the skirt was drawn up with a complicated series of tapes and ties, falling in a graceful cascade to train after her, unless she used one of those clever little dress-holders to loop it up. "Not the sort of dress to wear when milking a cow or digging in the garden!" Magda observed aloud to her own reflection, just as Lottie returned with a tiny gold paste-paper box in her hand.

"I'll do your hair first," Lottie sounded terribly bossy. "And you ought to have a lap dog, if you keep on with this habit of talking to yourself, Mama! At least then you can say you are talking to the dog. And Auntie is loaning you her white opal necklace for the evening. We must hurry, Dolph has already gone downstairs to wait for us."

As soon as her hair was done, swept up onto the top of her head and fastened with the jet hair clips that Lottie affixed with all the care of a sculptor finishing her greatest masterwork, Magda stepped into her dress. She pulled it carefully up over her hips, and the little pad tied at the back of her over-petticoat which would make the dress drape as beautifully as a waterfall.

Lottie fastened up the buttons and stood back, biting her lip. "Just one moment," she said. Lifting the hem of Magda's train, she made some adjustments to the tapes that gathered the back of the dress. "There. Here's Auntie's necklace. Fasten it quickly, and let us go, Dolph will be wondering what is keeping us! You look very nice, Mama. If it weren't for Dolph and Onkel Hansi, your path would be thick with gentlemen admirers." Lottie added, with an air of world-weary sophistication which sat very oddly with her youth, "Rich widows are terribly attractive to the gentlemen who come to Baden!"

Magda laughed. "I am sure it is the rich part which forms all the attraction, Lottchen."

The grand lobby of the Stephanienbad began to fill early in the evenings. Guests returning from a day at the baths, or excursions in the park, met and mingled with friends lingering over a late tea, or with other friends who planned to dine together. They circled gracefully, like golden fish in a placid pool—or, thought Magda irreverently, like the cattle in her husband's pasture—lazily wandering here and there, gathering with their fellows in some choice spot among the potted palms and cushioned settees, and then moving onward. Gentlemen in severe black evening dress, or uniforms hung with gaudy rows of medals, bowed over the hands of ladies in elaborate evening dresses with ruched and ruffled trains, all the colors of the flowerbeds outside. They glittered with jewels hanging around their throats, from their ears, on their wrists, and in their elaborately piled hair. Magda had not yet tired of watching them, such a flock of glorious birds—birds that she had no wish to fly among. Other ladies had just returned and hadn't changed for dinner, but their day dresses were no less elaborate and just as colorful.

Magda and Lottie looked for her son as they came down the grand main staircase. Here, where there were so many other tall and fair-haired men, he and Peter were not as easily picked out.

"Oh, Mama—is that Dolph with that Russian princess?" Lottie breathed.

"I might have expected it," Magda answered, "because of the dogs."

The old lady sat bolt upright in the middle of one of the window settees, as proud as a queen on her throne. Dolph was down on one knee, among her dogs. Only three of them this afternoon; all of them seeming quiet and well-behaved, fawning for his regard and attention. The boldest of the three stood up with its front paws on Dolph's knee, begging for caresses. The Princess and Dolph were laughing companionably together. When Dolph saw them on the stairs, he gave the dog one last pat, excused himself to the Princess with a respectful kiss of her hand, and came to meet them.

"Nice old girl," he remarked by way of explanation. "She wanted to thank me for rescuing her precious little fur ball. You remember we saw her in the station on the day we arrived? We talked some about her dogs—I was curious. They are a queer breed from China, meant only to be the pet of royals. They call them lion dogs, because they are actually quite fearless and very wise. The princess says they are fiercely loyal to their owners and want to be with them at all times."

"I'm not sure what use such a dog like that would have," Magda said, "aside from hunting rats, maybe!"

"Companionship," Dolph answered. "The littlest of the breed are carried around in the Emperor's sleeve. The Princess said they are also trained to carry his robes and sometimes little lanterns. The Princess rather likes them—she says they have the courage and heart of a wolfhound. Like me, she finds that dogs are better company than most humans she knows."

Magda thought nothing of that conversation, until several days later, as she waited for Liesel in the veranda of one of the spa-baths. The day was warm and she fanned herself and wondered how much longer Liesel would take, getting dressed after a prolonged soak in the waters.

"Your son is a delightful young man," remarked a voice at her back. Magda started to her feet, more in respect to age than to nobility, for which Vati had never had much good to say. The Princess had obviously finished her treatment for the day. Out in the gravel forecourt, one of the Princess' menservants waited with her wheeled invalid chair. Princess Cherkevsky leaned on a silver and ebony cane. "Manly without being a brute boor, courteous and well-mannered without being epicene. You did very well with him, Madame Becker. Alas that I am not thirty years younger, I might very well be tempted." Her bright old eyes flicked up and down Magda's figure, doubtless taking in every detail of her dress, the book she had been reading, and her fingers lightly stained with ink from writing Hansi's letters. The Princess spoke proper German; her voice had the deep timbre of an old bronze bell with a crack in it, the voice of a trained singer or an actress, perhaps. "You are one of those Americans, aren't you? I had never talked at length with an American woman before. American men, many times, but their wives bored me."

"I am sorry, Princess. I shall probably bore you also," Magda answered. Amusement flashed like summer lightning in the Princess' extraordinary eyes, a peculiar hazel-green, like new birch leaves and they were slanted almost like an oriental's. Her face was as wrinkled as an old apple and offered a jolting contrast to her hair, dyed vividly red and piled up in a complicated arrangement of rolls and knots under a small and fashionable hat tilted rakishly forward.

"I think not," Princess Cherkevsky replied thoughtfully. "I have noticed that you dress to suit and please yourself—not milord Worth and the other couturiers favored by the ton. It argues an independent mind, one not easily swayed by the herd. You have well-spoken children and devote yourself equally to the welfare of your sister and her husband's business." The princess chuckled knowingly. "Now, he would be a boyar in the old days, a swashbuckler and an adventurer. Rather a pirate, I think. New enough to riches to enjoy it thoroughly, clever enough to be welcome among those to whom it has grown to be something that has always been there. He would amuse me, and so would you, Madame Becker. Life can become very boring, once one has lived as long as I have."

"Princess," Magda began, feeling rather as if she had been run over by a stampeding herd of cows.

The old woman merely laughed. "You may call me by my name— Irina." Those wickedly knowing old eyes crinkled in amusement, "And I was not always a princess, my dear Madame Becker. I only married a prince after having been his mistress for years! So long ago that everyone has forgotten the scandal. I sang in the opera, not very well, I must confess. Another sort of career seemed to be a good idea. I think you also must have had an interesting life . . . a different life, anyway. You should tell me of it, little by little as we come to know each other better. I would very much like it if you would come to call on me, tomorrow, after breakfast."

Irina Cherkevsky consulted the little gold watch that hung from the lapel of her bodice-jacket on a gold pin shaped like a bow of ribbon. "They tell me that your family has interests in cattle in Texas, that you went from Germany to live there some years past—the servants do gossip, you know. And I am intrigued. There are so very few original people in my circle these days. Baden has become terribly dull, now that gambling is forbidden and all the most amusing visitors have fled! Will you pay a call on me, Madame Becker?"

Magda hesitated but a moment, drawn irresistibly by the lively curiosity and the charm in those eyes, queerly seeming as young and lively as Lottie's in her age-ruined face. "Then I shall, Madame Irina."

"Good! Until tomorrow then," and the Princess stumped down towards her waiting invalid chair and settled herself into it with the assistance of the manservant who sprang into assiduous attention as soon as the old woman emerged from the porch. He wheeled her away, just as Liesel emerged from the depths of the bath, apologizing for having been so delayed.

"You were not bored, Magda?" she asked anxiously, fanning herself vigorously with an ivory-handled fan.

Magda answered, "Oh, no, I brought a book and one of the other hotel guests struck up a conversation with me. The Russian princess with all the dogs. You remember, Lise—from the railway station."

"Oh, my!" Liesel fanned herself even more vigorously. "What would Vati have thought! You on easy terms of conversation with a princess! What did she say to you, then?"

"That she wishes for me to call on her," Magda answered and Liesel's eyes rounded in astonishment. "She says she would like very much to make our acquaintance. She is bored with the sameness of things."

"I think Vati would call her a sensation seeker," Liesel said, censoriously. "Aren't you afraid that she only wishes to make mock of us? Some of the others do, you know. I have heard them talking among themselves," and the familiar tears trembled on Liesel's eyelids. "They say we are naught but violent and vulgar, new to riches and quite without intellectual understanding of the world. The shopkeepers were so rude and disobliging, once they knew us to be Americans! I would rather not endure any more of such, Magda."

"I don't think that of her," Magda answered, thinking again of Irina Cherkevsky's lively green eyes. Dolph liked her for her love of dogs, and called her a 'nice old girl.' What had she said of herself—that she was an opera singer who married a prince, so long ago that everyone had forgotten the scandal of it? "I rather liked her, Lise. She was not snobbish like what I had expected of the Firsts. And she said nice things of my children."

"Oh, that would do it," Lise laughed, although her eyes still appeared worried. "The way to our heart—say flattering things of our children!"

In the morning—and as it turned out, many mornings after that—Magda went to Princess Cherkevsky's suite. The Princess' elderly senior maid admitted her to the chamber where Irina Cherkevsky sat in her chair, being made ready to face the day through the labors of three hovering maids. The dogs romped around through the Princess' rooms, a cacophony of shrill soprano barks greeting her; all but the fat one, who Magda now saw was a mother, nursing a litter of small, blind pups in an elaborate padded basket beneath the dressing table.

"Such labors, in making one fit to face the public," the Princess allowed with an oddly girlish chuckle to Magda. "Really, it's like being made fit to face an audience upon the opera stage. Would you care for some coffee?" Without waiting for an answer, she clapped her hands and spoke sharply to the most junior maid, who set aside the garments she was folding and left the room. Presently she returned bearing a silver coffee pot on a tray with two cups. "One of life's pleasures," the Princess sighed with frank delight as she took her own cup in her bejeweled hand, "the first drink of coffee of a morning! The second and third do not taste so sublime. I have always wondered why?"

"We were deprived of this during the last years of the war," Magda offered, by way of making genteel conversation. "And to have it again was such a joy for us, after drinking roasted acorns! To me now, the second and third cup always tastes as fine as the first."

"Roasted acorns?" The Princess' painted eyebrows arched in astonishment. "How extraordinary—you must tell me more, Madame Becker! Where did you spend those years? In the South, as it was? Was your husband away in the fighting or were you . . ." she hesitated and phrased it with careful delicacy, "already bereft of his company and affections?"

"He was taken from us in the second year of the fighting," Magda answered steadily, "and my children and I went to Friedrichsburg to live with my own father." Much later in their acquaintance she would tell Irina the whole story, of the Hanging Band, of poor Trap Talmadge and J.P. Waldrip. But that first morning, she only spoke of the small things, the deprivations and how Liesel and the children had brought food to Hansi by stealth, how they had hidden him on Christmas Eve under the very nose of the provost marshal. Irina listened intently, exclaiming with deep interest or pity. Magda thought the maids, for all their attention on their mistress, listened also. The hour passed very quickly. At the end of it, Irina pressed Magda's hand fondly in hers, and asked her to call again the next day at the same time. And so the habit was established, of rising early and accompanying Liesel to the spa-bath, then returning to Princess Cherkevsky's rooms at mid-morning. Sometimes Grete and Lottie came with her, entranced by the darling little golden lion-dogs.

Late in summer, Anna and Peter went on a Rhine excursion with their sons. When they returned, Hansi was afire with a restless intention to depart from Baden. He was bored, Magda perceived, bored with the amusements that Baden had to offer, ready to return to work. In this case, ready to go to England to survey and purchase blood-stock for the ranches. Peter and Dolph were also more than ready to go with him. This would be a project of months. They had thought of spending the winter and Christmas in Baden, assuming that Liesel would not countenance much travel or separation from her husband, but by fall she seemed much recovered, even daring to walk by herself outside in the Stephanienbad gardens.

Princess Cherkevsky impulsively invited Magda to spend the winter with her in Italy. "The girls and your sister, of course," she waved her hand airily. "I have a villa on Capri, with plenty of room for you all. Tell your buccaneer of a brother to come and spend Christmas in Italy."

"That is most generous of you," Magda began, but Irina only waved her hand again.

"Not generous, my dear, only to relieve my own boredom. I merely think of myself and how best to be amused! Christmas is supposed to be amusing, but it is usually only boring, unless there are children to take pleasure in their presents. And speaking of presents, it would please me to present you with one. Bella's puppies are ready to be weaned, and your handsome young son suggested that I gift you with a pair. They make the dearest little pets, you know."

Magda winced, hoping that Irina did not see. "Not more than one—I don't think I could endure the noise!" she pleaded and Irina laughed like a girl.

"Very well, then. Your knees are in better condition than mine. Kneel down and see which one you would favor." She patted Bella on her golden head, speaking soothing words as the little dog watched Magda with worried eyes.

There were six puppies, lively squirming little balls of fur; four of them gold like their mother, one black, and one piebald white with brindle spots. That one seemed to be more sedate, not as excitable as the others. Magda put her fingers around the pup—it was heavier that it appeared, no fragile little handful of bones and fur. It looked at her with curious eyes, as she said, "This one, Irina."

"Very good," Princess Cherkevsky nodded, regally. "That is a boy. Your son already brought a little collar and a bed and dish for you."

"You and he plotted behind my back," Magda exclaimed. She sat back on her heels, with the puppy cradled in her lap. "I know he loves dogs, but this is not a dog, it is more like a mouse!" And thus did the pup receive its name.

Lottie made much of it, of course. So did Liesel. Magda soon became accustomed to either carrying Mouse or having him sit quietly at her feet, intently watching her every move. He did not fuss much at being removed from his littermates or his mother. Eventually, Magda became quite attached to Mouse, and to his successors. Those little Pekinese dogs did indeed have the soul and heart of much larger dogs.

Anna took the boys to England with Peter, Dolph and Hansi. "I would adore staying at a villa on Capri," she said to Magda, "but I do not wish to be separated from Peter, or keep the boys with me and away from him. And anyway, Papa will need me to write letters and make all the suitable arrangements. You do understand, Auntie?"

"I do," Magda answered. "I would not have wanted to be apart from my husband for any length of time, or for any reason."

"You miss him dreadfully, still, don't you Auntie?" Anna's dark brown eyes were gentle with sympathy. "Now that I am acquainted with the married state, I find that I have a clearer understanding. Sometimes now, when I meditate on such a loss, I am amazed that you did not go insane with grief in the early months."

"I did, a little," Magda answered. Her hands moved, absentmindedly petting Mouses's head as he lay in her lap, snoring slightly, "until I came to realize that other women had the same grief, had suffered the same agonizing loss. And I had to see to the children, you know. One goes on living, Annchen. Go to England with Peter and the children—enjoy their company while you have it."

"Well, you and Mama should have fun," Anna remarked. "Mama is over the moon with excitement—traveling to Italy with a Princess. She is truly much improved in her mind now, isn't she, Auntie? I did not think that the water cure could have such good effect!"

"They made her stop taking so many of those dreadful tonics," Magda said, "which I think may have helped more than the baths. And with so many happy distractions, she has not had one of her crying fits for at least a month. This was an excellent stratagem of your father's!"

"And when we return in spring," Anna brightened, "there will be the Centennial exhibition and all those celebrations. Papa has a mind to attend them."

"He does think to go home, eventually?" Magda asked with some anxiety and Anna laughed merrily.

"Oh yes, laden with gifts and goods and all manner of marvelous things for his and Mama's house. We will go home as we planned, Auntie!"

"Good," Magda said. In her heart she was beginning to think of home, the stone house in the valley of the Guadalupe, of swathes of spring wildflowers and the look of the sky, of endless depths of clear light blue sky during the day and the way it was gloriously strewn with brilliant stars at night. Here, the sky seemed a dimmer blue during the day, the night's pageant not nearly so generous. Now that it was coming on to autumn, it was colder than she was accustomed to. Yes, Italy would be a good choice, now that Liesel was better.

They departed a week later, their own belongings barely to be noticed among the cavalcade of the Princess' luggage, servants and dogs. They traveled by sleeper coach, made up into luxurious little bedrooms at night. Lottie and Grete were glued to the windows all during the journey, marveling at the scenery, the mountains and lakes. Even Liesel took an interest. Princess Cherkevsky insisted on stopping over in Florence for several days, to show them the glories of that city, and again in Rome for the same. It seemed that cold winter followed them. Magda longed to fall asleep in a bed that didn't constantly move.

On a brilliant autumn morning, they took a steam ferry from Naples to the enchanted island, to Capri, where the Princess had her winter home. It proved to be a place of cliffs and grottos, and vine-hung pergolas, open to the soft sea breeze and a view of the blue Mediterranean, a place of narrow footpaths and stone staircases rather than roadways and sidewalks. Only a tiny fraction of it could be described as level ground; like swallows' nests, all the buildings clung tightly to slopes that sometimes achieved nearly vertical, the windows of a house looking down on the mellow terracotta roof tiles of its next door neighbor. The Princess' pocket-villa was down a little side street by the main town square, the Piazzetta. Her house seemed hardly larger than the stone house that Berg had built on the Becker lands, but vertical rather than horizontal. Magda felt at home almost at once for that very reason. There was a tiny paved courtyard behind an iron gate that was a miracle of iron latticework, a miniscule garden with a fruit tree neatly pleached against a sunny wall. The Princess' housekeeper had all in readiness for their arrival, beds made and lamps filled, everything scoured clean and vases filled with late wildflowers in every room.

"We are cut off by storms, now and again," Irina said comfortably. "But who would mind, when we have four strong walls and a sturdy roof? I have books enough, who would need a newspaper from the mainland? Of all my homes, this is the one I love the best. I know you think it plain . . . quite spartan by comparison, but there are so many interesting people here," and her tilted eyes sparkled with lively interest, "so many of them artistic! Some of them a little strange, even. But never boring, my dear!"

"I do not think anyone you have anything to do with could ever be boring, Irina," Magda said affectionately.

"You should not be bored, either," Irina said. "When you take the little Mouse for a walk tomorrow, go to the café on the Piazzetta. Sit at a table which overlooks the Marina Grande and enjoy your coffee. They say that if you sit there long enough on a fair day you will see everyone you know on Capri."

"But I don't know anyone on Capri but for you," Magda protested.

Irina waved her hand airily. "Oh, you will before the week is out. You were attending to your sister all summer—now you should have a little of your own amusement. I think you will enjoy meeting the people here. Most of them are terribly amusing and very original, not ordinary in the least."

In the morning she did as Irina said; she took Mouse, who bounced from excitement at the end of his leash, and walked up the tiny alley towards the Piazzetta. It seemed to hang in the air like a balcony, open on one side to a view of the sapphire blue Mediterranean and a vertical drop below, straight down to the stone jetties of the big harbor where they had arrived. Just coming up to mid-morning, with the sunshine ameliorating the chill, there were plenty of people at the spindly little tables set out at the edge of the Piazzetta. She took a place at an empty table, mesmerized by the view; the two ends of the island rose up like the pommel and cantle of a saddle, the village spilling over the comparatively level land in between. Of course, since most of the island was vertical cliff, level meant anything less precipitous than that.

She asked the hovering waiter to bring her coffee and, daringly, an almond biscuit. Two gentlemen sat at the table next to her; they acknowledged her with a brief, polite nod. She thought they might be English; the older one had a heavy cane leaning against his chair. His companion was quite young, about Horrie's age. They had a resemblance about the face, the same wiry build and lively blue eyes. Sunlight was spilling over the tops of the buildings, and the young one shifted his chair to avoid having it fall into his eyes. Mouse, peacefully curled up like a dropped muff at Magda's feet, was startled awake at the scrape of his chair and began to bark shrilly. Magda picked him up, attempting to shush him into quiet, but from this higher vantage he perched with his forepaws on the table and barked even more loudly.

"I am sorry," Magda said to them in English. "My dog is ... uncontrollable. I shall take him home."

"Worry not, Madame," said the older gentleman, with humor and in the same language. "That is no dog, but rather a barking rat with long fur. My nephew and I will endure."

"Thank you." Magda sat down again, still attempting to hush Mouse. He had calmed down, settling himself onto her lap, when the waiter brought her coffee and biscuit, which set him off again. Embarrassed, she bolted the coffee and put the biscuit in her reticule for later.

The following morning she returned. This time Mouse behaved, sitting alertly at her feet, while she drank her coffee and enjoyed the achingly beautiful vista spread out before her. The old Englishman and his nephew were not there on that morning, but they were on the following day.

On the fourth day, when she approached with Mouse, the old man struggled to his feet, removed his hat and sketched a bow.

"Madame," he said, "might you permit me the liberty of assuming that the roof, such as it is, constitutes a proper introduction, after three days? Colonel Roland St. John Bertrand, at your service—Rollie, to m'friends. M'nephew, the Honorable Sebastian Bertrand."

"Mrs. Carl Becker," Magda allowed him to bow over her hand. "We are guests of Princess Cherkevsky for the winter."

"Ah, the lovely Irina—she was a pip in her day." Colonel Bertrand's face lit up. "Knew she had houseguests—no secrets on Capri, y'know. The bush telegraph had it that her guests were Americans, but you sound like a German. Rather like Her Majesty, matter of fact. Friend of mine got seconded as the Prince's ADC, way back in the day, that's how I came to be reminded of that."

Magda tried to explain, as the nephew shyly bowed over her hand, "We are—German, that is. We emigrated many years ago."

"If you would join us," Colonel Bertrand urged her, gallantly pulling out a chair for her with a smile, "and your dear little rat-dog as well."

"Not a rat," Magda said, "a Mouse. His name is Mouse."

"Is it, by Jove!" and Colonel Bertrand laughed cheerfully. While he gestured to the waiter, Magda wondered why he seemed so familiar, with his weather-burnt face and bright blue eyes. It came to her that he reminded her of Charley Nimitz; irrepressible Charley with his magic tricks and outgoing charm, who never met a person he didn't like at once. They enjoyed their coffee and biscuits together and, when Magda took her leave, both of them rose and bowed again over her hand.

"Tomorrow, my dear Madame Becker?" Colonel Bertrand rumbled. "Same time, same table?"

"Of course," Magda answered, surprising herself. The next day, she brought Lottie with her; she supposed afterwards that it was some kind of unspoken instinct and defense. Young Sebastian Bertrand blushed as deeply as a girl himself upon being presented to her, but Lottie soon had him laughing and chattering away, as any girl having the same easy familiarity with brothers and male cousins would know how to do.

"Lovely gal," Colonel Bertrand observed, across the table. "Put the lad right at ease. He's a good lad, too. Family sent him to me—got thrown out of school. Doesn't know what to do with himself. But he's a good lad. He'll come up with something."

"Do you have children, Colonel?" Magda asked. He seemed so very fatherly; affectionate yet realistic with his nephew. Oddly enough, that casual question put a shadow over his face.

"I did, Madame Becker," he answered at last. She thought his eyes had the bright appearance of tears subdued and unshed. "Two sons and a little daughter, just a babe she was. They and their mother, my dear Molly— her name was Mary, but we called her Molly—were taken by the cholera in '56. All my little chickens and their dam!"

"I am so sorry," Magda said, in a rush of apology, horrified that she should have inadvertently trodden on a painful subject.

"No, Madame Becker, for I came to see the loss of my dear ones in that year as a mercy. We were stationed at Cawnpore then and the very next year the pandies rebelled. Molly and the babes—if they had still been living!—would have gone into Wheeler's encampment with all the other families. Their end would have been doubly, triply as agonizing. I was on detachment when word was sent to me that they had sickened. Came back long enough to see them buried, then back to the frontier. I was safe enough—had some dicey moments here and there. Would have given up my own existence to have seen them safe, though," he added, with some little difficulty, as if he struggled with some deep and awful emotion.

Magda confessed, "My own husband did so, to ensure my safety and that of our children."

"Stout fellow." Colonel Bertrand seemed to have recovered some of his cheerful spirit. "A proper officer, was he?"

"A sergeant of Rangers," Magda replied, "one of Jack Hays' men. That is something to be reckoned with, where we live!"

"Rightfully so, I daresay," Colonel Bertrand answered with restored cheer. "Backbone of the Army, the sergeants are. What hey, I think they only let the officers go ahead of all in order to be shot at first. Couldn't run the show without them, o'course. I'd not heard of the Rangers, or your Jack Hays, though—would that be like the Guides, maybe?"

"Something like that," Magda answered.

Colonel Bertrand smiled, his whole face lighting up. "I wish you would tell me of that, Madame Becker—I always like to hear of mad adventure and daring in far places."

"I thought at first," Lottie ventured, as she and her mother sat in the parlor, late at night during the fall of the plague year, "that you had fallen in love with him, or he with you. But it was not like that, was it, Mama? Dear lovely Auntie Irina told me that I should have no fear of that, that you only cared for each other as fond friends."

"So we did," Magda answered. "I could not love another man as I loved your father, but Rollie became very dear to me."

"A regular beau," Lottie nodded, "someone to escort you to parties and dances."

"More like walks and picnics," Magda corrected her daughter, "or even just long evenings in Irina's drawing room. He offered nothing more complicated than undemanding friendship."

"And laughter," Lottie added. "He made you laugh. I think he rather cared for you in the same way. Sebastian has often reminded me of that time, saying that your company was good for his uncle, giving him an interest. Otherwise, he hibernated in the winter like a grouchy old bear."

"He was rather gruff, sometimes," Magda allowed, "but always considerate, and he took such joy from the smallest things. Every day was an adventure; every walk to the Villa Jovis was a marvelous expedition! And he was one of those men who are in no doubt of their own qualities. Such men have the strength to be as tender and sentimental as women on occasion and feel no embarrassment over it. He took me to see the grotto, on one sunny day when the sea was calm. Such a beautiful, ethereal sight, but on our return the sea became rough and I caught the worst of it. I was wetted all through, but nothing would stop him from wrapping me in his own coat, and then insisting that the boatman give up his as well! I fretted all the way back to the villa that he might take harm from being so chilled, but he insisted that no harm would come to him. 'I'm as tough as old boots, Maggie. I went all the way from Peshawar to Landi Kotal in m'shirtsleeves once and never took harm. Well, sniped at by a Shinwari deserter, but he missed clean. Rotten shot!' That was all he said, but Irina had her cook make us both some sort of herb brew and drink it down as a sovereign preventative and remedy."

Magda set down her own sewing, smiling with great fondness. "He was very fond of a music hall song, one of those popular songs that they sing on street corners and music halls: 'When You and I Were Young, Maggie.' He would sing it and laugh, and then he would call me Maggie. 'Let's go up to the hill, Maggie, and look at the rusty old mill,' he would say! He gave me a very precious gift, Lottie dear—one that I was so grateful to receive, although I never had a chance to thank him for it."

"What gift was that, Mama?" Lottie asked.

"He showed me something of what it would have been like to grow old with your father." Magda rubbed her shoulder. There was an unaccustomed ache there, another to add to the collection sustained by her many long years of life and work. "Enough of a taste to let me know that it would have been sweet, indeed."

Chapter Twenty-One: *The World in a Grain of Sand*

Late in November, a letter from Anna arrived, along with a packet of American newspapers for them all and a smaller packet wrapped separately and addressed to Magda. *"Do not let Mama read any of these,"* Anna wrote. *"She will in any case be distracted by the happy news of my condition. But a dreadful storm struck Indianola last month, leaving much of the city in ruins. Jacob and Elias were in the city during the storm with three wagons and teams, all of which are lost, together with one of their wagon guards. He was a young man with family in Indianola, not known to you and I and Papa, but recently hired. He felt obliged to see to the safety of his family in their house near to Powder Horn Bayou. Jacob urged him to remain within safety with them, in their lodgings in a house in the older part of town, which was on higher ground. At the height of the storm the wind changed direction, and all the water in the marshes and bayou behind the new town immediately rushed forth and carried all away into Matagorda Bay. Please assure Mama that my brothers remain safe and insist they were never in any acute danger, although the storm was quite violent. All the town is devastated. Papa has only lost three wagons, six teams of horses and a portion of fine goods stored in one of the warehouses near to the Morgan Line docks—but not nearly what has been sustained by our many friends within that town! Please, assure Mama as regards the survival of her sons—they are unharmed and quite unaffected."*

"Sounds like a proper box-wallah!" Rollie Bertrand grunted when Magda read this portion of Anna's letter aloud to him. They were sitting together on a stone bench along one of their favorite walks, near the cliffs by the ruinous Roman villa located at the point of the island. A crumbling wall at their back gave shelter from the cold breeze. Below the cliff at their feet the ocean sparkled as if strewn with millions of tiny silver sequins. At Magda's look of puzzlement, he expounded, "Merchant-chappie . . . in trade. Always fussing about their accounts and shops."

"Fussing about our accounts and shops is what gave us our start," Magda answered. "And continuing to do so is what keeps our children from suffering the sort of poverty we endured during the war."

"Ah, Maggie, you talk like a shopkeeper," Rollie chuckled.

She returned crisply, "I am a shopkeeper, Rollie—not a woman of leisure."

It did annoy her sometimes, Rollie's blithe assumption that trade was vulgar, something that ought to be beneath her notice and concern; she who had always taken care of the shop and its accounts! She who had been genuinely fascinated by the intricacies of buying and selling, who together with Anna had helped Hansi spin his complicated web of commerce in cartage, cattle and land. She couldn't fathom why continuing an interest in such matters ought to be dropped like an unfashionable garment once one had reached a certain level of prosperity. Such notions seemed to be an unspoken assumption in the social circle that Rollie and Princess Cherkevsky moved within. Privately Magda thought an elaborate disinterest in the means by which a fortune was made and maintained was a sure guarantee of returning to the mean degree from which a family had sprung. She refrained from saying so to Rollie. He was a dear man, but such matters were as far beyond his understanding as a liking for grand opera was beyond the comprehension of a Comanche Indian.

But he did understand some things very well; Liesel's fragility was one of them. Now he ventured, with a care which suggested that he had really considered the matter, "I suppose you will have to tell her a little at a time, Maggie. You can't keep the whole of it from her—even if it is on the other side of the world. It will have made a great show in the newspapers and among your friends back there. It's a bit much to hope that it will all be rebuilt by the time you return. But I've seen marvelous things done, after storms along the Bengal coast!" He patted Magda's hands, where they held the letter in her lap, and added comfortably, "They'll get cracking away, Maggie. They're probably putting in foundations even as we speak. If there is still land to build on, they will have too much at stake in a place to move away. But still," He squeezed her hands. His eyes were the same blue as the sea, guileless as a child's. It was moments like this that he reminded her so piercingly of her husband. He continued, "I daresay it will be the boys that she worries about most. Once she hears of them, all else will be secondary, and you can let all the rest of it trickle out by drops."

"That is what I had thought to do," Magda agreed. Doubtless, Anna was right. And Liesel would be more distracted by the news that Anna and

Peter were expecting another child, a child that would be born soon after their return to the States. But Rollie's advice was not only sensible, it confirmed her own thoughts on the matter. They sat comfortably side by side, their shoulders just touching, and watched the sea-birds wheeling in the crystal air. The curve of the Bay of Naples lay far distant and half veiled in mist. A sprinkling of islands trailed off the farther end, and at the nearer end the Sorrento peninsula reached out towards Capri.

Magda's thoughts were not on the view before her. Rather, she saw Indianola in her mind's eye, that bustling wooden Venice set on its shell-sand spit between the bay and the bayou. So hard to think of all that, smashed into splinters by the sea. She could hardly bear to read the newspaper stores which Anna had sent to her. All those warehouses where she and Anna and Hansi had gone to buy goods for the store in that first year after the war, the Casimir House and the Morgan Line's dock—all of it swept out into the bay, leaving it as empty as it had been when the Verein settlers had been landed there. It was a comfort to lean against Rollie, who was kind and sensible; sensible enough to know when not to talk.

Presently, they heard Lottie and Sebastian's voices at some distance. Lottie and Sebastian had gone a little farther into the ruins to look for an inscription that Sebastian claimed to have seen.

"He's a good lad," Rollie suddenly remarked. "Doesn't quite know what to do with himself. Younger son, y'know. Not interested in the Army. Doesn't get good marks, so the Church is out. Told me himself he doesn't want to fiddle around doing nothing in England." Magda listened patiently. Having given her his advice, now he was working around to ask it of her. "He's interested in this Western cattle business," Rollie said at last. "Your little gel has told him this and that. He's read some books about it."

"I'm not sure what he needs to know about it all would be in a book," Magda replied. The Honorable Sebastian was a good lad but he was also only sixteen; added to that, he seemed younger, softer and less fully-formed than her sons had been at that age. At sixteen, Dolph had helped defend Friedrichsburg from the Hanging Band, had gone and joined Colonel Ford's Western Cavalry. Magda could no more imagine Sebastian doing such things then she could imagine Mouse metamorphosing into a wolfhound.

Rollie continued, "Thing is, Maggie—he's m' godson as well as nephew. And sole heir as well. I'll do right by the lad, o' course, in due time, but if he comes out to Texas when he turns eighteen, I'd like to know someone has taken him in hand, see that he starts off on the right foot." He smiled sideways down at Magda, a glint of mischief in his eyes. "I know some of you colonials are a canny lot, not beyond playing games on a young griffin, fresh out from home."

"Of course, I will recommend him to my brother-in-law," Magda answered, swiftly, "or to my own son. You've only to ask."

"Thank you, Maggie." He took her hands into his once more. After another comfortable silence, he added, "I'd like to think of him with something of his own that he can work at. He's too serious a lad to waste away his days as a society drone. No better thing for him than for you and Mrs. Liesel to introduce him around, see that no one takes undue advantage. Hullo, boy—your ears must have been buzzing, we were just talking about you," he added, as Sebastian and Lottie appeared on the path. Lottie's hat hung by its ribbons and her hair was disarrayed from an encounter with one of those gnarled little juniper trees that grew all over the upper island.

"Nothing bad, I hope, Uncle," Sebastian answered with an affectionate smile.

"No, Madame Becker has promised to take you in hand, if you should decide to go ahead with that cattle venture, once you're of age. Time to stir the stumps, lad—that wind has a bite to it and I am sure the ladies feel the chill now."

"I'd like that, Marm," Sebastian said quietly to Magda, as he helped his uncle rise from the stone bench. "It interests me, very much."

"I will show you some of my younger son's letters," Magda found herself saying. "He does the most amusing drawings, and that might give you a better idea than your books of what you would find—if you pursue this venture."

"Miss Lottie has already told me much," Sebastian answered. His eyes went towards Lottie as he said her name with such affection. Magda looked between them, chilled by something that was not the wind, recognition that there were feelings between the two of them. Just so had Rosalie and Robert Hunter looked at each other on that long-ago morning, when Rosalie pointed him out to her sister from an upper window of Vati's house. Magda had known at once that they were bound to each other with shining bands, bands that neither distance, war, nor death could never shatter. Just so now was her own daughter bound, and Magda felt suddenly old, as empty as a hollow tree, as empty as the shell of old mad Emperor Tiberius' ruined palace, here on the cliff that overlooked the Tyrrhenian sea. In another year, Lottie would put up her hair and be a young lady. She would be courted, would marry soon after that, and Magda's arms would finally be empty. The last of the children Carl Becker had given to her, the children she promised to care for, would have taken wing and departed the nest.

"Mama, are you unwell?" Lottie asked with sudden concern. "You look chilled."

"The wind is cold, little miss," Rollie answered. "It will affect those whose blood is thinned by having lived in hot climes, such as your dear mama."

"Oh, Rollie, please don't be gallant and give me your coat again," Magda begged. "You were in India as long as I have been in Texas, you should feel it just as much!"

"I assure you, I do not," Rollie insisted, but then he snapped his fingers. "Aha! I just had an idea, Maggie. It's almost Christmas and I have a present for you. Better have the use of it today than wait until Christmas. We'll stop at our digs and I'll fetch it for you!"

They walked sedately along the trodden path, through the scrub woods and tumbled ruins, back towards the close-packed houses and villas. At Rollie's tiny bachelor cottage, hardly more than three rooms and an apron-patch of garden, Rollie went in, while they waited by the door.

He emerged, unwrapping crackling brown paper from a length of brilliant fabric; a shawl of printed wool challis in rust red and gold, as light as feathers and as warm as an embrace.

"Kashmiri weave, of course," Rollie said, unfolding it. "Bought it years ago, meant to give it . . . to someone. Never did. But I thought the colors were a treat."

It was indeed a magnificent shawl, with a deep silken fringe and an intricate border of scallops and roundels, stylized flowers, in rust and gold, green and black. Rollie shook it out and with a flourish, settled it around her shoulders.

"But Rollie—I cannot accept this, I do not wear anything but mourning," Magda protested.

Lottie said, "Oh, Mama, but it is gorgeous! Please, Mama—just this once."

"For me, Maggie." Rollie drew it closer around her and lowered his voice. "I would like to see you in bright colors, just for this little while. Your dear old chap—I'll wager that he would have liked that too. For us, Maggie—a bit of cheer on a winter day?" And he smiled at her with such sweet affection that Magda could not bear to cast a shadow on it by refusing his gift.

"And you did wear it often, Mama" Lottie pointed out.

Her mother admitted reluctantly, "But only at home, Lottie—in my own rooms. His gift was a private matter, something I preferred to keep to myself."

"It was not long after that . . ." Lottie began.

Magda answered, "Yes . . . just before Christmas."

One morning, Rollie was unaccountably absent at the little table in the Piazzetta where they had become accustomed to meet for their morning coffee. Magda waited with mounting impatience, wondering if she should walk over to Rollie's little house, or return to Princess Cherkevsky's villa. Before she had completely made up her mind as to what she would do, with Mouse looking up at her with worried eyes—he was a creature of habit, was Mouse—her daughter emerged into the Piazzetta. Lottie stepped from the archway of the alley that led by the villa, hand in hand with Sebastian and followed by Irina. As soon as she saw their faces, especially the moment she saw Irina, who was never out of her room before 10:00 a.m., she knew what had happened, why Rollie was late.

"It all happened quite peacefully, my dear." Irina took Magda's hand in own. Her hands felt like cold little claws, stiff and bent with arthritis. "Sometime last night. The boy says his face was quite serene, nothing of the bed disarranged, and he never heard his uncle cry out. He was just asleep, never to wake. Not such a bad way to go, I think—even for a soldier."

"He would have been surprised," Magda answered. She was not as shocked or grieved as Lottie and Sebastian seemed to think she should have been. Neither was Irina. "Surprised and gratified to know that he was fated to live long. He told me of some of his alarms and hairbreadth escapes in India."

"There, you see?" Irina's eyes lit, happily. "He might have preferred that, all the same. But still—a good man, and a good end. You are not distraught, my dear?"

"No, I think not," Magda shook her head. No, she was not distraught, but rather saddened for herself, at the losing of a friend and being deprived of his good company. "I feel rather as I did when my own father died—he also peacefully, after a long and useful life."

"Just so," Irina nodded. "A good end, among good friends. Nothing better. I wonder what sort of funeral the boy has arranged? I expect he will be buried in the English cemetery on the mainland. He had lived here for so long. I can't help thinking he would have preferred something very martial."

"A Viking boat," Magda suggested, "with all his weapons and trophies around him, pushed out into the sea and set on fire?"

Irina clapped her hands. "Oh, he would have liked that," she agreed, laughing, "but I do not think the British Consul would have approved!"

Magda uttered a small and wistful sigh. She pulled more tightly around her shoulders the brilliant Kashmiri shawl that Rollie had given her only a few days before. "I shall miss him, Irina. Somehow, there is not as much to savor of these places as there once was. I might almost wish myself at our home in Texas."

Curiously, at nearly that very hour, Dolph Becker was saying almost the same thing. He had left his uncle and his cousins in London, the town winter-dark and choking with coal fire smoke. He couldn't stand cities; a city the size of New York or London made him feel as though he were choking on the air, on the constant noise and the inescapable presence of so many other people. It was, he reckoned, the exact opposite of Auntie Liesel's megrim about being out in the open, alone under the sky. She feared that so much, preferring to revel in the constant city bustle. The city oppressed him, made him long to be away. If it weren't for the chance to look at fine blood-stock, he would have turned around and left for home as soon as Auntie Liesel was settled.

"Don't forget," Uncle Hansi said, as he packed his single valise, "we must depart next week, if we are to be in Italy for Christmas. Where do you think to go, Dolph?"

"Anywhere but here," Dolph answered. "Someplace empty, and not too far away. I'll be back in a week, Uncle—don't worry about me."

"I wouldn't stay awake for a moment," Hansi smiled, a knife-edge smile. "What hazards could lay in wait for you, after trailing cattle in all weather for ten years, eh?"

"Can't picture any," Dolph said, but he had his revolver in the bottom of his valise, just in case.

The cabman looked askance at him, clad in rough work clothes, kerchief knotted around his neck rather than a collar and tie, carrying a single valise with a heavy travel blanket strapped on top of it.

"Where to, squire?" the cabman asked. He would have been less respectful, but Dolph had first tossed him a couple of large coins.

Dolph answered, "Take me to the railway station, for any trains going west."

"Waterloo Bridge Station?"

"That'll do," Dolph agreed. "Just someplace to the west, someplace out of here."

"Bristol's in the west, squire—will that suit?"

"Anyplace." He tossed his valise into the cab and climbed in.

"Well, look out for the funeral trains, then." The cabman laughed coarsely. "You don't want to be put on the coffin-car, do you? They run the funeral trains to Brookwood out of there."

"I'll pay double, if you don't talk to me," Dolph said, and thereafter the cabman maintained a rather miffed silence.

He bought a ticket to Bristol, but got out at Reading and, finding a livery stable, rented a dog cart and a single horse. The liveryman looked at him strange, though, when he insisted on inspecting every available horse before making his choice. The best of the lot was a small beast, trained to harness. Dolph did not even wish anything to do with English saddles, upon which you were apparently expected to perch with your knees up around your ears.

"I'll be back in a week," Dolph told him, "and if not—I'll leave a deposit on the nag and cart. If you don't see us again, consider him sold to me." The liveryman protested, but only as a matter of form.

Winter in England seemed no colder than winters in the hills around the Becker place. He went north, towards Abington and the start of the Downs. English Jack had once said something about that place, when they had been spinning yarns around the campfire; English Jack had talked of a horse carved into a chalk hillside and a stone smithy nearby, where an invisible smith would shoe a horse if payment was left along with the beast. He said it was an empty land, the Downs, a line of chalk hills where you could look out at the land below, all quilt-patched with fields and little towns, stitched together with white roads. But up on the Downs, underneath the sky, the wind blew so hard it fair forced the grass to curl over and take cover in the ground again. Aye, Dolph wanted to see a place like that.

An old road, an old trail threaded its way across the chalk uplands, the oldest road in England, so Jack said. Dolph thought he would rather spend a week in the open there, than another day in London, breathing the air under that murky sky and listening to the incessant city din. No, give him the empty sky and quiet fields and hills. Reading was just place where that impulse overwhelmed him.

Dolph felt better almost at once, as soon as he and his horse were out and alone, away from cobblestone streets, away from red-brick buildings darkened with soot, away from city voices, city noise. The air blew sweet, clean and cold. This was a fair land, even winter-blasted and with trees bare and shapely under the sky, adorned by frost in the morning that left every leaf edge glittering with ice. At the reins of the dog cart, he meandered north along narrow lanes lined with thick hedges, overhung with trees, guided more by instinct and the sight of the glittering stars than by the signposts at crossroads or at the village greens. Darkness seemed to come in late afternoon, now that it was winter. That vaguely offended him—it didn't seem quite right, that it should be pitch-dark so early. He chose to spend most nights in villages, wherever there was an inn or a pub with a small room to rent for the night, spending the long evening in a corner of the public room, sitting in a corner with a tankard of ale and watching the regular habitués. He didn't like to talk much; the country-folk spoke in accents almost impenetrable to his ears. His own excited too many comments and questions, questions about who he was and what business he had in coming to wherever it was; a situation which also vaguely offended him. Where he came from, it was considered unpardonably rude to ask anything beyond what a man volunteered about himself. As English Jack himself once observed patiently, *"It is not the done thing, old chap."* But English Jack's countrymen asked question after question, and Dolph found it very wearying. After a couple of evenings, he found it expedient to speak German and pretend that he only had a little English, just to ensure that he was left alone. There were foreigners and then there were foreigners; one sort didn't have to answer so damn many rude questions.

On the fifth day of his self-claimed holiday, he drove into a small village near to Abington. It was midmorning and he found it already overrun with horsemen milling about in the high street in front of the inn. He reined in, tying his horse to a handy set of iron railings. The horses and some dogs fascinated him as always, but Dolph was not nearly so interested by the people, save for noting that they all seemed considerably overdressed for a morning in the saddle. It looked to have been a hard morning even so; the horses' legs were splashed with mud and some of the men's tight red coats were rather the worse for wear.

The dogs were corralled together by two men wielding long whips. They barked in an excited chorus, hounds of all the same breed if the colors were anything to go by: white with black or dark brown spots, a seething mass of backs and wagging tails. Dolph realized they had been out hunting,

hunting for foxes and probably without any result. From the half-heard talk, they were pausing in the village before going out to quarter the woods on the other side. It seemed to him to be a very inefficient way to go about hunting foxes. But still, Dolph leaned his back against the railings and watched the scene with great interest. Presently he noticed three other dogs, dogs that did not go with the pack but seemed to trail after one of the red-coated men; huge dogs with rough grey coats. Dolph whistled in astonishment to himself; the smallest was the size of a pony. When one of them wandered out from its orbit around the hunters, Dolph whistled softly and wooingly to it.

The dog's head lifted and turned towards him with dark intelligent eyes. He whistled again and held out his hand, and the dog came obediently and nudged trustingly at it.

"Why you lovely fellow," Dolph said in wonder, for when the grey dog lifted his head, it came up nearly to the middle of Dolph's chest. He stroked its ears. The dog seemed to gather itself together, and in a single swift movement it had its forepaws on Dolph's shoulders and began licking his face most affectionately.

"Luath!" shouted a nearby commanding male voice. "I say—down, boy!" The dog abruptly dropped to the ground; its eyes swam with a mixture of guilt and affection. The commanding voice belonged to a big man in a red coat with brass buttons. "I do apologize for Luath," the huntsman continued. "No manners at all, I'm afraid."

"No matter," Dolph answered; his hand found the dog's shaggy head again, caressing as it pressed its head against his hip and looked adoringly at him. "I don't mind—I like dogs. And this one is a lot of dog to like. What sort is he?"

Luath's companions joined him, shouldering in to beg for a caress as well, with their great tails waving like plume-grass fronds in a light breeze. Their master slid down from his own horse. Dolph read some mild astonishment in his face. He guessed that most strangers would have been nervous about being backed up against an iron fence by three huge dogs. Not with these boys, though. Dolph could read their great shaggy bodies and their dark eyes; there was nothing in them but curiosity and affection.

"Irish wolfhound," answered their master. He extended a hand over the dogs' backs, shaking Dolph's with a firm grip. "Lindsay-Groves. Behave yourself, you beggars!" The dogs instantly sat down on their haunches, still looking at Dolph with friendly interest. With their owner now on the ground, they seemed disposed to spread some of their affections in his direction.

"Rudolph Becker."

"Ah." Lindsay-Groves was about Onkel Hansi's age, a short snub-nosed man with a ruddy face. He squinted thoughtfully at Dolph, seeming to see him for the first time. "Not from around here, then?"

"No." And then because Lindsay-Groves had not pressed any farther than that, Dolph reasoned that such good manners deserved some kind of explanation. "M' uncle and I have property in Texas. We came to England to look for good blood-stock, cattle and horses both."

"Ah." Lindsay-Groves's face lit up with interest. "See anything here you fancy?" He gestured expansively at the horses. "Some damned good blood-lines in the Hunt."

Dolph shook his head. "Good stamina among your hunters for an all-out chase, I guess. But we work cattle from horseback—what we need is brains and agility."

"More like a polo pony." Lindsay-Groves nodded in perfect understanding. They leaned against the railings in pleasurable amity, scratching the dogs' heads. "I see—right tool for the right job. I know all about that, y'see. Build bridges, m'self."

Presently Dolph ventured, "One of the other big ranch-owners—Captain King at the Santa Gertrudis—he's bred a very good line. Quarterhorses, they call them. Run a quarter-mile race, dead on. But he's been at it for thirty years, more or less."

"Head start?" Lindsay-Groves ventured, sympathetically. Dolph nodded. It looked as if the Hunt was gathering itself together for another round. The hounds spilled out into the street, yapping in chorus. One of the red-coated men blew a horn, in a series of short notes.

"I wouldn't mind one of these fellows, though," he added, ruffling Luath's shaggy grey ears.

Lindsay-Groves looked positively jovial. "I've a bitch that just whelped a litter of pups by him—you should come up to the Hall this afternoon and see them."

"I'd like that," Dolph answered.

Lindsay-Groves clapped him on the shoulder. "Four o'clock then, shall we say? Anyone here will tell you the way." He whistled to his three wolfhounds and swung up into his saddle. "I take it you're staying here? Good—they set a decent enough table, but look out for the landlord's cider!"

Goes down like water, but first thing you know you're lying under a hedge singing love songs to the stars overhead."

"Thanks for the warning," Dolph answered. He watched the man clatter away, with the three wolfhounds loping after him. He was followed by two young men in plainer jackets and a young woman in a black riding habit, draped gracefully over her side saddle. Dolph shook his head pityingly at the sight. One might as well sit sideways on one of Daddy Hurst's flapjacks than ride like that; but any woman who did must have a hell of a seat. He rather thought the woman was Lindsay-Groves' daughter; she had the same round face and snub nose.

On the whole, Dolph had more interest in Lindsay-Groves' dogs than the girl. Dogs like those were definitely worth staying overnight in this village for, even though he could have traveled on for another five or six miles.

"The Hall?" the landlord looked at him with no little curiosity when he asked for directions. "Go along the wide road past the church and on a little way to the lodge gates. Can't mistake it, sir—it's the largest house around."

Dolph thought little of that; back in Texas he lived in the largest house around, but it wasn't really all that large. Onkel Hansi's house in San Antonio, now that was large. That was what he unconsciously expected of Lindsay-Groves' residence, even though the gate lodge was about the size of Opa's house in Friedrichsburg. He drove along a fine graveled road, in which the dog cart's wheels crunched pleasantly, through parkland so subtly arranged that the house itself came as a surprise. It seemed as if the trees parted, and there was a mellow golden stone pile with pillars across the front and a lake that reflected it like a mirror. Dolph drew rein and whistled softly, wondering how many people lived in a place like that and why on earth they didn't rattle around like a peas in a gourd.

There seemed to be no one about; although with a house that big there could be a whole cavalry company knocking around inside, spare mounts and supply wagons and all. Dolph made a good guess at what must be the front door and pulled at a metal ring next to the door. Deep within the house he heard a faint chime. He waited patiently, the horse and cart waiting with equal patience but considerable less interest at his back. The door opened, and a very superior gentleman in a black frock coat looked down his nose at Dolph.

"I was told to come see a man about a dog," Dolph ventured. He was not terribly surprised by the condescension or the barely concealed sneer that he was met with. He had, in fact, gotten in a lot of quiet fun over the summer, by appearing to be an ordinary laborer. The way that people's faces changed at the moment when Dolph paid for something in gold or large notes provided him with a lot of amusement. Dolph detested snobs and people who lorded it over others.

"Tradesmen and servants go around to the back," the very superior gentleman drawled. "To the kennels, the stables and the servant's entrance."

Dolph shrugged. "Very well. Tell Mr. Lindsay-Groves that I'm here, then." he said.

The very superior gentleman looked as if he had bitten into something bad-tasting, and answered, "I will inform his lordship." The door closed with a little more than necessary force, as Dolph raised an eyebrow. A lordship, eh?

"Well, he didn't have his lordship suit on this morning," he observed to the closed door. Really, if it weren't for the dogs, he would hardly have bothered.

He returned to the dog cart and followed the graveled drive, which wound around to the side of the house. There was a terrace there, edged with a balustrade and urns big enough to boil a whole cow in. Farther along, a wide gateway led into a ramble of lower buildings and yards. From here, the Hall looked a bit more jumbled, with oddments of wings and lower rooflines sticking out. That must be the stables, he thought—windows with the shutters standing open, and horses looking out into a cobbled yard.

He drove through the gateway; there were two people and another horse there, a horse whose head hung down with exhaustion, or maybe pain—it favored its off foreleg and stood with the hoof barely touching the ground.

A groom held its bridle, and was saying anxiously, "I don't know rightly what Mr. Arkwright will want to do, Miss Isobel."

Dolph cleared his throat. The other person was the young lady he had noticed that morning, but now she appeared much less modish and considerably disheveled. She had lost her hat. Her hair, light brown and the color of coffee-sugar, hung half loosened around her shoulders. She looked as if she had been pulled backwards through a particularly thorny hedge, her habit was richly splashed with mud, and there were blood-oozing scratches on her cheek.

"I was invited to come and look at the puppies," Dolph ventured, as both the groom and Miss Isobel turned to look in his direction.

Miss Isobel distractedly combed her loose hair back from her face with her fingers. "Oh, dear—the American gentleman. I saw you with Fa this morning. I'm afraid they're still out—they picked up a good scent and it was view-halloo and away. Fa and the others should be almost to Harwell by now!" She seemed almost tearful with disappointment.

Dolph ventured, "I'm Rudolph Becker, but everyone calls me Dolph. What happened to you that you're not almost to Harwell, Miss?"

"Isobel," she sniffed, "Isobel Lindsay-Groves. Actually, it's Lady Isobel, but I don't care much for that. A ditch happened to me, a ditch on the far side of a hedge, and poor Thistle tried his best, but he landed short . . . And our head groom, Mr. Arkwright, is off taking the spare horses to meet the Hunt."

"Ah," Dolph said, as if he understood. Not that he did, exactly, but acting as if he did seemed to make Isobel fell better. She was a sturdy, square-shouldered girl; not in the least a slender and ethereal lady of fashion, for all that she was cruelly corseted and stuffed into clothes that did not suit her at all. Her eyes were the only beauty in her round and snub-nosed face; hazel and surrounded with thick lashes. "I do know a bit about horses, if you would like me to look at your poor old Thistle."

"Would you?" Isobel breathed, and looked at him mistily. Oddly enough, it made Dolph feel very much like a knight errant. "I'd be so grateful. Fa bought him for me for my eighteenth birthday."

Sighing, Dolph tied up the reins to the dog cart, and jumped down to look at poor old Thistle's leg. Isobel hovered anxiously.

"Miss Isobel," he said, as he leaned into Thistle's shoulder, "if you took a tumble yourself, shouldn't you . . . ."

"Not until I am assured that Thistle is all right." Isobel laughed, an oddly strangled laugh, before stating firmly, "And I came to no lasting harm, which is more than I can say of my riding habit. Mama will be distraught—which is as good a reason to remain here as any that I can think of."

Another Mama like Auntie Liesel, Dolph thought—given to endless worries and megrims. He didn't blame Miss Isobel in the least for taking refuge in the stable.

"It looks like you landed in some nice soft mud," Dolph observed, and to Thistle he added, "All right, boy . . . let me have it. There you go." He lifted up the horse's hock, and felt along the bone and tendons with gentle fingers. "Umm. Feels like he's torn a tendon. Not much you can do, except let him rest. A hot bran poultice might make him feel it a bit less." He let Thistle put his leg down, and straightened up to face Isobel's trusting hazel regard. "I don't know that he'll be much good for jumping and all that, after this. You'll want to go gently for a couple of months, until it heals."

"At least it's nothing broken." Isobel beamed with honest relief. "Thank you, thank you so much, Mr. Becker. I adore Thistle—he was a bribe to me, you should know. Fa promised me a horse of my very own if I should behave myself for the Season."

"The Season?" Dolph asked, having only a vague notion of what that might mean. It sounded horrendous, if an apparently sensible and honest person like Isobel had to be bribed into participating.

"Oh, you know, being presented at Court . . . all the balls and events and that. Mama insisted."

"It was that awful?" Dolph asked, sympathetically.

Isobel made it sound like a prolonged round of torture. "Picture me, in a white dress with three plumes on my head, being brought into court, before her Majesty," she explained. Dolph could; it was like imagining an ungainly young heifer being dressed up in a ball gown. He did not have to imagine the sneers and the sniggering behind raised hands. He had put up with a sufficiency of that over the last six months. Isobel continued with determined cheer, "I endured for imagining coming home and Fa's promise of a horse of my own and being able to play with the dogs and go out among Fa's tenants. It almost made up for Mama not being able to marry me off and have a grand society wedding at the end of it."

Dolph couldn't think of much to say to that save, "We don't do much of that where I come from. I have two sisters and I can't imagine my mother doing that to them."

"How lucky!" Isobel sounded deeply envious. "Where is that—you must tell me more, Mr. Becker. It sounds like paradise!" The young groom led away the limping Thistle, leaving the two of them momentarily alone in the stableyard. Isobel smoothed back her hair again and brushed nervously at a patch of mud on her skirt, venturing as she did so, "You've been very kind. Fa was fearfully impressed—the dogs usually don't take to people so readily. Quite honestly, they terrify most. He so wanted to speak to you, you should know—he had ever so many questions!"

"Your butler didn't know that," Dolph observed wryly and Isobel clapped her hand to her mouth, horrified.

"Oh! You went to the front door and Spencer sent . . . ."

"He said that servants and trade went around to the back," Dolph answered.

To his horror, Isobel looked about to weep with embarrassment. "I am so sorry," she blurted. "Sometimes I think Spencer takes more care for propriety and the honor of the house than we do. Certainly more than Fa or I do. I am so sorry," she said again and Dolph regretted saying anything at all about his reception.

"Think nothing of it, Miss Isobel," he said, taking her hand. "I didn't—except for the inconvenience." And he kissed her hand as elegantly as they did in Germany although Isobel's hand wasn't elegant at all; just capable, with sturdy, blunt fingers, slightly callused and fairly dirty. "Besides, I was promised another look at the dogs. Wolfhounds, your father said. I suppose they were used to hunt wolves with. Are there even wolves left in England?"

"Yes . . . and no," Isobel colored. "They were once used so. They're an ancient breed, nearly extinct. The dogs, I mean. The wolves <u>are</u> extinct. Fa adores them—the dogs, not the wolves! He and some of his friends are trying to revive the breed. I adore them because . . . ."

"Because dogs are trustier than most people you know?" Dolph ventured and Isobel cried, "Exactly! Oh, you should come and see Deirdre's puppies—Deirdre's the dam, you know. They all have Irish names."

"Only logical," Dolph observed. Isobel grasped his fingers in the hand that he had not let go of, and led him through another gate beyond the stable into a farther, smaller courtyard. This yard was swept and clean, but still smelled faintly of dog dung. A number of small ornate houses stood elevated on pilings a little distance from the ground. Isobel went to the nearest of them and knelt on the ground by the doorway, which was tall enough for a child to walk through without stooping.

"Deirdre," she crooned, lovingly. There was a scrabbling sound within; the shaggy head of the wolfhound bitch emerged warily. "Come and pay your respects, dear pretty girl!" Deirdre emerged all at once; obviously reassured by the presence of one person that she knew, not terribly apprehensive of the one she did not. She licked Isobel's face and came to sniff with immense dignity and care at Dolph, who went to one knee; dogs always seemed to be reassured by someone who took the trouble to approach on their level. The pups also emerged from the kennel-house, tumbling over each other in their eager curiosity; grey and brindle, sand-colored and brown.

"How old are they?" Dolph asked; being larger than any other breed that he had experience with, size was of no use in gauging age.

"Six months," Isobel answered. "They really are not quite fully grown until over a year old. Fa says it's because they are so clever. I do so like dogs!" She sighed happily. Incredibly, she had gathered Deirdre into her arms, as she sat with her legs curled under her, on the cobbles of the dog-kennel yard. The great ungainly wolfhound bitch curled lovingly into her lap, looking with adoration into Isobel's face as if she were as dainty as one of Princess Cherkevsky cherished little pets. Poor Isobel, muddy, awkward and disheveled, devoted to dogs and horses. She belonged in this place, or at least the front aspect of it, as much as he did.

Dolph looked at her, as two of the pups engaged in playing tug-of-war with the sleeve of his coat. He cleared his throat and asked, "Miss Isobel, if I might ask—how well do you like cows?"

Her answer pleased him very much. Three days later, when he returned to London, wanting to tell Onkel Hansi of it and about her, his cousin Anna looked up from the floor of their living room suite. She was engaged in rolling clothes in layer upon layer of tissue paper, packing them into a steamer trunk. Like his mother, she did not like being fussed over by maids.

"Oh good," she said. "You've returned just in time. We're going home."

"We are?" he asked, puzzled. "Not to Italy for Christmas?"

"No," Anna shook her sleek head. "Papa received a telegram. My brother Willi is alive. He has been recovered from the Indians."

Chapter Twenty-Two: *Llano Estacada*

"So we came home," Lottie shook her head. "Our departure was so very abrupt, Mama. I confess I was most distraught, thinking I was deprived of Sebastian's company forever—only eighteen months, but it seemed forever at the time! It meant so much to me. He had lingered in Capri quite purposefully, and not only to see to his uncle's affairs and property. Auntie Liesel's joy just seemed like turning the knife in the wound!"

"And she was joyful," Magda allowed. "She could think of nothing else—her child was restored to her and she to her former spirits! It seemed like a miracle, of course. She insisted upon leaving at once; we would have departed the very day that Cousin Peter arrived with the good news, save for the difficulty of making arrangements!"

It was a hurried and harried Christmas, for they were now to depart during the week after. Hansi had arranged for passage from Hamburg on the regular packet steamship, and to meet them there with Anna and the children. Magda felt she was being tugged in all directions; her usually sunny-tempered daughter moped and sulked in corners, Liesel was over the moon with excitement, chattering exuberantly of the miracle of Willi's return and her plans for when he was restored to the loving arms of his family, and Peter fretted impatiently, eager to be reunited with Anna and the boys.

"I am sorry that we are all become such uncongenial company," she lamented to Irina on Christmas Eve. At the Princess' direction she set out the Christmas presents in the tiny parlor, with the tall window that looked towards the swallows nest houses clinging to the cliffs that fell straight to the harbor below. "I know you had planned such delights on our behalf, now all that effort is come to naught!"

"No matter," Irina shrugged, carelessly. "Such is life, my dear—that which happens when you have made plans!" She rummaged through the pile of brightly wrapped gifts in her lap. The two maids had carried in a wicker laundry hamper packed with larger parcels. "At least the girls will have a pleasant Christmas Eve!"

"You think?" Magda sighed. "Lottie is upstairs crying her eyes out."

"Pish!" Irina said, shrugging eloquently. "She is merely a girl in love for the first time. It is like one of those tiresome children's ailments; once recovered, one doesn't catch it so badly again. Either young Bertrand will come to Texas when he turns eighteen and they will still fancy themselves in love, or not. I think," she added with a shrewd look at Magda, "that you have another worry. Is it your niece? She fares well, does she not?"

"No, she is marvelously well," Magda answered. "It was her idea to send Peter to shepherd us all back to Hamburg to take the packet home. My son was taken with a fit of wanderlust, otherwise he would have come in his stead."

"Pity," Irina said with a sparkle. "And a pity again that I am not thirty years younger! It is your sister then, about whom you are fretting, my dear Magda?"

"Yes," Magda nodded somberly. "She is ecstatic with joy. I know that may seem a trifle strange."

"She is intemperate in her moods," Irina agreed. "So you have said often and so have I observed. Surely this is nothing new. After a time, she will be as melancholic as she has been happy. So what do you so fear about this inevitable descent?"

"You have not listened to her talk of her son as I have," Magda explained. "She speaks of Willi as if he were a child still."

"All children remain children to their parents," Irina answered. "My stepson has grey hair and a mustache like a walrus—yet to his dying day, my husband thought of him always as a boy."

"It's not like that." Magda hung the last of the small presents from the branches of a small cedar pine which had been set in a corner of the parlor. She sat on her heels at the base of the tree and explained, "Willi was a child of six when he was taken by the Indians. He turned seven a few short months afterwards. Grete was taken also. She was four, but she was recovered from them almost at once, within a year or two."

"Oh, my!" Irina clapped her hands almost with excitement. "Grete! Your niece, Grete? The quiet little thing who hardly has a word to say for herself? How terribly interesting that is, Magda! You had never spoken of this to me before!"

"My sister and brother-in-law did not wish it to be known," Magda answered, with slight reproof. "They wanted her to forget that ghastly experience as thoroughly as possible and for other people to forget it as well. There can be a considerable scandal attached, especially for older girls taken captive and later recovered to their families. It is always feared that they have been made," Magda searched for the right word, "into concubines. And our younger sister and her husband were most piteously murdered when Willi and Grete were taken. They would have witnessed that horror, you see."

"I see." Irina sighed regretfully. "And I quite agree. Poor child! I will govern my terrible curiosity for her sake. But why do you fear for your sister? Surely it is cause for rejoicing to have her son restored to her, at last?"

"Yes, but it has become plain to me that she is thinking of him as a child, a child only a little older than when he was taken captive. Irina," Magda knotted her hands in her lap, hardly aware that she did so, "that happened almost ten years ago, in the first year after the war ended! He will not be a child, he will be nearly a man grown!"

"Surely your sister can count the months and years." Irina's eyebrows lifted. "She is surely aware of how much time has passed, and that children grow!"

"I am sure she is aware of that," Magda answered. "For she and Hansi have seven still living, of whom Grete is the youngest. But she persists in this odd delusion! She talks of school and toys and amusements more fitting for a child, and—"

"You fear that she may be disillusioned." Comprehension dawned on Irina's countenance. She nodded slowly. "Once she comprehends the reality, you fear another descent into sorrow."

"She almost went mad, when they were taken," Magda whispered, for she could hear Liesel's voice and step on the stairs. "I do not think she would be so afflicted by this new disappointment. But she has truly been almost made well again. I dread anything that may disturb the balance of her mind."

"Perhaps she will come upon the realization slowly," Irina suggested.

"So I hope," Magda whispered, as the parlor door opened.

Liesel called cheerfully within, "Are the presents ready? May I call in the girls now?"

"Yes of course, my dear," Irina answered. "And call everyone—it is my great joy, you see, to see all their faces when they behold their gifts. I have had a care with yours, knowing that you were going to be traveling; they are small and portable. It is my hope that you will think of me whenever you gaze upon them."

"I am sure we shall," Magda answered. "I only hope that such gifts as we have brought for you will do the same!"

"Think nothing of it," Irina answered, her wise old eyes alight with mischief and vitality. "You have already given me a gift of inestimable value—companionship and amusement for the most of this year. I vow I have not been bored for more than two or three minutes at a time."

When they departed the island, only Magda and her daughter looked back. Sebastian Bertrand waved sadly across the widening water. Princess Cherkevsky had said her farewells at the villa, as she was too old and frail to be carried by her menservants all the way down the winding hill to the quay more often than absolutely necessary. She and Magda had exchanged promises to write; Magda was already forming the sentences of her first letter to Irina before Capri dissolved into the mist behind them.

"And now," Liesel clasped her hands with joyous fervor, "we are going home!"

It wasn't until much later that Magda realized how very peculiar that sounded, especially from Liesel. Home, as they had spoken of it for so long, was no longer Germany, no longer Vati's house in Albeck. Home was in Texas, home was Hansi's sprawling mansion, or the stone house on the Guadalupe ranch. Home was there, where their hearts were, and where were buried so many of those whom they had loved. Albeck was the place they had outgrown, as a bird first outgrows an eggshell and then the nest it was laid in. They could no more constrain their wings and return to it than a bird could return to an egg. A week later, they watched Hamburg diminish in the distance behind the swift steamship that would bear them home.

To Magda's initial puzzlement, Dolph remained behind, in England.

"He's finishing up the business of acquiring blood-stock for the ranch," Hansi said when he met them at the Hamburg main station. He kissed Liesel enthusiastically once again, and explained to Magda, "He will return as we originally planned, once he has arranged passage for the cattle and horses."

"Not to mention one particular filly," Peter added slyly. "No great beauty for looks, Cuz says, but much to his taste and very spirited, with a stout heart and good bloodlines."

"A horse?" Magda looked from Hansi to Peter as they both laughed in the superior way of men who know something. "I have brought him a horse, as a present from Princess Cherkevsky!" That was a little bauble, beautifully carved out of quartz with bright eyes in some dark brown gem. True to her promise, Irina's Christmas presents had all been small things, in exquisite workmanship and taste: for Liesel, a rock-crystal vase with a sprig of an orange tree, the flowers and fruit in enamel and gold, with leaves of green nephrite; and for Anna a sprig of enamel and gold forget-me-nots in a similar vase. The girls were gifted with parasol handles, beautifully worked in enamel and gold. Magda had a little dog, carved in stone, which looked so like Mouse; so spry and lifelike that she laughed in affectionate amusement every time she looked at it. For Hansi, being expected for Christmas, Irina had bought a cow, also carved out of quartz, from the same atelier and artist.

"Carry her gift home with you," Hansi chuckled. "You may give it to him as a wedding present, perhaps!"

Aggravating man, he said no more. Magda went below to her cabin, reflecting upon the mixed emotions attending on their first departure, so many years ago. Only Hansi and Vati had been eager to shake the dust of the old country off their boots, then. Now they were all quite cheerful at departing for home, all but poor Lottie, still moping after Sebastian.

At least, this time they traveled in very much more comfort. It was the same journey in reverse, although through Galveston rather than Indianola. It astounded Magda how swiftly they arrived in San Antonio, barely four weeks after departing from Hamburg, their passage by steamer, train and coach seemingly greased by Hansi's generosity and repute.

Fredi and Porfirio waited upon their arrival at Hansi's house; along with Liesel's household staff. All were made welcome. Another reason to be glad to be rich, Magda reflected; it made arrival after so long a time away so easy, even though they had outdistanced the wagon which carried their heavy trunks. Porfirio had a cup of coffee in his hand as he came out to the porte-cochere. Fredi held a piece of Mexican flatbread rolled around scrambled eggs and sausage, and he crammed it into his mouth at the last minute before embracing Liesel and Magda, and all the rest. They were caught in a happy clamor for quite some time.

"I hear that the young Patrón has been courting." Porfirio kissed Magda's hand with all due gallantry. "Does the young lady meet with your approval, Madame Becker?"

"I can hardly say," Magda answered, "for I only know what my son wrote to me, before we sailed from Germany. He is most hopeful as regards his suit. The young lady's family looks upon him with favor—all but the distance that she would be removed from them."

"Ah," Porfirio patted her hand, consolingly, "I see. That is an obstacle that may be overcome with time and persistence. One hopes that her family may prefer to see her married to a fine young man like the young Patrón, rather than a wastrel close at hand."

"We had them put on late breakfast for you all," Fredi said. "Ah, good to see you all! My God, it's good to see you safely home. You would not believe what has been happening all this time!"

"What of our son?!" Hansi demanded. "What of our Willi—your letter said that he had been brought into the agency months ago! Where is he, what have they done with him?"

"Ah," Fredi finished chewing and swallowed a great mouthful. "Well, that's the thing, you see. He's been at Ft. Sill for months, with all the rest of the band that he was with. At first, they didn't even recognize him as a white man. It seemed that he managed to stay in the background, never letting any of the soldiers take a good close look at him. Couldn't keep that up for long, though; presently someone noted he had grey eyes and light skin. They took him to the agent, Mr Lawrie Tatum—the Indians call him Bald Head. He's the man in charge of the Comanche Agency." Fredi chewed and swallowed the last of his breakfast. "Look, can we go back inside and have something more to eat while I tell you the rest? He had him cleaned him up a bit, cut his hair . . . Johann wrote that it took half a dozen soldiers to hold him down for a bath, he fought like a wildcat the whole time."

"That does not sound like Willi!" exclaimed Liesel. "He was always so good and biddable." Suddenly her face was shadowed by doubt. "Could it be truly our boy and not some other child? Might they have made a mistake? Perhaps our son has been claimed by some other family!" She appealed frantically to Hansi, who set his arm around her.

"No, they are certain of it," he responded at once. "I have letters from Agent Tatum, outlining all the particulars. Johann also made a journey to Fort Sill to confirm such details as could not be expressed in letters. They both questioned this boy very closely. It was not Tatum's fault that when he wrote to me, we had already departed for Germany."

"All these months!" Liesel lamented. "We thought him dead for all this time, yet he was alive!"

Magda met Anna's eyes, knowing they shared the same thought; that the exertion of travel and their arrival home might be pushing Liesel from the heights of her tower. Liesel continued, "And why did he not recollect who he was, tell his proper name to this agent?"

"I'll take the boys upstairs," Anna murmured to Magda. "I am sorry, Auntie—I have so little patience for Mama, when all my attention is bent towards my own children!"

"Take Lottie and Grete also," Magda answered in the same tones. "I do not think it can be good for her to be reminded anew."

Meanwhile, Hansi was reassuring Liesel yet again. Magda and Anna had heard him patiently repeating almost by rote what he had read in letters forwarded from Mr. Tatum in Kansas and from Johann, so many times during their journey home. "We are certain of this, dearest. Do you not recollect that Willi was born with a strawberry mark on his back, just under his shoulder blade? This boy has an identically shaped scar in that same place. He remembers some German but no English. He also has some memory of Friedrichsburg and of living with many other children in a house that sounds like your father's house. He said also that he was taken captive along with his younger sister. It can be no other, Lise!"

"In any case, the lad arrives with an Army supply train at the end of the week." Fredi dealt out that information as if slapping down a playing card. "If he does turn out to be the wrong one, you can always send him back." There were times, Magda reflected, that she still wished that she could just turn her younger brother over her knee and smack him, as she had when he was a small child. This was one of them; a man full grown and responsible, with all the blundering tact and manners of one of his own cattle.

"It's our lad," Hansi quickly reassured his wife, who wavered on the edge of tears for one fraught moment. "I am as sure of that as I am of anything. You should write to the other lads, let them know that their brother is about to return home, eh? What about a party, Lise? One of your splendid parties to welcome him home—to welcome us home! What about that, hey?"

And that was all it took to restore Liesel's high spirits, although Magda's apprehensions were not relieved. She feared that Liesel, in wondering if this boy found among the Agency Indians really was her son, had inadvertently hit on a very real consideration, only to be jollied out of her apprehension by Hansi. As Magda settled back into the little guest cottage that evening, she pondered once again how long it would take for her sister to cope with the knowledge that her lost child had not remained a child. And how long before Willi would be able to claim his former life, after having been among the Tribes for so long? Seven years old, Magda thought; surely that was of an age enough to retain something of his upbringing, memories of the love and affection lavished on him by his parents and Vati! Hadn't Vati often quoted that grim old Jesuit scholar who said, *"Give me a child until he is seven, and I will show you the man?"*

Breathlessly they waited for news of the Army supply caravan, drawing closer day by day. Indeed, several of Hansi's wagons were among them. Hansi had importuned one of his teamsters to send word by messenger when once they approached San Antonio. It was Fredi who brought word of their actual arrival, in the dusty plaza before the rambling old citadel ruins. He had been fretting impatiently and whiling away the days at the Vaudeville Theater and Saloon until he could return to the Live Oak ranch with a clear conscience and commence the spring round-up and branding.

He came pounding up the gravel drive, shouting, "The wagons from the north are here! They're just coming down the Salado Creek road!" It was but a moment for Hansi and Peter to put on their coats, for they had been expecting word all since sun-up. The barouche was already waiting under the porte-cochere. Liesel had been fluttering around the house all morning, alternately getting into the house maid's way as they prepared a bedroom for Willi, and pleading with Hansi to take the barouche and follow the road north, to meet the wagons bearing her boy somewhere along the way.

Magda caught up her shawl, looking around the door into the parlor. Anna lay on the chaise, with her small portable writing desk balanced over the bulge of the new child, writing letters for Hansi.

"We're going now, Annchen," she said.

Anna closed her eyes wearily. "Take Harry and Christian," she begged her aunt. "They are eaten up with curiosity—I have explained a thousand times that Willi will not be dressed as an Indian. In the next hour I would have to explain it a thousand times more. What is it about children, when they don't get the answer they want, they think that asking the question yet again will get them a different answer?"

"Human nature," Magda replied. She had never had much difficulty in getting Harry and Christian to mind. She had the advantage over their parents of seeming stern and grim, and relatively impervious to childish charms. She made them behave, sitting quietly between herself and their father, opposite Hansi and Liesel.

"They say that the railway will reach here within two years," Hansi remarked jovially as they rolled towards town. "What a difference it will make for us! Think of how we walked from the seaside, or rode in ox-wagons! And now, it's just a matter of riding the iron horse for a day or so. What times we have seen, Lise!"

"Do you think we are fully prepared for such miracles?" Magda asked.

Hansi laughed, a hearty and knowing laugh. "I hope so—for I have been advised to buy property within and just without the city! Won't it be handy, to own warehouses and stock corrals close to where the railyards will be!"

"Didn't waste your time in Kansas, did you?" Fredi called from where he rode alongside the barouche.

Peter laughed as well, when Hansi replied, "Once the railway is finished with a town, everything changes. It connects to the rest of the world, which might be a change for the worse, but mostly for the better. Once the railway comes, there are no more wildernesses, unless it is beyond the sound of a steam whistle. When things change, we must change also."

But what of those who do not wish to change, Magda thought, *those who cannot change and cannot bear to see the world changing around them—what fate is theirs?*

They came out into the plaza in front of the sprawling old Citadel, the disused mission chapel with its stone façade arched like a bedstead. Columns twisted like lengths of barley sugar framed a pair of empty niches where statues of saints would have stood. Magda wondered which patron saints would have rested there when it was a church. It was decades since it had gone from that to becoming a barracks and then a warehouse. Carl Becker had fought there as a boy volunteer with the Texian militia, before he and his brother Rudi went away to the Goliad citadel with Colonel Fannin's garrison to guard the road from the coast. Porfirio's father had died here, early the following year, as one of Colonel Travis' artillerymen. Then it had been a bastion, filled in at the altar end to serve as a platform for cannon. Now it was a warehouse, and on this day the plaza and the old churchyard before it become a vast wagon park, deep in churned mud and horse dung. Blue-clad soldiers bawled orders at each other, snapped whips and reins over the necks of their team animals. Crews of laborers had already begun to empty out the wagons. How on earth to find one young civilian among all this bustle?

"We need to find the man in charge," Peter suggested quietly to Hansi. "Look for the one with the most gold on his shoulders."

Hansi stood up, then scrambled up onto the seat, shading his eyes. "Over there," he said, with satisfaction, "three or four of them—one of them has to be our man."

He had his coachman drive as close to the knot of gold-laden officers as he could, angling close between the heavy drays and ambulances. Fredi rode ahead, his horse threading an easy way through the controlled chaos in the plaza. There were a handful of women and children among the soldiers, travel-worn and very weary. Magda's spirits rose; so Willi would not have had to travel with the soldiers, perhaps he would have accompanied an officer's family, traveling in what spartan comfort an ambulance might provide.

Once close enough, Hansi cupped his hands and shouted, "Colonel— Richter, here! I've come for my son! The boy sent by Agent Tatum and the Butlers from the Agency school! We were told to expect him today! Where is he—the Indians stole him away ten years ago this spring and his mother and I have wanted him home every day since!" Hansi's voice carried easily over the raucous shouting in the plaza; not for nothing had he been a teamster himself.

The man with the most ornate braid and the most gold on his shoulders turned abruptly towards the sound of Hansi's voice. He spoke a few words to the man at his side and came up to the barouche with the lounging, slightly bowlegged stride of a man who spends most of his time on horseback. "You Richter, the cattle man?" he asked tersely.

Hansi answered, "Yes, yes . . . but of our son? Where is he? You have not let him get captured again, have you?" Hansi added, with a heavy attempt at humor.

Magda could not quite read the expression on the officer's face; a curious mixture of relief and much-tried exasperation. "No such luck, Mister Richter. We've got your boy, and you're welcome to him." He sketched a salute, adding, "I've sent Sgt. Donnelly to fetch him and his traps."

"Thank you." Hansi leaned down from the barouche to offer his hand. "This means so much to us! I cannot begin to tell you how grateful we are, for all you have done!"

"You're welcome. I'll make a list, directly," the colonel added. Magda looked in much puzzlement towards Peter, who seemed amused.

"What did he mean by that?" she whispered.

Peter answered, "It sounds like Willi has been quite a handful."

"There he is!" cried Liesel, clutching Hansi's arm as a soldier with a great many stripes on his jacket sleeves appeared from between two wagons. "Hansi, there he is! Our boy!" She sprang up, hardly waiting for Fredi to slide down from his mount, or the coachman to leap down from his seat, to open the barouche door and help her to the ground. She shook off their hands, and flung herself at the wiry boy whom the soldier led towards them. She enfolded him in a frantic embrace, crying out endearments, half sobbing as she stroked his face.

Magda, helped down by Peter, stood back a little, watching warily. Yes, it was indeed Willi, although his face was bonier, more angular. His hair was darker than it had been as a child, and cropped brutally short. Magda saw two things almost at once—that his expression was perfectly controlled, almost rigid, as his mother wept over him, and that one wrist was tethered by a length of clothesline to the wrist of the soldier who led him.

"Aye, here he is," the soldier explained cheerfully, as he took out a knife and tactfully slashed through the tether at his own wrist. "Just a bit o' precaution, y'see. He's a bit of a lively one, this lad of yours. He tried a runner three or four times before we crossed the Red River, so we had to put him in restraints, y'see, sor." He handed the end of it to Hansi, contorted his pug-Irish countenance in a deliberate wink, and added, "I recommend you keep a good hold on your end, sor, so I do. Here's his bits o' things. Sorry, those heathens did not leave him with very much. Lord bless him, the Army could not give him very much more." He handed over the rough gunny sack which he carried over his shoulder. By the way he handled it, there was not much inside. He sketched a salute and walked away, although he watched over his shoulder. Other soldiers were also watching, with mild interest. Hansi looked down at the gunny sack and the clothesline in his hand with an expression of mild puzzlement, before he enfolded both Liesel and his son in a rough embrace.

"Oh, Willi," he said, his voice rough with emotion. "We came after you, as God is my witness. We followed the tracks until the rain ruined the trail. Then I hired a man to search for you as I could not! I promised your mother that I would find you and Grete, and bring you home—can you forgive me that it took this long? They told us that you were most likely dead and I agreed with them, but your mother never stopped believing, never stopped hoping."

Magda's heart sank, for Willi's face remained perfectly blank, as if he had schooled himself to show no emotion at all. Did he not understand? Magda wondered. Could he have forgotten the language that he spoke as a child? Grete had been mute at first, or so said Fredi. But she had recovered her speech within a few months, as if she had never put it out of her mind entirely. Surely, Willi had not forgotten everything!?

Hansi stood back after a moment, still quite overcome, holding the weeping Liesel in his arms. The boy stood alone, his face absolutely still. Magda's heart was quite wrenched by the memory of the last time she had seen him, the day that Robert Hunter had driven his trap away from Vati's house. Willi had waved happily from the back of Robert's trap and his sister stood up on the seat as Rosalie held the back of her dress—an unbearably poignant memory. Robert was buried in a closed coffin, so brutally mutilated he had been, and it sickened Magda still to recall Rosalie's abused body and the long torture of her death bed. Grete—perhaps Grete had been least damaged of them all.

Magda touched Willi's cheek with a delicate touch. "Willi, little one," she whispered, "do you remember me? Auntie Magda?" It seemed to her that something lit in his eyes, something far back, like a tiny light at the end of a long dark hallway. He nodded briefly and she continued, "We have missed you so much, Willi. You would not believe how much has changed. Hannah—you recall Hannah? My daughter, who played with you? You could not say her name properly, you called her 'Nannie' and so that became her pet name among the family. She has gone to be a nun. Your sister Anna, she is married to our cousin Peter; the two little boys are hers. Your brother Jacob is married, so is Marie. Vati—your Opa, in whose house we were living? He is dead. Your father is a rich man—they call him a cattle baron. He lives here now. Will you come with us? We have so longed for your rescue. Your mother was driven nearly mad with sorrow. Willi, dear heart—do you understand? Will you give me some sign that you understand?"

The boy nodded again. His lips moved very slightly. "Auntie," he said, almost experimentally. With that she had to be content, for he did not say anything more, even as Hansi and Liesel urged him into the barouche. That was when Magda saw that he was lame; he walked with a limp and a lurch for those few steps to the barouche. She recalled what Grete had said about his leg being broken while riding an untamed horse.

Willi sat as rigid as a stump between his parents, through the short drive to Hansi's mansion. Liesel's hands fluttered like butterflies. She could hardly keep from touching him, holding his hand, exclaiming over his rough clothes, and how very thin he appeared. Harry and Christian exclaimed excitedly, asking a million questions, while Peter and Magda could but watch, as if an audience at a play.

"Ma'am Becker, he does not look anything the age he is supposed to be," Peter murmured quietly. "He is very spare of flesh—if I were to note him in passing, I would say that he barely appears older than twelve or so."

"He is the same age as Horrie," Magda answered in the same low tones. "You are right—he does not appear anything close to that age. Which I think may be a relief to my sister; she thinks of him as a child still. But that he did not have enough to eat, among them! What hard use they gave to their slaves!"

"Ma'am Becker," Peter ventured, with much care, "I do not think he was a slave. I think he was one of them. It was told to us, by the Apache tracker, that he would be tested by his captors. If he was weak, he would be killed, or perhaps ransomed back. But if he was strong, they would keep him and make him a warrior." Peter took up the oddly-shaped burlap bag from the floor of the barouche, experimentally feeling the shapes within. Magda caught a sudden flare of alarm in Willi's eyes. "It feels like a quiver and a bow, with one of their shields. I think those would be his, Ma'am. He was a fighting man among them and the Army let him keep his side arms—they're very generous that way," Peter added with a twist of cynicism to his voice. He set the burlap bag on the floor again. In an infinitesimal way, Willi relaxed, although he continued to watch them warily.

"You should not say any of this to my sister," Magda warned.

Peter whispered, "No, I would not ruin her joy. But that he remained among the band, long after they were removed to the agency, and he did not make himself known as a captive? That would indicate that he did not think of himself as such." Peter sat back against the cushions. "He was such a dear little chap, Ma'am. He followed after us, after Cuz and me. I recollect that so very clearly."

"He was timid as a child." Magda was thinking out loud, as she so often did in front of Lottie or Mouse. Peter was as thoughtful as either of them, a careful and courteous listener. "Hansi dressed as Father Christmas— that frightened him dreadfully. He hid himself under the chaise, behind our skirts, rather than take his Christmas present from Father Christmas!"

"So we all assumed that because he was such a shy and polite little creature, that he would not fare well in such cruel captivity!" Peter shook his head as his eyes went towards his own young sons. "Oh, Ma'am, I do not think this will turn out well! Talk about a cuckoo in the nest! Ma'am Richter will be distraught and Papa Richter will tear himself to pieces, thinking over all he ought to do for this last and least of his sons. They did not deserve this," Peter added.

Magda couldn't help but think it might have been easier for her sister and Hansi if their son had really died in that first winter of captivity, as they had all come to accept, or never caught the attention of the soldiers at the Comanche Agency in Kansas. Peter obviously thought so. But for poor Willi, she thought, looking at his rigid and desperately expressionless countenance; he did not deserve this, either, cruelly wrenched from the bosom of one loving family and then capriciously returned. What must he think of all this, of the barouche and his fussy and fluttering mother, of the gaily painted mansion and the park around it, the garden and the trees, the wooden-lace and ornate shingles and porches of the All-The-Rest-of-The-Week-House just barely visible at the other end of the garden. No, Cousin Peter was right—this would not turn out well.

She took refuge in pouring out her thoughts and fears in a letter to Irina. How she missed Irina, her acerbic intelligence and her experience of the larger world. She recollected those mornings in Irina's parlor suite or in the villa on the enchanted island. It seemed another world now. But Irina was a safe refuge, a sensible voice removed from the immediate crisis, yet knowledgeable and sympathetic about the people involved. Now Magda comprehended Vati's attachment to his correspondence with Onkel Simon.

* * *

Letter to Irina Cherkevsky, from San Antonio, 27 January 1876:
My dear Irina,

We are safely arrived without any untoward or unexpected incident. My sister's son is recovered from captivity, returned to his parents with much joy on their part. He is alive and whole, unscarred so we assume from the experience, although he is quite lame and very spare of flesh, almost malnourished. Brother Hansi has consulted with Doctor Herff and his expert associates, sparing no expense. There is nothing to be done about the lameness, having been incurred early in his captivity. Surgical remedy would be painful in the extreme. My sister refuses consideration of that option, most stridently. It is almost the least of our concerns at this point.

My nephew is completely illiterate and rejects with considerable determination any attempts to remedy that lack. He can barely bring himself to converse with us! We would hire a private teacher, but to no avail! Brother Hansi would eagerly purchase for his son any enterprise at which he would work and be happy. He has done the same for all of his sons by birth and marriage according to their inclination, each of them being trained up to enterprise and industry—but this youngest of them stubbornly resists!

His habits are most peculiar. On the first night that he spent with us, Brother Hansi saw him to the bedroom allotted for him.

But shortly thereafter, he climbed out the window and, taking a single blanket, preferred to curl up in a corner of the garden! He speaks little, in monosyllables; he seems to comprehend what we say to him, as long as we speak in simple words. Although he tried speaking the Indian tongue to Grete upon his return with us, she did not understand, and the attempt appeared to distress them both. I would not say so to any but you, but Grete seems to fear her brother. He took no other notice of her or Anna, seeming to be indifferent to his female relations—and dare I say, quietly contemptuous of his mother. He brought with him some few things from the Agency which he was allowed to keep: a knife in a beaded leather sheath, a bow and quiver of arrows, and a painted shield of buffalo bull-hide which he seems to treasure most particularly.

Irina, my dear friend, Hansi and my sister hardly know what to do with him. He is sullen and disobliging, has no interest or inclination towards any of the family's business affairs. He has some small interest in the stable of horses and an affinity to the hunt, but my sister's cook almost gave notice yesterday—he will not eat pork and flung yesterday's dinner roast to the floor! This after dropping whatever he has hunted and slain on the kitchen floor, expecting someone else to skin and clean it! And our nearest neighbors have given complaint, for he has been shooting at their ducks and chickens in their own yard. Hansi is distraught, fearing that he will take the usual Indian disdain for private property as regards horses and help himself to whichever he fancies. This is no small crime, in this part of the country; the theft of a horse may mean life or death. The penalty for horse thievery is severe; all of Hansi's riches may not defer a capital penalty, should it be demanded, as it no doubt would. In this country, the perception of one rule for rich and another for poor is publicly disputed, although honored in actuality as much as in every other place. My brother-in-law worries that Willi may have some dreadful misadventure through his disinclination to pay attention to proprieties or law! But the boy is so clearly unhappy, it quite breaks my heart.

They were so joyful about his return—and, also I believe, quite joyful at their return to their home, to their known comforts after an excursion that was in some instances, rather more awkward that expected. My sister put on a grand party, welcoming all their friends to their house; all of his brothers attended, all of his father's associates, the ton of San Antonio! Oh, Irina, it was painful in the extreme! Willi submitted to being taken around, being introduced to all their friends, appearing more haggard and desperate with every encounter. Shortly after I bade my farewells and withdrew to my own little cottage, we heard a small noise on the verandah. My little Mauschen gave voice of course, most bravely! It was my nephew, with his blanket. I gestured him inside, where he slept on the parlor floor for the rest of the evening.

I do not know what will come of this, Irina—truly I do not.
Ever thy dear friend,
Margaretha Becker

Chapter Twenty-Three: *The Prodigal*

"No one would tell us at first, what happened then," Lottie mused. "Grete and I arrived home from school one day to find Doctor Herff's carriage in front of the house and Auntie Liesel in a fit of the vapors upstairs in her room, while Cousin Peter was giving Harry and Christian a talking-to in the hallway. I had never seen Cousin Peter so angry. Was that when they decided that they could not cope with Willi any longer?"

"It was not something that your Onkel Hansi wished to do," Magda answered, carefully. "He loved his children. He loved Willi even after everything. But Lise and Anna, and Cousin Peter, all insisted. He had to agree, especially with Anna and Peter. What he did imperiled the boys—and after that incident, his presence was no longer something Anna could endure. She was near to time with her daughter, your cousin Rose. If she had not been in the family way when Willi first came home, Hansi might have been able to reason with her. But as it was," Magda sighed. "Anna was adamant. Hansi could not stand against all three."

On a mild spring morning three months after their return, Hansi had convened a family meeting in his study. The French doors which led to a small porch overlooking the lawns and garden, stood open to admit the fresh spring breeze and the distant voices of Harry and Christian as they played on the lawn. It was time to plan for the yearly drives north, and to put final touches on stocking the Friedrichsburg store for the summer trail season. The painted mansion was full to bursting, for all Hansi's sons were there. Jacob had come from Friedrichsburg, Elias from Neu Braunfels, and George had returned from Indianola, having gone there to report on the rebuilding and whether anything of the goods and property had been or could be recovered. Peter and Anna had stayed since their return, awaiting the birth of their third child, mostly because Liesel would not hear of them going anywhere else. Fredi came with great reluctance from Live Oak, making an elaborate show of his disinterest in city business while he had another herd to assemble for the trail to Kansas. Sam was present, cheerful and full of questions about when Dolph was to return. He also was gathering a herd for the trail north.

"Not for too many seasons longer," Hansi had pointed out over dinner the night before. "In another few years, when the railroad reaches San Antonio, we'll be able to ship beef cattle straight to the east from here."

"What about trailing north to the Montana territories?" Peter ventured. "Not for beef, but for blood-stock. Lots of Eastern investors are looking to start ranches in the north. They have to stock it with western cattle, and they have to get stock from someplace."

This morning, though—they were attending to what George told them of Indianola. "There's not a whole building left between Powder Horn and the railroad tracks, but for Mitchell's Hardware. Most everyone who plans to rebuild is going to do so on higher ground—or even farther up the bayou. I think if we do choose to rebuild there," he suggested, "we should look at purchasing a tract in the old town or inland where the new site is. Not anywhere near the present town. Or better yet, relocate entirely to Port Lavaca." George looked around them with serious eyes, the same dark coffee-color as Anna, as his father. "Or even Galveston. It seems that Morgan is not going to rebuild the piers, or dredge a new channel into a new site farther inland. It is rumored that his steamship and rail interests are going to bypass the city entirely."

"Had you read anything of this, Annchen?" Hansi asked his daughter, who frowned thoughtfully. She reclined on the study chaise with a shawl over her lap. The baby was due any day. If this were not a family meeting, she would have been upstairs, resting and awaiting its arrival.

"Many newspaper editors are most unhappy with Morgan and his company of late," she answered, "for it seems that he is attempting a monopoly. Having once had the advantage of a railway, most are unwilling to return to transport long distance by wagon . . . indeed are willing to pay almost any price—oh, my God!" Suddenly her face went ashen; she sprang up from where she sat and shrieked, "Harry!"

All within Hansi's study were paralyzed for at least an instant as she ran towards the tall windows. She was clumsy with pregnancy and tangled in her shawl. She fell to her knees on the very threshold. As Magda and Peter followed after, they in turn were struck to immobility by the shocking sight revealed to them.

Harry stood in the middle of the lawn, tremulously holding Willi's round bull-hide shield before him. Christian stood a little apart, watching with intent interest. Willi stood about fifty feet distant, with his bow in his hand and quiver of arrows on his back. There were three or four arrows stuck in the shield already. Even as they watched in horror, Willi swiftly drew out another. With a sound like a single harp note from his bowstring, he sent the wickedly barbed arrow towards the child.

"Thunder and lightning!" Hansi shouted. "What game is this!"

Anna cried out, an anguished cry cut short as Peter, cursing like a madman, shot out of the French door. He leaped the balustrade in one swift rush and fell on the younger man. He wrenched the bow out of Willi's hands, casting it one-handed with all his strength, far across the lawn and away from his sons.

"Not my boys, you filthy savage!" he shouted. Before Magda could even help Anna rise to her feet, before Hansi and the other men could even pull them apart, Peter bunched his good hand into a fist and drove it into Willi's face. The force of the blow landing like a thunderbolt knocked the younger man to his knees, sending blood gushing from his nose. He went down with Peter's knees on his chest, Peter's hand at his throat squeezing without pity or mercy. Willi fought, tearing at Peter's face and arms with his fingernails, kicking spasmodically. If Peter had two good hands, Willi would have died within seconds; Magda knew this without a doubt. Although wiry and fit, Willi was still a boy in comparison with Peter, older, heavier and stronger.

"What is he doing! Peter! Peter! You're killing him!" Anna wept hysterically, one arm around her aunt, the other clutching her belly.

"Stop them!" Magda shouted, while she tried to set Anna on her feet. "For the love of God, stop them!"

Mercifully it was over hardly before it was begun, although it didn't seem that way. Hansi and George dragged Peter off, breaking his one-armed hold on Willi's throat by brute force. But the minute Peter was pulled away, releasing the boy from the ground, Willi sprang up as swiftly as a rattlesnake striking, a knife appearing in his fist like a conjuring trick. Anna shrieked again, but Sam and Fredi had deftly captured his arms before he could launch himself at Peter. Fredi twisted the knife away, turning the hand which held it behind his back and near to hoisting him from his feet with the force of that grip.

"Stop that!" Fredi snarled between his teeth, "or I swear to God, I'll let him kill you. What kind of game were you playing at?!"

"No game," Willi gasped. He spat blood from his mouth. "No game. They wished to know, to use a shield against an enemy. I showed them. No harm."

Peter's face was ashen. "No harm?" He breathed in deep gasps, as if his chest were a blacksmith's bellows. "I'll be the judge of that kind of game and what sort of harm might come to them. You will stay away from my sons." His eyes bored deep into Willi's. "You will not speak to them. You will not come near them and most of all—you will not endanger their lives teaching them your filthy savage ways. Not now, not ever. Or I swear I will finish the job I started." He shook off Hansi's and George's grip and looked towards his sons, standing white-faced and with mouths agape with shock. "Harry—put down that . . . that thing. Go up to your room."

"But Papa," Harry began to plead, but Peter snapped, "Now, Harry!" His expression brooked no argument.

Hansi's shoulders slumped as he looked between his son and his son in-law. "Take him up to his room, also," he commanded Fredi and Sam wearily. "Lock him in until I have a chance to talk to him." Peter had already turned his back on Willi, hanging in Fredi and Sam's grip like a puppet, like a rag in the mouth of one of the dogs, and went straight to Anna. Magda relinquished her niece into her husband's arms. "Anna-love. I am sorry—I couldn't think straight, when I saw him shooting at Harry."

"I know." Anna scrubbed at her cheeks with one hand, and hiccupped slightly. "I know. Harry and Christian . . . ." She began to weep again, silently.

"They are unharmed, Anna-love." Peter answered. He lifted her tenderly, and turned to face Hansi, who had followed him back into the study. "Papa Richter—if it weren't for the baby, we would leave at once. He's a danger to the boys and I will not permit that. Anna-love, do not cry!"

Liesel's footsteps pattered in the corridor. She looked into the study and cried incoherently, "Hansi—what has happened? Willi is hurt and his face is bleeding! Should I send for Doctor Herff?"

"A slight disagreement," Hansi answered.

Magda sighed; no, this was not turning out well. All of hers and Peter's fears about Willi's prodigal return were being realized. She explained, very calmly amid the clamor in the study from the other boys, "Lise, Willi was shooting arrows at his shield, and Harry was holding it. I do not think he meant harm—"

"I don't care if he meant it or not, we will not stay under the same roof," Peter interjected, white-lipped. "He is a bad influence on the boys, Ma'am Becker, and I will not have it."

"It gave Anna a terrible fright," Magda added. "I think you should send for Doctor Herff, Lise."

"The baby!" Liesel went nearly as pale as Anna. "Oh, my God, the baby! Carry her upstairs to her room, Peter . . . oh, I knew she should have stayed upstairs!"

"Mama, you were always out and about your business," Anna gulped, "why should not I?"

"Because we are respectable folk now!"

Liesel fluttered away and Peter added, tenderly, "And also because I put down my foot, this time, Anna-love." He turned in the doorway, Anna still gathered up in his arms, and added, "I meant it about the boy, Papa Richter. Either he goes, or we do."

The family meeting reconvened some little time later; with Liesel instead of Anna and without George, who was sitting on guard outside Willi's bedroom door. Anna was resting in her room, attended by Liesel's maids. White-faced and already struggling with birth pangs, she had been just as adamant. "He is my brother, but I am in agreement with my husband—we will not permit him to be anywhere around Harry and Christian. Tell Papa, I am sorry—but I do not want him anywhere near us."

Doctor Herff had promised to call in the afternoon, as neither of them looked to be in imminent distress, although Willi's eyes were both blackened and his nose still leaked blood.

"Obviously," Hansi concluded heavily, "Peter and Anna cannot leave at this moment. So where does that leave our son, Lise-my-heart? What is to be done with him?"

Liesel huddled wretchedly on the chaise where Anna had lain that morning, weeping into an already-sodden handkerchief. "He is our son," she quavered indecisively. "So everyone insisted, so I believed at first. The agency, the Army, everyone says that this boy is ours. I have come to think that he isn't really—they returned to us someone who has his coloring, his likeness, even to the scar on his back. He is not anything like our little Willi—such a sweet and good-tempered child, so kind and loving! He was stolen by the goblins and they have sent one of their changelings in his stead. He is sullen and disobliging and when he looks at us—he hates us! He hates us! This is not Willi, this is not our son!" she dissolved into incoherent sobs, out of which Magda could discern the only the words, ". . .he is dead, those savages killed him! They sent back his likeness only to torment us!"

"I always did say you could have sent him back." Fredi looked embarrassed and defensive. "Well, I did!"

"Not much help, Fredi," Hansi sighed. Magda noted that for once, he looked his age, weary beyond words. "He is not happy. I will be the first to admit. We had such hopes that all would be as it should have been; that he would become ours again as readily as did Grete, and it would only take some little time."

"You do not have enough time." Magda spoke kind and stern; things were past the time of sparing feelings. It was time to be honest, for everyone's sake. "Grete was a little child, still. This one thinks he is a man, and he will not be kept wrapped in cotton-wool while he forgets five times the number of years that his sister spent among them. Will you wait until he harms someone, fighting? Or steals a horse and meets up with a posse, a rope and a strong tree branch? I think not, Hansi." Hansi sighed again, acknowledging the truth of her words. "So, what do we do with him? He cannot work in any of our stores. He knows no more of letters and numbers than a baby."

"I'd take him north on a trail drive with me," Fredi allowed, "just to get him away from the city. He knows horses, doesn't he then?" He chuckled at his own wit.

Hansi immediately looked more cheerful. "That would knock some of the idiocy out of him, hey? Nothing like working a young sprout stupid to keep him out of trouble!"

"Save that once we crossed into Indian Territory, I could trust him with one of my own horses no farther than I would throw them both," Fredi added, depressingly. "No, not such a good idea, perhaps. Sorry, Hansi. "

"He could come up to our place and work the round-up, though," Sam spoke for the first time. He seemed quite cheerfully surprised when everyone turned to look at him. "I'd make sure he was busy enough. Setting him to work with horses and cattle—it's not like letters and numbers would do him any good anyway. I think Mama and I could convince him to stay and work . . . wouldn't you, Mama?" he added with an anxious look in Magda's direction.

Hansi chuckled, with heavy wit, "None dares disobey your Mama, Samuel! I daresay she can even make our wayward son behave himself!"

"So what do you say, Mama?" Sam looked as pleading as he had, that summer day that Mr. Berg the hermit brought them a puppy to train up as a watchdog. The Hanging Band had poisoned their former watch dog before Carl Becker's murder. "May we take Cousin Willi home with us?"

"Please, Magda?" Liesel whispered. "You will take care of him? Please? For me? I cannot bear to have him with us, but to think of him outcast . . . ." She dissolved into tears again. There was nothing for it but to acquiesce.

"We will take him to the ranch," Magda sighed. "But I should like to speak to him, now that this has been decided. And we must remain at least until the baby is born."

"Of course," Hansi agreed, already much cheered, "I will have George bring him down."

"No," Magda answered, "I will go to him. If you will excuse me," She rose, as all the gentlemen arose, and took her leave of Hansi's paneled study.

She climbed the stairs, rehearsing in her mind what she might say to her nephew. She dismissed George, and tapped lightly on the door. Receiving no answer and thinking that he might very well have climbed out the window again, she turned the cut-glass knob and went in. Willi lay flat on the bedstead, looking up at the ceiling overhead with eyes which clearly saw something other than ornate plasterwork. He didn't speak or look in her direction and Magda snorted—so that's how he wished to play it. She had no doubts about him being Hansi's true son. All of his brothers had been sullen and disobliging at that age.

"Willi," she commanded crisply, "I have something to tell you. Samuel and I are taking you to our ranch in the hills, in a day or so. You have had enough time to loaf around. This is not good, when there is work to be done."

"Women's work!" he answered scornfully, still not looking in her direction.

"Not women's work," she corrected him sternly. "Men's work. Not silly games with bows and arrows. Work with horses, hunting for our cattle."

His face, she noted, was still smeared and crusted with blood. There were already purple bruises under his eyes, and bruises from Peter's fingers on his throat. He appeared appallingly young, terribly lost. She took a towel from the washstand and dampened it from the water pitcher. He flinched away from her, still scowling. "Hold still!" she commanded him again and began daubing at his face.

"Not a game," he insisted, screwing his face up as she scrubbed at the dried blood. "Practice. My father showed me the same."

"Hansi? Shot arrows at you?" She was astonished. "Don't be silly, he never did any such thing.

"Not him," he answered, scornfully, "my Indian father, Pahchokotovt, the Black Otter." To that, there was very little to say, since it was so plain already. Magda squeezed out the cloth and again daubed at his face. Really, he was another one such as her husband had been, not much inclined to talk about those things and people who mattered most to him. In all of Carl

Becker's life he had only brought himself to speak to her more than two or three times of his older brother Rudi, cut down in the massacre at Goliad when he was a boy hardly older than this one was.

"You should tell me about him, then," Magda commanded. "About that family. Which I hope does not include the husband of a sister who tries to choke the life out of you. Otherwise, you will not gain much in returning to them."

"No," he made a sound which she thought might have been a laugh, but that it made his face and throat hurt. "Only a brother. He is dead at the Adobe Walls fight. He believed the medicine man who said he had painted himself with a magic paint. Bullets would not harm him. He lied." Willi shrugged, his voice flat and toneless as if he had squeezed all emotion, all grief out of it. "I did not want to come here. But Bald Head of the Agency, he said I must. So did my father. He came to me and said, '*Oh my son, the Bald Head says you have a father living who has searched long for you. As I have loved you, so must this white father love you also. As I grieve so will he have grieved.*' My mother, Ta'yetchy—She Who Rises at Dawn—she wept and cut her arms, hearing this. But my father was not moved."

"He sounds like an honorable man," Magda commented, although the words nearly choked her, to say such about a man who might very well have been one of the raiders who had tortured Rosalie.

"He is a brave warrior," Willi affirmed stoutly. "He took many horses, led many raids against our enemies."

"How did he come to be your father?" Magda asked. She could not bear to ask if this Black Otter was one of those who had led the raid into the Pedernales, in that year after the war.

"He gave a horse to the man who owned me. I could not carry wood or water, having broken my leg. The old woman who once was wife to his father thought I showed promise." Willi shrugged again, his face still expressionless, "If I did not, she still would have a slave. I crawled to the next camp. The old woman helped me. She told Black Otter I might make a warrior after all. He gave a horse to my owner and brought me to his lodge. He said that I would be brother to his son. That is all." And he pressed his lips together and would not say any more. Magda reflected philosophically that it was more than anyone else had ever gotten him to say. When his face was as clean as she could get it, Magda returned to her original plan.

"My sons and I returned to our land. We have many cattle there now. We think you should come to work there. We also have many horses," she added, with calculation. "And my sons say the hunting is very fine. Would you like to do that?" His response was an indifferent shrug. Remorselessly she pressed on. "We will pay a salary of thirty dollars a month. If you choose instead, you may have a horse every two months. Are we agreed?" Another indifferent shrug. Magda rose from the chair where she had sat to clean his face. "Then I ask a promise; that you work for us loyally. You will not run away. You will not treat my sister so."

"My Indian mother is Ta'yetchy, She Who Rises at Dawn. The fat white woman is nothing," he explained, with cruel indifference. "But horses are all. I will work so."

And with that, she had to be content.

* * *

Letter to Princess Irina Cherkevsky, written from the B-R Ranch, Near Comfort, Kendall County, April 15, 1876:

My dear Irina;

My fears regarding my prodigal nephew, miraculously returned from captivity amongst the savage Indians, were in the end fully justified. He has been given into my care, by my sister and Brother Hansi, following upon a series of unfortunate events and one propitious one. Anna has given birth to a healthy daughter, who has been christened Rose, in dear memory of our own younger sister, so cruelly slain when he and his sister were first taken captive. Upon her safe delivery, my younger son and I took our departure with Willi in custody, leaving Lottie to remain at school until the end of term.

I own that I am not particularly solicitous upon his needs and his moods, as my sister was wont to be—indeed I am most indifferent. Do I seem a cruel and distant parent? Perhaps—but I have been inclined to treat my children as adults as soon as they gave evidence of responsibility and consideration to others, and they have so richly rewarded me! But my nephew; such are the oddities of his present character that he has been—if not particularly amiable in his address to me, at least considerably less hostile than he was to my poor sister! As you have counseled me, such are the ardors of men—nothing excites like indifference, romantically or otherwise!

His older brother George departed with us. He is taking over management of a mercantile establishment in Comfort—do we not appear to be the very Rothschilds or de Medicis of commerce? Indeed, I think that Brother Hansi's plan is to have a son, a nephew, or a grandson or some other connection or relative conducting profitable commerce in every important town of this part of Texas.

I own that I am very glad to be returning to the ranch and the house that my husband built for me and that my son has so enlarged upon. Summers in the lowlands are most uncomfortably hot, but the hills are always somewhat cooler, so green and beautiful. There was a most curious incident, when we passed through Comfort and spent the afternoon at the store . . .

Willi was not much interested in the shop, or what it contained, halfway along Comfort's main street. They paused there at midday to let down George and his study valise. Willi and Sam had gone on horseback from San Antonio, but George rode with Magda in the sturdy old two-horse ambulance that, for all of Hansi's riches, everyone vowed was still the most comfortable and commodious way to journey over a long distance. George had so little in common and less to say to his own brother, Magda realized sorrowfully. They drew up in front of the store building, already organized and opened by some local lads whom Hansi, at her advising, had hired as clerks. No, it was a mad dream that Willi would ever fall in with Hansi's grand mercantile plans. She saw that now, by the contemptuous disinterest of expression as he looked at the place; tidy and stone-built, the very epitome of the German towns. The shop had rooms over it, already furnished, in which it was planned for George to live. Like Jacob and Elias, George was trained up to commerce and transport, having worked for Hansi since he was tall enough to climb into a wagon and take up the driving reins.

"We will break our journey here and see to getting George settled," she commanded the boys, as the tied their horses to the railing in front of the store building. "An hour or so, at most."

"We're nearly home, then." Sam clapped his cousin on the shoulder. "So let's go find a drink, something to cut the dust!" Willi didn't look terribly enthused about the prospect, but he followed after Sam.

The inside of the store was dim, even though the double doors stood open to the street for light and fresh air. Magda looked around with approval; very tidy, as were all of the stores which she, Hansi and the boys had opened. The air was redolent with the smells of cheese, cured meat, coffee, dry goods, and a faint tang of kerosene. At the back of the store one of the young clerks was deep in discussion with a customer, a farmer in work clothes worn and threadbare. He was pleading in English for some consideration, for which the clerk shook his head. Both of them turned around at hearing George and Magda's footsteps.

"Oh, Mr. Richter, Madame Becker," the young clerk blurted with relief, "I am glad you are here. I cannot make Mr. Tackett understand that I may not extend credit to him, since his farm is outside this district and I do not know him."

"It is our customary practice," George answered, unhappy at having to admit it. "And we cannot make too many exceptions."

He did not like doing this; no young person of sensitivity liked to turn away someone in need. But if this young farmer was not known in the district, then who knew anything of his ability or inclination to pay his debts? It was a fine line, Magda knew to her cost. Too many a shopkeeper had been bankrupted by extending credit where it was not deserved.

The farmer turned his shapeless wide-brimmed hat in his hands. "I'm Sullivan Tackett—folks call me Sul—and I ain't asking for all that much." He was a young man, his face and hands sprinkled with mud-colored freckles, but already aged by hard labor in the out of doors, seeming proud but already diminished by the necessity of pleading with a shopkeeper. "Ma'am," he nodded towards Magda with the courtly courtesy that the Americans usually extended towards women, "we're just looking for just enough to tide us over the summer, till the crops come in an' I bring the corn to the mill. I wouldn't ask for myself, Ma'am," he swallowed, seeming to steel himself for the ultimate abasement, the final dismantling of his manly pride, "but that I have three chirren, ma'am. We're down to eating mush, with nettles and greens and cactus fruit. I dasn't go hunting for game, can't afford any more bullets no-how."

Sul Tackett turned his hat once more in his hands; just so had the Browns always looked so poor and no-account, rich in nothing but pride. But the Browns lived their hardscrabble life because they chose to, and this man had no choice. Magda wondered briefly if he was a connection of theirs, for he looked familiar enough.

He turned his face full to hers, and she felt a prickling sensation down the back of her spine. Yes, she knew him—or not precisely knew him, but recognized him. She had stared at his freckled face, over the sights of Carl

Becker's Paterson. This was the young Confederate soldier who with his fellows had played a game of tormenting their dog, who had pointed their weapons at Sam as other soldiers looted the Becker place of everything valuable; even turning the chickens out of their pen, tumbling the filled milk pans onto the cellar floor, and smashing every stick of furniture. And then they had fired the barn and the bunkhouse, sending Magda and her children away in the dung cart, having taken from them in the space of less than an hour all that it had taken fifteen years of patient and careful labor to acquire!

Magda felt as if she were turned to stone, turned to ice, her own heart frozen in her chest. It would hurt her to breathe. How dare he! How dare he come begging, after having cheerfully taken part in that robbery? *"Oh, yes, be afraid,"* she had raged on that awful day as she held the Paterson on him, *"you in your homespun grey uniform... Be afraid, so afraid you are pissing yourself like an infant. Be afraid. You thought to amuse yourself tormenting a child and his pet, and now you see retribution, a fury in widow's black . . . Your friends also frightened; they stand there uncertainly, not knowing what to do. They could shoot me, but then everyone will laugh at them."*

"Ma'am?" queried Sul Tackett uncertainly. Magda made herself breathe, once and then again, realizing with a sense of both wonder and annoyance that he did not recognize her at all. In fact, George and his young clerk were now looking between them, not quite daring to say anything at all before Magda spoke. No, this was her decision.

Just then, there was another light footstep in the doorway and Sam's cheerful voice, "Mama, are you nearly ready? I can't talk Willi into a drink at all, so why waste the time?"

Magda looked towards her younger son; no, he wouldn't have recognized this man. He had been a child, a child too caught up with rescuing his pet to pay much attention otherwise. The constriction around her throat loosened as Sam strolled farther into the store. What a contrast there was between them at this moment! Her son, with his open, happy face, his work clothes trail-dusty and worn but not to raggedness; full-blessed with prosperity and going to a comfortable home, the home they had reclaimed. This man, Sul Tackett, once one of their persecutors, now was marked with defeat and poverty. He was, Magda realized, going home from here to—as he said in his plea—a meal of corn mush and whatever wild greens his wife and children had been able to glean. Who could have foreseen such a reversal of fortunes, when the Beckers had been robbed in a single hour of home, property, and land? Now they had prospered and the

Confederacy's adherents had suffered, tasting to the last drop the bitter dregs of a cup of defeat and humiliation, of disenfranchisement, of slavery being abolished for once and all. Even the much-scorned Union Army, upon their return to the frontier, had been able to force the Indians to abandon their raids into Texas for once and all. It was over, Magda realized, accepting the final proof with a sense of wonder and relief—it was at last over. She and her children, why, they had won! Could anyone doubt that, looking between the two young men?

"Mama?" Sam ventured uncertainly, just as young Tackett asked, with a worried note in his voice, "Ma'am?

"George?" Magda turned to her nephew. "I am acquainted with Mr. Tackett. I shall authorize an account for him, up to five hundred dollars. As long as," she added with a severe look at the farmer, "regular payments are made, in cash or kind; wild game or pecans, or even cut shingles."

"Thank you, ma'am." Tackett was, to her relief, too proud to make an abject display of his gratitude. "That will make all the difference in the world to my wife and the chirren, it surely will, ma'am!"

"I am sure of that," Magda answered. Queerly, she felt almost lightheaded with a feeling akin to joy, as if the sun had just come from behind the clouds, or the first cool breeze of autumn had just begun to stir the trees, banishing the sullen heat of summer. "You should always have a special care for your children, Mr. Tackett."

"Are we going now, Mama?" Sam asked with impatience.

"Yes, we are," and she added, in a whisper to George, "Give Mr. Tackett a little penny candy for his children. Don't charge his account; just write it off as my gift."

Having done that, I felt a most curious sense of well being, she wrote later to Irina Cherkevsky, *which I cannot quite account for. I have always been advised that it is better to return good for evil, although admittedly his actions so many years ago were not precisely evil, more a matter of indulging himself in a careless and brute impulse. My dear Vati's oldest friend, the Reverend Altmueller, once preached a sermon on how hate not only destroys the person hated, but also subtly destroys the person who hates. I did not entirely comprehend then—but now I do! For I had hated so many men, some with cause, and one in particular to whom I was finally able to mete out justice—but still I hated them. This hate did no great harm to anyone but myself! Now, having put it aside with some small effort, I can see clearly and without rancor.*

I still despise the Comanche raiders who murdered our sister and stole Liesel's children from her. But there is no future in dwelling overmuch on that emotion, no more than if I should waste my emotions in hating the little wild wolves that raid the chicken coop and slaughter our prized chickens out of sheer wantonness. It is what they do, it is in their nature. There can be no other explanation; it is what it is.

Regarding my nephew; he has been working these last months as a horse wrangler with the spring cattle round-up. I have scarce laid eyes on him above two or three times, always with the other drovers and hands, but he seems happy enough among them. My son tells me the other wranglers have nothing but the highest praise for him, in his abilities to ride and tame the wildest pony! I should tell you that our native custom of conversation, especially among those men hired as drovers and cattle herders, tends to the laconic. So a man who is few of words and vouchsafes little of his origins is not thought strange or eccentric. He rides most adeptly, a perfect centaur! Once in the saddle his lameness counts for nothing. Mr. Inman and some of the others who have lived here long know that he is Samuel's cousin, but know not of his return from captivity or his disinclination to rejoin white society. Long have been the sufferings of settlers here, fifty years of depredations, murder, and pillage! Those who have been affected so are not inclined to look kindly on such whose natural sympathies seem to be with the raiders!

Irina, I do not know what will become of him. His words about his "Indian father" weighed upon my mind—as if all the care and affection that his parents have lavished upon him are for naught. . .

* * *

Magda sat in the parlor of her husband's stone house, the house with the bird and branch carved over the door. It was early on a summer evening in June. The windows stood open to their farthest extent to catch the fitful breeze. She had a letter from England in her lap, but it was a secondary matter to her. Dolph had found a bride for himself, the not-so-pretty filly with a good heart who loved dogs and horses and, with luck, would come to care for cattle and for this place as well. She had never doubted that he would, never doubted Dolph's ability to take care of himself. No, she had another care tonight; Sam and his men would take the herd north in the morning, north to the railheads in Kansas. Hansi had already decided this would be the last year they would take that momentous journey. By next trail season, they would have a railhead in Texas; no more the months-long adventure to the Red River, through Indian Territory and into Kansas with thousands of head of cattle. Hansi was already looking ahead to the future, accepting and adapting to the changes brought to him by time.

But what if one didn't want to look ahead, what if one wished things to remain as they were? She sat with the letter and daguerreotype of Dolph and Isobel, stiff in their fashionable wedding finery, lying in her lap. Not a pretty girl, but capable and determined, Magda had decided upon close examination; a girl who would suit this place, this country. This Isobel would probably meet with all the customary shocks and disturbances—but she had the look of someone who would prevail.

Magda lifted her head from the daguerreotype, gazing out the tall parlor window. When Dolph had added onto the house, he had Mr. Berg build a tripartite window in the new parlor; a double glass window, with two smaller windows on either side, the whole of it framing the view all the way down to the river, over all this part of the ranch. There was the orchard below, the long meadow, the river slipping between its veil of cypress trees, and the hills beyond, diminishing dusty green and pale blue as the setting sun touched them with gold and orange highlights.

Carl Becker would have loved this aspect upon his property, Magda thought. She hoped that her son's wife would come to do the same.

There was a horseman in the lower meadow, riding a pinto pony at a dead gallop back and forth across the meadow, weaving between the few sparse trees. She set the letter and the daguerreotype aside, and went to stand at the window. Yes, it was Willi, flying across the same meadow where her husband, together with Porfirio, young Matt Brown, and Trap Talmadge, had taught her brothers to ride; to ride as true horsemen and Texians did, fearlessly and as one with their mount. She closed her eyes for a moment, nearly overcome with the memory of her husband riding across the meadow and laughing, slipping to one side of his horse and scooping up his hat from the ground. Just so was Willi slipping from one side of the spotted pony, and then the other, clinging with one foot to his saddle. Willi had his bow and quiver, and he was shooting under the neck of his horse at the tree trunks as he flashed past at a gallop. Magda clicked her tongue as she saw that—he should not do such where anyone could see. They would know then where his true sympathies lay, which was not good. But still she lingered, inexpressibly saddened by the sight; it was like watching a caged bird. Even if the cage was large and the conditions commodious, it was yet a cage.

The door opened at her back, and she turned; Sam, exuberant and sketchily washed for the evening meal. Tia Leticia's daughters would serve it, as appropriate, in the dining room. Magda felt a brief pang of regret. In the old days, the days of the smaller house and when her husband lived, they would have eaten in the kitchen. No, that would not have suited her new daughter, the very proper English Isobel.

"Hello, Mama! I see you have a letter from Dolph! So have I! He says she loves dogs and is bringing two more with her!" Sam kissed her cheek, and picked up her letter and the daguerreotype. "Dolph said he had sent you this. I expect that I shall meet her when I return in the fall. What fun—she sounds like a proper wife for him! At any rate, she got him to wear that proper monkey-suit. Oh," Sam's gaze followed hers, to the boy on a pinto horse circling the meadow. "Looks rather sad, doesn't he, Mama?" Sam added, with astonishing perception. Then she reminded herself of how Sam was the artist—his insights came from his brush on the canvas! Of course, he would have observed such matters; at some point they must have flowed through his intellect!

"He is, Samuel," Magda answered. "It's enough to break the heart. Call him in. Leticia's girls will want to serve supper soon."

Sam stepped to the open window. He put two fingers to his mouth and whistled piercingly. Below in the meadow, Willi swung to the top side of his pony and looked towards the house. Seeing Sam in the window, he waved casually. He turned his pony towards the lane, presently vanishing from sight.

"He's coming." Sam turned grave eyes towards his mother. "So, Mama, what do you want to tell me, before he puts away his horse and washes up enough for supper?"

"I think you should take him on the drive to Kansas," Magda intoned. "I think we should let him take the wages that he has earned. And once you have reached the Indian Territory, let him do what he likes."

To her astonished relief, Sam nodded in acquiescence. "I think that would be the best thing, Mama. Onkel Hansi wants to do the best thing for him, but I do not think Willi looks to his family at all."

"He looks to his family," Magda corrected him, "but not to your aunt and uncle; rather towards the family he has in Indian Territory." She sighed heavily; Liesel and Hansi would be disappointed, even grieved. But she couldn't help thinking that they would also be relieved, and accept what she had done. Willi might be their son in blood, but in his heart he had long since chosen his father, Black Otter of the Quahadi Comanche. Just as her own husband had chosen to honor Vati with filial devotion, rather than that harsh, unloving man in whose house he had lived until he was nearly grown. No, Willi would put off his white clothes, his white family, and remain in Indian Territory. His heart was already there and Magda was in no doubt that he would have gone as soon as he was able anyway.

She looked out the window at the broad valley of the Guadalupe. This was her home, this had always been home. It was time to let Willi go to his own, where he was loved, where were those whose hearts would not be in their throats every day and every hour, fearing for him or the trouble that he might make for himself in a world where he didn't belong, didn't wish to belong. He should be allowed leave to go to his true home, to wherever Black Otter might have set up his skin lodge on the Reservation.

"Shall I tell him, Mama? He will need to pack his traps for tomorrow, then." Sam lingered uncertainly in the parlor door.

"Yes—tell him that he may go home." Magda again looked out the window as her son left the parlor to find his cousin. She rejoiced once more in the beauty of the evening, the look of the setting sun burnishing the limestone of the walls, glowing pink and amber, as blue shadows crept out from the trees.

"May my son's wife come to treasure this," she said out loud, "and might Willi come to treasure that place he goes to."

From his basket in the corner, Mouse lifted his head, hearing the sound of approaching footsteps in the hallway. He barked once, his warning bark, and came to sit adoring at her feet.

"Yes, I know, Mauschen," Magda responded cheerfully. "Suppertime."

* * *

"*He did return to Texas now and again, although never as Wilhelm Richter. He came as Ase-Tamy, Grey Brother of the Quahadi Comanche, son of Black Otter, sometime war chief. He married—for all we know he might have been married when the Agency returned him to Hansi and Liesel! He came to Hansi's funeral, years later, with his two sons. I think it was his sons who made him come to Texas. They were curious about his white family. And once their curiosity had been satisfied, they went away, saying little to any of us. He was courteous to me, though. I have often wondered why.*"

"*Because of all of us, you saw clearly what had to be done, Mama,*" Lottie answered. "*You had saved his life, I think. Onkel Hansi would have been stubborn, tried to keep him close and turn him into the son that he should have been. And he would have made trouble, been put into prison, or maybe wasted away like these poor lads today.*" Lottie's eyes brimmed and her mother snorted.

"*Don't be a sentimental goose, Lottie. Fredi said as much, but being Fredi, everyone thought it a joke.*" She stared unseeingly into the fire. The ache in her shoulder and her arm intensified; she would have to ask Lottie for a hot poultice, to sooth away the pain. "*I merely saw things clear, Lottie. That is one of the few benefits of getting old—seeing matters clearly, and knowing when you should let go.*" She stood, carefully leaning upon her cane, and walked over to the window to open the heavy curtains. A pale watery light was just dawning in the eastern sky. "*Look, my dear—we have talked the night through and now it is dawn. Is it not glorious?*"

Under the trees across the road, the familiar, tall young man held the reins of his brown horse in his hands and smiled at her. The sun blazed on his fair hair like a beacon. His eyes were as blue as the sky, and lit with joyful welcome, still brighter than the white blaze of the sun that was coming up in the sky behind him.

Historical Notes:
Cowboys, Comanche Tribes, and other Texiana

In his magisterial one-volume history of Texas, T.R Fehrenbach suggested that Texas evolved a unique identity out of fifty years of bloody and bitter war with the various Indian tribes that also claimed it as a home; in other words, being forged by constant and unrelenting conflict. Other states seemed to follow the carefully choreographed steps of a minuet: settlement, conflict with the Indians, resolution of the conflict followed by dispatch to a reservation, statehood, and subsequent peace and quiet. Wars with the local Tribes were usually short, sharp and decisive. Within a few years Indian/settler disputes were resolved to the advantage and satisfaction of the settlers and soldiers. Not so in Texas—where war between the Comanche, Kiowa, and Apache against Mexican and later Anglo settlers continued with unrelenting ferocity from the time of the first settlements until late in the 19th century. Any spot along the frontier—which by the time of the Civil War was a rough arc stretching northwards from Rio Grande Station, bisecting the Hill Country, through the headwaters of the Brazos and Trinity Rivers, to Red River Station—could in the blink of an eye become a war zone. This was simply a reality for generations of settlers; not only the first-comers.

Although John Meusebach's treaty with the Penateka Comanche, as described in the first volume of this story, was made in good faith and honored by all parties involved, it had been made with only a small portion of those tribes and divisions who roamed at will throughout Northern and Western Texas. The German settlers of the Hill Country were at just as much at hazard of sudden brutal murder, rape and capture as any other settler on the frontier in the time that I am describing.

I should also reiterate that the various Comanche tribes and, to a lesser extent the Kiowa, adhered to a warrior culture. Their societies were built around it, no less than that of the Spartans of ancient Greece. There was literally no honorable way to live other than by hunting and raiding for horses, plunder and slaves. There is no politically correct way to soften those facts or to soft-pedal the truly horrible situation that anyone taken captive found themselves in. A large part of the detestation which those on the Texas frontier came to feel for their Indian foes was due to the fact that the standards of 19th century chivalrous conduct required that if war be waged, it should not be waged on women and children. In this long war along the Texas frontier, the cruelest sorts of atrocities were frequently perpetrated upon just those—women and children—whom Victorian propriety held to be noncombatants.

Another book which I read by way of doing research—and to which I kept coming back, over and over, was Scott Zesch's *The Captured*, which followed the experiences of a number of children taken from the Hill Country settlements at about this time. Some of these children described therein so absorbed the values of their captors that they identified ever afterwards with their Indian families. As a parent, that struck me as a particularly refined cruelty: to lose a child, have that child miraculously returned, only to discover that your child is indeed lost to you. The experiences of Grete and Willi Richter are based roughly on those of Minnie Caudle, Rudolph Fischer, Hermann Lehmann and Adolph Korn, as outlined in *The Captured*. The deaths of Rosalie and Robert Hunter are loosely based on the deaths of Johanna and Henry Kensing, although the Kensings were the parents of a number of older children. Mrs. Kensing was indeed pregnant, was treated with particular brutality by her captors, was not told of her husband's death, and miscarried shortly before she herself died of her injuries. The pursuit of the war party which had taken the Richter children is based on Captain John W. Sansome's pursuit of a raiding party that had taken his cousins Jeff and Clinton Smith from their home on Cibolo Creek, northwest of San Antonio, in the spring of 1871. For a week, Captain Sansome's Ranger company chased the raiders all the way to the Llano River, until they lost the trail in a rainstorm.

Britt Johnson, teamster and frontiersman, did indeed ransom his wife and younger children from captivity in Indian Territory, as described. He is thought to have made four trips into Indian Territory, attempting to locate and ransom other captives. Along with two other teamsters he was killed, also as described, by raiding Kiowa Indians in 1871, near Salt Creek. Those who came upon the aftermath counted nearly two hundred empty rifle and pistol shells where Britt Johnson had made his last stand, behind the body of his horse. His efforts to rescue his family and others are supposed to be the inspiration for the movie *The Searchers*.

J.P. Waldrip, the leader of the Hanging Band which particularly plagued those of Unionist sympathies in the Hill Country, mysteriously returned to Fredericksburg two years after the war. He was killed by an unknown assailant in broad daylight according to local legend, and fell under the tree by the side of the Nimitz Hotel, which still exists. His last words were reported to be, as I wrote in Chapter Ten: "Please don't shoot me any more!" The identity of his assailant has been a mystery ever since, although I suspect that at the time, it was common knowledge. Philip Braubach, the son-in-law of Mr. Scheutze the schoolteacher, did indeed take a shot at him and missed. By one obscure account, Mr. Fischer the cobbler confessed to his wife on his deathbed that he had killed J.P. Waldrip, had sniped at him from an upper window of his workshop and home on Magazine Street (now Washington Street), but swore his wife to secrecy out of fear of Waldrip's friends and relations. That was a very real consideration, post-Civil War. The bad relations established between German settlers and their Anglo-American neighbors before and during that war did not die down for decades.

One of my lucky finds at a San Antonio Library book sale was a paperback edition of a collection assembled by J. Martin Hunter. *The Trail Drivers of Texas* is a vast collection of first-person accounts put together in the 1920s. It proved to be a goldmine; who knew that cattle herds had been taken from Texas to Gold Rush-era California? Many of the adventures experienced by Hansi's and Dolph's drovers were drawn from that book. There was a long history of trailing cattle out of Texas to profitable markets elsewhere in the west. Texas longhorns were brought north beginning in the 1840s, along what was called the Shawnee Trail, between Brownsville and variously, Kansas City, Sedalia, and St. Louis. Another trail, the Goodnight-Loving trail, went from west Texas to Cheyenne, Wyoming, following the Pecos River through New Mexico. The most heavily trafficked trail was the many-branched Chisholm Trail. Its tributaries gathered cattle from all across Texas into one mighty trunk route which began at Red River Station, on the river which marked the demarcation between Texas and the Indian Territories of present-day Oklahoma. The Chisholm Trail crossed rivers which, thanks to storms in the distant mountains, could go from six inches to twenty-five feet deep in a single day, and farther east skirted established farmlands whose owners usually did not care for large herds of cattle trampling their crops and exposing their own stock to strange varieties of disease.

Once into Kansas the trail split again, coming to an end variously at places like Dodge City, Newton, Ellsworth, and Abilene—depending on the year, how far the railway had advanced, and the exasperation of local citizens with the behavior of young men on a spree after three months of brutally hard work, dust and boredom. The cattle were loaded into railcars, the drovers paid off, and next year they did it again. The tracks can still be seen from the air, all across North Texas and Oklahoma. In the twenty years after the Civil War about 10 million cows walked north; most to the Kansas railheads, but a smaller portion went farther north, into Wyoming and Canada, to be used as brood stock for ranches that eager but late-coming entrepreneurs were falling all over themselves to establish.

The classical free-range cattle ranching and long-trail-drive era ended in the mid-1880s when bad weather and a glutted market brought prices for beef crashing down. The cattle towns depicted in western movies and television shows actually were limited to a very small time and space. They were also not nearly as lawless as presented then, or now. Many of the towns were in economic competition with each other, and each having a fairly freewheeling press and enthusiastic economic backers, any ruckus in one town was quickly magnified by detractors in another. Two cowboys indulging in a bit of relatively harmless gunplay outside a saloon in Newton could be magnified into small war, riot, and murder by a rival town's newspaper. Murderous gunplay in cow-towns generally involved members of the professional gambling fraternity or local law enforcement professionals. Often, they were the same body of personnel. These were small towns any other time than the cattle trailing season, and people doubled up when it came to jobs.

The young lady with the pet prairie dog described in Chapter 13 was an enterprising dance hall girl and lady of the evening who later went by the name of Squirrel-Tooth Alice. Her real name was Mary Elizabeth Haley. She died of almost respectable old age, in a Los Angeles nursing home, in 1953. She had also, as a child of nine or ten, been a captive of the Comanche, until ransomed by her family.

Other curious things noted as regards the golden age of western cattle ranching: The average age of a cowhand/drover was about twenty-four. About one in six or seven was black and one in six or seven Mexican. The work was seasonal and most did it for only about seven years before moving on to something that paid a little more, or setting up as ranchers themselves. They usually did not own their horse, just their saddle. Horses were provided as a necessary tool by the cowhand's employer, to be swapped out when necessary. At the end of a long trail drive, the horses were usually sold and sometimes the cook wagon too, as I have made note of in this volume. The cowhands returned to their starting point by rail, a ticket home being provided along with their wages.

One would think that to write about cowboys and the cattle trails is to venture upon extraordinarily well-trod territory, but there still are stories to be told. In this one I have tried to emphasize that it was a business, and sometimes a chancy one, especially for those who came late to the party. Men like Hansi Richter and Dolph Becker got into it because it looked like it would turn a profit, in taking a commodity of which they posessed a lot to a place where they could get a better price for it. I have modeled the R-B Ranch and Hansi's and Magda's various businesses after Charles Schreiner's Y.O. Ranch near Kerrville. Charles Shreiner also ran a bank and a general store and experimented with other herd animals than cattle. The general store became a department store, which closed in 2007 after 138 years of business in Kerrville.

Finally, the birth and death of the city of Indianola: the Queen City of the Gulf coast, which flourished for merely a half century. It rivaled Galveston as a port and a mercantile center for that time, before being destroyed by a hurricane. Although the city fathers tried very hard to rebuild and revive their town, another hurricane ten years later made the end inevitable. There is nothing left of it now but a scattering of holiday homes on very tall stilts and a monument. Indianola's nearest rival, Galveston in turn was nearly destroyed by another hurricane at the turn of the century. At least 8,000 residents were killed. Among the institutions destroyed was a Catholic orphanage, where the sisters tied the younger children to themselves with clotheslines and led them in singing a hymn to Mary, Queen of the Waves, as the building fell apart around them.

> *If we shadows have offended,*
> *Think but this, and all is mended,*
> *That you have but slumber'd here*
> *While these visions did appear.*
> *And this weak and idle theme,*
> *No more yielding but a dream!*

Wm. Shakespeare, A Midsummer Night's Dream Act 5, Scene 1

Celia Hayes
San Antonio, 2011

Steinmetz – Richter Family

Robert Hunter 1841-1866

Rosalie 1844?-1866

Christian Friedrich "Vati" Steinmetz (2) b.? d. 1866

Hannah "Mutti" Schmidt b.? d. 1845

Heinrich Vogel (1) b.? d. 1823

Margaretha "Magda" Vogel 1823-1918

Carl Becker 1819-1862

4 surviving children

Johann 1838-1895

Friedrich 1838-1902

Annaliese "Liesel" 1826-1888

Hans "Hansi" Richter 1823-1887

Anna 1843-1925

Peter Vining 1839-1910

3 children

Elias 1852-1923

George 1848-1896

Jacob 1847-1905

Joachim 1844-1845

Christian 1857-1864

Marie 1850-1886

Wilhelm "Willi" "Grey Brother" 1859-1930

Margaretha "Grete" 1862-1943

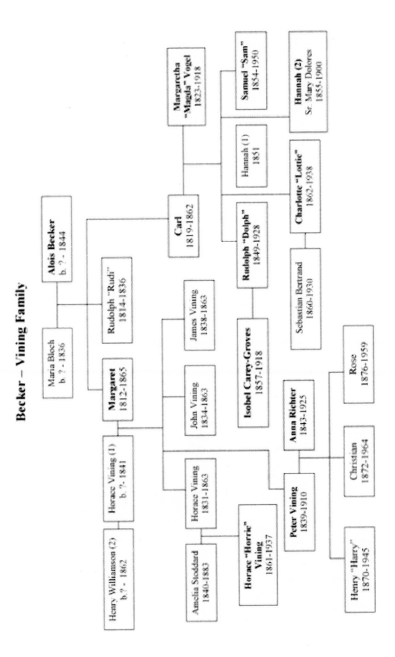

Becker – Vining Family